BLOOD
AND
SABLE

BLOOD
AND
SABLE

Carol J. Kane

McGRAW-HILL BOOK COMPANY
New York St. Louis San Francisco Bogotá Hamburg
Madrid Mexico Milan Montreal Panama Paris
São Paulo Tokyo Toronto

1 2 3 4 5 6 7 8 9 D O C D O C 8 9 2 1 0 9 8

ISBN 0-07-037866-5

Library of Congress Cataloging-in-Publication Data

Kane, Carol J., 1946–
  Blood and sable.

  1. Soviet Union—History—Revolution, 1917–1921–
Fiction.   I. Title.
PS3561.A467B56   1988   813'.52   87-25978
ISBN 0-07-037866-5

Designed by Eve Kirch

*To my generous parents, who made the writing possible,
and to the friends who encouraged me,
with special thanks to Paula and Claire, who
believed in Blood And Sable from the first draft.*

"Victoire, c'est la volonté."
—*Marshal Foch*

GLOSSARY

barin, barinia	a nobleman, noblewoman; direct address
Batushka Tsar	Father Tsar
boyar, boyarina	nobleman, noblewoman
Byelochka	Little Squirrel
dorogai	dear, darling
Do svidanya	Good-bye
dushka	little soul, dearest
izbas	wooden peasant huts
kvass	popular drink made from fermented rye bread, similar to sour beer
kovsh	drinking vessel
lubovnik	lover
malenkaya	little one
Maslenitsa	mid-winter holiday before Lent
matiushka	little mother
milochka	darling
Na zdarovye	a toast
Nichevo	It's nothing
nyanya	nanny
proschai	farewell
pyraniki	gingerbread treat
stanovoiy	country policeman
starets	holy man
traktir	tavern
verst	Russian measurement; about 3,500 feet in length
zakouski	hors d'oeuvres
zemstvo	local government organization
zhid	Jew (derogatory slang term)

✤ PROLOGUE ✤

Paris, 1900

"Mama," whispered the blonde girl in the doorway, "are you sleeping?" She wanted to talk.

Varia Andreevna lay sprawled on her elaborately carved and gilded mahogany bed, her blonde hair in a neat, careful plait, her face half-hidden in the pillow. One hand was curled around the heavy lace of the pillowcase; the other dangled over the side of the bed. Although it was four o'clock in the afternoon and she was expected downstairs in the blue salon where the family customarily gathered for tea, she showed no sign of going anywhere. She was dressed in a sable-trimmed green silk negligee and a pair of black silk stockings. In the soft honey-colored shimmer of sunlight flooding across the bedroom, she looked very peaceful, very young, the loveliest ornament in the elegant room.

Slowly padding across the thick Aubusson carpet, past her mother's ornate dressing table draped with soft pink tulle and littered with a dozen beautiful silver and crystal perfume bottles, golden monogrammed hairbrushes and hand mirrors and an open jewel box carved from a single chunk of amethyst, the little girl approached the bed and timidly extended a hand.

"Mama," she insisted. Failing to get a response, the child tried again, harder, shaking Varia's shoulder. Still nothing. Bewildered, Anya realized there was something terribly wrong. Mama was always easy to wake up. This time, nothing would budge her.

"*Mama!*"

Thoroughly frightened, the girl tried once again to awaken her sleeping mother. Failing again, she turned and ran from the room, calling for Aunt Ksenia and Grand-père as she raced down the corridor past Louis Quinze tables, giant malachite and ormolu vases as tall as she was and endless rows of paintings, mostly eighteenth-century landscapes.

Footmen in the blue and gold Malyshev livery smiled as the tiny princess rushed past them and flew down the white marble staircase, shouting for her auntie. She was a playful child; they all adored her.

I

"Anyushka," laughed Princess Ksenia as her niece entered the room with a gasp, "whatever is the matter? Where is your Mama?"

"She won't wake up," stammered the child. "Please go see."

Surprised, Ksenia glanced at her sister Lisa, who was reading *Le Figaro*'s account of a party she had given two days earlier.

"She *said* she was tired," shrugged Lisa, more interested in the description of her party than in her sister-in-law. "Why don't you let her be? You know how she's been lately."

"Please," demanded Anya. "Come and try to wake her. She won't move."

Prince Sandro Sviridov, Anya's grandfather, leaned forward in his armchair and stared at the child. "Did your mama move at all?" he asked.

"No," wailed Anya. "Not even when I tried to shake her."

Startled, Princess Ksenia rose from her chair and began racing toward the stairs, her father on her heels, followed by the girl. Lisa continued to devour the paper, smiling in delight as she read that the elegance of her black velvet dinner gown with its black jet spangles was matched only by the slender purity of her white throat, half-hidden under six descending rows of pearls. Ksenia, she noted with annoyance, was "a green-eyed beauty of the purest Slavic type, ablaze with diamonds from the vaults of Boucheron."

"*Zut!*" pouted Lisa as she flung the newspaper over her shoulder, sending a footman scurrying to fetch it. It was the green eyes. They always mentioned the green eyes! Damn.

Upstairs in Princess Varia's bedroom, Sandro was calling to his daughter-in-law, roughly shaking her. It frightened the girl to see her grand-père slap her mother's face several times, trying vainly to rouse her.

"Ksenia," Sandro said, the fear rising in his voice, "call the footman and tell him to send for Dr. Lebrun. Right away. It's grave. She's taken a bottle of sleeping draught."

"We should never have left her alone," murmured the princess as she hurried to get help. "We should have known!"

Sending the coachman to fetch the doctor, Ksenia returned to the room and was shocked to find her niece still there, watching in terror as Sandro tried desperately to find some sign of life in his daughter-in-law, propping her up against the pillows, shaking her, shouting at her while Varia remained a large, disheveled doll, her green negligee in disorder, her neatly plaited blonde hair coming undone.

"Varia," shouted the tall, white-haired prince, "you have a child to think of! You can't do this!"

But she had done it. She had done it as easily as falling asleep, leaving behind the child who was beginning to wail, burying her face in her mother's soft silken negligee, her cheeks stroked by the dark, glossy sable trim.

"Anya," whispered Ksenia, kneeling beside her on the soft, thick carpet with its pattern of interlacing garlands, "your mama can't hear you."

"But she's sleeping. Why can't we wake her?" sobbed the child. "I don't want her to sleep like this."

Raising her eyes, Ksenia saw Sandro shake his head, gently smooth down the rumpled green silk fabric and lay Varia down on the bed with dignity. Her arms folded on her breast, her long blonde hair gently smoothed back, she looked almost peaceful.

"My only son is dead," he said, his voice beginning to crack, "and now his wife. We'll spend our time in cemeteries this year—"

The girl buried her face in her aunt's silken tea gown and sobbed, uncomprehendingly, brokenhearted, alone.

"Anyushka," whispered Ksenia, stroking Anya's head, her tears falling on Anya's tangled blonde hair, "you'll live with me from now on. Mama can't take care of you any longer. She's going to sleep forever."

"But I don't want her to be asleep."

"Yes, but she was so tired, Anyushka. So tired. She had to sleep."

Ksenia had known Varia as well as she knew her own sister and liked her more. But Varia was fragile. When Ksenia's brother had died in a hunting accident last autumn his young widow had died with him in everything but the body. Her body she had kept going until this afternoon, although how she had managed to last as long as she had was a mystery to Ksenia. It had finally taken a bottle of sleeping draught to extinguish the spark that remained.

"Whose little girl will I be?" whispered Anya, looking with huge eyes at her mother.

Ksenia kissed her tenderly on both cheeks. "You'll be mine," she replied softly.

1

Byelaya Beryozka, Russia, 1911

"Anyushka! Where are you? Your uncle wants you to get ready to go to the train station to meet your auntie. You mustn't let her see you looking like a peasant."

Princess Anya looked out from beneath a fluffy bough of lilacs and thought, Oh, Lord! If the housekeeper found her here without her shoes and stockings she'd have to hear another lecture on propriety. Why was it Praskovaya Feodorovna, who wasn't a princess, always had such ironclad views on proper behavior for *her*? It wasn't fair. And yet she was fond of the old woman.

Struggling to slip into her soft leather shoes before she was spotted and reprimanded, Anya found herself overtaken by the housekeeper as she was stuffing her dark stockings into her skirt pocket.

"Prashkosha," she smiled cheerfully, "was that you I heard calling me?"

Facing her was a stately, gray-haired dragon who didn't appear to be amused. Praskovaya Feodorovna's sharp eyes took in the shoes hastily put on Anya's bare feet, and she noted the suppressed giggle in Anya's voice.

"Don't be cheeky with me, young lady," she intoned. "Just look at you. If your auntie ever saw you like this, she'd think I was letting you run wild. Now off with you. I've told Sonia to put out a white skirt and shirt-waist for you. And brush your hair before you and your uncle leave for the railway station!"

"Anything else?" she smiled. There was always something else.

"Yes," replied the housekeeper. "Mind your manners. People who make such fine plans for their presentations ought to know how to behave themselves like ladies."

There was a sly gleam in Prashkosha's eyes that puzzled the girl. And then she gasped. "You know something! What is it? Is it the gown?"

"I know lots of things, *malenkaya*," smiled the housekeeper. "And if

5

you can manage to bring your auntie home from the station some time today, you'll know them too."

"Oh, Prashkosha!" she giggled, flinging her arms around the woman's neck. "You're as bad as I am at heart! It *is* the gown!"

The gown had been the main topic of conversation among the women around the manor house ever since Princess Ksenia's departure several weeks earlier for her father's residence in Paris—where he had been spending the greater part of each year since the death of his son years before. In anticipation of Anya's presentation in St. Petersburg this winter, Princess Ksenia had once said something about a Paris gown to her chambermaid, Daria. Daria had repeated her mistress's words to Anya's maid, Sonia, who in turn had assured Anya that Her Highness was going to order it. And then Princess Ksenia never mentioned it again, confusing everyone.

But Anya knew her aunt well enough to expect something spectacular. Or at least she hoped so.

"Never tell your auntie. Let her have her surprise."

"Of course. But thank you."

Hugging Prashkosha once more, Anya turned and raced across the lush green lawn, thrilling with anticipation. She headed for the white-columned entrance of the butterscotch-and-white Palladian-style manor house. Now she was eager to get ready.

Smiling fondly as she watched the girl, Praskovaya Feodorovna calculated that within the year, little Anya might be engaged to some important gentleman from St. Petersburg and within the next two or three years become a married lady with children. What a thought! Anyushka a mother! She was such a child, as carefree as a playful kitten, ready to create havoc at a moment's notice and then wonder why everyone was so upset.

Well, a sunny nature was a good thing to have, the housekeeper thought. Thank God Anya wasn't like her Aunt Lisa, a tall, dark-haired shrew who was the terror of her household, a virago whose temper tantrums were legendary among her unfortunate staff. Princess Ksenia was a lady. Anya would be the same.

As Anya ran toward the house, carrying an armful of fragrant lilacs wrapped in a linen cloth soaked with water, she thought excitedly about the gown and wondered if she'd ever become an authentic *grande dame* of St. Petersburg. Somehow she doubted it. A proper lady was something she never wanted to become, although, she thought with a mischievous smile, she stood a good chance of becoming a genuinely improper one in the great Sviridov family tradition.

She couldn't wait for that!

◆　◆　◆

At exactly two o'clock, Prince Andrei Malyshev was pacing the foyer, pocket watch in hand, waiting for his niece. A tall man, Andrei was elegant in a navy-blue linen blazer, light-gray tropical wool trousers and a straw boater. At forty, he had scarcely any gray in his black hair and his deep-blue eyes looked out peacefully at the world. He was the owner of five estates from Moscow to the Urals, a mansion on the Moika Canal in St. Petersburg, a residence in Moscow and various properties in Europe. The only thing he missed at present was his beautiful wife, Ksenia, and that would soon be remedied.

"Anyushka!" he called up the staircase. "Are you ready?"

"Coming!" a voice echoed from upstairs.

"We mustn't keep Auntie waiting!"

"I know!"

Yes. But that didn't seem to make any difference, he thought.

Just as Prince Andrei was about to shout once more, his niece came bounding downstairs, her hair neatly brushed, shoes gleaming, looking like an angel in a white linen-and-lace shirtwaist and white skirt.

"Very good," he said. "Now let's go."

Helping Anya into the back seat of his shiny new red Fiat touring car, Andrei climbed into the passenger seat in front and waited patiently while the chauffeur got out to start the motor. Sometimes the engine turned over on the first try, sometimes it took longer. Much to Andrei's surprise, today was one of the good days, and within minutes they were off to the train station, waving goodbyes to the servants who had been standing around taking bets on how long it would take to get the foreign contraption going.

"Hurrah!" shouted two or three peasants as the princely party got off to a noisy departure, the motorcar backfiring a few times as it rolled grandly down the tree-lined *allée*, past tall oak trees and through the ornamental entrance gate bordered by the little red flowers known as firecrackers.

"I can't wait to see Auntie again," declared Anya, curling up on the caramel leather seat. Or her presents, she thought.

◆　◆　◆

On board her private railway coach, joined to the tail end of the Moscow express, Ksenia Alexandrovna was glancing impatiently at the small pink-enamel-and-gold traveling clock on the table of her salon compartment. Twenty minutes to go before reaching the station at the village of Byelaya Beryozka. She hoped Daria, her chambermaid, had packed everything properly. From past experience she knew how Andrei's peasants would fling her baggage into rough carts for the trip to the house. Daria knew it too.

Looking around the pretty compartment decorated in honey-colored paneling inlaid with mother-of-pearl and lighted by French crystal fixtures, Ksenia relaxed in a striped pink-and-cream cushioned armchair and thought of the surprise she was bringing home. It was marvelous.

Ksenia Alexandrovna was tall, black-haired, green-eyed, with enormous, long-lashed eyes and delicate features. Twenty thousand francs worth of gros point de Venise lace ornamented the collar, cuffs and bodice of her cream-colored tailored suit. Three strands of long pearls cascaded over her lacy bosom while another frosting of finer lace, augmented by a ruching of black-and-white-striped silk moiré ribbon, trimmed her broad cream picture hat. And all this elegance would be coated with the grit of Russian backcountry roads within half an hour.

Thinking of the shimmering white evening gown packed securely in one of her trunks, Ksenia smiled with delight at the thought of her niece's presentation ball at the Sviridov Palace this winter. Anya would outshine every other debutante of the season, dazzling society in the setting of white-and-gold marble columns, huge crystal chandeliers and tons of specially cultivated flowers shipped in from the Crimea and the hothouses of Tsarskoye Selo. There would be an orchestra from Paris, an opportunity to wear the family's most lavish jewels—Mama's diamond necklace if Papa was in a good mood, several rows of pearls if he wasn't—and, of course, the opportunity to allow Aunt Ksenia to preen as well. At thirty-seven, she was as elegant as ever.

Anya was lucky she had no sisters, thought Ksenia as she smiled into the mirror. She had, and she had the scars to show for it. On the evening of her presentation ball—and Lisa's—Lisa had burst into her bedroom to demand to wear the elaborate diamond and pearl necklace, bracelet and earrings Prince Sandro, their father, had designated for Ksenia. A resolute *no* had greeted that suggestion. Undeterred, Lisa had made a grab for the necklace, pulling Ksenia off balance. Both sisters had ended up in a free-for-all amid screams of horror from the chambermaids, shouts of "Hooligans!" from Prince Sandro and cries of anguish from Ksenia, whose hand was badly bitten in the fray. Not that Lisa had escaped unscathed. She had black-and-blue marks on her shin that took weeks to disappear. And Princess Ksenia had to grit her teeth and wrap the hand in ice for an hour before the music started. But when she had entered the ballroom that evening, she was wearing diamonds and pearls.

Anya's presentation would be far less dangerous.

◆ ◆ ◆

On the station platform twenty minutes later, Anya and Prince Andrei were staring into the distance, trying to make out any sign of the express from Moscow. Not a puff of smoke in the clear, cloudless blue sky.

"It's late," muttered Andrei, nodding politely to the distressed station-master who was perspiring in his uniform of heavy blue serge and blue cap.

"It's the fault of Moscow. This train is always late."

"Yes," agreed Andrei. "It always is."

Anya smiled at the small blond peasant children clinging to their mothers' calico skirts, looking like chicks around mother hens. The mothers were waiting quietly for the most part, their wide, sunburned faces patient and passive under brightly printed kerchiefs or shawls, their feet bare and calloused or shod in cheap birchbark shoes wrapped in linen. The dark people. The calm and uncomplaining Russia from centuries past. Princess Anya saw one of the women glance timidly at her and Prince Andrei and then just as timidly look away. Peasants didn't impose on *boyars*—aristocrats. Not even with their eyes.

"Look, Uncle!" exclaimed Anya. "I think I can see Auntie's coach."

"Then your eyes are better than mine," he joked. "All I can see is dust."

When the grimy black locomotive came gasping and groaning into the Byelaya Beryozka station, hailed by ragged cheers from the crowd, Anya and her uncle raced impatiently towards the red-and-gold-painted private coach at the end of the train, the one bearing the Sviridov family crest.

Andrei boarded the train with a bound, surprising his wife as she hurried down the corridor. She greeted him with a delighted embrace, nearly losing her hat.

"Andrushka, darling! You look wonderful. Oh, I'm so happy to be home. Anyushka! Come and kiss me. It's so good to see you again."

"Hello, Auntie. How is Grand-père?"

"Grand-père is in splendid shape," she smiled ironically, raising her eyes to meet Andrei's. "In fact, that's our problem." "Papa's bad heart" was Ksenia's code for Sandra's romantic problems. She used it to shield Anya from a rather embarrassing family secret in Paris.

After the men on the platform had stowed Ksenia's twenty leather trunks into rough carts for the trip back to the estate, the prince and princesses were helped into the dust-spattered red Fiat by the bearded station-master while the uniformed chauffeur entertained the onlookers by trying to start the motor.

"Does this new toy work?" Ksenia asked skeptically, trying to look dignified amid catcalls of derision directed at the struggling chauffeur. White-bearded peasants in dirty linen shirts and birchbark shoes hooted with pleasure as the city-bred chauffeur cursed ferociously under his breath.

"Aha!" the chauffeur shouted at last, finally getting the right response. Before the car could change its mind, he was in his seat and rattling down the dusty country road, jolting his elegant passengers every foot of the way.

The Fiat rolled past wheat-colored fields dotted with tall haystacks and peopled with the small, sturdy figures of kerchiefed women hard at work with primitive wooden pitchforks, singing ancient, plaintive country airs their mothers and their mothers' mothers had sung before them. The car churned up impressive clouds of dust, causing the peasants to look up and making the passengers choke.

Anya saw a tiny, barefoot girl of about ten beside a small stream, swaying as she balanced two buckets of water on a wooden yoke, a relic from the days of the Mongols. Beside her waddled a family of downy yellow ducklings, taking their lead from her.

"The harvests are good this year," Andrei remarked to Ksenia. "No trouble so far."

"Good," nodded the princess, clutching her lovely hat as the Fiat took an especially bad bump.

Stubbly fields of gold gave way to green fir trees as the now-grimy motorcar began to approach the outer limits of Byelaya Beryozka estate, ringed by acres of dense green. The chauffeur had to toot his horn several times to clear the road of a flock of sheep, the animals splitting into two shaggy groups as the shepherd tried frantically to divert them to the side of the road before they were run over.

Bowing low before the princely vehicle, the young shepherd wondered where His Highness had ever got such a machine. It was like magic.

By the time Andrei, Ksenia and Anya arrived at the manor house, the ladies were coated with a fine brownish grit, making them look as if they had taken a dust bath. Andrei shook himself like one of his borzois and tapped his boater against the palm of his hand.

"Welcome home, Highness," smiled Praskovaya Feodorovna as she presented the princess with a huge bouquet of wildflowers. She received a genuine smile in return. "We all hope His Highness, Prince Sviridov, is well, please God."

"He is. Thank you, Prashkosha. And he always asks about you."

Wearily climbing the stairs, Ksenia and Anya went straight to the princess's apartment on the second floor, kicked off their shoes and collapsed onto the blue overstuffed silk sofas in her boudoir, relaxing while Prashkosha sent two servants to bring them tea in a Sèvres teapot, served

Russian style in glasses in gilded and enameled holders. Small buttered sandwiches appeared shortly afterward, carried in on a silver tray.

When Daria, Ksenia's maid, appeared with the first of the twenty trunks, the princess told her to get the presents. Anya's heart started to pound.

As Daria went to fetch the treasures, Prince Andrei entered and took a seat at Ksenia's side, delighted to watch the show about to unfold.

"Auntie, are all these for me? There are so many."

"Yes, *malenkaya*, all for you. But only one is the special one. Can you guess?"

Starting with a medium-sized package done up in pink tissue paper and silvery ribbon, the girl opened a box containing a blouse almost entirely covered with delicate Alençon lace. Magnificent.

"Oh, thank you, Auntie."

"Keep going," instructed the princess, opening her newest cigarette case—pink *guilloché* enamel on gold with her monogram in Cyrillic letters studded with diamonds.

"Oh, a silk nightgown! It's too elegant for me. All this lace."

"Nonsense, *milochka*. You'll simply save it for your trousseau. Do you think you won't need these pretty things sooner or later?"

The suspense was killing Anya. She and Ksenia both knew the largest box contained the long-awaited gown, but the girl also knew it was Auntie's surprise, so it wouldn't be fair to spoil the effect by going straight to it. Ksenia Alexandrovna liked the recipients of her largesse to be properly astonished and grateful. And if they had any sense, they were.

"This is too much for me," declared Anya, ripping through more presents, lace-trimmed handkerchiefs, white kid gloves, a parasol.

Pushing aside the tangle of ribbons and wrapping paper, Ksenia handed her niece the last box. "I can't seem to recall what's in here. It is rather large, though. What do you suppose it could be?"

With beating heart, Anya began to rip off the large silk bows and the gleaming pastel paper. If this wasn't the gown, she'd die. Could she have misunderstood? She wondered.

Oh, Lord, prayed Anya as the lid came off, let it be—

As the girl carefully parted the white tissue inside the deep box, she let out a joyous shriek that brought Ksenia's maid running back into the room.

"Oh, Auntie! I can't believe it!"

Rising with the white gown in her arms, she flung herself into Ksenia's embrace. Both of them began to laugh and cry at the same time, Anya being careful not to crush her gown, Ksenia trying hard to keep her cigarette out of the way.

"Stop all this chattering and try it on," commanded the maid. "We've waited long enough, haven't we, Highness? Tell her to put it on."

"All right," giggled Anya. "Come on, you two. You have to help me." Since Andrei was there, Anya retreated behind a silken screen. She quickly wriggled out of her clothes, then held up her arms while Ksenia and Daria slid the presentation gown over her head.

"Careful," warned the princess. "It's very delicate. We'll hang it up as soon as you take it off."

"Oh, how beautiful! How French!" exclaimed Anya as they guided the silky dress over her head and fitted it over her rigid form. She was almost afraid to breathe for fear of harming the dress.

"Put your arms down now, *milochka*, and look in the mirror."

Until that moment, Daria had never believed there could be another lady as beautiful as her gorgeous, black-haired mistress, but looking at Anna Nicolaievna standing there in front of the mirror, her camisole showing above the low-cut bodice of the gown and her hair in a tangle all over her shoulders, the maid knew there was going to be another beauty in St. Petersburg this winter. A blonde one.

"Oh, Daria. Look at her!" cried Ksenia, misting over with tears. "She's too beautiful for words! Andrei, just look."

"She'll be the girl of the season," declared Prince Andrei, feeling like the father of the bride. "We'll be besieged by all sorts of young men in Petersburg this winter. I'll have to become very stern, I fear."

Anya smiled at her uncle and threw her arms around his neck. "I'll always find a way to get around you," she reminded him.

"Yes," agreed Andrei with a rueful smile. "I know you will!"

Princess Ksenia took her husband's hand playfully and whispered, "But she'll have to work a lot harder to get around me!"

Standing in the middle of the pretty, sunlit boudoir, shimmering in white, Anya looked at her reflection in the mirror and marveled, "I can't believe it fits so well, Auntie. How did Monsieur Poiret ever manage that without me?"

"We sent him a wire form from the dressmaker in Petersburg," laughed Ksenia. "It was a big secret."

"Oh, he did it so beautifully. It even has a little train. It actually ripples into a little train." To demonstrate, she spun around to see the full effect.

"It creates a nice touch when one dances," explained Ksenia. "Although one has to take care not to fall down if one treads on it in the middle of a waltz."

"Of course."

"But then, *milochka*, you haven't spent all those afternoons at dancing class for nothing, have you?"

"No, Auntie. I understand how to handle a train." She did, too.

"Good."

Watching Princess Anya, her aunt and uncle knew the winter season was destined to be even more exciting than usual.

That night, after all the excitement of the homecoming was over and Anya had gone to bed to dream about parties and gowns and sparkling jewels, Ksenia lay in bed with Andrei, talking about more serious things. She was deeply disturbed by what she had seen in Paris and even more disturbed by what the future might hold. The problem was her father, Prince Sandro Sviridov—or more precisely, his mistress Zenaida Kashina.

Andrei smiled. "I'm glad the old fellow is so robust. I'm fond of him, you know. It can't be as bad as all that."

Ksenia propped herself up against two thick, lace-trimmed white pillows and sat up, her arms around her knees, looking pensive. "Andrei," she said. "I think Papa has lost his mind. He's talking about marrying Zenaida."

"What?"

"He hinted at it. He said he was tired of being a lonely old widower whose children were too busy to care about him and he was thinking of marrying again."

"But you know your father. He loves to be dramatic. He always claims he's old and lonely. He even says this in the middle of parties where he's surrounded by women who are practically clawing each other to get his attention. I hate to say it, chérie, but Sandro adores self-dramatization. He always has."

"I know that," laughed Ksenia. "That's very true of Papa. But," she added, "he's even talking about children this time, and that's not at all like him. He wants an heir. He never really recovered from Nicki's death." Nicki, Anya's father.

"He's in his sixties. He ought to be content with being a grandfather. There are some things even Sandro ought to accept."

"Darling," sighed Ksenia, "the only grandchildren he has are both girls—Anya and Tasha—and he's on the worst possible terms with Lisa and her husband, so little Tasha hardly counts. He seems to be obsessed with the possibility of the Sviridovs becoming extinct as a family. Zenaida's young. She could give him a son."

Startled by that revelation, Andrei sat up too, staring at his wife. "I can't believe he'd actually marry her. And I truly can't believe she'd take time out from her career to have a child. She's never done that for anyone else. And God knows she's had enough lovers. Besides," he said, "I don't think a ballerina would risk the wear and tear of childbirth. It has to affect the muscles."

"If it came down to a choice between becoming Princess Sviridova and remaining Madame Kashina, you think she'd prefer to keep Sandro as a lover?"

"Yes. He can offer her money—which she loves, clearly—but he'd want to put a golden leash on her and keep her as an ornament, the mother of a little prince. I doubt that would have much appeal for a woman like that. She's tiny and looks fragile enough to shatter, but did you ever look into her eyes? They tell more about Zenaida than all the stories ever created by her admirers."

"When did you spend time looking into her eyes?" teased his wife. "I'm not sure I like the sound of that."

Andrei laughed. "Don't worry," he said. "I have no ambition to be a patron of the arts on *that* scale."

"I'm still concerned about Papa. He keeps an apartment at the Ritz on the Place Vendome in Paris all year round for her to use whenever she's in town."

"That's not dangerous, just expensive," smiled Andrei. "A truly dangerous sign would be the news that Zenaida's canceled her engagements for the next season. That would be the only way of knowing she's willing to go along with Sandro's plans. And I don't think she will."

"Why? Half the women in Europe want to marry Papa. Mothers drag their young daughters across his path in the most disgusting fashion. It's a throwback to the days of ancient Muscovy and the bridal parades before the old tsars."

"And your father revels in it."

Ksenia leaned back against her pillows and sighed. It was true. He did. And he always enjoyed playing off one against the other—Lisa against Ksenia, the girls against his late wife, or Madame Zenaida Kashina against his daughters. She didn't want a scandal to erupt just in time to embarrass Anya during the coming season. That would be unbearable. Princess Ksenia could already picture the scene in the ballroom of the Sviridov Palace this winter, with Zenaida stealing the spotlight from Anya and ruining her presentation.

There was no way she'd allow that to happen—not if she had to stoop to offering the woman a bribe to get her out of St. Petersburg for the week. And she knew Zenaida's character well enough to know she'd succeed if she could meet her price.

"Darling," whispered her husband, "why don't we worry about your family tomorrow. I'd rather concentrate on you tonight."

Ksenia smiled at him. She thought that was a splendid idea.

2

When Anya awakened the next morning, she was still thinking of the beautiful white ball gown lying carefully wrapped in tissue paper and ready for the St. Petersburg season. She was startled to hear a sharp rap at the door, followed by the appearance of Princess Ksenia's maid, Daria, whose glossy black hair was gathered in a neat chignon. She wore a white starched apron over her dark-blue dress. Strange. Why not Sonia, her own maid?

To Anya's surprise, the woman was visibly upset. "Highness," she said in a strange voice, "there's been trouble. Your aunt sent me to tell you to stay close to the house today, just in case there's more. Last night someone broke into the stables and mutilated one of the horses."

"What?" Anya gasped. She couldn't believe what she'd heard.

"The men are prowling the grounds and the forest looking for whoever did it, but, of course, nobody knows who the culprit is. It's sickening."

"Which horse?" Anya demanded, shaken.

"Byeli."

"My God." Uncle's champion trotter. Anya felt her stomach turn.

"The men are ready to kill," said Daria. "He was a fine animal. Please God, they find the maniac."

"And hang him," the young princess said.

In the stable, Prince Andrei was standing outside Byeli's stall, staring at the bloodstained hay, his eyes refusing to look at his dying horse. The vet had just left after mumbling his sympathy, and now Andrei, with his best hunter, Lev Petrovich, standing beside him, had to give Byeli the *coup de grace*. He wouldn't let the vet do it; Byeli was his. It was his responsibility. And it was tearing his heart out.

Lev, a gray-bearded forty-five-year-old peasant who looked at least ten years older, stuffed his hands in the pockets of his baggy trousers under his belted red linen shirt and shifted uneasily from foot to foot. Every moment His Highness hesitated meant another moment of misery for the dying horse.

"Highness," he said finally. "It's time."

"I know."

Taking a Smith & Wesson .38 from his belt, the prince looked down at Byeli, his champion, and was overcome with pity at the sight of his favorite animal. This splendid creature, this sleek, well-tended trotter was reduced to a shuddering wreck, thrashing feebly in his stall, his eyes rolling wildly in his head, half dead from the savage slashes someone had given him a few hours before. Full of pity as he was, Andrei had to force himself to kill the horse. It wasn't lack of resolve; he knew he couldn't let the poor beast linger. It was simply shock before the finality of death. This is ignoble. You don't deserve this, he thought.

Caressing the animal's twitching shoulder, Andrei Nicolaievich whispered softly, "*Proschai, dorogai.*" And then he carefully placed the barrel of the revolver against Byeli's head.

As the muffled sound of the shot echoed through the stable, which had been cleared of other horses for this grim event, Lev Petrovich silently crossed himself and bowed his head. If the man who had mutilated Byeli ever fell into his hands, he promised himself, the fellow would suffer longer than the horse.

It was over; Byeli was at peace. And his owner felt as if he had just lost a son.

"This is a bad sign, Lev," he said at last. "It's how the trouble began in 1905."

"Lev Petrovich nodded grimly. Both men were only too aware of the similarities between what had happened to Byeli and what had happened six years before to dozens of horses and cows belonging to wealthy landowners. And to some of the landowners themselves.

Remembering that horrifying episode, the prince recalled the fears he'd had then for Ksenia and Anya, who were alone at Byelaya Beryozka while he was stranded in Moscow during the general railway strike. He had gone there on business at precisely the time the revolt broke out. The entire city had been in the streets, erecting barricades, challenging the soldiers, parading down Tversky Prospect with red banners. Half the populace was talking hysterically about overthrowing the autocracy; the other half was shuddering behind locked doors, fearful of a mass bloodbath. Andrei was desperate for news of the events out in the province and frantic when he received it.

Agitators from the city had gone to the area, trying to incite a peasant revolt. Suspicious of outsiders, the peasants had shunted them aside at first—until the agitators had begun to talk about Prince Andrei Maly-shev's vast reserves of grain. It had been a bad year for the peasants.

Lev Petrovich, hearing the talk, had gone to the manor house to alert the prince, found that he was in Moscow and decided things were too serious to leave the princess and her small niece alone. With Ksenia Alexandrovna's consent, he and four of his older boys had taken up positions on the ground floor of the house at night, armed with Andrei's rifles. Two nights before the prince's return, a mob had begun milling outside the gates, calling for the landlord.

At that point—here the story always varied, depending on whether Ksenia or Lev was relating it—Ksenia had walked out to confront the people, flanked by Lev and one of his sons. She had shamed them into listening to her instead of to "those strangers who don't even sound like you"—this from Ksenia with her pronounced St. Petersburg accent—and she had succeeded in turning the peasants against the outsiders from Moscow with generous promises of extra grain from her storehouses and protection from the soldiers who were advancing on the area. She hadn't added that the soldiers were coming to protect the landowners from people like themselves.

That last remark had been pure inspiration, since part of the problem was the very lack of soldiers, but Princess Ksenia had been clever enough to play on the eternal fear of the peasant for the army and had used it to rid herself of the agitators.

By threatening the very people who were threatening her, Ksenia Alexandrovna had reinforced her authority. Lev Petrovich had admired her nerve. He'd also personally shot four of the agitators, just to make sure his brother peasants didn't have second thoughts. Before daybreak the agitators were floating in the River Moskva and Ksenia was issuing orders to facilitate a generous distribution of grain.

Now, six years after those troubles, was it all beginning once more?

That afternoon the whole estate was on edge, the peasants whispering of old grudges as they paused, hands clasped on top of primitive wooden pitchforks, or rested beneath the trees to take a moment's relief from the hot sun. It's started again, they said, recalling the old troubles. Peasant corpses had swung from trees all over the province in those days, after the soldiers had put down the rebellion. They remembered that part especially well. They also remembered how Ksenia Alexandrovna had rewarded them for their loyalty with extra supplies of food. They had no interest in rebellion. It only harmed the peasants.

Now Andrei called in some of his friends from a few of the neighboring estates to tell them what had happened to the horse and to warn them to prepare for something similar. Each man was concerned. They all had sharp memories.

"Should we alert Petersburg?" asked Count Boris Scherbatkin, a stocky, nervous man with wavy brown hair and dark eyes that always seemed to be appraising whatever lay in his field of vision. "This could be the beginning of another revolt."

"I don't think it's that serious," replied the prince. "One dead animal does not mean a revolution is on the way. We'd look pretty foolish if we asked for a battalion of soldiers this afternoon."

"But if we hesitate," murmured someone else, "we might not be able to get help in time. They burned my house last time. They damn near burned me with it. These are savages, Andrei Nicolaievich. We have to remember it."

"Times have changed," said the prince. "In 1905 the people were angry about the war and starving because of the poor harvests. My peasants are fat and content today. I can't believe they're preparing an uprising."

"Lev Petrovich," nodded Boris to the hunter who was quietly sitting in the background, "what do you think? You know the people's state of mind."

The gray-bearded peasant shook his head. "I've talked to my brothers. No one has a grudge against His Highness. And everyone remembers the soldiers." He looked at the group of men watching his expression and said, "No peasant did this. I'm certain of it. That horse was our pride. Everyone is against the one who mutilated him."

The men in their white linen jackets listened to the hunter, wondering who the attacker could be if not a peasant.

Andrei spoke up. "I've already issued orders for Lev Petrovich and his sons to patrol the area with rifles. If they spot a stranger, they are to bring him in for questioning. I'd advise the rest of you to do something similar."

Nodding grimly, the visitors said they would.

On the terrace behind the manor house, Anya and Ksenia were sitting under the striped canvas awnings, quietly discussing the horse. Everyone was grieving. Byeli had been the fastest trotter Byelaya Beryozka had ever produced, and his string of victories at the St. Petersburg hippodrome had set records.

"Who hates Uncle enough to do this?" Anya asked.

"If we can find the answer to that question, we'll have the culprit," replied her aunt as she gently straightened the lace collar of Anya's white blouse. "In the meantime, darling, don't go too far from the house without a companion. It wouldn't be wise."

Glancing sideways at Princess Ksenia, Anya was surprised to see how serious she appeared.

"But Auntie," smiled the girl, "I've got two feet, not four."

"All the more reason," replied the princess. She wasn't smiling a bit.

One of Prince Malyshev's neighbors who hadn't been invited to the conference at Byelaya Beryozka had heard about the mutilation of the horse and was worried about his own property. He was a lot less popular than Andrei Nicolaievich. And having risen from field laborer to landlord on the strength of his own backbreaking, relentless effort, he mistrusted the peasants, knowing they resented his success and wished him all manner of misfortune.

Well, let them be jealous, thought Ivan Ivanov. And if they dared to touch any of his animals, it would be the end of them. He hadn't spent most of his life working like a madman to accumulate the money to buy land just so some lazy loafer who never did more than the minimum could take what belonged to him. He'd kill before he gave up so much as a stray pig.

Clad in a typical linen shirt with a rough cord at his waist, his beard almost white despite the fact that he was only fifty, his boots scuffed and spattered with manure and bits of hay, Ivanov looked like an ordinary peasant; it was the eyes that gave him away. Those deep-set, piercing blue eyes could look straight through an opponent, giving Ivanov a ruthless aura, as if murder itself wouldn't be too remote for him to contemplate. He wasn't a man who made friends easily. He lacked a good nature. He knew it and didn't give a damn.

The one soft spot he had was for his wife, Maria Andreevna, a devoted companion who had entered their marriage with a small tin box full of silver rubles, a nice little flock of chickens, two decent pigs and two featherbeds. A local girl, she had looked him over when he'd arrived in the area from Kazan province, bought a farmstead and let it be known that all he needed was a wife. A small, buxom blonde with a turned-up nose and glowing pink cheeks, she'd had a strong desire to escape from her parents. Ivanov had admired her straightforward approach to marriage as well as her ability to organize his house into something clean, cozy and comfortable. It had been a good marriage.

Except for the child it produced, a miserable misfit of a son, Oleg, unfortunately the only one of their three children to survive infancy. Oleg was a terrible disappointment. It was as though, with all of his mother's splendid qualities and his father's tough determination, he was a throwback to some earlier, fuzzy-minded ancestor, a boy who was given to daydreaming about impractical, bizarre theories, a born loser. In Ivanov's more susceptible moments—not that there were many—he sometimes thought that it was because the child had been on its way before the wedding and this was their punishment.

Damned young wastrel, he thought, spotting his son crossing the fields on horseback, returning from a ride.

Urging his horse over the wooden fence separating the field from the court-yard, young Oleg cleared it easily, cantered over to the wooden hitching post in front of the long, rambling front porch and dismounted, giving his parent a curt greeting before he ducked into the house, eager to read the letter he had just received from a friend of his in Moscow, Pavel Scriabin.

Heading for his room, with its icons in the corner just over a stack of his books and its neat, rolltop desk near the window, Oleg stretched out on his bed and slit open the envelope, glad to be in touch with Pavel once more. He was bored and restless here in the backwoods; Pavel always had something exciting in mind.

In fact, he thought, it was because of a lot of commotion that he had crossed paths with Scriabin in the first place. And then two years in remote Tobolsk province had cemented the friendship and had introduced Oleg Ivanov to a group of radicals steeped in Marxist theory and willing to undertake class warfare with the sworn purpose of overthrowing the Russian autocracy. He had been thrilled to be included in their plans. But now it all seemed like a happy dream.

Except for what he had carried out this morning—that was no dream. That was delightful revenge on the man who had sent him to faraway Tobolsk in the first place—Prince Andrei Nicolaievich Malyshev.

And before the prince had finished lamenting the death of that nag, His Highness himself would be the object of lamentations by his beautiful, overdressed, arrogant and insufferable women. Oleg had sworn it; he would carry out his mission and use it to impress Pavel Scriabin and his group when he joined them in Moscow.

Reflecting on those brief Siberian summers and the endless winter nights, Oleg decided that his exile had actually served a purpose. A punishment without prison, internal exile transported a man—or woman—far beyond the borders of his place of origin, banished for a predetermined length of time. Free to make his own living arrangements, Oleg had boarded with a peasant couple in Tobolsk. He'd had plenty of time to hunt and fish—and attend political sessions presided over by Pavel Scriabin and his intimidating mistress, Katia Petrovna, a red-haired shrew who could never remember his name. Oleg had found her less than appealing; but he had admired Pavel, a thin, wiry intellectual from Kazan with sharp gray eyes and a brisk, efficient manner. His long nose gave him a disdainful look, especially whenever he encountered portraits of the tsar, which he secretly used for target practice in the woods.

Thinking about the nag, Oleg decided it really wasn't enough of a revolutionary act. No. But striking down the biggest landlord in the province would be grandiose enough to impress anyone, and that was what he intended to do.

At heart, Oleg wanted desperately to impress someone, especially the girls. But he never succeeded, mostly because of his bad temper. Never taking rejection lightly, he frightened girls with displays of fury which only led to further rejection and a general feeling of frustration. As a genuine, dedicated revolutionary who had shed blood for the cause, he had vague hopes of emulating Pavel Scriabin and attracting admirers like Katia, who, although she was hard to take, was undeniably lovely to look at. He adored the pretty ones. But once they knew him, they shunned him like death.

To Oleg's mother, a practical woman endowed with common sense, her son's troubles had been caused by those Moscow friends of his who had filled his head with foolish notions of liberty and justice for all. They had talked her boy into expressing his solidarity with the peasants—as if he wasn't one himself—and had got him to cause a disturbance on the largest estate in the area, haranguing the laborers about social justice until, bewildered, the peasants had called the constable and turned him in. And while Oleg was being treated with the severity due an insurrectionist, his fine Moscow friends had run for the nearest train station, leaving him in the lurch. Holy Mother, the boy could be stupid.

To his father, the episode had been proof there was something wrong with the boy, some terrible mental quirk that rendered his son unfit to inherit what he'd worked all his life to build. Perhaps it had been lurking there in the back of Oleg's brain all the while he was growing up, ready to flower in the dark recesses of Moscow University like some poisonous weed. Books only confused a man, Ivan always maintained. Oleg was evidence of that. Worse than that, they'd made him stupid!

"Well," demanded Ivanov senior as he entered the dining room and found his wife and son in deep discussion near the gleaming brass samovar, "have you decided what you're going to do with the rest of your life? You have to do something."

"Leave the boy alone. Let him take his time," protested Ivanov's wife. "He just came home to us. Why can't you let him be?"

"Because he's had two years to decide what to do with himself. That's plenty of time if you ask me."

Seating himself at the head of the table, the father took the small copper kettle from atop the samovar, poured a glass of tea and looked sternly at his son.

"Well," he persisted, "give me some kind of answer. Don't I deserve that much from you?"

"I told you, Father, I don't know what I want to do."

"Well, why the hell don't you know? By God, at your age I knew what I wanted and I went out and got it."

"Nobody questions your success, Father. You worked for it. You deserve everything you have."

"Yes, damned right I do. Everything. Every cow, horse, pig, building and pile of shit on this land belongs to me. Not to some aristocrat from Petersburg who plays at being a farmer, or to some half-destitute member of the gentry who hasn't got the brains to make a success of an inheritance, but to me."

"We all know how hard you worked, Father. Nobody questions it."

"No, Oleg. That's a lot of shit. You don't know the half of it. You don't know what it means to be born a serf, a thing a nobleman can sell. I do. I'll never forget it."

"Why do you have to shout at the boy? He's not arguing," Maria said.

"Because our son needs somebody to remind him of what he comes from. And where he ought to go."

Oleg glanced at his mother in the light of the hanging gas lamp. She shrugged almost imperceptibly, her round, lined peasant face patient underneath her calico kerchief, a reminder of her years in the fields.

"Your father and I sent you to the university because you were a boy who liked books. We were proud of you for that. But then you got into trouble at Prince Malyshev's estate. And my boy, you don't know how that foolishness broke my heart. For my sake you must make up for that stupidity. It's time you put your life in order, Oleg. High time."

Young Oleg sullenly lowered his head and looked into his half-finished glass of tea.

"I'm not meant to be a farmer," he muttered, shading his eyes. "That much I know."

"All right," nodded the old man. "I've always known it, too. It tears the heart out of me to think everything I've worked for all these years means nothing to my only son, but that's the way it is. I'm a realistic man. Now just what the hell are you going to do with yourself?"

The son ran his fingers through his thick blond hair and kept his eyes on the embroidered tablecloth, his mother's work.

"I'm going to dedicate my life to the Revolution," he mumbled, glad to get it out in the open but rather embarrassed to sound so pompous.

"Shit," retorted old Ivanov, "you're a fool if you really believe any of that. And you must think I'm a bigger one to tell me this."

"Father! It's the truth."

"That's a fairy tale. This is the revolution—the Ivanovs living in the house that once belonged to Count Denisov. That's something worthwhile, not some stupid fantasy."

"It's not a fantasy to want to overthrow the tsar's government. Everyone wants it."

"Who wants it? Not me."

"People want it. People who are clever and educated and progressive. People I met in Siberia—lawyers, teachers, engineers. All kinds of people."

"If they were so clever, what were they doing in Siberia? Something's not right with that, can't you see?"

"Something's not right with our Russia if a man can be exiled for speaking the truth before a group of farm workers," replied Oleg, the anger rising in his voice. "I was shipped to the icebox just for telling Prince Malyshev's peasants not to pay his price for grain."

"Yes, you fool! And it was the peasants themselves who called the *stanovoiy* because you had no reason to create trouble for them. Malyshev has held his prices so low it's almost a joke. Do you think they want to change that? Of course not. I exploit my peasants, Oleg, because I need every kopek I can get. Prince Malyshev doesn't have to survive on his income from Byelaya Beryozka because he owns four other estates, but I have to live on what I can wring out of this place. If you want to preach against exploitation, look a little closer to home. Exploitation is what supports you, my boy. And don't ever forget it!"

"You have to break away from these scoundrels who want to cause you trouble, Oleg," Madame Ivanova said quietly. "They've already made you waste two years of your life—and for what? Things are improving for us, not getting worse. And," she added softly but firmly, "never think of Prince Malyshev as your enemy. It's not so, in spite of everything."

"I can't see any kind of improvement when a man can be exiled for speaking his mind."

"You're damn lucky you didn't do it here," retorted his father. "By the time I got through with a fool like you, there wouldn't have been anything for the *stanovoiy* to arrest. You'd have been dead."

"But don't you see, they've got you thinking the way they want you to think. You'd side with them against your own kind."

"Listen, Oleg, and get this straight. I'm on the side of whoever's in a position to help me. And I know damned well that man's not going to be some soft-headed fool who wants to start a revolution in his own backyard. It's time you learned this too."

Ivan Ivanov glared at his son, rose from the table and gestured with a broad sweep of his arm, taking in the sturdy, carved dining-room furniture, the heavy cabinets, the knicknacks, the new gas lamps and other signs of his affluence.

"Your stupid revolution will never come to life, Oleg, not because of the tsar or the aristocracy or the soldiers, but because of men like me. Yes, that's right," he nodded with fierce emphasis. "Because of men like me."

"Father—"

"Don't interrupt me. I'm not through," he ordered.

Lowering his head, Oleg stared sullenly at the floor.

"I've profited by the government's policy of making land available at cheap rates. I'm content with the policy. Do you think I want to change it?"

"But there are millions of peasants who have to leave the land to work in the cities because they can't live in the countryside any longer. Millions starve to death...."

"Oh, for God's sake, Oleg, what't the matter with you? You tell me where on earth smart people don't succeed and stupid ones do? It's the way things are in every land. Maybe God loves fools but nobody else does."

"I can't make you understand anything, can I?"

"I think you're the one who needs to understand," replied Ivanov senior as he turned to leave the room. "It makes me sick to think I fathered an idiot."

Madame Ivanova looked at her son and said nothing for a minute. She studied him carefully, running her eyes over his thick, straight blond hair, hanging in an untidy fringe over his forehead, and at his beardless, round young face, not yet lined by hard work or weathered by the elements. She shook her head.

"What, Mama?" he asked.

"Life could be so easy for you if only you didn't want to spoil it for yourself. Yes, you do, Oleg. You spoil it. Can't you see how stupid that is?"

The boy poured himself another glass of tea and drank it peasant-fashion, with a lump of sugar between his teeth.

"I want to be very successful," he muttered.

"You can't win by opposing the ones in power. You have to make use of them like your father knows how to do. He lets them help him. Then he helps them. Everyone's happy that way."

"What about the ones who don't know how to do that, and who just die by the wayside?"

Maria Andreevna looked pained. Her boy was thick. No doubt about it.

"Oleg," she said patiently, "life is not equal. If it were equal, we'd all be in the gutter. That's where equality gets you. And nobody wants to be equal with the man in the gutter. Except maybe some young fool who's never been there." Maria Andreevna looked significantly at her son, then rose to leave the room. "Think about it," she said.

Alone in the dining room, Oleg poured himself a shot of vodka from the collection of homemade liquors on the sideboard and thought of the man he hated most, a man who surely didn't believe in any sort of equality.

Andrei Malyshev, he thought bitterly. There had been bad blood between the Ivanovs and the Malyshevs for as long as he could remember, not that it was open and honest. No. It was more of an instinct than anything else, a feeling that the Malyshevs were off limits for the likes of them. Even as a child, Oleg had been aware of it. It had been brought to his attention in a most painful way during a village fair when he was scarcely more than a baby, a playful five-year-old who didn't know his place.

Strolling with his mother among the colorful stalls, he had spotted a tall, beautiful, green-eyed lady walking with a tall man and a small blonde girl. Attracted by the pretty lady and her child, he'd pulled away from his mother and run to them, impulsively offering the little girl a *pyraniki*, the gingerbread creation customary on all festive occasions. Suddenly a strong hand had caught him by the shoulder and pushed him away. Prince Malyshev had prevented him from making a present to the women.

He could still remember the feel of that hand. Its force would have knocked him to the ground if his mother hadn't come rushing forward to snatch him back and flush bright red as she apologized for her son's behavior.

"*Nichevo*," the princess had smiled, a little puzzled by her husband's anger. But Oleg's mother had continued to blush as she dragged him off, telling him fiercely never to approach the Malyshevs again.

"But why, Matushka?" he'd wailed, hurt and resentful.

"Because they're *boyars*," she'd replied angrily. "And nothing good ever comes from mixing with them. Always remember that. Your father knows it."

"But the lady and the little girl were so nice."

"It doesn't matter. I want you to have nothing to do with them. Ever."

So after that, Oleg had disliked all *boyars*, just as his father did. But he always remembered his longing to be friends with that beautiful lady and the child with her.

And then his first revolutionary act had been directed against Prince Malyshev, a disaster that became all the more embarrassing when his mother went to plead with the prince for mercy.

"You ought to keep your son on a leash," the prince had hissed in exasperation as Maria Andreevna stood before him, tears in her eyes, begging for his pardon. "It's beyond my comprehension how he could do this to me."

As an act of kindness to the poor, stricken mother, Prince Malyshev had put aside his intention to sentence her son to five years in a penal colony and had commuted the sentence to a mere two years in Tobolsk province, Siberia. A slap on the wrist—no chains, no prison, merely a great distance between himself and Oleg. As the local magistrate he could not have done less without losing the respect of the countryside.

"Damn him," muttered Oleg to himself as he gulped down a shot of vodka. Reaching into his pocket, he touched the letter he had just received from the Siberian acquaintances who were trying to organize a revolutionary cell in Moscow, with the sworn purpose of overthrowing the established order represented by both his own father and Prince Malyshev.

His father! What a joke. A former serf, he had the social conscience of a bandit. All he cared for was getting his. Let the rest of the world go hang.

To hell with them both.

But he wasn't done with Malyshev. The only comfort he could derive from his visit was the chance it had given him to strike out against his old enemy and to inflict a painful loss on his famous stud farm. That had been a pleasure.

Now after tasting blood, Oleg was hungry for more. What he had done to the horse was nothing compared with what was to come.

After several days of bickering with his family and writing long, complaining letters to his Siberian associates, Oleg finalized his plan. He would join Pavel Scriabin in Moscow after pulling off a revolutionary coup at Byelaya Beryozka that would be sensational enough to reach the Moscow newspapers and establish his reputation as a serious revolutionary. He would assassinate Andrei Nicolaievich Malyshev, local landlord, magistrate and bloodsucker.

"Be careful if you ride out alone," warned his father as Oleg saddled up and prepared to set forth in search of his victim. "There's been trouble in the neighborhood and the people are jumpy. In times like these, they'll shoot at anything, so don't surprise any of our friends."

"What kind of trouble?" asked Oleg, slyly feigning innocence.

"There's a maniac on the loose in the district. He's slashed one of Prince Malyshev's best trotters in his stable, and everybody's waiting for him to try something else."

"Oh? And what are they going to do if they catch him?"

"Shoot the bastard. What else?" shrugged Ivanov senior.

Oleg smiled oddly, then dug his heels into his horse's side and cantered off.

3

At Byelaya Beryozka, guards had been posted to head off any further intrusions but so far, nothing peculiar had occurred. Yet each man in the village as well as each one on the estate went about his business with some sort of weapon. Nobody wished to be the horse slasher's first human victim. It was an uneasy time; everyone felt the strain.

To try to help her husband recover from the loss he had suffered, Princess Ksenia decided to organize a house party and invited some of their more intrepid friends to join them in a hunt for the slasher. If nothing else, it might strike fear into the lunatic.

One of the guests who made the trip to the country was a young American, Adam Lowell, third secretary of the United States Embassy in St. Petersburg and a friend of Princess Ksenia's since the day in Paris several years before when he had fished ten-year-old Princess Anya out of the boat basin in the Luxembourg Gardens and returned her, dripping with fury, to her aunt. That had led to an invitation to the next party Prince Sandro gave, which led in turn to the American community's favorable assessment of the young man's potential as diplomatic material. Even the Americans had heard of Sandro's wealth.

As Adam Lowell was on his way to Byelaya Beryozka from St. Petersburg, he had plenty of time to reflect on what had happened between that meeting in the Luxembourg Gardens and the present. For one thing, he had been married and widowed, and he was still recovering from the loss.

At thirty, Adam Michael Lowell was enjoying a modestly successful career in the foreign service that had begun with a stint in Cuba after that country had been liberated from Spain, continued with an assignment to the Philippines, then Paris, and now St. Petersburg. The only important part of his life apart from his work had been his wife, Catherine, and he

27

had lost her to an attack of influenza while she was home in Pittsfield, Massachusetts, on vacation the year before.

Since then, his life had been a monochromatic wilderness, spent in St. Petersburg's elegant palaces and in his rather drab office at the embassy. The newest arrival there, William S. Whitmore, was probably the only other human being who ever managed to breach the wall Adam had built around himself. Unfortunately, it was the sort of relationship that was likely to lead to bloodletting, since Billy was his much-loathed younger half brother, a thorn in Adam's side for years and a perpetual problem for his family.

Charming, lazy and cheerful, Billy had an inborn aversion to hard work, which sometimes led him to attempt shortcuts. Just before Adam had departed for Byelaya Beryozka, he'd threatened to throw his sibling down a flight of stairs for claiming credit—for the third time—for a report Adam himself had prepared!

And if he lived to be ninety, Adam would never forgive Billy for having got thrown out of his second university. The day Billy had arrived home in Boston to announce the news and plead for forgiveness, their mother had suffered a massive heart attack and died. The news had arrived while Adam was in Paris, and nothing would persuade him that his brother hadn't been the direct cause of her death.

Although Billy professed to be quite fond of Adam, the feeling was not returned. In fact, Adam was trying everything he could to put the little poacher in his place. And that place was far from St. Petersburg. Having lost the only person he truly cared for, Adam felt oddly lost himself, like a living ghost. Princess Anya was to be a revelation.

As Adam and a party of visiting Muscovites came clattering down the tree-lined *allée* leading to the stately manor house surrounded by its profusion of flower beds, trees and statuary, the young American waved to the familiar figures at the entrance, Andrei and beautiful Ksenia who had come outside to greet their guests. And then he stared at the tall blonde young lady standing next to the princess. At first he didn't recognize her.

"Anya," he murmured, half-hesitating, staring as the carriage brought his party closer. Anya? My God, she was almost grown. That lovely girl dressed in white linen and lace was little Anya! That stunning blonde beauty with the magnificent cascade of wavy hair was the child he had fished out of the Luxembourg pond not too many years ago. After a year of seeing the world through a bleak gray haze, Adam felt as if he had just discovered color.

Anya stood beside her aunt, waving gaily to the guests as she watched the carriage approach the house. Recognizing Mr. Lowell, she gave a gasp of delight. It had been three years since she had seen him. Elegant in his navy linen blazer and straw boater, he somehow appeared to be a different person from the gentleman she remembered.

Or perhaps she was the one who had changed, she thought with a suppressed giggle. He no longer looked like an older person to her.

In fact, she thought, waving with what Ksenia noted as extreme animation, he looked just right.

As the party alighted on the steps of the manor house, Prince and Princess Malyshev greeted them with kisses on both cheeks. Ksenia kept her eye on her niece as she came face to face with Mr. Lowell, watching with amusement as the young diplomat gently kissed the girl and stood back a little to look at her.

"Welcome to Byelaya Beryozka, Adam Mikhailovich," smiled the young princess, lowering her long lashes ever so sweetly. "It's wonderful to see you again." And then she looked up playfully, directly into his liquid dark eyes. Anya was an adorable little flirt.

That evening, as the Malyshevs and their guests sat on the terrace behind the manor house, making plans for the next day's hunt, Adam and Princess Anya were deep in discussion of his Paris days, her elaborate plans for the presentation ball this winter, Uncle's new motorcar—all sorts of nonsense that was delightful to hear from a pretty girl on a lazy summer evening.

That night in his comfortable featherbed, listening to the sounds of the Russian countryside, Adam felt both restless and happy at the same time.

The next day, when Anya and Princess Ksenia were having their morning cup of tea in the princess's sitting room, the girl found herself thinking that Adam Mikhailovich's presence would be a definite asset to her ball this winter.

As Ksenia proposed various activities for their guests, wondering about the marksmanship of the Muscovites and about what would be appropriate for tomorrow's luncheon, Anya sat dreamily staring out the window overlooking the garden. She watched Mr. Lowell as he made his way down the sweeping terraces to the riverbank for an early-morning walk.

"Auntie," she said suddenly, "do you think we could invite Adam Mikhailovich to my presentation ball this winter?"

Startled, Ksenia paused and looked oddly at her young niece. She had just been talking about meat patties. Obviously Anya's mind was on something quite different. "Well, I suppose so. Diplomats are always useful for rounding out a ballroom. And some of them can actually dance. Yes. Why not? That would be a splendid idea."

"Oh, thank you, Auntie," smiled her niece. "It's going to be grand."

Ksenia had no doubt about that and thought with a twinge of regret that the girl was growing up. Despite the plans for the presentation and all the chatter, the princess had never really *felt* the excitement until last evening when she'd noted that Adam Mikhailovich could not take his eyes off Anyushka. And he was a dignified person of sound mind.

Tall, handsome, dark-haired, dark-eyed Mr. Lowell had looked at her young niece as if Anya were a grown-up! It made the princess think she knew what her mother must have gone through twenty years earlier at the time of *her* presentation. And now she was about to play that role. Oh, Lord!

After two days of beating the bushes in search of any sort of game, Count Boris Scherbatkin had invited Prince and Princess Malyshev and their guests, the American and two gentlemen from Moscow, to his estate to shoot quail. Not sighting the slasher had disappointed Boris, and he intended to take out his frustrations on the small birds of the region.

"Anyushka," said Adam as he saw her that morning in the yellow salon on the first floor, "aren't you joining us?"

She shook her head and looked stubborn. "No," she replied. "I can't abide Irina Scherbatkina. And I know if I go there, I'll have to be polite and listen to her chatter on and on about her fiancé from Moscow. He's even more boring than she is. They're truly a well-matched couple."

The young man laughed, then said, "Well, why don't you come along and keep me company and save me from listening to Irina?"

"I would like to," she admitted. "But it won't work out that way. "I'll be forced to stick close to Auntie and Countess Scherbatkina and Irina because the men all think there'll be an accident if they can't keep an eye on us in a group. And Count Scherbatkin will want to tell you all his stories from the time he was an officer in the Guards during the Japanese war. I'd rather stay here."

"I'd much rather listen to your stories," he smiled, looking straight into her light eyes, making Anyushka's heart skip a beat as she looked back, almost about to change her mind.

"Well then," replied the girl, glancing at him flirtatiously from beneath her long, dark, feathery lashes, "you must make sure we sit together at tea this afternoon when you return."

"I will," he promised.

Princess Ksenia and Prince Andrei gave orders to the chauffeur to bring round the motorcar for their party while Anya watched from the front steps with Praskovaya Feodorovna to wave them off. The prince, princess, Mr. Lowell and the wife of one of the Moscow gentlemen got into the Fiat. The two Muscovites and two servants set out on horseback behind them.

"Now behave yourself while we're gone, Anyushka," called the princess as the party started off down the tree-lined drive, "and don't wander off."

"Yes, Auntie," she smiled obediently. "I don't want to be mistaken for a colt!"

"Anyushka!"

But before Princess Ksenia could add anything, the motorcar was already halfway through the entrance gate and on its way out to the road.

Watching Anya wave after the departing hunting expedition, the housekeeper sternly brought it to her attention that nice gentlemen didn't like to see young ladies being cheeky with their elders.

"Oh, Prashkosha!" she laughed, still looking towards the gate, "Auntie has a sense of humor. And so do the gentlemen."

Smiling grimly, the housekeeper informed her that what gentlemen do and what they think were often two entirely different matters, and she ought to learn that now before it could do her any harm. Especially with foreign gentlemen, she added darkly.

"You make life sound so gloomy," sighed the young princess as she disappeared inside. "It's not meant to be that way, I'm sure."

Since nobody had reported any further crimes by the horse slasher, the girl decided to spend the morning searching for mushrooms in spite of all the carrying on. The cook had been complaining about not having enough for the prince's favorite sauces, and Anya wanted to ensure the household's supply of this important tidbit. Besides, it was fun.

Selecting a fair-sized basket, she started looking for a companion. Unfortunately, the kitchen help were in the process of polishing the silver, and Daria, Princess Ksenia's maid, was lying down with a headache. Since the best help was unavailable, Anya decided to look for a partner wherever she could find one. She knew there had to be someone willing, since Uncle's peasants excelled at finding edibles and avoiding strenuous labor. But who?

Walking through the French doors out onto the terrace, Anya spotted Petya, the twelve-year-old son of Lev Petrovich, who was amusing himself with a dangerous-looking knife, throwing it quite accurately against the painted wooden pillars of the rear facade.

"Stop that," she ordered, surprising him. "If Praskovaya Feodorovna sees you doing that, she'll whip you for it. The men just repainted these.

"Oh, please don't tell," begged the youngster, a handsome little blond fellow with gray-green eyes like a cat's. "I'm already in enough trouble with her. Please don't tell her or Papa. I'll do anything for you."

Pulling the knife out of the pillar, Anya handed it back to him and smiled. "How good are you with that?"

"I don't miss," he replied. "You saw me hit my target every time."

Looking at the youngster, Anya had an idea. Petya was the perfect companion. He knew the estate and the surrounding grounds like a creature of the forest, and he knew how to use that sharp knife. Although a boy, he was too young for anyone to raise objections about the lack of a chaperone. Besides, boys were always better than girls for an excursion like this. They knew all the shortcuts.

"Do you know where there are any good mushrooms?" asked Anya.

"Of course," he nodded. "Mama and I go to hunt for them all the time."

"I would like to find some today."

"Then I'll go with you," he said quickly, eager to redeem himself for putting the nicks in the pillars. "Mama taught me how to identify more than twenty different kinds. The old woman who picks the herbs to make magic showed her where the best ones are."

"The witch, Matryona Petrovna?"

"Don't say it aloud!" he gasped. "She can hear you."

All the peasants believed in strange folk magic, and sometimes these beliefs were strong enough to demand respect from even those who had doubts, so Anya said nothing, not wishing to upset Petya—or to draw down any unnecessary trouble upon herself. Nobody bothered the witch— not if they had any sense. She hoped she had not already caused some bad luck.

Not far from where Anya and Petya had decided to go exploring, Lev Petrovich was stalking something else. Despite the fact that the slasher hadn't returned to strike again, there was still no guarantee that he wouldn't. And Lev was almost counting on it.

With memories of 1905 in mind, the stocky, gray-haired peasant had repeatedly canvassed the locals, trying to determine whether or not there was something in the air, some current of restlessness he ought to be aware of. There was not. Everyone was just as worried as he was, and nobody rejoiced over Andrei Nicolaievich's loss—a good sign.

Suddenly Lev hesitated, sniffing the air like a hound on the scent of a rabbit. There was a peculiar odor close by, tobacco, but unlike any used by anyone in the area. Calculating that he could summon half a dozen armed men within five minutes, the peasant slipped quietly away to gather reinforcements and return to capture whoever was lurking close by, no matter how many culprits there happened to be. Andrei Nicolaievich and his guests were far away, he thought in consternation. They would have been useful right now.

At precisely the time Lev Petrovich was trying to gather his men, Oleg Ivanov was returning to the place where he had tethered his mount, not far from a clump of five ancient birches. Ivanov was about to give up his hunt for Prince Andrei; he hadn't been able to approach the grounds of the manor house or even the outbuildings. After smoking one of his favorite English-tobacco cigarettes, he was on the verge of leaving the area when he heard voices coming toward him. He hid behind a gigantic pine tree to observe the newcomers, thinking they might prove dangerous. Instead, he found something that delighted him.

It was a young girl, a beautiful girl with long, thick blonde hair caught back in a fluffy white bow, dressed very attractively in a white lacy blouse and white skirt. She was accompanied by a boy, obviously a peasant. She herself was no peasant. This was a lady, Oleg thought in amusement. And either a very brave one or a very foolish one, since the whole region was wandering around armed to the teeth and ready to shoot the very man who was now looking at her. The idea made him proud.

But who was she? he wondered, devouring her with his eyes. And who would be idiotic enough to allow this beauty to wander around while the famous horse slasher was on the loose? Didn't they care about her?

"You see," declared Petya proudly, "look at all these huge mushrooms. Didn't I tell you I knew about them?"

"This is wonderful. Oh, we'll get lots of them right here."

"There are even more farther on. You try under those birch trees while I pick these."

Anya hesitated. They really had come a little too far, and she felt ashamed of herself for blatantly disobeying Ksenia Alexandrovna in this fashion. Auntie would be furious and wouldn't hesitate to punish her for this transgression. She might even banish her to her room for the rest of Mr. Lowell's visit! That thought filled her with such apprehension that the girl said nervously to Petya, "Let's hurry, shall we, so we can get home quickly? And how on earth are you going to carry the mushrooms you pick?"

"I'll take the basket. You can make a pouch out of your skirt like Mama does. It's easy."

"All right," shrugged Anya. "Here." But she felt oddly apprehensive.

As the youngster headed off in the opposite direction and then vanished from sight, Oleg stepped out from his hiding place and began to creep up on the girl as she bent over a clump of tender chanterelles.

The boots were the first thing Anya noticed and at the sight, she started in shock. She became even more alarmed as she rose to her full height, face to face with a beardless young blond man in a linen shirt.

"Who are you?" she demanded, taking a few steps back as he advanced on her, staring at her with a lupine intensity that frightened her.

She was the most beautiful girl he had ever seen. Even in Moscow he had never seen anyone like this; she was exquisite. Suddenly it occurred to him who she was, and the discovery jolted him.

"You're Prince Malyshev's niece!" he exclaimed, staring.

"Yes. Who are you?" demanded Anya, quite bewildered.

Oleg thought back to the day years ago when he had been a child trying to give a girl a present at that village fair. And her powerful uncle had come between them. He couldn't do that now. No one could.

"You really are beautiful," he murmured, reaching out to stroke her hair, pulling away the white silk bow as Anya protested, angrily hitting his hand. Her defiance angered him, making him want to hurt her.

"Don't do that," he warned her. "No woman hits me." She reminded him of one of his favorite prostitutes.

Looking the young man in the eye, Anya watched him uneasily, waiting for him to make the next move, horrified to be so unprotected.

"I asked you who you were," she said, gently edging away from him, trying not to look frightened, although she knew there was something very wrong with him, something in his eyes so far from normal it chilled her. Those narrow, slanting blue eyes were like small icy slits.

"Oleg Ivanov," he replied, advancing on her. "I think you and I are going to get to know each other a lot better."

And then he lunged.

"Petya! Help me!" she screamed, her voice shrill with terror.

Oleg stifled the girls's screams with one hand as he dragged her to the ground, jumping on top of her to pin her down while starting to rip off her skirt and petticoats.

Anya responded by kicking him in the stomach, but this only enraged him further. He hit her savagely as she thrashed under him. The struggle excited him; he enjoyed it when they fought back, and this one had a lot of fight in her.

She was better than his favorite prostitute.

"Petya!" Her heart felt as if it would burst with racing, desperate fear.

Oleg caught hold of the girl by her long hair, now a tangled mass of gold among the pine needles, and he yanked her so hard she yelped in pain. "Listen, *barinia*," he panted, struggling with the bursting buttons of his fly, "if you say another word, I'll kill you." He was going to have this little aristocratic bitch if it was the last thing he did.

At that moment Petya came running into the clearing, alerted by Anya's cries. Seeing Oleg on top of her, he pulled the knife from his basket and gripped it as though he intended to use it.

"Get away from Anna Nicolaievna or I'll kill you," ordered the boy, brandishing the weapon. "I mean it," he said as Anya broke free.

"What the hell?"

"You heard me. Let her go!"

Oleg rose unsteadily and advanced on the boy as Anya scrambled to her feet, white-faced and shaken, clutching at her torn clothing.

"Petya! Be careful!" Her first thought was of Petya's safety.

"Give me that knife," commanded Oleg, holding out his hand as he walked toward Petya.

The child backed up nervously as the man came nearer; Petya was frightened but did not want to show it.

"Petya! Run!"

"Get back or I'll use it," shouted the boy, twelve years old and feeling older. Sweat began to bead on his forehead as he stared into the cold, cruel, light-blue eyes of the man only a few feet away.

"Give me the knife, boy. Give it to me." The voice was as cold as ice.

Dodging Oleg's feint toward him, Petya ran behind a clump of birches, forcing the man to play cat and mouse with him while he dodged and lunged among the tree trunks. Anya was terrified, desperate to run away but unable to abandon Petya to this monster. She had brought the child here; now she was praying she could find a way to get them both safely home. What a fool she was. What a fool not to have listened.

Suddenly Petya made a break for it, pulling back the branch of a birch tree and letting it crash into Oleg, knocking him briefly off balance.

Seizing the opportunity, Petya and the girl ran, Petya screaming for help as he raced toward Byelaya Beryozka, Anya right beside him. But Oleg was furious and determined not to be cheated of his prize. The uncle had escaped him; the niece would not.

Hurtling through the forest like a wild boar, he furiously pursued Anya, covering ground much faster than she could with her torn clothing catching on everything in her path.

Just as Anya was beginning to hope she could reach a shortcut to safety she knew, her foot became entangled in a patch of vines and she fell. "Keep going, Petya!" she shrieked as Oleg pounced on her. "Get the men!" If not, he would surely kill her.

Thrashing wildly in the underbrush, Anya nearly dislocated her shoulder as she fought to throw off her attacker, but she was too desperate to worry about the pain. She *must* win this fight. She had no choice.

"You're out of luck today, aren't you?" Oleg grinned as he struggled to control her.

"Let me go! Prince Andrei will hang you if you hurt me."

"You're not very friendly," grunted Oleg, tearing at her blouse. "You're a little vixen." He was getting excited again.

Anya sank her teeth into her attacker's hand, drawing blood, biting as hard as she could.

"Bitch! Do that again and I'll smash in your head," he shouted.

Anya cried in horror as the man smacked her viciously across the face several times to subdue her while he ripped away at her underclothing. Fighting back despite the terrible pain, she knew her only hope lay in attracting the attention of those armed men not half a mile from here. Lev Petrovich would save her, she thought frantically. He would do it.

Screaming as though her throat would burst from the effort, the girl clawed her attacker across the forehead as they fought. Anya flailed desperately to scratch anything within reach. Oleg tore at her skirt, shredding her fine, lace-trimmed batiste petticoats. The ground was littered with pieces of Anya's clothing now, bits of delicate Brussels lace fluttering across the grass.

Looking directly into Oleg's eyes for a split second as they lay tangled on the ground, the young princess saw a passion so raw, so irrational it wiped out all traces of humanity. Those eyes were glassy; this was a beast ripping at her, no longer a man.

"I hate him," Oleg hissed into her ear as he grabbed her blonde hair. "I hate that *boyar* and all his kind. You think you're better than I am. I'll show you...."

Anya sank her teeth into Oleg's wrist again before he silenced her by hitting her head ferociously against the ground. Unconscious now, Anya was defenseless at last.

The man stared at his victim lying so helplessly, so deliciously before him, her long strands of blonde hair streaked with bits of dirt and leaves from their struggle, her clothing torn and disheveled. And she was still beautiful. Except for the violent pattern of scratches and bruises he had left on her face and shoulders during their fight. That almost spoiled the effect. But he was more excited than ever now.

You shouldn't have hit me, he thought. We could have been friends... we could have been lovers.

Suddenly he heard a sound that nearly froze his blood. Men's angry voices were coming toward him, a lot of them. And dogs. In the distance he could hear the voice of the boy leading them.

If she survives and identifies me, they'll hang me, he thought. She's spoiled my plans to kill Prince Malyshev and now she'll hang me over to the hangman. No. She can't.

Stumbling toward the spot where he had tethered his horse, Oleg ripped the reins from the branches of the birch tree he had used as a hitching post, hoisted himself into the saddle and turned briefly to glance back at the girl. He couldn't kill the boy who had seen him, but he could and would eliminate the little aristocrat.

Aiming nervously, he fired at the unconscious girl, drawing blood. With no time to spare, Oleg dug his heels into his horse's sides and galloped off in cold terror.

Barking furiously, the dogs were the first to reach the battered young princess, the long, shaggy white borzois racing around Anya as Petya beat them away from her, pushing them in the direction of the fresh tracks made by the horse. While three of the hunters headed after the fleeing attacker, Lev Petrovich and his young son flung themselves on the ground next to Anya, trying to discover whether or not she was still alive, listening frantically for a heartbeat, attempting to determine if the head wound was as grave as it looked. The older man was praying it was just a flesh wound, but the flow of blood made it difficult to tell. Petya was wailing.

"I'm going to take Anyushka back to the house," Lev told his men. "Petya will come with me. You—Grigory, Anatol, Sasha—get the horses and go after him. I'll join you as soon as I send word to Count Scherbatkin to bring His Highness home."

"And when we catch him?"

"Do everything but kill him. We'll save that for Andrei Nicolaievich."

Petya wept as he accompanied his father. He should have used his knife on that monster.

4

When Prince Andrei was located at Count Scherbatkin's estate and finally brought to the telephone, he hardly recognized the voice at the other end of the line.

"Andrei Nicolaievich," said Lev, knowing the local operator would be listening in, "there's been some trouble here. I think it would be a good thing if Your Highness returned home immediately."

"The animals?" cried Andrei. "He's struck again?"

"It's Anna Nicolaievna. She's been injured."

There was a gasp at the other end of the line—whether it was the prince or the operator, the peasant couldn't tell. It was only the second time in his life Lev had ever used the contraption, although he understood the need for discretion on the line. And then he heard a click, cutting him off from his employer.

Once the call was completed, the peasant left the manor house and headed for the forest to join his men. Dr. Krimski was already in the house; there was nothing further for him to do here.

As Praskovaya Feodorovna sat by the girl's bed, weeping with despair she wondered if the unconscious child would recover. She looked terrible, her face a swollen mass of bruises.

When Prince and Princess Malyshev finally arrived home after a frantic race along some of Russia's worst backcountry roads, they found the household in an uproar and Dr. Krimski waiting in the hallway.

"My God, what's happened?" demanded Ksenia as she ran inside. "One of the maids just said something about a shooting."

The princess hadn't even removed her motoring duster, hat or veil, all of which were finely coated with grit. She was white and shaken as she stared at Krimski, hoping he'd tell her it was all a terrible mistake.

"Where's His Highness?" replied Dr. Krimski, abruptly forgetting his usual good manners. "I must speak to him first."

"No! Tell me whatever you're going to tell him. For God's sake, let me know whether the child is alive or dead!"

Krimski and the princess both looked relieved to see Prince Andrei striding through the door.

"Something dreadful has happened, Your Highness. I must speak to you in private."

"You can tell my wife anything you can tell me. Anya is alive, isn't she?"

"Yes."

Ksenia felt a premonition of disaster as Krimski kept glancing at Andrei, seeking a way to speak to him out of earshot of his wife.

Oh God, thought the princess, the child's been crippled. That's what he's trying to hide from me!

Darting up the gleaming carved-wood staircase, Ksenia ran impulsively to the girl's bedroom before the doctor could restrain her and burst in on a startled group consisting of Sonia, Praskovaya Feodorovna and Daria, who were all standing quietly near the bed, watching Anya.

"Anya! Anyushka!"

"She's still unconscious, Highness," whispered Daria, badly frightened.

"What did Krimski tell you?" demanded Ksenia, anxious for information. "He examined her, of course."

"Certainly. We called him as soon as they brought her home. Then we called you and His Highness at Count Scherbatkin's."

Ksenia couldn't believe the damage to Anya's face. This morning she had been beautiful, lively, dazzling with youth and gaiety. Now the contours of her face were so misshapen, her eyes so puffy and purple, that she looked like a monster. And there was a bandage around her head, showing bright red stains. Blood.

"Oh, my God," murmured Ksenia, sinking into a chair. "What have they done to you?"

"Anya and young Petya went to pick mushrooms after you and Andrei Nicolaievich left this morning," explained Daria. "In the woods, they were surprised by an intruder. The boy tried to frighten him off with a knife when he started to menace Anya, but the fellow had a revolver. Still, the two of them tried to make a run for it. Petya was able to get away and head for home. He managed to alert his father and a party of hunters. They're out right now, beating the bushes, ready to string him up when they catch him."

Ksenia could only stare at *Daria*. "Who did this?" she whispered. "Who could do such a dreadful thing?"

"The boy saw the attacker and gave us a good description. But we still don't know his name."

"Was Anya able to say anything?"

"No, Highness. She's been unconscious ever since the attack."

Distraught, Princess Ksenia knelt down by the bed and buried her face in her hands.

In Andrei's study, the prince had just been told the full extent of the girl's injuries. For a couple of seconds he didn't react at all. He appeared quite blank. And then he went to the mahogany gun cabinet where he kept his imported English rifles and began arming himself. Those he had used this morning were useless for this hunt.

"I'll kill him, whoever he is, and when I get done with him there won't be enough left of the body to feed to the dogs!"

Taking two of his high-powered imported rifles, the prince strode angrily into the hallway to confront Adam Lowell and the other members of the hunting party who had returned from Count Scherbatkin's with him. "The bastard's tried to kill my niece," he said. "We've got to find him now. No delays."

"How seriously is she hurt?" demanded Adam. "Will she live?"

Prince Andrei nodded grimly as he handed him a rifle. "She'd better."

The Russians crossed themselves and prepared to follow Andrei.

"Where are you going?" cried Ksenia from the stairs.

"Where do you think? I'm going to kill the man who did this."

"I want to come with you!"

"No. You stay here and watch the girl. Krimski will stay with you."

"Andrei! I want to find this animal," she screamed, chasing them down the stairs. "Let me come along! I should never have left her here!"

"No," replied her husband as he restrained her. "You belong here with Anya. It's my duty to hunt the man and kill him. Our friends and I will do what has to be done."

"Highness, we're about to kill a man. It's not fit for a woman to see such a thing," Adam said under his breath.

"Neither is that sight in the room upstairs," Ksenia flung back, furious with them. "I want to see him put in the same condition."

"I'm sorry, Ksenia, you stay here," exclaimed Andrei angrily. "I don't have the time or the inclination to argue with you. Goodbye!"

"Andrei!"

Before the princess could further delay them, Andrei and the men were out the door and heading for the stables. The motorcar was useless in a chase like this. Only horses could take a man through the backcountry where they'd have to go.

"Lev Petrovich already has his men in the field. And they also called the *stanovoiy*," the prince said to Adam. "That was good."

"What about the neighbors?"

"My people sent out the news when Lev brought Anya home. By now the region knows there's a fiend on the loose once more."

Lowell nodded as they saddled up. "Good. We'll run him to ground wherever he tries to hide. And when we get done with him, he'll wish he had never been born."

As Ksenia watched from the upstairs window, she saw her husband and Adam on horseback, racing down the *allée* and out onto the country road beyond. When she lost sight of them through the trees, she bitterly regretted not being able to ride with them. It would have been far easier to shoot the man responsible than to have to look at the damage he had done to Anya.

"It's a good thing you're here, Your Highness," said the doctor. "She'll need you when she regains consciousness."

The princess looked wary. "Will she recover? Will there be scars?"

Dr. Krimski's round, bearded face assumed a peculiar expression— half-fearful, half-devious.

"May I speak to you alone?" he asked quietly.

Ksenia's heart almost skipped a beat. She motioned to the three servants to leave.

Dr. Krimski looked serious. "Please be seated, Highness. I am going to give you the full extent of your niece's injuries."

My God, thought Ksenia. What is he going to tell me?

With Princess Ksenia looking in anguish at the girl, Krimski began pacing up and down the room, hardly aware of its elegant decor—the furniture of Karelian birch, the long lace curtains at the windows, the pink-hued Chinese carpet on the floor—as he searched his thoughts.

"Please, Doctor," begged Ksenia. "Tell me the truth. Has she been crippled, for heaven's sake?"

"No, Highness. Or at least she doesn't appear to be. But you must understand that she received a brutal beating—worse than anything I've seen since the troubles."

"Yes," nodded Ksenia, wishing he'd get to the point.

"And since she hasn't regained consciousness, it's difficult to make a thorough assessment of her condition, but I'd be shirking my duty if I didn't tell you I'm afraid she may have sustained a fractured skull...."

A stunned gasp greeted the news. Krimski wished Andrei Nicolaievich were standing beside him. He hated breaking bad news to a woman. Women had a tendency to dissolve into hysterics—or faint.

"Highness, it may be," he continued. "The bruises indicate a tremendous blow to the back of the skull. Everything else—contusions, sprains, cuts—can be treated with ordinary care. But if the young lady has suffered a skull fracture, it could prove fatal. At best, it will mean a long recovery, possibly under the care of a specialist in Europe."

"You must be wrong," Ksenia replied, unwilling to accept his diagnosis. She'd known people who had died from skull fractures. She refused to accept his assessment.

Krimski sighed, shaking his head. "If I'm wrong, I will apologize from the bottom of my heart, Ksenia Alexandrovna. It gives me no pleasure to have to tell you this terrible suspicion of mine. But if I'm right," he said softly, "I have to prepare you to face reality."

Reality, thought the princess. He may as well have said death.

"I'm sorry, Highness," Krimski said gently as he left the room. "I'll be downstairs if you need me."

Alone with Anya, Ksenia felt numb. She drew her legs up under her like a child and sat there in the large upholstered armchair, staring at the pattern in the Chinese carpet, at the bowl of wildflowers on the dressing table, at the pink silk coverlet, anywhere she wouldn't see that battered child.

"My poor darling," she whispered to Anya. "How could this terrible thing happen to you?"

And then with a shock of fright, Ksenia wondered how the girl would ever come through it. For that matter, how would she?

Hours later, when Andrei returned home empty-handed, he found his wife still keeping her vigil in Anya's room. Seeing her husband, Ksenia rose from her chair and went to hear his news.

"How's Anya? Any improvement?" whispered the prince.

"She woke up about an hour ago. She seemed coherent. Krimski nearly put me in my grave with dire predictions of a fractured skull but it's really too early to tell. She recognized me and the maids. She spoke to me. And she can see. Now Krimski is saying it's probably not as bad as he feared. He's calling it a concussion now."

"Thank God," murmured the prince. "Adam Mikhailovich was worried about her losing her sight."

Ksenia looked steadily at her husband with eyes that were unusually red and puffy. "Did you find him?" she asked pointedly.

The prince shook his head in disgust, bone-weary from riding through the backcountry, jumping fences, fording streams, beating the bushes in pursuit of the elusive attacker. "We combed half the region but we lost him," he admitted. "Damn the luck."

Ksenia Alexandrovna glanced outside at the bright patches of light cast by the lanterns strung along the darkened *allée*. It must be quite late; she had lost track of time hours ago.

Turning to Andrei, she said, "Anya knows who it was. She kept repeating his name over and over, once she awakened." Ksenia's mouth was taut with anger.

"Who, for God's sake?"

"Oleg Ivanov," the princess replied, looking straight into her husband's eyes.

Andrei turned dead-white. He looked as if he had been struck.

"You were too lenient with that vicious young monster two years ago, *dorogai*," said Ksenia. "Ten years at hard labor near the Arctic circle would have prevented this. You were too soft then because you pitied his mother and now he shows his gratitude by trying to murder Anyushka! Now kill him!" she hissed. "Make him pay for this, Andrei. Make him suffer like a beast for a long time before he dies, just as my niece is suffering now!"

The prince did not say a word, but he had death in his eyes. As he grimly departed, he called for the horses to be saddled up once again. Now he knew who it was and how much that young bastard must hate him. There would be no mercy this time.

In the darkened room, Anya wept quietly as she listened to Andrei and Ksenia. They didn't realize she was awake, but she could hear everything they were saying, and her aunt's harsh words shocked her to the depths of her soul. She couldn't imagine Ksenia Alexandrovna speaking like that to her husband. And it was her fault Ksenia was so enraged. The shame nearly overwhelmed her. She should have listened.

I hate you all, the man had told her as he tried to kill her. So much hatred frightened Anya. In all her life she had known only love and affection. This morning had changed that forever.

He had truly hated her, hated her enough to murder her without even knowing her. The thought of it filled her with a horrified disbelief. He had come close to killing her simply because she was a *boyar*. Just because of that. It made no sense to her.

And she had been rescued because of Petya's devotion and his father's—peasants—just like the man who had attacked her. They didn't hate her for being a *boyar*. They loved her because she was Anya.

The episode repeated itself in her mind as Anya tried to comprehend it, trembling again and again as she recalled those hate-filled blue eyes piercing into her very soul. An animal's eyes.

As the girl tossed restlessly in her bed, her whole body aching from the struggle in the forest, she heard the sounds of men and horses in the courtyard, preparing to ride out again even at this late hour. The noises blended with the pain in a hazy mist and finally they were gone.

Trembling in the darkness, Anya knew her childhood was over. It was a long time before she felt safe enough to retreat into the happy oblivion of sleep.

Less than an hour later, the horsemen arrived at their destination, ready to administer justice. It was well before dawn. "What the hell is this?" demanded Ivanov senior as he was awakened by someone trying to pound in the front door.

"Maybe it's the boy," murmured Madame Ivanova, turning over in bed. "He must have forgotten his key again."

"Damn fool. He must be drunk, coming home like this."

With several colorful oaths, Ivanov senior stumbled through the darkened room and into the parlor, expecting to find his wayward son on the other side of the front door. What he found there was closer to a lynch mob.

"Shit!" was all he could say.

Rushing the old man before he could slam the door shut in their faces, six armed men led by Prince Andrei Malyshev poured into the unlighted front parlor and surrounded Ivanov, demanding to know where Oleg was.

"Turn on the lights," someone ordered in the darkness.

Suddenly the room was illuminated by the light from a gas lamp, and the intruders found themselves facing a nervous Madame Ivanova, clad in an old nightdress and shawl and pointing a shotgun at them.

"Put that down before someone gets hurt," ordered her husband, astonished to find himself confronting Prince Malyshev, a dark-haired foreigner, Lev Petrovich and three of Lev's sons, all angry and seemingly looking for trouble.

"What the hell are you doing here at this time of night?" demanded Ivanov as his wife lowered her gun.

"We're looking for your son. He tried to murder my niece this afternoon in the forest on my property."

Gasping, Madame Ivanova clapped her hand over her mouth, stunned. "No," she stammered. "I can't believe that."

"We have two witnesses," interrupted Lev. "My boy Petya, whom he damn near murdered, as well as the girl. She's lying in bed now, beaten to jelly and shot in the head by your son!"

Oleg's mother stared in shock. The old man shook his head in disbelief, but soon his anger returned. "Get the hell out of my house," he ordered. "The boy's not here. And if he were, I wouldn't hand him over to you."

"Maria Andreevna," said Andrei, looking her straight in the eye, "I am going to kill your son tonight. I am going to be his executioner."

Facing the prince, Madame Ivanova stared into his eyes, tears beginning to course down her cheeks, grief-stricken and mute in her horror.

"Oleg's not here," she replied at last. "He's gone, God knows where."

"Then," said Andrei, "we're going to have to search the house. My little one's half-dead from what he did to her. When we find him, he's going to pay the penalty for his crime."

"No!" wailed the horrified mother. "For God's sake, don't do this!"

Pushing her aside while Adam took her gun and Lev Petrovich held his Winchester ready, Andrei and his men—Grigory, Anatol and Sasha, burly young men with rifles—went from room to room, turning on gaslights, opening cupboards, doors, chests, poking around in the storeroom where the household's supply of preserves, pickles and vegetables lay stacked on shelves near bottles of homemade vodkas and brandies. They found nothing.

"Where's the ice cellar?" asked the prince, returning to the parlor in frustration, his face white with fury.

"Underneath the kitchen," sobbed Madame Ivanova. "But you're just wasting your time. My boy isn't in the house. I swear he's not."

"Show me."

She followed the prince down into the chilly, ice-lined stone repository for perishables. Just as she'd said, Oleg was not to be found.

Exploring the cubicle in angry silence, Andrei had to admit defeat. As he rejoined the others, he found Ivanov senior nose to nose with Lev, fulminating against the *boyars* in general and Prince Andrei in particular. Lev, still outraged by the viciousness of Oleg's attack on the girl, and furious at not being able to find him, growled at the other man to shut up while he still had his front teeth.

As Madame Ivanova flung herself between the two gray-haired men, fearful of bloodshed, Prince Andrei snapped, "Lev Petrovich, he's not the one we want. We won't soil our hands with his blood."

"But you wouldn't hesitate to kill my child," said Oleg's mother bitterly, looking him straight in the eye.

"Maria Andreevna," he replied quietly. "It's my right."

"Only God has that right," she answered him, refusing to accept his claim.

"You can debate the point with the local priest," he said coldly. "I know what I must do."

A swift but thorough check of the grounds, including the barns and storehouses, yielded nothing. Having failed to locate Oleg, the hunters left the Ivanov estate, dissatisfied and angry.

Watching them from the long wooden front porch, Ivanov clutched his flowing beard and wondered whether or not he should shoot Oleg himself or let that arrogant *boyar* do the job for him. What a brainless moron he had raised! If the story were true—and his neighbors were furious enough to make him believe it—then Oleg was as good as dead anyway.

The worst part was the harm it could do his father's standing in the community. Prince Malyshev's influence was far-reaching, both in the local *zemstvo* and in business transactions. If Malyshev decided to launch a boycott against him, he could lose what he'd spent a lifetime building.

Damn Oleg! How could he have sired this jackass?

"Come inside," said his wife. "Comfort a mother about to lose her son."

"Maria," he replied, looking sadly at his wife, "I wish to God you had never had this child."

Madame Ivanova leaned sadly against the porch rail and stared into the darkness beyond her husband. Then putting her arm around his shoulder, she silently nodded her agreement.

Finally the unhappy woman said brokenly, "He's a bad one. In my own heart I don't want to believe Prince Malyshev, but I know it's the truth."

"Why?" muttered her husband. "Because some *boyar* says so?" But he knew it too.

"No," she replied. "Because I know in my heart he's cursed. All his life, in spite of all you and I have tried to do for him, he's been stupid and hateful. Even Siberia taught him nothing. It's as if he has nothing good in his soul."

Maria Andreevna looked at her husband's heavy profile in the darkness and saw a faint reflection of the sturdy young peasant who had mar-

ried her, already pregnant with Oleg. Ivan had spent a lifetime struggling
to give his family more than any peasant had a right to enjoy. Now her
son's stupidity would erase the decades of patient, backbreaking labor.
Where was the justice of it all? Did justice exist for people like them?

Her eyes overflowing with tears, Maria said quietly, "We must go to
Prince Malyshev and tell him how heartbroken we are over the harm our
son has done. If he finds our boy, he will shoot him, but if Oleg escapes
him he might take his revenge on us, just because he's been cheated of his
pleasure. He's like all the gentry. He must have his way."

"Oleg will make a fine hunting trophy for His Highness," Ivanov reflected bitterly. "God damn the boy, he's such a fool!"

Unable to hold back her tears, Maria Andreevna leaned against the
porch railing, shaken by sobs that threatened to tear apart her chest.

"You were a good mother to that boy," Ivanov said to his wife as he
encircled her in a warm embrace. "None of this is your fault."

Shaking her head violently, the woman sobbed so hard her husband
was afraid for her. Never in all their married life had he seen Maria
Andreevna lose control, not even when she had buried her parents, surrounded by hysterical female relatives wailing like lunatics at the graveside.
Not in childbirth either, even though her labor dragged on for two long
days and the midwife was afraid she wouldn't survive.

Only Oleg was able to do this to her.

When the sobbing had finally stopped, there was nothing more to do
except go to bed and try to forget everything that had happened. But it
would never go away; this disgrace would have to be faced every day for
the rest of Maria Andreevna's life.

Wrapping herself in the quilted coverlet her mother had made for
her as a wedding present, Oleg Ivanov's mother sank back in her pillows
and stared at the flickering votive candle in front of the icon of the Christos
Pantocrator in the corner of the bedroom. The gentle face of Christ seemed
to radiate love and forgiveness. But for whom?

5

Anya was waiting for him in the yellow salon that faced the back gardens, her face pale and drawn, her eyes ringed by faint bluish shadows. Her head ached. It always ached—ever since the attack. If Ksenia Alexandrovna hadn't told her Mr. Lowell had stopped at Byelaya Beryozka expressly to visit her during a brief trip to Moscow, she would never have come downstairs. It had been several weeks since the attack, and Anya had not seen Adam since that morning when everything was so deceptively lovely.

She was ashamed to see him now. It wasn't vanity, but shame over what her playful disobedience had led to that made her feel so dreadful.

As the American entered the silk-hung salon, decorated with two centuries of the Malyshevs' collective taste, he came to a shocked halt in front of the girl. Nothing could have prepared him for this sight.

It had to be Anya, and yet this pitiably bruised girl had little relation to the lively young woman he had known. It was as if all the life had been brutally crushed out of her in one horrifying morning. He ached to see her like this; it was unnatural.

"You know that Auntie and I are leaving for Paris," said Anya. "And I didn't wish to leave without saying goodbye. And to thank you. I know that you and our other friends tried to capture that man. It was very brave of you. I'll never forget it."

The bruises were dreadful. They had toned themselves down to a sort of gray-green patchwork, but since they were still highly visible, Anya refused to set foot outside the house without a large hat draped with veiling. Not that she went out very often. This was the first time she had been seen by someone who was not a member of the household.

"When will you return?" he asked, not knowing what to say, tongue-tied and struggling with so many bewildering feelings.

"I don't know. Not until next year perhaps." She felt displaced, almost as if she were dead and watching from above.

48

"Next year?"

Anya looked miserable. "Auntie and I are going to visit Grand-père in Paris for a while. They want me to visit a doctor there because of the headaches."

Anya looked at him and smiled ruefully. "If I had only gone with you that day, I never would have met that madman. Praskovaya Feodorovna says it was fate. I suppose she's right."

"Praskovaya Feodorovna says more than her prayers," replied Adam, making Anya laugh a little. "Don't ever believe it's your fate to be unhappy. You weren't made for tears, Anyushka. Don't ever let anyone make you think so."

Surprised by his tone of voice, the girl looked at him, straight into his deep brown eyes. "I wish I could believe that," she murmured. "I used to. Now all I can think about is that maniac. And they can't even catch him. He may be out there waiting for Auntie the next time, or for Uncle. Or for Petya, who was so brave...."

"Anya," said Adam gently, "they *will* capture him. And then he'll never be able to harm anyone again."

She gave him the briefest sketch of a smile, trying to make him think she felt better, but it was useless. She couldn't pretend something she didn't feel.

"You'll be visiting your grandfather," he said, trying valiantly to sound cheerful. "That ought to be wonderful."

"It will be dreadful!" Anya burst out, breaking down and flinging herself into his arms. "I don't want to go to Paris. I don't want to be poked at by foreign doctors and I don't want to be chased away from here because of a madman!"

The tears flowed easily once they started. She buried her face in Adam Lowell's dark-gray tweed jacket and sobbed, clinging to him like a small child, her whole body shaking with the force of her misery. The man closed his eyes and held her very close, unable to calm her, wishing with all his heart that he could.

"Anyushka," he whispered, cradling her in his arms, "you must not think it's the end of the world. We were so terrified for you when it happened, convinced you might die. You didn't. And you're a very brave girl. You fought back so hard he wasn't able to kill you. You saved your own life. You were stronger than you realize. And," he added, "you identified him."

"But he's still *alive!*"

"That won't last for much longer. They'll find him and kill him. I promise. There's not a man here who wouldn't like to shoot him if he could."

"Would you shoot him?" She knew he was a man of peace.

"Yes," he said softly.

The warmth of his response made her lift her head to search his face. She was deeply moved. Adam's beautiful dark eyes were so expressive, she understood his feelings instinctively. He cared for her and it had nothing to do with his affection for her as a child. This was a new sensation. The sudden discovery awed her as much as it delighted her, making her feel grown-up and giddy at the same time.

"I don't want to leave," she whispered, nestling against him.

"Anya," he murmured, "it will only be for a time. Those doctors will take a good look at you, tell you you'll live to be eighty and send you home smiling."

"Do you really believe that?"

Adam looked at her tenderly and smiled. "Yes, I do. Your Aunt Ksenia tells me all the Sviridovs are tough. It takes more than an Oleg Ivanov to break them." He wanted her to believe it.

As Anya smiled back, she suddenly remembered her mother. She buried her face against his jacket as if she were taking shelter.

Holding her tenderly, he said quietly, "Listen to me, *dushka*. I want you to promise me something. Will you?"

"What?" she whispered.

"I want you to promise that if things get very bad, so bad that you don't know what to do, you'll ask me for help. No matter where you are or what you need. Do you promise?"

"Yes." She was so grateful she almost broke into tears again.

"Remember," he whispered. "If you need me, Anya, I'll be there. No hesitations. No excuses. Just say the word."

For a minute Anya said nothing, gazing into his eyes. And then hesitating just a second, she reached up and kissed him softly on the cheek. And before he could restrain her, she was out the door, scampering upstairs, delighted, but shocked at what she had just done.

On the train ride back to Moscow and then overnight to St. Petersburg, the young American wondered how he was going to explain his sudden disappearance from the capital. If he had been in the army, he would have been considered AWOL. He was glad he wasn't in the army.

He didn't care. He would take the consequences, if any. What was important to him was seeing Anya with his own eyes to know that she had survived the attack and that she would recover.

In a world that had become cold and gray with the death of his young wife, Adam Lowell cared passionately about protecting the rare beauty he had just rediscovered.

St. Petersburg

While Princess Ksenia and her niece were on their way south to Paris and Grand-père, Prince Andrei performed a self-imposed duty. He kept an appointment with a gentleman he knew from society circles—a man who was hated by half the country, feared by most of it, and who was every bit as formidable as his reputation.

At the end of his wits and still unable to run Oleg to ground after two weeks of pursuit on his own in Moscow, Prince Andrei had decided to wage an all-out war against the animal who had attacked Anya. To begin the campaign he conferred with Simon Petrovich Beletsky, the head of the dread Okhrana, the tsarist secret police—or as the prince himself had once remarked, the devil's aide-de-camp.

When Andrei Nicolaievich left his interview with Simon Petrovich, he had little faith remaining in the moral purity of the Okhrana, not that he'd had much to start with. It simply seemed indecent that he, Prince Malyshev, should be placed in the position of buying an execution. It seemed a sin against justice. Nevertheless, he intended to keep the appointment Beletsky had made for him.

A week later, at the place of the rendezvous—the gold-domed St. Issac's Cathedral on Nevsky Prospect—Andrei was still moving like a man in a dream. What I'm about to do, he thought, is the very worst sort of sacrilege. There can't be any hope of forgiveness for this, not in this world or the next. Yet he also knew that nothing would deter him from his vengeance, even if he were to spend the rest of his life regretting the manner by which he'd gained it.

To his discomfort, wherever the prince glanced, crowds of gilded saints peered down at him, soft-eyed and pure, dozens of them, all passing judgment. On the ceiling, a magnificent Christ flanked by the most illustrious members of the Orthodox pantheon smiled down on him in tender contemplation. It made him feel queasy.

Even more startling, the executioner for hire recommended by Beletsky turned out to be the most unlikely one imaginable, a totally nondescript type named Roman Vasilievich Petrov, who could easily have passed for an overworked accountant or a village schoolmaster.

But anyone who mistook Petrov for either of those was a fool. Petrov was in fact, a fifty-five-year-old Okhrana operative with the rank of inspector. His career had been as varied as it had been deadly. In his time, Roman Vasilievich had betrayed Georgian bandits, Serbian royalty and innumerable plotters in the provinces. And he had engineered an unsuccessful plot with the German police to kidnap and detain a group of known radicals in Bad Homburg during an international socialist conference. He had been careless there, shooting one of the radicals himself, which had caused a flap with the foreign ministries of both Russia and Germany. Petrov had fallen out of favor for that, but he was cunning, excellent at blending in with the woodwork and very dependable—in most cases. Right now, he was assigned to tracking low-level revolutionary vermin.

Pale, stooped, balding, of medium height and shabbily respectable appearance, Roman Vasilievich's only distinguishing feature seemed to be his wire-rimmed spectacles. He had the air of a baby owl. He smelled of cheap tobacco and cabbage soup. He was not at all the sort of fellow one could picture pulling the trigger on another human being.

Yet he did it and he did it for the money.

As the prince stood gazing at the iconostasis, a quiet voice murmured, "Andrei Nicolaievich?"

Surprised, he spun around and glanced down into the glittering eye-glasses before him. "Yes. Who are you?"

"Petrov. You already know my credentials, so we don't have to go into that here."

Encircled by a moving mass of worshippers, kneeling, praying and lighting candles in a swirling mosaic of peasant calicos, Paris frocks, official uniforms and the black robes of professional holy men, the two conspirators looked at each other and nodded. Each knew the other was in deadly earnest. So much the better.

"I've been made aware of the particulars of the case," declared Petrov, keeping his eyes straight ahead. "This Ivanov shouldn't be too hard to locate, given his background and mentality. Sooner or later he'll join up with some group of radicals and we'll pick him up."

"But what if he doesn't link up with anyone? He acted alone as far as I can see. And he's vicious. My God, he nearly killed my wife's niece, and he mutilated and destroyed one of my horses. We're dealing with some sort of lunatic here."

"No," Petrov replied softly. "He's no lunatic. Or at least not any more than the rest of them. He's merely vicious. He's the kind who will commit any act of violence to make his presence felt. By himself, he's a zero, but with a gun in his hand he feels important and capable of anything. The country's full of his sort these days. It would make you sick to see our files."

That was a damned depressing thought; Andrei hoped Petrov was exaggerating but he didn't appear to be.

"Before Ivanov was arrested for disturbing the peace at Byelaya Beryozka two years ago, he attended Moscow University," said Andrei. "Did you know that?"

"Yes. It's all in his file. That's where most of our radicals find their calling—in the universities. They should shut them all down for ten years and start all over again with a fresh crew."

"They should at least do a better job of getting rid of these agitators."

"We try. There are only a handful of us compared with thousands of them. It's a never-ending battle. And you'd be shocked at the family background of some of them. For example," he sighed, "there's Katia Petrovna Solovina. My God! She's a red-haired beauty from a wealthy family in Nizhni Novgorod, and she nearly murdered the governor-general of St. Petersburg. Fired a Browning at him at point-blank range and missed."

"Missed?"

"Missed. It misfired and he escaped with powder burns. Katia simply escaped."

"My God."

"A friend is working on her case right now. She's tied into a lame-brained terrorist group centering on herself and her lover. They're reorganizing someplace and they've gone underground. We'll get them, though. It just takes time."

"How much time do you think you'll need?"

"I can't possibly give you a prediction. It depends."

"I'm willing to offer 20,000," Andrei stated softly but clearly. "Five for expenses now and the remainder when you show me the body."

That was more than generous, reflected Petrov. The man must be rabid to kill this Ivanov. "Well, Andrei Nicolaievich," he said, "I'll take it. Yes. Certainly. I'll get on it right away."

"Do it quickly," warned the prince. "I can make arrangements to have my banker transfer funds to your account if you wish."

"I'd prefer cash," responded Petrov, without the slightest embarrassment.

"Don't you trust me, Roman Vasilievich? I assure you, my credit's quite good."

"Oh, I'm sure your credit's excellent, Highness," smiled Petrov. "It's just a personal preference. I hope you'll humor me."

Andrei glanced at him. "When shall we meet to arrange it?" he asked crisply.

"Could you meet me with the money tomorrow morning at ten?"

"Where?"

"The east portico of Kazan Cathedral."

"Fine. Are you religious, by the way? You seem to have a preference for churches."

"Good camouflage," responded Petrov. "Everything seems so innocent with the cross looming over it."

Andrei smiled. He had a point. "All right. Tomorrow then, at Kazan Cathedral. And bring me his file. I'd like to see it."

"All right. It can be copied. It's not really that long."

"And I want results."

"Yes, Highness. I promise."

As Andrei crossed himself and left St. Isaac's, the sweet, dry smell of incense felt suddenly oppressive, cloying. Out in the sunlight once again, the prince put on his straw boater, sighed and signaled for his chauffeur. He had done his duty; now it was up to Petrov to do his.

Since the Ivanov affair had brought Andrei back to St. Petersburg, he decided to pay a few calls while he was in town. But almost everyone he knew was either in Europe or at his country house, and the prince had to settle for a reduced circle of friends.

To his surprise, he found his pretty cousin, Natalya Grekova, still in the city and on the afternoon Petrov received his preliminary 5000 rubles, Prince Andrei paid her a visit. She was terribly agitated, he discovered, and on bad terms with the entire family.

"It is too stupid for words," declared Natalya as she poured tea in the conservatory, among the potted palms. "Gregory Efimovich is a saint, and yet here he is persecuted by this rabble. It makes us so sad."

"Us" was Natalya, her good friend Anna Vyrubova, and none other than the tsaritsa, Alexandra Feodorovna. "The rabble" were members of the government, including the prime minister.

"But Talya, dear, why do you waste your time with this Rasputin fellow? He's a very dubious character from what I hear. They say he even raped a nun, for heaven's sake! What sort of *starets* is this?"

"Lies, Andrushka. All lies. He's purity itself."

"Oh, come on, Talya! Even you can't believe that."

Countess Natalya angrily shook her blonde head, making her pearl earrings wobble in her earlobes. "Gregory Efimovich is Christ reborn. He is incapable of sin. He takes our sins unto himself and absolves us of our guilt."

"Yes, and from what I've heard he especially likes adultresses! In fact, if they need a partner for their transgressions, there he is. It's all terribly convenient for everyone concerned, isn't it?"

"You're being sarcastic."

"Damned right, I am! God Almighty, what a perversion of religion."

"Nonsense. When Gregory Efimovich takes on people's sins, it's a mystical expression of God's love."

"It's a lot cheaper for him than going to a whorehouse, you mean!"

"Andrei!"

"Excuse me, Talya, but it's the truth. And I hear you're making Volodya quite angry because of your devotion to this charlatan. I even saw your name mentioned in the newspapers as one of this *starets'* inner circle. Don't you understand how insulting this is to you—and to your husband?"

"It's an honor."

"It is most definitely not an honor. It's like branding you a loose woman. My God, can't you see it?"

The countess put down her teacup and looked directly at her cousin, her friend since childhood. "Perhaps you'd better go, Andrei. I won't sit here in my own home and listen to your insults. You're beginning to sound like the rest of them."

"And who, dear Talya, are the rest of them?"

"Volodya, Mama, Belle-Maman, everyone—"

"Darling, they all love you and don't like to see you being abused by this Rasputin character. I know you, Talya, and I know how pure you are. But this fellow is so debauched that merely linking your name with his is enough to ruin your reputation. That's why everyone is so upset." His voice radiated concern.

"Gregory Efimovich is received by the highest in the land," Natalya reminded him petulantly.

"Yes. If by that you mean our tsaritsa who seeks out every religious fake in Russia."

The countess stiffened visibly and put down her teacup. "I won't permit you to say these things to me. You're talking about your tsaritsa and my friend."

"I'm sorry, dear, but what I'm saying is the truth, and you'll do well to heed my advice. Give up Gregory Efimovich. He can only do you harm."

Natalya rose in a shimmering swish of violet silk and creamy pearls. The tea was over.

"I'm sorry, *malenkaya*," smiled Andrei as he rose, bowed politely and started to leave. "But if you don't listen to good advice from those who love you, you'll end up very badly used by this trash from Siberia who only wants to abuse you."

"Goodbye," she retorted. "And please don't return until you find your manners again."

"Yes, dear. *Au revoir*," he nodded. Well, thought the prince, that was a charming little tête-à-tête. Dear Natalya was as daft as everyone was saying she was. Poor, pretty, foolish little Talya. She never did have any sense.

As Prince Malyshev accepted his hat from the footman, departed through the marble and gilt entrance hall and stepped out onto the sidewalk, he was stopped by a cry from someone fifty feet down the street.

"Andrei! Wait!"

"My God. Volodya! How have you been?" Andrei exclaimed in delight as Natalya's husband caught up with him and engulfed him in a friendly bear hug. "It's good to see you. I thought you were away."

"Ha! That crazy woman wishes I were away," he grunted, clapping the prince on the back. "God, she's gone 'round the bend this time with all her religious drivel. Sometimes I think I ought to divorce her and start all over again."

"Oh, come on. It can't be that bad!"

"Andrei, she's crazy. They all are, these mystical ladies who run after that *starets*, Rasputin. From the tsaritsa on down, they all ought to be sent to an asylum."

Count Volodya had very little sense of humor, Andrei knew, so he was speaking straight from the heart. "Well," he declared, "I'm only in town for the day. I'm leaving on the last train this evening for Byelaya Beryozka. If you're free, why don't we have dinner tonight at the club? I have some bad news to relate, too."

"Ksenia?"

"No, and I don't want to discuss it on the street. Shall I meet you at my table at the Imperial Automobile Club? Say eight o'clock?"

"Fine. Until later then."

That evening, after a day spent mostly with bankers and members of the Duma, the tsar's fledgling parliament, Andrei met for dinner with Volodya at the club. They were both rather surprised to see several government officials gathered for a conference dinner. *Caneton à l'orange* and Mumm champagne were featured on the menu, but whatever had drawn these gentlemen together for a meeting in one of the small private dining rooms must have been of greater importance than the house specialty. All the other diners were commenting on the gathering and speculating wildly.

"It's him," shrugged Volodya, tucking into a bowl of sturgeon soup. "It has to be."

"Who?"

"Rasputin. You've been out of touch, I see. He dominates the tsaritsa."

"A common backwoods tramp? It's hard to believe."

"Oh, you haven't been treated to a recitation of Rasputin's virtues, I see. I'm surprised. Usually Natalya bores everyone within earshot with a long litany of the master's so-called miracles. They all go about telling people how holy he is and how Russia needs him. At the Alexander Palace, they talk of almost nothing else."

"Is everyone mad?"

"Not entirely. They just want to be in the good graces of our tsaritsa, who totally controls our tsar. It's a case of monkey-see, monkey-do. It's comical in a way, isn't it? But it's pathetic, too."

"And Natalya is part of this."

"Natalya's a fool. She spends her time praying and visiting, but she has entree to the palace and encourages the tsaritsa in her lunacy. If the tsar had any sense at all, he'd exile the whole lot to a monastery in Siberia."

Spooning a bit of top-quality caviar onto a round of buttered toast, Prince Andrei munched thoughtfully.

"We've fallen pretty low, Volodya," said the prince.

"Oh, it's only the beginning, if you ask me. When she succeeds in dumping the prime minister—and I think she will—we're liable to end up with Gregory Efimovich Rasputin heading the government."

"My God, what a warped sense of humor you have!"

"I've been married to your cousin for too long," replied Volodya.

Both men glanced at each other and thoughtfully sipped their iced vodka. Finally Volodya asked about the trouble at Byelaya Beryozka. He was stunned to hear of the attempted murder. "But a child like Anyushka? Why?"

"Because he's a maniac. I also think he's the one who slashed one of my horses. It's all unbelievable."

"Are they still looking for him?"

"Of course. The police suspect he might join a group of radicals. They intend to catch him when he does."

"Good luck."

"You don't sound as though you have much confidence in the police."

"I haven't. I don't trust them any more than I trust the terrorists. In fact, I suspect the two play at the same game. It's been done, you know."

"Anything's possible. But I still have a certain amount of faith in the police. After all, they're on our side."

"So they claim. Actually, everybody infiltrates everyone else to such an extent that even they don't know who's who any longer."

"If that's the case, poor Russia."

"Yes," agreed Volodya as he drained his glass. "Poor Russia indeed."

6

He'd seized the best opportunity he would ever have to avenge himself on Prince Andrei, and he'd made a terrible and embarrassing fiasco of everything. What was the matter with him, Oleg demanded of himself as he sat huddled in a second-class seat on the Moscow train he had boarded several miles down the line from Byelaya Beryozka station. Why was he so damned unlucky?

He had wanted to kill the prince. He had been living for the moment when he could take his revenge for all those months in Siberia, and what had happened? He had changed his mind, aimed for a lesser target and then botched things so horribly that he had actually left a witness behind who would be telling everyone in the province exactly what Princess Anya's murderer looked like. Christ! That was stupid! What was the matter with him?

Trembling a little at the memory of his fury, Oleg almost wished he hadn't killed her. She was so beautiful, so feminine. But arrogant like all the *boyars*.

She looked at me as if I weren't human, he thought bitterly. He had been to the university. He had read books. And still to that beautiful girl he wasn't on the same level as she was. The damned arrogance of them! To her and all the *boyars* he was nothing. He had no meaning for them.

The bitch, he thought. Well, now he would have meaning for her, or at least meaning for her surviving family.

At the thought of her family's reaction, Oleg shifted uneasily in his seat. He had really done the worst possible thing in killing the girl. To have killed Prince Andrei wouldn't bother any rightthinking person, he told himself. Nobody loves a landlord. Kill them all, the peasants would say. But a girl. . . .

People would get themselves all worked up over something like that. Prince Andrei, who had escaped his just punishment, would be showered with condolences from all over the province and every able-bodied man in the area would ride up to the manor house, armed to the teeth and offering the prince his assistance in tracking down the fiend who had attacked his family.

To Oleg's intense shame, he realized he had not only cheated himself of his revenge on the prince; he had just provided his worst enemy with the motive—and the justification—to have him hunted down and killed like a wild beast. With the blessing of the entire community!

They would call him a fiend. Oddly enough, that idea made Oleg smirk a little. Well, at least people feared a fiend, he decided. It was a good thing to have Prince Andrei afraid of him. He wanted desperately to terrorize the prince now that he hadn't succeeded in killing him. He wanted to strike at him in any way he could.

And yet the memory of that beautiful girl disturbed him, haunted him, made him tremble. He had murdered something finer than himself and he knew it. Worse than that, he would always know it.

The hell with Byelaya Beryozka, thought Oleg as he puffed on a cheap Russian cigarette in the rickety second-class coach. It's all behind me. I've outgrown them. I've finally killed....

Yes. And by leaving behind a witness, he had just put himself under a death sentence. For as long as he lived he and those *boyars*, those arrogant bastards, would live for the day the score was settled, one way or the other.

Moscow

When Oleg reached Moscow, he cautiously found his way to the current address of his Siberian comrades and informed them of his revolutionary coup. He was greeted with coolness rather than the outright admiration he had expected. Pavel Scriabin, the long-nosed, pale-blond creature with lank, straight hair falling into his gray eyes, asked the new arrival why they should welcome him back to their circle. Now he would surely be a magnet for the police.

"The hell I will," retorted Oleg. "I killed the only witness to the act. All they have is a body. No one will come looking for me, or for you because of me. I can guarantee it," Oleg lied easily. Annoyed at his lackluster reception, he decided to emphasize the positive. There was no point in mentioning the youngster he had left behind. He wanted to be admired and accepted as a revolutionary. Besides, having killed one aristocrat, he was prepared to kill more. It had a certain excitement, like hunting wild animals.

"I never liked him in Siberia," declared a voice from the back of the room. "And I don't like him now. Anyway, we're looking for someone who can help us rob banks, not murder little girls."

Oleg glanced sharply at the speaker, who was lounging on a musty divan. Katia in turn regarded Oleg with a long, oblique, rather catlike gaze, totally unimpressed.

Bitch, he thought. Arrogant little snob.

"Robbing a bank is a crime," he said defensively. "If we get caught, we'll all go to jail as common criminals. How will anyone ever know our motives are pure?"

"My God, will you listen to this one?" demanded Katia. "Are we recruiting from kindergarten these days?"

"I've served time in Siberia for political agitation, just like you," answered Oleg, with dignity. "I consider myself a revolutionary on active service."

Katia guffawed, then rose, stretched and lit a cigarette as she looked casually at Pavel Scriabin. "He thinks he's in the army, maybe?" she said with icy sarcasm.

Oleg gave the young woman a cold look, peering at her from beneath a tangle of unkempt blond hair like a beast of prey before it has decided to strike. He wanted to give her a taste of what he could do.

"You killed a young girl in Moscow province. That's the act of a pig, not a revolutionary," stated Katia. "What sort of pervert are we dealing with?"

"It was a political act. She was from a family of prominent landowners who'd sent me to jail for speaking out on behalf of the peasants." Oleg was outraged at this lack of respect.

Taking a long drag on her cigarette, Katia glanced with contempt at the scruffy young man in the red Russian blouse and black trousers.

"You're not a very impressive candidate for our organization. We expect our people to be able to assassinate more difficult targets than little girls. My God!" exclaimed Katia. "You have all the moral sense of a cannibal!"

"It was an act of outrage against a specific social order," protested Oleg. "Why should it matter if the victim was young or old, harmless or dangerous? The attack was aimed at the class of our oppressors as a whole."

"It was the act of a cowardly swine."

From his place of honor at the head of the table, Pavel Scriabin glanced across the room at his mistress, shrugged and sighed. "We need an extra man for the expropriation," he explained apologetically.

"It's like dealing with someone who rapes babies," retorted Katia. "He's not our kind."

"Well, we can't be too fussy these days, Katiushka. The fellow Oleg is replacing was locked up by the police last week. If we're going to pull off the job, we need this help."

The redhead took another drag on her cigarette—a specially blended Turkish variety, purchased in one of Moscow's fanciest tobacconists—and disdainfully blew a series of smoke rings into the air.

Pavel's brother Dimitri glanced at Katia and declared himself in favor of Oleg's admission to their revolutionary cell. He was supported by the other members present: a Georgian and two Russians. They seemed agreeable to Scriabin's proposal simply because it was so difficult to recruit new blood. The Moscow police were having one of their periodic cleanup campaigns, and several comrades had ended up in leg irons at the Kazan station, set for the long trip east. Oleg might be a less-than-splendid specimen, but he did have one outstanding attraction—he was ready, willing and out of prison.

"Do you want him?" demanded Katia in disgust. "I think you're all insane."

"We're practical, Katiushka. If we limited our membership to the pure of heart, none of us would be here tonight."

"If you want him, use him," retorted the redhead. "But remember when he turns out to be incompetent that I was opposed."

Angry at her tone, Oleg glared at the woman but took a seat at the table next to Dimitri Scriabin, while the other members of the group introduced themselves. Pyotr, Valery and Josif resembled each other with their shabby Russian blouses, round, flat-brimmed caps and dirty black trousers, casually stuffed into scuffed boots of inferior leather. They looked like typical Khitrovka thugs.

"Well, comrades," smiled Oleg, trying to sound businesslike, "what is the target of our expropriation?"

"The Bank of Azov and the Don on Malaya Sadovaya Street."

Oleg nodded studiously, evaluating their chances. Why not?

"We've observed that they leave the vault open during the day as a normal practice. There's a guard stationed at the entrance. He has to be lured away before we strike. Then, while part of the group holds the tellers and customers at bay, the rest of us will rush in and clean out the vault."

Oleg wondered what his services would be.

"Are you a good shot?" Katia asked Oleg as she joined the group at the table.

"Well, I—"

"Don't waste our time. Just yes or no."

"Well, yes."

Katia's slanted green eyes sought out Pavel's. He smiled.

"You can distract the guard," she decided.

"Wait a minute. What do you mean by 'distract'? How am I sup-posed to distract him?"

"Hold a gun on him. Shoot him if he gives you any trouble. I'm sure you can handle it."

"But why me? I mean, I've just joined up. Why not someone with more experience?"

"Because we all have a part to play and that one's yours. Either you're in or you're out. There's no middle way."

"It's a little hard the first time," said Dimitri, trying to sound like an expert. "But then again, you've already killed once before, so you've had your baptism of fire. It shouldn't be too hard for you a second time."

"Well, this is different. For one thing, the guard will be armed."

"Oleg, we know you prefer your victims young, female and defense-less, but if you want to make your mark, you'll eventually have to progress to more difficult targets." Katia's icy green eyes looked straight into his, freezing him with disdain.

"All right," Oleg nodded angrily. "If you want me, you've got me. I'll show you all how a real revolutionary operates. You'll find out what kind of man I am."

"Wonderful. You'll be responsible for neutralizing the guard," said Pavel Scriabin. "Josif will take care of our transportation. Dimitri, Pyotr, Valery and Katia will go into the bank with you, hold the customers at bay and clean out the safe. I'll be waiting for you at the appointed place after you've successfully completed the operation."

Looking round the table at his coconspirators, Oleg thought they seemed too pleased. There was something going on here that he didn't like, but he couldn't quite figure it out.

It was only when he was on his way home that he realized they had delegated him to deal with the *only* person in the bank likely to be armed. Startled by this revelation, Oleg felt a chill of suspicion slither up and down his spine as he recalled the dislike in Katia's eyes. What was the green-eyed witch plotting? Could he trust these people?

As the blond, well-muscled, shabby young man meandered through the dark, steamy Khitrovka slum, fending off drunks, beggars and bleary-eyed prostitutes amid the black and treacherous streets stinking of stale urine and horse manure, he remembered his very first excursion into rev-olution at Byelaya Beryozka. He had trusted a pack of well-spoken young comrades from the university, and they had left him in the lurch to face the local *stanovoiy*—and Andrei Nicolaievich Malyshev. This bank robbery could be more of the same, he thought sullenly. That green-eyed bitch was trouble; he could feel it.

When he thought of her arrogant face he could remember how angry he had been that day in the woods. He could see that frightened little aristocrat. Ha! She hadn't been frightened enough. She'd fought back like a tigress, scratching hard enough to leave scars. But it hadn't done her any good. She was gone, and her family must be half-demented with grief. He could take satisfaction in that, he thought. But of course his own life was now in danger, a fact that caused him a certain queasiness, although he didn't like to dwell on it.

In reeking Khitrovka, lost among the company of shrieking drunks and gaudy whores, with the dense river fog swirling around him, Oleg wandered among the damned and felt utterly at home.

7

Paris

s soon as she and Ksenia entered the cobbled courtyard of Prince
Sandro's town house, Anya knew something was wrong. Very wrong.
The familiar eighteenth-century white limestone edifice, designed by
the architect Gabriel for a royal mistress, looked as imposing as ever, but it
was missing its chief ornament—Grand-père was nowhere in sight. He had
always met them at the Gare du Nord before. It was peculiar.

"Hello, Pierre," smiled Princess Ksenia as the old butler greeted them
effusively on the doorstep. "Is there anything wrong with my father? Where
is he? He's not ill, surely."

Lowering his eyes in embarrassment, the white-haired servant murmured something about His Highness having a previous engagement, preventing him from being there for their arrival.

"Ah," responded Ksenia, suspicious of Pierre's manner and of his excuse. She had known him since childhood and had never heard him lie so
badly before.

"There's something strange going on here," Anya whispered to her
aunt as they climbed the white marble staircase to the upper floors. "Do
you see their faces? The servants are hiding something from us."

Unwilling to admit her own fears, Ksenia smiled and said perhaps
they were planning a surprise. But she was uneasy; the atmosphere *was*
strange.

Dressing with great care, Anya chose a high-necked gown for dinner
with Grand-père. The fading bruises could be disguised in that way, although the ones on her face were going to be visible. A veiled hat had
hidden her face from view on her arrival, but now she had to bare it, as
distasteful as that was. The marks were terribly humiliating.

At dinner Prince Alexander Alexandrovich—Sandro to his friends—
informed Anya that he had heard from his daughter of the tragic events at
Byelaya Beryozka and that they had caused him tremendous sorrow.

Seated at the head of the Louis Seize dining-room table, flanked by two liveried servants whom he abruptly chose to dismiss, Sandro looked grim and massive this evening. Six-four and built like an athlete, with a white Vandyke beard and mustache, the prince had the manner of a *grand seigneur* and the temperament of a tyrant. He also appeared to be in a somber mood, a fact Ksenia found unsettling after her lackluster reception earlier.

"Yes, Grand-père, it was dreadful," said Anya. "But the doctor said if the headaches go away, I ought to recover. The sprained arm doesn't hurt so much now. And the bruises are disappearing."

Sandro looked steadily at his beautiful young granddaughter and said nothing, gazing into her face as if he were trying to decipher a puzzle. Those faint traces of gray-green were disturbing.

"I really am beginning to feel better," Anya added nervously, glancing at her aunt, who was seated opposite Sandro at the far end of the table, her sapphire necklace reflecting the lights of the large chandelier.

"This is so painful for me, I don't know how to begin," declared the prince at last. "You must realize how this will alter our plans for you. Prior to this, I had envisioned a brilliant alliance with an heir to some great European fortune. Now, in one day, everything I had hoped for is in ruins. My poor child."

Was he mad, wondered Ksenia, exchanging perplexed glances with her niece, who was as puzzled as she was. What was he chattering about?

"Papa, Anya suffered a brutal beating but she survived. You're going on as if she'd been killed. I don't understand this. You can see her here before you."

Fixing his beautiful daughter with a ferocious stare, Sandro said angrily, "How can you keep up this repulsive charade, Ksenia? The child might as well be dead. Do you think people haven't been talking about it, here and in Russia? Do you think word doesn't travel? Gossip can cross borders faster than a speeding train."

"What are you talking about, Papa? You aren't making sense."

Furious, Sandro stood up and shouted across the table at Princess Ksenia, "I'm talking about the fact that your niece was raped while she was in your care, that every gossip from Moscow to Paris is spreading the story that you—my favorite child—have been trying to hide from me. That's what I'm talking about!"

Stunned, the two women gasped simultaneously. Then Ksenia rose from her seat at the far end of the table, pushing the chair angrily aside as she headed toward Sandro. So this is why he had dismissed the servants, she thought. He was waiting to open his can of worms in private.

"It's not true, Grand-père," protested Anya, staring at him in disbelief. "The man beat me, he shot at me, but he didn't do that!"

"How dare you talk to us like this, Papa?" raged Ksenia, her dark-blue satin dinner gown shimmering beneath her sapphire necklace. "It's the vilest sort of slander! Even from you I won't tolerate it!"

"Remember you're speaking to your father, *chérie*," he replied, rising to tower above his tall daughter. "And I won't permit any disrespect."

"Neither will I. Whoever told you this story is a shameless liar. Anya has nothing to be ashamed of, unless you consider being nearly murdered cause for shame!"

"You're lying, Ksenia. The story is all over town. The damage is done. We'll never succeed in finding her a husband. You've both disgraced our family."

"*I've* disgraced our family? You're the only one to be ashamed of if you actually believe these vicious lies, Papa. And I'm ashamed to be your daughter!"

At that, Prince Sandro flushed a deep red and, shaking with anger, slapped his daughter across the face.

Picking up the first thing that came to hand, an elegant eighteenth-century Sèvres figurine, an outraged Ksenia sent it flying across the room. Knocking a fine Watteau landscape onto the floor, the figurine damaged the gilded frame before it shattered in several pieces on the parquet.

"*That's* what I think of your story, Papa," declared Princess Ksenia as she swept out of the room with Anya following. "And if I ever meet the man who started that rumor, I'll kill him."

Before she crossed the threshold, Princess Anya turned for a moment to glance at Sandro, who was leaning on the dining-room table, badly shaken by his outburst and even more so by his daughter's.

"I'm ashamed of you, Grand-père," she said quietly. "I never thought someone I loved could treat me so badly." And she was out the door.

Anya was so devastated nothing could comfort her. What had happened in the forest that day was going to be a never-ending horror, a disgrace dragging on for the rest of her life, haunting her until the day she died.

It was insane. She had been nearly murdered by a lunatic who hated her because he was jealous of her class. Now she was about to be rejected by that very class as an outcast because of the gossip that had apparently accomplished what Oleg Ivanov couldn't. How could it be possible? Who had spread such a hideous lie?

None of it made sense to Princess Anya. Lying on the green and gold bedspread of her heavily carved French-empire–style sleigh bed, Anya absent-mindedly traced the pattern of the gilded rosettes in the woodwork behind her head, her mind in a daze, her vision half-blurred with pain.

My life is over, she thought, staring at the heavy green-silk hangings above the bed, a shining mass of Napoleonic symbolism, all imperial bees and laurel leaves in gold thread against the silken background. For a moment she was six years old once more and kneeling beside this very bed with Aunt Ksenia and Grand-père.

"Whose little girl will I be?" she had asked her beautiful aunt, and the answer had come without missing a beat. Now no one would want her. She faced a wilderness alone, aching with pain and in disgrace. And she didn't even know who was responsible for her misery.

Princess Ksenia was so furious with her father she refused to go to her room and brood over his accusation until morning—when he would probably escape for a drive and keep her waiting until late that night. She wouldn't rest until she'd had a talk with him; she couldn't let him slander her and Anya like that and come away unscathed. Even if he was her father.

When the princess located Prince Sandro, he was in his ground-floor library, peacefully reading one of the exquisite leather-bound, gold-embossed volumes from the collection of French novels that lined the shelves of an elegant glass-paneled Louis Seize cabinet. *Le Rouge et Le Noir* was his choice of the evening.

"Well, *chérie*," smiled the prince, hardly lifting his eyes. "Have you come to destroy more of your inheritance?"

Ignoring the sarcasm, Princess Ksenia seated herself beside him and said, "Papa, we have to talk about this. It's too loathsome to accuse me of such a terrible thing. I can't believe you actually believe any of it."

"Why not?" he replied, slamming the book shut and laying it on his desk, a fine Louis Seize piece; like the cabinet, it was from the workshop of Georges Jacob, an eighteenth-century cabinetmaker with a royal clientele. Everything in the mansion had a fine pedigree except himself, Sandro used to joke. His ancestors were thieves, bandits and sackers of cities. But they had sublime taste.

"Papa, if the story were true, you would have been the first to know. That in itself ought to say a great deal. You know I don't lie."

"All women lie. Some more than others."

"Was it a woman who told you this outrageous slander!" demanded Ksenia, having two or three in mind, Lisa foremost among them.

The prince looked at her with his cool light-green eyes and said finally, "I don't care to discuss it."

"Well, *I* do."

Sighing, Sandro shrugged his shoulders. "You've all failed me," he said. "Nicki died in a ridiculous accident without an heir to carry on our name. You've never even given Andrei a child, let alone an heir. Your sister," and he intoned the words with grim dislike, "has only succeeded in giving that perverse little dwarf a daughter. The entire family has failed me. We're well on our way to becoming extinct, Ksenia. The last thing I want to hear is gossip about Anya's honor. I had such plans for her. Now they've been utterly destroyed."

"You are a selfish old man, Papa, and if you keep on this way, you'll die alone and unlamented among servants, lackeys and fickle hangers-on."

"I want a male heir. I had hoped my granddaughter might provide me with one. How does that make me a villain, Ksenia?"

The princess stared at him. He reminded her of a child who's been told he can't have his own way. "Papa, even if Anya married, she'd cease to be Princess Sviridova and she'd take her husband's name. Any son of hers would bear his father's name, so I can't see how that would solve your problem."

Sandro was annoyed. To him it all seemed perfectly clear.

"I wish to cite a precedent," he stated, sounding a little like a lawyer. "In the case of Princess Zenaida Yusupova, there was an exception to that rule. She was the last of her line and the tsar allowed her husband to adopt her name. The princess gave birth to two little princes and the family continued. *That* was what I wished to do. Now your carelessness has prevented it."

"Then wait a few more years for Lisa and Seriozha's daughter," replied Ksenia angrily. "Perhaps Tasha will find you an obliging grandson-in-law."

"I may. Or I may marry again," he said coldly. "And I think you know the young lady."

"Don't be coy, Papa. Zenaida is no longer in the first bloom of youth."

"She's seven years younger than you, *chérie*," retorted Sandro with more than a touch of malice.

"And she's had seven times seven lovers," replied his daughter, unwilling to let that last remark slip past. "If you marry Zenaida, you'll regret that decision for the rest of your life."

"If I don't, the Sviridovs will go the way of the dinosaurs."

"Papa," she said with a wry smile, "people still talk with respect about those dinosaurs."

Sandro shook his head. "I'll provide for Anyushka. She'll certainly never starve. But she'll never bring me what I want now."

"She's not a chattel, Papa. She's a young girl whose life is going to be ruined through no fault of her own. If you can accept that, I can't."

"Then try to fight the gossip, and see how far it gets you. She is ruined, Ksenia. And if you intend to go through with your plans for this winter, you'd better be certain she can stand the strain."

Ksenia was, in fact, genuinely frightened for her niece. The old man was right about one thing—society would be absolutely vicious and in the girl's fragile state, it would be a mistake to subject her to a winter of humiliation in St. Petersburg. But if they didn't fight this slander, Anya's life would be utterly wrecked forever afterward. There was no choice. Either fight or run.

Princess Ksenia sighed and decided they'd better arm themselves if they hoped to see the spring.

The next morning the princess was surprised to find her niece dressed and serene, ready to go shopping. Happy to distract her, Ksenia ordered the chauffeur, Paul, to bring the motorcar around for an excursion to the *grands boulevards*. It was a pleasant summer day, exceptional for Paris in July, pleasantly warm and sunny and perfectly cloudless, like the nicest day in May.

As Sandro's chauffeur drove the black Mercedes out the wrought-iron entrance gate and onto the Rue du Faubourg St. Honoré, Ksenia noticed the usual assortment of pedestrians, nannies with young children, servant girls running errands, delivery men with packages, most of them dark-haired, dark-eyed people, small in stature with sharp, lively features, so different from her fellow countrymen with their broad cheekbones, pink, glowing cheeks and blond hair. No Parisian coachman resembled the fat, bearded Russians who raced proudly down the Nevsky Prospect with their blue caftans and round hats, perched grandly behind fine horses to whom they chattered constantly. No parade of guards officers in white summer tunics and flat white caps, only an occasional *flic* in a short dark cape. The French seemed to save their showy *Gardes Republicains* for decorating the stairway of the Paris Opera on gala evenings and for the annual celebration on the fourteenth of July.

Sitting beside her beautiful aunt, Anya noticed nothing, saw nothing, felt nothing. The only thing on her mind was a void where her future had once been.

Ksenia enjoyed the classical beauty of Paris, with its stunning eighteenth-century public buildings and private mansions and its fine parks and broad avenues, but in her heart she was glad not to have to live there, preferring the mixture of splendor and exuberance back home. The French seemed too preoccupied with form for her taste. And too heavily structured. Ksenia's Slavic soul hated content over emotion.

Watching Anya out of the corner of her eye, the aunt decided that she looked quite content. Perhaps everything would work out after all. Eager to humor her, Ksenia said they could browse through her favorite shops on the Rue de Rivoli and have Paul meet them. And afterward they could go to Boucheron's, Ksenia's Paris jeweler.

"Yes," agreed the girl. "That sounds wonderful." But her voice was toneless.

Two hours later, after walking in and out of a succession of smart shops and failing to notice anything set out before her, Anya was ready to go home. Unwilling to force her niece into further pointless activity, Princess Ksenia suggested they walk to the spot where the chauffeur had been told to expect them. Nodding listlessly, Anya agreed.

Because of a ceremony in the Madeleine Church, not too far away from the rendezvous point, the city traffic had become quite dense. Huge omnibuses, smart automobiles from various government ministries and sleek private motorcars joined with the occasional open carriage with liveried coachmen—a relic from the not-so-distant past. All were caught up in a swirling mass as they negotiated the huge Place de la Concorde, its white and gold obelisk gleaming like a beacon in the center between two splashing fountains.

Standing beside Ksenia but not hearing anything she was saying, Princess Anya saw Paul and the Mercedes at the same time she noticed the large omnibus heading toward her.

It wouldn't take much, Anya thought. All I have to do is walk out there and stand still. It will all be over in a minute. Glancing at Ksenia, she saw she was momentarily distracted by the cries of a street vendor. All right, thought Anya. It's now or never.

The whole crowd became a blur as she stepped into the line of traffic, a tall, slim figure in a white summer suit, white-kid ankle boots properly laced, her face hidden beneath a small straw hat draped in light veiling.

Staring straight ahead at the oncoming vehicle, Princess Anya was utterly devoid of feeling. She no longer felt fear or unhappiness; she had gone beyond that. Now all she courted was oblivion. If her life was no longer worth living, she herself would put an end to it. Besides, it had actually ended that day in the forest; there was nothing left to do but make it final.

People stared in horror as they saw the girl standing in the path of the bus.

"Anya!" Ksenia turned and saw her too. Horrified, she started into the street to pull her out of the way.

"Princess!" shouted the chauffeur, frantically honking the horn, convinced Anya must have gone crazy.

While his forty-three passengers screeched and clung to their seats in terror, the bus driver managed to avoid Anya by mere inches, maneuvering the ungainly vehicle around her and crashing into the streetlamp at the balustrade near the Tuileries Garden. Pedestrians screamed and raced for cover, scattering like a flock of pigeons.

As the omnibus careened out of control, a black Renault in its wake grazed Anya as it whirled around her, neatly flipping her like a toy doll into the gutter. She landed with a sickening thud, a wounded white bird.

"Paul saw the whole thing," Prince Sandro snapped at his daughter. "She deliberately placed herself in the path of that omnibus. She was trying to get herself killed."

Princess Ksenia had given her father a somewhat different version of the accident, claiming carelessness on Anya's part as she crossed the street. Damn the chauffeur, she thought, lighting a scented cigarette.

Father and daughter stood by the French windows of the upstairs salon overlooking the rain-swept Rue du Faubourg St. Honoré, its streetlights glittering under a steady downpour. It was a perfect complement to their mood.

"The doctor told me she escaped from her foolishness this afternoon with nothing more than bruises and a sprained ankle," Sandro declared. "She's very lucky."

"Foolishness?" mimicked Ksenia. "That's a clever way to speak of it."

"Don't be flippant with me. It disturbs me deeply that Anya would do this. She must have lost her mind."

"If she has, she had ample provocation," Ksenia replied bitterly.

Alone in her bedroom, Anya stared up from her bed at the elaborate moldings on the ceiling, still trying to understand what had happened that afternoon. She had deliberately and cold-bloodedly placed herself in the path of an omnibus. Yet it had not killed her. It had refused to take her life—it had rejected her!

That was so comical it made her laugh aloud, covering her mouth with her hand so nobody would hear; after all, it was scarcely a humorous thing to try to hand over one's life to a large, crowded omnibus in the middle of the Place de la Concorde. But it *was* funny!

She had been rudely rejected by death, bounced around enough to receive some additional black-and-blue marks, but nevertheless flung unceremoniously back into life. Well, she thought, tears from her laughter coursing down her cheeks, I've survived the very worst now. From this day on, whatever happens, disgrace, insanity, total ostracism by society will be nothing in comparison. If Grand-père thinks I'm a scandal, let him. It no longer matters.

All that mattered was the new-found freedom she had won that afternoon. Sandro would probably let her do anything she wished now. Having had his selfish plans undone, he would no longer find her a useful pawn in his little games.

The only dreadful thing about the afternoon—aside from her ridiculous attempt at suicide—was the fright she had given Ksenia. That was very bad. Ksenia was her best friend and closest ally, a mother in everything but name. She didn't deserve to have been put through that.

Suddenly Anya was determined to go downstairs. She needed to talk with her. She also had something to tell Grand-père—and she didn't care how he took it.

Making her way painfully down the long white marble staircase, startling the footmen on duty, Anya discovered Sandro talking with Ksenia in his library. Both held glasses of cognac; both looked bereaved.

"Anyushka! What are you doing here? The doctor told you to stay in bed!" exclaimed Sandro. "Are you trying to finish what you started on the Place de la Concorde?"

"Papa! That's not fair," protested Princess Ksenia, helping Anya to a chair. "Leave her alone."

"It's all right, Auntie. Grand-père can say whatever he pleases. It's his house. I just hope he doesn't expect anything he says to bother me. It won't ever again."

Glaring at the girl, Sandro was about to say something to that, but he restrained himself. After all, the girl couldn't be in her right mind.

Looking painfully delicate and still quite resolute, Anya looked her grandfather in the eye. "I was a fool to have tried to kill myself this afternoon. Well, I learned my lesson. And now I'm not about to let myself be intimidated by vile slanders from unknown liars. From now on I have better things to do with my life. A lot better."

"Well, listen to the little tiger," said Sandro, regarding Anya with amusement.

In spite of his sarcasm, Princess Anya kept her head up and looked straight into his eyes. "What's the best way to put down the slanders about my being dishonored?" she demanded.

The old prince hesitated. In the old days he would have said, "A duel in an isolated section of the Summer Gardens," but things had changed. His Highness hadn't fought a duel in thirty years, and he had scars to remind him to beware any more of *that* madness.

"I'm not certain, *chérie*. Would you have anything in mind?"

"Marriage," replied Anya, taking him totally by surprise.

Sandro was so astonished by that suggestion he couldn't believe he had heard correctly. "Marriage?" he repeated. "Well, Anyushka, this must be proof you've lost your mind. Ksenia, take her upstairs and put her to bed. She's raving."

"I am not raving. I'm quite rational, Grand-père. And if you can't think of a better way to safeguard my honor, then I want you to support me in carrying out my plan."

"Are you serious? No one in Europe or Russia will even consider you now. You've been irreparably damaged, Anyushka. You're beyond hope."

The girl looked at Sandro and for the first time in his life, he saw a trace of iron in her light-blue eyes. "I was beyond hope this afternoon," she replied. "I'm not any longer. I refuse to be dishonored by slander, and I don't intend to give up without a fight. And if you let these unknown liars intimidate you, you're no better than they are."

Princess Ksenia wondered if the injuries had affected the girl's mind. She would never speak to her grandfather like this under any other circumstances. She was on very thin ice. And she was also absolutely right.

"Anyushka," said Sandro patiently, forcing himself to be kind to the unfortunate child, "marriage is the very thing that's been rendered impossible by these stories."

Unimpressed, Anya shook her head. "Marriage is the one thing that will prove them false."

Princess Ksenia had been watching her niece and her father very carefully, and she was struck for the first time by how alike they were in their stubbornness. But Anyushka had just given them the perfect strategy. She was remarkable.

The old prince looked carefully at his granddaughter. "I don't suppose you happen to have the bridegroom in mind, by any chance."

"I have," she replied, her heart starting to pound a little.

"Well," demanded Sandro, "who is this fellow?"

Anyushka looked stubborn. "That's my secret," she answered, a little daunted by her own recklessness. "Of course, I haven't asked him yet, so I don't know what his response will be."

"Of course," nodded Sandro, fearing the worst but wishing to humor the girl. She was obviously suffering from the aftershock of the afternoon's folly. But she thought like a Sviridov; she was bold.

"Grand-père," said Anya, "if this gentleman says yes, will you stand by me and let the world know the slanders are nothing but wicked lies?"

"If you can find a husband under these circumstances, I'll set you up in your parents' former apartments in the Sviridov Palace in Petersburg and make you the lady of the house. I rarely use the place except during the winter season and it seems a pity to keep it vacant for months at a time. Keep your end of the bargain and I'll keep mine."

When Princess Anya returned to her room, she was appalled by her own audacity. Well, she thought, I have absolutely nothing to lose. If I'm rejected, at least I've tried my best. If I don't take the risk, I'll never know. I have no choice.

Anyushka sat down at her small inlaid rosewood writing desk and began composing a letter on fine, gold-embossed stationery, taking great care not to ruin the effect with untidy ink blots.

"Dear Adam Mikhailovich..." the letter began.

When Anya had finished, she showed her letter to Princess Ksenia, who read it in astonishment, glanced at the young niece who appeared to have grown up so quickly and asked, "Are you certain?"

"Yes," she replied, even as she prayed she wasn't mistaken.

"Then, darling," sighed Ksenia, "I wish you good luck with your choice. And I'll support you against Papa if it comes to that."

As she gently embraced the young girl, Princess Ksenia wondered if they weren't both a bit mad. But it was a very appealing madness, she thought with a smile. It was daring, resourceful and brilliant.

If those vicious slanderers in St. Petersburg thought they could get the better of a Sviridov, they had a lot to learn.

Lord, thought Anya as she hugged her aunt, this was a desperate gamble. If she had chosen well, she'd be content for the rest of her life. And if she had made a mistake, she'd never cease to regret this day.

But she didn't plan on making a mistake. She didn't dare.

8

"Y ou, Ivanov," said Katia Petrovna, "do you understand what you have to do?"

"Yes. Of course I do."

"Repeat your instructions."

Cleg gave Katia a glare and through clenched teeth replied, "Go into the bank with the rest, walk over to the guard and pull the gun on him."

"And?"

"Order him to stand aside or be killed on the spot. Hopefully he'll decide to move over."

"And if he doesn't?"

"Shoot him."

Katia's cool green eyes darted a glance at Pavel Scriabin to her right. Scriabin nodded his approval.

"Remember one thing, Oleg," he warned. "If you lose your courage, don't come back. We'll kill you. We're not interested in cowards."

"Don't worry about me," he replied coldly. "Watch yourselves."

His fellow bank robbers looked at him with skepticism which did nothing to instill confidence. Nobody seemed to think too highly of him, he noticed with annoyance. Their mistake.

"If we succeed, we'll be able to purchase a regular arsenal," Scriabin reminded them. "And with the money that's left, we can travel easily from city to city, striking at the heart of tsarist rule in every province."

"Bravo," smiled Dimitri, Pavel's younger brother. "Enough talk. Let's go get the money!"

Katia Petrovna nodded, extinguished her cigarette and clapped her hands. "All right," she ordered. "To the bank!"

While the band of bank robbers filed out of the room and down the rickety dark staircase of the dirty tenement, Pavel Scriabin remained behind long enough to pick up his papers, pack his valise and cover any traces of his presence.

75

As leader of the gang, he would meet his henchmen at a prearranged rendezvous on the outskirts of town—after they had done the dirty work. He considered himself too important to risk the robbery itself.

Josif, a quiet fellow who had once worked as a tram operator, took charge of transportation, having stolen a good-sized coach as well as the horses and the driver's uniform—a long dark-blue caftan, a round hat and a belt. There were dozens like him speeding through the streets; nothing would look more innocent or attract less attention.

It took longer to get to the bank than they had planned. To make matters worse, an army coach from the Moscow garrison was parked near the entrance, just where the robbers had intended to leave their stolen vehicle and its nervous driver.

"I don't like this," muttered Josif, who had the responsibility for their getaway. "These soldiers—"

"Shut up and don't be nervous," retorted Katia. "Just do exactly as we planned and nobody will suspect a thing. Pull over to the side now and let us out. We'll walk the rest of the way to the bank. You pull up about twenty feet short of the doorway and stay there. Talk to the nags like a real coachman and keep your eyes on the door."

With misgivings, the driver brought the vehicle to a stop and discharged his passengers. As the five bank robbers—Oleg, Katia, Valery, Dimitri and Pyotr—proceeded down Malaya Sadovaya Street, blending into the usual Moscow crowds of linen-shirted workmen, officers, housewives, street peddlers and itinerant beggars, their driver slowly continued on to his prearranged destination, twenty feet short of the bank. Nervously he watched his comrades proceed to the imposing granite beaux-arts-style building.

"Remember," warned Katia as they passed through the heavy brass doors of the Bank of Azov and the Don, "Oleg goes for the guard before the rest of us do anything."

"Right," agreed Oleg, strangely excited. Walking into the elaborate marble-columned interior, he noted the small number of customers. Good. They were mostly elderly people and harmless-looking types. No problem.

Behind their brass cages, the tellers briskly counted banknotes with the efficiency of carefully drilled automatons.

Well, thought Oleg, pulling a muffler up around his face as he saw his companions do the same, let's get moving. Looking impatiently at Katia across the room, he gestured toward the tellers. What the hell was the matter with the bitch? It was time.

"Hands in the air!" shouted Katia, stamping her foot in agitation. "Nobody move!"

Startled by the shrillness of the tone and the sight of weapons appearing from beneath coats and jackets, the bearded guard obeyed, glancing nervously at Oleg's revolver, which was not too far from his chest.

"Come on," yelled Oleg. "All you people, hands up!"

One elderly lady in a faded-green dress and a pincenez took one look at the weapons and collapsed in a heap. Some people gasped or screamed, but most just stood staring like fools, shocked at the idea of being robbed in the middle of the afternoon in such a perfectly respectable location.

"You," gestured Oleg to the guard, departing a little from Katia's original plan, "go inside the vault and start bringing out the money. Hurry!"

Glancing at the bank manager, the guard received the go-ahead and proceeded into the open vault in search of cash.

"You too," ordered the burly young man, pointing his revolver at the manager. "Help him."

"Dimya," commanded Katia, angry at the departure from orders, "help them both. And make it quick!"

Madly stuffing wads of banknotes into the bank's own canvas bags, the manager, the guard and Dimitri Scriabin all worked as rapidly as possible, while Oleg, Katia, Pyotr and Valery held guns on everyone else.

"Hurry!" repeated Katia nervously while the captives stared and waited with their hands raised and their hearts beating wildly.

"All right!"

"Hey!" shouted Oleg, pointing to an elderly army officer, "he's got a gun!"

Furiously Katia took aim and fired at the man who was reaching inside his jacket. As people screamed and ran for the other side of the room, the wounded man rolled onto the floor, clutching a pillbox.

"You savage!" shouted an outraged bystander, safely hidden by a post.

"Shut up! Come on, Dimya. Let's get out of here!"

Obeying at once, young Scriabin grabbed the canvas sack crammed with ruble notes and ran from the vault, leaving the guard and the manager standing amid a pile of scattered banknotes, fallen at their feet like autumn leaves.

"Out, out, out!" shouted Katia, still keeping the crowd covered with her revolver as her comrades ran past her through the wide brass entrance doors.

Then, as she too turned and fled, the bank guard drew his gun and fired, missing the girl but catching Valery in the neck. The young man screamed and went sprawling onto the marble floor, wedged between the heavy doors, trapped by their weight and his own wound.

Without even looking back, Katia burst through the outer doors and onto the street, racing frantically toward the waiting coach. To her horror, it wasn't anywhere in sight.

"What's happened?" she shrieked at Oleg, Pyotr and Dimitri, who were running down the street, weaving in and out through the curious crowds.

"Who knows? Just get the hell out of here on the double! They'll be after us in a minute," replied Oleg, shouting over his shoulder.

Terrified at being caught in the middle of the city with the marked bag stuffed with the bank's money, Dimitri ripped off his coat as he ran and wrapped it around the sack.

"Down that street," ordered Katia, panting. "We'll catch a tram. Keep that thing covered, for God's sake!"

"Why did you have to shoot that old man?" Oleg panted angrily, puffing to keep up the pace. "That was brainless and stupid. Senseless!" These tearoom bandits might be able to talk rings around him in matters of Marxist theory, but they were fools. And a definite danger to him.

"If you hadn't shouted about a gun, I wouldn't have," retorted Katia, gasping for breath. "It's all your fault! And you don't listen!"

"We should have tried to bring Valery with us," groaned Dimya beside her, "it was disloyal to leave him like that."

"Idiot! We didn't have time. We all knew the risks. What I'd like to know is what happened to that fool with the coach!"

Stopping to catch their breath, they leaned on the stone fence in front of a wealthy merchant's home, a typical Moscow mercantile extravaganza of robin's egg-blue with graceful white molding. With the crazy zigzag path they'd taken, nobody would have been able to trace them; still they couldn't linger too long. Already the porter of the house was casting suspicious glances their way.

"We have to split up," directed Katia. "It's too ridiculous to run around in a pack. Get to the rendezvous on your own and tell Pavel what happened. And," she added fiercely, "shoot that damned Josif if you ever see him again!"

"Right," agreed Dimya.

"God," thought Katia, watching her henchmen depart, "what a pack of incompetents. Pavel will be furious."

She brushed aside the entreaties of a strolling *kvass* vendor who waved a glass of his brew in her direction, insisting it would lift her spirits.

"No thanks, old man," she replied sourly. "Today I need a lot more than that to pick me up."

And silently cursing Josif and his vanished vehicle, Katia Petrovna cast aside the old shawl she had worn during the robbery, flinging it into a dark courtyard as she rushed to catch a passing tram. She was infuriated by the afternoon's performance and ready to tear Pavel Scriabin limb from limb if he dared to say one critical word about it.

St. Petersburg

"So, Mishkin, what news do you have for me?" asked Petrov as he and a colleague met for dinner in one of St. Petersburg's noisier restaurants. "Anything interesting?"

"Delightful," chuckled Mishkin as the white-aproned waiter deposited a gleaming brass samovar on their table. "It concerns a lady we both know and love."

"The tsaritsa?"

"Don't be amusing, Roman Vasilievich. I'm talking about our favorite redhead."

"Ah, Katia Petrovna you mean. Yes, that *is* interesting."

Petrov placed a cube of sugar in his teeth and picked up a steaming glass of tea in its metal filigree holder, sipping the dark-amber brew carefully.

"What did our beauty do now?"

"Robbed a bank in Moscow almost a month ago with some friends."

"Who?"

"The dead one they left behind was an ex-student who attended Moscow University with Katia. From eyewitness accounts, one of the Scriabins was involved too—Dimitri, the lesser of the two evils," he said.

"So?"

"I'm getting to the good part, Petrov. One of the eyewitnesses I interviewed only last week swore he recognized that Ivanov of yours at the scene. He says Oleg Ivanov was the one who ordered the guard to help clean out the vault. He was able to identify him from pictures on wanted posters, purely by accident. We had no idea Ivanov knew Katia. And, by the way, he now sports a rather sparse beard. Just thought I'd let you know."

"Christ! Why didn't you tell me this when it happened? I've been looking all over for him."

"Well, Petrov, I only just received the word myself."

Roman Vasilievich removed his spectacles and nervously polished them with a soiled handkerchief. "Damn," he muttered.

"At least we know he's thrown in his lot with Katia and those Scriabin idiots. If we find one, we're likely to find them all."

"Where are they?"

"Nobody knows. They've gone underground again. By the way, they made quite a nice withdrawal from the bank. Over 200,000 rubles."

"Very impressive."

"But, of course, they lost one of their members."

Petrov shrugged. "A nobody."

"A nobody with interesting connections," replied Mishkin, an old colleague, a chubby little fellow with a gap between his front teeth.

"Really?"

"Yes indeed. This one was involved with the sons of two very prominent aristocrats. All three boys dabbled in revolution and used the Finnish villa of one of the fathers as a hiding place for smuggled weapons. We raided it last week and gave a certain prince the shock of his life when we questioned him about it. He professed total ignorance, of course."

"Of course."

"In a way, it's too bad this boy was killed. We were anxious to grab him for questioning. He might have been able to give us some useful information about their arms supplier."

"Pity," mumbled Petrov. "Did Oleg escape?"

"Oh yes. Along with Katia and the others."

"Funny. She used to consider herself too fancy to bother with a brute of Ivanov's type. He's not like her regular cronies, head-in-the-clouds intellectual misfits. From what I heard about his behavior in Moscow province, he's a savage. That horse...."

"There was also an attack on a young girl. Very violent." Mishkin leaned across the table confidentially. "I heard it was rape as well as attempted murder. And the family is trying to hush up all the grisly details."

"Where did you hear that?" demanded Petrov. The prince hadn't said anything about rape. Had he missed something? He was annoyed.

"One of my contacts in court circles told me the story. He was in the area visiting when the crime occurred. He was told about it by someone else," explained Mishkin. "Too bad. They say she's pretty too."

"There was no rape. It was a *beating* she suffered," declared Roman Vasilievich firmly. He wouldn't allow Mishkin to brag about his superior knowledge like this. He could be quite irritating when he started giving himself airs.

"Suit yourself," replied Mishkin. "It's what I heard."

The two Okhrana men looked across the restaurant with its shiny brass samovars, racks of painted lacquer trays and noisy balalaika band, and they wondered about Katia Petrovna's plans for the future.

"I need to find Katia," said Petrov, making a stab at a plate of *zakouski*. "She'll lead me to Ivanov."

Mishkin eyed him suspiciously as he popped a pickled mushroom into his mouth. "Passion for justice?" he inquired.

"You could call it that."

"Ivanov is pretty small potatoes."

"Let's say he has interesting possibilities."

A wild shout went up from one of the corner tables where a jolly group of caftan-garbed merchants from the Gostiny Dvor, one of St. Petersburg's largest bazaars, were staging a drinking contest. One fat man had just slumped slowly to the floor, completely inebriated and out of the running.

"What's in it for me?" demanded Mishkin, looking Petrov in the eye.

"Five hundred rubles for accurate information leading to Ivanov's capture by me."

Mishkin calculated that if Petrov were offering him 500, his own expectations must be at least three times that. And that was a conservative estimate.

"One thousand," replied Mishkin.

"Six hundred."

"Eight hundred."

"Six fifty."

"Make it 700 and you've got a deal."

"You drive a hard bargain, Mishkin."

"But you can afford it, Petrov, or you wouldn't make me the offer."

"I'm a poor man. This is a terrible sacrifice for me."

"You have such a passion for justice, Roman Vasilievich."

"Yes. Just so."

They broke the seal on a bottle of vodka to cement the deal. Roman Vasilievich was pleased to have saved so much money; he had been prepared to risk at least 1500 to buy Mishkin's cooperation; this bargain rate was a pleasant surprise.

"*Na zdarovye!*" he smiled, hoisting his glass. "Let's drink to the success of our hunt."

When Adam received Anya's letter, he had been both relieved and worried. She informed him of an accident she had had while crossing the Place de la Concorde and asked him to come to see her in Paris as soon as possible. It was of the greatest importance, she'd written, and he hadn't waited to be asked twice.

Informing his colleagues he was taking some overdue vacation time and pointedly avoiding Billy's prying questions about the sudden decision to go to Europe, Adam had packed that afternoon, taken the overnight train to Moscow, boarded the *Nord Express* at Nicholas Station, then headed south to Paris by way of Warsaw, Dresden and Berlin.

As the flat, monotonous landscape of European Russia slid by the windows of his first-class compartment, Adam saw nothing of the peasants laboring in the fields, ignored the occasional troop of soldiers riding by, failed to observe the charming little roadside shrines where devout country women placed bouquets of wildflowers on the way to or from their chores. All he saw was a delicate blonde girl standing in the salon of her uncle's house, covered with bruises and terrorized by the attack of a mad-man. Anya needed a protector, all the more so since he had overheard unsavory rumors about the incident.

In his eagerness to reach Paris, Adam ignored every stop along the line. At the Warsaw station he was furious to find the train running twenty minutes behind schedule because of the delayed arrival of an important lady who was to take the famous express to Paris. Nobody knew who it could be, but everybody had his or her own theory. Members of the im-perial family were high on the list of possibilities. There was a great deal of running about on the part of railway officials, who had cordoned off a section of the platform to contain the growing crowd that was restlessly pushing and shoving in their eagerness to see a tiny woman in an elegant peach-colored coat, half-hidden by two towering policemen.

"My God!" exclaimed the gentleman to Adam's left. "Look who it is! No wonder they held up the train!"

Adam glanced out the windows of the dining car, taking in the crowd, the lady and her escorts. "A grand duchess?" he ventured.

"Grand duchess!" laughed his companion. "Sir, you can't be serious. You mean to tell me you don't recognize her?"

"Should I?" replied Adam, quite annoyed that this little creature should have set him back twenty minutes, going on twenty-five. "Is she a person of some renown?"

"I should say so. It's Zenaida Kashina."

Since that was said with such an authoritative air, Adam supposed the appropriate reply could only be "Aha!" But he didn't feel like obliging.

"She's the reigning queen at the Maryinsky ballet," explained the gentleman. "And she left St. Petersburg in the middle of a terrible scan-dal. She's the reason one of the younger grand dukes was just banished to his estates in Moldavia. Now she's on tour in Europe and playing to packed houses in each city. Fabulous woman!"

"Ah," nodded Adam, "the lady's a dancer."

"My dear fellow, Zenaida Kashina is *the* dancer of our era. You ought to see her if you can manage to secure tickets. How could you possibly not know about her?"

"I've spent the past several years in the jungle," replied Adam, not entirely lying, considering his service in Cuba and the Philippines.

On the platform, the ballerina was making her way toward the near-est railway carriage with the assistance of her police escort. People were waving to her, shouting after her, frantically trying to get her attention, if only for a brief smile. Struggling to keep her balance among the crush of hysterical admirers, Kashina graciously tossed roses from the bouquet she held in her arms to the more vocal members of the crowd, distracting them from screaming in her pretty ears while she and her escorts fought their way aboard the train.

Once safely on board, the woman was joined by a tall man in the uniform of a Russian general who led her into the dining car on his arm, amid the general applause of the passengers. Kashina smiled as though she spent most of her time pleasing strangers, albeit obviously relieved that these people showed no inclination to maul her.

As the ballerina passed Adam, she glanced briefly at him, taking his curious expression for wonder-struck admiration and rewarding it with a genuinely beautiful smile. And then she was gone, settling into a corner table with her general and reaching with great determination for the menu.

"What a life she must lead," whispered Adam's companion as he watched Kashina in rapt adoration. "Isn't she superb?"

She certainly was. But she also looked very much like a pretty girl who needed a good night's sleep—and who wasn't likely to get it that evening. Studying the tiny, dark-haired, dark-eyed ballerina, Adam wished he were already in Paris.

Paris

When the Nord Express finally pulled into the noisy, bustling train station in the French capital, the American was leaning out the window of his compartment, anxiously scanning the platform for any sign of Anya. There were several people standing there, straining to see into the windows of the incoming train, but so far, no Anya.

Well, he thought, disappointed, perhaps the delay at Warsaw threw everyone's plans off.

And when he saw her, standing next to Princess Ksenia, both ladies slim and elegant, wearing fashionable silk afternoon frocks from the house of Poiret, Ksenia in pale green, Anya in pink, each with a matching toque. Anya was waving to him, dismayed he hadn't recognized her yet.

"Anya!" he shouted. Delighted to find her there after all, the young man waved frantically, making both princesses smile as they returned the greetings.

Anya tried hard to appear dignified. What she wanted to do was rush to the train's open window and throw her arms around him as some young Frenchman was doing with a lady in the next car, but it wasn't proper. Strange how so much of human nature always seemed to be at odds with propriety, she thought with a guilty smile.

As the porter took his luggage, Adam kissed Princess Ksenia's extended hand and then took both of Anya's hands in his as he looked tenderly into her light eyes, wanting to take her into his arms. "How are you, Anyushka?" he heard himself saying as if the circumstances were quite ordinary instead of rather mysterious and tinged with an emotion all three could feel.

"I feel much better," she smiled, her eyelashes fluttering only slightly as she looked up into his dark eyes. "Adam Mikhailovich," she murmured, "I'm so glad you're here. As soon as we go home, we must have a talk. It's important."

"Of course," he replied. And he sensed from her expression that whatever they were about to discuss would be extraordinary.

Princess Ksenia smiled a lovely, enigmatic smile and prayed silently for success.

Outside the Gare du Nord where the Sviridovs' black Mercedes was parked in a long line of other private motorcars and taxis, some sort of confrontation was going on. In a stylish black and white frock with a black tunic, Madame Kashina was tapping her foot at curbside while a tall gentleman stood next to her, talking in low tones. In front of her, the Sviridov ladies recognized another automobile belonging to Prince Sandro. And inside it was the prince himself, almost hidden from view. Only the chauffeur was visible.

It appeared that Madame Kashina had a surplus of admirers today. She was caught between two of them and quite sulky about it.

How can he do this to himself? thought Ksenia, taking in the scene. It's a surrender of all dignity. Foolish old man.

Paul, the driver of the ladies' automobile, a stocky Frenchman with a permanently worried expression, winced and hastily helped his passengers into the motorcar before they could view any more of His Highness's little drama. Paul was old-fashioned; he hated to see a man behave badly before the eyes of his children. And he liked the two princesses.

Once the party arrived at the Sviridov mansion, Adam was shown to his room, an empire masterpiece in shades of gold whose decor owed a great deal to an Egyptian craze of a hundred years earlier. Most of the rosewood furniture bore carvings of the heads and paws of bronze sphinxes, and on two of the silk-paneled walls were hung masterpieces by Delacroix and Géricault of Napoleon's Egyptian campaign, featuring the emperor in heroic poses. If the young man hadn't been so worried about Anya and eager to know the reason for his invitation to this place, he would have been impressed.

After a luncheon that seemed to last forever, Princess Ksenia suggested to Anya that Mr. Lowell might wish to see the gardens. She would join them later, she said. To her annoyance, her father still hadn't returned; he was obviously busy elsewhere. And if it had escaped Anya's attention, the young American had understood the situation perfectly. She could tell from his careful avoidance of any potentially embarrassing questions.

Anya, lovely in her pink silk frock, had surprised Adam by wearing her hair up, a grown-up touch that was very appealing. In all the time he had known her, she had always worn it loose or caught at the back of her neck in a wide bow. Now, displaying a double strand of pearls with a small diamond catch and fine pearl earrings, she was elegant.

Seated on a marble bench in the shade of a huge chestnut tree, the young couple was alone except for two gardeners trimming an ornamental hedge. Princess Ksenia was nervously but discreetly keeping an eye on things from her upstairs sitting room as she sat writing to Andrei at her small escritoire near the windows.

"Adam Mikhailovich," murmured the young princess, "I'm so happy you were able to come visit me. It hasn't been a pleasant time."

The young man looked at her tenderly. She was struggling.

"I told you that day at Byelaya Beryozka that if you ever felt things were so bad that you didn't know what to do, I would help you. I meant it, Anya." He looked at her beautiful face and saw just a faint trace of the bruises under her natural glowing color.

Suddenly she said, "Adam Mikhailovich, you know what happened to me at Byelaya Beryozka."

"Yes. I was there."

Anya's eyelashes fluttered a little, and he saw the pearls rise and fall on her bosom.

"Well," she faltered, "someone told Grand-père that it was worse than what it was. It's so dreadful. Unbelievable. Terrible stories are spreading...."

"Anya," he whispered, taking her hand, "I know what you are referring to. Do you think I would ever believe any of that?"

"I know you wouldn't. It's other people who would. They do, in fact."

The young princess felt her throat tighten as Adam gently pressed her hand. Her idea had seemed brilliant when she thought of it, but now, with him right next to her, she was very scared.

"Anyushka," said Adam, looking at her intently, "I care for you very much. I liked you when you were simply the little girl from the Luxembourg Gardens. But when I saw you at Byelaya Beryozka, I saw you for the first time as a grown woman."

Startled, Anya's blue eyes widened slightly and Adam saw the pearls rise and fall rather rapidly.

"This gossip means nothing to me—except that it hurts you. If I can do anything to stop it, I will," he promised.

"What I would like to ask is enormous," she said, almost inaudibly, her fingers entwined with his, her eyes meeting his.

For a moment Adam stared at her, half-understanding but not quite ready to believe what he was thinking. It couldn't be.

"Adam Mikhailovich," she said quietly, "I have a lot of affection for you. If you truly mean what you said, I would like you to ask Grand-père for my hand in marriage."

For a second the young man was speechless. And then he forgot himself and, leaning closer to Princess Anya, kissed her gently on the lips. The girl trembled with emotion as he drew her close to him for an instant. Hesitating for a long, tense minute, Adam murmured "I will." Then, "When?"

My God! Had he actually said it? He felt dazed, as if he had only dreamed it.

"Soon," whispered Anya, giddy. Her hand was fluttering at her pearls as she gazed in amazement at Adam Mikhailovich, who had just astonished her. "As soon as possible."

Ksenia was standing at the window now, brought to her feet by the surge of emotion in the garden. I think he must have said yes, she speculated, smiling wistfully.

"Anya," said Adam, still holding the girl's hand, "I love you and I want you to know that I intend to be a good husband to you. I'm not a man who would enter into marriage lightly. If I give my word, it's for life. And I expect the same from you."

"Yes," whispered Anya. "I wouldn't want anyone else. Ever." Well, she thought, she had done it. And he had said yes! Looking with wonder at the handsome dark-haired man beside her, she knew that he loved her and that he would do anything she wanted at the moment. So much power was a new experience; it was also a little alarming. She was only seventeen!

"I love you," whispered Anya, almost to herself, fascinated by the sound of it. It was ridiculous but she couldn't remember which language she had been speaking when she had proposed to him. French was what she ordinarily used with non-Russians, but Russian was the language of the heart, the truest expression of her feelings. Her inner self.

"I love you," came his answer in Russian, and from that moment on she knew she was right. The feeling had come straight from the heart; there was no mistake.

Adam was almost as startled as Princess Anya by his quick response to her marriage proposal. On the train down, he had been speculating on the reason for the invitation, but this had never entered his mind. And yet it was the very thing he himself wanted. He was in love for only the second time in his life, and his feelings for Anya were just as strong as they had been for Catherine several years earlier.

When this engagement was announced in St. Petersburg, the whole town would say he was a fortune-hunting foreigner who was marrying Princess Sviridova for her money. What a joke. The gossips of the capital were far too sophisticated ever to suspect the truth. It was too simple for them. Adam Michael Lowell, formerly of Boston, Massachusetts, was in love with a beautiful girl who had just given him back the world.

When Anya and her fiancé paid Princess Ksenia a visit in her rooms immediately after their tête-à-tête in the garden, the princess kissed them tenderly on both cheeks, wished them happiness and promised to prepare the way for Adam's formal request to Prince Sandro for Anya's hand in marriage.

"A word of advice, Adam Mikhailovich," murmured Anya as she, Princess Ksenia and Mr. Lowell enjoyed their afternoon tea among the lovely blossoms of the formal garden. "Approach Grand-père as if you were a prince asking the tsar for the hand of a grand duchess. It's the best way." As if he would say no! she thought mischievously.

Casting a sly, sidelong glance at her aunt, Princess Anya received an amused smile in return.

God help this poor fellow, thought Ksenia. He doesn't know what he's in for! "I'll do my best to arrange things for tomorrow," she promised. "And good luck."

Squeezing his hand, Anya looked sweetly into Adam's eyes and smiled endearingly.

Prince Sandro's interview with his granddaughter's suitor took place in the classic manner. At a formal meeting in Sandro's private apartment— while Anya and Ksenia waited expectantly in an adjoining room—Adam Michael Lowell asked Prince Alexander Alexandrovich Sviridov for the hand of Princess Anna Nicolaievna Sviridova in marriage.

To nobody's surprise, he was accepted. Three days later, the betrothal was celebrated with a flood of champagne at a private party where Sandro had gathered fifty of his most intimate Paris cronies. Notable for her absence was Zenaida Kashina, to the great relief of Princess Ksenia.

It was noted that the groom-to-be wore a slightly dazzled expression each time he glanced at his fiancée. His betrothed wore a diamond necklace that could have equaled the state treasury of one of the smaller European principalities.

St. Petersburg

When Aunt Lisa read the story a few days later, she was wild with rage. That necklace was her mother's and it had been promised to her years ago. Estranged from her father or not, she meant to have it. And God help that blonde brat, Anya, if she thought she was going to walk off with even a single stone!

"It's all your fault, Seriozha!" screamed the countess, hurling the newspaper at her husband. "If you hadn't tried to swindle Papa, he wouldn't have threatened to disinherit me!"

Countess Lisa looked especially fetching, wearing a black afternoon frock of fine wool crepe trimmed with satin at the cuffs and bodice. Black lace set off her lovely white bosom, and three strands of large pearls encircled her beautiful slender neck. Large diamonds flashed fire each time she tossed her head, which was often, since Lisa was quite dramatic and thoroughly enraged.

"Swindled?" exclaimed Seriozha. "It was hardly that. I admit it was less than legal, but when I told the director of the Crédit Lyonnais that Sandro would cover me if our plans fell through, I was speaking as a son-in-law. I assumed he wouldn't wish to expose his family to the embarrassment of a lawsuit over defaulting on a loan."

"You should have asked him. When he was told by the director of the bank, he was furious. And now he holds it against *me*. You have enough money. Why do you have to use *his?*"

Count Derzhavin sighed. His beautiful wife didn't understand finance. He had earned millions by letting other people finance his textile holdings.

"You are a weasel, Seriozha," Lisa said contemptuously.

That remark struck a nerve for Seriozha was terribly short and wiry, with the face of a ferret. While Sandro usually referred to his son-in-law—behind his back—as a perverse dwarf, Lisa called him a weasel to his face. His tall, beautiful, blackhaired wife tolerated him only for the sake of the endless treasures he bestowed on her.

"If I'm a weasel, darling, you're a parrot, insinuating all sorts of nasty things about that unfortunate child and her misfortune on your brother-in-law's estate. If Ksenia ever finds out who started those rumors, she'll kill you. She's quite maternal, you know. Unlike you."

At that, the countess flung a cushion from the sofa at him, making him laugh. The drawing room was done in red and gold with decorative objects plundered from Etruscan tombs. Seriozha was grateful Lisa wasn't hurling those.

"The worst thing about your rumors, darling, is that they didn't work. The child's apparently become so alluring, this young diplomat can hardly wait to marry her. According to the article, the wedding's scheduled for September," he noted, glancing at the paper lying scattered on the sofa.

"Yes," replied the countess, "but they ought to know the folklore. No true Russian would ever marry in that month. It's bad luck."

"Perhaps Americans are immune to these things," he smiled.

Well, Anya shouldn't be, thought the countess as she stamped her foot in a spasm of frustrated rage. How could that blonde brat have turned things around so beautifully? She was only a child, no match for an experienced schemer like herself. Since when was *she* able to manipulate the old man so skillfully? Little Sainte Nitouche!

"I can see another influence at work in this," announced Seriozha, practically reading his wife's mind.

"Yes," she agreed bitterly. "Ksenia."

Both Derzhavins looked quite glum at the thought. The combination of Princess Ksenia and Princess Anya allied with Sandro against them had always haunted Lisa's dreams. Ever since childhood, she had feared her sister's influence with the old man, secretly dreading the time when Ksenia would succeed in gaining the upper hand and persuading the old fool to cut her off without a ruble.

Now Sandro's fury with Derzhavin seemed to be fulfilling her worst fears. If he should ever discover who had started those rumors, there would be no hope for her.

Countess Lisa's huge diamond earrings were sparkling more than usual as she carefully studied her reflection in the gilded mirror to her right. She was beautiful—at least that satisfied her. And the old man liked to surround himself with beauties. Perhaps she ought to make a show of great sorrow over dear Papa's coldness, weep a few tears in his presence and declare she had made a mistake to have married such a scoundrel as Seriozha. Papa had never liked him. She had married very young. And impulsively.

Yes. That was the right approach to take now, thought the countess, glancing with disdain at her smiling husband as he watched her from across the room. She would blame everything on Seriozha.

9

Moscow

Katia and the Scriabin gang were not the only ones interested in Oleg. R.V. Petrov had put out feelers among the lowlife of the Khitrovka district. He had given them a fairly recent description of Oleg and the promise of twenty gold rubles for information leading to his capture. So far, he had had no takers.

Then one night in late August, the policeman received a tip from a young streetwalker named Sonia that a fellow of that description had accosted her near the river, taken her home with him and roughed her up. She was a young blonde, rather arrogant, still pretty but bearing scars from the encounter. She wanted his hide.

Delighted to be making such rapid progress, Petrov alerted his friend Mishkin and together they arranged to meet with Sonia, who was to lead them to their boy. But when Sonia's pimp had heard she was talking with the Okhrana, he had beaten her so viciously that she'd been taken to the charity ward of some unspecified hospital. Petrov found this out from a competitor of hers, an alcoholic whore named Masha, who told them the story when they arrived at the grimy *traktir* to keep their date with Sonia.

Plying Masha with vodka, Petrov and Mishkin listened carefully as the woman rambled on and on, her frizzy blonde head sinking occasionally to the table as she clutched her precious bottle of vodka, caressing it as lovingly as if it were a child.

"But did Sonia ever tell you where the man lived?" sighed Petrov, rolling his eyes in annoyance. Mishkin chuckled as he watched him, a small professorial figure with his glittering round frameless spectacles and fussy little mouth. He knew how Roman Vasilievich was restraining himself from grabbing the damned girl and shaking her until her teeth chattered. He was that frustrated.

"She said something about the rooming house near the Three Thieves," muttered Masha, her eyes bloodshot and barely focused, fearfully searching the dark, noisy, smoky room for any sign of her pimp. "That's all."

Fixing the drunken whore with a cold stare, Petrov said quietly, "Think, girl. Where?" He pointedly dropped a five-ruble piece before her half-closed eyes to stimulate her shaky memory.

That had a miraculous effect on Masha's powers of recollection. Reaching for the gold, she muttered, "The green door."

"Which green door?" demanded Petrov.

"The green door," repeated the woman, trying to wheedle another drink out of the policemen. "Sonia said, 'the green door.' That's all."

And her frizzy head sank down onto the table once again.

"Christ!" muttered Petrov. "There could be a dozen green doors on the tenements near the Three Thieves. That's worse than nothing."

But it was all they had.

In his filthy room, Oleg was pacing the floor, pondering his future as a member of Pavel's gang. He was in a state of panicked confusion. Not only did his suspicions gnaw at him, eroding his trust in his comrades, but there was something even more bizarre, something that left him nearly disoriented. Katia Petrovna, Pavel's arrogant mistress, had nearly seduced him this afternoon, carrying on like a cat in heat as she crawled all over him, telling him she wanted him to accompany her to Kiev where they would carry out the assassination of the century—Bloody Nicholas and his reactionary prime minister at one swoop. There was a comrade already in place, an unknown quantity named Mordka Bogrov with connections to the Okhrana, who would help them. Jesus!

Oleg had been so excited by Katia's passion, he was at the point of taking her when her damned boyfriend started pounding on the door, forcing Oleg to make a run for it. He still couldn't quite believe Katia's sudden about-face. She wanted *him* to make history with her. *Him!* He longed to be adulated by a woman like that, but Katia made him so vulnerable before his own desires, she frightened him. Besides, he thought cautiously, it was a big step up from the Malyshevs to the Romanovs. And the tsar would be surrounded by soldiers.

The whole idea was insane, he thought. Maybe Katia was too. But *God* she was beautiful. She got him so excited he couldn't think straight any more.

Basically he distrusted the whole gang. They appeared to have little faith in him. But they were the only people who were offering him a way to realize his ambitions and put his past failures behind him. They were stuck with each other.

It was an association that brought him little comfort. And tonight his uneasiness was torturing him, making him a little crazy.

The people in this house stare at me, he thought to himself. They can't be trusted. He recalled an incident from earlier in the day, involving an old hag who lived two doors down the hall. Oleg remembered how she had gawked at him, peering at him with hideous, hollow eyes as he passed her in the corridor. Was she a police spy? Was he in a house of spies?

He couldn't take a chance on having his suspicions confirmed. He would leave this place, he decided. And he would leave immediately. They would have to work hard to turn *him* over to the police. He wasn't about to be betrayed by some decrepit old crone who would drink away her reward in one of the district's seedy *traktirs*. He was too clever for that.

Determined to outwit his neighbors, he reached for the canvas bag he used to store his possessions.

Outside on the street, Petrov and Mishkin were grumbling as they located the Three Thieves tavern and proceeded to scout the area for a boarding-house with a green door. There were three of them in the vicinity, all tenements with peeling paint and broken windows, filthy rattraps catering to the dregs of the population.

"You try the one on that side of the street. I'll start here," said Petrov. "If we locate him, we signal each other. Don't try to take him alone."

"Right," nodded Mishkin.

And they both reached instinctively for their Brownings, hidden beneath their jackets.

As Roman Vasilievich returned to the street after talking with the landlady of the first building, he decided Mishkin was taking too long and ventured cautiously inside the tenement he had seen his friend enter.

On the second floor, Oleg was making his way downstairs when he heard his landlady in a muffled conversation, talking nervously to a stranger who was asking questions that made the hairs of his neck stand on end.

Overcome with fright, he cursed under his breath and nearly tripped over his own two feet as he scrambled backward up the stairs in total panic.

They were after him! Terror-stricken, he fled down the hall and collided with a boozy couple staggering into one of the rank-smelling rooms frequented by prostitutes and their customers.

"Watch it!"

"Watch yourself," muttered Oleg, shoving aside the drunks as he raced toward the back stairs, clutching his bag and sweating with terror.

Alerted by the noise upstairs, Mishkin and the landlady came running just as Petrov appeared in the hall.

"Is there a back entrance?" shouted Petrov, a little out of breath.

"Yes."

"I'll cover it."

In the smoky darkness of the tenement stairwell, Oleg was groping his way down the rickety back stairs, desperate to flee to the relative security of the narrow, twisted streets and alleys he knew so well. Once out on the street, he would be safe from any pursuer, especially one unfamiliar with the sprawling maze of the Khitrovka.

Roman Vasilievich rounded the shabby wooden building, tripping over a collection of broken bottles and garbage festering in the back courtyard, his revolver in his hand. And then he saw a well-built young man clambering down the wooden stairs, bag in hand, the pale moonlight illuminating his light Russian blouse and pale, shaggy hair.

"Oleg Ivanov," muttered Petrov to himself. It had to be. This was easier than he had hoped. He was about to make his fortune.

Petrov darted under the open framework of the stairs, unseen in the shadows as his prey made his way down. Then without warning he reached out and grabbed Oleg's foot as he planted it on the step in line with Petrov's chest. Oleg sprawled headlong down the stairs and onto a pile of filth in the yard. Cursing in fear, the young man staggered to his feet only to find himself facing a small fellow in a shabby suit. His most distinctive attributes were his glittering round spectacles and the revolver in his hand.

Desperate to avoid capture, the young man seized the first thing at hand, the bag that had come tumbling down the stairs behind him, and hurled it violently at the stranger, catching him squarely in the middle and knocking him off balance, his revolver discharging in the air as he staggered in the darkened courtyard. Recovering, Petrov lunged after Ivanov.

"Mishkin!" screamed the inspector. "Help me!"

But before reinforcements could arrive, Oleg flung himself at Petrov, sending both of them sprawling in the mud. Ivanov bashed the inspector's head savagely on the step, stunning him.

As he broke away from Roman Vasilievich's faltering grip, he grabbed his sack of possessions, leaped over a nearby fence and was out of sight and heading for a safe night's lodging halfway across town.

Now he had all the motivation he needed to accompany Katia Petrovna wherever she wanted to take him, provided it was far from Moscow.

St. Petersburg

The tinkling sound of the bell brought the hall porter to the entranceway, and he bowed as he greeted the visitor, ushering the lady into the foyer where her exquisite black and white ensemble matched the large marble tiles of the floor. For a second, Countess Natalya Grekova resembled the queen on a chessboard. She paused on a square, then walked with little clicking steps to the white and gold salon where Princess Ksenia and Anya were waiting.

Greeting Natalya with kisses, the ladies declared themselves glad to be home once again after the dreadful scare Sandro had given them in Paris. That had been the *official* reason for their trip to Paris, a useful fabrication.

"It was his heart," said Ksenia as Anya tried hard not to smile. "We were so worried about him. But he seems better now." Sandro had the healthiest "bad heart" in the world! Very convenient!

Displayed like jewels on the white and gold silk-and-gilt sofas of Ksenia's white-paneled salon that was hung with eighteenth-century French tapestries designed by Boucher, the ladies were worthy of their setting. All were beautifully dressed and gracious—and all hid their own secrets. Natalya was causing as much talk lately as Anya.

"Still," said Ksenia piously, "the scare made Papa so anxious about Anya's wedding, we've had to rush like maniacs. It's now set for September."

"September!" squeaked the countess. My God! Sandro must be dying, she thought. September was a bad omen.

Fully aware of the tradition, Ksenia merely shrugged. "Anyushka is too modern to worry about old wives tales. So am I."

"It's Grand-père I care about," replied Anya. "I want him there."

"Isn't she extraordinary, Natalya? When we learned of Papa's condition, it was Anya herself who insisted on forgoing a more elaborate wedding, just to be certain of having Papa attend."

"But how will you manage? Who's going to prepare the bridal gown? That at least has to be done well."

"Auntie was kind enough to allow me to use hers," said Anya. "It was something I've always wanted."

"Ah," murmured Natalya, "I'm sure you'll be an elegant bride."

"Yes," replied Ksenia, "and Madame Brissac here in Petersburg can do the necessary alterations. Everything is arranged."

"Oh, this is too exciting!" bubbled Natalya. "I can't wait to tell Gigi!"

At the mention of that name, Ksenia tilted her head thoughtfully. Everyone had heard several startling rumors concerning Natalya and her spiritual mentor, Gregory Efimovich Rasputin, but lately Princess Ksenia had heard an astonishing story involving Natalya, her husband and her brother-in-law, Gigi. "Oh, is he back in Petersburg, *chérie?* I thought he was still wandering around the Balkans?"

"He returned two weeks ago."

"Ah. He must come and have tea with me. I'd love to hear about his adventures."

Ksenia and her young niece both noticed a vague uneasiness in the countess, but couldn't account for it. Her normally pale cheeks were becoming ever so slightly pink.

Natalya started talking quite rapidly, regretting having mentioned her brother-in-law. "He dug up some lovely ancient Roman graves in Bulgaria. Piles of jewelry. And he had a chance to spend three days in Montenegro with Stana and Militza's papa, King Nikolai," added the countess.

Anya sat dreaming of romance and weddings. Still, she noticed that Countess Grekova's voice was rising with emotion as she argued with Ksenia Alexandrovna over the merits of her spiritual mentor, Gregory Efimovich Rasputin. She was astonished to see Natalya so thoroughly stirred up over this fellow. The countess had always struck her as a rather mild, soft creature, utterly devoted to her vast wardrobe and her young son. This was a revelation. She was absolutely passionate about Rasputin. Even more so than about Count Grekov the digger, Anya noticed.

"You sneer at him, Ksenia," declared Natalya, her voice quivering with feeling. "You, Andrei, my husband, my mother-in-law. But none of you knows how saintly he is. Why, that good soul is purity itself. He's the living reincarnation of Christ."

"That's blasphemy."

"That's the truth," retorted Natalya, making Anya's eyes widen. "He's Christ reborn!"

"For God's sake," fumed Princess Ksenia, "you've heard the same stories we all have. The animal's just been accused of raping a nun."

Gasping at that, Anya stared at the ladies, astonished that Auntie would be so outspoken. It reminded her of Ksenia's explosion of fury on the night she had been attacked.

Now Natalya was pacing the floor, shaking with righteous indignation. "You are all so warped in your outlook. Gregory Efimovich pities you, even while you persecute him."

"Natalya, I have never persecuted him. Don't blame me for his present troubles. It's the prime minister who's banished him from Petersburg."

"That wicked man. Believe me, Ksenia, the day of reckoning is at hand for that one. And sooner than he suspects."

"Yes. I hear the tsaritsa is pressing for his dismissal."

Natalya paused in midstep and shook her head. "No, you don't understand," she said, as if she were speaking to a child. "It's God's will. Alexandra Feodorovna is merely serving as His instrument. It's all in God's hands, and He will not abandon His faithful servant."

Wide-eyed with amazement, Anya stared at Countess Natalya. For all her elegant attire—her beautiful cream-colored, lace-trimmed linen suit, her white ostrich plumes waving above her picture hat, her pearls, her gold and diamond crosses—she had all the religious fervor of an illiterate peasant girl, unwavering in her belief in miracles, holy men and divine intervention.

Anya could almost imagine the gorgeous Natalya, ostrich plumes sweeping the ground, on her knees before this *starets* of hers, bowing and kissing his rough hands just as the peasants did with the wandering pilgrims who passed through Byelaya Beryozka, begging for alms and praising God. But those men were harmless. This Gregory Efimovich sounded like no holy man on earth!

Caught staring, the girl smiled uneasily and suggested that if it was God's will, they'd all just have to wait and see.

"Ah, there, Ksenia. The child understands it better than you. Only the pure of heart can comprehend his message."

Ksenia knew Anya was only trying to humor Natalya, but she let it pass. She hated arguing with Andrei's cousin over Gregory Efimovich because there was no point to it. Natalya was quite primitive where religion was concerned. Primitive, gullible—and boring. It made the princess sad to think about it, since the two women had been friends for years. She liked Natalya despite her odd ways, and she rather pitied her.

In the American Embassy on Morkhovaya Street, the third secretary was sitting in his office, looking out the window at the army barracks across the street, seeing nothing, neither the soldiers nor the pedestrians. It annoyed him that the building was in the way. If someone had leveled a path at a 90-degree angle, he would have had a clear view of the Sviridov Palace on the French Embankment, his future home.

Adam had assumed he and Anya would make their home in the spacious apartment he lived in on the Millyonaya, a stylish neighborhood near the Winter Palace. Instead, Prince Sandro informed him he wanted Anya to have her parents' former apartments in his St. Petersburg residence, which he visited only during the winter season. Shortly after her eighteenth birthday, Princess Anya would become mistress of a house that was half the length of a long city block. It was all a bit unreal to Adam.

He had often driven past the Sviridov Palace on the way to or from parties at the neighboring French Embassy, one of the capital's most impressive foreign enclaves, both buildings splendid examples of eighteenth-century Russian classicism, with high windows that reflected the lights of glittering crystal chandeliers each night during the St. Petersburg season, and gilded wrought-iron gates that sent forth elegant motorcars, sleighs, carriages and sledges.

He had been inside the Sviridov mansion during the winter season on three different occasions and had danced there with Catherine as well as with countless Russian ladies, one grand duchess and Ksenia Alexandrovna. And except for Catherine, the only lady whose company Adam had really enjoyed had been Princess Ksenia, possibly the only beautiful woman in St. Petersburg who was faithful to her husband.

Smiling at the recent photograph of Anya on his desk, very chic in its blue-enamel-and-gilt Fabergé frame under rock crystal, the young man thought of her tenderly and was grateful Ksenia had raised his future wife.

As his wedding day approached, Adam Lowell began to understand he had taken an irreversible step the day he'd asked Prince Sandro for Anya's hand. In his first marriage he had been an ordinary husband. Now he would be a prince consort.

It was Sandro's idea. Delighted to see Anya married to someone so presentable in the face of those unsavory and scandalous rumors, the old prince had returned to St. Petersburg for the wedding and had made it known to his dear friend, the Empress Dowager Maria Feodorovna, that he wished to have Mr. Lowell create Prince Sviridov upon his marriage to Anya. Citing a precedent, Princess Yusupova, the last of her line upon her marriage to Count Sumakarov-Elston—and the subsequent birth of two prince Yusupovs—Sandro claimed the same privilege for his granddaughter. Obligingly enough, Maria Feodorovna agreed to ask her son to sign the ukase authorizing Adam's transformation, and a week before the wedding, a liveried court messenger arrived at the imposing yellow-and-white Sviridov mansion bearing the gilt-sealed imperial degree.

Adam was struck speechless. Nobody had asked him if he wanted to become a prince—as a matter of fact, he didn't. As a lifelong republican, he couldn't imagine such a thing. He wondered if it were even legal. It seemed preposterous.

"His Majesty Nicholas II signed the decree," replied Sandro. "There is no question of its legality."

Perhaps not in Russia, thought Adam, but I'm not Russian. After a check with the legal department at the embassy—which Anya and Ksenia thought terribly amusing—Adam Mikhailovich could find nothing that prevented the Russians from calling him whatever they wished, provided he didn't relinquish his American citizenship. And so Mr. Adam Lowell became Prince Adam Sviridov, a title his colleagues found either impressive or hilarious, depending on their nature. After all, said Anya, changing a name isn't such a tragedy. Women did it all the time.

Religion was the second problem. The parish priest had informed them that the wedding would have to be a poor, scaled-down version of the full ceremony if Her Highness married a Protestant. As the priest uttered the words, Anya and Ksenia both turned to Adam and looked at him with such horrified expressions that he knew at once what they intended to ask him to do.

"I was baptized in the Episcopal church," he said defensively.

"What sort of church is that?" asked Ksenia.

"Nearly Catholic."

"That's not so terribly far from Orthodoxy. Truly," murmured Anya.

It took the princesses two days of unrelenting hectoring to wear him down, but finally Adam had to admit he wasn't a fanatic about his religion, and although he went to church services each Sunday, he had been known to attend Methodist, Lutheran, Baptist and even Catholic services if a church of his own denomination was unavailable.

And so Prince Adam underwent the most rapid conversion to Orthodoxy in the history of the church in Russia and hoped that God and his Lowell ancestors would be understanding.

Once the religious problem had been settled to the Sviridovs' satisfaction, they turned their attention to the more mundane business of the wedding dinner, an enormous undertaking involving hundreds of gold and silver plates, antique Sèvres china, massive silver epergnes and other table appointments the Sviridovs had acquired over the centuries. The entire Sviridov mansion was one vast treasure trove. Several kings and emperors would have recognized their favorite possessions there, all resources to be used for Anya's wedding.

"Will Yeliseyev supply the caviar and the *zakouski?*" asked Prince Andrei.

"Of course. And Papa's chef has already told the butcher exactly what we need for the dinner menu. Natalya's man Leroux will take care of the fish dishes and our own pastry chefs will handle the cakes and desserts," replied Ksenia.

"What about the wines, champagnes and vodkas? Have they checked the cellars?"

"Yes. The butler took inventory and ordered what he needed to make up any deficiency."

"Splendid."

The bridegroom was impressed. There had been a pleasant wedding breakfast at the home of Catherine's parents in Pittsfield, Massachusetts, the first time he was married. This was a different story entirely.

"How many guests are you inviting, Ksenia Alexandrovna?" he asked, expecting a fairly conservative number, given his lack of family—except for his half brother, who might not even show up if he were busy enough in Paris, where Adam had recently had him transferred.

"About 200. You must understand that people don't return to Petersburg this soon," she said apologetically.

Adam smiled and wondered what the guest list would have been like at the height of the season.

The news of Adam Lowell's transformation to Prince Adam Sviridov made the rounds of the St. Petersburg salons within twenty-four hours, and not everyone who heard the story offered congratulations. Countess Elizaveta Derzhavina was so outraged by this new caprice on the part of her father that, upon hearing the news at a gathering at Countess Lili Vorontsova's, she gasped, turned on her heel and headed out the door without even a farewell.

She was wild with fury. Prince Sviridov indeed!

The servants couldn't signal her chauffeur quickly enough. Too angry to wait a second longer than necessary, Lisa startled the footmen on duty by rushing out to the street to get the chauffeur herself, causing him to bring the motorcar across Liteiny Prospect in record time, cutting off two horse-drawn cabs and a government vehicle in the process.

"The Malyshev mansion on the Moika Canal," snapped Lisa to her driver as Countess Vorontsova's servants hastily helped her into her automobile. "I want to visit my sister."

I want to kill my sister, she thought grimly, tapping her fingers on the soft leather cushions. And I'd especially love to kill that blonde bitch. How can they do this? After those stories started spreading to Europe I thought I had succeeded in putting her out of the picture forever. Now Papa does this! It's an outrage!

The man must be an out-and-out fortune hunter, thought Lisa. I can remember him vaguely. Tall, handsome. He speaks English with a peculiar accent. An American. Now I can understand why he wanted to marry her! He probably told Papa he'd take her off his hands in exchange for a title.

Glancing out the window, the countess saw a troop of Chevalier Guards ride past in white tunics and white caps and mounted on black horses, heading down Liteiny Prospect to Kirochnaya Street and out to the barracks district. Fine shops and houses mingled with lesser ones on the street. All the shops followed the Russian custom of having the owner's name and the name of the establishment in both Cyrillic and roman letters. Some of the places followed the even older custom of displaying the symbol of their product above the doorway—watchmakers exhibiting a gigantic watch, bakers a loaf of bread. There were many illiterates in Russia as well as an educated class that was fluent in several languages.

In the back seat of her automobile, Countess Lisa was swearing silently in both French and Russian.

Arriving at Ksenia's home, an impressive late-eighteenth-century mansion in yellow and white designed by Quarenghi for one of Andrei's ancestors, Countess Lisa brought the dozing hall porter to his feet with a fierce jangling of the bell. Sweeping past him, she angrily demanded to know where Princess Malysheva was; receiving a nervous response, she headed upstairs.

Passing many Malyshev portraits on the wall beside her as she ascended the white marble staircase, the countess glowered as she paused for a split second to glance at the last two—both portraits of her sister, one by the Italian Boldini, the other by the Russian Serov. There was Ksenia in all her beauty, depicted in the first as an unmistakable *grande dame*, covered with jewels and idly caressing a slender white borzoi as she sat in the gold and white salon downstairs. In the second she was sitting on the terrace at Byelaya Beryozka in a simple white linen frock, her black hair cascading down her shoulders, looking at the observer with an expression of amused skepticism; this was a pretty girl at her leisure.

You scheming bitch, thought Lisa, sweeping past the portraits and making a right-hand turn at the top of the stairs. Passing several large Chinese vases and a footman in livery, the countess came to a halt at a gilt-paneled door and flung it open, rattling the crystal sconces on the wall.

"Hello, Lisa," smiled her sister. "I imagine you must have heard the good news."

"Half an hour ago at Countess Vorontsova's. Why wasn't I told before the whole town knew?"

"You've been avoiding us since your quarrel with Papa. I've made three telephone calls to your home since the tsar sent Papa the decree. You never returned them."

"This is irresponsible," snapped Countess Derzhavina, magnificent in a green and black silk afternoon frock created by Worth in Paris. "First Mama's necklace, now this. It's monstrous!"

"There's nothing monstrous about it," replied her sister, rising to face her, equally elegant in a dark-blue silk frock by Paul Poiret, its fluid lines emphasizing her height and slenderness.

The sisters, almost eye to eye, had nearly identical profiles. Both were delicately beautiful, with large, dark-lashed eyes—Lisa's deep blue, Ksenia's sea-green—fine straight noses and sensual, but rather determined mouths. Neither one would ever give an inch in an argument.

"Papa wants an heir from Anya once she's married, and she's young enough to supply him with one or several. Therefore, he's decided to have her future husband take her name. There is a precedent for it."

Lisa wasn't satisfied. "He hates me for what Derzhavin did," she said bitterly. "I don't deserve to be humiliated in this way."

"Lisa! This has nothing to do with Derzhavin's dealings with the Crédit Lyonnais. It's simply a matter of Papa's wanting to see the family survive. Can you blame him for that?"

"Yes," retorted the countess. "Why should a girl like Anya—with what happened to her—be showered with favors? If Papa wants someone to continue the line, why not my daughter? She, at least, is a virgin!"

"How dare you say that? Don't you ever accuse Anya of being less than that! It's an infamous lie!"

"Then why is it the talk of the salons?"

"Because some lying tart jumped to conclusions," retorted the princess. "That girl has gone through hell. She was beaten by a madman but managed to fight him off. She shouldn't have to put up with these slanders too. Especially from you!"

Lisa was so angry her pearl earrings were beginning to tremble in her earlobes. She resented being called a "lying tart," even if Ksenia didn't realize the truth—and especially if she did!

"And what about Mama's necklace?" she screamed. "Is that brat going to inherit the diamonds too? Or will you divide the stones evenly, like two accomplices in a robbery?"

"What a loathsome accusation! You must be insane!" replied Ksenia, her complexion deepening with rage. "You're consumed with jealousy because your niece was permitted to wear a particular piece of jewelry to a party when you have a vault filled with the jewelry your husband's bought for you! It was a kind gesture on Papa's part, Lisa. Those stones went back into the safe at Boucheron's the next day."

"I don't care. I want everything that ought to be mine. And so, apparently, do you!"

At that, Princess Ksenia reached out and slapped her sister's face hard enough to send one of Lisa's earrings flying across the room.

"Don't ever accuse me of anything like that. Or of neglecting my duties to Anyushka either," she said in a low, furious tone as her sister gasped under the force of the blow. "That little creature you married is nothing but a crook. Papa wouldn't trust him with a single kopek after that business with the bank. And that's the least of it!"

"What Derzhavin does has nothing to do with me!"

"Thank God for that! It's being whispered that your husband's peculiar tastes are likely to lead to his being arrested if he continues to frequent a certain establishment on the Nevsky Prospect."

The countess stared at her sister. She didn't think Ksenia knew about that. And despite her own cynical tolerance for whatever Seriozha did on his own time—as long as she didn't have to hear about it—the idea of that sort of scandal appalled her.

"I know Derzhavin would probably bribe his way out of any punishment, but it would scarcely be flattering to you, Lisa, if your dear spouse were taken into custody during a police raid on a bordello staffed by twelve-year-old children. Especially since little Tasha is almost the same age."

"How dare you insult my family!"

"Your husband ought to be locked up as an affront to the public morals. And if you can't put a stop to this sort of activity, I'd keep a close eye on your own daughter!"

"You have no right to say such things!"

"Why not? I've known you since you were born. And be thankful I'm discreet. To this day Papa doesn't know how you and Seriozha used to cavort in the hothouses behind our garden in Paris when you were fifteen! And I won't even mention all your other lovers! You're lucky you weren't carrying Tasha when he finally married you!"

"You sanctimonious witch!" shrieked Lisa. "I hate you!"

"Why, Lisa," replied her sister with a smile, "I never would have guessed."

That was too much for Lisa. Crossing the room in an instant, she grabbed wildly at anything within reach and hurled four antique Dresden figurines in rapid succession at her sister, the beautiful little statues shattering noisily as they crashed into the walls, the floor, an inlaid cabinet. To her fury, all of them missed Ksenia, who was laughing at her from behind a sofa.

"Your aim used to be better," she declared, appraising the wreckage.

"You'll find out how good my aim is," snapped Lisa, making an exit over the littered remains of four porcelain ladies. "And when you do, you'll be weeping!"

After the countess's departure, Ksenia's maid Daria entered the sitting room where the princess was staring sadly at the bits of porcelain on the floor.

"Are you all right, Highness?"

"I'm fine, Daria. It was just a family discussion."

But Ksenia really didn't like the tone of her sister's voice. There was something new, something frightening in it.

10

On the first day of September, 1911, Anya's wedding day, Oleg Ivanov and Katia Petrovna arrived in the ancient city of Kiev to keep their rendezvous with fate and Mordka Bogrov. The streets were filled with jolly citizens ready to catch a glimpse of their Batiushka Tsar, the Little Father. The police were hard at work, trying to safeguard the parade route against what was officially labeled "unpleasantness"—or more plainly, threats of violence from the populace who were never, under any circumstance, to be trusted.

Today, however, the populace seemed docile enough. Many of the people were waving flags or handkerchiefs as the colorful parade passed by, the citizens glad for an opportunity for a day's holiday in the fine September weather.

"Well," said Katia Petrovna after she and her bearded companion returned to their rooms at the Hotel Dnieper, "what did you think of that disgusting spectacle?"

"What disgusting spectacle?" inquired Oleg as he munched on a warm meat pastry.

"You pig! All you can think about is satisfying your baser appetites," snapped Katia. "I'm talking about that ridiculous display of imperial arrogance."

Oleg looked pained. "I thought it was a good show," he replied. "I mean, even if it was only a silly extravaganza mounted to hoodwink the masses, it was a good show. People *like* parades. *I* like parades."

Katia wished this peasant had already served his purpose; she could hardly put up with him. His simpleminded world view, his repulsive table manners and especially his increasingly violent attempts to seduce her had taken a toll on her highly strung nervous system. She had been a fool to think she could ever tolerate him for more than ten minutes at a time.

"You are so typical of the shallow, dilettantish, pseudo-radical, bourgeois mentality," hissed Katia, with all the force of a shriek. "You are not a revolutionary, Oleg! You are not even close to being a revolutionary. You are merely someone who deludes himself into thinking he's a revolutionary! A nonentity!"

Swallowing the last bit of meat pastry, Oleg wiped his fingers on his trousers and looked sullenly at the red-haired shrew before him. Katia Petrovna was reverting to type, he told himself. She was the insufferable witch he had always known her to be.

"I'm sorry I bothered to come," he said, barely disguising his mounting anger.

"So am I," replied Katia, slamming shut the door to her room. "I'll let you know when I need you."

Infuriated by that curt dismissal, Oleg banged the door, cursed Katia Petrovna loudly and departed to console himself with whatever distraction Kiev had to offer him until their evening's work.

With several hours to kill, Oleg took a stroll through town, rather enjoying the excitement created by the imperial visit. Each street lamp and storefront was draped with white, blue and red bunting, the colors of the Russian tricolor, and vendors of all sorts of edibles roamed the streets, enticing passersby to partake of their offerings. Tea and *kvass* vendors with their products carried piggyback style and their glasses in special belts were ready to provide something with which to wash down the food.

This will all be changed by tomorrow, thought Oleg as he walked along the banks of the Dnieper River. Tonight he would make his mark on history and by tomorrow, Russia would be in turmoil, ready for revolution.

After spending the rest of the afternoon in the company of a very vulgar prostitute, Oleg returned to the Hotel Dnieper calmer but still angry with his red-haired comrade. She was as autocratic as any damned aristocrat, he thought. Christ! Princess Malysheva couldn't be any worse. Katia needed to be taken down a peg. She was intolerable.

Had he spent two years in Siberia dreaming about the revolution merely to play lackey to Katia Petrovna? It was maddening.

While he was brooding in his room, he was startled by a quiet knock, signaling Katia's presence. Sullenly he rose and answered the door, and was surprised to find a small, very dark and sickly-looking young man standing beside the girl. Unimpressed, Oleg suddenly realized he was face to face with their revolutionary comrade, Mordka Bogrov.

Bogrov, dressed for the occasion in evening clothes, had the air of a man who would do anything as long as it paid well. He radiated a smarmy good will, producing a large bouquet of roses and a small package, which he began unwrapping after he had closed the door and locked it behind him. Inside the package were two Brownings, gifts for his Moscow colleagues.

Earlier in the week he had met with his fellow plotters in the police security detail, he said, and they had given him the revolvers and worked out the plans for the evening. When all the shooting had died down, the same members of the security detail would speed their exit from the theatre and spirit the comrades from Moscow to safety over the border. Nothing could go wrong.

"So," said Katia, "everything is set?"

"The police who are in on the plan have taken care of everything."

"Did you get the passes for the opera?"

"Here," he replied, handing Katia two tickets for the evening's gala. "These came courtesy of Kiev's ranking Okhrana chief."

"Wonderful," smiled Katia.

Oleg noticed that Bogrov was ignoring him, scarcely paying any attention to him. The little creep addressed all his words to Katia.

"Check the bouquet carefully," he was saying. "We've made holders for the Brownings inside, hidden among the flowers. Here, let me show you how to hide them."

"Ah. Very clever."

"Can the Brownings be traced?" inquired Oleg, trying to sound professional.

"No," responded Bogrov, finally glancing at him. "They're from the police and they're meant to disappear after this evening. It's all arranged."

"Can we trust them to get us out of there after we kill our targets? I find that hard to believe."

Bogrov seemed annoyed. "The highest level of the Okhrana is involved in this," he stated firmly. "All will proceed as planned."

Oleg was unconvinced. "But why should they want to help us kill the tsar and his prime minister? I mean, they're on the same side. Against us."

His two coconspirators give him the same look of intense dislike. These people hated having him question their plans. "The Okhrana will attempt to use anyone to further its own aims," declared Bogrov. "And sometimes, without its wishing to, its aims and ours coincide."

Katia snapped impatiently, "Do you think the reactionaries of the far right love our prime minister? Our German tsaritsa hates him because he refuses to tolerate that degenerate miracle worker she adores."

"And another group of ultra-rightists is dying to remove Nicholas II from power and replace him with one of their own candidates for the throne," explained Bogrov, "whereas we don't like either man and want them both out of the picture for totally different reasons."

"So we're working hand in glove with the forces of reaction."

"Precisely."

"My God!" Oleg was truly perplexed.

Katia and Bogrov ignored his bewilderment and made their final arrangements. Immediately following the intermission, Bogrov would be standing in front of the prime minister while Katia and Oleg would have worked their way toward Nicholas.

After the shots were fired and the uproar began, agents of the Okhrana—their fellow conspirators in ordinary police uniforms—would spirit them outside and speed their escape. Corpses from the morgue would be exhibited in their place to show to the board of inquiry which would naturally follow.

And while the tsar and the prime minister were moldering in their graves, Katia, Oleg and Bogrov would be celebrating their exploit in some distant European capital, admired, famous and safe.

"Perfect," smiled Katia Petrovna.

I'm dealing with madmen, thought Oleg. He wondered if he could still manage to escape from Kiev before going through with the plan. This double assassination was beginning to sound like a bad dream. He couldn't comprehend Katia's insistence on his presence. For all the notice she and Bogrov paid him, he was a mere cipher. Yet the girl had practically raped him one afternoon in Moscow to get him to agree to accompany her. It made him horribly apprehensive.

When Bogrov left to make his final preparations for the evening, Oleg turned on his partner, seized her by the arm and roughly pulled her close to him.

"Something stinks here, can't you smell it? This Bogrov is crazy if he thinks the Okhrana's going to help us murder the tsar. What's the matter with you, Katia? Can't you feel a trap being set?"

"The only thing that stinks here is you. Let go of me!"

"No!"

"Damn you! Let me go!"

Suddenly Katia found herself being dragged across the room to the bed despite her flailing arms and screams of outrage. Pavel Scriabin was most inconveniently hundreds of miles away.

"You bitch," Oleg grunted, "if I don't get anything else out of this trip, at least I'm going to find out what it is between your legs that keeps Pavel so fascinated!"

Throwing Katia down on the bed, he ripped off her blouse and tried to pin her down as she thrashed about, striking at him with both hands. Grabbing her by the shoulders, Oleg forced her down and knelt on top of her to keep her down.

"Let me go!" screamed the girl, punching him as he almost crushed her beneath him. "There's no time for this!"

"There's always time," grunted Oleg, his light eyes staring straight into Katia's as she struggled with him, shrieking with helpless fury. "I hate these tricks you women play. You're all alike. All little whores."

Katia's face became Anya's for an instant and the hotel room the forest at Byelaya Beryozka. The red-haired girl's shrill cries became Anya's as she fought him, biting his hand, tearing at him with her sharp nails in frantic desperation.

My God, thought Katia Petrovna, he's absolutely mad. Those eyes are demented. They were so strange, fixed on her face and not even see-ing her. She'd been a fool to think she could control him, and Pavel was a bastard for sending her off on this mission. He should have taken charge! If he had, she wouldn't be in this spot now. How could Pavel not have foreseen the danger? This madman might fit in perfectly with the plan she, Pavel and Bogrov had concocted to assassinate the tsar and the prime minister—and leave behind Oleg's body for their police coconspirators to show the court of inquiry that would follow—but he also might just kill her before they ever got to the opera.

Oleg was so determined to subdue the girl—Katia, Anya, whoever—that he smacked her across the face and knocked all the fight out of her temporarily while he unbuttoned his fly and struggled out of his trousers.

Dizzy with pain and momentarily free of Oleg's weight, Katia forced herself to hop off the bed and rush toward the revolvers Bogrov had left lying beside the bouquet of roses. Seizing one she turned to face Oleg who had climbed off the bed and had come lurching after her, half-dressed and furious. If she showed the least sign of hesitation, he would overpower her.

Staring in bewilderment at the Browning, Oleg felt cheated. Katia Petrovna had lured him to Kiev. Now she was threatening him for claim-ing what was owed. Damned whore. She was like the other one, the blonde who thought she was too good for him. The one he'd killed at Byelaya Beryozka. Staring at Katia with glassy eyes, he heard her tell him to put his trousers back on.

"You're in no position to threaten anyone," Katia was saying to him, still pointing the weapon straight at his heart. She had also released the safety catch. "What you have to do is obey. You have to help me tonight. That's all you have to do. Fail me and I'll set the police on you."

She would kill him, he thought, slowly returning to his senses. This cheat, this whore who had deceived him wouldn't hesitate to kill him. He glared at her as she edged toward the door to go to her own room, carrying the Browning now hidden by the bouquet. Watching her go, Oleg knew he was finished. If she had threatened him like this, he knew she was capable of anything—even turning him over to the police if he showed any sign of faltering. The thought of the Okhrana cooperating in an imperial assassination was so unlikely as to be insane. No matter what Katia and that little *zhid* said, it was all lunacy. Worse, it had to be a gigantic trap. He saw it now that they were only hours away from the crime.

Looking at his pale, frightened face in the mirror above the dresser, Oleg felt trapped. It was his own stupid lust that had got him into deadly peril twice in three months. This was not the act of a revolutionary, he told himself. It was the act of a stag in rut, just like the other time.

What happened to him? It was as if a demon possessed him at moments like those—the desire for the woman driving every other thought from his mind. It went beyond sex. It was madness. With other women, he enjoyed himself; with these two—with the two women he hadn't been able to possess—it was as if contact with them was an incitement to insanity.

They were beyond him forever, taunting him, cheating him, making him feel the way he'd felt as a child when Prince Malyshev's hand had swooped down on his shoulder, barring him from coming near his women. Keeping him in his place.

Well, he thought, he had killed the one. Perhaps he could kill the other. If he wanted to survive this night, he knew he'd better.

But this red-haired vixen would take a lot of killing. It wouldn't be easy.

St. Petersburg

In her bedroom in the east wing of the vast Malyshev mansion, Anya was nervous, weepy and irritable. In spite of wanting to marry Adam, she felt unaccountably terrified at the thought of going through with the actual ceremony. It was irrational, she knew, but the idea of being a grown-up, married woman was so overwhelming, it made her knees feel as if they were made of cotton.

She was living the last moments of her childhood and was about to make the transition into adulthood without even the usual midway point of a presentation and a glamorous winter season. To Anya's horror, she didn't know if she was up to it. What if Adam—who already knew what it was like to be married—found her too childish? Good Lord! What if he actually sent her back to Ksenia Alexandrovna and departed for America?

He wouldn't do that, thought Anya. That wasn't like him. But perhaps he might take a mistress. That was even worse! Oh Lord! This was dreadful!

"Where is Auntie?" she demanded as her two maids tried to drape the bridal veil for the third time. "She promised to help me and now she isn't here. Oh, Masha, let Sonia arrange the lace. Maybe she can find the way."

Sonia, the chambermaid, sighed and thoughtfully handed Anya an icy-cold wet handkerchief to hold over her reddened eyelids.

Placed in charge of Anya's gown, veil, underwear, shoes and stockings, Sonia had done a splendid job of dressing the bride. The wife-to-be of Prince Adam Sviridov looked like one of the women in the magnificent formal portraits in her grandfather's eighteenth-century gallery, a blonde beauty in a high-waisted satin gown copied after one her great-great-grandmother had worn for her wedding in 1798. The antique French lace veil had come from the Empress Josephine's wardrobe, a gift to an ancestor.

Ksenia had worn both gown and veil at her wedding sixteen years before and they had apparently brought her luck, Sonia hastened to point out to Princess Anya. She mustn't worry so.

Masha carefully arranged the four yards of creamy pearls around the young lady's neck and shoulders and agreed with whatever Sonia said.

"Are you dressed, *malenkaya?*"

That was Auntie. Finally.

"She's a beautiful bride, Highness," declared Sonia. "But please tell her to stop crying. She's ruining her eyes."

"Anya."

"I don't know what the matter is. I'm so nervous."

Shaking their heads, the two Russian maids gave the princess a fatalistic shrug. Perhaps Her Highness could succeed where they had failed.

Dismissing the maids, Ksenia embraced her niece and gently kissed her forehead. "You are a beautiful bride, *malenkaya.* Be happy. You're going to dazzle everyone."

"I don't want to do it," whispered Anya, overwhelmed by her emotions.

"Anya, you don't have a choice. Besides, you love Adam Mikhailovich. How could you possibly leave him waiting at the church?"

"I'm afraid, Auntie. I know I love Adam, but even that's not enough. This wedding is so rushed. I know we wanted it this way because of those scandalous stories, but I feel so frightened right now. Perhaps it would have been better to wait." It suddenly seemed so terrifying!

Princess Ksenia put her arms around Anya and held her very close. "Darling," she said, "we can never predict the future. Perhaps things won't be as easy as we hope for you. Perhaps Adam will be unkind. Perhaps you'll fall in love with another man. Nobody knows. But we can't let these fears prevent us from doing what we have to do."

"I don't know what's the matter with me," murmured Anya. "I do love him. I think he loves me. And yet I still have such fears."

"Darling, sit down and listen to me," Ksenia said quietly, motioning Anya to join her on the green-silk empire sofa near the fireplace. "I know you're frightened and worried; you wouldn't be human if you weren't. But all this will pass. Let me tell you, Anyushka, that on the day I married Andrei Nicolaievich, I was so hysterical with nerves that I threw up three times, couldn't find the necklace he had given me as a wedding present and went through the entire ceremony in a state of semiconsciousness. And I've had a very happy marriage—for the most part."

Anya was astonished. Nerves were never Ksenia's style. "Why were *you* nervous?" she asked.

"Because I knew how happy my life was at home with my parents, and I was afraid to face a life of my own with all its responsibilities. I was as terrified as you are now."

"But Uncle is so good."

"Of course, he is. And I knew that. But it didn't make any difference to me at that awful moment when I found myself facing a new world all by myself."

The princess was so gorgeous in her white silk gown covered with silver embroidery and diamonds that it didn't seem possible that she had ever been afraid of anyone, let alone Andrei Nicolaievich, but Anya felt comforted. She knew Auntie didn't lie.

"It will be fine, *malenkaya*. Wait and see."

"I don't know."

"Well, I do. Besides, Anya, we must leave soon. And I still have to give you something."

Going to the dressing table, Ksenia returned with a large blue-velvet box bearing the stamp of Boucheron, her Paris jeweler. Kissing her niece on both cheeks, Princess Ksenia said, "Wear this with our love, darling," as she ceremoniously handed it to the girl.

Startled, Anya carefully opened the gift and gasped in surprise. Lying on a bed of soft white satin was a triple-strand necklace of large milky pearls. It was a magnificent present. "Auntie, thank you! They're too beautiful."

"Nonsense. They're perfect. And unlike the ones around your neck, you can keep these," she teased, gently poking fun at her father's rigid dictum of "back to the vault in the morning." Sandro permitted the women in his family to borrow any piece of jewelry they wanted, but he always made it quite clear it was all his; they had to await his death before they would acquire any of the pieces in his possession. It had spared him much fighting during his lifetime. What they did after his will was read was up to them.

Placing Anya before her full-length mirror, Ksenia stepped away to survey the effect of her new pearls among the others. It was overwhelming. And in the midst of all the pearls sparkled a small diamond cross, Adam's present to her.

"Remember, darling, our love goes with them. Think of us when you wear them."

"Always," replied Anya. "I'll treasure them as long as I live."

Both women stood before the tall, gilded mirror, lovely images in white. The slightly taller black-haired Princess Malysheva glittered with diamonds, her arm around her young blonde niece. Both were fearful for the future, both hopeful too, faced with all the promises and deceptions at the dawn of a new life.

And then Ksenia broke the silence. Embracing Anya very gently, she said firmly, "*Allons-y!* We can't keep them waiting any longer."

Taking a long look around her dressing room with its gilded empire decorations and green-silk-upholstered furniture that one of Andrei's ancestors had bought in Paris in 1816, Anya realized it was the last night she would ever spend in Ksenia's home as part of the household. From now on, once she returned from her long honeymoon, her address would be the butterscotch-and-white Sviridov mansion on the French Embankment where she had spent her early years, before moving in with her aunt and uncle. And at eighteen, with a husband, and perhaps even a child on the way, she would become mistress of the house. It was a sobering thought. And yet she felt a new strength.

"I'm ready, Auntie. For whatever happens."

Departing for the marriage ceremony at the nearby Church of St. Nicholas, Anya closed the door on her childhood and accepted whatever fate had in store for her as a woman.

The marriage ceremony at the Church of St. Nicholas took place on schedule, despite Princess Anya's last-minute fright. The guests commented on the bride's youthful beauty, on her magnificent cascade of pearls and on the uncommon good looks of the bridegroom.

Standing beside Adam under the silver filigree bridal crowns, Anya couldn't even remember why she had been so terrified. All she could see were friendly faces, wishing them well, in a mosaic of uniforms, Paris gowns and lavish jewels. The company stood out against a gilded background of ancient altar screens, venerable saints with jeweled halos and thick columns of semiprecious stone, while incense swirled around the church, accompanying the chanted prayers of the splendidly garbed priests.

At the point in the Orthodox marriage ceremony when onlookers watch carefully to see who steps upon the red carpet first, Princess Anya surprised everyone by reaching it at the same time as her husband, leading some relatives to speculate that the American wasn't familiar with the folklore. According to tradition, the first one to set foot upon the carpet will rule the household.

Married at last, a dainty gold band on her finger, Anya and her new husband were conveyed to the Sviridov mansion in an antique coach worthy of an imperial pageant, gilded wood and painted panels behind four prancing Orlov trotters. Passersby cheered the newlyweds; some peasants thought they were the tsar and tsaritsa, much to Adam's amusement. He adopted the dignified posture of England's King George and waved his gracious acknowledgment to the masses while Anya held his free hand and blew kisses.

Greeted at the entrance to her new home by Ksenia, who had driven with Andrei in a motorcar to reach the Sviridov mansion before her niece in order to carry out her duty of presenting the bride with the traditional bread and salt, Anya was swept away on a wave of music, perfume and enchantment. The Sviridovs, mindful of recent gossip, were doing everything in their power to put on a display of splendor such as would prevent even the most entrenched scandalmongers from finding something amiss.

And Prince Sandro was letting it be known that little Anya was as dear to him as his own two daughters, a strong hint to one of them.

In the twilight of a St. Petersburg autumn, interested onlookers stood on the pavement to stare at the succession of elegant carriages and gleaming motorcars depositing their sleek passengers at the entrance of the Sviridov mansion. The tall windows above their heads were glowing with the lights of dozens of heavy chandeliers, and each crystal prism reflected the flash and sparkle of the jewels on the guests inside. The entire facade seemed on fire with light and movement as the last feeble rays of sunlight came dancing across the Neva to gild Sandro's mansion once more before they vanished into the dark river and died.

Working under Ksenia Alexandrovna's very specific instructions, St. Petersburg's leading florist had transformed the Sviridov mansion into a gigantic garden. Garlands of flowers festooned the marble staircases, corridors and galleries. The ballroom itself had been so lavishly banked with gardenias and roses it appeared to be an extension of the garden.

Inside, the guests, whose appetites had been tempted with lavish *zakouski*—hors d'oeuvres—of caviar, smoked sturgeon, reindeer tongues and a dozen other delicacies from the vast reserves of Yeliseyev's, were sitting down to a lavish feast on the golden plates Ksenia had chosen for the first course. Goblets of Baccarat crystal were arranged beside the plates and were constantly refilled with the variety of French wines which accompanied the meal.

The footmen in their gold-braided livery were attentive to the needs of the guests, and there wasn't an empty glass anywhere. Always on the alert for a sign of displeasure from the master, old Matvei, Sandro's St. Petersburg butler, commanded his troops with iron discipline.

In the vast kitchens, the chefs and their ranks of subordinates had cooked, baked and decorated themselves into a culinary frenzy. From their hands streamed an endless supply of soups, jellies, sherbets, roasts, fowl and fish. Even those among the guests with the heartiest appetites found themselves hard put to do justice to this bridal feast.

To Ksenia's extreme annoyance, Zenaida Kashina had made a stunning entrance in palest gray silk—and over a million rubles' worth of pearls, all gifts from Sandro, putting an unfortunate end to the princess's speculation that the affair was over.

Andrei smiled as he observed a number of budding love affairs among the guests, including two Romanovs and several princes. A certain grand duke was irritating his plump wife with all the attention he was paying to a lady in white charmeuse and ostrich plumes. And on the far side of the room, the Grekovs were studiously ignoring each other; Countess Tamara and her older son Gigi were at one table and beefy, sandy-haired Volodya at another with his pretty Natalya. From time to time, the prince noticed, Gigi would dart a lingering glance at his emerald-covered sister-in-law, who would anger her husband by smiling sweetly and pretending not to see.

Natalya has the mind of a child, thought Andrei. She has absolutely no idea of the effect she has on poor Gigi. He's utterly besotted and ready to commit any foolishness for her. She doesn't deserve such devotion. And he's a fool, Andrei reflected, to provoke his brother.

Prince Adam's guests were a small group, mostly from the diplomatic colony, with the American ambassador, Mr. Marye, the highest-ranking member. A political appointment from the midwest, the ambassador delighted the Russians with his eccentric ways and good humor. Sitting beside him was Mrs. Marye, his good wife, and next to her was William S. Whitmore, on leave from his new duties in Paris.

On perpetually uneasy terms with Adam, Billy had been astonished to hear the news about his marriage and was delighted to receive an invitation. He was under strict orders from his older brother not to disgrace him in any way or else he would suffer total banishment. Kicked out of both Yale and Princeton in major cheating scandals, Billy had settled upon diplomacy as his life's calling, thanks to Adam. He was twenty-four, slim, blond, good-natured and absolutely untrustworthy. Adam was going to try to get him sent to Morocco if he could. Americans had been kidnapped there recently.

Waltzing with Adam under the sparkling crystal chandeliers, her handsome, dark-haired husband the center of every woman's attention, Princess Sviridova smiled when she remembered asking Ksenia if she could invite him to her presentation ball. She had planned on dancing with him here in this very room, if not quite on this occasion.

"Are you happy?" he whispered, holding her close as they swirled to the music of the orchestra in a colorful pattern of rich silks and jewels, the glittering necklaces and bracelets of the women flashing red, blue and green fires with each movement.

"I'm very happy, Adam," replied his bride, slipping her fingers through his. "This is the most beautiful day of my life."

To nobody's surprise, the Derzhavins failed to appear until well after the supper, and then only because Seriozha was afraid to absent himself from the festivities for fear of offending his sister-in-law, who was on good terms with her ferocious Papa and who might one day be persuaded to intercede with Sandro on his behalf.

Countess Lisa was more pragmatic; she wanted to keep an eye on who was wearing what. When she beheld the rows of pearls reaching well below Anya's waist, she wanted to scream, but restrained herself to a few acid remarks about looking like a heathen idol—which she repeated in the vicinity of Madame Kashina who was equally adorned.

Kashina was a sore spot with Lisa. It had been the countess herself who had introduced her to Sandro at one of her parties in connection with the Ballets Russes in Paris. The attraction had been instant. The old man had not only fallen out with his own daughter, he was now talking about marrying the ballerina. It was even worse than what he had done for Anya. Zenaida had already destroyed several fortunes at home and abroad and would look upon the Sviridov millions as a real challenge.

Lisa would let her do *that* only over her dead body!

When at last Ksenia took her niece aside and whispered it was time to leave, Anya glanced shyly at her new husband. They departed in one of Grand-père's English motorcars, Adam's arm around her, nestled together in the comfortable back seat.

Arriving at Ksenia's mansion on the Moika Canal, Anya and the new Prince Sviridov were ceremoniously greeted by Andrei's old butler and shown to the bridal chamber, Anya's girlhood room.

While Adam undressed in the small room next door, Sonia helped her young mistress out of her beautiful, lace-trimmed gown, unlaced her satin corset, lifted off her layers of petticoats and went to fetch her night-gown and peignoir while Anya peeled off her stockings, modestly keeping on her drawers until Sonia slipped the white silk nightgown over her head.

When Adam knocked on the cream-and-gilt double doors of the bed-room, Anya was standing in front of the fireplace, her long blonde hair flowing down her back, her slim, lace-drenched peignoir clinging to the soft curves of her body. "Come in," she whispered, blushing a little as he entered in his silk dressing gown and tenderly embraced her in the firelight.

"You are the most beautiful woman I've ever seen," he murmured, kissing her gently. "I'm very proud to be your husband."

Shyly, Anya slipped her arms around him and allowed him to press her very close, feeling the warmth of his body against hers, timid but want-ing more than anything else in the world to belong to him.

For a terrible second, she remembered that day in the forest, and the ugliness of it made her tremble. Adam drew her closer to him and kissed the little blonde tendrils at the nape of her neck, her ear, her forehead.

"You mustn't be afraid," he murmured. "I'll never harm you."

She wasn't afraid of him. She was thinking of that day in June, that madman. Even now it unnerved her to think of how much that man had wanted her. She wondered if all men were capable of such violence.

"Anya," Adam murmured, caressing her gently, exploring soft, silky curves, kissing her tenderly as she shyly started to respond, stroking the back of his neck and moving her hand down his back, murmuring en-dearments.

Without another word, Adam lifted his bride off her feet and carried her to the large mahogany bed, which was carved in the shape of a sleigh and curtained in dark-green silk with a scattering of golden threads.

Burying her head against his shoulder, Anya wrapped her arms around her husband as they both slid onto the soft bed among a pile of lace-trimmed silken pillows.

"*Dushka,*" he murmured, kissing her firmly on the mouth. My God, how he wanted her. He was absolutely intoxicated with her, her skin, her eyes, her hair, her scent, all beautiful, all sensual.

Anya felt terrified and aroused at the same time as Adam kissed her, caressing her all over with gentle, firm, loving hands. He burrowed closer to her in the softness of their bed, moving into her silky embrace as she closed her eyes and remembered that afternoon in Grand-père's garden.

"I love you," she whispered as he unfastened the satin bow at the neck of her peignoir, sliding the filmy garment off her shoulders and onto the Chinese carpet on the marble floor.

Leaving a trail of warm kisses across her neck and shoulders and down her breasts, Adam wanted to lose himself in her. He held her close to him, murmuring endearments as Anya put her arms around him and caressed him with a dreamy sensuality that was sweet and exciting at the same time. Inexperienced and provocative, she aroused him unbearably.

Sliding his hand under the silky nightgown, he felt her gasp as he caressed her bare skin, his touch exciting her as his fingers glided along her body, gently exploring what no one had ever touched before.

"Adam," she murmured, kissing him as he lay next to her. As he covered her breasts with kisses, his fingers entwined with hers, pulling her closer to him.

When he took her, it seemed to him he had never been so overwhelmed before. She was possessing *him*, making him hers in the most beautiful way possible, tenderly, deliciously.

"I love you," murmured Anya, burying her face in his chest. "I never want anyone else."

"I love you more than I've ever loved anyone," he whispered, cradling her in his arms, kissing her gently.

The girl closed her eyes as she listened to the steady beating of his heart, much calmer now, just like hers. Adam belonged to her, she thought, nestling against him, and he seemed to understand it.

Now there was nothing that would ever separate them; this was for life.

In the early hours of the morning as the festivities at the Sviridov mansion were beginning to break up, an incident occurred in the courtyard that was to cause quite a bit of talk the next day in the salons of the city's biggest gossips.

Leaving the party with Natalya, Count Volodya Grekov reacted sullenly when his brother Gigi said goodnight to Natalya with the customary kiss on the cheek, telling her he'd see her the following day at his mother's house.

"You're not going," replied Volodya, rudely hustling his wife into his automobile. "You're not to make assignations in my mother's home. What kind of whore are you?"

Even given Volodya's rough manners and the level of alcohol he had consumed, this was a bit strong. Gigi grabbed his larger, heavier younger brother by the collar, demanding that he apologize to Natalya.

"I won't stand by and let a woman be insulted like that. Apologize!" he shouted, turning bright red in the light of the street lamps, the veins standing out in his temples. "You have no right to say that!"

"No, Volodya!" screamed Natalya as her husband struck his brother a tremendous blow to the jaw, sending him sprawling on the ground.

By now there was an enormous crowd gathering around the two brothers, with chauffeurs shouting, guests pleading for a truce and the mother of the two combatants, Countess Tamara, stamping her foot in anger as she watched her two grown sons disgrace themselves in public.

"This woman is mine," shouted Volodya, hitting Gigi again. "She may be stupid and scatterbrained, but she's mine. And until she isn't any longer, you keep your hands off her!"

Natalya burst into tears and hopped out of the automobile to comfort Gigi, but her husband flung her bodily back into the back seat, shouted to his chauffeur to get going and left the scene with his wife wailing her distress at the top of her lungs, a fury in green satin and emeralds.

"My God," muttered Tamara Mikhailovna as she took out her lace handkerchief to dab the blood streaming from her elder son's cut lip. "I've raised two savages. Volodya takes after his father. What is your excuse?"

Gigi glanced at the curious crowd in the courtyard who had witnessed the family squabble and were no doubt going to discuss it with embellishments all over town. He was to present a paper at the Imperial Historical Society on the morrow. How could he possibly do it with the bruises from this brawl? My God, he was a disgrace.

"I don't know, Mama," he replied, rubbing his jaw. "Love?"

"More like sheer stupidity," retorted the countess, unimpressed.

11

By the time Oleg and Katia left for the opera house that night, Ivanov was convinced it was either himself or the girl. If he could kill her before she attempted to murder the tsar, he could still escape a free man with plenty of space between himself and the Scriabins—not to mention the police. Katia's remark about turning him in had unnerved him. From that moment on, he'd known what he had to do.

Of course, it was damned ironic that he—a dedicated revolutionary— was going to save the life of a tsar by murdering a comrade. Well, life was full of small ironies, he thought, patting the knife he had concealed beneath his trouser leg. In a way, it was even amusing.

"Are you mentally prepared for what you have to do?" demanded Katia Petrovna as she and Oleg stepped out of their cab and proceeded through the crush of people outside the opera house, a large, impressive beaux-arts structure. "It's going to depend on split-second timing."

It seemed as if all the elite of the city were gathering here. The ladies were wearing fortunes in jewels and splendid gowns, their escorts were in the colorful dress uniforms of various Kiev-based regiments or in civilian evening dress with the red or blue sashes denoting government honors. Anybody with social ambitions had wrangled tickets for tonight's performance; the pleasure of the tsar's company was a thrill nobody wished to miss, since it was so rare.

"I'm prepared," nodded Oleg, concealing his own plan. "At the intermission, we rush outside our box to greet the tsar as his party leaves the imperial box for refreshments with the director of the theatre and the local notables."

"Exactly."

Katia Petrovna was right at home among these aristocrats and high-ranking government parasites, noted Oleg, who was trying to carry himself well in the unaccustomed evening clothes. She had also become a blonde for the occasion; her red hair was too distinctive to escape notice.

Dressed in a high-waisted emerald-green satin gown edged with gold lace and bejeweled like the rest of the ladies, she clearly showed her origins— the only daughter of a wealthy provincial lawyer. She was among her own here, blending in well enough to escape detection by even the most experienced policeman.

Beside her, ascending the wide marble staircase between rows of over-decorated guards officers, Oleg was a nonentity. "Where did you get these clothes for us?" he asked, trying to take his mind off his desire to murder her.

"They were stolen from a theatrical costumer by a comrade who used to be a tailor. He has a good eye for measurements, so that helped."

"And your jewelry?"

"From the vault of the bank on Malaya Sadovaya Street. It makes a nice touch, don't you think? We're going to sell it when I get home."

Oleg didn't like the sound of the "I." She had already written him off, he thought angrily.

The place was swarming with police. Uniformed policemen and soldiers were visible on the outside, clearing a passageway from pavement to entrance; inside, a network of cold-eyed gentlemen in shabby dark suits and frayed cuffs prowled the aisles and corridors, exhibiting extraordinary vigilance. If Katia thought this lot was on their side, she was out her mind, thought Oleg. She and Bogrov were both crazy. He had no faith in anyone who worked hand in hand with the Okhrana; that kind betrayed both sides in the course of a day's work.

"The tsar's party hasn't arrived," Katia noticed, pausing at the top of the grand staircase and casting a glance backward at the sight of elegant couples climbing the red-carpeted marble stairs behind them. "The police may seat the whole house before he enters. They've done that in Petersburg."

"Let's go to our box," urged her companion, feeling uneasy in the midst of so much overdecoration. Wherever they went they passed their own reflections in the mirrored corridors, mixed in between gilded sconces, crystal chandeliers, colonels with a multitude of medals and the bejeweled ladies of Kiev society who glittered like Christmas trees with the contents of their jewelry boxes. Oleg detested them but had to admit he found the atmosphere fascinating in a bizarre way. So much opulence was beginning to affect him, rather like strong wine.

Katia nodded in response to his idea. She wanted to put down her loaded bouquet since it was beginning to feel heavy. If she should drop it by accident, she couldn't possibly explain away those two Brownings that might come loose.

As the old lady in charge of the boxes on their level opened the door for them, Oleg was pleased to find himself inside a fair-sized anteroom, with a mirror, a coatrack and a couple of seats. The actual box lay behind a closed door, hidden from sight. Once the door to the box was shut, the anteroom was hidden from sight. Oleg had an interesting thought about its possible use later on.

As Katia opened the door to take her seat, she was delighted to find herself near the imperial box. It would be easy to overtake the tsar's party when they left during intermission. Suddenly she beckoned to Oleg. She had just spotted Mordka Bogrov down in the parterre, deep in discussion with two gentlemen who could only be members of the Okhrana.

"There he is," she said quietly.

"Looks like a little monkey, doesn't he? All he needs is someone with a barrel organ next to him."

Ignoring him, the girl seated herself in her velvet armchair, putting her bouquet on her lap.

"Why don't you lay that on the floor?" suggested Oleg.

"All right."

"We leave when the lights come up for the intermission?" he asked, glancing around the rapidly filling house.

"No," replied the girl. "As soon as the orchestra plays the final note before the curtains go down. I'll tell you when."

"We rush out together?"

"Yes. We'll both shoot as soon as he comes into view. Remember— don't think. Just fire."

Yes, thought Oleg. That's all I'm supposed to do—not think. You bitch! What a fool I was to have thought you were ever on my side.

Regarding Katia's jewelry with sudden interest, he asked casually what kind of stones they were. If they were as expensive as they looked, he would be able to live comfortably for years on the proceeds from their sale, thought Oleg. It was the least Katia could do for him.

"Emeralds and diamonds," she replied. "Why?"

"Just curious. They must be worth a fortune." Yes. He could probably find a fence for them, no matter where he might find himself. The world was full of crooks.

"Remember," instructed Katia, "just rush out and do your job. No hesitations."

"And the Okhrana will rescue us from the outraged bystanders," he added sarcastically.

"Yes."

If she actually believed that, she was a fool, he thought with disgust. He knew Katia was not a fool. She was a deceitful, lying little witch who undoubtedly planned to escape while turning him in as the one and only assassin. He could imagine her plotting the whole thing with Pavel and that little *zhid*. It was his only reason for being here. Damn her!

Oleg's hatred for Katia Petrovna was momentarily deflected by the excitement created by the entrance of the tsar and his party in the imperial box. Almost in unison, the glittering audience rose with the first sonorous notes of the imperial anthem and began to sing. Katia pulled Oleg to his feet beside her as they joined with the rest of the crowd.

Only a few boxes away from theirs were the tsar and his party, all in full dress, the men in red tunics lavishly trimmed with gold braid and glittering epaulets, the women in slim, cream-colored gowns, heavily embroidered and decorated with the blue silk sash of the Order of St. Catherine.

The anthem completed, Tsar Nicholas sat down, followed by the rest of the audience, and the conductor brought down his baton, signalling the start of the overture to Rimsky-Korsakov's *Tsar-Sultan*.

As the colorful extravaganza of the opera unfolded onstage, Katia began removing the revolvers from her large bouquet, obscured in the semidarkness of the box. One she stuck back among the roses, the other, she handed discreetly to Oleg, who promptly shoved it into his jacket pocket while he gritted his teeth, hard at work unwrapping the stiletto he had taped to his leg beneath his black trousers.

Shooting Katia would be too noisy, he had decided. A knife would be much better. All he needed was a minute alone with her in that anteroom and he would be rid of the witch forever. Let that monkey Bogrov trust in the complicity of the Okhrana. Oleg would wish him all the best— from a safe distance. There was assassination and there was suicide; he knew the difference.

Finally working the knife free, he felt it slide down his leg, landing noiselessly on the carpet at his feet. Casually letting his program flutter to the floor, he bent down to pick it up with the weapon beneath it, keeping an eye on his companion all the while. Good. She was watching the tsar. She hadn't seen him do anything.

Finally, after what seemed an eternity of earsplitting sounds, the noise lessened and Katia was swatting him. "This is it," she hissed. "Get going!"

"Right."

Rushing into the anteroom, Katia Petrovna never made it to the outside door. As soon as Oleg was inside the room with her, he grabbed her from behind, clamping his huge hand over her mouth while she fought back, clawing in fury. Then with a loud grunt as he thrust, Oleg drove the sharp stiletto deep into the soft flesh beneath the girl's ribs, twisting the blade, forcing it in as far as it would go. There was no corset to deflect the blow, and the knife pierced straight through to the heart.

Katia was so astonished, she never had time to make a sound except for a muffled sort of groan as she slid slowly to the floor, a rivulet of blood staining the deep rich green of her gown.

As she lay there on the carpet, her eyes wide open, face registering stunned disbelief, Oleg felt a savage satisfaction. She had tried to trick him and he had outsmarted her. The witch had been so sure of her power over him, she never even suspected her fate—Katia, the intellectual, had been outfoxed by a peasant. He liked that.

Oleg stripped the girl of her emeralds, stuffed them into the velvet handbag she had carried and placed her revolver beside her on the floor. Threading his way nervously through the crowd in the packed corridor, he found himself within twenty feet of Nicholas II, a slim, bearded gentleman in the uniform of a colonel, surrounded by aides-de-camp, all of them looking a little like a set of toy soldiers, all bright red tunics, heavy with gold braid and medals. The women in the party were lovely dressed-up dolls in jewels and bright sashes. They were not quite of this earth, thought Oleg, reminded suddenly of Prince Malyshev's niece.

Desperate to escape before anyone discovered Katia—or before Bogrov carried out his part of the plan—Oleg increased his pace, moving rapidly in and out of the crowd, heading for the grand staircase and freedom outside. Descending the red-carpeted stairs at a clip, mingling with other operagoers on their way to the champagne bars, Oleg heard a loud crack from deep inside the auditorium.

He's done it, thought Ivanov, increasing his pace. The fool has fired at the prime minister.

The noise of the revolver was followed by a strange silence, which gave way to cries of horror and shouts for the police. As hysterical voices rose inside the still-crowded hall, Oleg reached the wide doors of the ornate entrance and passed quickly through, brushing elbows with a contingent of policemen on their way in.

Hailing one of the hackney cabs near the opera house, he was on his way before some of those inside even realized what had just taken place. And long before Mordka Bogrov was finally wrestled away from outraged citizens intent on lynching him, Oleg was at the Kiev railway station, ticket in hand, boarding a second-class coach for Warsaw.

Well, he thought, he was through with that bunch. The only drawback was that Pavel would now want to murder the man who had killed his beloved, and things being what they were, Oleg was the only possible suspect. He didn't like that.

But he could worry about it later, he thought wearily as the train pulled out of the station, heading across the flat, broad plains of the Ukraine, bound for Russian Poland. At that moment, tired and overexcited as he was, Oleg Ivanov felt safer than he had in weeks.

He felt something else too. Seated in the shabby second-class compartment among the peasants, soldiers and poorer commercial travelers, Oleg felt a certain satisfaction at having outwitted Katia and having had the nerve to kill her in the midst of a crowded opera house in the throes of a spectacular political assassination. Granted, the assassination would have been more spectacular if the second part had been carried out, but it was impressive enough.

Lighting a cheap cigar, Oleg inhaled deeply, wondering where he should go now. No matter. He would join a new band—without any damned female members this time—and try his hand at something more reasonable than what he had just come from. Assassination was fine; suicidally incompetent fantasies were not.

But of one thing he was certain: Faced with a kill-or-be-killed situation, he knew how to react. No one would ever threaten Oleg Ivanov again and live.

About a week later, strolling through the main square in Warsaw, Oleg spotted a Russian newspaper carrying the final chapter of Mordka Bogrov's story. JEWISH ASSASSIN HANGED, screamed the headlines of the *Novaya Vremya*, which went on to fulminate against the threat to the empire posed by its Jewish citizens, and strongly praised the value of the pogrom as a deterrent to this kind of activity.

Okhrana cooperation, thought Oleg with an evil grin; that's their cooperation. And tossing a few kopeks to the news vendor, he picked up a copy and took it to the table of a nearby cafe to enjoy his revenge.

St. Petersburg

Two weeks after Anya's wedding, Natalya Grekova's shaky marriage came to an end, collapsing under the weight of its own problems. The countess's young son had fallen ill, the illness had become raging fever, and the fever had proved fatal. The parents, facing each other over their child's deathbed, found themselves strangers who wanted only to be free of each other.

Devastated by her loss, Natalya turned to the two men who mattered most in her life—the two men the short-tempered Volodya blamed for the breakup of his marriage: her brother-in-law Gigi and Gregory Efimovich, her spiritual adviser. She knew she could count on each man in his own way for support and comfort in her bereavement. Rasputin had made a recent and spectacular return to St. Petersburg after the death of his most implacable enemy, the late prime minister, which seemed to indicate whose side Almighty God was on. But it was beyond her ken why the good Lord, whom she adored, should take Nicky from her. Nothing could ever make her accept that loss, she thought sadly.

"It's no use, Gregory Efimovich," declared Natalya one dark, rainy afternoon as she and the *starets* sat having tea in her blue and white salon. "I try to pray, I try to understand, but I can't. My beautiful Nicky was so young, so sweet. Why was he taken like that? It's cruel, Gregory Efimovich. It's not the act of a loving God."

"God judges man, little dove, not man, God. Try to remember that."

"All I can remember is my Nicky."

She saw the *starets* rise from the table and place himself in front of her. He gently raised her chin with his hand as she looked at him, tearful and miserable.

"You must pray, Natalya Alexeevna."

"I do. I pray all the time, but it isn't doing me any good."

Taking Rasputin's hand in hers, Natalya kissed it and pressed it against her cheek. He bent down and softly stroked her hair, kissing her tenderly on the forehead.

"Come," he whispered, "you can't live like this. You must accept what you cannot change."

"Help me," she murmured, gazing into those strange eyes boring into her own. "Help me, Gregory Efimovich. Don't let God abandon me." She had faith in him. He had to help her. He must.

"Let us kneel and pray before the holy icons," he replied, carefully maintaining the calm expression of a man of God as he studied the countess's full bosom. "Where are the icons?"

"Why, in my bedroom," answered Natalya, puzzled that he had to inquire. Every believing Russian had an icon corner there.

"Take me there," he said quietly, "and we will pray together and ask God to bless you and comfort you in your misery."

Hesitating at first, Natalya rose obediently and led her mentor upstairs to the beautiful yellow and white bedroom she used to share with Volodya. She now placed her fate in Rasputin's hands.

Once inside, she watched him bow low, as reverent as any monk, before her rows of holy images, some of them jewel-encrusted antiques dating from the fifteenth century.

"Let us kneel and pray," said the *starets* in hushed, respectful tones as he motioned to his hostess to get to her knees on the Persian carpet.

As Natalya followed his directions, she watched in wonder as he gazed down at her thoughtfully, as if he were meditating, his small, piercing, light-blue eyes nearly shut, his rough hands grasping her by the shoulders. Then he suddenly knelt beside her, intense in his red embroidered Russian shirt, fine black trousers and shiny, expensive black boots, all gifts from wealthy admirers.

"Look at the holy icons, little dove. See how beautiful and kind is the face of the Madonna. Look how she sees into your heart and soul."

Watching him as he blessed her, Natalya let him direct her eyes to the saintly pictures, each with its own small candle in a silver holder. He wrapped his arms around her to allow her the privilege of drawing on his strength. At the touch of his alarming warmth, Natalya quivered, feeling oddly light-headed. It was overwhelming. She felt faint.

"What would make you happy, little one?" asked Rasputin as he gripped her shoulders, sliding his hands down her arms, pressing hard.

"I want to understand Nicky's death," she murmured, looking at the icons, feeling a little stronger, her soul in Rasputin's hands.

"If God were to send you another little boy, would that make things easier for you?"

"Yes, but that's impossible. My husband is going to divorce me."

"But you told me of another man who loves you, my dear. This brother-in-law of yours could serve as God's instrument and give you a child."

"It would be a terrible scandal, Gregory Efimovich. My husband would never accept the child as his, and Gigi can't very easily marry me without a special dispensation from the Holy Synod."

"You have friends who could help you arrange that. I would help you."

As Natalya pondered that, the *starets* suddenly enveloped her in a passionate embrace that was overwhelming in its intensity. "Believe, little Natalya, believe," he whispered. "If you believe in God and in Gregory Efimovich, your prayers will be answered."

Natalya buried her pretty face in her mentor's red silk shirt and sighed. "I wish I could believe again," she murmured. "I wish it so much."

At that, Rasputin pulled away angrily and rose to his full height, towering over the kneeling woman, looking like a stern prophet of the Old Testament, wrathful and indignant. "It is your sinful pride that prevents you from receiving God's blessing. I can see it quite clearly now. You are an unrepentant sinner, Natalya Alexeevna. You must humble your pride in order to be saved."

"How?" wailed Natalya, looking desolate, imploring him with her eyes.

To her astonishment, the peasant slowly began to unfasten the combs that held her coiffure in place, allowing her long, glistening blonde hair to cascade down her back like a river of gold in the glow of the icon lamps.

"Come," he intoned solemnly. "Humble your pride. Repent with me. First you must begin by stripping off your garments. Let yourself be clothed only in the pure light of the soul."

Startled but willing, Natalya allowed Rasputin to unbutton her black silk dress. She trembled as he slid it and her layers of petticoats to the floor. Then came the corset, panties and black silk stockings, which all landed in an untidy heap on the carpet, a few feet from where the countess now lay, watching her mentor hastily tear off his splendid red silk Russian shirt, his black trousers and his boots.

"These are all part of our sinful pride, little dove," he explained. The countess regarded him nervously from the carpet as he stood over her, displaying an unusually large and erect organ. Accustomed only to Volodya's penis, Natalya was awed and rather uneasy.

"Remember, little dove," said Rasputin softly as he settled down on the carpet beside the countess, "even pride in your own virtue is a sin against humility. Look at the holy icons and feel my prayers enter your sinful soul."

Uneasy, she tried to put herself in a prayerful mood. She trembled as Rasputin took her in his strong arms and embraced her full length under the eyes of twenty-eight saints.

"Gregory Efimovich," she whispered timidly, "I don't know—"

"Hush! I'm praying."

Shocked, Natalya felt her religious mentor grab her full breasts with rough paws and squeeze her so hard she cried out in pain. As he began to climb on top of her, she gasped in surprise, not quite prepared for this sort of spiritual communication, although she had heard other women tell whispered stories of Rasputin's odd religious practices. Only the specially blessed received the *starets'* attentions, they said. To be united with him in flesh and spirit was to be almost assured of heaven on earth. But somehow it seemed shocking!

"Gregory Efimovich!"

"Humble your pride," he commanded, trying to enter the startled young woman, who seemed to lack a certain fervor in her devotions. "If you make yourself humble before the Lord, he will grant you peace in your troubled soul. Come," he ordered, out of patience with this stubborn indecision of hers, "open to the Lord! If you humble your wicked, sinful pride, the Lord will fill you with his blessings!"

Terrified by the feeling of being submerged in the arms of this wild Siberian, Natalya cried out as, grunting and panting like an animal, he entered her.

"Oh!" moaned the countess, closing her eyes as her mentor burrowed deep inside her, hungry for her soul.

Then, rather thrilled once the first shock had subsided, Natalya warmed to her repenting and astonished the *starets* by the violence of her self-mortification, nearly overpowering him as she climbed on top of him, caressing him from head to toe with her mouth, her hands, and her long, silky hair. Natalya was so determined to make the most of her chance to save her soul that even after the panting *starets* had taken her three times, she was still climbing all over him, trying for more.

"No," he said at last and raised himself on an elbow as the woman knelt beside him, whipping him with her blonde tresses. "God will listen to your prayers, little dove. He will, I promise you."

"Tell me God will send me another son, Gregory Efimovich. Tell me!"

Natalya was a most aggressive penitent. Breathless, she was really quite pretty, totally disheveled, pink and white, clothed only in her long blonde hair—and in the pure light of the soul, of course.

"Natalya Alexeevna," murmured the bearded *starets*, "I can say from the depths of my heart that God will hear your prayers and bless you with another son to ease the pain you feel. I see it quite clearly."

"Then you must help me marry Gigi," she replied. "Make the Holy Synod grant me an annulment through the influence of the tsaritsa, your patroness. The tsaritsa can do anything she wishes."

"Yes, little dove," whispered Rasputin, stroking her hair. "When the Lord gives His blessing through His intermediaries, man cannot refuse."

"Yes," murmured Natalya, nodding solemnly. "I do believe that."

Making the sign of the cross over his latest convert to repentance, Rasputin wearily suggested that Gigi seemed a likely choice as the father of her second son.

"You mean Gigi could be God's instrument, Gregory Efimovich?"

"Yes, little dove. Why not?"

Natalya liked that. It was precisely what she herself had in mind.

12

Several days after the wedding, with Anya and Adam packed off to Europe, Prince Andrei had an appointment with Inspector Roman Vasilievich Petrov. Since Petrov had seemed so hopeful about a speedy end to Oleg's case, Andrei was anxious to hear his report. Unfortunately, the little inspector was disconcerted and gloomy. From the expression on his face, Andrei guessed he had bad news.

Strolling through the long corridors of the Gostiny Dvor, Andrei glanced at all sorts of offerings in the tiny cubicles presided over by sturdy peasant traders in traditional blue caftans. He bought nothing. He was merely listening to a running commentary from Petrov, who was discreetly trailing at his elbow. His Highness was not pleased.

The noise in the great rabbit warren of a market was distracting. In the little shops, cages of songbirds twittered gaily over the voices of haggling housewives and the enticements of the merchants. Sellers of everything from dried fruit to new kerchiefs to wax candles displayed their wares inside the yellow-and-white merchants' bazaar located on Nevsky Prospect. Gostiny Dvor was one of St. Petersburg's leading emporiums, and its great size and long halls packed with crowds of shoppers made it an ideal place for a meeting. It almost guaranteed anonymity.

Unfortunately, Petrov had nothing of real interest to offer his employer today. He omitted a report of the Moscow incident when Oleg had eluded him, ashamed of his lack of success, but he did tell Andrei that Katia Petrovna, one of Oleg's companions in the bank robbery, had been discovered stabbed to death inside an anteroom at the Kiev opera house on the night of the prime minister's assassination. It was an odd coincidence.

"Yes, but what about Ivanov? He's the one we want. Was he involved?"

Petrov hemmed and hawed, merely stating that the old lady who opens the boxes reported letting a man of his description into the box along with a woman. He disappeared around the time of the shooting, according to the report.

"Is that all? We don't even know for certain he was there?" asked the prince, bitterly disappointed. "Do you think he might have had a part in the assassination?"

"That would be pure speculation, Highness," murmured Petrov, his round eyeglasses glittering with embarrassment. "We would need more than that to say yes."

Andrei instructed him to continue the search and reminded him of the reward. He wasn't so wealthy he could afford to pass it up, was he?

Roman Vasilievich appeared nervous. "No, Highness," he assured him. "Believe me, the full weight of our organization will be brought to bear on this case. I imagine we'll have our man before the snows fall."

With a skeptical smile, Andrei remarked that didn't leave very much margin for error, St. Petersburg weather being what it was. Taking his leave, he handed Petrov an address in central Russia where he could be located during the following week—just in case. After that, he would be in the Crimea at the Villa Rosa near Yalta, then back to St. Petersburg to the Malyshev mansion on the Moika.

And he hoped he'd hear something soon. He didn't want to grow old waiting.

As Petrov watched his tall, dark-haired client disappear into the crowded corridors of the vast market, he wondered if Prince Andrei Nicolaievich Malyshev had ever experienced failure, defeat or discomfort. He didn't look it.

That made the policeman both envious and uneasy.

Moscow

Contrary to Prince Andrei's gloomy assessment of the situation, not only was Petrov trying to track Oleg as quickly as possible, he was even prepared to offer a reward for information. He went so far as to make a deal with the Scriabin brothers in exchange for good solid leads.

Getting in touch with the Scriabins had been easy, once Mishkin had put the word out on the streets of Moscow. Shortly after the rumors began circulating that fall, Dimitri, the younger brother, arranged a meeting at which Mishkin and Petrov explained their offer—2500 gold rubles and a chance to patch up past misunderstandings with the police if they could locate their former colleague, Oleg Ivanov, and deliver him to the Okhrana—to Petrov.

At first, the Scriabins had demurred, suspecting a trap, since their usual sort of activity attracted all the wrong kind of attention from the police, but upon consideration, the idea began to show some merit. They wanted Oleg dead and although their contacts with the Okhrana in Bogrov's case had been disastrous, they felt morally obliged to avenge Katia, all the more so since Pavel felt guilty for having sent her to Kiev with a man she so mistrusted.

Pavel had been deeply in love with the beautiful redhead, and he took her death hard. Dimitri, his younger brother, who was taller, even thinner than Pavel with light-blue eyes and lank blond hair, had admired Katia too, but he was especially concerned now about Pavel, who appeared to be on the verge of a breakdown.

Not daring to claim the body after Katia's murder at the opera, they had let her grieving parents go to the morgue after the police had notified the shocked couple in Nizhni Novgorod. Trailing them like a couple of stray dogs, the Scriabins had attended the funeral as friends of the deceased, thrown their handful of earth into the open grave and headed back to Moscow, determined to avenge the girl, no matter what that entailed. It appeared now that their revenge was going to entail working with Inspector Roman Vasilievich Petrov and his chubby friend Mishkin. The Scriabins concentrated on their revenge and on those 2500 gold rubles.

Meeting Petrov and Mishkin outside the Great Hall of the Nobility on Tverskaya Street, the Scriabins showed up looking like any ordinary lower-class Muscovites—shabby dark-blue jackets and flat caps. Both of them paced up and down, awaiting the arrival of the Okhrana inspectors, unaware they were being observed as they paced.

Petrov and Mishkin appraised them with professional interest and silently classified them as maggots, their slang for that category of criminal who is neither impressive nor special, merely run-of-the-mill. As they remarked later, they had both shot more interesting specimens than Pavel Scriabin. But they didn't disdain using him if he served their purpose.

Although Pavel refused to admit that Katia's presence in the Kiev opera house had any sinister connotation, he was quite adamant about stating that Oleg Ivanov was the man who had shared the box.

"Both opera fanciers, were they?" asked Petrov, managing to keep a straight face.

Pavel ignored him, while Dimitri coughed. The four men proceeded down Tverskaya Street as if they were a group of old friends discussing plans for a drinking party.

"Pavel Ivanovich," declared Petrov solemnly, "we both want to bring this murderer to justice. Cooperate with us and do yourself and the Okhrana a service."

"You send me to Europe and I'll find him, Roman Vasilievich, no matter where he's gone. Our network of mutual acquaintances ought to make it short work."

Petrov wiped his spectacles and nodded. "Good," he said. "I'll provide the train tickets and you'll provide me with Oleg's carcass."

"Here's my hand on it," replied Pavel Scriabin. "But there's one thing I'd like to request."

"What?"

"Send Dimitri along with me. Together we can cover twice as much ground."

Petrov glanced at Mishkin. Mishkin shrugged as they paused just outside Red Square, near the drab red-brick History Museum with the gaudy multicolored cupolas of St. Basil's peeking out from behind its facade.

"Why not?" sighed Mishkin. "It's the agency's money."

"All right, Pavel Ivanovich. You and your brother will leave in two days. If you play us for fools, you'll live to regret it. Understand?"

The Scriabins nodded.

"Well then, I wish you luck," smiled the little policeman as he clapped them on the back. "And happy hunting!"

St. Petersburg

Lisa Derzhavina was furious with her father for threatening to cut her out of his will while he proceeded to make a fool of himself with Zenaida Kashina. She thought the old man was out of his mind. And she loathed the idea of Zenaida coming in contact with any part of Sandro's fortune that ought to go to her within a matter of years. It was worse than a scandal. It was ridiculous!

There was one other thing that was perplexing the countess, and it involved her jewelry cabinet. Just recently Lisa had begun to notice subtle alterations in the placement of her jewels in their velvet-lined trays inside the rosewood and mother-of-pearl inlaid cabinet. At first she had attributed this to her own carelessness, but soon she began to note the position of each necklace, bracelet and pair of earrings quite carefully so she could spot any changes. And each time she looked, there was something ever so slightly off. The day she found her largest diamond necklace lying in the tray reserved for her sapphires, she knew something was dreadfully wrong, although it puzzled her that nothing had been taken. That was obviously the next step. And it made the countess wild to think about it.

On a wintry afternoon shortly thereafter, while taking her daily drive along the Nevsky, participating in one of St. Petersburg's favorite snowy diversions, Lisa felt a sudden desire to return to her magnificent neoclassic mansion on the Fontanka. She wished to speak to Seriozha and hoped to catch him before he left for his club.

Finding she had missed her husband by mere minutes, Lisa flung her glistening sable coat at her butler and headed upstairs, petulant and edgy. As the countess opened the doors to her apartment, she heard a little cry of surprise from inside, like something one would expect from a small animal. And then the sound of running feet.

Startled, Lisa called for one of the footmen and boldly walked in to confront the intruder, too furious to be cautious. When she proceeded into her yellow and white boudoir, its panels and ceiling a delicate tracery of eighteenth-century plasterwork, she glanced around cautiously and then gasped at the sight of a large emerald-and-diamond necklace lying on the carpet, discarded by the prowler in his apparent haste to flee.

But unbeknownst to the countess, the intruder was now just a few feet from where she stood, hidden from sight and shaking with fear. At her mother's approach, beautiful little Tatiana Sergeevna, a dainty creature with long black hair and enormous blue eyes, had scampered into the small room next to the boudoir and had taken refuge in a large Chinese armoire, pulling the door closed after her as she trembled inside, terrified of discovery.

As Lisa prowled the area, an agitated figure in an elegant black wool-crepe tailored suit with four strands of long pearls, the child held her breath. Then just as her mother was about to return to the bedroom of the suite, a heavy diamond bracelet slipped from Tasha's hand, landing with a loud, brittle sound on the wood beneath her feet.

In an instant Lisa was back, flinging open the lavishly inlaid door to confront the thief. She was bewildered to find her own daughter.

"Get out!" she ordered, as soon as she could find her voice. "Get out at once!"

And then as Tasha scrambled out of the closet, she grabbed the bracelet the child had dropped, tore a heavy necklace from her hands and sent the little girl sprawling on the carpet at her feet.

"Please don't hit me, Mama!" wailed Tasha, covering her head with her arms to ward off the blows as Lisa slapped her repeatedly, viciously, not caring if she drew blood.

"Get up!" ordered the countess. "Get up right now!"

Sobbing, the child rose and looked out from under her arm at her mother, who was now frantically searching her jewelry case for missing pieces.

"I just looked at them," sobbed Tasha, disheveled and thoroughly contrite. "Please don't be angry. I didn't lose anything!"

"What is the matter with you, you little beast? Have I raised a thief? Is that what you are? How did you ever get in here?"

Still sobbing, the child admitted she had stolen the key to the cabinet. It was wrong. She was sorry. Really.

Brushing aside her apologies, Lisa demanded to know why she had done it, puzzled and still furious even though nothing had been taken. It was bizarre, not to mention devious. Really, she didn't understand this child at all.

Wiping her eyes with her fists, Tasha whimpered as Lisa towered over her, shaking her in annoyance and demanding to know the reason for this outrage.

Looking up at her beautiful, angry mother, Tatiana Sergeevna replied, "Because I wanted to be like you, Mama."

That was so unexpected it seemed to amuse the countess. Releasing the girl, she looked at her oddly. Clever little brat, she reflected, observing her frightened daughter. It was a very astute reply, just what she herself might have said. The child resembled her in many ways. That irritated her. Tasha was too deceitful already, too spoiled by her father. She didn't wish to hear this cleverness.

"You're a bad girl, Tasha," Lisa said at last. "And I'm going to punish you for this. You are never, never going to have any of these pretty things when you grow up. Never. I'll see to it. And then everyone will know what a bad little thing you are and how little your mama thinks of you."

Sneering at the child who was trying to keep from crying, Lisa smiled inwardly as Tasha broke down and sobbed again, imploring her forgiveness.

But as she stood there weeping, Tasha was also vowing revenge. She *would* have all these pretty things, she promised herself, and she would have them with or without Mama's blessing.

As if her daughter's appalling behavior wasn't bad enough, Lisa now heard the happy news from her sister that Anya, who was still in Europe on an extended honeymoon and seeking medical treatment in Switzerland because of recurring headaches, was expecting a child. The little bastard was due in June.

"If it's a boy, Anyushka will be able to get anything she wants from your father," said Seriozha. "Ksenia is lucky she always treated the girl well. What a shame *you* were less than a loving auntie."

Glaring angrily at Seriozha who was sitting with their daughter when she entered the room, Lisa considered the child's presence a blight and an intrusion at the moment.

"I have better things to do with my time than amuse little nuisances," replied Lisa as she sat down to have a serious discussion with her husband. "Tasha—go upstairs. Your father and I are busy."

Tatiana Sergeevna, their wayward eleven-year-old, pouted, removed herself from her father's lap and fixed her mother with a sullen glare, recent grievances still fresh in her mind. "Papa and I were talking too," she said.

"It can wait until later, darling," smiled Seriozha, giving the girl an affectionate kiss on the back of the neck. "Mama has something important to say."

Lisa and her daughter looked each other in the eye and felt a strong mutual dislike. The girl was beautiful like the countess and small like her father, a slender child in a cream-colored sailor blouse with a navy-blue silk scarf, fine navy-blue woolen skirt, dark stockings and ankle boots. She was enough like Lisa to make her mother suspicious of nearly everything she said or did. And she still had several years to go before she could marry off the little witch.

"I don't think you ought to hold her on your lap," remarked Lisa once the child was gone. "She's getting too old for that. She's not a baby."

"Merely a fatherly gesture," murmured Seriozha. "Since you dislike showing the child much affection, I feel I should. I'm very fond of my daughter. I wish you were."

"She has a nurse and a governess. Let them fuss over her. I've always found it odd for a man to be too fond of children."

That was said with such an edge, Seriozha's expression altered subtly, as if he had been kicked in the shin and was trying hard not to let it bother him.

"You underestimate the capacity of the human heart, my dear."

"I don't underestimate yours," replied Lisa. "I know you too well. But I haven't come here to discuss that. I want your help."

"Of course."

They were sitting in Seriozha's elaborate study, a dark and cavernous room with paneling and ceilings taken from an Italian palazzo that had once belonged to the Borgias. Opposite his heavily carved and inlaid desk—decorated in Florentine Renaissance style with hundreds of semiprecious stones in the shapes of flowers—was a portrait of Niccolo Machiavelli, Seriozha's favorite author, another short and crafty man whose philosophy the count found most congenial.

"We have to get rid of Kashina," said Lisa.

"That is too extreme. I don't intend to go to the gallows for your jealousy."

"I'm not talking about killing the woman. I have something better in mind."

As Seriozha listened, he had to agree it might work. The only reason the ballerina had anything to do with Sandro was the amount of money he spent on her. If someone else showed clear signs of giving her more, then Sandro would be left in the dust, hopefully in public.

"But who?" asked the count.

"Your Moscow friend, Vinogradov."

"My God. I think it might work."

Unfortunately, they would have to prime the pump.

It was a rather elaborate scheme. Knowing how much Alexei Vinogradov admired the ballerina, Lisa had her husband write Kashina a letter—supposedly from Vinogradov—extolling her artistry, expressing undying admiration for her superb Esmeralda, and inviting her to a private party at the Villa Black Swan in Moscow following one of her performances. It was delivered by one of Lisa's servants along with a basket of orchids containing a diamond bracelet-Seriozha's sacrifice.

When Count Derzhavin met Vinogradov in Moscow to outline the plan, he claimed it was for old times' sake. Both he and Vinogradov were fervent supporters of new trends, patrons of the arts and, like many other wealthy industrialists, secret contributors to revolutionary organizations abroad and at home that preached the overthrow of the autocracy.

Derzhavin saw the revolution in quite different terms from a radical like Scriabin. To him and people like him—wealthy men cut off from a real opportunity to influence the all-powerful tsar—it meant the chance to rid themselves of an outdated tyranny and bring the country into line with the progressive and parliamentary states of western Europe. Once in power, such men would then find ways of suppressing the grubby little men who had helped bring the revolution about.

Each revolutionary had his own vision of Utopia.

To Seriozha's delight, Alexei Vinogradov was so taken with his gesture he reimbursed him for the bracelet the day he received a delighted thank you from the dancer. She remembered him as one of her Moscow admirers, she said, and would be pleased to accept his invitation after the fourth performance, the only evening she could spare.

Vinogradov was ecstatic. A notorious ladies' man, he had been a devoted admirer of the famous Italian soprano Lina Cavalieri, lavishing her with a fortune in jewels before their breakup. Following that came an interlude with the dancer Carolina Otero, who had received several diamond necklaces and a sable coat before jilting him for a grand duke. And now Kashina! He was beside himself.

As a guest artist at Moscow's Bolshoi Theatre, Madame Kashina was welcomed with all the ceremony due one of the stars of St. Petersburg's Maryinsky, transported to Moscow in a private railway coach and met at the station by the director of the theatre and several hundred admirers who presented her with multiple bouquets, creating an illusion of springtime in the freezing Russian winter.

As Vinogradov anxiously awaited his rendezvous, Seriozha, directed by Lisa, organized the final part of the plan. They hired a photographer and his assistant and instructed them to meet him at the notorious Villa Black Swan on the night of Alexei's appointment with Kashina. They were to follow Seriozha's directions and deny they'd ever met him if questioned. He would have a sleigh waiting for them to speed their getaway.

The night of his private party—the guest list was limited to two—Alexei Vinogradov went to the Bolshoi to applaud Kashina in *Paquita*, covered her dressing room with flowers and proudly escorted the ballerina to his sleigh after the performance.

Utterly enchanted with Kashina, Vinogradov, a handsome fellow with black hair and green eyes, was already planning their second meeting. Zenaida, who had heard of his affairs with Cavalieri and La Belle Otero, had checked his financial standing with reputable sources in St. Petersburg and was listening with interest.

Arriving at the nightclub—the scene of more than one scandal—Madame Kashina was greeted with wild applause as she and Vinogradov made their way to the private dining room he had reserved in the rear of the place. For the occasion, Kashina wore a violet gown with a six-strand diamond choker and diamonds scattered over her upswept black hair, her fingers and her wrists—just to let Vinogradov know what she expected.

The small room was like a jewel box, an appropriate setting, all beveled mirrors and gilt paneling, with a magnificent chandelier of ruby and gilt crystal hovering over the round table, draped with fine damask. Fresh flowers bloomed in vases between the mirrors and on the table itself, their scent competing with Madame Kashina's favorite perfume, *Le Fruit Défendu,* specially blended for her by Poiret in Paris, a rich, exotic and rather heady scent.

First came a dinner that was notable for a delicious consommé Célestine, an elegant poached turbot with hollandaise sauce, a superb pheasant Souvaroff, and Kashina's favorite dessert, *poires Bourdaloue,* a concoction with frangipane cream, poached pears and chopped pistachio nuts. Then Vinogradov made his move.

To Kashina's surprise, her admirer pulled a large crocodile satchel from under the damask-draped table and told her he wanted to cover her with the contents—an enormous pile of banknotes.

Impressed by the man's originality, Zenaida laughed and told him to go ahead. No one had ever thought of this before and she loved the idea.

"Take off everything but the diamonds," whispered Vinogradov, pulling out a handful of hundred-ruble notes, followed by another. And another....

As he did, Derzhavin's two nervous henchmen in the small room next door kept him in their sight, peering through the keyhole, camera ready.

Leaving her violet evening gown draped over the back of a chair, Zenaida scattered her gray silk-and-lace lingerie over the red carpet. Stretched out on the silk empire sofa, she was curious to see how many rubles Vinogradov was prepared to devote to art.

As the textile magnate was lovingly depositing a fortune in cash on every available curve of Zenaida's lovely form, the photographer's assistant suddenly pushed open the door, held the flash for his boss and enabled him to capture on film the country's leading artist of the dance in a new role.

Then leaving Vinogradov and Kashina stunned by the sudden intrusion and still blinking from the blinding flash, the photographer and his assistant grabbed their heavy equipment, helped by two waiters who were also in on the prank, and rushed from the nightclub, carrying the evidence of Zenaida's perfidy.

Going straight to the studio, Derzhavin waited for his man to develop the incriminating photograph, then departed for the train station and St. Petersburg.

The next morning, Countess Derzhavina paid a surprise visit to her Papa, who was in town for the duration of the winter season. As she and Sandro strolled in his favorite Gallery of the Ottocento, the long corridor on the mansion's second floor, devoted entirely to his fine collection of eighteenth-century paintings, Lisa told him how she worried about him constantly, especially since he had acted so coldly toward her—for reasons not her fault—and because he was allowing his good nature to be abused by those who didn't truly love him.

"I'm a good judge of character, *ma chère*," murmured Sandro as he and his lovely daughter sat down for coffee in the green salon just off the gallery. "I don't think there's much in life I'm unaware of."

That was when Countess Lisa presented him with the photograph.

Startled, he looked at it, turned slightly pale and abruptly dropped it on the small rosewood table, next to the silver coffeepot and tray.

After what seemed an eternity, Sandro asked, "Where and when?"

"Last night at the Black Swan in Moscow. The man is Alexei Vinogradov, an industrialist. He's very wealthy."

"I would imagine."

That was all Sandro said to anyone about the matter, but that day he took the train to Moscow, traveling in his private coach, and went straight to the Hotel National where Kashina was staying.

When he arrived, he headed for her suite, forced open the door and found his mistress sitting in an armchair, having a manicure.

"Sandro!"

"I have something that belongs to you," he said, flinging the picture in her face. "A vulgar present for a vulgar woman."

And while Madame Kashina scrambled to pick up the photograph before her maid could get a look at it, Sandro turned and left, heading back to St. Petersburg, having said the last word he ever planned on saying to Zenaida.

To the general astonishment of nearly everyone in town, Countess Lisa suddenly appeared to be on much friendlier terms with her Papa than she had been in months, and no one could understand why—except for Kashina who managed to piece the story together from what the horrified Vinogradov told her.

But Zenaida had a long memory. One day, she vowed, she would pay back the Sviridov ladies for the humiliation the episode had caused her. And her revenge would come when they least expected it. She was Kashina. No one insulted her and escaped the consequences.

Not even the Sviridovs.

13

Paris

After a brief sojourn in Warsaw, during which time he'd devoted most of his time to fencing Katia Petrovna's stolen jewelry, Oleg Ivanov had decided the Polish capital was not the place for him and had made up his mind to venture farther away from home. As the center of Russian administration in that subjugated country, Warsaw was crawling with police, not an ideal place for a man on the run.

Besides, the Poles Oleg had had to deal with disliked Russians. They had made him feel as if he always had to watch his back, an unnerving sensation, especially if one was spending time prowling the narrow, crooked back streets of the old town, that medieval cluster of tenements, shops and churches that lay like a maze of stone in the center of Warsaw, in whose side streets Oleg had searched for the men who would turn Katia's jewels into cash.

Though disappointed with what he had managed to raise, Oleg still had a more-than-respectable nest egg with which to build a new life. The only trouble was, he hadn't yet quite given up on the old one. He still wished to carry on the fight against the autocracy, the *boyars* and Prince Andrei Malyshev. The episode with Katia had been an aberration; he had learned from it that he could not trust people who chattered constantly about theories while they allowed themselves to be duped by the likes of Mordka Bogrov—who was in turn deceived by the Okhrana.

No. Oleg's innocent days of faith were over. He still considered himself a revolutionary, but now he would tolerate no bosses. He had his own plans.

And he saw no reason to deny himself any of life's small pleasures while he waged his personal war on the autocracy and aristocracy. That would be absurd. If he was going to take the risks, he wanted the rewards.

After all, he thought when he reflected on that morning at Byelaya Beryozka, his life span might not be that long. With the episode at the opera added to that, he just might not live to see twenty-five. Or even his next birthday.

With this in mind, he'd left Warsaw for Berlin and then Geneva, stopping only briefly in both places, disappointed by the level of discussion of the comrades there, mostly intellectuals with whom he had little in common. He wanted action, not theories, and a chance to go back to Russia to prepare a new assault against Andrei Malyshev—or any member of the prince's family he could reach. Oleg thought it was a shame Malyshev and that wife of his had no children. It would have been a real pleasure to kill a string of little princes, one by one, while the parents went mad with grief—until they too were killed in the end. Prince Malyshev would be the last to go.

Well, he thought, he couldn't have everything. He had murdered the pretty niece; he had to be content with that. But he didn't like to think about the way she had affected him. She had driven him a little crazy, just as Katia had. That was frightening. It made him think he was losing his mind.

Finally settling in Paris, Oleg made contact with Jacov Bernstein and entered a new phase of revolutionary endeavor—smuggling. He liked the excitement of it and he liked working with Bernstein, a quiet man who refrained from asking personal questions. As long as Oleg did his job, Bernstein didn't want to know anything, not his world views, not his opinion of the weather. He was a strangely impersonal fellow, devoted to his second family and to the revolution. Everything else was of small concern.

In a way, it was Bernstein's protection against disappointment. A tall, bearded man with a limp, he still carried the saber scars from the bloody pogroms of 1905, memories from the days when he believed the people could change the tsar's ideas and modify the autocracy. He had listened to other peoples' opinions then and had lost a wife and two children when those beliefs had proved erroneous. Now, having been in Paris since 1906, he listened only to his own feelings and said very little. And when he did speak, it was generally to talk of business—the print shop that supported his new wife and children and the contraband that supported the revolution.

Living for the day the motherland would be free of the tsarist autocracy, Bernstein forwarded shipments of propaganda pamphlets and Brownings to comrades back in Moscow, St. Petersburg, Kiev and Helsingfors, relentlessly, tirelessly. And if the Okhrana picked up his couriers or confiscated the weapons and the pamphlets, there were always more where those had come from, ready, packed and waiting for shipment. For Bernstein, the fight would end only with death or revolution. And truthfully he wasn't unduly optimistic about his chances of seeing the revolution.

For the present he was satisfied with the work of his new operative.

"Well, Oleg, back already? Any trouble with the last shipment?"

"None at all. I'm getting a little suspicious of the customs officers on the Swedish border, though. They've started poking around inside the suitcases. I think they've been tipped off."

"So? They can't confiscate what they haven't found. If they find anything, we'll change points of entry for a while. It's good to vary them anyway. Routine is the kiss of death in operations like ours."

"That's the truth," agreed the younger man. "I believe in variety too."

Oleg Ivanov was rather good at the work, Bernstein thought, a willing daredevil. He seemed to thrive on the thrill of eluding the police as he crisscrossed Europe with his false-bottomed suitcases loaded with Brownings and propaganda. He also seemed to have some source of private income, since he dressed fairly well and spent his free time in the bars and music halls, always accompanied by a pretty female companion.

"Jacov," Ivanov said one day early in the new year, "that last shipment of rifles was a little tricky. We thought we had been set up by the police, but it all worked out in the end."

"What was the problem?" asked Bernstein, taking out a cigarette and offering one to Oleg. "Did someone betray you?"

"Nothing like that," laughed the young man, now disguised with dyed brown hair and a drooping brown mustache. "It was comical, almost like something out of a boulevard farce. When my Russian contact and I got to the address of our delivery—a deserted summer villa in Finland—we knocked and knocked, waiting for the comrade to open up. We must have hammered away for at least ten minutes. We thought we had made a mistake. Finally we heard a lot of laughter inside, and after more delay, out came a little man, pulling up his trousers and trying to hide three naked girls who were hanging over the stairs, completely drunk and giggling like mad. There wasn't one of them older than eleven, I swear." Oleg took a long drag on his cigarette and shook his head in pious disbelief. "What are we dealing with these days?"

Bernstein smiled. "Seriozha Derzhavin is what you were dealing with in this case, and he has enough money to buy any playmate he wants. He's also one of those liberal fools who hands us money to wage war on the system that makes him rich. Don't ask me why. It's a sort of game with his kind, I think."

"Derzhavin. The name sounds familiar. Is he famous?"

"He is to readers to the financial news. He owns textile factories in Moscow and St. Petersburg, plus a whole string of other interests. And this is the ironic part—his factories always manage to get fat government contracts while Seriozha spends thousands of rubles trying to overthrow the tsar."

"Is he crazy?" Oleg demanded, staring at his associate.

"Who knows?" shrugged Bernstein. "It's considered fashionable among some members of the aristocracy to help those who want to destroy them. Personally, I find it ludicrous, but I never refuse their contributions."

Oleg shrugged. "Of course not."

"They think they can control the revolution by giving us money," smiled the printer. "It is a false hope. Once we take power, we will allow them nothing but the privilege of loading the rifles for their own executions."

Bernstein inhaled deeply on his cigarette and looked thoughtful. In the dingy printshop he had put up a collection of secular icons—Marx, Herzl and Kropotkin. He looked at them for a long, serious minute.

"We will use anyone who can be of use to us, Oleg. Always keep that in mind. But never be deceived by momentary alliances brought on by necessity. Know your enemies, my boy. Know them and study them so that you may destroy them."

It was sensible advice.

Oleg felt entitled to a good time in Paris, so when he was in the French capital between trips to Russia, he frequented the cafes and music halls, usually with a *poule*; they were all interchangeable to him. They all seemed to be named Marie, and they offered him nothing more than a brief physical release utterly devoid of emotion. The only emotion he ever experienced in these days in Paris came from an appointment he'd kept with a beautiful blonde girl at a high-priced house on Avenue Victor Hugo. And he'd nearly murdered her.

The memory of that night made Oleg break into a cold sweat. He had gone there tempted by the luxurious surroundings, the beauty of the girls, the distinguished ambience—in a way it reminded him of the things he had seen at the opera, the luxury, the beauty, the elegance. He had gone there in a good suit, trying to blend in, and had spotted the girl he wanted almost at once. She'd had an uncanny resemblance to Prince Malyshev's niece—fair, blonde, with a trace of arrogance.

Taking her upstairs, he'd felt himself reliving that day in the forest. It had been eerie. His head had started to pound. The girl became Anya for him.

"Put up a struggle," he'd told her when she'd asked him what he liked.

But then he'd been carried away, beating her with his fists, causing so much commotion the madam had come bursting in to investigate.

"You're a maniac!" she'd shouted at him, picking the girl up off the floor, shocked at the damage he had done to her face. "I'm calling the police!"

That threat had seemed most unlikely under the circumstances, but

Oleg wasn't taking any chances. He was down the stairs and out on the street before either of the house's two sturdy bouncers could respond to the cries of the madam.

He had walked the streets for hours, trying to understand what had provoked him. It was as if that kind of woman was a siren, luring him to destruction, provoking him with the temptation of a life that was beyond him forever, taunting him, enjoying his anger as he tried to subdue her. He hated them all—Prince Malyshev's niece, Katia, the blonde he had nearly murdered here. They all knew his weakness, humiliated him because of it. They laughed at him, forcing him to feel small, despised, forever apart from them.

Just as he was convinced he was about to go mad, something would pull him back to reality and rescue him from his torment, changing his mood so rapidly Oleg himself didn't understand it, although he was relieved. And then he was cheerful once more, eager for adventure and feeling as frisky as a colt.

He was in one of those happy moods when he encountered Wanda Zumbrowska.

Small, curvaceous, blonde and blue-eyed, Wanda was a Russian-speaking Polish girl who worked in a small, neat, almost bourgeois establishment on the Boulevard des Italiens, a house catering to minor bureaucrats and commercial travelers. Hardly the star attraction, Wanda exuded the sort of good cheer found in barmaids or talkative concierges. She was a sharp-featured, lively girl with a sense of thrift and a willingness to sew buttons on shirts—for a minimum charge. She was as much a peasant as Oleg and used to remark upon the similarities, putting him at ease as she chattered about her village near Krakow and the local characters, so similar to those he had known.

Wanda never made him feel inferior, and he quickly became fond of her. She was good company in much the same way a dog is good company. In fact, her only flaw as far as Oleg was concerned was her tendency to rattle on and on, never pausing for breath between stories.

According to Wanda, she had been a poor, devout novice at a convent, assigned to the laundry, when her downfall took place. Lured to a remote section of the vast gardens by a visiting monsignor, she had been pounced upon; she had then been dismissed by the mother superior as immoral, lazy and lewd. She disagreed with the first charge, was incensed over the second and didn't know what the third meant. She discovered the meaning of that term later, in Warsaw where she was befriended by a Russian captain attached to the governor-general's staff. The captain's attachment to Wanda lasted very briefly, and when it was over, the Russian handed her some money, bought her a ticket to Paris and wished her good luck. Deciding to try her talents in Paris, she'd ended up in the laundry of the house that now employed her. And then one night there had been an oversupply of clients, and the Polish girl had been called upstairs. She'd stayed there from that point on, saving her tips and acquiring a friend, her pet cat Koshka, a white angora she adored.

Oleg listened patiently to all her stories while Wanda demonstrated half a dozen different ways to drive him nearly out of his mind with blissful torment. His favorite called for her to spread caviar over certain private parts of his body and then slowly lick off the little gray beads while he moaned in ecstasy.

One night, Koshka had pushed his way into the room while Wanda was entertaining Oleg. When her back was turned for a moment, the cat had leaped upon the bed, greedy for what was smeared over the man, whose eyes were closed in anticipation. The cat had attacked the caviar with gusto; its small tongue, with a texture like sandpaper, was definitely a new sensation. The first touch had brought Oleg to a sitting position, screaming that he was being mauled by a beast. He'd knocked the frightened cat off the bed and greatly embarrassed its owner. From that moment on, Oleg and Koshka became mortal enemies.

The Scriabin brothers were determined to find Katia's murderer. Toward this goal they worked with frantic determination, talking with one comrade after another who might have heard something, seen something, guessed something. By Dimitri's calculations, they must have climbed thousands of back staircases in half the slums of Europe, wherever Russian political exiles were to be found.

Moving relentlessly from Warsaw to Berlin, Berlin to Geneva, Geneva to Paris, the Scriabins tracked down all available leads until at last, quite by chance, their persistence paid off. One day in Paris they ran across an old friend of the printer Bernstein.

Peter Mikhailovich Drabkin was the fellow's name. Like the Scriabins, he had attended Moscow University. Delighted to meet the new visitors from the motherland, Drabkin cheerfully invited them to join him at a nearby cafe to talk about the situation in Russia and what was going on in Paris.

A large, jolly person, rather bald, with high Slavic cheekbones and sharp eyes, Drabkin picked out a table inside the glass enclosure that protected clients from the winter chill and called over the waiter to order a bottle of wine, surprising the visitors, who'd expected vodka. "It's hard to get the good stuff here," Drabkin explained.

"So," smiled Pavel, hoisting a glass, "you know our old friend, Ivanov—big blond fellow, built like a wrestler? How is he these days?"

Drabkin looked a little puzzled. "Blond?" he said. "Ivanov's not blond. He has brown hair and a dark mustache. Are you sure you have the right man?"

Dimitri's eyes flicked a wary glance at his brother. "Of course," he smiled. "Pavel has him confused with another Ivanov I think."

"Ah yes," nodded Pavel. "That Ivanov."

"What's he doing now?"

"Working for Bernstein as a courier. Oleg takes shipments of contraband into the motherland and returns with donations for the cause. They say he's good at it too."

"Ever hear anything about a job he pulled off in Kiev?" asked Pavel in a tone so casual Dimitri wondered how he could manage to keep the emotion out of his voice. Only Scriabin's gray eyes gave him away, but Drabkin wasn't watching that closely.

"No. Anything special?"

"Only rumors," replied Pavel.

Not knowing Drabkin, Pavel was afraid to say too much for fear of having the man repeat his remarks to Oleg. He and Dimitri hadn't used their own names and he wasn't about to say anything that would tip off Ivanov. Drabkin had told them where Oleg worked and where he could usually be found. They didn't want to do anything to invalidate the information.

By the time Pavel and Dimitri left the cafe in a narrow back street near the huge white-domed Sacré Coeur, they had learned more about their former colleague's new career than they had ever hoped to know.

"Shouldn't we just ambush the bastard once we spot him?" asked Dimitri, pulling up his collar as they descended the slopes of Montmartre close to dawn.

Early-morning folk—milkmen, tradesmen, and factory workers—hurried by, bound for their daily chores. The clip-clop of horses' hooves on cobblestones and the mechanical rumble of a motorcar lent their own variations to the street noises—the human cries, whistles and shouted greetings—that filled the air as working-class Parisians prepared to face another day.

The younger Scriabin glanced admiringly at the pretty dark-haired French girls descending the steep streets; it was odd to see so many brunettes, he thought. They looked so different from the girls back home.

"If we ambush him here, we run the risk of arrest on charges of murder," Pavel explained. "If we do it at home, the Okhrana will consider it a public service. Since we need the money, we'll wait until we get home."

"Do you think we can trust this Petrov?" asked Dimitri, suddenly worried.

"About as much as he can trust us."

"That's not too reassuring."

"At this point, I'd say it's the best arrangement we can expect."

Actually, it seemed the sole possibility open to them, a situation that always made Dimitri nervous, for it could lead straight to disaster.

St. Petersburg

"Ksenia, *chérie,* look at this. Isn't it exquisite? My God, how he must love me!"

Ksenia Alexandrovna smiled her approval. Natalya's wedding present from Gigi was magnificent—a sapphire and diamond necklace with stones the size of quail eggs.

"It's breathtaking," declared the princess, hugging her friend. "I wish you much happiness with it."

"Oh, Gigi is so good to me. If it hadn't been for him and Gregory Efimovich, I know I would have died after the Lord took my poor, dear little Nicky. They saved my life."

Unwilling to discuss Rasputin, Ksenia gently advised Natalya to finish dressing so she wouldn't be late for the wedding that was already causing such a scandal.

Though four months pregnant, Natalya was deemed a virgin once more in view of her recent annulment, and as such, she was about to marry her former brother-in-law, Count Georgi Kyrilovich Grekov.

Gigi's mother wouldn't be attending the wedding; neither would certain other members of the family who looked upon the whole affair as a slap in the face to the Orthodox church and a public humiliation for the long-suffering Volodya, who should have been entitled to divorce his adulterous wife in peace and put the blame squarely where it belonged.

Erring wives were hardly an uncommon species in St. Petersburg; in fact, the breed was rampant, but they generally paid the price for their adventures. Brazenly thumbing one's nose at a spouse's justifiable retaliation like this was unique. Some gentlemen were overheard to mutter about Rasputin's shaking the foundations of society and destroying the sacredness of family life. The Metropolitan of St. Petersburg must be daft, they declared, to countenance such outrageous pressures from the Rasputin clique—the tsaritsa and her intimates.

If a man couldn't shame a disgraceful little trollop like Natalya by divorcing her in a display of high moral dudgeon, what comfort could he possibly derive from his religion? It was all very irregular and smacked of dirty politics and unbalanced intervention in the nation's spiritual welfare.

As Princess Ksenia watched the countess smile blandly at her own lovely reflection, she wondered whether the girl realized she was providing more material for the tsaritsa's enemies to cite as proof of Rasputin's warped influence on the court.

Natalya's curious annulment was mentioned in every newspaper in Moscow and St. Petersburg, with the implications of the *starets'* involvement made plain for all to see. The journal *Golos Moskvy* was the most outspoken in its condemnation of both Rasputin and the Holy Synod's kowtowing to him. The censor had fits but surprised everybody by passing the article anyway.

After the wedding, swathed in sables against the cold night air, Count and Countess Grekov dashed in a troika through the dark streets of the capital to the Petersburg High Road and then on to the suburb of Tsarskoye Selo, fifteen miles to the south. Reaching the white neoclassic villa that had been the scene of much prenuptial passion, Gigi and his bride were let in by an old servant who tactfully disappeared after he had prepared a fire in the bedroom fireplace.

Alone with Natalya for the first time as her husband, Gigi kissed her softly in the glow of the fireplace and caressed her tenderly as they sank comfortably into the warmth of the featherbed. Natalya murmured endearments, running her fingers through his curly hair.

As he made love to his new wife, Gigi was consumed by guilt, a relentless nagging in the back of his mind that taunted him even as he caressed his lovely bride. He loved Natalya. He wasn't proud of the fact that he had first taken her while she was still his brother's wife, but he had been too overwhelmed by a combination of affection, sympathy and, he admitted it, sheer lust, to have behaved any differently. When his beautiful sister-in-law had lost the child she adored and turned to him for sympathy, how could he have refused her the comfort she so desperately needed? It was long after Volodya had accused him of it. Perhaps it was a natural response? If he had the name, why not the game?

That was all in the past, and now this lovely, fragile, gentle girl was carrying his child, and with it, their hope for the future.

Had he made the right choice? he wondered, brushing her cheek with his lips as she lay in his arms, soft and warm. If he hadn't, then all the family scandal, his mother's anger, and his brother's fury would have been for nothing.

"I love you," whispered Gigi, breathing the words so quietly he almost missed them himself.

Natalya smiled sleepily, murmuring in reply.

Kissing her, Gigi hoped she loved him. If not, he would have a lifetime to regret his actions of the past few months.

And he would also be the biggest fool in town.

14

Back in St. Petersburg, Pavel Scriabin wrote Bernstein, pretending to seek help for a group of radicals in Narva, the city's factory district and a well-known hotbed of agitation. The workers, he alleged, wanted two dozen rifles for defense against the police. The money—provided by the Okhrana slush fund—accompanied the letter.

Bernstein wired back a response, saying the package was on the way. Petrov was ecstatic.

The night the meeting with the gunrunner was scheduled, Petrov met with his henchmen, Mishkin, Pavel and Dimitri, to plan their final strategy. It had been arranged that Oleg would rendezvous at the Anichkov Bridge with Mishkin, a St. Petersburg comrade, and would then direct him to the place where he had hidden the shipment of weapons. Mishkin was chosen because he was unknown to Oleg and looked more like a worker than Petrov, who had a distinctly scholarly air.

At precisely nine-thirty on a chilly spring night, Oleg Ivanov appeared at the far end of the bridge and lit a cigarette as he peered into the dark and swift-flowing Neva, waiting for his contact, who was to make his presence known with the phrase, "Lots of good fishing from this spot." He didn't have to wait long. Within five minutes Mishkin was sauntering across the bridge, dressed in a shabby dark-blue jacket, worn trousers and scuffed boots, whistling "Kalinka" and heading straight toward him.

In a parked cab not far from the bridge, Petrov and the Scriabins were watching with nervous fascination, ready to spring into action the moment Mishkin gave the signal. They saw him approach Ivanov, exchange a few words and clap him on the back.

"It's our boy," chuckled Roman Vasilievich. "Let's get going."

Disguised as a coachman, right down to the blue caftan and round hat, Petrov released the brake, took the reins and chirupped to the horses. Moving in the direction of the bridge at a sedate pace, Petrov had to wave away a couple of customers who tried impatiently to hail him.

On the bridge Mishkin, still in conversation with Ivanov, saw the cab, then saw Pavel open the door from the inside. Without warning, Mishkin grabbed Ivanov, caught him off balance and shoved him in, hopping in after him.

"What the hell's going on?" was all Ivanov had a chance to say. Punching him in the face, Mishkin silenced him. Both Scriabins pounced on their victim, pummeling him fiercely. Mishkin took out his revolver, just in case.

Petrov drove as fast as he could across the bridge, down Nevsky Prospect and toward the quays of the Neva, intending to cross the Bourse bridge and head for the Okhrana's safe house not far from the Bourse. A traffic accident involving a motorcar and a horse-drawn cab prevented him from crossing at the spot he had chosen, and it took longer than anticipated to arrive at his destination. It was an eternity to the group of men inside the cab.

Once at the safe house, Petrov braked the vehicle, attached the reins to a hitching post and hopped down from his seat, giving the horses a pat as he reached for the door of the cab. Before he could open it, Mishkin beat him to it, tossing a battered Oleg Ivanov out onto the grass.

In a secluded area—the house was surrounded by a tall wooden fence—nobody was going to see or hear what they did to their guest this evening. And the official interrogation hadn't yet begun.

Ordering the Scriabins to carry Ivanov into the house, Mishkin walked in after Petrov and lit the gas lamps, revealing a small, plain area with four chairs, a table and a sofa. The walls were plain unfinished pine, giving off a spicy, resinous aroma. Not a picture or even a cheap print enlivened them. It wasn't a dwelling, but a house of special purpose, and its visitors didn't need too many distractions.

Dumped unceremoniously on the wooden floor, Oleg Ivanov felt his head pounding as he blinked a few times, trying to focus his eyes on the gang who had abducted him and beaten him nearly senseless in the cab. Inside the vehicle, it had been almost impossible to tell anything about them. Two of them hadn't spoken; they'd merely pounded the hell out of him. The one who did speak was a stranger—Comrade Stepanovich who had wanted the rifles. He couldn't figure out their game.

The game became quite clear the moment he at last recognized Pavel and Dimitri Scriabin standing above him, ready to maul him again. "Christ!" squeaked Ivanov.

It was the only comment he made before the two Scriabins were at him again, kicking him with their heavy boots, cursing as they struck him while the other two men watched as if it were a wrestling match. Bastards.

"You filth!" screamed Pavel. "You murdered Katia. I'm going to kill you for it!"

Letting Pavel and Dimitri take out their rage on Ivanov to soften him up a bit, Petrov stood off to the side, watching intently, neither enjoying the spectacle nor disdaining it. He had been through too many of these little scenes to care much about them at all. They were all part of the job. He was permitting the Scriabins their satisfaction, that was all.

When Oleg was a groaning, bleeding wreck, stretched out on the wooden floor like a corpse on a lab table, Petrov snapped his fingers. Turning to him, the worn-out Scriabins looked for directions.

Even though he was half-numb with pain and disoriented from the beating, Oleg could follow what they were doing. He was lifted onto one of the chairs and allowed to fall across the table. His head banged on the rough wood. And then three of them—the short one with the round spectacles, the one who had posed as a worker and Pavel Scriabin—sat down for a conference. Dimitri stayed behind his brother's chair, his hands gripping the back, his eyes boring into Ivanov. His former comrades. Bastards. They'd sold him out. For a moment Oleg actually thought he saw Katia with them, laughing.

"Oleg Ivanov," began the balding fellow with the spectacles, "you are being detained here this evening for an interrogation. You are accused of an attempted murder and an assault at Byelaya Beryozka estate in Moscow province last June. . . ."

"And of a murder in Kiev in September," Pavel cut in, drawing an irritated glare from the one with the spectacles.

"I'm in charge here," said the man, mildly, but with an edge to it. "Please don't interrupt."

Pavel shut up and seemed to slink down in his seat, annoyed but uncomplaining. It must bother him to take orders, thought Oleg.

"You're wrong about the attempted murder," he managed to say, defiant now that he could lift his head. "I killed that little aristocrat."

"You only injured her," replied the one with the spectacles. "She's alive and well and newly married. Let's get our facts straight."

"Liar!" shouted Ivanov, his face as bruised and battered as Anya's had been that day. "I killed her. She didn't survive."

She had to be dead, he thought wildly. If she were still alive, that meant she had cheated him, just like Prince Malyshev. No. He couldn't accept that. He had struck down both Katia and the princess. It was true. "I killed her," he repeated stubbornly, looking his interrogator in the eye. "She was dead when I left her."

Mishkin and Petrov exchanged glances. It wasn't often they encountered criminals who made the charges against themselves worse than they already were. This one must be mad as well as vicious.

"Be that as it may," muttered the one with the spectacles, "her family has put out a reward for you and we are about to collect it."

"Who put a price on my head?" screamed Oleg, half-rising from his seat. "Those *boyars?*"

Pushing him back into his place, Mishkin grinned. "Yes. Exactly. They were wild to bring you to justice. They spared no expense. It's just unfortunate that His Highness is out of the country right now. Or he'd be here loading his revolver, ready to blow your brains out."

Petrov nodded gloomily. He was already thinking of the proof they'd need to present to Prince Malyshev since he wouldn't be able to witness the execution. He'd expect something.

Rising from his chair, he ripped open Oleg's shirt, looking for anything he might be able to use. Some identifying mark he could cite. No, that was no good. His Highness wasn't likely to have seen him shirtless, after all. Marks like that would be useless.

And then he glanced at the medallion hanging from a gold chain around his neck.

"What is this?" he demanded.

"A present from my mother," came the surly answer.

Pulling it off, the man with the spectacles read the inscription on the back, TO OLEG FROM MAMA, 1909. He glanced at Ivanov. "Pretty," he said.

"Give it back. It's mine."

"You won't be needing it where you're going. Don't worry about it." The little man put it in his pocket.

Oleg felt increasingly fearful as he glanced around the table, watching his captors. They would kill him when they were ready. He knew it. In terrible pain from his beating, he knew he was powerless to fight all four. He was doomed.

"Ask him about Kiev," he heard Pavel say impatiently.

"You murdered a girl in Kiev at the opera," obliged the fellow with the glasses. "What happened?"

"The bitch. We were supposed to murder the tsar in connection with Bogrov's attack on the prime minister. I wasn't about to die for those fools," he replied with contempt. "Brainless idiots."

"I told you he would try to blame us," said Pavel quickly. "You see. Almost the words I predicted too."

"I saved the life of Nicholas II," retorted Ivanov. "I'm a true Russian patriot, not slime like these two. I killed the little witch before she could murder your tsar. Most people would tell you I ought to be honored for that."

Even Petrov had to smile at that one. This specimen was as brazen as anything he had ever seen. False bravado. It reminded him of a few gallows speeches he had heard.

"Unfortunately, Ivanov, you are going to die for other things you've done."

And with that, the little man with the spectacles rose from his chair and looked at the Scriabins, who were only waiting for the word to take over. "He's all yours," smiled Petrov. "Do what you wish. Just make sure you finish the job."

Realizing what was to come, Oleg tried to leap from his chair but fell to the floor, knocked down by Dimitri who'd tackled him while Pavel was taking out a butcher knife about twelve inches long. The last thing Oleg remembered was struggling with Dimitri. The rest was blocked out by screams of pain.

When Petrov was satisfied the Scriabins had done the job, he and Mishkin walked over to the battered, bleeding remains and prodded it with their boots. Nothing.

"Well, Roman Vasilievich? Where to now?" asked Mishkin, lighting a *papirosa* cigarette as the Scriabins stood looking down at their victim. Both men were still breathing hard from the fury of the fight, their eyes a little glassy, unsteady on their feet. Wiping the blood from his knife, Pavel kept staring at Ivanov, as if he were still waiting for some further movement.

"To the Neva," replied Petrov. "I have a boat waiting. We'll dump him in behind a factory in the Vyborg district."

To Petrov's surprise, he saw a small flesh-colored thing not far from Ivanov's head. Curious, he bent down to examine it. A finger, he noted, glancing at the corpse's hands. It had been lopped off in the struggle. Like a bullfighter taking the ear as a trophy, the little inspector picked it up and put it in his pocket along with the gold medallion.

"Gathering souvenirs, Roman Vasilievich?" inquired Mishkin, grimacing. He didn't like that kind of thing. It seemed ghoulish.

The inspector shrugged. "Proof," he replied. "It will make it more convincing for His Highness, I should think."

Mishkin said nothing but he found the idea repulsive all the same.

An hour later, Petrov had driven Mishkin, the Scriabins and their cargo to Oleg's final destination, loaded him into a boat and rowed out into the Neva under a fairly cloudless sky. The splash he made when he landed in the water was rather loud, but it disturbed no one. Oleg was finished.

And Petrov and company were anxious to collect their reward.

Geneva

Although Andrei and Ksenia had arrived in Geneva expecting to attend the birth of Anya's baby within a few days, nature kept delaying the event. After more than a week of hovering close to Anya, the Malyshevs decided to take a day's excursion around the lake, to enjoy a luncheon on board one of the sightseeing boats that cruised past various scenic spots and allowed for a brief side trip to the casino on the French side. Two hours after Ksenia and Andrei left their hotel for the boat, Anya experienced her first labor pain.

It came upon her so suddenly, she gasped, bent in two. She stared at Masha, her maid, who promptly called for Monsieur at the American consulate, where he had gone to visit an old acquaintance. While Adam was frantically trying to reach their temporary home on the Rue Calvin, Anya sent their manservant for the doctor, a small, fatherly Swiss named Moreau, who looked wise and reassuring with his white hair, white beard and mustache and pink cheeks.

Ordering Masha to put the sterile sheets on the bed, the princess clutched the nearest chair as another pain ripped through her lower body, making her weak.

My God, after all our preparations, they've left me alone when I need them, thought Anya, making her way upstairs. She knew this was going to be bad; she hadn't planned on having to contend with the baby all by herself. Adam ought to be here, she thought. It was frightening to be abandoned at precisely the moment she needed everyone around her. It was heartless.

Another pain stabbed at her, doubling her over in agony as she reached the bedroom on the second floor. Horrid pain, she thought with a gasp. My God! And this is only the beginning. She would never have any more children, she decided. If she were lucky enough to survive this, she would consider her family complete. Just pets from now on, thought the young princess. Perhaps a dog.

When Dr. Moreau arrived, looking very cheerful—disgustingly so, thought Anya—he examined her and put her to bed, telling her it was just the start. The whole process would go on for several hours, he said, trying hard to make it sound less terrifying than it was. He would tell her what was happening at each step, he promised, patting her hand.

When Adam finally reached the house, he took the stairs two at a time. He arrived in the bedroom in time to hear his wife scream so hard Masha put her hands over her ears and burst into tears, annoying the doctor, who didn't want his patient disturbed by anyone else's fears.

"How are you, Anyushka?" asked her husband, bending over to kiss her on the cheek. "Is everything all right?"

"No," came the reply. "Everything is *not* all right. I'm in pain. And I don't want to be here. Where's Auntie? I want her here. I'd feel better if she were with me."

"But, Madame," smiled Moreau, "your husband is here with you."

Fool, thought Anya. It's his fault I'm in pain. I hope he feels terrible about it. He doesn't know what it's like.

Anya watched as the men went outside into the hallway for a conference—probably deciding what to do with her in case she died, thought the princess. She wondered if Adam would marry again as quickly as he had after the death of his first wife. She supposed so.

Looking around the bedroom, Anya let her eyes wander over the cheerful decor, the white lace curtains, the charming blue and white wallpaper, the masses of flowers in crystal vases and the icon she had brought with her from home. As she cringed, experiencing a smaller pain, she looked at the Madonna and wondered if *she* had had such pains. But that, of course, was a miracle. This was merely run-of the-mill.

"Oh, Masha!" she wailed. "This is so dreadful!" Didn't they care?

Hearing Anya cry out, Adam returned to comfort her, taking a seat at her bedside to hold her hand and talk to her, doing his best to make her feel better as she gritted her teeth and tried hard not to scream.

"Anyushka," he whispered, kissing her hot forehead, holding her hand quite tightly, "I love you and I know this is going to be painful for you. I promise I'll stay here until it's over and we have our baby."

"You won't run off?" she asked, looking very frightened.

It was her worst fear, being abandoned to Dr. Moreau and Masha. Moreau was a nice man, but he was a comparative stranger; Masha was as nervous about babies as her young mistress, no help at all. She was over in the corner, folding sheets and sobbing, looking utterly helpless. Adam was the only person in the room she had any faith in. Besides, she thought, it was his baby. She hoped he would be properly impressed by all her pain and suffering.

"I'm not going to run off," he replied, trying not to smile. She had such peculiar notions sometimes. How could he possibly leave her alone now?

"Some husbands do."

In Moreau's experience, *all* husbands did. This was quite novel. Perhaps His Highness was eccentric, he thought.

"Well, I promise to stay by your side. You're far too dear to me to abandon you like that." And he leaned over to tenderly stroke her hair.

Scandalized by that remark, Masha nearly dropped the pitcher of hot water Dr. Moreau had asked for. A husband who would stay and *watch*? Staring at the prince, she wondered what sort of person Her Highness had married. It was most peculiar. She was even more startled when Moreau chose to humor him. Really, these foreigners were an odd lot! Ladies normally sent their spouses to their clubs to kill time until they could exhibit squalling offspring decently wrapped in soft linen and lying in their nurses's arms. What would Princess Ksenia say when she returned?

While Adam held his wife's hands in both of his and assured her it would soon be over, Dr. Moreau got ready to administer the painkiller he had been preparing, a mixture of strange-smelling potions he now dripped onto a clean sterile cloth and held carefully over the princess's nose, telling her to breathe in deeply. Anya hastened to obey, taking in a deep gulp of the odd fumes as she clung to her husband's hand.

Then as Adam studied her expression intently, he saw her begin to relax. She slowly released her grip and sank back into the pillows, no longer feeling any pain. The effect of the drug was remarkable. Laughing gaily, Anya appeared to forget her pain as she began to chatter about all sorts of nonsense, including several scandalous bits of St. Petersburg gossip which Moreau couldn't understand since his patient had reverted to Russian, but which nearly convulsed Adam and Masha. The maid, in particular, was so astonished to hear her young mistress going on like this that she had to cover her face with her hands to hide her laughter. Her Highness had a wicked, wicked tongue!

"She's going to be fine, Prince," Moreau stated as he glanced at the husband. "No need to worry."

As if to confirm the doctor's opinion, Anya laughed at them both.

Relieved, Adam suddenly remembered a promise he had made two weeks before, while he and Anya were discussing the coming birth. Nervous about giving birth so far from home, the young princess had asked her husband to make certain he remembered to light the wax candles they had carried during their marriage ceremony. In keeping with an old Russian superstition, she had carefully packed them away for just this purpose.

While Dr. Moreau attended his patient, Adam slipped out to search for the slim white tapers. To his horror, he had completely forgotten their location. Afraid to let his wife come out of her stupor, notice their absence and become frightened, he sent the cook out to the nearest church with orders to beg, buy or steal two white wax candles. After twenty fretful minutes, the prince was happy to see his fat cook return bearing the required candles, courtesy of a Catholic priest.

"This is your first," the doctor observed as he watched Prince Sviridov place the candles in the silver candlesticks on the mantle, no doubt a custom of his native land. All the Russians he had ever known were incredibly superstitious, including members of the aristocracy.

"Yes," replied Adam, taking Anya's little hand in his once more.

"It will go smoothly," said Dr. Moreau. "Princess Sviridova is a healthy woman. This ought to be the first of many."

Stroking his wife's flushed cheek, Prince Sviridov thought that sounded like a fine prospect in theory. But he recoiled from seeing Anya like this, utterly helpless and detached from reality as she labored to bring forth this child. It overwhelmed him, leaving him in awe of the whole process. The child would be beautiful and precious to its father. Just let it be healthy.

Four hours from the time her labor began, Anya finally heard the words she had been longing for.

"I see the head," declared Moreau. "It's almost over. Just a bit more."

Groaning, Anya held onto her husband's arm and tried with all her might to do what they were telling her to do. The painkillers were starting to wear off and she was beginning to feel the pain once again, nipping around the edges of her dim consciousness, hazy and misty.

"I want it to be over," murmured Anya, clutching at Adam. "Stop it!"

"Just a little more," replied Adam, kissing her forehead. "Just a bit."

"The head is out!" announced Moreau smiling. "One more push!"

Panting, Anya dug her nails into Adam's arm and closed her eyes hard. Suddenly she felt a tremendous release and the whole baby was out, red, messy and covered with mucus, feebly trying to move its tiny arms and legs as it lay between its mother's thighs.

"Oh," she gasped, "is it finally over?" The room was dancing strangely.

"Yes, Madame," announced the doctor, lifting the baby to show her. He gave it a hard pat on its small buttocks. "You have a healthy little boy."

Princess Sviridova was so dazed from her ordeal—the strangeness, the disorientation—that, peering carefully at the red and wrinkled little creature, she decided it looked like a baby squirrel. Imagine, she thought, all that fuss for this. It didn't look like the pretty blond babies one could see with their nursemaids in the parks. It looked, well, like a squirrel. And it was hers. She wasn't sure she wanted it now.

Exhausted, she lay back and closed her eyes, grateful the birth was over. Nothing seemed real. It was all so strange. The room swam before her as if she were dreaming, and Dr. Moreau was standing there proudly exhibiting a small red creature that was beginning to screech rather unpleasantly.

"Anya," whispered her husband, kissing her forehead, "we have a fine Prince Sviridov. You've given me a beautiful son."

That was how it appeared to him, she marveled. A beautiful son.

The little thing looked so comical, it hardly appeared to be human. Fascinated by it, Anya held out her arms to take the little creature from Moreau, who relinquished it with a big smile, placing it gently in its mother's arms as its father bent over, whispering tenderly.

"Darling," he murmured, "he's beautiful. He looks just like you."

Looking up at Adam, Princess Anya wondered if he were mad. It most certainly did not look like her, or anyone else. She noticed for the first time that Adam was crying; tears were streaming down his face.

"Maybe he'll look better when he grows a little," said the princess, still uncertain about the results of her labor. Was that why he cried?

"My God, Anyushka," laughed her husband, "it's the happiest day of my life. I adore him!"

Anya felt terribly strange and fascinated. He was her son. He was tiny and red and wrinkled and hers. She had carried him all over Europe inside her, jostled him, bumped him, felt his little kicks in her side, and now here he was, lying comfortably in her arms, flexing tiny fingers and toes.

"He really is our son," she murmured to Adam after a closer inspection. The idea took some getting used to.

As his young wife shyly cuddled her softly mewing firstborn, Adam Sviridov realized she had done a lot more this afternoon than give him a son. She had secured a dynasty, giving her grandfather the heir he had been praying for since the death of his only son, Nicki, so many years ago. Looking down at the beautiful sight of Anya and her child, Adam wondered if she even thought about the rewards awaiting her for that remarkable feat.

If Adam knew anything about Prince Sandro, his gratitude would be flamboyant. And while Princess Ksenia would be delighted for her young niece, that other one, Elizaveta with the bad temper and beautiful blue eyes, would be filled with rage. In a harem, she probably wouldn't hesitate to kill the favorite's child, he thought. Adam Mikhailovich reached for Anya's free hand and gently kissed it, looking protectively at his wife and baby.

"I love you," he murmured. "And I'll take good care of you both."

Looking up at him, Anya smiled wearily and gently squeezed his hand. She had no doubts that he would. But she wished her baby looked human!

When Prince Sandro arrived in Geneva to offer his congratulations, the first thing he did upon reaching his granddaughter's house was to visit the nursery. There, nestled in the arms of his plump blonde wet nurse, was Prince Mikhail Adamovich Sviridov, the child he had been waiting for ever since Nicki's death, so many years ago. Sandro was in a state of bliss. Now, he thought, he could die happy.

While the men were opening bottles of Moët in the dining room, the new mother and her Aunt Ksenia were in the nursery, bending over the bassinet, fussing over Anya's tiny son. Despite Ksenia's great disappointment at having missed the actual birth, she was thrilled with this small Prince Sviridov, the newest member of a great family that traced its origins back further than the Romanovs and had stood beside the rulers of Russia since the days of Alexander Nevsky. With this baby, the family would continue well into this century, thought Ksenia with pride. Anya had given them all something very precious.

"My little squirrel is a pretty thing, isn't he?" smiled his mother. "I've nicknamed him Byelochka because he did look like a little squirrel at birth. He's beautiful now, though."

Laughing at Anya's choice of pet names, her aunt hugged her. "Oh Anyushka," she said, "you've made your Grand-père happier than he's been in years. This little squirrel of yours is going to climb higher than any of his ancestors, I'm sure."

Thinking of the group that had preceded him, Princess Anya was deeply moved by her aunt's prediction. He was certainly a beautiful child, all blond and pink, his wispy hair barely covering a perfectly shaped head, his little fingers and toes delicate and fine. She adored her son. "Do you think he takes after his father?" she asked tentatively, smiling as Ksenia let the baby clutch her little finger in play.

"Not at all," came the reply. "He's a Sviridov through and through."

"Poor Adam," murmured Anya. "He thinks our son looks like him."

And she and Ksenia exchanged a look of unabashed triumph, shamelessly happy in this unmistakably Sviridov baby.

To demonstrate his delight in his great-grandson, Prince Sandro presented Anya with a magnificent token of his esteem—a seven-and-a-half-carat diamond pendant, commemorating Byelochka's birth weight. The rest of the official christening presents, all lavish, awaited the young parents when they brought their son home. Among them was an emerald parure so dazzling, so exquisite that it was spectacular even by Russian standards.

It was a measure of Prince Sandro's gratitude.

St. Petersburg

When Prince and Princess Malyshev arrived back in Russia's capital after spending several weeks in Europe with the family's newest addition, the first person Prince Andrei chose to see was Roman Vasilievich Petrov, who had left a discreet note requesting a meeting. Prepared for more excuses, the prince was astonished to hear the news. Petrov had actually brought it off.

Walking with the inspector along the pleasant tree-lined banks of the Swan Canal, the prince listened to the details of the capture, nodding intently as Petrov explained their ruse, the use of the Scriabins, the final interrogation and the end of Oleg Ivanovich Ivanov in the cold waters of the Neva.

To the inspector, his distinguished employer appeared almost subdued. Then again, he thought, it would hardly be proper for him to whoop with joy, even if he felt like it. He was a prince and a gentleman, not the sort Petrov was used to dealing with. The only real emotion His Highness displayed was at the moment Petrov presented him with the evidence of the kill—the gold medallion taken from around Ivanov's neck. And the finger that had been hacked off in the fray.

At the sight, Prince Andrei became white and stopped walking. He seemed to turn to stone at the sight of Petrov's trophies; he became speechless beneath the trees of the canal, the sunlight flickering across his pale face.

Damn, thought Roman Vasilievich. I should never have shown him Ivanov's finger. Watching the much taller prince, Petrov saw him stare at the remnant of Ivanov as if it would bite him. Andrei was utterly fascinated and throroughly repelled. Then, with unsteady hands, he reached for the gold medallion and inspected it closely.

"It was from his mother," explained Petrov, rather superfluously since Andrei could read the inscription for himself.

"Yes. I can see." OLEG FROM MAMA it read. Maria Andreevna had given this to her son with her love, thought the prince. It dated from the year he had sent him to Siberia. A token of a mother's affection. Brusquely, he handed it back to the inspector, as if prolonged contact with it would contaminate him.

"Yes," nodded Andrei. "I accept this as proof." My God, he thought. He could picture Maria Andreevna three years ago, sobbing in his study at Byelaya Beryozka as she pleaded with him to be merciful to her son.

And then he saw Anya, beaten nearly to death that afternoon by that vicious animal *because* he had been merciful. Her injuries had been due to his bad judgment, thought Andrei, still ashamed. It had all been his fault.

But now he had made amends.

Turning to his henchman, the prince announced he would make arrangements for payment through the Bank of Azov and the Don. Briskly shaking Petrov's hand, he turned and strode off, a tall figure in a dark-blue blazer, gray trousers and jaunty straw boater.

Watching His Highness as he vanished into the group of strollers farther down the path, Roman Vasilievich was amazed that anyone as low as an Oleg Ivanov had ever managed to get close enough to any member of his family to do her harm.

Polishing his spectacles as he stood by the side of the canal, observing the passerby, Petrov thought proudly that it was the first time in his life he had ever shaken hands with such a highly placed member of the aristocracy. He would enjoy telling that to his wife that evening as she ladled out the cabbage soup, complaining as usual. Naturally, the circumstances would be artfully disguised, he thought as he sauntered off, heading toward Nevsky Prospect. One couldn't reveal too much.

But it gave Petrov great satisfaction to be able to brag about anything he could.

When Prince Andrei returned to his home on the Moika Canal, he went to his study and locked himself in for half an hour, not wishing to be disturbed while he considered how to break the news to Ksenia. For months he had been waiting for this very moment, but now that it had arrived, he felt oddly reticent about announcing it. Why? he wondered, thinking of the gold medallion Petrov had handed him. Was it because he had bought a murder? Or was it because in his heart he knew he should have done the job himself?

He had no regrets. The memory of Anyushka lying in bed, nearly beaten to death by Ivanov, hardened his heart against any thoughts of mercy. Justice had been served by killing the criminal, and from now until the day he died, Andrei Nicolaievich would never believe he had done wrong to bring about that end. It was the *manner* of the killing that left him disturbed. He ought to have been able to do it himself. That was what bothered him, gnawed at him, irritated him.

When the prince emerged from his dark-paneled study and arrived upstairs to announce the news to Ksenia, he appeared so composed that his wife didn't understand what he was talking about at first. She paused in her work—selecting a new color scheme for her music room—and stared.

"He's dead," repeated Andrei. "Petrov killed him while we were in Geneva. It's finally over."

Flinging herself in the prince's arms, Ksenia wept tears of gratitude. Finally she sank into a sofa, overcome with relief. "We must tell Anya," she said when she could speak. "We must do it at once. Andrei, this is one of the happiest moments of my life! I only wish I could have been there to witness it."

He understood her perfectly.

It was Princess Ksenia who announced the news to Anya in a diplomatically worded letter that could be construed as innocent if opened by the wrong person. In it she revealed the end of the "problem that began last June at Byelaya Beryozka" and praised Prince Andrei for his wise handling of the solution, having had the *bête sauvage* hunted down to prevent a recurrence of similar problems in the future. The livestock was safe now, she said, especially the young colts.

When Anya read the letter, she went to sit with Byelochka, who was being bathed by his nurse and screeching in protest. Silently watching her son, who was screaming con brio as his pretty nursemaid poured warm water over him, Princess Anya thought of that day in the forest and of its aftermath. If anyone had told her that afternoon she'd ever be happy again, she would have said they were crazy. Right now, if anyone dared to suggest she'd ever know sadness again, she'd say the same.

She had Adam, she had Byelochka and she had just been given the news she had been praying for since that June day. The nightmare was over and life never looked more beautiful.

"Your son has good lungs, Madame," smiled the Swiss maid. "He'll be another Caruso if he keeps on singing like this."

Singing, thought the princess. That was a nice way of putting it. This girl had a sense of humor.

"My son will be anything he wants," she smiled, taking the baby from her to wrap him in soft linen. "He's a Sviridov. There are no limits."

She meant it.

While Princess Anya was receiving the news of Ivanov's death, one of her relatives in St. Petersburg was discussing another death, and not a pretty one either. Count Derzhavin was in conference with a left-wing friend of his, an associate from the radical movement. The man's name was Roman Malinovsky, a fiery speaker and well-known agitator. Malinovsky was a Bolshevik member of the Imperial Duma, and unbeknownst to anyone at the time, the leading double agent in town. He was on the payroll of both the Okhrana and the Bolsheviks, a claim not too many men could make, not even in Russia's bizarre political jungle.

Derzhavin, a supporter of the left when it suited his purposes—which were to see his class take control of the government, send the autocrats packing and replace tsarism with the rule of plutocrats—had many contacts among the leading leftists of both Moscow and St. Petersburg. Like several members of Moscow's most distinguished mercantile families, he was an active supporter of the underground journal *Iskra*, not to mention others of the same kind. Their stated goal was the overthrow of the Russian autocracy. It brought him into contact with odd companions; Malinovsky was one of the more presentable.

"Bernstein is dead," declared Derzhavin's guest as he accepted a glass of Madeira from his host.

"My God, I had no idea. How did it happen?"

"Someone turned him in. The resident Okhrana chief in Paris got hold of the prefect of police and suggested a raid. Jacov shot one of the French police when they began smashing his presses and the rest opened fire on him."

The industrialist glanced nervously into his wineglass. He hadn't known Bernstein personally, but he had dealt with him over the past year and a half, funneling small shipments of arms to various radical groups via Roman Malinovsky.

After Malinovsky departed, Derzhavin poured himself another glass of Madeira and pondered the unwholesome possibilities of an investigation of Bernstein's associates at home and abroad. The idea filled him with terror.

As he was staring grimly into the flames of the carved marble fireplace, he was startled by soft footsteps behind him on the carpet, then by two hands clasped over his eyes.

"Tasha, darling," he smiled, "you sweet child."

"Oh Papa! You were supposed to be surprised," replied the girl as she wrapped her arms around him. He picked her up and carried her to a large comfortable armchair, settling down with the child in his arms. He caressed her playfully under her layers of white batiste petticoats while she draped her long legs over the side of the chair, kissing Seriozha like the young strays he found in the city's alleyways.

"Darling Tasha," he murmured, stroking her slim little thighs, "do you love Papa?"

"Oh yes, Papa," she replied as he nuzzled her pink ear, gently caressing her long, silky black hair. She pillowed her pretty head on his chest. "I love you more than anyone."

"More than Mama?"

"I don't like Mama," said Tasha, kissing his cheek. "I don't like Mama at all."

That made him smile. Neither did he at the moment. Mama was a lovely shrew whose father was one of Russia's wealthiest aristocrats. Her disposition left a lot to be desired, even though she herself was quite beautiful. She would have been perfect in marble, a silent art form.

On the other hand, he adored Tasha. Tatiana Sergeevna Derzhavina was a beautiful black-haired angel who might prove useful in securing money from Sandro one day, since he was rather generous with his ladies—one of his finer attributes.

Entwining her arms around his neck, Tasha nibbled his ear the way he sometimes did to hers, poking her small pink tongue in and out like a cat.

Aroused by the warmth of her soft little bottom on his lap, Derzhavin smiled and pressed his hand against her inner thigh, stroking the thin batiste material as Tasha buried her face in his chest and wondered nervously what he was doing that for. Her nursemaid had told her never to let anyone touch her under her clothes, but since this was her Papa, she supposed it must be all right. Still, she found it troubling as he kept caressing her until she timidly pushed away his hand, embarrassed to be so defiant, puzzled by that hard thing poking her from underneath his trousers.

"Sweet little kitten," whispered Count Derzhavin as he kissed Tasha's neck. "Someday soon you and Seriozha are going to visit a special place where we can play all by ourselves, without anyone ever knowing what we're doing. Would you like that?"

The child looked up from underneath her fringe of black bangs and nodded. "Yes, Papa."

"Good."

Covering Tasha's neck and cheeks with kisses, Seriozha held her tightly in his arms as he slipped his hand underneath her drawers to caress her smooth, bare bottom. She was like velvet. And soon, he would get to explore the rest of her in splendid seclusion at one of St. Petersburg's most elegant brothels, his home away from home.

"Sweet innocent," he smiled, stroking her gently.

❧ 15 ❧

Moscow

In September 1912, the tsar and his country celebrated the one hundredth anniversary of the battle of Borodino. The government planned to commemorate the famous battle with ceremonies, the laying of wreaths, and several galas, all culminating in Borodino Day, a spectacular military review at which the tsar would be present.

To celebrate the Borodino centenary, Princess Ksenia was giving a huge party at Byelaya Beryozka, her husband's estate outside Moscow, not far from the site of the battle. Besides giving her relations a chance to tell all the old family stories about Gen. Denis Borisovich Sviridov, one of the heroes of the battle, it would give the princess the chance to show off Anya and her new husband, just back from their European trip.

A week before the big day, an unpleasant incident took place at the Bolshoi Theatre that cast a shadow over the festivities, at least from Anya's point of view, and enraged Sandro and Ksenia.

At his wife's death, Prince Sandro had kept many of her jewels—valued in the millions—and had given his daughters very little, except for the necklaces and bracelets the princess herself had willed to them. Consequently, while Lisa and Ksenia inherited the small but glittering hoard of diamonds, rubies, emeralds and many other less precious stones their mother had brought to her marriage, they still hadn't been presented with the splendid collection of baubles Sandro had purchased for his wife. These reposed in bank vaults and in a series of inlaid cabinets in the Sviridov mansion, periodically checked by Lisa and Ksenia to make certain Papa hadn't given them to his mistresses.

By Sandro's standards, the gift of rubies he had given Anya as a wedding present was extraordinary, but in September 1912, he went one step further. As a further demonstration of gratitude for her little blond princeling, he sent her the most dazzling parure of emeralds Boucheron had ever designed for his late wife—a necklace, bracelet, earrings and diadem all worked in the largest stones the jeweler could find. The effect was astonishing, all fire and green ice. When the beautiful young princess appeared at a Bolshoi gala wearing the parure, she created a sensation.

That evening, the artists of the imperial theatres were staging a patriotic performance, and all Moscow seemed to be present, the men who were eligible dressed in full-dress uniforms, the women in their own version of full dress. Every lady in the audience was fashionably weighted down with a fortune in jewels. Rubies, diamonds, emeralds, sapphires, beryls, opals, pearls, amethysts, topazes, aquamarines, peridots and garnets were casually scattered through the theatre like pebbles on a beach. And even in this sparkling crowd, Princess Sviridovs's emerald parure was remarkable enough to turn heads.

As Anya and her party ascended the grand staircase of the Bolshoi, the princess smiled graciously in response to the sounds of admiration that greeted her green treasures, displayed quite beautifully on her neck, ears, arms and head. The jewels looked very fine with the gown she had had made in Paris for the event—cream satin and lace with a hobble skirt and a deep neckline, the better to show off the emeralds. Anya was radiant.

"*Dushka*, you're receiving more attention than the tsar," smiled her husband as he observed half a dozen pairs of opera glasses trained on his wife as they took their seats in the family's box.

"The women envy your jewelry and the men envy your husband," joked Andrei. "What a success."

Looking out over the crowd from the Sviridov box right next to the imperial family's, Princess Anya would have been delighted with her first appearance as a married woman in her own country if it hadn't been for the expression on Aunt Lisa's face. The countess was watching her from the Derzhavin box directly opposite hers. At the sight of those emeralds, Anya's grandmother's, Lisa was filled with a violent rage. Seriozha was seen trying to calm her, and not succeeding too well. If it hadn't been for the dimming of the lights, Anya knew Aunt Lisa would have been at her side in an instant, wild with fury.

Oh Lord, she thought, fluttering her feathered fan as the vast theatre began to go dark, she's going to make a scene. The idea appalled the princess, making her shudder briefly. She knew what the countess was capable of, and it was quite a bit more than she was prepared to handle.

"Darling," whispered Adam, taking her hand. "Are you all right? You're shivering."

"It's nothing," she replied, feeling her stomach quiver. What will we do? she thought as Chaliapin began an aria onstage. What will Auntie Lisa do? She didn't really want to think about it.

At intermission, the Sviridovs and Malyshevs strolled the promenade, sipping champagne and greeting friends, managing to avoid the Derzhavins who were together on this particular occasion and edging closer.

As Countess Lisa was about to pounce on her niece, Billy Whitmore appeared in company with the American ambassador and his wife—having wrangled an invitation from them for the occasion—and was warmly received by his sister-in-law, who was grateful for the arrival of anyone who might block Lisa's approach and deter her from violence. Even Lisa wasn't likely to cause a scene in front of a foreign ambassador, she thought.

Thwarted for the moment, the countess did an abrupt about-face and, with Seriozha whispering nervously at her side, ascended the grand staircase, intent on something else.

"What is your sister up to?" asked Andrei as he and Ksenia stood watching her retreat. "She looks like she's about to commit murder."

"Keep your eye on her if she tries to get within three feet of Anya. She's going to make trouble. Tell Adam Mikhailovich."

Anya chatted gaily with Billy as Adam smiled pleasantly, making conversation with his ambassador and his wife, who—God knows why—found his young brother perfectly charming.

Adam kept an eye on Billy as he talked with Anya, studying her beautiful face and those emeralds. He could see the glint in his brother's eye as he took in every detail, including the depth of her décolletage. The little bastard.

Billy was invited back to the Sviridovs' box by Princess Ksenia, who was, ironically, trying to be gracious to Adam. Billy was amazed to hear his beautiful sister-in-law say that Adam was now Russia's newest pilot; she described the airplane her grand-père had given Adam as one of his son's christening presents. She was excited by airplanes and had wanted him to learn to fly.

"Airplane?" murmured Billy. My God, he thought. His present for the little prince had been a silver mug. How embarrassing.

As the group was discussing the air race that had just taken place from Paris to London, they were so engrossed in the details that nobody noticed another visitor in the box until she was right on top of them.

"What do you mean stealing my mother's emeralds, you conniving little brat? Who gave you permission to wear them?"

Startled by the virago in deep-blue silk and sapphires, they simply stared.

"Lisa!" squeaked Seriozha from the door of the box, a little out of breath from pursuing her, "for heaven's sake, don't make a scene! People are looking!"

"Let them look."

Facing her angry aunt, Princess Anya turned white and replied that Grand-père had given them to her. They were a present.

"Liar!" replied Lisa as she slapped her across the face.

Then, before the young princess could recover from the surprise attack, Lisa attempted to rip the heavy necklace from her throat, but succeeded only in leaving a series of angry red claw marks.

Seriozha thought he'd die. His wife had just assaulted her niece in full view of the entire audience, including members of the imperial family, and was now doing her best to steal her emeralds. She was out of her mind.

As Lisa reached for Anya's throat, Adam grabbed her from behind and pulled her roughly away, while his wife staggered back a little, clutching her brother-in-law's hand for support and trembling. Auntie Lisa was insane, she thought.

Princess Ksenia put her arm around her niece and tried to steady Anya as she sank into one of the gilt chairs.

While Adam picked up Lisa and carried her, struggling wildly, from the box, he was joined by Andrei and Seriozha who were adamantly barring the door to prevent her from forcing her way back inside. Billy remained with the ladies, trying to calm the young princess who was still trembling from the attack.

To Anya's intense embarrassment, the entire audience was reveling in the spectacle and buzzing with excitement. Nothing like this had happened at the Bolshoi in recent memory, and it was delightful to have the thrill of a scandal on such a splendid occasion, making it even more noteworthy.

In the corridor, the scene wasn't yet over. Demanding that Adam release her or have his eyes scratched out, Lisa ordered Seriozha to help her. And now!

"Lisa," he pleaded, "will you behave yourself? You're disgracing us."

"You," she hissed, glaring at Adam, "were you the one who put that blonde brat up to this? Let me tell you you're mistaken if you think you've made your fortune by marrying her. You began as a nobody and will end up the same way!"

Straining to keep his composure, Adam tightened his grip on the countess's arm and then pushed her away, for fear he might throttle her. "Countess Derhzavina," he said, quite pink, "I don't care what you call me or what you accuse me of because I've seen your kind before and I know what you are. But I swear, if you ever touch my wife again, I'll tear you apart."

Lisa's head spun around so quickly, she felt momentarily dizzy. Giving the nobody who had just threatened her a withering look, she suddenly retreated, flouncing off down the hall in search of safer territory. She preferred to terrorize those who didn't retaliate.

When the group rejoined the ladies and Billy inside the box, Seriozha hastened to dissociate himself from Lisa's actions; he loudly proclaimed his innocence and offered abject apologies to the husband.

"Anya, are you all right?" was Adam's reply, neatly sidestepping Seriozha as he went to his wife's side.

"Yes. I think so. My God," murmured the princess. "She's a horror. Look how all those people are gawking at us now."

It was true. The entire house appeared to be fascinated by the Sviridov family disturbance, even more than they had been by the emeralds. It was humiliating, thought Anya. Lisa had to be absolutely mad.

"Adam," she whispered fiercely, "I wish to go home. Please!"

"No," replied Princess Ksenia. "Don't you dare leave and give her the satisfaction of driving you away."

"Anya," whispered Billy in her ear, "nobody can make you feel humiliated unless you let them. Believe me, I'm an expert." And raising her hand, he bowed over it and kissed it.

That gesture would have annoyed Adam if he hadn't seen the effect it had on Grand Duke Alexander Mikhailovich, an acquaintance from the St. Petersburg airfield. Responding to Anya's distress, having witnessed the altercation with Lisa, His Imperial Highness made a slight bow in the direction of the Sviridov box, letting the audience know whose side *he* was on.

And as Ksenia noted with justifiable glee, it was Lisa who decamped, descending the grand staircase at a feverish clip, drawing curious stares from the normally impervious Chevaliers Guards decorating the route.

This was a disgrace, thought Seriozha. After this episode, he never wanted to show his face in Moscow again. As he shouted for Lisa's evening cape and his overcoat, he saw his wife run out into the street, without even glancing behind her.

All the way home to their Moscow residence on Arbatskaya, Count and Countess Derzhavin argued so loudly that the chauffeur could hear what they were saying right through the glass partition that separated them from him. And from what he was hearing, Count Derzhavin was clearly getting the worst of it.

Once they reached the blue and white house behind its high walls and garden, Countess Lisa pushed open the door of the motorcar and flew into the entranceway, her long black evening cape billowing around her like a sail. Derzhavin followed like a pet dog.

From the top of the stairway, Tasha was observing the whole scene. Having been awakened by the sound of the motorcar on the gravel of the courtyard, she had sneaked out of bed and had looked out to see Lisa's dramatic exit from the vehicle. She wondered what the trouble was now. It seemed as if there was always trouble with Mama.

Crouching down behind the marble railing overlooking the entrance hall, Tasha saw Papa try to take Mama's arm, only to be soundly rebuffed. Lisa flailed at him wildly as she broke away and turned in the direction of the staircase.

Seeing her angry mother heading toward her, the little girl yelped, jumped up as quickly as she could and ran for her bedroom, but she was too late. She had already been spotted.

"What are you doing there?" demanded the countess as she reached the top of the stairs. She cornered Tasha against the wall, halfway down the corridor to her room. "I heard you come in. I wanted to know if you had a good time," the child lied, trying to look sincere.

"Does it look as though we had a good time?" shrieked Lisa, slapping Tasha hard enough to knock her head against the wall. "Go back to your room!"

"Leave the child alone," shouted Seriozha, enveloping Tasha in a protective embrace. "You'll hurt her."

"I don't care if I kill the brat," replied Lisa as the little girl sobbed in Seriozha's arms, burying her face against his starched white shirtfront. "I may have given birth to her, but there's nothing about her that means anything to me. She's completely yours, isn't she? In every way."

At that remark, Seriozha reached out and did something Tasha had never seen him do before. He slapped his wife smartly across the face, stunning her. "Don't ever accuse me of that," he hissed, quite ashen. "It's not true."

Shocked by the violence, Tasha looked at both parents as if she were seeing them for the first time. They hated each other, she thought. She was fascinated by the vicious feline expression on Lisa's face as she picked up a large crystal vase of eighteenth-century origin from one of the gilt tables along the corridor and let it fly at her husband. Missing him, the vase shattered against the wall.

Tasha cringed as the shining particles of crystal showered over her, glistening on her long white batiste nightdress, lodging in the rows of smocking and in the embroidered flowers. Seriozha received his share too, shaking himself to clear them off his tailcoat and trousers.

As Lisa flounced off to her bedroom, Seriozha turned his daughter over to her frightened governess and followed the countess to her room. Lisa removed her heavy sapphire necklace and earrings, throwing them at her chambermaid who winced as the jewels hit her, not daring to say one word in protest. Dismissing the woman with a wave of his hand, Seriozha took a seat and told his wife to do the same.

"You have nothing to say to me, you little weasel!" raged the countess. "You were disloyal to me tonight. And in public! I'll never forgive you for that. Never!"

"You were mad to do what you did! Don't you realize how important that girl is to your father? She's managed to outdistance both you and your sister, but Ksenia's intelligent enough to treat her with great care. You haven't the brains to imitate your sister!"

"Don't lecture me, you little weasel! All you have to do is stand by me. *That's* your proper place. Or perhaps," she sneered, "your true place is in prison. Remember, Seriozha, I know all about your revolutionary friends. And your baby whores. In fact, I know all your secrets."

"Oh," he replied in mock amusement, "now we're showing our little claws, aren't we?"

"Yes. And just remember how deep we can scratch," retorted Lisa arrogantly. "I can draw blood in more ways than one."

Alone in her bedroom, curled up in a frightened ball with the coverlet pulled over her head, Tasha felt the pain in her cheek where Lisa had slapped her. Closing her eyes, she wondered how Papa could stand her mama. The child wished he had married someone else, almost anyone else—Aunt Ksenia, for example. Perhaps it would have been easier with her.

Sighing, the girl buried herself in the covers and wished she were far, far away, anywhere Mama didn't exist.

St. Petersburg

In a gaily decorated, shiny red sleigh, behind a pair of glossy-black Orlov trotters, Prince and Princess Sviridov were laughing as they rounded the corner and sped onto the French Embankment. Adam had the team as expertly in hand as one of the professionals on the Nevsky. Bundled into thick fur coats beneath warm fox rugs, the young Sviridovs were enjoying the fine winter weather like a couple of children, just like other Petersburgers of their acquaintance.

Winter in St. Petersburg was magical, a time of nonstop amusements in the snow, visiting the traveling carnivals in the great parks, sliding down huge mountains of ice, whooping like twelve-year-olds for the joy of it. Snow turned Russia's imperial city into a fairyland every year; everywhere were dazzling images of pastel palaces above frozen canals, ablaze with crystal chandeliers in snow-drenched nights, fragrant with Crimean roses and crowded with fur-covered beauties who drifted by on ice skates or between the fur robes of passing sleighs. For those who had the means to enjoy it, winter was the happiest time of the year.

When the young couple arrived in the inner courtyard of the Sviridov mansion, after a sharp turn into the entrance gate that left a few pedestrians breathless, servants hurried to assist them out of the sleigh as soon as the horses had come to a halt in a great whoosh of snowflakes.

"I'll race you," whispered Anya as soon as she and her husband were inside the house and heading toward the stairs.

Laughing, Adam nodded. In a burst of speed that startled him, Princess Anya gathered her skirts in both hands and sprinted ahead. Laughing like a child as she took the great wide stairs two at a time, she arrived at the doors of their private apartment before him, exhausted and cheerful, absolutely delighted to have beaten him.

While Anya called her maid for a change of costume, Adam sank down into one of the comfortable armchairs to watch her. She was fairly bursting with high spirits today and she had good reason. On this particular snowy St. Petersburg afternoon, his beautiful wife, Princess Anya Sviridova was about to receive a rare honor, a distinction so seldom given as to be more prestigious than a diamond-studded imperial decoration—she was about to be received by Her Imperial Majesty, Alexandra Feodorovna, tsaritsa of all the Russias, for tea in the family quarters of the Alexander Palace at Tsarskoye Selo. Anyushka was thrilled.

As the young princess sat at her dressing table, trying to choose the proper outfit, she was intimidated by the prospect of meeting her tsaritsa. She wanted to behave properly; that frantic race up the stairs was her last concession to high spirits. From now until she left the august imperial precincts, she would act with all the dignity one would expect from a princess, a mother and a *grande dame*. The only problem with that, thought Anya, was that inside she wanted to giggle madly.

As her chambermaid Sonia brought forth dress after dress, the princess despaired of ever finding the right one. She needed something that would make her look dignified, she insisted. Dignity was very important to Alexandra Feodorovna, according to Natalya, the one responsible for her invitation.

"Somehow," Adam had said when they learned of the invitation, "I find it hard to imagine Countess Grekova as the confidante of royalty."

"It's her love for that man Rasputin," his wife had replied. "Natalya and the tsaritsa both consider him a saint. Everyone who thinks the same is welcome; everyone who dislikes him is barred. I hope I can keep my mouth closed when they begin talking about his miracles. Grand-père keeps saying he ought to be hanged for corrupting the tsaritsa."

"He'll never be invited out to Tsarskoye," Adam had said, smiling.

"He wouldn't want to go," answered his wife. "He thinks the tsaritsa is mad."

Now as the American sat watching the elaborate process of preparing for an imperial invitation, he wondered if he were living in the real world. His lovely eighteen-year-old wife who liked to romp in the snow and slide down the long ice chutes in her grand-père's garden was about to step into a Paris frock that cost more than a year's salary for a minor bureaucrat. The triple strand of pearls destined for her pretty neck was enough to feed a small town for a few years. And he had nothing to do with any of that. It was all part of the life she had inherited from those Sviridovs whose fine portraits hung on the mansion's walls—grand and splendid and untouched by ordinary troubles.

It sometimes made Adam wonder how Anyushka had remained as charming and unaffected as she had. And it occasionally made him wonder how they had ever allowed him to marry her.

"Well," asked Anya after she and Sonia had contrived to make her as grand as possible. "What do you think?"

"Beautiful, darling. You look as if you just stepped out of a portrait by Velázquez. Great dignity."

"Now tell me what you think of my curtsey," she said, demonstrating.

"Perfect."

"Is it really?"

Princess Anya wanted to believe him, but she would have felt better if Auntie were here to rate it. Ksenia had been presented at court and she was an expert, unprejudiced witness. Adam loved everything she did and came from a place where ladies didn't have to curtsey, so that made him a poor judge of imperial protocol. She'd practice later with Natalya, she decided.

As Princess Sviridova swept down the grand staircase of the family mansion, she was absolutely magnificent, resplendent in a black velvet frock by Worth and covered with a fortune in pearls on her bosom, ears and wrists. Over all that went a fine coat of glossy sable. On her husband's arm, Anya headed for the train station and the express to Tsarskoye Selo.

While the princess was spending her time making conversation and nibbling tea sandwiches with Her Imperial Majesty, Adam was going to join Gigi Grekov at his Tsarskoye villa. Natalya was a guest of the tsaritsa too, and Adam wanted to talk with her husband to find out the extent of Rasputin's influence on the imperial inner circle. The most peculiar stories were spreading in the foreign colony about the peasant; some of them were so bizarre, they were unbelievable.

When the Sviridovs arrived at the special platform at Tsarskoye meant for court guests, Countess Grekova was waiting to collect the princess. Bidding Adam farewell for a few hours, Anya got into the automobile sent by the tsaritsa and settled down beside Natalya, trying hard to look composed. Her heart was starting to pound already.

The princess made polite conversation with her companion but inwardly she was wondering why she had been honored by an imperial invitation. Alexandra Feodorovna disliked St. Petersburg society. She remained secluded at Tsarskoye Selo unless it was an absolute necessity to present herself in the capital. And she had let it be known how little she thought of her glittering city on the Neva, referring to the great Russian families as "loose" or "frivolous."

As Anya traveled the path from railway station to the gates of the plain, severely neoclassic Alexander Palace, she wished she were somewhere else, almost anywhere else. What on earth would she say to Alexandra Feodorovna? She had never met royalty before, except as a small child, when she had been patted on the head by various members of various royal families visiting Grand-père. It was an entirely different matter now.

Stepping out of the imperial motorcar with Natalya, Anya clutched her soft furs and made her way into the Alexander Palace past liveried footmen. The women progressed from one room to the next, each magnificent, each leading directly to the next while heading toward the private apartments.

Following the majordomo in his splendid knee breeches and gold braid, Princess Anya took in the sumptuous paneling, the thick silken draperies, the tall porcelain stoves, the fine crystal vases filled with rare flowers from the imperial hothouses, the exquisite Persian carpets. She began to calm down. It was rather familiar in a way. She might as well have been in a long hidden wing of the Sviridov mansion.

Of course, she thought with a smile as she saw herself reflected in one of the tall, gilded mirrors, the tsar of Russia did not live in the Sviridov mansion. He lived here. And that was why she had butterflies in her stomach.

When at last she and Natalya arrived in the private apartments, Anya took a deep breath and held her head up. In two seconds she would meet Alexandra Feodorovna. Her heart began to pound again.

As she and Countess Grekova stepped through the doorway to the tsaritsa's mauve boudoir, Alexandra's favorite room in the entire palace, Anya came face to face with her empress and quickly followed Natalya's example by dipping into a deep and reverent curtsey, wishing Ksenia could have been there to admire it. Perfect.

All she could remember from those first moments in the imperial presence were pearls, lots of them, as Alexandra extended her hand to be kissed. The long ropes danced before her eyes.

When the princess stood up again, she found that she was almost as tall as Alexandra, who was a few years older than Aunt Ksenia and yet appeared to be much older. She didn't resemble the official portraits which depicted her as a young bride; she looked like a woman who had suffered—her mouth was a taut little slit, her nose a thin beak. Even her large blue eyes seemed unbearably sad, as if life was a tremendous burden.

Fascinated by the presence of the woman who was being accused of destroying the monarchy by some of the most fervent monarchists in Russia, Princess Anya noticed how friendly she was toward Natalya. There was nothing sinister about her, contrary to what Anya had heard in some St. Petersburg salons; she seemed genuinely interested in hearing about the countess's infant son and Anya's. "Maternal" was the word that best described Alexandra, decided the young princess.

When the tea was over, Her Imperial Majesty told Princess Sviridova she was pleased to meet a young woman who was so obviously unspoiled by the fast living all around her. Anya thought she must have heard all the stories about Auntie Lisa. Alexandra wished more young ladies were as devoted to their children.

And then Alexandra graciously presented the princess with a beautiful formal photograph of the imperial family framed by Fabergé in a blue-and-white-enamel frame under rock crystal, a very lovely memento of the occasion.

As Princess Anya curtsied her way out, clutching her imperial presentation photograph, she felt as if she had just passed some sort of examination, although she didn't know which kind.

When she and Natalya joined their husbands, Anya noticed that Gigi was polite but quite unimpressed by his wife's access to the highest station in the land. Privately, he thought both Natalya and Alexandra were candidates for the asylum. "Did Her Majesty ask you if you were a follower of her peasant wonder-worker?" demanded the count of Anya.

"No. She never mentioned him. I was waiting for her to say something but she never did."

Natalya looked annoyed. "Her Majesty only speaks of Father Gregory if she knows believers are present."

"She was very kind," said Anya, somewhat defensively. "It's difficult to credit the stories one hears."

On their way back to the railway station, Prince and Princess Sviridov were chatting happily in the back of Gigi's motorcar when Anya suddenly asked. "Did Gigi tell you why he opposes Natalya's friendship with the tsaritsa? Her Majesty seems very kind."

"Darling," laughed Adam, "he's afraid they've let themselves be duped and deceived by this charlatan. It's a national scandal."

"But why?" wondered the princess aloud. "What can he possibly do to Alexandra Feodorovna or Natalya?"

Prince Sviridov smiled. Anyushka could be endearingly naive. "People suspect it's a sensual attraction," he said at last. "That's the general consensus of opinion."

"Then people are wrong. Her Majesty isn't like that."

"Darling," he suggested, "people are different things with different people. You've only met her once."

The princess stubbornly shook her pretty head. "Auntie Lisa is a sensual woman. Alexandra Feodorovna isn't. And," she pointed out, "you've never met her at all."

He laughed. She was right.

All the way home, Princess Anya wondered what made Alexandra Feodorovna the way she was. She hardly seemed the wicked empress depicted in gossip; if anything, she was gentle and kind. She had to be kind to befriend Natalya Grekova, thought Anya. Natalya could be very trying when she got going on Rasputin. But of course, they both thought highly of him, so that made all the difference.

"Well, darling," said Adam at last. "You've done something today that no other member of your family has done."

"What?"

"Have tea with Alexandra Feodorovna in her private apartment. You'll be besieged by every hostess you know to come and reveal all the details. Was it very grand?"

Anyushka smiled. "It was...cozy," she said, using one of her favorite English words as she nestled against him, brushing him with her sables. "And that's what I'm going to tell all the gossips. That ought to puzzle them."

⟡ 16 ⟡

The young countess Tatiana Sergeevna Derzhavina—Tasha to her family—was so excited she could hardly believe her good luck. Following a series of family fights, Mama had decided she needed to rest at one of the spas on the Italian island of Ischia, so off she'd gone with her personal maid, thirty-two red-leather trunks of clothing and a slim, dark young man who was introduced as her secretary, although Tasha didn't know why she needed a secretary. She never wrote.

To celebrate their liberation, the remaining Derzhavins went to a very chic restaurant, where they dined on *caille farcie aux raisins*, exquisitely arranged hothouse vegetables grown in St. Petersburg nurseries while the Russian snow swirled around the roofs, French champagne and, for dessert, delicate spun-sugar baskets of ripe berries shipped by train from the Crimea.

To the girl's surprise, after the meal was over she and Papa didn't return to the huge Derzhavin mansion on the Fontanka Canal, but to another large house located on one of the side streets off Nevsky Prospect. Dozens of expensive-looking sleighs were parked outside, presently joined by the Derzhavins', and the attendant coachmen were warming themselves over little fires at curbside while they waited for their masters to come out.

Hopping out of their sleigh, protected from the snow flurries and the frozen pavement by fur coats and warm, fur-lined boots, the count and young countess were quickly admitted to a lavishly decorated foyer blazing with the light of glittering crystal wall sconces.

A neatly dressed maid smiled a greeting as she took their coats and boots while they put on the expensive shoes they carried from the sleigh. Then, after Derzhavin had whispered something to an elegant, elderly woman in green silk and pearls, they were taken upstairs and shown to the oddest room Tasha had ever seen in her life.

With Papa smiling at her, the girl in white lace and white stockings

177

stared up at the mirrored ceiling reflecting a bizarre decor lavish with hot-house plants and flowers, several florid Persian carpets, piles of plump, embroidered pillows strewn casually about, and at least five gilded cages of little yellow songbirds. If this wasn't impressive enough, a huge, swan-shaped bed of gilded wood reposed among a veritable jungle of potted ferns, orchids and palms. On the walls—between the greens—were brightly colored murals of naked savages in the most incredible positions.

"Papa," Tasha asked in bewilderment, "what sort of place is this?"

Seriozha smiled again but he didn't answer. Instead he seated the puzzled child on the elaborate swan bed and began to undress her. A little frightened, Tasha protested but yielded to Derzhavin's gentle tone and soft caresses.

"You love Papa, don't you?"

"Yes," she replied, still uneasy. Everything here was so odd. Scary.

"Good girl. Then you must be nice to him and make him happy."

Suddenly a blonde girl slipped into the room, bearing a tray with a bottle of Moët and three champagne flutes on it. As Derzhavin uncorked the wine, the blonde wrapped her arms around both of them and smiled reassuringly at the child. And then in the space of a few seconds, the woman and Derzhavin had disrobed and were lying on the swan bed beside Tasha. She was terrified as her father and the woman exchanged whispered confidences above her head.

When they decided Tasha had had enough to drink, Seriozha and the blonde began to caress her as she struggled to escape from their strange game, wriggling all over the satin coverlet like a trapped animal.

"Tasha, you're going to be nice to Papa, aren't you, my angel?" he asked, kissing her tiny, budding breasts as the blonde held her gently but firmly.

"Yes," Tasha replied, frightened to the bottom of her soul, glancing wildly at the woman, then at her father.

Derzhavin and the blonde exchanged glances as he slowly climbed on top of the terror-stricken child, forcing her slender thighs apart. Nathalie, the blonde, pinned her to the bed, murmuring instructions about how to accommodate a man as Tasha thrashed wildly, biting both Seriozha and the woman.

Derzhavin slapped her hard and put an end to her struggles as he entered her suddenly and painfully. The child felt as though she were being ripped apart. The whole room seemed to swim before her eyes as she screamed, staring at the disgusting scene overhead that depicted every step of her agony.

"Good girl," murmured Count Derzhavin, crushing her with his body while Nathalie nearly suffocated her with kisses, exuding the mingled scents of sweat, heavy perfume and champagne. It was a repulsive mixture of perversion and squalor in the luxurious heart of Russia's most civilized city.

Two hours later, as Derzhavin and Tasha were en route home, the girl was still mute with fear and racked by a terrible, throbbing pain between her thighs. When Seriozha put his arm around her and asked her to promise never to tell anyone—especially not Mama—about their private games, she cringed and tried to withdraw from his embrace. Annoyed, her father shook her until she made a reply.

"That's better," he murmured, accepting her strangled *yes* for a guarantee of complicity.

"That's my good girl," he smiled, kissing her cold cheek. "You love Papa, don't you?"

Tatiana Sergeevna let two tears fall, then quickly brushed them away with her gloved hand in the icy night air so they wouldn't freeze. "Yes," she sobbed.

"Good."

Suddenly she said, "You hurt me, Papa. I didn't like that. I didn't like that Nathalie, either." She felt something new toward her father. Disgust.

"It wasn't that bad," he replied, irritated. "I thought you enjoyed our private game. I know I did." She was the best little lover of all.

"You hurt me, Papa. I didn't like that."

"Well, you'll get used to it, *chérie,* and then it won't hurt. You'll see. That's what they all say at first."

"I don't want to do it again. Ever!"

But they did do it again, and it became a kind of sport with Derzhavin. Tasha found herself trapped in a hurtful, frightening private nightmare, too ashamed to tell anyone out of fear of not being believed and out of fear of her mother. She was dragged into a strange netherworld of disgusting games and peculiar people, forced to accompany Papa into the most infamous houses in the city.

It had all started so innocently, she thought. She hadn't even understood what he was doing at first. He had said it was all right.

She knew it wasn't. And now she didn't know how to avoid it. Worst of all, there was no one to turn to; she couldn't tell the servants. Mama was on the worst possible terms with the Sviridovs. Why should they help her? Tasha reasoned. Besides, everyone would say it was her fault. She had been bad and this was what happened to girls like her.

In total despair, she even started wishing Mama would come home, something she had never wished for in her entire life. If she were here, Tasha thought, Papa would stop. Yes, that was it.

With this in mind, the little girl began writing long, loving letters to Mama informing her of how much she missed her and begging her to return. Mama was her only hope.

Back in St. Petersburg after his trip to Moscow, Roman Vasilievich Petrov was more nervous than ever. Mishkin had been killed in mysterious circumstances. Now Pavel Scriabin sought him out to tell him a similar story: "Dimitri had been found blown to bits in his small attic room in a cheap boardinghouse in the Haymarket district. There was a note left outside the wrecked room. Some gibberish."

"That was it?" demanded Petrov as he and Pavel Scriabin stood on the snow-covered Singer's Bridge overlooking the frozen Neva.

Pavel frowned impatiently, looking half-frozen, thumping his gloved hands to keep his circulation going in the cold. "That was it."

Petrov shuddered in the icy afternoon air while smart-looking private sleighs and less elegant public ones sped past, bells jingling as they raced over the ice, horses' hooves pounding the frozen snow. Pretty girls under robes of costly fur laughed as they headed down the prospect, passing grave bureaucrats and elderly officers heading for appointments at the general staff headquarters on Palace Square. All St. Petersburg appeared to be out for a sleigh ride this afternoon, enjoying one of the pleasures of winter. Nobody noticed the two shabby men on the bridge.

"Who do you think could have wanted to kill your brother?" Petrov asked at last.

"I haven't the foggiest idea," snapped Pavel. "I just want to be certain the killer doesn't come looking for me next."

That struck Petrov as a decidedly self-centered viewpoint. He would have expected the elder Scriabin to show more sorrow. Long-nosed bastard.

As he took his leave, turning to cross the bridge and catch an oncoming tram, Petrov called back, "Be careful, Scriabin!"

Pavel laughed as he watched the small, shabby man in the moth-eaten fur hat run after the tram. "You too!" he shouted after him.

But Petrov was too far away to hear. Anyway, he was apt to take that bit of advice without any prompting from Pavel Scriabin. He wasn't stupid.

If the family was placing Anya on a pedestal, talking of a love match that delighted them and lavishing money and affection on Anya, her new husband and baby, society concluded, somebody had made a dreadful mistake the year before—namely, Countess Lisa who was recalled as the source of the story about the rape. Everybody knew what a tyrant Sandro was. If his granddaughter had disgraced him, she would have been out on the street, not occupying one of the grandest mansions in St. Petersburg. Indeed, the one who seemed ostracized was Countess Derzhavina herself.

Despite the rift in the family, the birth of little Byelochka had brought so much happiness to Sandro that he hardly seemed aware of having lost a daughter. His great-grandson upstairs in the nursery more than made up for her absence. He adored the child, commissioned Boldini to paint a life-sized portrait of the little one in Anya's arms and had the four-room nursery suite decorated with murals of old Russian folktales for Byelochka's amusement. Adam worried what Sandro would do when the baby could actually make requests, and he spoke to Anya about spoiling the child, to no avail.

In her first year as a married woman, Princess Anya had come to realize there were rather sharp differences between her upbringing and her husband's. He was inclined to take a possessive view of her. If she danced too long with other gentlemen at a ball, for instance, he became irritated. If she wanted to learn how to fly an airplane, he said it was too dangerous for her. If she wanted to leave a party at four in the morning and spend the rest of the night at gypsy nightclubs in Novaya Derevnaya before returning home to sleep until the afternoon, he said she could make better use of her time. Everyone did these things, protested the young princess. Well, replied Adam Mikhailovich, they didn't do them in Massachusetts.

"Ha!" sniffed Anya, "be grateful you don't live there any longer. It sounds dreadfully dull." And off she went to visit Ksenia and complain about the tyranny of husbands.

When Adam thought about his friend Gigi Grekov's marriage, he knew he had relatively little to worry about, but the more he got to know St. Petersburg society, the more it bothered him to see Anya, whom he adored, adapt so readily to the prevailing pursuit of endless pleasure. If she hadn't been as straightforward as she was and so devoted to their son, he would have been greatly concerned. Unfaithfulness was all too common in St. Petersburg. If Anya had been unfaithful, it would have killed him.

From what he could see, it appeared to be killing Gigi Grekov.

One afternoon Adam and the count were discussing the recent troubles in the industrial districts when he noticed a large number of oil portraits and photographs laid out in Gigi's study. In response to Adam's question, Gigi replied that they were pictures of members of his family, dating back to the early 1700s.

"Are you planning to hang them together?" Adam asked, thinking the count had a great interest in genealogy.

"No," replied Count Grekov. "I was trying to find a resemblance.

Some hereditary trait passed down through each generation. Just curiosity on my part."

As Prince Adam studied the collection, he remarked upon a tendency of the Grekovs toward dark complexions, dark eyes and a refinement of feature. Gigi was a typical example. Volodya took after Tamara Mikhailovna's family—blonder, heavier descendants of a German who had fought for Peter the Great and received splendid compensation for it. Gigi's mother had been born Tamara von Gartner.

The last Grekov, Gigi's son Nicky, didn't look like anyone in the family. Worse than that, he didn't look like anyone in Natalya's family either. The baby who had been the reason for the marriage resembled nobody.

Nobody but Rasputin's teenage daughter Maria.

Gigi knew this because one day while he and his wife were driving down Nevsky Prospect, Natalya had seen the girl out with a friend and had remarked to her husband that the Holy One wouldn't like it if he knew his daughter was out unchaperoned.

"How very proper of him," the count had laughed. And then he'd studied the girl. She was friendly looking, with light-blue eyes, fair complexion and a flat peasant nose. His son looked enough like her to have been her brother. To Gigi's horror, the resemblance was so strong it unnerved him. That was the reason for the examination of the family tree. And to his despair, Nicky didn't favor any Grekov—or any member of Natalya's family, living or dead. He looked just like Rasputin's daughter.

From that moment on, Count Grekov began to hate the sight of the child. He was convinced he was a bastard but was too proud to admit the possibility and utterly wretched because of it. To add to the count's humiliation, Alexandra Feodorovna was so fond of his empty-headed wife's company, she had her appointed *dame à portrait,* an honor that entitled her to wear her sovereign's miniature portrait surrounded by diamonds on court occasions, a singular favor and probably the first step toward creating Natalya lady-in-waiting. In a way, Gigi almost wished she would become one. That way, Natalya would be so occupied with her duties to her sovereign that her husband wouldn't have to put up with the sight of her.

If Adam felt sympathy for the Grekovs, he had absolutely none for his brother Billy, who finally managed to get himself appointed to the St. Petersburg embassy toward the end of 1912. In spite of high praise from the ambassador and Billy's own claim to have finally grown up, his older brother still looked upon him as a great liability.

The idea of having this charming wastrel associating with Anya and their son filled Adam with loathing. To Prince Adam, Billy Whitmore was a damned albatross, even if he was his brother, and it would take more than an outsider's testimony to convince him otherwise.

With the end of the year approaching, Princess Anya was busy with preparations for the holidays and the beginning of the St. Petersburg season, which began officially with the tsar's New Year's day reception in the Winter Palace and went on until the start of Lent. She had ordered a few dozen gowns from Poiret in Paris for special balls, dinners and the theatre and felt satisfied with them. Now she was thinking of Christmas presents.

In the lull before the start of the official season, Anya enjoyed herself by playing with Byelochka, her beautiful blue-eyed blond six-month-old and by joining in one of society's favorite winter diversions, an afternoon's sleigh ride down Nevsky Prospect. She often saw the Dowager Empress Maria Feodorovna and her daughter, Grand Duchess Olga Alexandrovna, leaving or returning from the huge Anichkov Palace halfway down the prospect, as well as other ladies whom she was beginning to know from her round of parties. She even spotted Madame Kashina one day in a very smart sleigh and pretended not to see her—but she couldn't help noticing that the ballerina was now accompanied by a grand duke, confirming recent gossip.

One snowy afternoon when Anya was enjoying her daily drive, which generally consisted of a swing down Liteiny Prospect from the French Embankment, a right-hand turn onto the Nevsky and then up the long Nevsky to return home along the quays of the Neva, the young princess saw something that made her order her driver to halt just past Kazan Cathedral. There, alone and on foot, was her little cousin Tasha.

Oh Lord, thought Tasha as she heard her name. Turning in the direction of the voice, she was even more startled to see who was calling her. If she hadn't been afraid of creating more problems for herself, she would have fled; but as it was impossible to avoid Anyushka now, she simply smiled and went toward the sleigh, pretending to be delighted to see her.

"Get in at once," ordered Princess Sviridova. "What on earth is the matter with you? What are you doing here alone?"

"Taking a walk," replied Tasha.

"Without even a servant? No, darling," smiled Anya. "You're not going to make me believe that story. Shall I take you home?"

"No. Please. I don't want to go home. I'm supposed to be in school."

Anya tilted back her head and looked skeptical. "Then what are you doing wandering the streets?"

To her surprise, Tasha only shook her head, not really knowing what to answer. The princess reached out and took the child's arm. "Get in," she said quietly. "We'll drive back to the French Embankment and you can tell me the whole story over tea. Come. It's all right."

Even with the hostility that existed between the Sviridovs and Tasha's parents, the princess wasn't about to leave the girl where she found her. Even if Aunt Lisa were an insufferable shrew, Anya had nothing against Tasha and was not going to allow her to roam the city unaccompanied. Anya knew only too well the dangers of unsupervised strolls.

As the cousins settled themselves into the sleigh for the drive to the Sviridov mansion, Anya noticed how listless the girl was. She had dark circles under her blue eyes and a terrible pallor, as if she were perpetually sleepless. The last time she had seen Tasha, the child hadn't looked like this. Something was dreadfully wrong with her.

"Grand-père hasn't returned from Paris," Anya announced as she and her cousin entered the foyer. "He's not expected back until just before Christmas."

Tasha didn't seem to care. She didn't ask about him, merely murmuring in response as her older cousin chattered about this and that as they headed for Anya's sitting room on the second floor where the princess had requested her tea. When they reached the pretty yellow and white room with its cheerful garden murals and rococco plasterwork, flowered silk sofas and thick brocade draperies, the girl sat down rather sulkily and sighed as her cousin asked once again what she was doing alone on the Nevsky.

"I decided not to go to classes," replied Tasha. "So I waited until the coachman was out of sight after he dropped me off and simply walked away."

"What time does he take you to classes?"

"At nine."

"And you've been walking all day?" exclaimed Anya. "Good Lord! That's very foolish. Someone might have harmed you." The thought appalled her.

The look Tasha gave her cousin was so full of contempt, Anya was taken aback. She couldn't imagine what prompted it.

"I didn't know you attended classes outside the house," Anya said at last, delighted that Matvei had just brought in their tea. Perhaps if the child ate something she would feel better. She was in a terribly strange mood, thought the princess, not knowing what to make of her. She and Lisa's daughter had never been close, but as cousins they had been acquainted with each other. She didn't remember Tasha ever being so sullen before. The whole thing was so bizarre it upset her.

"Mama got rid of my governess and decided to let me have my lessons with other girls. Now I study with Countess Bariatyn's two daughters."

From her expression, Tasha was completely indifferent to it all. Looking at her small cousin sitting opposite her in a white middy blouse with a navy-blue kerchief, navy-blue skirt, dark stockings and black kid ankle boots, Princess Anya thought she looked quite a bit younger than twelve. She also looked extremely tired.

"Tasha," said the princess gently, "you still never explained why you were wandering the Nevsky by yourself. Are you ready to tell me now?"

The small countess seemed to curl up into a little ball, wrapping her arms around herself and drawing up her knees to rest her feet on a nearby footstool. She wasn't volunteering any information.

"It's dangerous for a young girl to roam about on her own. People are not always good and kind, you know. There are men out there who might harm you," persisted Anya.

For an instant, Tasha looked at her cousin with such pain in her eyes that the young princess didn't know what to make of it. The girl appeared to be on the verge of saying something but then seemed to think the better of it and merely shook her head. Finally she said she wasn't afraid of strangers. People could just as easily come to harm inside their own homes.

"But they usually don't," replied Anya.

"Anything is possible," retorted the child, fixing her with those beautiful icy-blue eyes, so filled with anguish it was upsetting to look into them. "People aren't really safe anywhere."

Not wishing to quarrel with the girl about the hazards of life in the capital in a pointless argument that would certainly lead nowhere, Anya politely inquired about Auntie Lisa and Uncle Seriozha. That seemed to strike a nerve. Tasha sighed and looked distraught for a second.

"Mama is going away for a week," she said, wrapping her arms around herself again. "I don't want her to leave."

Now, thought Anya, that was something she never expected to hear from another living being. The idea of anyone missing Auntie Lisa was so novel it made her smile. Besides, Tatiana Sergeevna had never been close to her mother; it was her father whom she adored.

"Well, a week isn't such a long time," said Anya. "She'll be back sooner than you think."

"But I don't want her to go. I don't want to be alone."

"Tasha, we all have to do things we don't want to do from time to time." Lord, this child was spoiled, thought Anya. That had to be it.

Looking at Princess Anya, who was so kind, so normal, the girl despaired of ever making her understand what Lisa's departure meant. She couldn't tell her. For one thing, Anyushka wouldn't believe her. Who would? It was so shameful it was a disgrace to talk about it. As a last resort Tasha looked hopefully at the princess and asked if she could stay with her while Mama was away.

Feeling sorry for the child, Anya said she could, but in view of the recent family quarrel she didn't know if the Derzhavins would agree. After that horror at the Bolshoi, Anya couldn't imagine Auntie Lisa allowing her daughter to spend any time with the Sviridovs.

"But will you write to Papa and ask him if I could stay here for a week?" pleaded the child. "I would like that."

Touched by the girl's sincerity and sorry for her unhappiness, Princess Anya smiled and promised to extend an invitation. Then she and her cousin went upstairs to the nursery so Tasha could admire Byelochka, whom she had never seen. "Pretty," murmured Tasha. But Anya could tell she had no interest in him, and she was disappointed. Most visitors fell in love with her little squirrel on sight and couldn't bear to leave him. Tasha didn't care.

Still, she had promised to invite her to spend a week with them; after she'd returned home from depositing her small cousin outside Countess Bariatyn's so she could be picked up at the usual time, Anya went to her dainty escritoire and composed a very polite letter to Seriozha asking to entertain his daughter while he and Auntie Lisa were away for the week, deliberately omitting how she had come to learn about their travel plans.

Two days later a response came back, a very charming letter, thanking "dear Anyushka" for her tender concern, which had moved him deeply, but also informing her that little Tasha was most certainly not going to be left alone while her dear Mama was absent from the family hearth. Count Derzhavin was remaining in St. Petersburg, so there was no reason to send her to visit, although he personally looked forward to more cordial relations between himself and the Sviridovs in the future and expressed his gratitude for Anyushka's magnanimous spirit of reconciliation.

"But why did she lead me to think she'd be alone?" Anya asked Ksenia as they both took an afternoon drive a few days later, the ladies sheltering Byelochka between them, blanketed in furs—Ksenia in sable, Anya in chinchilla, the child in fox.

"I can't imagine," replied her aunt. "I also can't imagine her missing her mother. Nobody misses Lisa. One is grateful for Lisa's absence."

"She seemed so unhappy. As if she were expecting some terrible disaster to happen. Was I ever that unhappy when I was twelve years old?"

Princess Ksenia smiled. "Only once, when your old poodle died. You wept for a week and couldn't eat."

"This is different. This is fear. I feel very sorry for her."

As the sleigh raced down the long Nevsky, past its palaces, shops, mansions and churches, Princess Anya thought of that frightened child and wondered what she could do to help her. There didn't seem to be much she *could* do, since she didn't intend to place herself within striking distance of Auntie Lisa ever again. But she would have liked to do something, anything to remove that look of despair from Tasha's face. It wasn't normal for a child to be so reckless and so oddly fearful at the same time. It was very peculiar.

Holding Byelochka close, the young princess silently thanked God fate had sent her Ksenia and not Lisa to replace her own mother. Utterly content with her husband, her son and her life right now, Anyushka wanted to see the whole world smiling. It truly bothered her that Tasha couldn't.

"Whatever is disturbing the girl will sort itself out," Ksenia said gently. "That's all we can hope for."

"Yes, I suppose you're right."

But Ksenia hadn't seen those huge, terrified eyes. Anya had, and she wouldn't forget them so soon.

17

The Christmas holidays of 1912 were celebrated with the usual round of parties, dances and theatrical galas. The American ambassador to Russia gave a grand party for the children of his staff members, and Byelochka attended, one of his first social occasions. His mama's elegant outfit of dark-blue wool with fine black soutache trim was much admired, as was her sable coat, hat and muff. Anyushka herself was very much admired, in fact, which made her husband quite proud.

To please Adam, his wife decided to try to find out what Americans were likely to do at Christmas and discovered the quaint custom of making ropes for Christmas tree decorations by stringing together red berries and popped corn. Nobody in the kitchen knew anything about popping corn, but the parlor maids were pressed into service to string little red berries to drape around the Christmas trees. When Adam witnessed the effect he declared it was just what he remembered from Massachusetts. He was very pleased, Anya reported to Ksenia, and they had a wonderful time decorating the tree with glass balls from Germany, wooden ornaments from Switzerland and lots of little silvery icicles purchased at the Gostiny Dvor, plus the dozens of small red candles that gave it the finishing touch. To make things even better, they celebrated both the western and the Orthodox Christmas, prolonging the holidays delightfully.

Prince Sandro returned home a week before Christmas and held his yearly presentation of gifts to his staff, with Anya and Adam assisting. Gifts kept arriving from family and friends, keeping Anya busy with her thank-you notes, but nothing reached the French Embankment from the Derzhavins, which was considered a grave affront to Sandro.

To everyone's surprise, the day of the tsar's New Year's reception at the Winter Palace was the day Countess Natalya Grekova confided a secret to

Anya and Ksenia that nearly made the ladies blink with astonishment. She and Gigi were going to have a second child.

"What!" exclaimed Ksenia as she stood next in line to Natalya, awaiting the approach of the tsar and tsaritsa; she was prepared to bow almost to the ground as the sovereigns passed.

"It was confirmed three days ago," whispered Natalya, her eyes on the approaching Romanovs, while Ksenia whispered the news in Anya's ear, making her head spin.

As the tsar, tsaritsa, dowager empress and all the available Romanovs went down the line, leaving a row of bowing subjects in their wake, rather like the wind sweeping over a field of wheat, the two princesses both had an identical thought. Either Natalya or Gigi, or both, were utterly mad. Gigi loathed his son. Why would he ever chance a second one?

"Perhaps he was overcome by passion," suggested Adam that evening. "It has been known to happen."

"But Natalya and her husband hardly ever sleep together. She told me so."

"Good Lord! I hope you don't discuss these things."

Anya smiled as she glanced at Adam, settling into the covers. "No," she replied. "But I can't help hearing what Natalya Alexeevna tells me."

"I'd say Natalya tells more than she should. The woman has no sense of propriety."

She tried hard to suppress a giggle. Her husband would probably be shocked by some of the things ladies told each other when they were alone, not that Anya ever contributed to the general store of knowledge; she was too busy listening. Besides, after what she had heard, she feared that ladies might begin to pursue her husband if they ever discovered how happy she was with him; she knew that discontent was rampant in St. Petersburg.

Anya looked upon Adam as a harbor of security in a mad whirlpool. She enjoyed watching him play with Byelochka, liked to see him getting on so well with Grand-père and took pride in his success with the airplane Grand-père had given them. He was really quite good at swooping from tremendous heights and rolling over in the air, a feat that always made her gasp. In fact, he was so good, he was going to enter the St. Petersburg-to-Moscow air race, one of the highlights of the Romanov tercentenary.

March 1913 marked the three hundredth anniversary of the Romanov dynasty, and for the occasion the season was especially brilliant, extending itself into the spring with all sorts of balls, processions, Te Deum services and military parades in most of the empire's cities. Naturally, the St. Petersburg festivities were the most splendid, with the nobility of the capital given the rare pleasure of entertaining the tsar and tsaritsa at a great ball, being entertained by them at a series of receptions and parties at the Winter Palace and attending a stupendous round of activities dedicated to the glorification of the dynasty.

As a concession to the importance of the tercentenary, the imperial family moved back into the Winter Palace for the first time since the season before the Japanese war. Although the tsaritsa appeared to be in poor health and left many of the ceremonies early, her two elder daughters, Olga and Tatiana, made an enormous impression on society, somewhat making up for their mother's flaws. The rest of the Imperial Family appeared to enjoy the celebration as a well-deserved tribute.

In the general whirl of parties, balls, luncheons and more parties, the whole capital was wild. Anticipation mounted each time another gala affair was announced; the most frenzied efforts were made by the ladies to outshine each other. Dressmakers and jewelers were in heaven, florists were giving thanks for even more business than usual and the citizens of St. Petersburg enjoyed the glamour like spectators at a parade.

To cap a wonderful season, Princess Anya gave one of the most original and chic parties of the year, an eighteenth-century Venetian romp in which Grand-père assumed the costume and dignity of a doge and Anya and Ksenia appeared in powdered wigs and antique brocades as masked revelers at the casino the Gallery of the Ottocento became. Costume balls were all the rage and this one drew the grandest names in St. Petersburg. Guests came decked out in reproductions of what their ancestors would have worn, complete with family jewels that dated from the same era. It was stupendous. A set designer from the Maryinsky created backdrops and even a miniature lagoon with scale-model gondolas. Nothing was left out.

On the night the Sviridov mansion was turned into a doge's palazzo, most of St. Petersburg was present, or at least most of those who counted, including the Grand Duchess Maria Pavlovna, the Grand Duchess Elena Vladimirovna, Grand Duke Alexander Mikhailovich and his wife, the Grand Duchess Xenia Alexandrovna, as well as several members of international society, including a rather overly dramatic Gabriele D'Annunzio who decided to dedicate his next poem to Princess Ksenia, and several of Prince Sandro's Paris intimates who had been transported east on a special train just for the occasion. It was a wild success, and Princess Anya established herself on the social scene as a worthy upholder of the family tradition for lavishness and a fitting successor to Princess Tatiana, Sandro's wife, who had been known from St. Petersburg to Paris for her great style, jewels and penchant for parties. This was all very pleasing to Anyushka, but she would have preferred to have the whole family present, which was impossible: The Derzhavins had been banished from the Sviridov mansion, probably forever.

◆   ◆   ◆

With each event even more elaborate than the one that had gone before, the highlight of the season was to be the great costume ball at the Winter Palace, a re-creation of the Romanov court of 1613, with all the guests in period dress. Opportunities for extravagance were limitless.

One evening at a dinner party at Count and Countess Grekovs', Adam had remarked to Gigi that he wished he knew what ancient *boyars* wore. The whole idea rather daunted him, he said, since Americans of that era tended to wear buckskin, feathers and beading, none of which seemed appropriate for an imperial evening.

"Well," replied the count, "we can't allow Prince Sviridov to turn up as a red Indian, can we?" And he offered to design a *boyar*'s costume for him, which led to a similar request from Princess Anya, Princess Ksenia, Prince Andrei and even Prince Sandro. Before Gigi was done, he had been drafted by the whole clan and ended up spending hours in long discussions with the ladies and their dressmakers. With the combined resources of the Grekovs, Malyshevs and Sviridovs, they found enough pictures of their predecessors in *boyar* dress to make consulting the imperial archives needless, and when they were finished, they were magnificent. The cost of the fur trimming alone would have fed several families for a year.

Borrowing from Sandro's hoard of jewels, Gigi decked the ladies in ropes of pearls over richly embroidered, gold-laden brocades, with head-dresses covered with freshwater pearls and sable-trimmed sarafans and jackets, copying Muscovite matrons of the seventeenth century. The men were more subdued than their women, but not much more, all of them resplendent in golden brocades and cut velvets as Muscovite *boyars*, the whole lot growing beards for the occasion over the protests of their wives.

Prince Sandro looked especially imposing with his white hair and beard. The fact that he carried several pounds of antique gold chains—all family treasures sent to an ancestor from Renaissance Italy—gave his costume an added touch. The best Adam, Gigi and Andrei could do was to borrow a few brooches from their women.

Gigi appeared to be happier than he had been in several months, which had to do with Natalya's pregnancy. Despite his dislike of little Nicky, he was trying desperately not to believe that his wife had deceived him with Rasputin and was anxious to see what this baby looked like. If this child was blue-eyed with a flat potato nose, he would kill both the baby and the mother. If not, he would be satisfied. Fortunately for Natalya, she hadn't the slightest idea of what her husband intended and took all his displays of kindness as signs of reconciliation.

Adam enjoyed the round of parties along with everyone else and wondered privately how the Russian people, who had been showing signs of such alarming discontent for nearly a decade, could take the Romanovs to their hearts the way they did. Perhaps, thought the American, it was a strange kind of truce between ruler and ruled, a welcome respite from so much mutual antagonism. He hoped it would last.

On the night of the long-awaited costume ball, Princess Anya, her husband, her grand-père, Aunt Ksenia and Uncle Andrei assembled in full seventeenth-century dress at the Sviridov mansion for the trip to the Winter Palace. Anya and Ksenia were breathtaking in long brocaded sarafans threaded with gold, trimmed with sable at the hems, short jackets edged with more sable over those and elaborate, crescent-shaped headdresses beaded with dozens of freshwater pearls as a finishing touch. Anya's sarafan was purple with gold; Ksenia's was dark green and gold; both were magnificent. Their men were suitably grand and rather impressive themselves.

As the two motorcars of their party approached the palace quay, Princess Anya exclaimed in delight at the spectacle of the Winter Palace— every window was illuminated, lines of elegant motorcars and sleighs were lined up to drop off costumed guests and a throng of spectators huddled in the cold outside, eager to watch the arrival of the city's notables.

Palace footmen in knee breeches and gold-braided scarlet jackets ushered the arrivals inside as group after group of *boyars* and *boyarinas* climbed the magnificent Jordan Staircase between rows of Chevalier Guards, the huge columns of blue-green marble with gilded Corinthian capitals towering above the guests at the top of the staircase, the plasterwork of the ceiling like gilded lace above their heads. Several thousand of St. Petersburg's nobility and upper classes poured through the great palace, a spectacle of light, color and music.

As Princess Anya and her party made their way up the sparkling white marble staircase, greeting friends and acquaintances as they headed toward the grand St. George Hall, the crush of people was so dense, Anya felt like a fish swimming against the tide. It seemed as if the entire capital were here, dressed in seventeenth-century silks and brocades. The world's oceans must have been drained to produce the harvest of pearls on these costumes, thought the princess. Every lady wore them draped around her headdress, over her robes, framing her face. It was dazzling.

When the tsar and tsaritsa opened the ball with the traditional polonaise, Princess Sviridova noticed Natalya and Gigi rather close to the imperial couple. Natalya's condition was hidden beneath her sarafan of red and gold brocade and its jacket of silver cloth edged with sable.

"She looks splendid," Anya whispered to Ksenia. "I hope everything is well with Gigi."

"He wants this child. He's being desperately agreeable," replied Ksenia.

During the course of the evening, Princess Anya and Princess Ksenia both had the honor of partnering the tsar at different times, and Prince Sandro led off a polonaise with the elegant dowager empress, Maria Feodorovna. It was a marvelous night.

Only the next day did anyone realize that one of the city's most flamboyant couples had been missing. Lisa and Seriozha had been nowhere in sight.

According to those who knew the countess, only an act of God could have prevented her from attending the ball of the year. It was something to wonder about.

The afternoon of the ball, Seriozha had cornered Tasha in her bedroom, thinking Lisa hadn't yet returned from her daily drive, and had proceeded to make advances, ignoring her pleas and even her threats as he ripped off her dress and pulled her onto the bed.

"I'm going to tell Mama," sobbed the girl. "She'll turn you over to the police. She said she would once. She will."

"The hell she will," replied Seriozha. "Come here."

To Tasha, there was no hope left. If he was no longer afraid to touch her while Mama remained in town, she was completely defenseless. Sobbing with anger, the child fought back, hitting him as hard as she could, scratching, biting, kicking. She was screaming so loudly the servants gathered in the hall outside the bedroom, listening to every shriek, not daring to open the door. They were still there when the countess returned, curious to know what was happening.

By way of reply, the servants looked down at the parquet floor, not daring to say a word.

"Open the door," Lisa demanded.

Nobody moved on either side of the paneled door. Inside the room, Tasha was still sobbing, huddled on the floor in a heap of torn clothing, nearly hysterical after the attack. Seriozha was ashen at the sound of Lisa's voice.

"Seriozha!" said the countess. "If you don't open the door, I'm going to order the footman to break it down. You have a choice."

When there was no response to that, Lisa turned to the nearest servant and gestured toward the door. The fellow put his shoulder into it, bashing against it as hard as he could. The force broke the hundred-year-old lock and sent him sprawling on the floor. In an instant Lisa saw the half-dressed, hysterical child and the expression on her husband's face. Closing the door behind her, she stood staring at Seriozha, speechless for a second. Then she reacted, pulling her daughter off the carpet by her long black hair and throwing her into Seriozha's arms.

"How long has this been going on, you little weasel?" she screamed. "Answer me, Seriozha. How long?"

When the count declined to reply, Lisa picked up the nearest object and flung it at his head, missing him but striking Tasha, who cringed in terror.

Derzhavin was pale with fear. Flinging his daughter onto the floor, he threw his arms around his wife, receiving a slap in the face for his efforts and threats of calling the police.

"Please," he begged. "Don't do that. It was her fault. She kept after me. I couldn't resist."

In her heart, Lisa had always known this would happen. She had known it when Seriozha began to fondle the child years before. Seeing proof of his infidelity with their own daughter was so revolting, it made her want to kill them both.

Sobbing as her mother turned on her, driving her across the room under a shower of blows, Tasha no longer saw anything but a terrifying red blur. Hearing Lisa's shrieks, Seriozha's cries and her own sobs, the girl crumpled up into the corner, wailing, her arms over her head, trying to duck the abuse.

"He took me to a terrible place when you went to Ischia, Mama!" she screamed. "I wanted you to protect me but you left me! You handed me over to him! You should have helped me!"

As Lisa paused to scream at Seriozha, Tasha leaped up and grabbed a pair of scissors lying on her dressing table. Seeing Tasha's sudden movement, the countess grabbed her, forcing her up against the dressing table, fighting for possession of the scissors. Smacking the girl repeatedly across the face until she had drawn blood, Lisa snatched at the scissors as her daughter doubled over, desperately trying to keep control of them.

Seizing a handful of Tasha's hair, the countess wrenched her head up, trying to grab the doublepointed weapon. As she did, the girl's arm went back in a violent arc and then up into her mother's breast. For a moment Lisa doubled over, her eyes on her daughter, her hands clutching at her breast. Fascinated by the sight, Tasha silently watched the stunned countess sink slowly onto the Chinese carpet, the two sharp points of the scissors sticking into her heart. Tasha had driven the blades in so deep, only the jeweled handles could be seen. Gasping from the fight and the pain, her face bleeding from Lisa's attack, the girl stared at the trickle of blood beginning to stain her mother's frock below her chest.

I've killed her, she thought, clinging to the dressing table for support. She's not moving. I've killed my mother. The thought made her numb; she would be punished for this. It would be dreadful.

"Oh my God!" screamed Seriozha, rushing across the room to his wife. "Lisa!"

Countess Derzhavina looked like a wounded bird, her long black hair spread out on the carpet like a sweep of glossy plumage, her bright-blue frock and pale skin splashed with scarlet. The scissors were embedded in her chest like two small knives, tiny but deadly. No sound came from her open mouth.

Tasha stared in fascination at her mother, her father, the bloodied carpet, the whole scene like something from a nightmare, and suddenly she knew how she was going to punish Seriozha for all those afternoons and evenings of shame. He deserved it.

"You killed Mama," she announced quietly, with malice in her eyes. "You stabbed her with the scissors and you killed her."

"Tasha, don't say that," he pleaded.

"You killed Mama," she repeated, enjoying the terror in his eyes. "I saw you."

"You little monster!"

Tasha was already running out the door, naked, screaming to the servants clustered outside the room that Papa had killed Mama and was now after her.

Dumbfounded, the footmen and maids looked inside, saw Count Derzhavin staring back at them and Countess Derzhavina lying on the floor in a pool of blood in the middle of her daughter's bedroom.

"I didn't do this!" cried Seriozha, forcing his way out of the room. "It's not my fault!"

Running downstairs after his daughter, the little man chased her into one of the drawing rooms on the first floor, but when Tasha saw him pursuing her with a poker he had snatched from the fireplace, she raced back upstairs to take shelter behind the crowd of servants, who were too stunned to do anything but stare.

"For God's sake, help me!" screamed Tasha. "He means to kill me, too!"

As the furious count took the stairs two at a time, waving his poker at the child, shouting obscenities, a young footman reached out to take hold of the weapon. Struggling with Seriozha on the stairs, he lost his balance and, clutching his screaming employer, plunged over the marble railing to the foyer some fifty feet below.

Before the horrified eyes of his staff, Count Sergei Derzhavin landed with a shriek on top of a grotesque seventeenth-century clock. The most interesting thing about this ornate timepiece was its sharp metal spire, a distant cousin to the spire atop Sts. Peter and Paul Cathedral. Now the spire was protruding through the middle of Count Derzhavin, causing him much agony. The footman lay silently on the marble floor, his neck broken in the fall.

As Seriozha lay pinned to the clock like an insect on a laboratory tray, Tatiana Sergeevna leaned over the railing to get a better look at his agony, hear his cries of unbearable pain, see the expression on his face. And then she fainted.

Two hours later, after the doctor had come and gone, unable to save the count, Tasha entered the room where he lay and cautiously approached the deathbed. Yanking off the blanket, she stood a long time in silence, looking at the man who had caused her so much misery, her first and last love. In death, he was harmless and rather a revolting mess.

"You were clever, Seriozha, but I was even cleverer. Now I have everything and you have nothing, not even your life or your good name."

Smiling in triumph, the girl did one more thing. Leaning over the corpse, Tasha bent her face close to Seriozha's and, trembling with emotion, spat violently two or three times at the corpse.

"*Adieu, cher Papa*," she laughed. "*Je vais te revoir en enfer!*"

As Countess Tatiana Sergeevna Derzhavina walked out of that room, she left behind whatever feelings she had ever had toward her family. She was a woman, alone.

Circumstances being what they were, Prince Sandro decreed that a double funeral was out of the question. Lisa's family would make the arrangements for the countess; what the Derzhavins did with Seriozha's perforated carcass was their own business. Tasha agreed. She never even bothered to inquire about the plans for Papa's burial, thereby allying herself with Mama's relatives.

As a witness to Lisa's "murder" by Seriozha and the survivor of an attempted murder, Tasha enjoyed quite a bit of sympathy, even though her mother's relations with her family had been on the stormy side. There was nothing like instant martyrdom to change people's opinion, and since the obnoxious Lisa wasn't around to irritate them any longer, her nearest and dearest chose to think of her in a favorable light. As her only surviving child, Tasha was to be carefully nurtured.

"Now I'm all alone," declared the young countess as she walked away from the graveside, supported by Aunt Ksenia and Grand-père. "I don't know what I'll do without darling Mama."

Dabbing at her eyes—although no tears could be seen—the girl got into the waiting motorcar with her Malyshev relatives and drove from the cemetery, abandoning Lisa to the silent company of her forebears. Seriozha was being interred beside his own relatives on the opposite side of the great necropolis; Lisa was keeping her distance in death as in life.

Settling into the soft leather seat of the Mercedes, nestling beside Ksenia in her sables and heavy veiling, Tatiana Sergeevna leaned her head on the princess's shoulder and sighed. Ksenia mistook it for an outbreak of tears and gently put her arm around the child. Andrei looked sympathetic. He supposed a daughter might find redeeming qualities in his late sister-in-law, even if they were less than obvious to him.

I've gone over to the enemy, thought Tasha as her beautiful aunt tenderly stroked her hair. She buried her face in Ksenia's sables, inhaling the exotic scent of fur mingled with *Jasmine de Corse*, Auntie's favorite perfume. In the small, enclosed space, the air was heavy with its fragrance.

"What happened to you was dreadful," Auntie was saying quietly as Tasha pressed her face against her sables. "But now you must think of the future. Grand-père would like you to stay with him at the Sviridov Palace now that your parents are gone."

"You can't very well stay at home by yourself," added Andrei. "That wouldn't be proper."

"Yes. And you'll have Anyushka and her family around to keep you company. She has a sweet little boy now. And her husband is very pleasant."

"You and Anyushka are both Sandro's granddaughters," Andrei pointed out. "And you're really not far apart in age."

"Anyushka and Mama weren't on good terms," Tasha demurred. "She might not want me."

"Nonsense," replied the prince. "Anyushka's a very kindhearted creature. She wouldn't let that bother her."

Tasha hoped so. On the other hand, she herself wasn't a kindhearted creature and didn't feel any compulsion to become one.

Countess Tatiana Derzhavina's new life at the Sviridov Palace was in curious counterpoint to her former existence with Lisa and Seriozha. The initial euphoria of her triumph over both parents in one bloodstained afternoon and the knowledge she had perpetrated a ghoulish hoax on Seriozha gave way to loneliness as she tried to adjust to a more conservative household.

Despite Tasha's revulsion for what Seriozha had done to her, she missed the thrill of exploring the darker side of the capital where everything was so bizarrely fascinating. She hadn't hated *all* of it.

Anya and Ksenia shuddered at the idea of life with Lisa and Seriozha and tried to mother the strange little blue-eyed beauty they had inherited, but Tasha was too *sauvage.* She was like a wounded little animal, observed Anya, too much in pain to be tamed, far too mistrustful to allow it.

For her part, Tasha simply wanted to be left alone. She had no interest in Byelochka or his retinue, so there was little she cared to discuss with Anyushka, who adored her silly baby squirrel and spent hours romping with him on the Chinese carpets in her sitting room. Tasha would have liked to go to the theatre as she often had with Seriozha, but since they were all in deep mourning that was out of the question. Evenings spent in her relatives' company were wholesome, pleasant and dull.

Finally, Anyushka stopped insisting on her presence after dinner, gave up trying to entertain her and simply let her do as she pleased, which was to wander the huge Sviridov Palace like a ghost, alone and unimpeded, enjoying all the treasures her art-loving ancestors had gathered and comparing the vast collection with the smaller treasure trove Derzhavin had put together—hers now.

Tatiana Sergeevna had one other diversion. Like Lisa, Tasha was passionately fond of all forms of personal adornment, and now with her late Mama's impressive collection of jewels in her possession—at least the token pieces not kept in the bank vaults—she took great pleasure in dressing up and making up her face like the courtesans she had encountered on her escapades with Seriozha.

While Anya sat in one of the huge drawing rooms with Adam after dinner, chattering about airplanes, their son or the proper design of a flying outfit, Tasha often locked herself in her dressing room and practiced the art of illusion.

Using one of Anya's servants as a dressmaker, Tasha had the woman alter some of her mother's ensembles to fit her own budding figure and create for her a sophisticated wardrobe, straight from the house of Worth in Paris.

Taking over Lisa's enormous collection of wigs, the girl found she could change her appearance by adopting the hairstyle of a glamorous lady. But the final transformation came when Tasha began applying her mother's makeup. In twenty minutes, the demure schoolgirl in a dark dress and well-scrubbed cheeks could become a dazzling courtesan in silks, jewels and furs, reeking of exotic scent and gazing out at the world from kohl-rimmed eyes and sooty lashes, her red mouth smiling seductively at imagined prey.

Thrilled by the appearance of this fantastic and artificial creature of the evening, Countess Tatiana even gave her a name—Tata—something that sounded vaguely Parisian and insouciant, like an actress from the musical comedy, somebody Seriozha would have enjoyed pursuing.

Alone with her creation, Tasha perfected Tata's clothes, coiffure and makeup, practicing her gestures, her smiles, her little *moues*, patiently waiting for the time when she could take her out into St. Petersburg's nocturnal world of nightclubs and restaurants, which was filled with elderly gentlemen on the prowl for young girls and women eager not to be overlooked.

The first obstacle to Tata's immersion in the night was downstairs, stern, conscientious and over six feet tall—Uncle Adam. How the glamorous figure in Tasha's apartment was going to slip out past his watchful eye was a problem whose solution had escaped her. But, as her theology professor, Father Tikhon, was fond of saying, there was no problem so thorny that it couldn't be solved by careful, logical meditation. All she needed was time. For starters, she was already bribing the servants.

18

part from inheriting Tatiana Sergeevna, the young Sviridovs had experienced other difficulties lately. The St. Petersburg-to-Moscow air race was still on, but one of the other contestants had raised a surprising fuss over the entrance of Adam Sviridov in the event, since it was to be an all-Russian affair and Adam was scarcely Russian.

Prince Sandro's influence quieted the hullabaloo, but the old prince took it as a personal affront to have the status of his grandson-in-law questioned. That gave the gossips something to chatter about for a week as angry exchanges flew back and forth between Sandro and the racing committee in the dining room of one of St. Petersburg's most fashionable clubs. In the end it was agreed that if Adam was good enough for the Sviridovs, he was more than acceptable to fly from St. Petersburg to Moscow in honor of the Romanovs.

That taken care of, Prince Sandro and his newest mistress, Elena, departed aboard Sandro's private railway car for a trip south to the charming little Italian hill towns where the prince intended to hunt for paintings by an illustrious but relatively unknown artist of the quattrocento. He wanted the paintings for his fine Italian gallery in the Sviridov Palace and needed a decent excuse for absenting himself from St. Petersburg while he was officially in mourning for the Derzhavins, mourning being less onerous far from one's friends and the local gossips. It was left to the young Sviridovs and Malyshevs to be subdued in St. Petersburg.

"Grand-père certainly didn't waste time hanging about," commented Tasha as the family returned from seeing him off.

No, he didn't, thought Anya, and she really didn't like being left to mourn horrible Auntie Lisa while Sandro was having a good time, but there was very little she could do about it. It occurred to her that Grand-père, for all his good qualities, was a spoiled, selfish old man.

The one thing that wasn't out of the question during the mourning period was flying, since it was rather a recent pastime and therefore a gray area. Balls, parties and tea dances were forbidden, but risking one's neck in the air was perfectly acceptable, and therefore one of the few pleasures available. The whole family's hopes were pinned on Adam for the air race that was going to be the highlight of the Moscow festivities in June.

On top of that, Prince Sviridov was getting expert instruction from Count Franz von Murnau, a friend of Billy's from Paris, who was now also in St. Petersburg, assigned to the imposing German Embassy on St. Isaac's Square. The location of the embassy across the square from the popular Hotel Astoria was a fortunate coincidence, according to Billy, since it had one of the best bars in town and appeared to be a favorite night spot for actresses, dancers and other ladies who came to life after dark.

"And does Graf von Murnau spend most of his time supporting the arts?" inquired Adam as he and his brother sat talking in his office on drab Morkhovaya Street where the only big building in the area was an army barracks.

"No. Franz wants the Russians to think he's just a harmless skirtchaser, but he's actually taking a very careful look at their military defenses. His latest girlfriend is a lady who used to be quite close to half the general staff. Amazing what you can learn from listening to her. Russians can be very indiscreet."

"Generals or their girlfriends?"

"Both," laughed Billy.

"The Germans are preparing for another go at the French, aren't they? When Anya and I were in Europe last year, we spent a week in Berlin and found the atmosphere alarming. It's militarism run rampant."

"According to Franz, it's the general staff who wants the opportunity to start the ball rolling. The kaiser is being very pacific lately."

"You mean he's finally begun to listen to himself and decided he's not as warlike as he thought?"

"Something along those lines."

Prince Sviridov looked out the tall windows to the gray stone building opposite, a cheerless view. He knew Billy had been cultivating von Murnau for a year and claimed he was a good source of information about the Germans and their intentions toward their European neighbors. As the son of one of the heroes of the Franco-Prussian War of 1870, he had fine credentials. And from what he was saying—and sometimes not saying—Germany was preparing for a scrap somewhere.

"The German generals have the idea that Serbia is the viper of the Balkans," said Billy. "It's a view shared by their Austrian cousins as well. All they need is one false move from Serbia and all hell will break loose. I'm convinced of it."

And if that happens, thought Adam, Russia will go to the aid of her

Balkan brothers, France and England will honor the requirements of the recently signed Triple Entente and all Europe will be at war—France, Britain and Russia against Germany and Austria, with a secondary squad of lesser countries coming in on either side.

Billy glanced at his brother. He could tell what was on his mind.

"I don't think our country will enter a European conflict," he said. "It would be better for us to sit back and watch the fight, then attempt to play peacemaker in the end. When T.R. did that after the Russo-Japanese War, the people loved it. He was the only winner of that damned war."

Adam nodded in reply. "I don't expect to find the United States fighting in Europe any time soon. What scares the hell out of me is the idea of Russia fighting. If that were to happen, I'd want to evacuate my family to the Crimea."

"No faith in the Russian Army?"

"Not too much," Adam smiled.

The night before Adam and fourteen competitors were to take off for Moscow, Franz von Murnau accompanied his friend on a final inspection of his airplane, the *Four-Leaf Clover*, Byelochka's largest christening present.

"Now, Sviridov," warned Graf von Murnau, "just remember what I told you. No fancy business. Just speed and accuracy. Your objective is to reach that field before your rivals, so fly as low as you can on the approach and take care your motor doesn't stall when you drop altitude. We want you there first, but on the field, not *in* it."

"The landing is the only part that worries me. It could be crowded out there."

"Don't worry too much about that. The army will be there to keep order on the field. If some fool gets flattened by an airplane, it will be the fault of the officer in charge for not clearing the area properly, not yours."

"Somehow that wouldn't make me feel better."

Graf von Murnau chuckled. "Save your sympathy for yourself," he said.

Prince Sviridov grinned aimiably and pulled an iced bottle of Moët from the cockpit of the *Four-Leaf Clover*. "My dear Franz," Adam announced, "let's drink to our success in the race and to our continued friendship."

"Come what may," replied Franz as he cheerfully uncorked the bottle. "Now be a credit to me, Sviridov. Or I'll never admit to having given you the benefit of my expertise. The kaiser's air force does not train losers."

"Right."

And as they drank to success in the race, Adam was rather grateful he wasn't facing Franz up there.

Moscow

The early summer weather in Russia's ancient capital was magnificent. As part of the tercentenary ceremonies, the imperial family had paid a formal visit to their ancestors' former stronghold, one of the stops along their itinerary, but the tsar's schedule did not permit him to wait for the arrival of the airplanes from St. Petersburg. He had other things to do. Instead, Nicholas's brother-in-law, Grand Duke Alexander Mikhailovich, Adam's friend from the airfields and organizer of the Imperial Aviation Academy, was on hand to greet the flyers, the sort of chore Romanovs were used to.

The day before the flyers were due, the Malyshevs and Sviridovs, including Tasha, boarded Prince Sandro's private railway car for the overnight journey, arriving in time for a hearty breakfast at the prince's Moscow residence on Sadovaya Street, where they were joined by Billy Whitmore and Franz von Murnau. Sandro had returned from Europe for the event and was looking for a victory for his trouble.

As the gentlemen put away quantities of herring, ham, sausages and eggs, the ladies—too nervous thinking of Adam up there in the sky—contented themselves with cups of tea and slices of cook's special raisin baba, a childhood favorite. Tasha sat near Anya and studied the strangers.

"*Eh bien,*" sighed Sandro at last, "I suppose we had better be on our way. Are you ready?"

After a frantic last-minute search for one more pair of binoculars, everyone departed through the white-columned entrance of the mansion and climbed into Sandro's waiting motorcars, bound for Tverskaya Street, the route to the outskirts of Moscow.

When the Sviridov party reached the spot designated for the landing, the chauffeurs had to use their horns to clear a path in the crowd. Hundreds of spectators—many of them curious peasants—were all over the grassy field. Soldiers from the Moscow garrison were on duty to control the throng, the authorities mindful of past disasters not too far from this spot at the time of the tsar's coronation. Nobody wanted to see that happen again.

On the field was a typical mixture of Moscow society. At the edges, clad in rough Russian blouses, flat caps and wide trousers stuffed into shabby boots were the bearded peasants with their calico-clad women, attracted by the stories of men flying out of the clouds. Half-excited, half-suspicious, some of the more devout ones were whispering about the Second Coming; after all, the gentry were out in force, all staring toward heaven. Perhaps that was what had drawn them to the spot in the first place.

Circulating among the various groups were the soldiers, the men in good spirits, ready for the show, the officers smartly turned out in white summer uniforms, determined not to have a new disaster on their hands and interested in the great number of beautiful society ladies present.

The spectators who had driven out in shiny motorcars were mostly a blend of aristocratic and mercantile Moscow, with a stray bureaucrat thrown in for good measure. Princess Sviridova and Princess Malysheva were exquisitely dressed in light summer frocks, frothy with embroidery and openwork, their necks encircled by ropes of pearls, their heads crowned by wide-brimmed picture hats, fluffy with the plumage of jungle birds.

"There's nothing like a group of pretty women to dress up a sporting event, and I'd say our two princesses are the pick of the lot," declared Franz. "Your brother's a lucky fellow."

"He certainly is."

Billy exchanged pleasant greetings with several friends from St. Petersburg who had come to Moscow for the occasion, everyone wishing good luck to his brother. Prince Sviridov was a big favorite, it appeared, making Billy rather proud.

For the first time in their lives, the brothers were slowly beginning to like each other, or at least tolerate each other, something that had never happened before. Billy put it down to the good influence of that beautiful girl Adam had married. She was extraordinary. Imagine a princess marrying *his* brother. The effect on Adam was about the same as on the frog in the fairy tale, he thought. It had made him human.

Watching the Sviridov and Malyshev ladies from a distance of about a hundred feet, Billy noticed the beautiful young girl standing with them, the one who had accompanied them from Prince Sandro's residence, Anya's cousin. In six years she would be an absolute stunner. He remembered his chance encounter with the child's mother at the Bolshoi and wondered why that husband of hers hadn't killed her sooner. She was a terror. And now this dainty little miss with the large blue eyes and pouty mouth would inherit a significant chunk of the St. Petersburg textile industry. That was a friendship to cultivate—practically a relative, too, he thought in amusement.

As Billy and Franz joined the ladies, Andrei and Sandro, everyone was pointing binoculars skyward, searching for some sign of an airplane, anyone's. At this point, there wasn't even the hint of one.

Franz scanned the crowd, noting the presence of many high-ranking army officers, acquaintances of his from the St. Petersburg airfield. Like him, they regarded the airplane as much more than a rich man's toy. It was going to be the newest weapon.

Finally, after about half an hour had gone by and Princess Anya was almost desperate with concern for her husband, someone in the crowd popped the cork on a bottle of champagne and exclaimed, "Here they come!"

Anya's heart almost stopped as she aimed her binoculars up toward the first plane that came into view. It was still too far away for anyone to make out the insignia. But as it flew nearer, Anya gasped.

"It's him! It's Adam! He's here."

Shrieks of joy from his ladies made Prince Sandro wince a little. His favorite granddaughter was actually hopping up and down like a child, screeching in his ear, while his elegant daughter, a woman known for her refinement and good breeding, was whooping with unrestrained hysteria, kissing all the men in sight and doing her best to split her father's eardrums with her noise. Prince Andrei looked on in amusement.

"Oh, wait a bit," declared Billy, with the tone of a man who has just seen his horse go from first place to last, "there's another one."

Anya wailed in chagrin, sounding a little like her son, thought Tasha, who found it comical. "No!" she exclaimed. "He has to win!"

"Don't worry, dear lady. We've discussed this eventuality," said Franz. "He'll know what to do."

All around, people were making wagers, pointing field glasses skyward and opening bottles of champagne to go with picnic lunches packed by the city's leading caterers. Yeliseyev's had had to take on extra help for the occasion, said someone. Everyone in Moscow had gone there.

While her neighbors were helping themselves to refreshments, Princess Anya was too nervous to eat. She clung to Tasha for moral support and prayed.

Hundreds of feet above the crowd, the wind blowing fiercely into his face, his eyes protected by a sturdy pair of German goggles, Adam blinked as he tried to identify any familiar figures on the field. Impossible. Somewhere in that huge mass, Anya was looking up at him, excited and hopeful, waiting to see him land safely. Somewhere too, Franz was watching, mentally going through all his moves, repeating his instructions, advising accuracy and nerve.

In the cockpit of the *Four-Leaf Clover*, Adam checked his gauges and suddenly turned around, as if by intuition, to look behind.

"Damn!" he shouted above the roar of the engine. Terchenko, a highly touted pilot from St. Petersburg, the owner of a small textile factory in the Vyborg section, was right on his tail and gaining rapidly. Now the *Four-Leaf Clover* had serious competition. Terchenko was the only pilot Franz von Murnau considered a threat to Adam's chances, and there he was, cheerfully waving at him, grinning from ear to ear.

"Damn," repeated Prince Sviridov. "Well, it's now or never!"

With that, he seized the stick, gripping it with determination, and plunged rapidly, heading for the green field.

On the ground, Franz puffed nervously on a cigarette, intently following his pupil's moves, wondering whether Adam was aware of the airplane just behind him. His sudden dive could mean he had seen the other plane, or it could mean he was being reckless. In either case, he had better be careful or he'd stall the motor in midair and have to be scraped off the field. He didn't want to witness *that*.

"Isn't he beautiful?" cried Anya, following her husband's progress through binoculars. "Look at him go!"

Terchenko was right behind the *Four-Leaf Clover*, dropping just as fast, and now a third airplane appeared in the sky, far back on the horizon, just barely visible. Abruptly, with no warning, Adam swooped again. Franz was suddenly convinced Adam was guilty of bad judgment or temporary insanity. He had plunged too fast the second time. That could be fatal if he wasn't careful.

Prince Sandro wrapped his arm around Anya and pressed her to his massive chest. He could see she was frightened now; that husband of hers was too much of a daredevil for his own good.

Looking toward the sky, Anya felt weak. What she had just seen frightened her. It wasn't like the practice dives he had done. It was too wild, too uncontrolled. Adam must be having trouble, she thought, her heart pounding. It didn't matter to her any longer if he won the race. All she cared about was seeing him land safely.

Up in the sky, with the landscape passing before his eyes in a great blue and green blur, Adam saw to his horror that Terchenko was following his every move, right down to the last dive. If he wasn't careful, the man would cut him off in midair, sending them both to premature graves.

More determined than ever, Adam took one last look at the great blur that represented the crowd on the ground and dived in the split-S maneuver Franz always counseled in tight situations, avoiding the dangerous, nose-down plunge that sent so many pilots straight into the ground.

"Ah, good," sighed Franz. "He has it well in hand."

A brisk summer breeze was wafting in from the nearby River Moskva, ruffling the ladies' ensembles on the ground and providing some relief from the sun. Overhead, those pleasant breezes were more like gale-force winds pounding on the wings of Adam's Nieuport biplane, hitting his face so hard he had to blink behind his goggles as he headed for the field where now he could see human figures in uniform chasing some of the bystanders back to the perimeter in preparation for the landing.

"The other one's swooping again!" cried Anya, afraid he was going to cut off her husband. Was the man crazy? Didn't he see Adam?

"Bring it down now, Sviridov!" shouted Franz. "It's time!"

Thinking of Anya, Adam wondered again where she was as he surveyed the field intently, his eyes fixing on a spot for his landing. In a few minutes he'd be on the ground, coming to a bumpy stop in the middle of that huge meadow. Suddenly he noticed a great deal of movement among the crowd, too much, in fact.

"Damn. I hope the idiots in charge don't let them run wild," he muttered, not fifty feet above the heads of the spectators.

As Adam flew at them like a giant mechanical bird, Anya's heart was beating so fast, she was convinced it might burst. He was almost there! And he was going to win! There was no question now with the *Four-Leaf Clover* mere feet off the ground. People were already cheering.

"You owe me 10,000 gold rubles," laughed Ksenia to a friend.

Suddenly, with Adam only twenty feet off the ground on a steady course, the green-and-silver biplane appeared to lurch out of control. Instead of gracefully gliding to the finish, the *Four-Leaf Clover* dipped its right wing and careened crazily, buffeted by an unexpected gust of wind.

Anya was the first to realize the danger. Covering her mouth with her hand, the young princess was frozen to the spot, watching in horror as the biplane tilted perilously to the side, completely helpless.

In the cockpit, Adam wrestled with the controls, bringing all his strength to bear as he struggled to right himself. "Don't panic," he shouted to nobody in particular, gripping the stick. "Turn, damn you, turn!"

Looking on in horror, the crowd sent up a muffled cry of disbelief as the gaily painted Nieuport crashed with a resounding thud, splitting apart as neatly as if it had been sliced by an unseen hand.

In the air not thirty feet above the crash, Terchenko cried out in stunned shock as his colleague's machine shattered beneath him.

"Adam!" shrieked Anya. "Help him! Someone help him!"

Billy and Franz were already sprinting across the field, frantic to rescue him. If the fuel in the tank caught fire, he'd be roasted inside that wreck. On their heels raced Andrei, afraid his niece's husband had been killed in the crash, terrified he might still be trapped under the shattered airplane, barely alive and a helpless prey to flames.

As Terchenko's Sopwith glided to a graceful landing, nobody even bothered to notice.

With the crowd fighting the soldiers to get a better look at the disabled airplane, Princess Anya broke free of her grand-père's restraining arm and ran sobbing across the field with Tasha and Ksenia behind her.

All three were unaware of the possibility of fire, but desperate to know whether the prince was alive after the ghastly impact of the crash. All Anya could feel was terror, sheer, cold terror in her heart as she raced to reach her husband.

"Don't let him die!" she wailed as she dashed towards the plane. "Dear God, don't let him die like this!"

In the cockpit of the *Four-Leaf Clover,* Prince Sviridov was dazed but not disabled. He knew he had landed badly, blown off course by a strong gust of wind at the very moment of triumph. He was vaguely aware of some excitement on the field, of people running toward him, but it was only when he recognized Billy and heard his shouts that he realized he had to get out of the wrecked Nieuport. Fast!

Still dazed, he saw Ksenia struggling with Anya. Strange. Why was she doing that? Then he noticed red stains on his hands. Blood. Touching his cheek, he felt something warm and wet trickling down his face.

Managing to rise from the cockpit, Adam saw Billy and Franz materialize on the wing. Then he was being hauled out, supported between the two of them, being half-dragged, half-carried from the plane. He heard them shout at an officious gaggle of colonels who were screaming about fire.

As everyone ran from the area of the plane, Billy and Franz carried Adam out between them, sprinting as fast as they could. The explosion was only seconds away. Reaching the spot where Princess Anya and her relatives were being held back by a cordon of officers, Billy and Franz finally allowed Adam's feet to touch the ground, coming to a shaky stop as Anya threw her arms around her husband, sobbing with relief that he was alive.

"Oh my God!" wailed the princess as he collapsed in her arms, "I love you. Don't die on me!"

"Wouldn't think of it," he replied.

Two seconds later, the *Four-Leaf Clover* was a mass of flames, spreading black clouds of smoke into the clear June sky.

St. Petersburg

The St. George Hall of the Winter Palace was packed with the elite of St. Petersburg as Nicholas II made his entrance. The tsar, a slender, bearded figure in the gold-braided uniform of a hussar colonel, graciously acknowledged the homage of his subjects and proceeded to the business at hand— the presentation of the trophy to the winner of the St. Petersburg-to-Moscow air race.

It should have been a fairly simple business, but with the crash, Terchenko's claim that he had actually won the race because he had landed in one piece and the quibbling of the racing committee—who could not decide who ought to receive the prize—the whole thing had dragged on for weeks. Nicholas himself had finally solved the dilemma by decreeing two prizes—one for being the first to land and one for being the first to land intact. Everyone was pleased.

"Congratulations, Prince Sviridov," said Nicholas as he took a gorgeously enameled golden *kovsh*—a ceremonial drinking vessel of old Muscovy—from the hands of his aide and handed it to Adam. "I saw the newsreels of your landing, you know. It was a miracle you survived. Those who witnessed it said you showed remarkable sangfroid."

That was nice, thought Adam. I was so stunned, I didn't know what was going on. The autocrat of all the Russias was very gracious. The American also noticed that his English was effortless and quite polished, absolutely fluent.

"Thank you, Your Majesty," he replied, bowing the way Ksenia and Sandro had instructed him. "I have a lot to live for."

That made Nicholas smile. He knew the Sviridovs. It was certainly true.

Bowing was difficult when one had one arm in a sling and the other arm occupied with a heavy gold object, but protocol required it, so bow he did.

Anya watched proudly as Nicholas presented the Fabergé trophy to her battered husband while the newsreel cameras recorded the scene on celluloid to gratify Russian moviegoers, enrich the imperial archives and impress the Europeans in their cinema palaces in London, Paris and Berlin.

The entire tercentenary was being carefully filmed, and Adam's spectacular arrival on that airfield had made him the hero of the hour. People actually seemed to prefer the crash and the hair's-breadth escape from the flames to the flawlessly executed landing of the next-in-line.

It was romantic, said the viewers, especially when the movie screens flashed footage of Adam Sviridov, movie-star handsome, collapsing into the arms of a blonde society beauty, all framed by a thousand cheering onlookers and the plane erupting into flames just behind them. It was exciting. Perfection was dull.

"Good Lord," whistled Billy after attending a private screening of the newsreel in the Sviridov mansion. "It looked even more dangerous just now than it did then."

"I was totally out of my head," laughed his brother. "I can't recall a bit of it—except for you and Franz pulling me out of there. That I will never forget," he said seriously. "You saved my life."

Graf von Murnau chuckled. "But you looked so noble. That's the important thing. If you're only a hero by accident, never let on, because people don't want to hear it. They want to cherish their illusions."

Princess Sviridova rose from her seat, motioning to the footmen to serve the champagne. When everyone had a glass in hand, Anyushka, in shimmering black satin and with a glittering web of diamonds on her bosom, proposed a toast.

"To Adam, my darling husband. May he once again soar like an eagle without landing like an elephant. Congratulations on your triumph, and may it be the first of many. I've already ordered another airplane."

Kissing his wife's hand, Adam replied that he intended to do better once he got his arm out of the sling.

"And, by the way, *milochka,*" he smiled, "thank you for solving the problem of what to christen the new plane. You've just given me the perfect name."

"Well, Adam, don't keep us guessing. What is it?" demanded Billy.

Prince Sviridov ordered the glasses refilled and said solemnly, "I wish to propose a toast to my new flying machine—*L'Elephant Volant.* And to my dear wife for having enough faith in me to order a second one."

Princess Sviridova briefly closed her eyes and smiled. She certainly hoped she'd never have to witness another crash. She didn't think she could survive it. The sight of the poor *Four-Leaf Clover* splitting apart with Adam inside it was so ghastly that Anya's heart still raced when she recalled it.

Deliberately putting the horror aside, the young princess announced that they were all going to continue the celebration at the Strelna, one of St. Petersburg's most popular late-night spots. It was a lovely place far out on the Gulf of Finland, with the distant lights of Kronstadt sparkling in the distance before one's eyes. Billy and Franz applauded her choice. It was one of the city's most entertaining places because at the Strelna anyone was liable to show up, from grand dukes to demimondaines, and sometimes with each other. It could be a little racy but it was never dull. Franz offered his automobile immediately, in anticipation of a good time.

After the Sviridovs' party had reached the Strelna and were gaily toasting Adam's new biplane with bottles of Moët, a noisy group of revelers entered, greeting everyone with loud, jolly hellos as the leader of the merry company lurched across the room to the orchestra, requested his favorite song, and scattered gold coins to the musicians. It was Gregory Efimovich Rasputin, out for a night on the town with some of his St. Petersburg disciples—six of them, all pretty, all well-dressed, all without their husbands.

As the strains of "Barinia" filled the dining room, the *starets* flung out his arms in an expansive gesture of goodwill toward the guests. Without wasting any time, he spun one of his ladies into an energetic, bouncing peasant dance, clicking his highly polished heels on the gleaming floor as he and his partner whirled wildly around the room, applauded by the startled diners, all delighted at the chance to see one of St. Petersburg's most infamous sights in the flesh.

To her horror, Princess Anya found herself looking straight into the startling light-blue eyes of Natalya's religious mentor as the *starets* danced to an abrupt halt in front of her. To her amazement, he sat down without an invitation, smiling pleasantly at the company as if he had known them for years. Adam was amused but wary. He knew who he was.

"Good evening, brothers," said the *starets*, looking around the table. "And good evening, little dove. Are you married?"

"I'm her husband," Adam announced, taking Anya's hand as she blushed under Rasputin's intense scrutiny, embarrassed at all the stares she was getting form the other diners.

"Little dove," he smiled, never taking his eyes from her beautiful face, "you don't have to be afraid of me. I only want to bless you. Will you accept my blessing?"

Too bewildered to reply, Anya simply stared. Rasputin ignored her nervousness and gently placed his rough paw on her forehead as Adam, Franz and Billy watched, ready to tear him apart if he touched anything else.

To Anya's surprise, she felt an unusual warmth engulf her as the peasant's hand rested on her brow, an extraordinary sensation, similar to what Natalya had once described. Those mesmerizing light-blue eyes fascinated her, making her forget for an instant where she was and who she was. All she could see were those eyes.

Rising abruptly, the peasant slowly raised his hand in blessing, hovered over Princess Anya for a second and then was gone, vanishing into a crowd of people as the orchestra began a tango. When Anya saw him once more, an imposing sight in a bright-blue embroidered silk Russian blouse and fine broadcloth trousers tucked into polished boots, he was sweeping a dark-haired lady in the slow, sensuous glides of the dance, enjoying himself immensely.

"So that's the famous *starets*," murmured Franz. "Now I can truly say I've seen the sights of Petersburg. Fascinating."

"Those eyes are unlike anything I've ever beheld," murmured Anya.

"They go straight into one's soul. No wonder they tell such stories about him."

Watching Princess Anya, all three men thought she looked a bit dazed, as if she were just coming out of a trance. For the first time, Adam understood the power the man was capable of wielding and truly pitied Gigi Grekov, who was vainly trying to win Natalya away from him. If Gregory Efimovich were left alone with a woman, thought Adam, he hated to even consider the consequences.

"Let's go home, darling," said the prince, gently taking her hand. "I think it's time."

Anya didn't even protest.

In the automobile on the return to the French Embankment, Princess Anya nestled against Adam, trying to recall what the *starets* had said. Then she thought of Alexandra Feodorovna and Natalya, who lived by what Rasputin said. Perhaps he had told them things that actually came true. She had a difficult time picturing the tsaritsa, who looked like an excessively proper governess, and this rather flamboyant fellow in his bright silk shirt having anything to discuss.

"I hope I never see that man again," she murmured to Adam, resting her head on his shoulder.

He hoped so too.

19

To Prince Adam's growing concern, he was not making the rapid recovery from the crash he had expected. He no longer played with his frisky son; Byelochka had the bad habit of jumping on him whenever he sat on the carpet with him. The pain that sometimes resulted was unbearable.

Anya spent hours rubbing his back and soothing him in warm baths, but nothing seemed to work. Prince Sviridov had to see another doctor, as much as he hated to do so. And this time, he was seeking help from a European specialist. In Paris.

When the young couple departed in Sandro's private railway coach, Billy accompanied Prince and Princess Malyshev to the station to see them off. Byelochka was going to spend time at Byelaya Beryozka with his nurses and his great-aunt, who was very fond of him and was probably going to spoil him even worse than Sandro did. Andrei promised to restrain her.

Paris

The first thing the highly touted European specialist did upon examining His Highness was to insist that he wear a back brace.

"I'll be damned if I'll wear one of those things," protested Adam. "That's ridiculous."

"Well," shrugged the doctor, "if you're not serious about making a recovery, I can't help you. The back brace will realign the bones you injured."

The thing looked like a corset; Adam felt like an idiot wearing it. But he noticed after a week that his back was beginning to feel better.

One of the pleasurable things the Sviridovs did during their Paris sojourn was to attend the theatre, a pastime both Adam and Anya adored. Sarah Bernhardt was giving one of her performances of *L'Aiglon*, and Anyushka was thrilled to see it. Bernhardt had been a favorite of Anya's since the day she had met the great actress at Grand-père's Paris residence several years earlier. A slender figure with fantastic eyes and an imposing presence, the divine Sarah had looked at the small princess and pronounced her *pas moche,* favoring her with the compliment that she wasn't at all boring for such a tiny person.

The audience at the Chatelet was essentially middle-class that evening; the rich were summering at the spas, Biarritz and Deauville. Anya wore one of her more simple gowns, a lovely georgette with a raised waist, three-quarter-length sleeves slashed to show fine Brussels lace underneath, and a cluster of real gardenias at her bosom and in her upswept hair.

Adam thought she had never looked more beautiful.

As the young couple sat in their box to the right of the stage, chatting during the intermission, several young men in the audience trained opera glasses on the blonde beauty, wondering who she was. One of her admirers seemed quite unable to take his eyes off her.

Curled up in bed beside Adam later in their bedroom overlooking the garden, Anya felt like Mrs. Lowell instead of Princess Sviridova, something she hadn't thought about since their honeymoon. The idea made her smile as she looked at her handsome, dark-haired husband, asleep by her side, his arm around the pillow. Mr. and Mrs. Lowell, she thought. How funny. How American.

She loved Adam. At first she had fallen in love with him because she was desperately frightened and needed him, but that had given way to genuine affection. Byelochka's birth had created a bond nothing could change. And life as a married woman in St. Petersburg had convinced Anya that even if Adam Mikhailovich had unmistakably non-Russian traits—which he had— he was a prize compared with the general run of husbands.

She knew it wasn't Princess Sviridova he loved, but rather Anyushka. The only other man she knew like that was Andrei Nicolaievich.

One morning when Adam's back was beginning to feel almost normal, he and Anya decided to visit the Louvre. Prince Sandro had graciously lent a pair of field glasses, a uniform, a set of battle plans and a diary belonging to his ancestor Gen. Denis Borisovich Sviridov to the museum for its exhibit commemorating Napoleon's campaigns. Anya wanted to see how they were being displayed. During the Borodino celebrations at home, Anya and her family had unveiled a statue to the memory of Denis Borisovich on the site of the battlefield and in the presence of the imperial family. She hoped his former enemies were treating him with the same due respect.

Heading out the gates of Sandro's town house, not far from the Elysées

Palace, Paul, the chauffeur who had witnessed Anya's folly two years earlier on the Place de la Concorde, drove the young couple down the Rue
du Faubourg St. Honoré, past the British Embassy, the Hotel Meurice,
the Church of St. Roch to the Comédie Francaise and then made a right-
hand turn through the gates of the Louvre, crossing the courtyard to drop
the Sviridovs off close to the entrance.

"We'll take care of our own transportation on the way home," said
Adam as Paul handed Anya out.

"Are you sure, Monsieur? I could wait nearby."

"It's not necessary. We'll take a taxi home."

Actually Princess Anya had made her husband promise to take her
on the metro, which for some reason she considered exciting. Nobody
else had ever let her ride on it and she thought it would be great fun.
Grand-père would have had fits if he had known.

Entering the museum along with a group of German tourists, the
prince and princess—he in a navy blazer and gray trousers, she in a simple
lace-trimmed batiste shirtwaist and white skirt with a flower-trimmed straw
picture hat—wandered at their leisure past Greek and Roman antiquities
on the ground floor, up the *grande escalier* past the famous statue of Venus
de Milo and toward the Napoleonic exhibit on the second floor.

As Anya strolled through the section dedicated to the emperor's Russian disaster, she felt a thrill of pride remembering the famous final lines
from Denis Borisovich's diary as he and his men prepared to face the enemy: "Today at this place called Borodino, Field Marshall Kutuzov has
decided to engage the French, halting our retreat. Whatever the outcome,
no one will ever say we lacked the will to fight."

France had lost forty-seven generals in that battle, and Napoleon had
called it one of the toughest he'd ever fought. Both sides had claimed a
victory, and it had marked the turning point of the emperor's fortunes.
Borodino.

Standing before the display of Denis Borisovich's belongings, Princess Anya thought they looked so strange here, with little place cards in
front of them explaining what they were.

"It was a Russian victory," whispered Princess Anya, irritated at the
French claims on the wall poster.

"I'd say so," replied Adam, thinking of all the Napoleonic memora-
bilia in Sandro's mansion. "But be tolerant, *milochka*. It's a French museum, so they see things differently."

"Yes. The wrong way."

A large poster near the exit from the room had crisscrossed French
and Russian flags over a flowery paen to Franco-Russian friendship and
the Triple Entente, emphasizing the nation's alliance with the enemy of

100 years earlier. Handsome portraits of Tsar Nicolas and President Poincaré marked the conclusion of the exhibit.

As the Sviridovs left the room, a heavyset man of medium height, apparently attached to a group of British tourists, looked carefully at the young woman, his eyes taking in every detail of her face. Neither Adam nor Anyushka noticed him as they headed downstairs, discussing the presentation of the exhibit. The princess was a lovely sight, well worth a look. She attracted several admiring glances.

On the ground floor, Adam saw a display of Roman artifacts that intrigued him and his wife, drawing them into a small room lined with glass display cases off the main corridor.

The heavyset bald man had them right where he wanted them. Alone. Surrounded by four walls. Cornered.

Shadowing them as they wandered through the museum, listening to snatches of their conversation for almost an hour, the man had kept out of sight, afraid to attract the attention of the husband.

It was the girl who was important to him. She had seen nothing. He would relish her surprise. It would be the last thing she would ever know before she died.

Arrogant little aristocrat. She *would* die this time. Nothing would go wrong now, thought the man, fingering the revolver inside his jacket. There was nothing to prevent it now. After what she and Prince Malyshev had done to him, she would have to die.

"What does this say?" demanded Anya as she and Adam stood admiring the workmanship on a Roman sarcophagus. "It has some sort of inscription."

Studying the words, her husband pronounced, "Helen, wife of Phineas, rest in peace."

"You're very erudite," smiled Anya. "Grand-père should be pleased to have another scholar in the family."

"Too bad he'll never know it," said a voice from close by.

Turning quickly to see who was speaking, Prince and Princess Sviridov were startled to see a stocky bald man staring at them, his bulk blocking the door, his face distorted with hatred. In his right hand he held a revolver. The last finger on his left hand was missing, amputated.

Princess Anya recognized him with the most horrible fear she had ever known. Face to face with Oleg Ivanov, Anyushka thought she had lost her mind. This had to be an apparition from hell.

And then she struck back.

Seizing the first thing that came to hand, the young princess hurled a priceless stone statue at the animal who had attacked her two years earlier and who was supposed to be dead. As Ivanov fired his revolver, the shot went wild, shattering one of the display cases and missing the princess, who had instinctively dropped to the floor with her husband, taking refuge behind the stone sarcophagus.

Cries from outside let the three know that the gunshot had been heard. Shouts and running footsteps meant someone was coming. Or letting others know of the commotion.

Her heart beating as if it would burst, Anya saw her husband lunge at their attacker, not realizing who it was.

"Be careful!" she screamed as she saw the men grapple with each other. Her husband tackled the aggressor, rolling him to the floor. They thrashed about wildly as the prince tried to make Ivanov yield the weapon he clutched in his hand, kicking and grunting in the most vicious free-for-all the young woman had ever witnessed.

He'll kill Adam, she thought, trembling as she watched it. He was supposed to be dead and he wasn't. He was capable of anything. This had to be a nightmare, thought Anya. It couldn't be real.

She was so horrified by what was happening, she couldn't think properly. All she could see was Adam and this animal trying to kill each other, scratching, kicking, punching each other in desperation.

Suddenly Anya saw her husband wrest the gun away from Ivanov, sending it skidding across the stone floor. She ran for it. Snatching it as fast as she could, the young princess screamed at her husband to let him go so she could shoot him.

Ivanov was outraged, infuriated, his ambush about to be undone by a mere woman. Giving Prince Sviridov a tremendous kick, he managed to scramble to his feet as the taller, slimmer man writhed in agony on the stone floor, groaning as if he would die. Facing the girl he had tried to murder, the peasant hesitated, frightened by the sound of running footsteps in the hallway. People were coming to find out what all the commotion was about. They would send him to prison for this, and all because of this damned aristocrat.

She was the cause of all his trouble. She was evil, he thought, staring at her with a glint in his light-blue eyes. She should die. And he advanced on her, determined to finish her off this time.

Trembling so badly she was almost sobbing with terror, Anya felt transported back to that nightmare in the forest at Byelaya Beryozka, her heart pounding with fear, her throat dry, confronting a madman.

Aiming straight for his heart, she pulled the trigger. To her intense shock, nothing happened.

Ivanov, momentarily stunned when he realized her intent, hesitated just a fraction of a second too long. Adam, half-staggering from the effort, lunged at him, knocking him off balance and into the corridor, along with the weapon Anya had flung at him, frustrated at not being able to shoot him with it.

Scrambling for possession of the weapon as he saw half a dozen guards heading for him, Oleg snatched it out of the prince's reach, sprang to his feet and fired wildly at his pursuers, forcing them to the ground as he turned and raced down the hall, scattering a group of British tourists in his path. Looking backward once more, he fired at random—keeping the guards at bay as he made his escape.

Shaking as she helped her husband to his feet, Anya was so distraught she wasn't quite certain that she had actually survived her second confrontation. Everything seemed a great blur—the people clustered around her and Adam, the guards racing down the hall to pursue Ivanov. It was too bizarre to be real, she thought, clutching Adam, holding on to him as if he were a life raft in a storm, trying to staunch the flow of blood from his wounds.

It was only afterward that she realized she had faced down Ivanov with a loaded gun and had tried to kill him.

Oleg had a good head start on the guards. Pushing people out of his way as he fled down the long corridors, he collided with a Greek statue, sending it crashing to the ground, splitting into several pieces. He raced away, leaving a series of astonished onlookers in his wake. Dashing down the stairs of the exit, he managed to elude a single guard who had been alerted by cries. By the time his pack of pursuers had followed him out to the courtyard, he had vanished, racing down the Rue du Rivoli to disappear into the metro entrance near the Palais Royal.

Terrified by the thought of capture, Oleg just managed to catch a subway, leaping on board as it pulled out of the station, heading toward the Place de la Concorde. Gasping for breath as he flung himself into an empty seat, the bald man couldn't believe he had actually come face to face with Prince Malyshev's niece. He knew he had killed her that day in the forest. But she wasn't dead. The arrogant little aristocrat had survived the gunshot wound and the beating and had returned to haunt him like an angel of evil. She was truly a vicious creature; she was even capable of killing him.

It wasn't over. No, thought Oleg. He would never allow himself to die without avenging himself on her and all her henchmen. Three of them were gone already. She ought to have been the fourth but she was too powerful. She was a devil. Katia Petrovna was her second self. He had been able to kill Katia because she had been careless, but now apparently the devil-woman had learned from that encounter and was better informed of his plans. Yes. She had been able to read his mind and plan accordingly. She was very powerful, he thought. Almost invincible. Like Satan.

But now she was dealing with one who was almost as invincible as she was. Stabbed by those Scriabin idiots, kicked into unconsciousness and dumped into the icy waters of the Neva, he had regained consciousness in the river and had managed to cling to a tree branch floating by, clutching it until he was spotted by a fisherman who had pulled him out before he froze to death.

Taken near death to the charity ward of the Emperor Paul Hospital, Ivanov was patched up and nursed back to health during a two-month stay. He had survived and had had his revenge on two of the men who had attempted to murder him.

He had no intention of giving up on his plans to finish off the rest.

Returning to Paris after his release from the hospital, he had let Wanda take care of him. He had become her pimp as she plied her trade near the better hotels on the right bank, saving what she earned. Between the proceeds from his career as a robber and hers as a whore, they were accumulating a nice little nest egg.

Now all that was in jeopardy because of that blonde devil who wanted his blood. He'd scarcely believed his eyes when he'd seen her at the theatre that night. She was supposed to be dead. He hadn't been able to follow when the man had put her in a taxi, but he had managed to get the number of the cab. Getting in touch with the driver, he'd found out that the couple was dropped off at a mansion on the Rue du Faubourg St. Honoré. From then on, Oleg had followed the princess and the dark-haired man, her husband. Their visit to the Louvre had given him his best chance to kill her but it had turned out badly.

He would have to be very careful the next time. Very careful.

Returning to the apartment he shared with Wanda, Oleg ordered the Polish girl to pack her bags. They were leaving Paris.

"When?" asked Wanda in surprise.

"Tonight."

Startled, Wanda demanded if he were crazy. And where the hell did he plan on going?

"Out of here. I don't care where we end up. You pick the place," he replied, throwing together his clothes. "I've got to get out of here. It's not safe any longer."

"The police?" she asked, suddenly frightened, clutching her white angora cat who reacted by spitting at Oleg.

"Yes," he lied.

That made the right impression on Wanda. By the following morning, Oleg, Wanda and Koshka the cat had vanished from their Montmartre apartment as if they had been swallowed up by the earth.

And just in time to avoid paying the rent too. Cursing his tenants, their landlord wished them bad luck and threw the remains of their existence out with the garbage—some half-finished rolls and a kielbasa.

The Director of the Louvre was aghast that someone had tried to murder Prince and Princess Sviridov in the midst of his antiquities. The damage was incalculable, at least to the statues. Prince Adam's injuries could be repaired with a lot less fuss.

With his wounds bandaged and his back aching all over again, Prince Adam had very little sympathy for the statues. He was too angry. He and his wife had been attacked by Oleg Ivanov, a supposedly dead criminal who had nearly murdered them. If they hadn't fought back, he would have killed them.

The fact that Anya had fought back astonished him, making him realize just how deep the anger and hatred ran beneath her placid surface. This gentle girl was capable of shooting an attacker point-blank without hesitating. Inexperience was the only thing that had prevented her from killing him on the spot.

It was something her husband would never forget, and it left him a little in awe of her. Beneath a fragile facade, Anyushka was a tiger. He would never look at her in the same way again, he thought ruefully. But, my God! he was proud of her.

Anya was devastated, especially when the Paris dailies carried the story, which was quickly picked up by the *Novaya Vremya*, St. Petersburg's leading newspaper. Even a reporter from the Paris edition of the *New York Herald* called, requesting an interview. Adam instructed the butler to bar the gates and hired two private detectives to guard the house for the duration of their stay.

To the young princess, it was all a horrifying repetition of those summer days when she had fled to Paris to recover from the lunatic's attack and had been faced with hideous and unsavory gossip over the incident. She was distraught at the thought of new gossip, almost as much as she was at the thought of Oleg's return to life.

Hardly reacting at the time, too stunned to put her feelings into words, she had returned home to the Rue du Faubourg St. Honoré, gone up to her room and stood there in front of her mirror, watching herself for a minute. And then she had hurled a vase straight into her reflection, shattering the glass into a thousand splinters.

Andrei had lied. Ksenia had lied. There was no killing. They had deceived her. How could they? It wasn't possible. And yet there he was, that demented expression in his eyes, trying to murder her all over again.

It was Ivanov. There was no mistake. Even without hair no one could disguise that hideous look in his eyes. He was still alive! she thought, almost weeping with desperation. How could that be?

The idea of Oleg Ivanov alive filled Anya with such horror it sickened her. How could she ever feel safe again? He had nearly killed Adam now. Would he attempt to murder her son next? The idea of seeing them harmed was so terrifying that the princess swore she wouldn't rest until she saw his dead body laid out in front of her.

But how? I had him before me and I failed, she thought bitterly. If only I had had a rifle instead of that revolver. I've shot ducks, deer. I could have shot him. I could have killed him. Stupid, useless revolver.

The memory of that day in the forest came flooding back to her. The man watching her. Lunging at her. Laughing as he humiliated her.

This time he hadn't got the chance to do that. But he had got the chance to try to kill her again, she thought angrily.

The men had failed her. Andrei had tried to kill him with no success. Adam had attempted to defend her and had been badly beaten. She knew she was going to have to kill Ivanov herself. It would come down to that—the princess and the peasant.

The next time they met, one of them would not leave the scene alive.

Byelaya Beryozka

When Princess Ksenia received the letter from Anya detailing her ordeal in Paris, at first she thought that her young niece had lost her mind. And then she realized Anya was quite rational, even though the contents of the letter were so incredible as to stagger the imagination. For a moment, recalling the terrible summer of two years before, she felt the room swim before her eyes.

And then the princess went in search of her husband.

"Andrei! Are you an imbecile or a liar or both?" she cried angrily, throwing Anya's letter straight at him. "Read this and tell me the truth."

Astonished by this totally unexpected outburst, the prince stared. He thought Ksenia had gone mad.

"Look at this letter and tell me I shouldn't be furious!" she exclaimed. "Read it!"

Halfway through the letter, the prince turned white and let out a curse that would have startled his wife under any other circumstances.

"There, you see? He's alive, Andrei, and you deceived me. How could you?"

"No. There has to be a mistake. They brought me the medallion his mother gave him. And one of his fingers, for God's sake!"

Flinging the letter on a nearby table, Andrei began pacing the floor, completely horrified. That damned little policeman had lied about the whole thing. The deceitful bastard!

"I knew I should have been there," he shouted, pounding on the table. "There wouldn't have been any slipups that way."

Ksenia was shaking with rage, a vein in her neck throbbing from sheer fury.

"He's alive and he tried to kill Anya and her husband. God knows what he's capable of next. I'll tell you this, *dorogai*, if he comes near Byelochka, I'll kill him myself," declared the princess. "And I won't make a hash of it either."

"Well, perhaps you could give me some pointers," he replied sarcastically. "How would you have gone about it?"

Pausing to look her husband straight in the eye, Princess Ksenia retorted, "I would have slit his throat, ripped out his heart and fed the rest of him to the dogs. That's how."

And without another word, she turned imperiously and left, slamming the door behind her.

Andrei would have to have a talk with Petrov.

St. Petersburg

When the Sviridovs returned home from Europe, the only thing Anya was looking forward to at the Malyshev mansion was her reunion with her son. She was still so upset over her encounter with Oleg Ivanov that she didn't know what to believe. On the one hand, knowing Andrei as she did, it was almost incredible to suspect him of deliberately deceiving her. On the other, Ivanov had attempted to kill her in the Louvre. What possible explanation he could have for that hard fact, she could only guess.

Anya's stomach was in knots as she and her husband drove through the wrought-iron entrance gates, arrived in the courtyard of Andrei's mansion and were handed out by the butler.

Having returned from Byelaya Beryozka for the meeting, Andrei and Ksenia were looking out into the courtyard with Byelochka as the little one spotted Mama and Papa descending from the motorcar.

"Mama!" he shouted.

Despite her encounter with Ivanov, Anya looked splendid, dressed elegantly in a cream-colored tailored suit with wide lace collar and cuffs, two ropes of pearls around her neck and a small, lace-trimmed toque jauntily perched on her blonde coiffure. And Adam appeared to have recovered his health, the princess noticed. His stride showed no trace of pain now. He looked rather dashing, in fact.

As the young couple entered the room, Byelochka toddled toward Mama and Papa, babbling in his excitement. Princess Anya was grateful for his presence. She was so tense, she needed an excuse to be cheerful, covering her small son with kisses as he insisted on being picked up and held.

As Adam greeted his son with a bear hug, he felt the tension in the room. Andrei and Ksenia looked on edge, and so did his wife. Oleg Ivanov had done the impossible, thought Adam. He had created problems of trust within one of the most loving families Adam had ever known.

Turning Byelochka over to his waiting nursemaid, Princess Anya greeted her aunt and uncle with kisses on both cheeks and seated herself on the yellow silk sofa beside Ksenia. Adam took a seat on a nearby Louis Quinze chair near the window.

"How could it happen?" demanded the princess once she and her relatives were alone. She was livid with rage. "I trusted you, Uncle. Did you lie to me?"

"Anya!" Her husband looked embarrassed. He didn't wish to be linked to an accusation like that. He knew Andrei's character. The man was absolutely trustworthy. This was insulting, something he never expected to hear from his wife, who knew her uncle better than he did. After all, Andrei and Ksenia had raised her.

"It's all right, Adam Mikhailovich," replied the prince, waving away his protests. "In our present situation, I'd be surprised if Anyushka didn't ask the question."

Princess Ksenia glanced at her niece as if she was suppressing a desire to swat her. She had been furious with her husband too, but this was upsetting. Anyushka had lost her manners.

"I arranged with an inspector of the Okhrana to track down Oleg Ivanov and kill him," said Andrei, pacing the parquet floor. "When we went to Geneva for your son's birth, he and his accomplices abducted Ivanov on the Anichkov Bridge, carted him off to a house they had prepared for the killing and beat and stabbed him until they believed he was dead. They then loaded him into a small boat and rowed out to the middle of the Neva where they tossed him in. Petrov, the one in charge, presented me with two items testifying to the kill when I returned home— a gold medallion they took from Ivanov's neck bearing an inscription from his mother and a severed finger."

At that, Anya gasped, revolted by the idea of Andrei having to deal with bits and pieces of her attacker. And one of his fingers *was* missing!

The prince smiled wryly. "Yes. That was how I felt too."

"You had complete faith in this Petrov?" asked Adam.

"He came highly recommended," replied the prince. "From the head of the Okhrana himself. There was no reason not to trust him."

Princess Anya rose and flung herself into her uncle's arms. "I'm so sorry," she whispered, "I was rude to you. You didn't deserve that."

Prince Andrei kissed her gently on the forehead. "I failed you," he said. "I tried and failed. I'm so ashamed."

Both ladies began to weep quietly, dabbing their eyes with lace-trimmed handkerchiefs, everyone feeling better for having cleared the air and miserable for having to start the hunt all over again, as if it were two years ago.

And now Princess Anya intended to take up marksmanship; she invited her aunt to join her. Revolvers. "It's him or us," she said quietly.

Ksenia agreed.

Billy was anxious to hear all the details about the state of Germany's war preparedness. He hadn't been cultivating old Franz for nothing, he explained. While von Murnau was snooping around the Russian military establishment, Billy was keeping an eye on him. The count was a gold mine of information. Especially when drunk.

"Are you dabbling in espionage?" demanded his brother, somewhat amused.

"In a manner of speaking," he replied.

Wonderful, thought Adam. Billy has finally found his niche in life—an embassy snoop. It was a bit comical, but he seemed to take it quite seriously. Well, he had to be learning something of the art in St. Petersburg.

The whole country was one large intelligence-gathering service. The Okhrana was the largest, but it had competition from various agencies attached to the imperial court, from the different ministries, the foreign embassies and all the armed services, not to mention individuals who employed private snoops to ferret out someone's secrets.

Each concierge in St. Petersburg was in the pay of someone, Adam guessed. So why shouldn't Billy join in the game? The Russian mania for spying on their citizens and foreigners was equaled only by their mania for withholding information from them. Perhaps he might pick up something useful.

"Did you meet General von Murnau when you paid Franz a visit in Germany?" asked Billy as he and Adam strolled along the quays of the Neva on their way to the Imperial Yacht Club, one of the capital's most exclusive.

"Oh yes. We were invited to a dinner where the old man spent the whole meal reviling the Balkan bandits—meaning Serbia. He hates the Serbs with passion and would like to exterminate them in their mothers'

wombs. Big admirer of the kaiser. In fact, he was kind enough to intro-
duce me to the All-Highest at an air show outside Berlin."

"The All-Highest?"

"It's what the kaiser likes to be called. Gives you an indication of his
modest opinion of himself."

"They're getting ready. The Russians are playing a dangerous game
in the Balkans right now, financing revolutionaries in Austria's backyard.
They're giving the anti-Slav faction in Germany and Austria plenty of
ammunition to use against them. Franz expects Russia to be dragged into
one hell of a mess because of Serbian stupidity there."

Reaching the granite-faced building that housed the yacht club, the
brothers entered, were greeted by the old doorman and had barely sat down
to enjoy a whiskey when they were distracted by the sound of a mob racing by outside on the Morskaya.

"Christ! Look at that," exclaimed Billy going to one of the tall, dark-
curtained windows.

On the quay, several mounted policemen were chasing a dozen shabby
workers down the street, swinging at them with heavy whips tipped with
lead and shouting curses as they charged.

"Strikers," commented an elderly owner of textile mills. "They're getting just what they deserve. The bastards have shut down half the plants
in Vyborg. It's all inspired by radicals."

As the thud of running feet and horses' hooves faded into the St.
Petersburg dusk, Billy and Adam returned to their comfortable armchairs.

"If the tsar doesn't manage to keep a lid on these labor troubles,
there'll be hell to pay. Too much of this and the barricades will go up
again on the Nevsky the way they did in 1905. Seventeen strikes at major
plants this week," declared Adam, informed by Andrei. "It's serious."

As if the problems with Ivanov weren't enough, Prince Andrei had
been gloomy about his country's future. With strikes mounting at an alarming rate, he was predicting total anarchy in St. Petersburg once more. He
had no faith in the government's ability to control anything. Nicholas II
seemed lost in his role as tsar-autocrat, allowing the tsaritsa to influence
his choice of ministers, herself under the influence of Gregory Efimovich
Rasputin, who claimed to be divinely inspired.

The prince said it was a joke, sort of a high-stakes game of musical
chairs. Prince Sviridov thought Russia would be lucky to survive the year
in its present condition.

Yet it had before, and it would again.

20

One member of Adam's circle of friends who had an inside view of the imperial family and court was Gigi Grekov. He was predicting total revolution—starting from the inside. Several imperial relatives were already advocating a coup d'état to send Nicholas II packing and seizing the tsarevich to establish a regency with one of the imperial uncles or cousins acting as regent until the boy reached his majority. The tsaritsa was to be denied access to her son for the rest of her days.

"Any chance of this happening?" demanded Adam, astonished.

"Probably not," answered the count. "The Romanovs' problem is the same as Russia's. Indecision. They can't decide who will replace Nicholas."

And from what Gigi could see, there weren't many who would really do a better job.

Frequently accompanying Natalya to Tsarskoye Selo, Count Grekov found himself quite often in the presence of the tsaritsa, not as often in the tsar's presence. His impression of Alexandra was dismal—neurotic hysteria, he labeled it: imperial powers combined with the blind and unswerving faith in holy men more suitable for a peasant. She and Natalya were fated to be friends.

The only thing Gigi was pleased with these days was little Constantine Georgievich—Kolya to his parents. The countess had given birth to a healthy boy who looked like a true Grekov, making his father ecstatic.

At his christening Kolya had wailed loudly as the priest poured the holy water over his fluffy dark curls, making his lovely godmother Princess Malysheva smile with bewilderment, having not the slightest idea of how to calm a shrieking baby. Ksenia remarked later to Andrei that it was a shame the mother was traditionally barred from the ceremony. It would have been one of the few times in her life when Natalya could have been useful.

As soon as the countess was beginning to recover from the rigors of

226

childbirth, Alexandra Feodorovna fulfilled Gigi's prediction by making her a lady-in-waiting, thereby alienating at least a dozen other candidates and causing further gossip over the evil influence of the Rasputin set.

Despite the gloomy predictions, Russia survived 1913 and headed into 1914 in the midst of a winter season that was more dazzling than any in recent memory. The final festivities of the Romanov tercentenary ended the year with a splash of champagne and the sparkle of thousands of diamonds as the leading hostesses of the capital tried to outdo each other in splendid balls, receptions and entertainments in their stately pastel palaces.

Some people who had access to certain unusual sources of information were preoccupied with the possibility of European conflicts that could lead to Russian involvement outside her borders and, in turn, to revolution within.

The Okhrana had come to more or less the same conclusion on their own, but nobody appeared to be paying any attention. It was as if talk of impending disaster was in poor taste, something to be avoided in polite society. The government was committed to the Triple Entente and had no intention of backing out.

In June the tsar and his court began preparations for the state visit of France's president, Monsieur Poincaré and Nicholas' annual summer cruise. Natalya was predicting peace in Europe because her mentor Rasputin was constantly telling his imperial patrons of the dangers of war.

Yes, thought Gigi with some irony, but they don't have a treaty signed with Rasputin. They do with England and France. And the European partners would hold them to it.

Meanwhile, people continued to go about their business as usual, including the workers in St. Petersburg's large factories who, true to form, participated in a series of wildcat strikes, causing the cossacks to patrol the Nevsky in anticipation of barricades rising once again. To everyone's surprise, nothing much happened, giving the lie to dire forecasts of doom and destruction.

In the aftermath of Ivanov's attempt on their lives in Paris, Princess Anya and her husband were drawn closer together than ever before. Hiring bodyguards on Andrei's advice, the Sviridovs were determined not to be taken by surprise the next time, and to Adam's astonishment, Anya began spending her afternoons practicing a new hobby—target shooting with the Smith & Wesson .38 he had given her.

He hadn't really expected her to take to it, but she was quite serious. In fact, she was becoming a splendid shot, demolishing whole rows of empty bottles—as did Ksenia and Tasha who didn't wish to be left out.

The one who worried Adam the most was Tatiana Sergeevna, who soon became bored with shooting inanimate objects and started firing at small birds and squirrels unfortunate enough to be in the area. Anya had a talk with her and she ceased *that* alarming practice, but not before she'd nearly caused a servants' revolt by shooting the cook's cat.

Despite the horror of Ivanov's reappearance, there was one thing that made Princess Anya extremely happy in the late spring of 1914. She discovered she was going to have a second child. This was the first sign of hope since that day in the Louvre. With all her fears for her future, she found herself forced to plan for a new life taking shape without being asked, imposing itself on her as if it knew she had the strength to care for it. Well, she thought, she would have to.

And truthfully, even after the ordeal of her first labor and delivery, Anyushka didn't want Byelochka to grow up alone. As an only child herself, Princess Anya had always wished for sisters. She was certain her son would welcome a brother.

And if he didn't, Grand-père would be glad enough for them both. So would Adam, but since they were going to be traveling to Germany for Franz's wedding shortly, Anya decided to postpone the happy announcement until they returned home. Otherwise he would worry dreadfully.

She did tell Princess Ksenia, who embraced her tenderly and took it as a sign the family was destined to triumph over any and all obstacles Oleg Ivanov could put in their way.

"Your children are our future, Anyushka," said the princess as she sat with her niece in the charming conservatory of the Malyshev mansion. "It's as simple as that. It means we will survive."

Yes, thought Princess Anya. We will. Her ancestors had outlasted the wrath of Ivan the Terrible, the caprices of Peter the Great, the jealousy of Catherine II. Oleg Ivanov was reduced to insignificance in comparison.

Lying in her husband's arms that night, Anyushka wondered how he would react to her news. He had become very protective of her lately, as if she were too fragile to survive without him. That amused her.

Pointing that revolver at Ivanov had given Anya a sense of just how determined she could be. With the tables turned, the animal had fled for his life. He had been afraid of *her*.

Stroking Adam's dark hair as he lay nestled close beside her, the young princess murmured endearments to her husband and plotted murder in her heart. It would come to that eventually, she knew. And she would be ready.

On the twenty-eighth day of June, 1914, with Byelochka handed over to Aunt Ksenia and with Anya's Paris wardrobe packed in twenty-four leather trunks, the Sviridovs entrained at St. Petersburg's Warsaw Station and headed south to Germany and Graf von Murnau's wedding in drowsy Mecklenburg.

While they were somewhere between St. Petersburg and Berlin, an incident occurred in far off Sarajevo that would alter their plans for all time, for on that Sunday afternoon in one of Europe's most remote backwaters, the heir to the Austrian throne was murdered by Serb terrorists whose bullets set off a war the scope of which would stun the world.

It was so odd, Anya thought later, but at the time of the assassination, nobody seemed terribly concerned except the French. Always sensitive to shifting political currents, Russia's Gallic ally had predicted trouble and manifested their uneasiness during the state visit of President Poincaré to the Russian court.

In the Austrian press, the death of the heir to the throne was received with less than hysteria, perhaps a reflection of the old emperor's dislike of the unfortunate archduke. Another Hapsburg simply replaced the unlamented Franz-Ferdinand in the line of succession and even the Vienna stock exchange scarcely wavered, a sure sign of stability.

La Guerre Européenne? inquired a staff writer on a reputable Paris daily, who then went on to explain how the national genius for diplomacy and the presence of such terrifying modern weapons as poisoned gas made war unacceptable to civilized man.

Mecklenburg

On the afternoon of Graf von Murnau's wedding to the lovely Sissi von Walthers, the bride and groom were upstaged by the arrival of General von Murnau, fresh from a two-day conference in Berlin. His presence seemed to unleash a frenzy among the young officers at the party, who deserted their ladies to swarm around the old general, eager to hear the latest news from Berlin.

"Two weeks at the most, gentlemen," winked the old man, his decorations flashing under sunny skies. "We're headed toward fateful times. Always remember to be worthy of your fatherland, no matter what."

On what ought to have been the happiest day of her life, the new Grafin von Murnau was close to tears. Her father-in-law's news meant she might lose Franz quite soon. It was heartbreaking.

"Anya," declared Sissi as she prepared to leave on her honeymoon, "you must leave at once. The general expects us to be at war with Russia even sooner than he told those boys at the party. I'm certain Franz will receive his orders to rejoin his regiment even before we reach our destination."

"It's inevitable, isn't it? But why do they want it so badly?"

"Personally, I regard it as a case of mass hysteria, but please don't tell my husband. My only hope is that they keep it short and don't kill too many people."

The two young women looked into the mirror and saw their worried reflections—two beauties in embroidered white linen, one girl blonde, the other brunette. Neither one saw the face of an enemy.

"Leave as early as possible and make certain you cross the border before nightfall. You wouldn't want to be caught here if they declare war," advised the grafin. "Believe me, it wouldn't be safe."

"I'm not going to take any unnecessary risks," smiled Anya. "I have too much to lose."

Grafin von Murnau put her arms around the Russian girl and embraced her warmly. She liked the pretty princess and truly regretted it might be their last meeting. Stupid war.

There was a knock on the door and Franz's valet wanted to know if the frau grafin was ready to leave.

"Coming."

Turning to Anya, Sissi gestured helplessly and embraced her once again. And then she departed, brushing away tears, a tall, slim figure in an elegant white summer suit, on her way to a very uncertain future.

Alone in the room, Princess Sviridova sighed as she thoughtfully replaced the stopper on the bottle of perfume Sissi had just used, *L'Heure Bleue*, a French scent very much in vogue. Out of the tumult of those July days, when politicians negotiated and generals threatened, while Europe clung to the pleasures of peace and braced for war, the scent of that perfume came to symbolize for Anya all the vanished beauty of a world that would never be the same.

The next morning, the princess awakened early so she could be ready to leave for home on the earliest train. Masha had packed the night before and the trunks were waiting in the hall, set for the ride to the station.

Feeling slightly dizzy upon arising, Anya attributed it to nerves and hurried toward the connecting bathroom, a wonderfully modern touch she appreciated right now.

"*Dushka*," Adam murmured sleepily, "are you all right?"

"No," she replied. "I don't feel well."

Clinging to the white porcelain doorknob, Anya looked at her husband and had a difficult time seeing him, since the whole room was swirling before her eyes, a spinning mass of blue and white flooded with bright sunlight.

This was so peculiar, she thought. It was as if she were seeing everything through a distorted lens. Adam, lying on the bed, appeared to her to be floating, speaking to her as if from a great distance.

What was he saying? It was so difficult to understand him.

"Your time of month," he repeated.

It was a few seconds before the words registered. Anya shook her head, making heroic efforts to speak as she leaned wearily against the door.

"No," she murmured, "that couldn't be. Impossible."

"Are you certain? There's a stain on the back of your negligee. What else could it be?"

When she finally understood what he was saying, Anya stared at him like someone who had just been handed a death sentence and slowly sank into a crumpled heap of embroidered white batiste, her legs giving way completely as the pain overwhelmed her.

"Oh God!" groaned the princess. "I'm losing our baby!"

In an instant, her husband was out of bed and across the room, managing to catch her before she hit the floor.

The whole thing was so fuzzy in Anya's mind, she no longer knew where she was or what was happening to her. The pain was making her feel as if she would die. The dizziness fogged her mind, making her incoherent, irrational.

She was aware of being placed on the bed, hearing Adam call for help, hearing cries in German from down the hall. And then she lost consciousness and took refuge in oblivion.

When Princess Anya awakened, a strange man was leaning over her, speaking quietly to Adam in German, a language her husband understood but she didn't. She felt like something on a laboratory tray now, being observed, palpated, discussed.

"Adam," she muttered, speaking in Russian, "what is going on? Who is this man?"

"The grafin's own physician. He says you came close to losing the baby but it's still alive."

Princess Anya blinked back tears. "Thank God," she breathed. "Now we can leave."

"Absolutely out of the question," replied her husband. "You'll need bed rest for a while. The whole thing is still touch and go."

"No!"

The force of that no startled the German doctor who glanced sharply at the prince. Adam coughed in embarrassment. Anna Nicolaievna was as stubborn as the rest of the Sviridovs. They wanted their own way and didn't acknowledge any other.

"He can't guarantee your safety if you leave now. Do you think I'd allow you to risk your life? We're staying."

The princess angrily pulled the covers up and threw one of the pillows at him, drawing a shocked stare from the grafin's elderly doctor. This was not appropriate behavior for a wife. She ought to listen. Making an excuse to leave, the short, chubby, bearded doctor bowed formally to his patient and departed, whispering sternly in German on his way out the door. "Deal with her," he said. "Be firm."

Adam sat down next to Anyushka and took her hand, causing her to pull away in anger. At that, he did something she had never seen him do before. He exploded.

To the princess's astonishment, her husband was furious. He seemed ready to do something wild, so unlike him. It frightened her a little, but she faced him down, unwilling to be intimidated.

"You were wrong to have concealed the pregnancy," he shouted. "It was the most pigheaded thing I've ever heard of."

"It was not. It was completely innocent!"

"Innocent? You let me bring you to what may well become a war zone. Nobody in his right mind would endanger a pregnant woman like that."

"But Adam, it didn't matter if I told you at home or after our trip. My telling you wouldn't have made any difference."

"I might have decided against the trip if I had known. My God! The place is rife with the most bloodcurdling rumors. It's insane for you to be here in your condition."

"Even if I had told you in Petersburg, it couldn't have prevented us from being here. The fellow didn't get shot until we were already over the border, so we wouldn't have heard the war talk until we arrived anyway. And then it would have been too late."

Prince Adam looked grim. "The grafin's doctor refuses to allow you to travel until the bleeding stops. He says you must be carefully watched. He also says he can't predict when it will finally be safe for you to leave. Meanwhile, our German friends are getting ready to sharpen their bayonets. It's a bad time to be stranded in Germany, *dushka.*"

"And it's all my fault."

"I didn't say that. I said you ought to have told me about the baby."

"Does the doctor think I'll miscarry or not?"

"He won't say for certain, but he admits it's a real possibility."

"He's hedging."

"He's being as honest as he can. I wish you had been the same."

At that, the princess gave a cry of indignation. "How could you? How dare you insult me like that? It's monstrous!"

Adam was struggling to keep his composure. At a time like this, the last thing Anya needed was provocation, he told himself. Be calm. You have a responsibility to her and your children. Don't let her become hysterical.

To his relief, his wife simply sighed and turned her face to the wall, unwilling to continue the argument.

There was a long pause. Then Anya said quietly. "If I lose the baby, how soon afterward will I be able to travel?"

"The doctor didn't say. He's not convinced you will either, but he's not about to put you on a train so you can miscarry in the middle of the night somewhere between Berlin and Petersburg. That would be pure folly."

"I want to leave," declared the princess. "I'm too afraid to remain here a day longer."

"Out of the question."

Anya looked around the room with its pretty art-nouveau decor and its vases of fresh summer flowers, and she felt horribly trapped. "They're going to go to war, and if we're caught here when they do, it's going to be dreadful."

Adam looked tired, his wife thought as he caressed her, tenderly stroking her long blonde hair. She noticed a grim expression she had never seen before. He was truly alarmed and she knew he was no alarmist.

"The diplomats have to exercise their skills before war can be declared. They haven't finished talking yet," he said at last.

"But in the meantime, the boches are already planning their moves."

"Hostilities can't commence until diplomacy fails. It hasn't. Yet. And if we're lucky, our foreign ministers will carry the day."

But truthfully, thought the princess, he didn't appear to have much faith in that. Holding Adam's hand, Anya smiled faintly and tried to look calm and cooperative, but in her heart she was looking for the first chance to get out of there.

He worried too much about her, she thought. It was good of him. He was a wonderful man. But she wasn't about to let that considerate trait of his hold them in this country for one second longer than necessary.

21

After three weeks of enforced bed rest, Princess Anya was even more distraught than she had been at the first threat of miscarriage. Her bedside table was covered with telegrams from Ksenia ordering her to come home as soon as humanly possible, warning of a growing war fever in Russia—the tsar was being pulled inexorably into the conflict. Get out of there while you still can, insisted the princess. Hesitate and all will be lost.

Well, thought Anyushka, it's time. This baby is not going to be born in Germany while his mother is being detained in some ghastly prison for enemy aliens. The first shots had yet to be fired, but they were just days away, according to the Grafin von Murnau, who was advocating a speedy departure to save herself the embarrassment of entertaining potential enemies of the fatherland under her roof.

Either they made their move to leave now or they lost all possibility of doing so in the very near future.

The last week of July, Princess Anya packed her bags, put on a tailored blue traveling suit and informed Adam they were heading for the train station.

"Grafin von Murnau just told me Franz was ordered to a Berlin barracks and Sissi's on her way to her mother's home," announced Anya, putting on a black feathered toque with a dotted half-veil. "And your medical genius told me I stand an 80 percent chance of keeping our baby, so Adam, I am leaving, with you or without you. The old general's told his wife to get rid of us. You know what *that* means."

"Anya, it's still dangerous. You have a temperature and you only just stopped bleeding."

"Stop talking like a nursemaid! I feel well enough to leave and nothing will keep me in this mad country even one moment longer than necessary. The motorcar is waiting downstairs and the baggage has been sent to the station."

Prince Sviridov looked closely at his wife. She was flushed with emotion, but otherwise she appeared to be better. Still, it was mad to travel under the circumstances. Unfortunately, they no longer had a choice.

"All right, Anya," he agreed. "We're on our way. But it's going to be dangerous."

"I've been through danger before and I've survived," replied the princess. "I'm ready to gamble on living, not dying, so let's go, darling."

Reaching for his wife, Adam kissed her tenderly, holding her close for a long, slow moment. He could feel her heartbeat through her white lacy blouse.

Anya put her arms around him and kissed him in response, holding him very tightly. "We'll be fine," she murmured. "I know we will."

To the immense relief of Grafin von Murnau, Franz's mother, the young Russian couple was finally out of her home after a nerve-racking delay during which the general was sending daily pleas to get rid of them. Events were moving quickly in Berlin, prompting him to wire messages similar to the ones Ksenia was sending from Russia, an ironic touch Anya found grimly comical. Both sides were arming, preparing, waiting for the signal to begin.

With their two worried servants, Masha and Feodor, beside them, the Sviridovs said very little on the trip to Berlin from Mecklenburg. In the German capital they would pick up the *Nord Express* and head home by way of Warsaw, finally reaching St. Petersburg and their worried relatives who had sent so many anxious telegrams to Schloss Murnau, pleading with them to come home.

As she sat at the window of their first-class compartment watching the beautiful late-summer German landscape go by, Princess Anya held Adam's hand and wondered what would happen to them all in case of war.

Ksenia and Andrei were safe at home. So was Byelochka, thank God. Volodya Grekov had recently rejoined his regiment, so he would certainly be in the thick of it. Grand-père was in France; as an Ally, France would probably suffer the ravages of a German attack. Anya was concerned for him and the elegant house on the Rue du Faubourg St. Honoré. Dreadful stories of the seige of Paris in 1870 sprang to mind, tales of starving Parisians eating dogs and cats while the German Army surrounded them, waiting for their capitulation. My God, thought Anya. Grand-père was not the sort to dine on cats. It would kill him.

As the German railway conductors passed by their compartment, the princess felt as if they were staring at them, planning something terrible.

"Good Lord, Anyushka," whispered Adam, "don't let your imagination run away with you. Stay calm. You have a baby to think of."

She nodded to reassure him, but she still didn't like the way these boches were looking at them. Neither did Masha and Feodor, who said nothing but thought the young princess was right. The master was not Russian; he came from a far-off place that had suffered invasion only during its fight for independence. It made a difference.

When the train reached the Berlin area, the Sviridovs and their servants saw convoys of troops on the roads within sight of the railroad tracks. Mercedes trucks with military insignia carried hundreds of troops to unknown destinations as the Russians watched, fearing the declaration of war had been made while they were halfway between Mecklenburg and Berlin.

"Adam," demanded his wife, "if it's already happened, wouldn't they have made the announcement?"

"If they had received word, I'm sure they would have. Don't worry. We're still at peace."

But he wasn't giving it very much longer before they were at war.

"Look, Princess," murmured Masha. "Hussars."

Coming down the road in single file behind the convoy of trucks was a detachment of hussars in elegant uniforms loaded with gold braid, rakish caps and carrying regimental banners fluttering in the breeze as they cantered by like toy soldiers on parade. Their mounts were fine black beauties, groomed to perfection and full of fire.

"I imagine the same kind of thing is going on in Petersburg and at Krasnoye Selo," noted Adam. "All the generals moving troops here and there, whipping up the fighting spirit."

"I wish we were looking at our own troops right now and not theirs," murmured Anya, pressing Adam's hand.

"We will be, very shortly," he smiled as he entwined her fingers in his. "Don't worry."

At last, the large, neatly lettered sign BERLIN came into sight, reassuring Princess Anya. Within the hour they ought to be boarding the Nord Express and heading home, she thought, relaxing in her seat. This wasn't so bad.

And then the door to their compartment was opened with a great crash, revealing the conductor and two uniformed German policemen.

"What's going on here?" demanded Adam as his wife froze, rigid with sudden fear.

As Anya stared at the Germans, she felt as if the bottom had dropped out of her stomach. It was the conductor who had been giving them suspicious glances all during the journey. And now he had the police with him. She had been right.

"Passports, please," demanded the man, ignoring Adam's question.

As the four travelers produced their documents, the three boches looked grim. "Sir, madam, please come with us. We will escort you off the train. Servants, too."

"Why?" demanded Adam. "What's the problem? I'm an American diplomat returning to my post in St. Petersburg. My wife is very ill and must return home at once for medical treatment. For God's sake, don't delay us."

At the mention of "American diplomat" the three Germans glanced at each other. Sensing a hesitation on their part, Adam demanded to speak to their superiors, loudly complaining about this "flagrant abuse of inno-cent travelers" and threatening to file a full report with the Wilhelmstrasse, the American Embassy in Berlin and the embassy in St. Petersburg.

The three looked at each other uneasily and then back at this Amer-ican who was threatening them in excellent German.

"Very well, sir. We will take you to our superiors," replied one of the police. "Come with us. The other three will remain in the waiting room at the station."

Anya was alarmed at the thought of being separated from her hus-band under the circumstances, but she also knew he was going to try to find out what was happening. If the Germans were merely going to hold all Russian travelers apart from the rest of the passengers while they awaited a train home, that wouldn't be so bad. But why had they called out the police? That was the part that was making her stomach go into knots.

Berlin

Taken to a small office in the railway station, Adam Lowell, diplomat, found himself face to face with an official sporting the same sort of up-turned mustache worn by the kaiser, whose large portrait hung on the green-painted wall behind the desk. The fellow's fat pink cheeks glowed with indignation as the American protested his treatment at the hands of the Germans railway authorities.

"Why are Russian nationals being singled out?" he asked. "Will this involve a lengthy wait? If so, who's issuing the orders?"

"The orders come from the head of German railways, seconded by the commander of the Berlin garrison. There is nothing we can do about it."

"How long do you propose to detain Russian travelers?"

"Until the order comes to release them." The fellow with the pink cheeks looked curiously at Mr. Lowell. "You are not within our jurisdiction," he said. "You are free to continue your journey whenever you wish."

"Then I'm assuming my wife and servants have the same rights."

"No. As Russians, they must remain here."

"I have diplomatic immunity. I'm claiming the same privilege for members of my household. They go with me."

"I'm sorry. They must stay."

"The hell they will."

The argument dragged on in the little office while the waiting room where Princess Sviridova and her servants were being detained began to fill up with other Russians, fearful, angry and voluble in their frustration. They had been taken off the train at the Berlin station and told there would be a delay. The boches were telling them nothing else, and meanwhile the *Nord Express* was about to leave.

Watching the activity on the station platform through the glass of the waiting room, Anya observed an unusually large number of soldiers, something she hadn't remembered from other trips. It couldn't mean anything good, she thought apprehensively.

All around her people were talking angrily. Children were crying, mothers begging them to be quiet, husbands snapping at their wives. It was dreadful. She had never had to put up with this sort of thing before. She didn't want to now.

When Adam finally returned, she and her servants were greatly relieved, expecting to be on their way. The news shocked them.

"I demanded to be put through to the American and Russian embassies in Berlin," he said. "I protested our treatment, claimed diplomatic immunity for my household and told the Germans they were acting counter to normal behavior for civilized nations. None of it did the least bit of good. They'll let me leave but not you."

At Anya's shocked expression, Adam hastened to add that he wouldn't even consider leaving her.

As the Sviridovs and their servants waited with the other detainees in the overcrowded room, Adam put his arm around his wife and held her close. She still appeared flushed, a bad sign. He hoped the damned Germans would just put them on the first train out and send them across the nearest border. What point was there in detaining these people? Not one person in the room had any connection with the government or the military as far as Prince Sviridov could tell. And by now, he knew enough of Russia's upper classes to recognize the prominent personalities. This was a bourgeois collection with a few stray aristocrats thrown in by chance. No grand dukes or generals.

Presently two German soldiers carrying rifles with bayonets opened the door to the waiting room; one of them called out, "All you people—this way. Depart by twos. Keep together and follow me."

Alarmed by the sound of the voice, Princess Anya exchanged worried glances with Masha, who was looking with the gravest concern at the bayonets.

"This way," ordered the German, indicating the proper path with a flourish of his rifle.

Slowly, uncertainly, the Russians filed out of the room, stared at by the Germans on the platform as if they were criminals.

Holding tight to her husband's hand, Anya was certain they were about to be sent to prison. This was so dreadful, she thought, so crazy. War must have been declared and they were unaware of it. That had to be why the boches were behaving so irrationally.

As the group was led through the main hall of the station, several passersby hurled insults at them, startling the Russians and frightening some of the children, who began to cry. Adam couldn't believe this was happening. It was inexcusable to detain a group of ordinary citizens in a still-peaceful country.

If his phone call to the American Embassy had any effect, there would be a protest to the Wilhelmstrasse. Not that he expected much help from that quarter, but a protest was better than nothing at all.

He had to get Anya home. If a claim of diplomatic immunity wouldn't do it, he didn't know what would. The chargé at the embassy in Berlin had said he would bring the situation to the attention of the ambassador. If they were lucky, thought Adam cynically. If they were very lucky.

Once outside the Berlin station, the Russians were loaded onto trucks for a ride to an unknown destination. The detainees were extremely apprehensive. Peering out from the cracks in the canvas of the truck's covering, Adam and his wife recognized the streets of downtown Berlin filled with the normal city traffic, pedestrians and streetcars.

"It doesn't look as if they're at war," whispered Princess Anya.

"They would have told us," replied Adam. Neither the Germans holding them captive nor the American chargé he had spoken to on the telephone had mentioned it. It was so bizarre.

Berlin in the late afternoon sunlight had the sleepy, prosperous look of a place unconcerned with threats of war. The strollers on the Kurfürstendamm showed nothing more than enjoyment of good weather, the men in lightweight jackets and straw boaters, the women in summer frocks and straw picture hats decked with ribbons. The only discordant note came when a troop convoy passed the detainees, drawing cheers from the pe-

destrians. The men waved their hats in the air, the women their handkerchiefs. The soldiers waved back, whooping a little, delighted at their
reception.

Passing the zoo and the Tiergarten, the Russians saw more troops go
by on foot, probably heading for a barracks.

"Where are they taking us?" Anya asked.

That question was answered within minutes when the trucks halted
before the Hotel Continental.

"*Raus, raus,*" shouted the soldiers gesturing for their passengers to
disembark. An officer in charge directed them to go inside, assuring them
that they would be given tickets for their baggage shortly.

"How typically boche of them," muttered Anya as she clung to Adam's
arm on the way into the hotel lobby. The combination of fear, anxiety
and heat had made her light-headed. She was afraid she might faint and
was quite determined not to.

As the Germans in the lobby stared at the incoming Russians, the
soldiers led them to the place where they were to be held—several large
rooms on the second and third floors, fifty to a room.

"My God," murmured Anya as she and Masha staked claim to a section of the floor near the windows. "This must be what prison is like."

"This is worse, dear lady," said a cultivated voice nearby. "At least if
one is in prison, one knows the length of the sentence. This is all very
irregular."

Turning to glance at the speaker, the princess smiled. It was an elderly gentleman elegantly turned out in a light summer suit and straw boater. He reminded her a little of Grand-père with his white hair, mustache
and Vandyke beard.

He introduced himself to the prince and princess and explained he
had been taken into custody in Berlin at his hotel. The boches were making a roundup apparently, although nobody would disclose the reason.

While Anya and her husband were chatting with the gentleman—
Stepan Felixovich Davidov, a professor from Kazan—a rock was thrown
through the window nearest to the princess, startling her and sprinkling
her with shreds of glass.

"My God, Anya!" exclaimed Adam. "Are you all right?"

"Yes. I think so."

Prince Sviridov pulled her away from the window and looked out to
see who could have thrown the rock. To his surprise, he could see a crowd
of tough-looking men and boys standing around near the entrance of the
hotel and across the street. A very bad sign.

"Keep away from the windows," he told the people around him. "If the boches are going to shower us with stones, it'll be safer toward the middle of the room."

Whoever threw that rock must have one hell of a pitching arm, thought the prince.

As the Sviridovs huddled together with Masha and Feodor, at closer quarters than usual because of the circumstances, Princess Anya thought of stories from the French Revolution, most notably the slaughter of the aristocrats in Paris during the September massacres. It made her shudder. Adam asked if she felt all right.

"I'm fine," she lied. She didn't feel fine. She felt frightened, hot and terrified for this baby who lay nestled somewhere below her heart, whose hold on life appeared to be so fragile. If she miscarried now under these conditions, she knew it would be a nightmare. The thought was so horrendous, she couldn't even permit herself to dwell on it or she might lose her mind.

When night came, the Germans brought up some food for the detainees but refused to answer any questions. Orders are orders. Eat.

Jammed together like sardines in a can, the Russians quarreled over space, complained about the skimpy rations and proposed endless theories as to why the Germans were holding them, all the while children were wailing, husbands and wives were bickering and everybody was getting on each other's nerves.

Leaning against Adam, Princess Anya whispered that this was the most awful trip she had ever taken. The people were so badly behaved. "It's as though all the women were like Auntie Lisa," she murmured, evoking a laugh from her husband. It was true. There were some notable shrews in this crowd, especially one loud Muscovite matron who was telling the entire world she had four servants at home who did everything for her and she had never had to lift a hand in her life.

"As if everyone doesn't have servants," remarked the princess in amazement.

Prince Sviridov gently pressed her hand and playfully kissed it as Anya smiled. She was holding up better than he expected. He was grateful for that.

Leaving the windows open for ventilation, the group of detainees settled down for the night, knowing sleep would be an elusive thing for most of them. Some of the children were curled up in their mother's arms or lying on the floor like puppies. Masha was too exhausted to care about anything any longer. She rolled herself into a sort of ball and dozed off on the carpet, using Feodor's jacket as a pillow while he quietly made conversation with one of his fellow detainees.

Princess Anya and her husband stretched out near Masha, talking as they propped themselves on their elbows, thinking of Byelochka and Ksenia, even Tasha.

"I'm glad no one we love is here to go through this," said the princess. "It would be too dreadful."

"I wish that damned chargé would contact somebody who might help us," murmured Adam.

"Darling," said the princess, almost hesitantly, "do you think Ksenia would raise Byelochka if anything were to happen to us here?"

"My God, don't even think of that. Nothing that bad will happen."

"Yes. But do you think she would?"

"Of course. Ksenia Alexandrovna would treat him as if he were her own son. You know that. You'd never have to worry about that. Although," he added hastily, "I can't imagine why the subject ever came up."

Anya didn't answer. She merely smiled into Adam's beautiful dark eyes, lovely and enigmatic. It was exactly what she thought. She simply wanted to hear it from her husband.

After a restless night during which hardly anyone except Masha and several children slept soundly, the Russians were awakened formally by a German soldier who announced they would be transferred to their embassy within the hour. Food would be served once they reached it.

Even the thought of food made Princess Anya ill right now. She prayed she wouldn't be sick, not in this mob, among these strangers. She looked ill, dead-white, with dark circles under her eyes. Her poor color alarmed Adam. She had been that white the morning she had nearly suffered a miscarriage.

"After we reach the embassy," Adam heard one Russian say to the guard, "how soon can we expect to leave Germany?"

"I do not know. You will be notified at the proper time, not before."

And then the moment for the transfer arrived. The Germans instructed the group to proceed downstairs to the hotel lobby and out a side entrance into waiting trucks.

"Feodor," said Adam, "you and I will each take Princess Anya's arm. Support her on the way downstairs. And Masha, don't let anyone separate you from us. Stick close behind. If any of the Germans give you a hard time, tell them you're part of the family. Tell them anything, but don't let them split us up."

Giggling at that unique suggestion, Masha nodded. Nothing would part her from the prince and princess. She was too afraid of the Germans.

Despite Adam's fears for Anya, he and Feodor got her safely downstairs, Masha bringing up the rear. The trip to the embassy was made without incident, except for a few angry shouts from the mob of Berliners watching the Russians enter the building, an eighteenth-century mansion dating from the time of Frederick the Great.

Once inside, the detainees were rudely welcomed by the staff, who looked upon this influx of their countrymen as an additional burden inflicted upon them by the boches. Nervous and short-tempered from constant alarms and lack of sleep, the embassy personnel were burning papers in several of the fireplaces, making everyone perspire in the already uncomfortable July heat. The last thing they wished to deal with was a mob of fellow citizens demanding to be taken home immediately. They had their own problems.

From behind the damask curtains of the embassy's ground-floor windows, Adam was watching the crowd across the street swell in size until there seemed to be hundreds of young toughs, shouting anti-Russian slogans, obscenities, threats. Too many of them were fueling their patriotism with bottles of schnapps, he noticed. The police were fools to permit that.

"They're supposed to permit foreign nationals to leave the country in the event of war, aren't they?" demanded Anya, finding a seat on the stairway.

"Yes. It's the usual thing."

She made room for her husband and nestled against him. Poor Adam hadn't been able to shave and he looked a bit unkempt, not at all his usual style. For that matter, they were both unkempt, thought Anya. She had caught a glimpse of herself in a mirror and was shocked to see the results of the past twenty-four hours. They both looked like beggars, not princes.

The heat was the worst thing. Unable to wash properly, the detainees were drenched with sweat in the clothes they had been captured in. To Anya, who was extremely fastidious and used to having several changes of clothing a day, it was disgusting. To her humiliation, she and Adam had both become grubby.

As the young princess was curled up on the stairway landing, staring at the painted cherubs on the ceiling, she was startled out of her reverie by a pleasant voice speaking to her about a cool drink. In her present situation, she thought she was beginning to lose her mind.

"Princess," insisted the voice, a real one with a Kazan accent, "may I offer you a glass of water?"

It was the professor from the hotel.

"Thank you," she replied, gratefully accepting his thoughtful gift. It was delicious.

"I was talking to one of the chargés a while ago," said the professor, "and he told me a piece of news. The Serbs are supposed to have agreed to an ultimatum by Austria, even though it was written in the most insulting language possible. They chose to swallow the emperor's insult rather than risk war."

"Well," smiled Adam, glancing at his wife, "Then everything is settled."

"No," the professor replied sadly. "At this very moment the Austrians are shelling Belgrade."

Horrified, Princess Anya gasped and clung to her husband, convinced Russia would be in the war within hours. Adam put his arm around her and reminded her that the conventions of international diplomacy called for repatriation of civilians caught in circumstances like theirs. The Germans were generally respecters of convention.

"Then why haven't they let us leave?" she answered reasonably.

Nobody knew.

Prince and Princess Sviridov became silent, staring at the carpet.

Finally Anya said, "This is the worst news yet. It means they really intend to have their war."

Trying to cheer them, the professor insisted no word had yet arrived about Russian mobilization, but two hours later, a code clerk announced that the tsar's orders for partial mobilization had gone through. Things were accelerating. The St. Petersburg, Moscow and Kiev military districts were on full alert and orders had gone out to border stations to be prepared for an attack.

Outside, across the street, the crowd of rowdies was increasing hourly despite the presence of helmeted police. Stones were beginning to sail through lower-floor windows, causing splinters of glass to scatter over carpets, furniture and Russians unfortunate enough to be within range. People began to congregate in the centers of rooms, afraid to venture too near the windows.

Rocks were one thing, but when a mob of excited, anti-Russian youths charged the embassy despite the presence of the Berlin police, the Russian guards replied with gunfire, causing the attackers to scatter, leaping over the fence to escape their bullets, even though the guards fired in the air.

Inside, Adam pushed his wife to the floor and threw himself on top of her at the sound of gunfire, fearful it was coming from the Germans. When it died down after a few minutes, he relaxed but insisted Anya stay upstairs and away from the ground floor. Shaken, she obeyed, taking Masha with her.

Finding an out-of-the-way spot on the second floor, Anya and her maid opened the jewel case Masha had been carrying for her and began sewing pockets inside their camisoles to hide the princess's jewelry—her lovely pearls and a diamond necklace, bracelet and earrings, plus a few smaller pieces. She was wearing a pair of large baroque pearl earrings which she now concealed inside her camisole, replacing them with a simple gold pair.

When they had finished, the women felt uncomfortable but glad the jewelry was out of the way. Princess Anya had no intention of giving up her beautiful wedding pearls to the boches. Or anything else.

On the ground floor, stones were still causing glass to shatter every few minutes, but there was no further sound of gunfire, making the detainees somewhat relieved. Nervous embassy staff relayed bulletins as they arrived from St. Petersburg, suggesting the inevitable.

In the chapel, women were praying with great devotion to the Kazan Madonna whose icon was displayed in a place of honor on the altar, the noisy Muscovite matron with the four servants louder than anyone else. A great many candles were lighted for deliverance from the boches and a quick trip home to a Russia still at peace, although that possibility appeared to be more and more remote with each passing hour.

At last, after everyone had given up all hope of leaving Berlin, a boche in uniform appeared, gathered the Russians around him and announced, "You will leave the building in exactly fifteen minutes, proceeding in groups of five; you will board trucks to travel to the train station. Have your baggage receipts in your possession."

That last order made Anya nearly hysterical with laughter. It was so typical of them, she exclaimed, so punctilious. So boche.

"Anya," said her husband, putting his hands firmly on her shoulders, "listen to me carefully. When we leave the building, I'm going to hold you on one side with Feodor on the other. Masha will walk directly behind you as she did before. Take my jacket and place it over your shoulders."

"It's too warm for that," she said in surprise. Was he out of his mind?

Adam looked her in the eye and repeated his directions. "Do as I say," he added, not wishing to have any arguments. "Wear the jacket."

"All right," shrugged the princess. With all their other problems, it was too absurd to quarrel over at this particular moment, so she decided to humor him.

When their turn came to exit the building to go to the waiting truck, Princess Anya and her companions looked out at the mob on the street and were appalled to see the most frightening collection of thugs ever assembled in that fine neighborhood. Barely restrained by the police, men and boys in rough caps and shabby clothes were shouting obscenities at the Russians, flinging empty liquor bottles in their direction, pelting them with stones, all the while the women in the group were chanting something that sounded like "kill the Russkies."

"Hold on to Anna Nicolaievna and don't let her go, no matter what happens," Adam ordered Feodor as they made their way to the truck under a hail of stones and insults. "Anya, pull the jacket up over your head!"

The harpies in the crowd had begun to pelt them with rotten vegetables and any other sort of filth that came to hand. This is not real, thought the young princess as she felt herself being half-carried to the vehicle by Adam and his valet. It was as if the world had gone mad.

Suddenly Anya wondered if Ivanov were out there. It was irrational, but somehow fitting. In all her life—except for her confrontation with Aunt Lisa at the Bolshoi—he had been her sole experience with utter and unreasoning hatred. Until this moment.

"My God," she murmured to Adam, "they want to kill us!"

Shielding his wife as best he could, Adam pulled the jacket all the way up over her head, trying to protect her from being spattered with garbage. All around them in the open truck, people were being hit with decaying vegetables and an occasional stone. Frightened children were wailing and clinging to their mothers, terrified by the screams of the mob and the sight of the faces distorted with hate.

Holding Anya close, her husband nearly despaired of escaping the angry crowd that milled around the convoy as it began pulling out. The drivers were proceeding at a pace guaranteed to allow the mob to keep up with the trucks, creating enormous risks for the passengers.

Surrounded on all sides by maniacs who were shouting the most vile obscenities, the Russians felt as if they might be murdered right there on the street in the heart of Berlin.

"Adam, I'm frightened," whispered Anya, sick at the sight of all those hideous, hate-filled faces. "Do you think they'll kill us?"

"No. The soldiers won't let that happen. They're responsible for our safety."

"They're not doing too much to hold the people back."

That, thought her husband, was frighteningly true. It filled him with the gravest apprehension, although he wasn't going to say so.

"Keep your head down," warned Adam as a rock went sailing past his left ear. "Don't look up."

A neighbor was struck by a well-aimed stone, knocking him unconscious at their feet. Adam could feel his wife tremble as he held her tighter, whispering to her to try to keep her calm.

"How's our son?" he demanded, pressing her closer. "Any problems?"

"No. He'll turn out to be a tiger after living through all this," she replied, trembling as she watched the mob surrounding them on all sides, screaming at them as if they meant to murder all the Russians.

Just then, a teenage boy came racing up to the slow-moving truck, eager to vent his rage on the nearest easy target. While Anya cried out in horror, he scrambled onto the vehicle long enough to lash out at the first person within reach—Adam. Hitting the prince viciously with several blows from a large, jagged rock, the youth finally lost his balance and slipped back off the truck, vanishing into the crowd, quite pleased with himself.

Struck in the left eye and temple, Adam staggered in pain and then collapsed in Anya's arms, knocked unconscious. As he fell to the floor of the truck, the princess flung herself over him, nearly hysterical with terror. She was splattered with blood pouring from her husband's wounds.

"Adam!" she shrieked, frantically beating at the people who were practically falling over him in the close confines of the moving vehicle. "Adam! My God, help him!" She had never seen so much blood.

But the others had their own problems; all the passengers were trying to avoid the same fate. Nobody except for her two servants made a move to do anything for the prince.

Feodor was convinced the master was dead. The blood gushing from his head was truly horrifying. Prince Sviridov had been hit so hard, the valet had heard the sickening thud of the rock as it made contact with the skull. He didn't believe anyone could survive such a savage blow to the head.

Pressing her ear to Adam's chest, Anya tried desperately to hear a heartbeat. Yes, she thought, half-crushed by strangers who kept jostling her with each movement of the truck. He's alive. He is. He can't die and leave me. I won't let him!

Doing his best to raise the prince to a sitting position against the side of the truck so he wouldn't be trampled on the crowded floor, Feodor fashioned a makeshift bandage of his clean handkerchief and wrapped it around Adam's head.

Princess Anya held her husband in her arms and nearly despaired. He needed a doctor. Fast. If these boche maniacs didn't get them out of this crazy mob, Adam would die. He was breathing but unconscious. And that head wound was vicious. Cradling him in her arms, Anya frantically stroked his hair, talked to him, tried to revive him, wailed with frustration, all to no avail. The prince was not responding.

As the princess and her servants huddled around Adam, doing their best to keep him from being trampled, the truck suddenly jolted them to the floor again as the driver came to an abrupt halt.

"Where are we?" demanded Anya, completely disoriented in the crush.

"At the train station," replied Feodor.

Indicating a coach in the second-class section, the soldiers pushed the Russians on board, carrying the wounded as if they were mere baggage.

"Get a doctor," ordered the princess as the Germans pushed her up the stairs, along with Masha and Feodor. "If Adam dies, I'll hold you personally responsible. Where are your officers? I demand to speak to them! Show me where they are!"

"Princess!" pleaded Feodor, "don't anger them. These are real brutes."

Anna Nicolaievna was too outraged to care. She was hot, dirty, tired and furious. Her husband might die because of these savages and she was no longer sure she would reach the Russian border without losing their child. All because of these damned boche bastards!

"Get on board the train!" shouted a sergeant, flourishing a bayonet in Anya's face, angering her all the more.

Without waiting for Anna Nicolaievna's reaction, Feodor took hold of her arm and nearly dragged her up the steps, too terrified of the Germans to worry about his shocking act of impropriety. Anya was so stunned by Feodor's action she let herself be carried along, up the steps of the train and into the second-class carriage right into the midst of a terrible crush of people, all jostling for seats, noisily calling for family members, wailing their displeasure at the loss of their baggage.

Adam and the other wounded man were designated by the Germans as "special cases" and removed to first-class compartments where their families were reluctantly allowed to accompany them. There was more space in a first-class compartment, but more importantly, the injured were hidden from view, enabling the Germans to state they were taking good care of the Russians.

As Princess Anya and her servants hovered over Adam, who was still unconscious, the train began pulling away from Berlin, heading toward Denmark rather than east.

Adam will die before we ever reach Copenhagen, thought the princess, staring at the blood-soaked bandage. If he wasn't taken care of soon, he would die. The cut was an ugly thing, a terrible gash across his eye and temple; it needed medical care and on this boche train there wasn't so much as a first-aid kit.

The thought of losing him nearly paralyzed Anya. As she stared at her wounded husband, she thought of the desperation she had felt at the time of her attempt at suicide—a ridiculous escapade. Now she felt that same sense of helplessness tearing her apart.

22

For a year the neighbors had noticed an unusual amount of activity in the formerly boarded-up mansion on Alexander Street as workmen repaired the roof, the tall French windows, the wrought-iron gates hanging off their hinges. Someone had obviously bought it and was willing to spend money restoring it. The only question was *who*.

One of the bolder neighborhood children had scampered up the wrought-iron fence, across the lawn and around the back to peek through a window at whoever was inside. Pressing his face against the windowpane, he had seen furniture covered with sheets, rugs still rolled up and a large crystal chandelier lying in a corner like a peculiar glass Christmas tree. But no people. Disappointed at not finding any trace of a family, the boy had retraced his steps and strolled home, telling his friends it was very strange.

Several days later, a carriage had pulled up to the entrance to let out a man and three ladies, or at least a man and three women, since the females accompanying him hardly appeared to fit anyone's description of "lady." They were loud, gaudy and garishly decorated. One of them carried a fat white angora cat. The other two toted carpetbags.

The man had carried nothing but an air of self-satisfaction.

Entering the foyer with its parquet floor and small crystal light fixture—electric, the blonde woman stated proudly—the party passed through the reception salon, all carved paneling and fancy flooring under an imitation Persian rug. After pausing for the man to admire the restoration, the blonde woman had led the group upstairs to the work area.

Chattering gaily, the small blonde the others called Wanda had thrown open the double doors to the four bedrooms along the corridor, one after the other, while the two dark-haired girls wandered in and out of the rooms, nodding in admiration at the accommodations—paneling, soft rugs, tall mirrors and enormous, richly carved beds piled high with fluffy goose-down pillows and silken comforters.

"Very aristocratic," the man had declared; he was a heavyset fellow in his twenties, but appeared much older, due to his freshly shaved head. He was the oddest thing in the house, more like a circus strongman than the owner of this fine mansion. He felt a little bit overshadowed by it. The missing finger on his left hand testified to a rough life. His hard-set face confirmed it.

"Well, Monsieur Mossolov," Wanda had demanded after her skeleton staff had gone to explore the second floor, "what do you think? Have I or have I not done a splendid job?"

"Good, Wanda. Very good. The only thing is, it'll be hard to get used to being Timofey Mossolov. I'm not sure I like it."

The Polish girl flicked him a disgusted glance. "I never figured you for sentimental," she said. "Oleg Ivanov is dead. And if he isn't, he will be if the Russian police ever manage to locate him. I thought we agreed on the new name."

"*You* picked it," he said. "It wasn't my choice."

"Well, I picked out the house and the furnishings and I did a damned good job with those. Believe me, being Monsieur Mossolov will add twenty years to your life."

Koshka the cat stared at the newly named Mossolov as if he were no better than the former Ivanov. That one had hated all cats, Koshka in particular. Mossolov would be no better.

Walking through the place, exploring it from cellar to attic, the new owner had had to admit his assistant had good taste. It had to have been her convent background, he thought, with a certain amount of annoyance. She must have acquired her pretensions there too. She'd changed. He had begun to notice it. And it all started when he had allowed her to talk him into putting their money into this house. So fancy. A real palace.

She had begun to remind him of Prince Malyshev's niece and Katia Petrovna. It had made his skin creep. It was a sign he ought to watch this little Polish cow very closely, very closely indeed.

Having acquired the building cheaply when the children of its original owners decided to get rid of it, Oleg and Wanda had set about refurnishing it, cleaning it and making it shine. Located in a small park set back from the street, surrounded by a fence for privacy, nestled among several beech trees, it appeared to be a solidly respectable house, a handsome addition to a fairly undistinguished neighborhood.

Exactly the appearance it needed for the business they'd had in mind.

Within a year, they had begun to make a name for themselves among the officers of the large Russian garrison of Warsaw. Now the unsettling news from Austria made Monsieur Mossolov wonder if it was all going to be swept away.

Perspiring in his overdecorated office, although the windows were wide open, Monsieur Mossolov, né Oleg Ivanov, sat contemplating the newest addition to his staff, all of her, as she slowly peeled off her corset cover. Smiling sweetly into Monsieur's tiny, piglike eyes, she began to unfasten the laces that held her full bosom in check.

"Very nice," muttered Oleg, motioning for her to come closer; she kept unfastening as she advanced, flicking her little pink tongue suggestively over her lips as she bent over her employer, allowing him a good look at the merchandise which was spilling out well beyond the confines of the pink satin corset.

"Ah, big ones," he smiled, his mouth mere inches away from the large pink and white breasts Olga was shoving at him. "Good, I like big ones."

Grabbing the girl around the waist, Oleg pulled her onto his lap, burying his face in her amazing cleavage, kissing her with greedy, sucking sounds, his mouth pulling on her nipples like an anteater going after his lunch. Olga sighed, resigning herself to his pawing as she began to search for the buttons on his fly.

"Take off your drawers," commanded Oleg suddenly, getting to his feet and shutting the door.

Tossing aside her corset, the voluptuous blonde stepped out of her lace-trimmed batiste drawers and waited for Monsieur to return to his seat. She knew what he wanted.

"Ah," said Oleg, his little eyes glittering as he took Olga by the shoulders and pushed her down to her knees on the carpet in front of him. He unbuttoned his fly as he leered at her, making little grunts of pleasure as the girl slowly reached for what was poking out of his fly, waiting to be stroked.

"Beautiful," murmured Oleg, his head back. His mouth stretched into an ecstatic grin as Olga took him in hand, caressing him between experienced, plump white palms as he quivered with pleasure, waiting for her to get to the part he liked best.

Sighing from boredom, the blonde let him grab her head in a sort of death grip as she suddenly applied her mouth to Oleg's member, evoking a series of deep groans of ecstasy as the big bear gripped her more tightly than ever, clutching her as if he meant to keep her there forever, despite her tendency to make strange noises.

"Go on!" he groaned. "Keep going!"

Now Olga was groaning, but she managed to finish, rewarded by the sound of Monsieur's animal cries of pleasure and the usual tip. While she sat on the edge of his Louis Quinze desk, her round bottom on the blotter, her full bosom heaving from her exertions, she wondered if Monsieur had always been as ugly as he was, or if it was an acquired affliction.

And then she noticed an intruder in the doorway, twitching with fury.

Wanda!

"Monsieur Mossolov!" exclaimed the girl. "You have company."

"Don't let me interrupt anything really important," hissed Wanda, dripping venom with each word. "I merely wanted to let you know that my guess last night was correct. My colonel from the governor-general's staff says it's almost certain we'll be at war within the week. But I see you have other matters on your mind. Sorry to have bothered you."

And with that, Madame Wanda was off in a flounce of white ruffles, followed by her fluffy white angora cat, who accompanied her everywhere, even into bed.

"Wait a minute," Oleg cried after her as he got rid of Olga. "If this is true, we'd better start buying all the liquor we can get our hands on. They may start rationing."

"You take care of it," replied Wanda as she disappeared from sight, heading for the front door, too angry to talk to him. "You're the man of the house, aren't you?"

Standing on the expensive Bokhara carpet, his trousers undone, looking rather foolish, Oleg thought about what Wanda had just told him. War. "Damn," he muttered. "This is either going to be very good for business or it's going to kill us all."

With Warsaw on a wartime footing, the Russians would send even more men into the city, taxing his house to the limit of its capabilities. Now would be the time to expand, before prices went up. He had two properties in mind, not far from his present establishment. With an increased number of officers on duty, two more houses could make him a millionaire.

"War," he muttered to himself. "I'll be damned."

And then he went to see about buying those two buildings. With all the money coming in from his establishment, he'd be a fool not to expand.

Copenhagen

When the Russians' train arrived in Copenhagen, Princess Anya wasted no time in having Adam taken to the nearest hospital. Aided by Danish officials of the International Red Cross, the princess got in touch with the Russian Embassy; the ambassador was an old friend of Sandro's from his student days and more than willing to help Sandro's granddaughter.

Within hours of arriving in the city, Princess Anya was moved into a guest room at the embassy and Adam was being operated on by the doctor who attended Denmark's royal family. Count Markov, the ambassador, was highly critical of his Berlin colleagues, attributing their bad behavior to the fact that the ambassador had been recalled to St. Petersburg for a special conference with the tsar.

As the princess waited for word of the operation's outcome, she was so exhausted from the experience of the past few days that she was unable to stay awake. She fell into a sort of stupor as soon as she bathed and lay down in the soft featherbed that had been prepared for her. It was the next morning before she awakened, ashamed to have slept through it all.

My God, she thought as she opened her eyes, what happened? How could I have fallen asleep? Glancing at the couch on the other side of the room, she saw Masha snoring away, keeping her company at the suggestion of Countess Markova.

Although Anya didn't realize it, the embassy doctor had given her something to make her sleep, he hadn't wanted her to stay up all night worrying. If her husband pulled through the operation, she would be relieved in any case. If he didn't, there was nothing she could do about it. And no expectant mother ought to be subjected to further stress after what Her Highness had already gone through in Berlin.

The doctor was amazed she was as healthy as she was.

After a hasty breakfast, Anya asked to be taken to the King Christian Memorial Clinic, where Adam was recovering from surgery. With Masha along for moral support and Countess Markova accompanying them, Princess Anya met with the doctor who had performed the operation and listened grimly while he explained the injuries the prince had suffered.

It was serious. The damage had caused a buildup of fluid within the brain, pressing on certain sensitive optical nerves. The surgery had drained the fluid, but the wound caused by the blow to the head had harmed the left eye, possibly causing permanent damage. And the prince was running a fever, not at all a promising sign, although it was not that uncommon either.

"Will he survive?" demanded Anya, shaking with fear as she listened to the Danish doctor, having a difficult time following his thickly accented French, their common language.

"He should, barring unforeseen circumstances."

That was less than the resounding yes Anya was hoping for.

Alone with her husband in his bare, white-walled hospital room, the princess stood next to his bed and wept. He looked so helpless, covered with gauze bandages that hid the upper part of his face. He might as well be a corpse. Underneath those bandages his head was shaved because of the operation, a hideous thing to do, thought Anya, regretting the temporary loss of his beautiful black hair. Why did hospitals do these things?

Please don't die, she thought as she took a seat beside Adam, caressing his hand although he couldn't respond. Don't leave me and our son. I love you. I want you to see this baby we're going to have. After what he's just been forced to endure, he ought to know his father.

There was no response.

When Princess Ksenia received a telegram from her niece telling her of their arrival in the Danish capital and of Adam's injuries, she called Andrei at his club and told him they were on their way to Denmark that evening.

Despite the fear of imminent war, Russia was still at peace and Denmark was scarcely likely to be on the opposing side, considering the intense dislike between the Danish royal family and the Hohenzollerns because of German incursions into Danish territory not too many years ago. If Anya's situation was even half as bad as it sounded, Ksenia reasoned, she shouldn't be left there on her own.

Making the trip to Copenhagen over the extremely tedious Finnish-Swedish route involved travel through Finnish forests after the railroad line ended, then a border crossing at the empire's most desolate outpost, a long train ride to Stockholm and then south, and finally across to Copenhagen by ferry. Even so, the Malyshevs arrived in the Danish capital quickly enough to startle their niece, who was grateful to see them and utterly worn out.

"What about Byelochka?" was Anya's first question as she and her aunt embraced in the Russian Embassy. "Who's taking care of him?"

"His nurse, of course. She won't let him out of her sight. She has strict orders not to take him outside the grounds until we return home. He's confined to the gardens."

"Good," sighed Anya. "He'll be safe then."

Explaining the situation to Andrei and Ksenia, Anya revealed the extent of Adam's injuries, shocking her relatives. He still hadn't regained consciousness and was still feverish. And now the doctor was saying the left eye was damaged almost to the point of losing its vision.

There was no good news. And Ksenia's reports of troop movements and war talk were just as depressing. Princess Anya was frankly amazed her country was still at peace.

Peterhof Palace

On August 1, 1914, in the private apartments of the Peterhof Palace, Countess Natalya Grekova was keeping the tsaritsa company while Nicholas II was holding an emergency meeting with members of the Imperial Council. The men looked as grim as the subject at hand. As Alexandra and her lady-in-waiting paced the floor of the tsaritsa's elegant boudoir, the tsar was announcing his decision to declare war on Germany in response to the Germans' own declaration of war delivered to the Russian Foreign Ministry that afternoon by the German ambassador to St. Petersburg, Count Pourtalès.

Both women were weeping, convinced war meant Russia's destruction; Rasputin was warning as much from his hospital bed in Siberia where he was in touch with Alexandra by telegram as he recuperated after an attempt on his life by a former disciple. This time, Nicholas was not paying any attention to his wife's religious mentor.

Making the momentous decision to go to war, knowing how ill prepared Russia was for a European conflict, Nicholas II placed his faith in God and his minister of war.

When Countess Natalya left the imperial apartments that evening, she still hadn't heard the news of the tsar's decision, but as she was driven to her dacha on the opposite side of the Imperial Park, her chauffeur remarked that there were an enormous number of generals in the area of the palace, all accompanied by their aides-de-camp, all wishing to be the first to know. The St. Petersburg bureaucrats were hovering around too, men from the Foreign Ministry right next to the generals.

When Natalya reached her dacha, the old butler handed her an envelope an imperial messenger had just handed to him. Ripping it open, the countess gasped, crossed herself three times and fled to her bedroom to take refuge with her icons, weeping inconsolably.

Watching Natalya Alexeevna's reaction with bewilderment, the old man reached down to pick up the letter she had flung to the floor. As soon as he started to read it, he understood. "The Tsar has felt compelled to respond to Germany's declaration of war by declaring war on them. Tomorrow we go to the Winter Palace for the formal announcement. Pray for us. Alexandra."

With the imperial enclave in an uproar, nobody noticed a lone officer pause briefly before the gate of the Grekovs' dacha, stare at the darkened windows and then move briskly on, heading for the home of a general in the vicinity. Volodya Grekov, newly commissioned and eager for the fray, was carrying a message to a member of the general staff from his colonel at Krasnoye Selo when he found himself in front of his brother's villa. Having recently made peace with Gigi he felt better, although he knew it was an emotional reaction to the frenzy of the past few weeks. He still bore a grudge for the way his brother had behaved, and no rapprochement could ever truly erase that memory from his heart. Still, he had wanted to do the right thing by his mother, so he had consented to go through a show of reconciliation for her.

But he had never made peace with Natalya, and that bothered him.

Pausing before Gigi's villa, Volodya wondered if his brother was there. He knew through mutual friends that Natalya was now a lady-in-waiting to Alexandra Feodorovna, so conceiveably she might be at Peterhof right now. He almost attempted to open the gate and go up the walk but something made him refrain. He really didn't know what to say to her.

She always made him angry. If she had that effect on him now, it would be a dreadful way to part with her, perhaps forever. He didn't want that. It would be far worse than not seeing her at all.

Damn, thought Volodya, drawing back his hand from the gate, Why should I even care? The woman's a lunatic. She drove me around the bend. She's having the same effect on my brother. She's beyond hope.

All the same, after Volodya had delivered his message to the general and returned to Krasnoye Selo to find his regiment preparing to board trains for the front, he regretted having let the opportunity go by. In spite of all their quarrels, in spite of Rasputin, in spite of his own common sense, Volodya loved Natalya as one loves a ridiculous, wayward child. He didn't know why.

On the following day, the second of August, 1914, after the official paperwork had been concluded by the ministers, a grim-faced Tsar Nicholas and his family arrived in St. Petersburg to declare war on Austria and Germany and to invoke the blessing of the Almighty in Russia's hour of need. His welcome at the Winter Palace was tumultuous.

While the people were greeting Nicholas and his family outside the huge palace, inside, the nobility of St. Petersburg were jamming the great Jordan Staircase to welcome him, as excited as the rest of the city. Packed in with the rest, Count and Countess Grekov were clinging to the marble railing of the huge white marble staircase, drenched with perspiration and almost oblivious to all discomfort. Everyone was in the grip of such strong emotion, Gigi thought, it looked like a gigantic funeral.

After a Te Deum service in the huge St. George Hall and after taking the oath not to make peace as long as a single enemy soldier remained on Russian soil—although none was yet there—the tsar and tsaritsa walked slowly through the packed hall, beneath heavy, triple-tiered bronze chandeliers and headed for the balcony overlooking Palace Square to present themselves to their people.

A roar of acclamation arose from the sea of upturned faces as Nicholas and his wife walked out onto the balcony. Cheers rumbled from the depths and echoed across the huge square.

And then suddenly, as Nicholas tried to speak to them, the people, as one great crowd, dropped to their knees as if obeying some primitive instinct and began to sing the imperial anthem, the words of the song rising upward like the voice of the motherland itself, fervent and rich with the sounds of all the Russian lands.

Far above the weeping, singing crowd, Nicholas was united with them in this extraordinary moment, nearly overcome by the torrent of affection after so many unhappy years of a reign cursed by one disaster after the other. At long last, he was truly their beloved tsar.

Copenhagen

Princess Anya was standing at her husband's bedside in the King Christian Memorial Clinic weeping tears of joy. At 10:50 that morning, Adam had regained consciousness and found himself wrapped in bandages. He had begun to speak, loudly demanding an explanation in German, while the duty nurse let out a cry of astonishment and went to call the doctor.

Anya, too moved to speak at first, began to weep as she sat down beside her husband and took his hand in both of hers, murmuring incoherently as she heard him say her name and ask her where they were.

"Copenhagen," she replied. "We're out of Germany."

"Thank God," he breathed. "But what's happened to my eyes?"

That was a more difficult question to answer; it required the doctor for that.

When the news of war reached the Danish capital, Princess Anya and her aunt and uncle attended services in the chapel of the Russian Embassy; all were deeply moved by the dreadful announcement. As the young princess prayed for a Russian victory, she added prayers for her husband's complete recovery from his injuries, fearful he might lose his eyesight permanently.

That would kill him. If Adam had to spend the rest of his life sightless because of that vicious street brat in Berlin, it was an end to his career as a diplomat. That made no difference to Princess Anya. He could stay at home and spend his time in his clubs for all she cared. But if his career were taken from him, she knew Adam would never recover. He had a need to work, to feel as if he were doing something useful with his life. Without that, he would disintegrate.

And in his career, he needed his sight.

As Adam's recovery progressed, Anya described for him their exit from Germany and he found himself grateful to be alive. It was ironic, he thought. He had been so worried about his fragile, pregnant young wife, and she was the one who had taken charge, rushed him to a hospital and—according to Feodor—behaved like a little tiger with the Germans.

Adam Lowell found himself looking at Anya with new respect. He had always loved her, but he had never suspected the strength of character that lay beneath the soft and silken surface. At the same time, it worried him. If Anya ever realized what she could do without him, she might just as well realize she didn't need him around any longer, especially if he was blind and a burden. The thought tore him apart. If he didn't recover, he may as well die. He had no intention of surviving as a burden to her and his children—or as an object of pity for anyone.

❦ 23 ❦

St. Petersburg

While the Russian capital was working itself into a frenzy of war fever and cheering the long troop columns marching down the broad Nevsky on their way to the railway stations and transport to the front, some of the citizens were more concerned with their own destinies than with Russia's.

For Countess Tatiana Derzhavina, this was the moment she had been patiently awaiting for months—the absence of both Aunt Ksenia and Anya from the capital at the same time. With both ladies gone, she was free to indulge her own caprices to the limit.

With the connivance of the servants, a venal lot, Tasha slipped out of the Malyshev mansion where she had been staying since Anya's departure for Europe and headed for the nightclubs, dressed in Lisa's remade evening gowns and ready for the glamorous life of a *femme fatale*. Beautiful, eager and careless, Tasha soon found herself in company that was too fast even for her, and ended up one morning in total disarray on the steps of the Gostiny Dvor, where her companions of the previous evening had dumped her, totally inebriated.

After that fiasco, she decided to choose her friends more carefully, not wishing to die young and in the gutter. One night while she and one of a growing collection of lovers—a young officer attached to the general staff who didn't know her real name—were drinking at a nightclub known as the Rose Noire, the young countess remarked that the featured singer sounded like a sick basset hound. Laughingly, her companion suggested that Tasha audition. To his surprise, she did. To hers, she was hired.

On the night Tasha was to make her debut as "Tonya," singing a repertoire of French songs of the my-love-has-left-and-I'm-in-despair variety, she had extravagantly high hopes for success. Self-possessed despite her mere fourteen years, Tatiana Sergeevna had been through enough in her life to make her relatively fearless. The only thing she truly feared was discovery by her relatives and, because of their trip west, that was impossible.

Accordingly, the young countess showed up at the Rose Noire in a magnificent black satin gown embroidered in a dazzling pattern of jet beads swirling around the neck and down the tight-fitting bodice, fanning out in a black sunburst at the right hip. The skirt of the gown was draped close to the body, making normal walking a bit difficult. But walking was not the purpose.

While the countess was perched on the rickety chair in her dressing room, squinting a little as she applied kohl to her eyelids to create Cleopatra eyes, her officer-friend knocked at the door, bearing a dozen roses and a bottle of Moët for a private celebration after the show.

"How sweet of you," smiled the countess. "Well, what do you think? Do I look the part?"

"Sensational. By tomorrow evening all Petersburg will want to see you," he lied gallantly, kissing her hand.

"I hope so," murmured Tasha, "although I have a feeling my career might be a short one." If Auntie ever found out, it certainly would be, she thought, although she didn't tell him that.

When her friend departed to go take his seat, Tasha smiled as she looked at the roses, lovely pink ones, still dewy, looking somewhat out of place in this dingy little dressing room where everything was covered with dust or broken. Well, she thought, it was a real dressing room in a real nightclub. If she wanted beauty she could have stayed home at the Malyshev mansion. This was different. This was life.

Adding more kohl to her eyelids and dabbing her cheeks with an extra bit of rouge, the countess then pulled the neckline of her gown a little lower until it risked revealing more than was decently permissible. Satisfied, Tatiana Sergeevna stroked the magnificent double strand of pearls that reached below her waist and posed briefly before her cracked mirror to survey the general effect. Marvelous. She was ready.

In the dark and smoke-filled room where Tasha was to sing, there was a mixed group that particular evening, mostly middle-ranking embassy staff from the French and British embassies and a few stray Americans. The men applauded cheerfully as the chanteuse approached her post by the piano where a very pink spotlight bathed her in soft rosy hues that did Tasha's sophisticated makeup a disservice.

Amid the sound of glasses clinking and bottles rattling, Tatiana Sergeevna began her first offering, something called "Bébé d'Amour," which had the effect of drawing delighted applause from the French contingent.

Meeting with success, Tasha launched into her second number with a great deal of verve. Starting to make the rounds of the tables as the manager had suggested, she looked into the eyes of the customers as she

dwelt on all the more unpleasant aspects of undying love, flirting shamelessly with young and old.

As the chanteuse lingered at his table, one young man nearly dropped
his drink. He thought he recognized her under the layers of paint. Jesus!
It couldn't be. Was he insane?

Billy Whitmore had been drinking with friends when they suggested
a visit to the Rose Noire, and he had gone along to pick up any useful
gossip that could be gleaned from them. The last thing in the world
he expected was to see one of Princess Anya's relatives working there in
black satin and too much makeup. Had she run away? My God! If Anya
ever knew about this she'd die of embarrassment, he thought with amusement. But, damn, this minx was an adventurous little trollop. What she
lacked in decorum she more than made up for in sheer nerve. And she
had money too.

Thinking about all the possible misfortunes that could await a young
girl in murky St. Petersburg nightclubs, Billy decided the young countess
needed a protector to escort her home and promptly made his way to her
dressing room after her act to offer his services.

Knocking politely on the door, Billy was surprised to hear a man's
voice inside. Undaunted, he knocked again, this time having the door
opened by some fellow in uniform who told him to get lost.

"Sorry," he replied. "I'm a friend of the young lady and she's going
home with me or I'm calling the police and having you arrested for im-
pairing the morals of a minor."

Startled by that idea, the officer, a fine-looking blond fellow with a
captain's insignia, turned to "Tonya" and demanded, "Do you know him?"

Turning white at the sight of Adam's brother standing there and
sounding so fraternal, Tasha nodded in shock and stared at Billy, terrified
by her rapid discovery. He would reveal her secret, she thought. She was
lost.

"I'd leave if I were you," said Billy to the officer. "Morals charges are
always so messy. Bad for the career."

Glaring at the intruder who spoke Russian with a strange accent, the
blond captain kissed Tatiana Sergeevna's little hand and departed without so much as a glance at her visitor.

"Will you tell my family?" demanded Tasha, white with fear as Billy
smiled at her, admiring her beautiful, overly made-up face and pretty figure.

"Not if you don't do this again," he said. "Get your things. We're
leaving this rattrap."

"Where are we going?

"He smiled at the girl. "That's entirely up to you. Your choice. You can go straight home. You can come with me for a drive along the Neva. Or," he hesitated, "you can come home with me."

For the first time it occurred to Tatiana Sergeevna that if Adam Mikhailovich was a paragon of virtue, it was not an affliction that ran in his family. This shorter, rosier, younger brother was a man she might be able to deal with, a man after her own heart.

Looking boldly at Billy as he smiled at her low neckline, Tasha tilted her pretty head to the side and declared she was terribly fond of midnight drives along the Neva.

"Anything your heart desires," he murmured, opening the door for her.

As the young countess left the nightclub, not without some harsh words from the owner, she got into Billy's motorcar and nestled against him as he started off in the direction of the Neva quays, ending up just before dawn in front of the Malyshev mansion on the Moika Canal.

"Will you be able to get in?" asked Billy.

"Of course. I've been bribing the servants."

"I should have known."

"Billy," she said softly, brushing his cheek with her lips, "will you tell?"

He smiled. "What do you think?"

"I think you're as bad as I am," she smiled back. "I think we're destined to be friends."

He certainly hoped so.

When Adam was finally able to return home from his enforced vacation in Copenhagen, he, Anya and the Malyshevs were surprised to see the effects of war upon the Russian capital. Suddenly there were no more strikes or even threats of strikes. Workingmen were proclaiming their love for the tsar and the need to crush the Germans before they could do any more harm. Soldiers parading down the Nevsky on their way to the train stations seemed prepared to give their all for Nicholas II and Holy Russia.

The streets were decked out with tricolored bunting in honor of the Allies—French and British colors were the same as Russia's own. To a casual observer it looked splendid, the very picture of a nation ready to win.

Arriving at the Sviridov mansion after a stop at Ksenia's home to pick up their delighted son, Anya and her husband were relieved to find Prince Sandro in residence. They had feared for his safety in Europe. Sandro too had come home via an unusual route—Italy to Romania on the *Orient Express*, and from Constanza to Yalta by ship, entraining at Yalta for St. Petersburg. Now he was bemoaning the evil fate that had nearly killed

Anya and her husband and was plunging his country into a stupid, badly planned war that was going to ruin them all.

Princess Anya was startled to hear Sandro express these defeatist sentiments. She was afraid Grand-père might get himself arrested if he went on like this in public!

Adam, weak as he was from his ordeal, was curious to listen to the old man. Sandro was a tyrant but no fool. His chief purpose in life was to see to his own amusement, and he naturally detested anything that interfered with that goal. In addition, he knew anybody who counted in Russia and in Europe, so his sources of information were usually quite good. If *he* had no faith in the great Russian victory everyone else was expecting, then Adam wanted to hear his reasons.

Speaking to his granddaughter's husband in Anya's sitting room, Sandro declared that the whole disgusting charade was the government's fault. "The tsar is weak as water to have given in to these ridiculous pan-Slav agitators. Nickolasha, our commander-in-chief, has been egging him on for years, spouting nonsense about Russia's duty toward her Slavic brothers in the Balkans. Duty indeed! We ought to have turned our back on those bandits and parasites years ago. They had no business murdering Austrian archdukes and expecting us to help them out. It's insane!"

"Then you don't think Russia's ready for this kind of war."

"My dear young man, Russia's not ready for any kind of war. The Europeans ought to have been left to cut each others' throats without our help. All this will do is accelerate our own disintegration while allowing England and France to get stronger at our expense. To them, we've always been nothing more than fodder for their cannons. It would be in our own best interests to return their feelings."

The younger man listened respectfully as Sandro spoke, silently agreeing with him. Very few people were bold enough to express such negative opinions at this moment, with Gregory Efimovich Rasputin the one exception Adam had heard about, via Natalya's letters to Anya while they were in Copenhagen.

"I've had a remarkably easy life," continued Sandro, "but I'm afraid for you younger people, especially my daughter and granddaughters. I'd hate to see them adrift in a Russia torn apart by war and devastation."

"Whatever happens, you don't have to worry about Anya and our son," Adam assured him. "I'll take care of them."

Sandro smiled as he poured a glass of sherry and handed one to Adam. "I don't worry about that," he replied. "I've come to trust you. Even Ksenia trusts you, and that's a great honor because my daughter is very astute in sizing up people. She has faith in almost no one, and unfortunately, she's generally right. The thing that does worry me is the real possibility of a

German victory, followed by an uprising that will make 1905 look like child's play."

Adam was so startled to hear the prince say it, he looked shocked.

"You think I'm an alarmist?" demanded the old man.

"I don't know, sir. You were in Europe when the war broke out and you've had a better chance to see the effect of the Germans' techniques."

"They're superb," replied Sandro. "They came close enough to Paris to scare the French into shipping their government off to Bordeaux. If our brave Russian troops hadn't been allowed to get themselves slaughtered at Tannenberg on behalf of our Gallic allies, the Germans would have had no problem taking the city. As it was, they were forced to rush several regiments east to deal with our advance into Prussia, and the French are bragging about their great victory on the Marne. It's ironic, isn't it?"

"You sound cynical, sir."

"I am. Our commander-in-chief is so busy trying to be a great Allied general, he's wasting Russian blood on the grand scale in order to save France. They ought to remember 1812 and allow the Europeans the privilege of bleeding each other so badly none of them will be in a position to do us much damage. We have our own problems to worry about."

At the mention of 1812, Adam smiled. The Sviridovs regarded the date with something bordering on mysticism, for in 1812 at the battle of Borodino, Prince Denis Borisovich Sviridov became a hero by leading a splendid if foolhardy charge against a French gun emplacement, ending up in so many pieces it was impossible to identify the body afterward. His wife, the beautiful, spoiled, willful Zenaida Nicolaievna astonished everyone who knew her by remaining in Moscow long enough to be the last Russian lady to flee the city only hours before the enemy entered, after setting fire to her mansion herself, in keeping with the scorched-earth policy decreed by Tsar Alexander.

Lovely Zenaida, raised by French governesses, clothed in French fashions, a francophile to the tips of her fingers, became more Russian than the tsar as Napoleon approached. Loading twenty carts with the pick of the family's art collection, Zenaida added to the flames what she couldn't take with her, rather than have even a minor masterpiece remain as booty for the French. And then with her three small sons, Princess Sviridova made a dangerous, painful, exhausting journey across Russia to the safety of her estate in the center of the country, not having lost a single major painting or small prince to the enemy on the way.

It was a feat never surpassed by any other member of the family, and in time, Zenaida's exploit became the subject of a poem by Pushkin, a painting by Repin, and an object lesson in courage for three generations of her descendants. Those paintings now hung on the walls of the Sviridov mansion in St. Petersburg, the nucleus of a collection that had increased in size from generation to generation until it was equal in value to the best private collections anywhere—which brought something else to mind.

"Your diplomatic status could be useful to the family," said Sandro, regarding the young man carefully.

"How, sir?" asked Adam, putting down his glass.

"I want to ship the best of our paintings and smaller artifacts to Sweden," replied the prince. "If the kaiser's troops ever reach this city, it would kill me to watch some fat boche take possession of your son's inheritance. Remember," he added grimly, "they burned the library of Louvain University when they stormed through Belgium—a neutral country! That's the respect those Huns have for law and learning."

True. It wasn't a comforting thought. And the conduct of the German troops in Belgium, even allowing for the exaggeration of Allied propaganda, wasn't anything a man would wish his family to experience. If worse came to worst, the Sviridovs themselves might need to look for a safe refuge in the closest neutral country. A cache of valuables could make things easy for them while they waited out the storm.

Looking Prince Sandro squarely in the eye, Adam replied, "I'll do everything I can to protect our family, through diplomatic channels or in spite of them," he added with a smile.

Sandro nodded. Adam Mikhailovich had been a good choice after all. That granddaughter of his had really been clever.

In the present circumstances, it was a comforting thought. If only the poor fellow were in better health. After his terrible experience in Berlin, he looked so ill the prince was beginning to worry about him.

He needed him in good shape for his plans.

To Anya's dismay, Adam's recovery seemed to be taking much longer than she had hoped. With all the activity in the capital, he chafed at the restraints placed upon him by his doctor and felt thoroughly useless. Although most of the bandages had been removed, his left eye was still covered and the prognosis wasn't good.

On top of everything else, to Adam's intense humiliation, his shaved head made him look like a Siberian convict while the regrowth was a dark and stubbly mess. Princess Anya tried hard to be tactful about the whole thing, but she was secretly amused that her husband had at least one small vanity. She had never suspected it before and found it rather endearing.

The possible loss of the sight in his left eye, however, was nothing to joke about at all. It worried the princess dreadfully.

With the excitement of the war now a bit subdued by the ghastly

losses at Tannenberg and the Masurian lakes and the posting of long casualty lists in the city, the government was trying hard to keep up people's
spirits. Toward that end the artists of the imperial theatres were pressed
into service entertaining the troops. The prima ballerinas of the Maryinsky
and the Bolshoi brought their art to the wounded during special benefit
performances the length of the front and in all the empire's great cities.

Reading about Madame Kashina's pledge to put together a program
of five performances in St. Petersburg, Moscow, Kiev, Warsaw and Tiflis,
Prince Sandro had to smile. Zenaida was always a fierce little competitor,
never more so than when she suspected another ballerina might get the
jump on her. If artists were now going to be patriotic, nobody would be
more patriotic than Kashina.

Truthfully, time had softened Sandro a bit in regard to Zenaida's
shameless infidelity, and he rather missed her, although he was too proud
to relent. Besides, she now had Constantine Andreevich, and if she were
running true to form, Zenaida would regard her Romanov connection as
too good to be lightly thrown away. A grand duke was the ultimate prize
for a woman of her type.

Sandro's problem was that he adored women of her type, a minor
flaw in an otherwise discerning character.

While Russia and her European allies were throwing themselves into the
war effort with a vengeance, there were others on the fringes of the war
who were eager to make some sort of contribution, inspired by a need for
action or simply by the need to find out what was happening. Billy Whitmore was one. He had a plan that would fulfill both objectives without
sacrificing American neutrality in the slightest. In fact, it could only be
looked upon as altruism of the highest sort, a wonderful cover for intelligence gathering.

Witnessing the outpouring of Russian patriotism at the declaration
of war against the Germans, Billy had also been present for the sack of the
German Embassy on St. Isaac's Square, an event that left him with a
healthy respect for what mob violence could do. Seeing the beautiful building looted by a vengeful mob that raced from cellar to attic, throwing
priceless *objets d'art* out second-floor windows, the young American decided it would be in the best interests of his government to demonstrate a
humanitarian concern for the Russian people in their time of national trial. Nobody could fault them for this, and the benefits would far outweigh
any amount of money invested in it.

Back home, people were quite keen on goodwill for the Allies any-

way—as long as America wasn't sending troops to them. A little war relief effort here could only increase American prestige among their hosts
and contribute to Billy's own standing among his colleagues in the diplomatic colony. And with Adam's connections, the Amer-Russian War Relief Agency could turn out to be his passport to an ambassadorship some
day—if all went well.

Paying a call on his brother in the Sviridov mansion, Billy expressed
appropriate concern over his brush with death at the hands of the Huns
and spoke at length about the spirit of support for the Allies now prevailing at the embassy—with all due diplomatic restraint, naturally.

But, he declared, the ambassador was already quite willing to give
him the go-ahead for the creation of an American-Russian relief effort
that would aid the wounded and provide help for the war-distressed in the
cities, much like the Red Cross. In fact, he said proudly, his idea had
support from a few senators whose constituencies were heavily Slavic.

"Who would run the agency?" demanded Adam, recalling his brother's natural disinclination for hard work.

"The two of us, with additional help from a mostly Russian team of
doctors and nurses, relief workers, secretaries and general staff."

"Who are your Russian contacts? Anybody close to the imperial
family?"

"The Dowager Empress, Maria Feodorovna, has expressed her desire
to help us as a patron. And Princess Ksenia just agreed to let us set up
headquarters in a property of hers on Liteiny Prospect. How's that for Russian contacts?"

"Very impressive," replied Adam. "But as soon as I'm able, I intend
to try to join the Russian Air Force."

That idea came to nothing when Prince Sviridov was thoroughly rejected by the doctors at the recruiting station who told him bluntly that
the vision in his left eye was so completely impaired, he would get himself
killed before he ever got off the ground.

To Anya's relief, the prince decided he would take Billy up on his
relief effort, and he set to work recruiting workers for all phases of the
operation, from doctors to kitchen staff.

Within a month, the first hospital was set up—a small sixteen-bed
affair—and after a luncheon during which the premises were blessed by a
priest in the presence of two grand duchesses who were honorary patrons,
the first detachment of wounded arrived. The Amer-Russian War Relief
Agency was on its way.

Princess Anya, now in the last few months of a difficult pregnancy,
was glad to see Adam starting to take an interest in the agency. As a neu-

tral, he couldn't share in the fighting, but as Prince Sviridov it was unthinkable for him to do nothing while Russia bled on European battlefields. The war relief agency was the perfect solution.

His fame as the hero of the St. Petersburg-to-Moscow air race did much to attract popular support, and the story of the young couple's tumultuous exit from Berlin—told and retold by Billy—did much to convince Russians that even if the prince was prevented from fighting Germans one way, he was dedicated to the struggle against them in another. And if Billy had his way, the relief agency would become as much a symbol of the fight against the Huns as the icon of St. Nicholas the Miracle Worker, under whose banner the Russian Army marched off to war.

With the wartime repudiation of all things German and the express desire of the tsar to wage the war as a holy crusade, two long-established Russian institutions had gone by the wayside. The name of the empire's capital had been russified to Petrograd, the Slavic version of Petersburg, and the sale of alcohol had been forbidden for the duration of the war, an extremely unpopular move in a nation of thirsty souls.

One beloved tradition that was still alive was the ballet, and it appeared to be in lively form. One gala after the other was staged to help the wounded, their families, refugees from the Baltic provinces or any other group in need of support.

Billy Whitmore was so entranced by the idea of a benefit on behalf of the Amer-Russian War Relief Agency, he entered into negotiations with several leading ballerinas, but got nowhere until he covered Madame Kashina's dressing room with extremely expensive flowers and sent her a note requesting an interview, stressing his diplomatic connections and his relationship with the Sviridovs. Suddenly Kashina had time to talk.

With her customary perception, the dainty ballerina dismissed this blond chatterbox as all talk and no substance, but she was amused by his name-dropping. And by the fact that he was apparently unaware of her liaison with Sandro. How could he not know? she wondered. All Europe knew. However, his denseness might be the vehicle she had been waiting for to strike back at the high-handed family who had caused her such intense humiliation. She wasn't going to let the opportunity pass her by. Countess Lisa was dead and out of her way for good, but Sandro had other descendants who could pay for that episode with Vinogradov and those damned photographers.

Kashina was beautiful, sensual and vindictive. It was her nature. And she didn't believe in repressing a bit of it.

♦   ♦   ♦

Several days later in Anya's blue and white boudoir in the Sviridov mansion, Billy's meeting with the ballerina was having unfortunate repercussions. Princess Anya was heart and soul for anything that would help the Russian war effort and her husband's prestige, but she drew the line at having anything to do with "that woman," as she called Madame Kashina.

Any woman who had ensnared Sandro, cast him aside to cavort with a lowborn Moscow millionaire and then tossed *him* aside for a grand duke who had scandalized the imperial family by abandoning his wife and children for her was not the sort of woman Anya cared to have Adam associating with. Especially not now, when Anya was enormously pregnant and waddling around like a gourd on two stalks.

In fact, thought the young princess, it was a pity Adam's beautiful hair was growing back so nicely right now. It would have made her feel better if he were going to meet the little man-eater looking like a recently released convict. Kashina seemed to be interested only in good-looking men. Perhaps the scar over his left eye would put her off.

Knowing how his wife felt about Billy's faux pas, the prince tried to get her into a better disposition, but he was having a difficult time. Princess Anya was bitterly opposed to the idea of having Kashina give a benefit for the agency, and that was all there was to it.

"Are you certain you don't want to accompany me into the lion's den?" he teased. "This is your last chance."

"Sorry, darling," she replied. "I don't feel well enough to sit through a luncheon with that woman. You and Billy will have to deal with her by yourselves." There was a stern glint in her lovely blue eyes.

"I hear she devours men for breakfast."

"Then she ought to be sated by the time she encounters you, although in an emergency, I give you permission to feed your brother to her."

"He'd love that," smiled Adam. "He has an eye for dainty little things like Kashina."

"Yes," nodded the princess, "and absolutely no discernment."

She was angry and not about to yield. Zenaida Kashina was *persona non grata* in the Sviridov family, and if Billy Whitmore was too stupid to realize it, Adam wasn't. He had no business going ahead with Billy's plan. What would Grand-père think? It was dreadfully gauche.

Although Prince Adam knew the story about Kashina's parting with Sandro, his brother didn't—until Adam told him. But then it was too late to do anything about it because Kashina had already given them her promise to perform. And she was one of the brightest stars of the Maryinsky. If they suddenly withdrew their offer, it would be an embarrassment for the agency and an insult to Kashina, a fine mess either way.

"If you go through with this," declared Princess Anya, "I will be absent from the performance and so will Ksenia."

Oh Lord, thought Adam. Another scandal.

"Anyushka," he said, kissing her neck, "if your Grand-père forgives me for my brother's bad judgment, will you consent to attend the benefit? It would be a disaster if you weren't there."

Anya turned to him and put her nose in the air. "If Grand-père were to display any forgiveness for that, yes. But under no other circumstances."

He smiled. It wasn't much of a concession, but it was better than nothing. And Sandro *had* been in love with Kashina, so he was apt to be more understanding than his granddaughter.

At least, that was what Adam was praying for.

Kissing his wife as he departed for his luncheon appointment with Kashina, the prince was almost out the door when the butler stopped him, explaining that a message had just arrived from Mr. Whitmore.

As Adam opened it in surprise, he had bad news. Because of an emergency meeting with an official in the Foreign Ministry, Billy was unable to attend the luncheon, so now it fell to Prince Adam to wine and dine the lady; he must be careful to be gracious and attentive so she wouldn't back out of her agreement. The Amer-Russian War Relief Agency needed the benefit.

"Damn," muttered Adam as he departed for the Medved restaurant, crumpling the note and sending it flying. Billy was the one responsible for this in the first place. Adam had only agreed to this luncheon to see if there was any way Kashina might not be able to fulfill her promise—and solve his problems with Anya. Now he had to deal with the prima donna himself, and he really didn't look forward to it.

Arriving at the restaurant, one of Petrograd's liveliest, Adam spoke to the headwaiter, received a discreet nod of the head and a smile and was ushered into a private dining room on the second floor where the table had been carefully set with fine linen, crystal, silver and a charming bouquet of Crimean blossoms, a touch that belied the late October snow flurries outside the tall windows. Glancing nervously in the mirror as he waited for Kashina, Adam wished he had been able to invite her to luncheon at home.

To his surprise, Madame Kashina didn't keep him waiting. He had been there less than two minutes when the door opened and in she walked, a tiny beauty in soft, silvery chinchilla, her cheeks glowing from the cold, her large, velvety brown eyes regarding him playfully from beneath the fur of her hat. As Adam rose to greet her, he was struck by her overwhelming femininity.

"*Enchanté*, Madame," he murmured, kissing her small hand. "It was most gracious of you to meet me."

Kashina glanced around the room and smiled with amusement. "I thought there were going to be two of you," she replied.

"My brother asks you to forgive him. He was detained by the foreign minister." Or at least by one of his minions.

That didn't bother Kashina; Prince Sviridov was quite charming. In fact, he had the natural grace of an athlete, she thought. As a dancer, she had always admired men who moved well. It was a rare trait, she found, and underestimated as a weapon of seduction. Kashina herself moved like a goddess—in furs, silks, or nothing at all.

As the waiter glided around discreetly, opening champagne, serving the lobster—Kashina's favorite dish—before disappearing through the heavily carved oak door, Adam had a chance to study his guest at close range under the guise of making small talk. She was delicately beautiful, with large dark eyes, fine features and a small, curvaceous figure with a tiny waist. It was a measure of distinction in Petrograd society to possess one nearly as small as Kashina's. Her gray tailored wool suit with black soutache trim was a creation of Redfern in Paris, and her ropes of pearls were a present from Grand Duke Constantine Andreevich, her official, though not legal, consort.

"Are there any problems with the proposed gala?" asked Adam, hoping to hear of some reason why it couldn't possibly take place as planned.

"Actually," said the ballerina, "it does come at a bad time for me."

"Oh?" inquired the prince, looking concerned. "Anything that would prevent you from appearing? Is it that serious?" He was hoping so.

Kashina smiled sweetly. She could imagine the scene at the Sviridov mansion when this American had told his wife what his brother had done. She wondered if Sandro had been told.

"Oh, nothing that bad, merely a matter of scheduling. On that particular evening I will have just returned from an engagement in Kiev. Under the circumstances, a full-length ballet will be out of the question. However," continued Kashina, "it doesn't mean we can't stage another sort of program, with a variety of artists. That's become quite popular at these kinds of affairs. I'm sure I could bring in several dancers. That way, the burden won't be on me and I can give you my best."

"Why, that would be most gracious, Madame. We would be in your debt."

And it would be much less of a struggle to get the Sviridovs to accept that—or at least Adam hoped so.

Kashina smiled. "I would like to do the pas de deux from *Paquita.* Nicholas Legat can partner me."

"Wonderful."

"Have you seen it?" she inquired, caressing him with her eyes.

"Unfortunately not," replied Adam, looking into those huge velvet orbs, so tender and predatory at the same time, a marvelous cross between the gentleness of a doe and the fierceness of a jungle cat.

"Then you must come to the Maryinsky this week and see me dance. I'm scheduled to perform *Esmeralda,* my favorite role, my signature. I'm a darling little gypsy who has her heart broken by a heartless aristocrat. Everyone weeps when I die, including me. It's marvelous," laughed the ballerina. "I adore it."

Watching the prince's reflection in the mirrors of the small dining room, Kashina noticed he was observing her discreetly in the same way, his dark eyes showing an interest his face refused to reveal. Magnificent eyes, she thought, dark and mysterious as those of an Arab or an Armenian. Not like that blond and blue-eyed brother of his who was nothing in comparison.

Then again, she thought, the Sviridovs had let him marry their precious little princess. That said a great deal. Kashina wondered if fidelity was one of his strong points.

"I'd like very much to see you dance *Esmeralda,*" said the prince. "But my wife isn't feeling well, so we haven't been able to go to the theatre as often as we used to."

"Ah?" inquired Kashina. "Is it anything serious?"

"Yes," he smiled. "Princess Sviridova is expecting our second child. She's been having problems with the pregnancy, so her doctors have ordered her to rest as much as possible."

"And you don't like to go out without her," she pouted.

Adam's beautiful dark eyes picked up the slight hint of annoyance in Kashina's expression as the ballerina smiled to mask her feelings.

"My wife is a very young woman who underwent an enormous amount of tension during the early stages of her pregnancy," he said softly. "It's important to me to make her as comfortable as possible right now. It would be quite unfair to you if you were kind enough to send us tickets for *Esmeralda* only to have us miss the performance."

Kashina smiled again, but this time her eyes were gleaming as she looked deep into Adam's—he wasn't uninterested, merely cautious. "Then perhaps your brother would enjoy seeing *Esmeralda.*"

"It would be the highlight of the season for him," Adam quickly replied. "He once told me he chose his box at the Maryinsky expressly because it gave him the best possible view of Kashina when she took her curtain calls. It was Billy who insisted we ask you to honor us with your presence at our gala."

Looking him in the eye, the ballerina laughed with amusement, enjoying the compliment, which she suspected was untrue, and liking the prince for thinking of it.

Reaching for his hand across the table, the beautiful brown-eyed creature boldly turned it over to look at his palm as if she were a girl from Novaya Derevnaya.

"Do you tell fortunes, Madame?" Adam smiled, surprised at how much he enjoyed Kashina's soft, electric caress.

"Yes," she replied. "My grandmother was a gypsy. All the women in our family have the gift."

"Do I have an interesting future?" he inquired with a smile, his eyes on the woman's lovely face.

"Oh yes," murmured Kashina, stroking one of the lines in his hand from top to bottom, arousing him with the light warmth of her touch. "I see a long lifeline, Prince. And here," she smiled, "is your loveline."

"Ah."

"Three cross markings. Three great loves."

Adam's eyes met Kashina's, looking back at him with the fire of a jungle cat.

"I've been in love twice in my life," he answered. "I think I've used up my allotted share of good fortune."

Kashina's slim fingers suddenly entwined around his, then released him just as quickly.

"Three is what fate allows you, Prince," she said meaningfully. "Don't dismiss it so easily."

His eyes on Kashina, Adam gently took her hand and kissed it.

"Thank you for the prophecy, Madame," he murmured. "Only a fool would dismiss the promise of love."

But, he thought as he held her pretty little hand, breathing in the rich, heady scent of her perfume, only a fool would rush blindly toward an uncertain new love when he had a treasure at home. Anya was real life; Kashina was a dream, a beautiful bright dream composed of champagne, perfume—a hundred characters impersonated by a beauty who had to recreate herself daily in the reflection of a thousand pairs of eyes beyond the footlights. A gorgeous, glittering myth with brown velvet eyes and the touch of an angel.

"I promise to see your Esmeralda one day," said Adam as the ballerina gently slipped her hand into his. "I'll look forward to it."

The long black lashes flickered slightly as the ballerina replied softly, "So will I."

Warsaw

While Russia went to war to protect her Slavic brethren, Monsieur Timofey Mossolov, né Oleg Ivanov, was making his own contribution to the war effort in the Polish city where he—or rather his staff—worked day and night to keep the army's morale high. With the casualty rates as appalling as they were, he started a Victors' Club at his poshest house, entitling a ten-time client to an evening on the house. It sounded patriotic, the officers were pleased and very few of them ever collected, which made Oleg happy. Word of it spread up and down the front, and it became the fashion to frequent Oleg's establishment, everyone hoping to be the one to cheat fate and collect his reward. At least it gave them a diversion, he piously maintained as the money poured in.

"You know, Wanda," he declared one day as they sat in his office going over accounts, "you were dead right when you suggested we'd make our fortunes here. If this war goes on for a few more months, we could almost retire on the profits."

That gratified Wanda, but then she presented her partner with an idea that ruined the whole mood.

"Oleg, *lubovnik*," she purred, looking at him with soft eyes over the large black ledger, "only one thing could make things even better than they are right now."

"What's that?" he asked, expecting something businesslike, alarmed by that seductive note in her voice. He hated that. It was a typical bourgeois form of entrapment Wanda used to nauseating excess, a pretentious device better suited to a bedroom farce than to business matters. It always meant trouble.

"Marry me," she whispered, slipping her plump white arms around his neck as she stood over him, enveloping him with the scent of roses, her favorite fragrance. "Then we can be partners in every sense of the word."

He looked at her coldly, his skin crawling as he remembered that same tone used one afternoon by that monster, Katia Petrovna, who had returned in the person of this Polish whore. His stomach rebelled at the idea. She was haunting him.

That did it. Oleg stood up abruptly and pushed Wanda aside, leaving her alone with the scent of roses mingling with the odor of his still-smoldering cigar in the ashtray.

What the hell was the matter with him? she wondered, sitting down with a discontented thud on the seat he had just vacated, casting an eye over the ledger. Everything was in tip-top shape. Their three houses were taking in more clients than they could handle. This elegant place catered to the officer class, the smaller brick house five blocks away took in minor bureaucrats and the meat rack near the railway station had one of the highest hourly turnovers in the city, dedicated as it was to the needs of the common man. Settling in Warsaw had provided this damned Russian with the opportunity for making more money than all the bank robberies he had committed while he was running around playing revolutionary. Didn't he realize it? she wondered. And didn't he ever stop to think of the part she'd played in his success? The bastard! She regarded marriage as a consolidation of their partnership. What was the matter with the man? Wanda couldn't answer that question, although she knew there was something very peculiar about him.

He had always been an odd duck, she reflected, picking up Koshka. He had always hated Koshka, a sure sign of bad character. Any man who could hate such a lovely little animal was inherently vicious, she decided. But now things were past mere hatred of the cat. Oleg actually seemed to look at *her* with such evil in his light-blue eyes that the Polish girl was sometimes afraid of him, especially when he began accusing her of betraying him with people whose names she didn't even recognize—some Russians he knew, apparently. Whoever Pavel and Dimitri were was a mystery to her. Same thing as far as Anna Nicolaievna went. Or the one he called the "glass-eyed monster." At first, whenever Oleg got going on these fantasies of his, Wanda had tried to reason with him. Then when that didn't work, she'd begun ignoring him—even when he started threatening her. She'd had other things to worry about.

But lately the threats had begun to get nastier and his crazy periods longer. Shuddering as she recalled the last time, the night he'd got drunk and held a knife to her throat, Wanda found herself wishing she had never teamed up with this wild Russian. If she wasn't careful, he might just carry through with his insane threats one night and end her promising career as one of Warsaw's most famous madams.

The thing that held her to him despite all the uneasy feelings was the money, piles of it. With Oleg, Wanda had a fancy white automobile just like the one driven by one of Warsaw's most elegant aristocrats, several armoires crammed with Paris gowns, real jewelry and a personal maid. It was the glue that cemented their partnership. It was worth putting up

with Oleg to make certain she kept it. Bad-tempered, mad or merely can-
tankerous, the Russian had a talent for the details of their trade that Wanda
preferred to delegate. While he attended to the ledgers and ordered supplies, she preened in the salon, enjoying her pretty blonde reflection in
the tall gilded mirrors.

Keeping Oleg, she was assured of continuing the life she had gotten
used to. Without him she might even have to take on someone worse.
That thought always prevented her from doing anything too final.

But the idea was always in the back of Wanda's mind, like a secret
escape hatch.

24

Despite Gigi's attempt to take comfort in the presence of his second son, Kolya, who was a reassuring replica of himself, he could never put the thought of little Nicky's resemblance to Rasputin's daughter out of his mind entirely. He loathed the child and showed it more and more. It reached the point where his son's nursemaid was afraid to let the child cross Count Grekov's path.

Late one afternoon in November, when Natalya was expected home for tea after spending the day at Tsarskoye, Sonia the nursemaid was preparing her two small charges for their mother's daily visit when she was startled to see the master appear in the door of the nursery, alone.

Knowing it meant trouble for Nicky, the girl signaled for him to come to her, hoping to keep him out of his father's way. Instead, the little boy rushed to greet Gigi, expecting to see Natalya behind him. It was a mistake. Coldly ignoring the small blond child, the count pushed him away as he went to pick up Kolya, the baby.

"Papa!" Nicky cried.

"Come here!" hissed the nursemaid, trying to prevent him from going near the count. "Don't bother your Papa."

"Papa, pick *me* up, not Kolya," Nicky wailed, tugging at his jacket.

"Get away from me," replied the count, seizing him by the collar of his little sailor suit. "Never do that again."

As the flustered Sonia rushed to take away the offender, Nicky did the worst possible thing. He threw his arms around Gigi and began wailing, begging for his father's attention.

Red with anger, the count grabbed the small child by the shoulders, shook him savagely and slapped him so hard he knocked him to the floor. To Sonia's horror, as the little boy lay wailing on the carpet, Count Grekov kicked him aside as if he were a troublesome stray dog, cursing him in language the girl had never in her life heard from this gentleman.

Ashen as he realized what he had done, Gigi stared at the screaming

277

child, doubled up in pain on the carpet, and started to say something to Sonia, who was now on her knees on the floor, trying to protect Nicky from his father's anger. Unable to find words, he simply turned and left, ashamed at what he had done and wondering at the same time how he had ever managed to restrain himself for so long.

My God, he thought, fleeing the screams in the nursery, I almost killed the little bastard. If that girl hadn't been there, I probably would have. It was a thought that unnerved him. It set him on the same level as a drunken slum dweller and made him doubt his sanity. He really had wanted to kill the brat. All his education and good breeding had meant absolutely nothing compared with his hatred for that two-year-old. It was humiliating. And frightening too.

This is what marriage to that lunatic had done to him, he reflected bitterly as he stood shaken in the hallway, unable to understand what had possessed him. And as he did, Gigi wondered how long it would be before he did the same to Natalya.

Volodya doesn't know how lucky he is, thought the count. Fighting the Germans was nothing compared with putting up with his ridiculous and unfaithful wife. He almost envied Volodya. Putting his life on the line to do battle with the boches was nothing compared with risking one's sanity in dealing with a woman who was so out of touch with reality she didn't even understand how much she was hated by her own husband.

And how much he wanted to murder her damned bastard brat.

In Petrograd salons, the child's resemblance to Rasputin's daughter was causing a great deal of malicious gossip, an item which did not escape the ears of Princess Anya, who was appalled at the possibility. Everyone knew how the influence of the Rasputin clique had helped Natalya get the divorce from Volodya to marry Gigi when she was pregnant with his child. But now it seemed as if Gigi had been an innocent dupe, and was not in fact the father.

People who disliked the tsaritsa were only too eager to vent their spleen on those closest to her, and since Natalya's rise to the rank of lady-in-waiting, she was a good choice, all the more so since she was an almost daily visitor to Rasputin's apartment—along with half a dozen other regulars.

One afternoon shortly before Christmas 1914, Natalya brought her son to visit Anya. As she, Anya and Ksenia had tea in the glassed-in conservatory while the boys played under the watchful eyes of their nursemaids, Natalya broke down and began to sob, startling her friends.

"He's so hateful," she wailed. "When I married him, I thought he was a good man who would be a wonderful father for my second Nicky, but he's a cruel, wicked man with no heart and no regard for religion!"

Startled by the suddenness of the outburst, it took the ladies a few seconds to realize Natalya was talking about her husband, a man of generally mild disposition.

"Natalya," asked Anya, "how did you know you were going to have a second Nicky before you married Gigi?"

Dabbing her eyes with a lace-trimmed handkerchief, the countess sniffed and declared tremulously, "Because Gregory Efimovich told me I would."

Princess Sviridova and her aunt exchanged glances.

"Did Gregory Efimovich do anything to ensure that you would?" demanded Ksenia.

"Yes. He prayed with me in front of the holy icons and told me God would give me a child to replace the one I lost. He said I ought to marry Gigi because he would be a good father for my son, but he was wrong. Gigi is becoming a beast. Yesterday he hit Nicky again and called me dreadful names, things so vulgar I couldn't even repeat them."

In the last stages of pregnancy, Princess Anya was horrified. The thought of Gigi beating the little boy was so distressing, it brought tears to her eyes. Gigi, of all people!

"I don't know what to do," sobbed Natalya. "My parents told me they would cut me off without a kopek if I disgraced them with another divorce, and Gigi's mother told him the same. We hate each other, he hates my poor Nicky and we're forced to live together in a dreadful situation, full of hatred and anger."

"Why don't you stop frequenting Gregory Efimovich?" Anya gently suggested. "I think that would help things."

At the mere idea of doing without her mentor, Natalya shook her head in fright. "No," she said. "I couldn't. He is everything to me. You don't understand."

Princess Ksenia hinted, rather unkindly, that perhaps Gigi understood only too well.

"No, he understands nothing," replied the countess. "He accuses me of such vile things, it would take your breath away. But he makes no effort to comprehend what Gregory Efimovich is trying to do for all of us, for Russia."

"I'd say Gregory Efimovich is doing his best to line his pockets," declared Princess Ksenia, unimpressed.

At that, Countess Grekova got up from the sofa, turned on her heel and left the salon, calling for her maid to get her son ready to leave.

"Natalya," called Anya. "Come back."

The countess refused to answer, busily putting on her fur coat and boots in the foyer while the maid struggled to get Nicky into his, ignoring Byelochka's plaintive demands that his friend be allowed to stay longer.

"Let her go for now," said Ksenia, placing a restraining hand on her niece's arm. "I'll talk to her later when she's calmer."

"But she said Gigi beats the child!"

"I'll send Andrei around to talk to Gigi," replied the princess. "And if he's been beating Nicky, he'll soon stop."

Both princesses looked upset, not really knowing what to do to help Natalya and her son. It seemed unbelievable that Gigi, whom Ksenia had known since girlhood, should become so vicious that he would beat a helpless child. On the other hand, perhaps there was really some truth to the claim that he wasn't the child's father. If that were really the case, nothing he did would surprise the princess.

"My God," said Anya, watching the departure of the Grekovs from the vantage point of her silk-hung salon windows. "Do you think it's even a remote possibility?" Her mind still refused to accept it.

"I don't know," replied Ksenia, "but I do know one thing. It would be better for that poor child to look like either Natalya or Gigi. He really doesn't look like anyone."

Anya hesitated. Then she said timidly, "Do you think he looks like Rasputin, then?" The idea had occurred to more than one court gossip.

Princess Malysheva shrugged delicately, evading the question. She didn't want to admit that Natalya's son could have been fathered by a peasant from Siberia. That would have been too much.

"Anya, *malenkaya*," she smiled sadly, "when I was a young girl visiting London for the first time with my father, I made one of the most dreadful faux pas of my life. Being young and ignorant of society's rules, I had the temerity to ask the Prince of Wales if he was the father of a certain young lady, because of the startling resemblance between them. It was in a crowd of people, and I really thought he *was* her father. My hostess turned a distressing shade of purple, the prince looked as if he'd like to strangle me, and Papa got me out of there so fast, we didn't even have time to finish our conversation."

Anya smiled. "You asked the right man the wrong question."

"Precisely. He and the girl's mother had been well-known lovers for years. Naturally, not being familiar with English society, I had no way of knowing, and it was there that I learned one of its firmest rules: Never comment on resemblance. It can cause trouble."

"And you think Gigi ought to follow this code?"

"Darling, if he doesn't, he'll lose all his dignity. What can he hope to achieve by labeling his son a bastard? It's too shameful all around. Either divorce Natalya or put up a brave front."

Turning her face away, Anya sighed, feeling sad for the countess and her poor little boy. Natalya was like a holy fool, she thought. Sweet and trusting and totally gullible.

The two princesses didn't see Countess Natalya for a while after their unpleasant discussion, but several days before Christmas, as the family was preparing for Zenaida Kashina's gala at the Maryinsky on behalf of the Amer-Russian relief agency, Natalya telephoned to say she would be there. With Gigi.

"Well, what a nice surprise," marveled Anya as she informed her aunt. "I wonder what happened." Perhaps a small miracle by her *starets?*

"Andrei paid Gigi a visit and had a long man-to-man talk with him, explaining that the Malyshevs would not stand idly by while he abused any members of their family—meaning Natalya or her son. If Gigi chose to ignore this warning, Andrei was prepared to call him out."

"My God! Would he really have fought a duel over Natalya?"

"Yes. My husband has a strong sense of family, as you well know, and since his cousin has no brother to defend her, he would if he had to."

"My God!" exclaimed Princess Anya. It was so melodramatic, like something out of Pushkin. It gave Uncle a certain panache.

"Naturally Gigi came to his senses, apologized for his past behavior and promised not to lay a hand on either of them—although he was the wronged party in reality. Neither one wants a scandal, especially since Gigi loves little Kolya and is willing to keep up appearances for his sake."

"Ah," murmured the princess. "I suppose that's the best solution to the problem."

But what a terrible existence, living such a lie, despising each other with a polite smile on one's face. Poor Natalya.

And poor Nicky, thought Anya with a sudden shudder. Thinking of Adam's behavior with his young son, the princess knew how lucky her child was to have a father who adored him. And he would be the same with the new one who was doing such a splendid job of kicking her in the belly right then.

Since the inception of the Amer-Russian War Relief Agency, Adam had been taken away from home much too often to suit Princess Anya. Although she was genuinely glad her American husband was beginning to make a name for himself as a great humanitarian, she was extremely unhappy that he was taking unnecessary risks on his visits to the front—which stretched for hundreds of miles. His wife needed him as much as the Russian Army did, and what is more, Anya thought he should have realized it.

In the last stages of the pregnancy, Her Highness was living in fear of a late-night telephone call from Billy, announcing Adam's death in some godforsaken trench in Poland.

That was another sore point. While her husband was tearing around the front in Prince Sandro's private railway car converted to a traveling command post, Billy Whitmore was enjoying himself in Petrograd, handling the less onerous tasks. Even though it had been agreed that they would split the areas of responsibility, Princess Anya wondered if Adam wasn't taking charge of the whole operation.

To Anya's amazement, Prince Sandro had had no objection to Madame Kashina's appearance at the gala the agency was planning as a benefit for its field hospitals. She couldn't believe it. How could he not object? It was so—inappropriate!

"Papa is very capricious," sighed Princess Ksenia over tea one afternoon. "I don't think he ever quite got over her. They say certain tropical diseases affect people the same way. They keep coming back at the most unexpected times."

"It's not Grand-père I'm really worried about," replied Anya. "I was hoping he'd object to Kashina's appearance, but only for another reason." She didn't wish to say so but she was very, very jealous.

"You don't want Adam to go near her," smiled Ksenia. "Well, I don't blame you. But somehow I don't think you really have to worry about him. He's too busy with his war work to have time for Kashina."

"He's too busy for his wife, which is worse!"

Princess Ksenia almost agreed with her niece, but refrained from expressing her opinion. The man who had nearly died from his Berlin wounds only months before was now spending more time on the various fronts than some generals the princess knew. It said a great deal for Adam's spirit, but Ksenia knew it was making her niece uneasy, especially with the baby due at any moment.

Princess Anya was surrounded by a houseful of servants and an assortment of relatives who would do anything they could to help her, but she wanted her husband near her. She found it unbearable to be deprived of his support right now.

On the night of the gala at the Maryinsky, Anya received a call from Billy who had heard that the prince had been delayed in Warsaw. If he could manage to catch a train bound for Petrograd, he would go straight to the theatre. If not, they were to present Madame Kashina with his sincere regrets—as well as a gold bracelet from Fabergé, specially engraved in honor of her contribution.

"But Adam promised to be back in time," said Anya. "What could have delayed him?"

"Trouble with the supplies. The depotmaster is cheating us and Adam wanted to settle the matter once and for all. The situation is very bad in Poland, Princess Anya. Unbelievable."

"Well then, will I see you this evening? One of you ought to be there to represent the agency."

"Of course," he replied. "Shall I meet you and your family at the theatre or would you prefer me to stop by the Sviridov Palace so we can all set out together?"

"Meet us here. Grand-père will escort me to the theatre and, if you don't mind, you can partner Countess Derzhavina."

"Countess Derzhavina?" Billy feigned ignorance.

"My little cousin," laughed the princess. "You met her at the air race last year. Don't you remember?"

"Ah, of course." Remember her? thought Billy. If Anyushka only knew!

"Since it's such a family affair this evening, we told Tasha she could come too. She's quite excited about the whole thing. Be a dear and treat her like a grown-up. She'd be so flattered."

Billy smiled on his end of the telephone line. "I'll do my best to ensure a pleasant evening," he promised.

That evening as Prince Sandro prepared to leave his apartment on the second floor of the mansion, he paused halfway between his bedroom and the staircase, his hand clenching into a fist as a pain shot through his chest. "Damn," muttered the prince. "Not tonight."

This was the third time it had happened in two days. If he didn't dislike his Petrograd doctor so much, he would have called him. As it was, Sandro decided to let it go until the next time. He had been through all this before in Paris; it was nothing new.

Anya and Tasha were waiting in the white and gold salon on the first floor. The princess was enormous in a plainly cut green silk gown. Her rounded belly reminded Sandro of a girl in a Botticelli painting, representing fertility. Her condition might cause comment, thought the prince, but let the gossips wag their tongues. He knew that modesty was taking second place to well-founded suspicions this evening. She was not about to leave Adam alone with Kashina. If he ever arrived!

"I'm certain this will be a memorable evening, a true Maryinsky extravaganza," declared Sandro, smiling to block out the pain in his chest.

"I have Madame's sworn oath to surpass even her own formidable achievements," announced a voice from the doorway. "It will be a great success."

"It would be a greater success if your associate were here," replied Sandro rather pointedly as Billy entered the room.

Kissing Anya's hand and greeting Tasha with an airy kiss on the cheek, Billy smiled at the old prince. "He's going to do his best, sir."

Even without Prince Adam, the evening was spectacular. Taking their seats in Sandro's usual box, his party looked out over a packed house, complete with Petrograd's most elegant women, all trying to outdo each other. Prince Andrei and Princess Ksenia, who had met them at the Maryinsky, were congratulating the American on the audience that had turned out—the cream of Petrograd society.

White shoulders, arms and throats sparkled with the flashing lights of diamonds, rubies, sapphires and emeralds as prewar Paris gowns mingled with lavish creations by Petrograd's leading couturiers, Brissac and Bulbenkova. Officers in the uniforms of all the Allied armies and at least a dozen Russian regiments—all in colorful full dress—escorted these angels, flirting gaily for perhaps the last time before returning to the front.

Despite Anya's previous reservations, she had to agree it was magnificent. And Adam was missing it, she thought sadly.

Countess Derzhavina, on the other hand, was so ecstatic with joy at being able to attend a grown-up affair without resorting to subterfuge that she reveled in Billy's attentions, ignored Anya's melancholy mood and carefully studied every young officer in sight, dreaming of the time when she would come out in society and spend the season dancing the nights away with just the sort of young men who filled the Maryinsky this evening—if the terrible war spared any of them. Needing escorts so badly, Tasha prayed daily for peace.

Applauding wildly as Kashina made her entrance, the audience greeted the small, dark-haired ballerina with customary exuberance as she smiled toward the box of her protector, Grand Duke Constantine Andreevich, before beginning her chosen piece, the pas de deux from *Paquita* with her partner, Legat.

"Isn't she beautiful?" Tasha asked, training her opera glasses on the dainty figure in a white and gold froth of tulle onstage.

As Kashina danced across the stage, half-floating, half-gliding, Sandro felt a sharp, stabbing pain in his chest; it nearly took his breath away. Stoically ignoring it, the prince kept his eyes on the dancer, determined not to give in to discomfort.

It was Anya who first noticed something was wrong. Seeing Sandro bow his head and nearly pitch forward, she gently took his arm.

"Are you all right, Grand-père?" she whispered. "Shall we call a doctor?"

"Don't be foolish. It's just one of my usual pains," he murmured. "Nothing to get alarmed about."

But it didn't go away. As the graceful ballerina delighted her admirers with the fluid purity of her motion, Anya saw her grandfather gasp, clutch his chest and fall from his seat, rolling onto the floor at her feet. Suddenly her heart froze.

"Grand-père! My God! Call a doctor!" Why had he come? she thought. Why?

Springing to assist the prince, Billy Whitmore managed to lift him to a sitting position, enabling Prince Andrei to help him get Sandro up from the floor and carry him out to the corridor, amid cries of alarm from their neighbors, who had witnessed the uproar in the Sviridov box and feared the worst.

Since members of the imperial family were in the audience, the wildest rumors began to circulate about the reason for the disturbance. But when the houselights didn't come up, it was assumed that nothing too disastrous had happened. In the event of an assassination attempt, all hell would have broken loose by this time, with the police rounding up suspects and the army surrounding the theatre.

All the same, Kashina had noticed something wrong from the stage and muttered to Legat, nervously checking the position of Constantine's box, momentarily afraid for him.

In the corridor outside the Sviridov box, Princess Anya was white with horror as she, Ksenia, Andrei, Tasha and Billy watched a hastily summoned house physician try to save Sandro, tearing open his shirt to allow him to breathe as he lay gasping and wheezing on the floor, his color bluish, his breath coming in long, frightening gulps, his eyes rolled back in his head, his body racked by a series of painful spasms. He was only semiconscious, unable to recognize anyone.

As Anya looked on, silent with grief, she knew he was dying before her eyes. For all the doctor's frantic attempts to save him, she knew they were losing him. Sandro Sviridov, heir to one of the greatest fortunes in Russia, connoisseur of women and the fine arts, was dying painfully while struggling with all his might against the inevitable.

As the prince fought to stay alive and the doctor worked on him, Princess Anya found herself recalling the dreadful evening of her arrival in Paris with Ksenia, the night Grand-père had told her she was a disgrace and would never marry. And how he had relented.

My God, thought Anya, tears falling onto the carpet as she studied Sandro's face, almost purple now, a terrifying sound coming from his throat, this isn't decent. It isn't fair. How was it possible for him to end this way? So weak, so pitiable.

Ksenia was kneeling on the floor beside her father, sobbing as she threw her arms around him, not caring who saw her, holding him as he finally stopped gasping and slowly settled down in her arms, lifeless.

"Papa!" Wailing, his daughter buried her face in his chest and prostrated herself on the floor, sobbing convulsively as she clutched Sandro, not believing he was gone.

In his entire life, Prince Andrei had never seen his wife so utterly devastated. In spite of the many disputes with Sandro, in spite of the major and minor explosions along the way, Ksenia Alexandrovna was his favorite child, and the strong bond between them had never been broken, although it had often been strained.

Losing Sandro was the loss of her childhood, her last link to the past, to the life she'd led at home with her parents and Lisa as a girl, to an entire way of life that could only return in memory. Princess Ksenia forgot everyone else in the world and sobbed for her vanished family.

"I'm sorry," said the flustered house doctor, turning his palms up in a gesture of total helplessness. "He's gone."

He had taken the pulse. Nothing.

Watching her aunt, Princess Anya suddenly went back in time to an afternoon in the house on the Rue du Faubourg St. Honoré, fourteen years earlier, the afternoon her mother died. "Whose little girl will I be now?" she had asked. Without missing a beat, Ksenia had replied, "You'll be mine." Now who could comfort Ksenia?

Gently helping the princess to her feet—with great difficulty because of her own pregnancy—Anya put her arms around her and tried to steady her. Prince Andrei took hold of Ksenia and spoke quietly to Billy and the doctor, telling them to cover Sandro before any of his friends saw him like that. For the prince was a dreadful sight, disheveled from the doctor's efforts to save him, his carefully starched collar and shirtfront ripped open, onyx and diamond studs lying on the faded red carpet, a stream of saliva extending from his mouth to his chin.

Still too shaken to speak, Princess Anya held her aunt as Prince Andrei told the doctor and Billy Whitmore to call the chauffeur and to find a couple of men who could help them carry the prince to his automobile so they could take him home to the Sviridov mansion.

While Billy raced off to round up help, Countess Derzhavina was coolly studying her emotional relatives, Ksenia and Anya; they apparently had actually loved the old tyrant. To her, now that he was dead, Grand-père was merely a potential source of income. She had never liked him in life and his death left her indifferent. Tatiana Sergeevna had seen her share of corpses before. When Princess Anya sank to the floor in a faint, it really came as no surprise to her. Anyushka had a kind heart, after all, thought her cousin. She would be affected by such a touching spectacle. With a sigh, Tasha wished she were capable of that kind of genuine feeling. But she wasn't. And then she began to help Auntie Ksenia revive her pregnant cousin.

It was three o'clock in the morning when an exhausted Prince Adam Sviridov arrived at Petrograd's Warsaw Station, crowded even at this late hour with troops waiting to go down the line to the nightmare of disorganization he had just come from.

Looking at the youthful, healthy new recruits, Adam pitied them, a pack of youngsters who couldn't even imagine what lay in store for them. Within days they would be ground into so much chopped meat, more raw material for the tough German war machine to absorb. There would be few survivors from this group of about 200—perhaps five or six. He knew it from his recent trips to the wounded at his first-aid stations.

Hiring a sleigh to take him to the Sviridov mansion on the French Embankment, Adam was almost glad he had missed the gala at the Maryinsky. Coming straight from those scenes of horror in Poland to the dazzling spectacle of a full-dress evening at the ballet would have been too much for him.

As the sleigh sped through the darkened streets of the Russian capital, illuminated along the Neva's embankments by the blazing windows of its mansions, crowded with party-goers, Adam wondered if Petrograd society even realized there was a war on. The general mood in town was a desperate, crazed gaiety. War profiteers mixed with the aristocracy in the city's gilded salons, everybody trying to outdo his neighbor in the frenzied pursuit of pleasure, the last gasp of a decadent culture. Compared with the atmosphere in Petrograd, the frontline hospitals were havens of sanity.

Watching a drunken band of revelers stagger from a brightly lit mansion on the Fontanka Canal, slipping on the snowy street, laughing as they went, Adam wondered why the four or five young men in the group weren't with their regiments. They wore the dress uniform of the Elizabethgrad Hussars, and the last time Adam had seen a group from that regiment was last week near Rovno, up to their necks in soupy mud, fighting Germans. No passes were being issued. If these young men had been invalided back home, they were the healthiest bunch of wounded the prince had ever seen. Someone obviously had an influential papa.

When Adam reached the Sviridov Palace, he was astonished to find the entire house in an uproar, with Andrei's Mercedes parked in the inner courtyard and the staff wandering through the corridors, weeping and moving furniture.

"What's happened?" he demanded in alarm as the old doorman admitted him, tears rolling down his wrinkled red cheeks.

"It's dreadful, Highness," sobbed the old man. "Thank God you're here."

Grabbing the doorman by the arm, Adam asked in alarm, "Is anything wrong with Princess Anya?"

"Oh no," he replied, "it's the old prince. What a tragedy. What a loss!"

"Adam!" Prince Andrei appeared from Sandro's study and quickly embraced him. "Thank God you've returned," he exclaimed. "It's unbelievable!"

"What's happened?" he demanded, fearing the worst. "Has Anya's grandfather had some sort of attack?"

"Yes," replied Andrei. "He was stricken at the theatre. It's all over. Anya and Ksenia and I were with him when he died. The little one went into labor when we got home."

Staring at Prince Andrei, Adam embraced him in sympathy and said quickly, "Is my wife all right? The shock must have been dreadful."

"Yes. Ksenia and the doctor are with her, but she's been calling for you. Go upstairs, Adam. She needs you."

Pausing before racing up the curving marble staircase, Adam asked quietly, "How is Ksenia Alexandrovna taking it?"

"She's trying to be strong for Anya's sake, but she's devastated. Nobody could have foreseen this. We're all in a state of shock tonight."

"I'm sorry." Sandro dead, he thought. My God! It didn't seem possible.

Sighing, Prince Andrei patted Adam on the shoulder and nodded. "Now," he said gently, "stop wasting time and go comfort Anya. I'll take care of all the arrangements for Sandro."

When Adam arrived at his wife's bedside, she gazed at him through eyes that were haggard with pain, grateful to have him with her at last.

"Anya," he asked quietly, taking her hand and kissing it, "how is it coming? When did the pains begin?"

But Princess Sviridova could only grimace, too weak from pain to do more.

Angrily turning to the doctor, Adam snapped, "Why are you allowing my wife to suffer like an animal? Give her a painkiller."

Shaking his head in the negative, the doctor startled Adam by explaining that there was some difficulty. If Anna Nicolaievna were unconscious, she wouldn't be able to push when the time came, and she needed to be able to do this. Otherwise the whole process might drag on interminably, weakening her still further and delaying an already difficult birth. The child was extremely uncooperative and turned the wrong way.

At the mention of the baby's position, Ksenia flinched. Her mother had gone through a terrible birth with her last child; it had been a three-day ordeal, nearly killing her. Ksenia was fifteen and old enough to understand what was happening. If Sandro hadn't ordered the physician to save the mother's life even if he had to kill the child to do it, Princess Tatiana wouldn't have survived. The baby, a girl, was the one who died, deliberately sacrificed by her father, but he'd made the choice and stood by it.

Looking at Adam, Princess Ksenia wondered what he would do. If he showed the slightest hesitation about putting Anya first, Ksenia was quite prepared to do whatever she had to do to take over—no holds barred. She wasn't about to lose two Sviridovs in one night.

As Princess Ksenia was observing her nephew-in-law with terrifying intensity, Adam Mikhailovich turned to the doctor and said quietly, "If there had to be a choice, do everything in your power to save my wife."

As he settled down into the chair nearest the bed, the prince gently kissed Ksenia's hand. "I was devastated to hear about Prince Sandro," he whispered. "I feel the loss very deeply."

"Thank you," she murmured. "He was very fond of you." She was numb.

As the princess sat down beside him, Adam remembered that day in Germany when his wife had nearly lost the child. What a fright this baby had given them then. But he had behaved himself beautifully throughout their dreadful departure from Berlin and their enforced stay in Copenhagen while his father recovered from the effects of a head wound. Now, at the last possible moment, he was being difficult again.

Poor Anya, Adam thought, stroking her flushed cheek. She had already suffered enough with this child. The idea of losing her suddenly crossed his mind, almost too terrible to contemplate. It couldn't happen. Not to this girl. Not after all she had been through.

As Prince Adam held his wife's hand and spoke softly to her, the doctor whispered to Princess Ksenia, making her go white.

"No," protested Ksenia. "It won't come to that!"

"Highness," murmured the short, dark-haired doctor, "I would be remiss in my duty if I didn't say this to you."

"What's the matter?" demanded Adam, having missed the exchange.

Princess Ksenia looked him in the face, absolutely drained. "He says we ought to call a priest," she replied. "For one or the other."

Far from the Sviridov mansion on the French Embankment, another member of the family was heading home after a night on the town. Clinging to Billy Whitmore in a troika jingling with a dozen little silver bells, Countess Derzhavina was laughing with delight as the sleigh raced through the darkened streets, churning up bits of snow and ice under the hooves of the three horses.

Slightly drunk on champagne and bundled into a thick, glossy sable coat, Tasha kissed Billy like a wildcat and gleefully shouted out an open invitation to all passersby to come with them to the gypsies.

Sullen factory workers, the only ones out in the freezing, predawn chill, watched the cheerful couple speed by and made no reply, silently cursing the rich as they trudged on through the snow, heading for fourteen or more hours of backbreaking labor in the great gloomy mills of Vyborg, Petrograd's industrial heart.

Rounding the corner of the Millyonaya, a fashionable quarter where Billy inhabited Adam's former apartment, the driver suddenly pulled into the courtyard of an elegant building and prepared to let the couple out.

"Where are we?" demanded Tasha. "Another nightclub?"

"No, darling," he replied, kissing her gently on the mouth. "My home."

Billy was living dangerously. Charged with conducting the young countess safely to the Malyshev mansion where she had been living with her aunt and uncle, he had calculated that Andrei and Ksenia would be so busy making the arrangements for Prince Sandro and seeing to Princess Anya that it would be midmorning before they ever reached home. By that time, Tasha would be dozing in bed and ready to listen to her aunt's report on Anya's condition and the funeral plans as if she had been there all night.

But this was a surprise for Tasha. She hadn't planned on this.

As Billy paid the driver, tipped him generously and waved him away, Tasha smiled, watching the American in the light of the street lamps. He was handsome enough, she decided. She could bear to have him crawling all over her the way Seriozha used to do; in return, she would extract as much use out of him as she could. The arrangement would benefit them both.

Greeted by an aged porter inside the building, Billy slipped the man a ten-ruble piece to buy his discretion. Tasha wondered if her friend brought home many underage girls. She probably wasn't the first, anymore than she had been the first for Seriozha.

Thinking of the evening when the American had found her in the Rose Noire, the young countess recalled his concern. Had he been worried about her? she wondered. Or was it just a variation on Seriozha's ruses?

He hadn't done anything except talk to her. Yet. The night he visited the nightclub, he had taken her for a ride in his automobile that lasted quite a while, but he had seemed more protective than amorous.

Perhaps the man actually had been concerned for her. Stranger things had happened. But in view of her past experiences, it just didn't seem likely. Pulling her fur coat closer around her, Tatiana Sergeevna shuddered in the early-morning chill and felt quite vulnerable.

Silently ascending to the second floor by means of an elaborate wrought-iron elevator, the couple held hands. Billy noticed Tasha's perfume, surprisingly heavy and oriental for such a young girl.

As the elevator cage squeaked to a stop, Billy handed her out, directly across from his apartment, and unlocked the door, ceremoniously ushering the countess inside where a servant had already laid a fire, the flames dancing gaily in the pink marble fireplace.

"It's a very nice apartment," said Tasha politely, surveying the large, comfortable salon, decorated in Russian empire style by one of Petrograd's leading antique dealers. It reminded her of her parents' home.

Without wasting any more time on formalities, Billy put his arms around Countess Derzhavina and kissed her passionately, pulling her so close to him she gasped, afraid he was going to crush her.

"Take off this gorgeous thing," he murmured, stripping her of her sables. "You're a little animal who looks better without her fur."

Throwing off his own fur coat, Billy kissed Tasha again, picking her up and carrying her to the fireplace where a pile of silk Chinese cushions made a comfortable nest on the floor. As they lay down in front of the glowing fireplace, he began to undress her, skillfully unbuttoning the row of covered silk buttons down the back of her white frock while he kissed her, caressing her with his other hand.

Suddenly, as she felt the thin silk fabric slide off her shoulder, Tasha sat up, confused, understanding what he was doing and yet hoping for something else. Nobody would do these things to Anyushka, she thought, half-hesitating.

Sensing her indecision, Billy gently stroked her shoulder, murmuring endearments. He wanted this girl. He would tell her whatever appealed to her, but he had no intention of letting her get away. She was far too important. She represented money, the kind of money Adam had acquired through his marriage to dear, sweet Anyushka.

"What's wrong, darling?" whispered Billy, kissing her once more. "I thought we were going to be friends."

"This isn't right," protested the countess, delicately pulling up her dress. "I don't think I ought to be alone with you like this."

"Ah Tasha. Darling little Tasha," he whispered, taking her in his arms. "Are you afraid of me? You don't have to be. I would never hurt you."

Stifling an impulse to laugh, the countess buried her face in his chest, nestling close to him among the pile of silken cushions.

"Tasha," he murmured, "you told me this evening you liked to get out of the house. If we were friends—good friends—I could help you do this without your having to resort to foolish and dangerous pranks like your experience at the Rose Noire. It would be so easy."

The countess tilted her head and regarded him carefully, as if he were a street peddler trying to sell her something useless, something he insisted was wonderful despite all clear proof to the contrary.

"We were able to get away this evening because of Grand-père's death. Ksenia Alexandrovna was half out of her mind with grief when she asked you to take me to the Malyshev mansion. She and Uncle Andrei will be at the Sviridov Palace until tomorrow morning, so we're safe. Other times won't always be so easy."

Gazing into the dancing, flickering flames, Tasha nestled against Billy and smiled. "They probably trust you with me because you're Adam Mikhailovich's brother and he's practically a saint. You're not at all like him but they probably don't realize it yet," she reflected. "And I'm surprised, because Ksenia is usually more perceptive than that. She'd kill you herself if she knew what you want to do with me. She's very medieval about some things."

"Well," murmured Billy, "then I think we ought to make certain Her Highness never finds out."

Turning toward the blond young man, Tasha smiled again, fixing him with her large, catlike blue eyes. "You'd have to be sweet and gentle with me," she said. "I'm only a child."

"Darling," he whispered, kissing her among the silken pile of cushions, "I would be as tender with you as if you were my own child."

To his astonishment, the small countess sprang to her feet, furious. "Don't ever call me your child!" she screamed. "You're not my father. He's dead and I don't ever want to hear you say that again!"

"All right, darling," he promised, completely unnerved by this violent outburst. "I'll never say such a thing again, word of honor."

Looking up at Countess Derzhavina, who had an uncommonly hot temper, a most intimidating trait, Billy wondered if he ought to give up and take her home. Once she calmed down, he could always try again, although tonight was an unprecedented stroke of good fortune that might never again come his way. The last thing in the world he wanted or needed was for Adam's little Russian relative to accuse him of rape. With her unstable disposition, she might do anything.

To his surprise and relief, Tasha returned to the pile of cushions and lay down beside him as if nothing had happened.

"Are you all right, darling?" he asked, wrapping his arms around her.
"Yes. I'm fine."

Uncertainly Billy kissed her on the mouth, stroking her full breasts. It seemed to be all right now. Tasha merely sighed a little and curled up in his arms like a cat, responding to his kisses like a woman who had a lot of practice, teasing him with her pretty pink tongue, finding just the right spot where he was especially susceptible to stroking.

And then he began to undress her once again, sliding the unfastened silk dress down over her reclining form as slowly as if he were unveiling a living work of art, gently, tenderly.

"You'll have to be very nice," whispered Tasha. "I've never done this before."

She didn't know how she managed that with a straight face. It was a lie they always wanted to believe, so they usually did. And she despised them for it.

Nodding emphatically, Billy began to undress, tearing off everything in his haste to reach his objective. "Dear Tasha," he murmured, "you make me very happy."

"Let's go into the bedroom," said the countess. "I don't want to lie here on the floor."

"Fine, darling," replied Billy, lifting her up and carrying her into his bedroom. "We'll be much more cozy here."

It was an unimpressive sort of room except for the luxurious lynx rug casually thrown over the bed. Billy saved all the other exotic touches for his salon; this room was almost spartan in its simplicity, a typical bachelor's abode with a minimum of frills.

"What a beautiful fur," marveled Tasha as she slid onto it, rolling around like a kitten at play, stroking the white and tawny fluffiness of it, letting the long, silky guard hairs tickle her breasts, her arms, her shoulders, her belly. She was excited by the texture of the lynx all over her bare skin.

Billy lay down on the rug beside her, enjoying the spectacle of soft fur caressing the undulating pink and white flesh before his eyes, aroused by Tasha's sensual pleasure in the texture of the animal skins.

"Come here," he whispered, taking her in his arms. "I want you!"

Trembling a little in spite of herself, Tasha felt the man quiver with desire as he touched her his warm hands stroking every part of her as if he were a blind man discovering a woman for the first time, reverent and a little impatient to possess her.

Looking up toward the ceiling as Billy started to kiss her breasts, Tasha opened her startled eyes wide as she felt his tongue descend into the downy region between her thighs, astonishing her as he began to probe the moistening slit, delicately but insistently. He was arousing her beyond anything she could ever recall with Seriozha or any other lover.

Stroking his tousled blond hair, Tasha shuddered, wanting him to do it all over again. She was absolutely fascinated, limp with satisfaction.

"Ah," gasped Countess Derzhavina, "you are a wicked, wicked man. You're killing me."

"Nonsense, darling. Only the good die young. You'll go on forever."

As Billy took Tasha in his arms, he saw a glimmer of laughter in her eyes that he found unsettling. "You're probably right about that," she murmured, allowing him to cover her with his warm body, resting as lightly as an eiderdown above her.

Enfolding her lover with trembling, slender arms, Tatiana Sergeevna closed her eyes as she felt him guide himself inside her vulnerable thighs, entering her as gently as he could, sensitive to her youth and her relative state of innocence.

"Don't hurt me," hissed Tasha, burying her face in his chest as she sank her fingernails into his back, sliding them across his bare skin with surprising effect.

"Yes, darling," he murmured, moving deeper inside her, excited by her gasps and the frenzied caresses she was beginning to bestow on him, as uninhibited as a cat among the pile of lynxes. Moving together with the girl in a rhythm that grew increasingly frantic, Billy found himself wondering if he were mating with a beautiful feline in human form, so supple beneath him, so greedy for the sensation of loving.

When at last he felt himself drained by a release of overwhelming proportions, deep inside Tasha, he nuzzled her tenderly, too tired to speak, and lay back beside her on the bed, sated and drowsy.

"My God," he breathed. "You're no child."

Smiling with satisfaction, Tasha knew then that from now on, she would be able to get anything she wanted from Billy Whitmore.

But there was one thing that troubled her. She had enjoyed making love with him. That was so unlike anything that had happened to her with Seriozha and the others that it frightened her a little; for if she actually enjoyed all this ridiculous thrashing about, it might lead her to make foolish concessions to this man.

And what was he after all, but a rather handsome little arriviste with one outstanding talent? She was Countess Derzhavina and she had no intention of being dominated by a mere nobody.

Although occasional interludes among the lynxes couldn't be ruled out with any great finality.

As Tasha had predicted, the terrible events of the evening had kept Princess Ksenia and her husband at the Sviridov Palace until well into the next day, so her dawn arrival never reached the attention of the princess, whose servants were always open to a generous bribe. Future excursions might be just a bit more difficult to arrange, but she had great faith in her own deviousness as well as Billy's.

And he was wild about her, thought Tasha; therefore he had an incentive to spur him on to further resourcefulness. He would be useful.

Across town in the Sviridov Palace, as the inky-black night merged into a sooty dawn, Princess Anya was going into her eighth hour of exhausting labor.

With a thoroughly uncooperative baby refusing to turn properly in spite of all the doctor's best efforts, it appeared that the child would be a breech birth if he were to be born at all. Anya was so weak from futile attempts to shift the baby into position that all she longed for was an end to her suffering. In terrible pain, the young princess saw death as a welcome release.

Breathing with difficulty as she lay with her head against a silken pillow, her eyes straining to keep Adam in view, Anya felt herself about to give in to her pain. This is how dying is, she thought, just drifting off. Why couldn't I go quickly like Grand-père? Poor Adam. He looks so overwhelmed. And Ksenia....She's losing us both tonight. How will she ever recover from this? And Byelochka....The room seemed to spin.

As one of the chambermaids led in the black-robed, bearded priest who had been hurriedly summoned to administer the last rites, Anya suddenly gave a sharp cry and clutched her husband's hand. Rudely jostling the holy father out of the way, the doctor quickly examined her once more and practically shouted, "The child's turned! It will be all right!"

And despite the mother's gravest doubts, it was. Half an hour later, a daughter was born, followed shortly afterward by her sister. Both were shrieking quite fiercely to everyone's great joy.

"*Twins,*" murmured Anya, gazing at them in shocked disbelief as Adam tenderly caressed her hand. Good Lord, she thought. No wonder this pregnancy had been so dreadful. There had been two of them lurking inside her! Practically a litter. Byelochka had been so easy by comparison.

Through a hazy mist of pain and emotion, Anya saw her husband standing beside the bed, holding the babies and speaking to her. She couldn't really understand what he was saying, worn as she was and weakened from loss of blood. Ksenia's hand clutched hers and Ksenia's voice was telling her everything was well. And then, as Adam handed his new daughters over to the waiting nurse-maids and bent over to kiss his wife, Anya looked into his eyes and slipped into a darkening void that loomed as a safe and seductive haven, far from all pain.

She had finally used up every last bit of strength she had.

25

The birth of Princess Anya's two baby girls—Alexandra and Victoria, called Sashenka and Tory by their parents—was such a tremendous strain that Anyushka was forbidden to exert herself in any way immediately following the event. Adam, who had been convinced his wife was dying when she fainted at the end, made sure she was left undisturbed while the rest of the household busied themselves with the funeral arrangements for the prince.

Andrei and Ksenia Alexandrovna took care of everything. One of the princess's first steps was to bribe officials of the railroad to dispatch a few carloads of Crimean roses to the capital—at a time when troop trains had the highest priority—in order to decorate the huge ballroom of the Sviridov Palace with fragrant blossoms as a fitting backdrop for her father when his friends came to pay their last respects. Prince Sandro's funeral was, after all, one of the highlights of the winter season.

Andrei, Adam and Ksenia received a flood of Romanov grand dukes and their spouses, among them Grand Duke Constantine Andreevich, Kashina's lover. The greatest surprise came in the person of a slim, bearded gentleman in the plain uniform of a colonel, escorted into the ballroom by a young aide. It was His Majesty, Tsar Nicholas II, just back from a visit to his army headquarters and wishing to pay his respects to an old friend of the family.

Speaking to Princess Ksenia with his usual charm and simplicity, the tsar consoled her on the death of her distinguished parent and reminded her of Sandro's many contributions to Russian culture, at home and abroad, especially his lifelong interest in the preservation and augmentation of the capital's finest private collection of art.

"The Sviridov collection is one of the jewels of our Russia, Ksenia Alexandrovna. It is his finest legacy to both your family and our nation."

"Thank you, Your Majesty," murmured the princess, enjoying the compliment, knowing that the tsar's family owned the collection in the Hermitage.

Retiring to one of the small salons on the first floor to rest for a few minutes, the princess almost missed another visitor who arrived by herself, magnificently garbed in glossy black sable with a simple black wool-crepe suit beneath. It was Madame Zenaida Kashina, appropriately solemn, but rather pleased to find herself in Prince Adam's presence. "Please accept my most sincere condolences, my dear Adam Mikhailovich," purred Kashina, her small, carefully manicured hand pressing firmly against his. "It was one of the saddest moments of my career when His Highness was taken from you in that way."

Glancing into the ballerina's velvety brown eyes, Adam smiled in spite of himself.

"Madame Kashina, what better way to go?" he replied. "I've just returned from a visit to the front where any number of poor devils would gladly have traded their death for his. At least Prince Sandro enjoyed life up until the last minute. How many men are that fortunate?"

Sighing sweetly, Kashina nodded, the diamonds sparkling in her earlobes, concentrating her soft yet penetrating gaze on the young man in front of her, so tall and handsome, more attractive than any other man she could recall. And Kashina could recall many.

Sandro had had the end he deserved, she thought. Perhaps it was the emotion of seeing her once more that had led to the fatal heart attack—a well-deserved punishment for his brutal and vindictive dismissal of her as if she were some sort of wretched servant. He had done the unpardonable and he had been humbled. That gave Kashina a great deal of satisfaction.

But she still wasn't finished with the Sviridovs. Lisa was dead, Sandro was dead, but that charming blonde girl whose husband was talking with her right now was alive and capable of being humiliated. She was quite lovely—and apt to be devastated with grief if Prince Adam became her lover. What delightful irony! thought the small dancer. What she hadn't gotten out of Sandro, she might very well get from this foreigner little Anya had married. And the pain her affair would cause the haughty Sviridov ladies would warm her heart all winter long.

Aware of the scent of lilies of the valley amid all the white roses, Adam felt a twinge of desire, dreadfully out of place here and embarrassingly ardent. The woman was beautiful; more than that, she was the living personification of the feminine spirit—graceful, charming and capricious. For a brief second, Prince Sviridov's brown eyes met Kashina's and both felt a surge of emotion that was inexplicable but real. And instantly repressed by the prince.

Holding his gaze, Madame Kashina smiled mysteriously, discreetly, accepting a polite kiss on the hand before she was gone, a lovely sylph in sable, trailing the scent of spring flowers.

As Ksenia entered the ballroom, she observed the ballerina's exit, including the veiled, predatory expression on her face as Adam bent over her hand. To her relief, she saw nothing alarming in the look he gave her, merely well-bred politeness. Good.

Two days after Sandro was laid to rest in a snow-swept ceremony at the Alexander Nevsky Monastery, which, out of concerns for her health, Princess Anya was forbidden to attend despite her bitter tears, Adam, Andrei and Ksenia had a conference.

Recalling her father's pessimism about the war, Ksenia echoed his concern for the safety of their family in case of a German victory and its consequences. Adam had reached the point where he was too familiar with the casualty lists to foresee anything but disaster. So had Andrei, keenly aware of the staggering losses at Byelaya Beryozka. All three realized the time had come to plan for the very worst.

Leaning forward in his chair, Prince Sviridov began to outline the plan he had been formulating in his mind ever since the day of his talk with Prince Sandro about this very topic, only a few months before.

Reminding Andrei and Ksenia of Sandro's shrewd assessment of the situation—and the possibility of civil strife following a disastrous defeat in the war—Adam said, "Since I've become involved in this Amer-Russian agency of ours, I've met many people who could be useful here and abroad. My brother and I have American diplomatic passports and access to the diplomatic pouch. I'm going to start smuggling valuables out of the country under cover of the agency—and just possibly in the diplomatic pouch."

Ksenia stared for a minute, enchanted with the idea.

"Wonderful! Papa once spoke to me about this. I think you're quite right. And I know my great-great-grandmother, Zenaida Nicolaievna, would approve too if she were here. She didn't risk her neck to have her descendants lose everything to a pack of rampaging foreigners in another war."

"Precisely," replied Adam. "She saw her duty and she did it. Now it's our turn."

Glancing around the magnificent gallery, Prince Andrei saw the results of several generations of collecting. "Paintings, jewels, *objets d'art*," he murmured. "The Sviridovs would be entrusting you with a fortune."

Adam nodded. "Believe me, I understand the importance of it. Anya's future and our children's is at stake here. I intend to be very careful."

Kissing him spontaneously, Ksenia laughed. "I know you will. Now," she said, getting down to business, "when shall we try a practice run?"

Another citizen of Petrograd who was starting to have grave doubts about the whole rash adventure this war had become was Roman Vasilievich Petrov. He was already predicting riots in the streets. As he confided to his favorite informer, Pavel Scriabin, it wouldn't be long before the burning fuse of people's anger reached the powder keg.

At the outbreak of hostilities, the government had decided on a round-up of what they considered the most dangerous elements, and many radicals had found themselves making the long trip east to Siberia, courtesy of the tsar's prison trains.

In the excitement of the raids and the constant hysteria over the war, some inspectors discovered their best operatives being arrested by ignorant colleagues, and the corridors of Okhrana headquarters were packed with dangerous Bolsheviks, protesting informers and, of course the police themselves, deciding who to ship east and who to release.

Pavel Scriabin himself had come close to visiting the big icebox at government expense until Petrov had spotted him, let out a cry of recognition and ordered him turned loose. Now he was working for Roman Vasilievich at a huge textile plant in the Vyborg district, spying on his coworkers and passing himself off as a late-blooming Bolshevik.

The factory, owned by the late S. A. Derzhavin, was one of those bellwether places that seemed to be accurate indicators of working-class opinion. It was necessary to have spies there to keep track of any genuine rebels among the workers, and frankly, Petrov couldn't think of anyone more suited for the job than Scriabin. A leftover from the futile Ivanov affair, Pavel had the soul of a whore, Petrov thought. He could be useful for a price.

These days, Roman Vasilievich rarely thought about the Ivanov fiasco, although he dutifully checked the files and sent Prince Andrei Malyshev monthly reports, to prevent him from taking back his retirement fund, the 20,000 gold rubles. No, these days, Petrov had other, more wearisome duties to make his life miserable. He had been assigned the onerous task of shadowing Rasputin, and at his age, he simply couldn't stand the pace.

Lurching from palace to cathouse to gypsy nightclub, the *starets* was considered such a precious imperial adviser that the tsar—or more precisely, the tsaritsa—had given orders for his round-the-clock protection. In this case, it was a good idea, for if Rasputin's own drunken sprees didn't kill him, an outraged husband might. Petrov's superior had put it plainly: "If anything happens to him, your job is on the line."

With the city filled with Russian officers and men, Oleg's establishments, or rather Monsieur Mossolov's, were doing more business than they could handle. He should have been wild with joy, but as he kept track of his books, noting the flood of money pouring in, he felt as if he were being stalked by some shadowy, evil presence within the walls of his first-class house. And he had a feeling it had settled inside a human form.

Wanda's.

As Monsieur Mossolov roamed the halls of his bordello, he walked stealthily over the fine Chinese carpets, paused to listen to the sounds of the old mansion creaking beneath its parquet floors, and watched the bright reflections of the chandeliers' crystal prisms on the light-colored walls and across the gilded boiseries. As he waited for an attack, he studied Wanda carefully while she spoke to him, ate with him and occasionally slept with him, never trusting her, always watching, always waiting.

It's the women, thought Monsieur Mossolov, never forgetting he was born Ivanov. They pursue me. That red-haired witch, she tried to kill me, but I was too clever for her. She was the one who got it that night in Kiev, not Oleg, the peasant, the fool. Katia Petrovna, the intellectual. Dead.

And that blonde, that aristocrat, she was even worse. Prince Malyshev's niece! She was more dangerous than Katia Petrovna, thought Oleg. She'd had been able to overpower him and seize his gun, turning it against him in that French museum. Christ, she was a devil! Katia Petrovna was nothing compared with her. And now she had come to Warsaw to haunt him, making his life miserable when he should have been so happy.

She was taking over Wanda's body, that was the worst part. Before arriving in Warsaw, Wanda had been a slightly plump, agreeable, good-natured whore, ready to humor him, quick to cheer him up when he felt bad. Now all that had changed. Wanda had become conscious of his eating habits—disgusting, she called them; of his clothing—garish, she said; and what she said about his lovemaking was unfit to hear. Piggish! Yes, that was her exact word for him. *Piggish!*

If it hadn't been for him, that plump little Polish cow would still be wearing out her tail in that mediocre place in Paris, still looking for someone to get her out of there.

No. Wanda was gone. And she had been taken over by those others, especially by Anna Nicolaievna. Who else would have given her those notions about class? It was unnerving to live with her, never knowing when she would reveal herself completely. Wanting her to. Waiting for it.

When Oleg started to think about these things, his face took on such a demonic expression that he terrified the girls. It sent them scurrying away in real fright as Wanda tried patiently to shrug it off as the result of overwork. But she too was beginning to steer clear of him when he went into one of these strange moods, when he would slam his way out the front door in the middle of the night and stalk off to wander Warsaw's deserted streets, cursing Katia and Anna Nicolaievna with an occasional bad word thrown in for Pavel, Dimitri and the "glass-eyed monster." It actually made Wanda's skin crawl to listen to him.

But as long as he limited his attacks to verbal skirmishes, she could live with them. What frightened her was the prospect of his becoming violent. And because of that, Madame Wanda was now sleeping with a knife hidden under her mattress, just in case.

But the really maddening thing about dealing with Oleg, as far as Wanda was concerned, was his unpredictability. One minute he was muttering about going back to St. Petersburg—he never referred to it as Petrograd, despite Wanda's many reminders—and killing those people he hated so much; the next minute he was asking her pleasantly if their liquor supplies were running low, just as normal as you please. With Oleg, you never knew.

It was hard to take, and if Wanda hadn't been motivated by sheer, unrelenting greed, she would never have been able to tolerate it. Luckily there were always enough problems to take one's mind off these matters, especially when one's clients showed up with their weapons. On those nights, the decor tended to suffer dreadfully.

"We're going to need a new mirror in the Chabanais room," declared Wanda. "Last night a general shot it to pieces during a drunken fit. Sonia said he was lying peacefully beside her in bed when he suddenly leaned over her, reached for his revolver on the night table and started shooting at the mirror. Nearly gave the poor girl a heart attack."

"What was the problem?" demanded Monsieur Mossolov, his shiny bald head glowing in the morning sunlight as he and Wanda sat in his office.

"I don't know. Nerves, I guess. It seems to affect them differently. Some men drink. Some men chase women. Our clients do both and like to destroy things as well."

Oleg gave a little grunt of amusement. For once Wanda had said something he agreed with.

"It's the tension," added Madame Wanda. "The damned war is going on and on. The clients keep dying. A man leaves here and goes back

to the front and three hours later they're sending home a letter of con-
dolence. I don't know how they manage to keep sane."

"Well, some of them don't," replied Oleg. "And now I can feel the
loss in my bank account. Call the glazier. We've got to get the thing fixed.
That room's too popular to let it lie fallow."

"I'll call today," replied Wanda as she departed.

"Damned aristocrats," muttered Oleg. "They get upset and destroy
the property of a hardworking man. Cowards. I hate them all."

Taking a bottle of vodka from a drawer in his mahogany desk, Oleg
sat down and calculated how much the general's caprice ought to cost
him. He would send a bill for triple the price. It was the only way to treat
the bastards.

As he brooded about the mirror, Oleg found himself worrying about
his companion and partner. He didn't trust her any longer, although he
knew she was doing a fine job with the house. Well, he thought, he could
handle her. Sometimes he didn't know why he thought the things he did.
It frightened him a little. On one level, he knew she was just a simple
Polish farm girl who had a knack for keeping a man happy. On another,
he saw in her the two devils from his past who had tried to kill him. It
was getting harder and harder for him to tell what was real and what was
only in his mind especially late at night when he was alone.

And as bad as all that was, there was something else that was driving
him wild. Picking up an old newspaper, he'd discovered that Prince Adam
Sviridov—the man he'd nearly murdered in Paris, Anna Nicolaievna's husband—was running some kind of Red Cross outfit with offices in Warsaw.
Christ! Their paths could have crossed right here at his own establishment by the most ridiculous kind of coincidence! What a disaster.

Once Oleg got over the shock of his discovery, he began to look at
it from a different angle. The advantage was his, not Sviridov's, for as
long as his enemy was on his territory without realizing it, nothing could
possibly happen to Oleg, while all sorts of things could befall the prince.
And if Oleg had his way, they certainly would.

Smiling at the thought of renewed opportunities for revenge, the Russian decided to give the matter the highest priority, and while he was arranging for a tragic accident to happen to His Highness, he might even be
able to do something about Wanda at the same time.

Petrograd

With the renewal of her friendship with Adam's younger brother, Countess Derzhavina was finding life much more interesting. Under the innocent guise of helping the staff at the Petrograd office of the Amer-Russian

relief agency, Tasha spent several afternoons a week in Billy's company, engaged in anything but harmless pursuits. Her relatives, suspecting nothing from Prince Adam's brother, allowed the charming young man to take the girl to the city's restaurants or accompany her on numerous shopping excursions, none of which they would have permitted with any other grown male.

Insinuating himself into the intimacy of their family, Billy won everybody's trust. Generally suspicious, Ksenia found him pleasant and extremely useful, thanks to his aid in setting up an underground railroad for the safeguarding of her family's treasures. Anya trusted him even more and often asked him to keep an eye on Tasha to protect her from the advances of the omnipresent, affection-starved young officers who filled the capital, all too eager to spend an exciting week's leave in the arms of a pretty girl.

If Billy had had a conscience, he would have been ashamed to look his friends in the eye. Luckily for him, he had no such thing. Nor did Tasha.

One afternoon, as the countess and her blond lover strolled along Nevsky Prospect in the area of the Yeliseyev gourmet shop, filled with stylish matrons in search of hard-to-find delicacies, Tasha finally revealed her hand.

"Billy," she purred, "I want you to do me a favor. Help me take some valuables out of the country."

Billy stopped short. He had never discussed the underground operation with anyone, least of all Tasha. And he was certain Adam hadn't either. That one was a man who could keep a secret.

To conceal his alarm he smiled. "I really don't think it's that serious, darling. I mean, your tsar's armies just won a huge victory over the Austrians at Przemysl. Things are starting to look promising."

"Hah!" replied Tasha with scorn. "If we were really doing well, we wouldn't be seeing those!"

Gesturing toward a long line of housewives outside a bakery, the countess pointed out the newest symbol of wartime Petrograd—the stolid women of the food lines, patiently waiting for provisions that might run out before they ever had a chance to reach the counter. It was the war's latest burden on the civilian population, and so far, they were displaying amazing forbearance. But how long could their patience last?

"Tasha, darling," sighed Billy, putting his arm around her, "you're a minor; the sorts of things you might wish to safeguard are already quite secure in the vaults of some bank. It's not necessary to store them elsewhere. Besides," he added, "it would require someone's permission to release such things. It would be impossible."

"Let me worry about selecting what I want taken out of the country," replied Tasha. "All you have to do is take them to someplace neutral—like Sweden or Switzerland. I'll take care of the rest."

"No, it's too ridiculous."

Furious with Billy, Tasha stopped in midstride and pulled away from him. "Billy," she said venomously, "either you do what I want or I'll tell Adam Mikhailovich about our little games. And then I'll have a nice long chat with your ambassador the next time I meet him at Auntie's house."

"You wouldn't!"

"Try me."

Shocked, the young man stared at the blackmailing little tart who was glaring at him as if she'd like to kill him, and he felt a chill run down his spine. Those cold, gorgeous blue eyes had absolutely no pity. If he didn't humor the bitch, she'd destroy his career without blinking. And that was the least of it. Adam would go after him with a horsewhip if the Sviridov ladies didn't get to him first.

"Why are you doing this to me, Tasha? I thought you loved me."

The countess gave him a look of astonishment. "I don't love anyone, least of all you!" What a preposterous idea, she thought.

At that, Billy felt hurt. He really did feel affection for her, even if it only lasted for the duration of their games on the lynx. And he had great ambitions for their future together, which meant even more. "You're blackmailing me," he said plaintively.

"Of course I am."

Damn. The creature had no heart at all. There was no way to appeal to her better nature. It simply didn't exist. "All right," he conceded, admitting defeat rather than risk his career. "I'll help you."

"Good," nodded Tasha.

As he hailed a sled to take her home to the Malyshev Palace on the Moika, Billy noticed no trace of nervousness on Tasha's part. They might have been talking about the weather for all the emotion she showed.

"You're a vicious little tart," he declared, putting his arm around her in spite of it. "You know that?"

Tasha laughed explosively. "Absolutely. And as long as we both know it, we can be happy."

Reflecting on that bit of wisdom, Billy Whitmore began to wish he had been born a eunuch.

Throughout the late spring and early summer of 1915, the German buildup in southern Poland had been so concentrated that the Russian Army was once more in retreat, losing all the ground they had so painfully gained in the previous year of fighting. Men sent straight from the troop trains to the battlefields died by the score under the withering barrage of German gunfire. For miles and miles, the land looked like a distant province of hell. According to some observers, it was the beginning of the end.

With the exception of the month after the twins' birth when Princess Anya was dangerously weak and feverish, Adam was spending most of his time in the field.

Despite Adam's injuries from the plane crash in 1913 and his more recent brush with death in Berlin, the man worked tirelessly for the Amer-Russians. He absented himself from home for days at a time, checking the various outposts of the agency across Poland and in the empire's great cities, returning to Petrograd exhausted and silent. He was also witnessing the decimation of the Russian Army and hearing the first rumblings of dissension among the troops. It convinced him all the more that Prince Sandro had been right, and it made him fiercely determined to do all he could to protect his family.

He loved them beyond anything else. In years past, as a junior diplomat trying hard to make a career for himself, Adam had thought of a wife and children as a pleasant refuge from the strains of his job, something that could be put aside at will when more important matters arose. He'd thought he loved Catherine and would have loved any children they might have had together. Now he knew he had been wrong. He had loved himself. What he experienced with Anyushka and the children was something so different from his old ideas that it made them seem pathetic, comical, utterly wrong.

Beautiful Anya had enriched his whole existence and had given him three children without any thought of putting him aside at her convenience. He didn't want to offer her less. And he hoped he never would.

Prince Andrei was engaged in a sort of warfare of his own with Count Boris Scherbatkin, his neighbor in the country who served with him on the war mobilization committee. Boris was shipping off far too many peasants, creating problems at Byelaya Beryozka. And everyone in the district was complaining about the exemption he had gotten for his new son-in-law, his daughter Irina's husband. It was causing bad blood.

Andrei, alerted to the problem by Lev Petrovich, who had lost one of his own sons in the first month of the war, was spending a great deal of time at Byelaya Beryozka challenging Boris's rulings, doing all he could to see that anyone with a proper claim to an exemption received one. He'd be damned if he'd let Boris ship out his peasants just to make himself look patriotic. Who would work the land if they lost all their men? And from the lists of names on the casualty reports, they were losing far too many.

"Highness," said the old tracker one day as he and the prince talked about horses and the fine stable Byelaya Beryozka had had before the war, "do you think the Germans will come to Moscow province?"

"I don't know any longer. They've overrun our army in Poland."

"Poland isn't Russia."

The man's patient face looked much older now than it had before he'd lost his son. The deep wrinkles around Lev's blue eyes were more pronounced.

"I know that," replied the prince, "although the governor-general of Warsaw would deny it."

"But will the Germans come here?"

"God only knows. At this point, I'd say anything was possible."

But the prince knew what the peasant was thinking. If the Germans didn't come to them, why should they kill his son in a far-off place the boy had never seen before and should never have been in? There really was no answer.

One of the few people who was still full of fighting spirit was Count Volodya Grekov, a newly created major. Seriously wounded in East Prussia at the battle of Tannenberg in 1914, he was now fully recovered from his wounds and ready to go back to the front. And he had just received the honor of an imperial invitation to appear at Tsarskoye Selo to be awarded the Order of St. Andrew.

It was a private audience. Conducted through the vast Alexander Palace by the master of ceremonies, Count Frederiks, an elderly gentleman with a beautiful head of fluffy white hair and an impressive gold-embroidered uniform, Volodya was shown into Nicholas's private study where the tsar was waiting, looking extremely tired in the plain uniform of a colonel.

As the new major approached, Nicholas shook his hand warmly and congratulated him on his recent recovery. He had read the dispatches and knew Volodya was one of the few survivors of the Elizabethgrad Hussars to come out of that battle. So typical. Very few of the officers who had gone off to war in August of last year were still around. This rugged-looking, sandy-haired fellow had beaten enormous odds.

Nicholas had heard about Volodya from the tsaritsa, who in turn had been given a detailed account of his exploits by his former wife, Natalya. The countess was now almost nostalgic for the past, when she and Volodya had first been married and he hadn't yet begun to complain about her religious excesses. When her mother-in-law had reported on Volodya's martial exploits and told her how he had fought at Tannenberg, Natalya had relayed the story to her imperial patroness, who suggested a medal. Unaware of all of this, the count was flattered by all the attention and deeply moved to meet his tsar in a private audience and receive the medal.

On his way out, Volodya spotted a familiar figure descending a staircase in the private apartments. For a minute, he hesitated; then, recalling the lost opportunity at the outbreak of the war, he spoke.

"Natalya! Is it you?"

The blonde woman turned, her face thinner than the last time they had met. "Hello, Volodya," she said warmly, looking at him as though a harsh word had never passed between them. "How are you?"

"I'm fine. I just received the Order of St. Andrew," he said, not quite knowing what to say. "How are you?"

"Oh," she smiled, "the same."

The overdressed footman who was conducting the major through the palace looked perplexed. The fellow was supposed to leave, not stand in the corridor talking with the tsaritsa's lady-in-waiting. This wasn't proper behavior.

Ignoring the servant in his red and black livery, Volodya looked at Natalya, who had caused him so much misery, and felt sad. He had heard all the gossip about her and Gigi, had heard the rumors about little Nicky's paternity, and he wished his brother had done a better job with her than he himself had. She needed someone to tear her away from Gregory Efimovich, and apparently Gigi was as incapable of it as he had been. Poor Natalya. She was a fool.

When Volodya and Natalya parted that day after taking a long walk in the park of the Alexander Palace, the count felt satisfied that somehow he had made peace with her. But the feeling she left him with was deeply unsettling. He knew now without a doubt that she was lost to him—and to Gigi too, for that matter—forever.

One day in late June 1915, in response to his repeated requests for an interview, Prince Sviridov received an invitation to have lunch with Grand Duke Constantine Andreevich, Inspector-General of Military Hospitals. To Adam's surprise, Madame Kashina was present, a startling departure from normal etiquette.

Over a magnum of Moët, *langoustes à la parisienne* surrounded by deviled eggs, and elegant little vegetables, followed by a magnificent bowl of *fraises Romanoff* and coffee, Prince Sviridov explained his position vis-à-vis the army. He was not desirous of incurring anyone's wrath, he stated, but he was also not about to stand by and see his field stations forced to close because some incompetents with good connections resented his agency. Russian soldiers didn't.

"Bravo!" exclaimed Kashina, the breeze ruffling the organdy frill around the low neck of her frock as she raised her champagne glass. "As the only nonaristocrat present, I salute you on behalf of the people."

At that, Constantine Andreevich turned to his mistress, smiled, kissed her free hand, and remarked that Kashina's nobility lay in her art, elevating her beyond mere rank or title.

Those long-lashed brown-velvet eyes met Adam's above Constantine's handsome head, and the dancer smiled, sending a shock of pleasure through Prince Sviridov's body.

"I would like Your Imperial Highness to help my agency keep its premises open, even if they displease certain gentlemen in the military establishment. Russian lives are at stake, not my personal prestige."

Settling back in his chair, Constantine Andreevich glanced out over the edge of the balcony of his charming pink-marble palace where he and his guests had enjoyed such a pleasant luncheon. The flower gardens were in riotous bloom, tiny red "firecrackers" making a border around dozens of carefully laid out flower beds. It was his favorite vantage point. So peaceful. So orderly. So unlike army headquarters.

"I understand what you're telling me, prince," he replied. "Believe me, it is not the army per se that opposes your good work, but merely a clique of jealous officers whose own endeavors fall so far short of the mark. And, of course," he murmured, "you are not a Russian."

"Can we do something about it, Highness?"

That provoked a wry smile. The clique His Imperial Highness referred to consisted of some of his own relatives and their friends. No. There was really not that much he could do, except to humor this Amer-Russian. That, at least, was within the realm of the possible.

"I will lend my support, prince," he declared, looking Adam squarely in the eye. "This is a matter of some consequence for the troops, and God knows, they get little enough consideration from anyone."

"Thank you, Your Imperial Highness," replied Adam, genuinely grateful.

"I would like to give a performance to help your agency," Kashina added seductively, "but on two conditions."

"Name them, Madame."

"That I can give it at one of your field hospitals and that you will attend."

His Imperial Highness looked startled. "Zenaida, that's not possible."

"What, Highness?" asked the dancer. "The performance or Prince Sviridov's presence?"

The exchange of glances was a study in icy hauteur. Kashina outdid her lover. She knew he had no intention of giving Adam any real support beyond a few words of encouragement.

"A performance at a frontline hospital is too dangerous. You would only get in the way, my dear. And besides, civilian travel in the war zone is about to be curtailed. It's too risky."

"It's also too risky for the soldiers, Your Highness. But they're there."

"I don't care to discuss this right now, my dear. We'll take it up later."

So this was domestic life at the top, thought Adam, studying the middle-aged grand duke and his youthful mistress. Kashina was at least thirty-four, Constantine around forty-five. Adam wondered where the grand duchess lived. Perhaps she had exiled herself to the south of France, so beloved of the Russian aristocracy.

When Adam reached the Sviridov Palace after his luncheon, he found a small envelope waiting for him on one of the Louis Quinze tables in the foyer.

Opening it, he found a lady's white calling card. On the back was a message. "I will do the performance at the front. K."

"My God," he murmured. "She won."

But truthfully he didn't know if he was pleased or worried. Tapping the card against the palm of his hand, he remembered Kashina playing gypsy with him at the Medved restaurant. "Three great loves," she'd said. Why did that thought make him so uneasy? There was nothing Kashina could offer him to make him want to deceive his wife. Was there? "Put the thought out of your mind," he said almost inaudibly. But it remained, along with memories of a lovely pair of brown-velvet eyes, predatory as a great cat from the steppes.

Without a second's hesitation, Adam tore up the small white card and handed the pieces to the footman, sprinting up the stairs to pay his twins a surprise visit in their nursery.

When Princess Anya heard of Kashina's proposal, she listened with polite interest and asked, "Why?"

"I suppose because she sees it as a patriotic gesture. She's been generous in her support of our agency."

"Yes," nodded the princess. "She has."

But they both felt uneasy about the idea, although neither would admit it. Both felt foolish to express doubts about something that hadn't yet happened.

Standing with Adam under the chandelier in their bedroom, Anya reached up and stroked his face, caressing him with the gentle touch she used with her babies. "I love you very much," she whispered.

"I know you do. I also hope you know how much I love you."

"That's good to hear."

He looked shocked. "Have you ever doubted it?"

"No, darling, never," she lied.

Pressing her tenderly against his chest, Adam picked his wife up and carried her across the antique Chinese carpet to their bed, a huge gilded Venetian structure from a palace that was slowly sinking into the Grand Canal. Sandro had thoughtfully rescued the building's decor years before.

Adam placed Anya softly on the silken coverlet and turned out the lights. "When I married you," he murmured, getting into bed beside her, "I was convinced I had the most beautiful girl in St. Petersburg. And it was true. But now I have someone even more beautiful—the loveliest married woman in Petrograd."

Laying his head on her breast, Adam nuzzled her gently as Anya caressed his dark hair, burrowing close to him like a child as she murmured endearments in his ear, kissing him softly among the soft, silken covers.

"Sometimes when I'm away from home, I clutch my pillow, pretending it's you," he confessed. "It makes me feel less lonely."

"Sometimes I wrap myself in your old dressing gown. The one you bought on our honeymoon," she said, stroking his back as he stretched out alongside her, cradling her in the crook of his arm and enfolding her warm body.

"I hate this war," he said, caressing Anya's soft curves under the lace-and-satin nightgown. "I could say I hate it because of all the bloodshed and the insanity of prolonging it, but that would be a lie, *dushka*. I hate it for the most selfish of reasons—because it's keeping me from you and our children."

He took his wife in his arms and kissed her ear, her neck, leaving a trail of warm, soft kisses down her bosom and across her shoulders. Slowly, voluptuously, he slipped his hands down her arms until he had taken hold of her wrists, gently pinning them above her head as she arched her body against his, her long blonde hair spilling across the lace-trimmed pillows, a golden river against the pale-pink silk bedcovers.

"I love you so much," Anya whispered, gently slipping her arms around him, kissing him softly as he enfolded her in his embrace.

Much later, as she and Adam lay nestled in each other's arms after their lovemaking, Anya pillowed her head on his chest and sighed softly, tremulously. She feared Adam's departure.

"I love you," she murmured, drowsily entwining her fingers in his. "Forever."

"Forever," he repeated, cuddling against her warmth, satisfied. "Nothing less, *dushka*."

At that moment, anything else would have seemed impossible. Yet was that really so? wondered Anya as she lay curled in Adam's arms. Did anything good last forever? She had been wrong before, when she thought she and her family were safe from that demented peasant, Ivanov. She could be wrong now.

Kissing Adam's tousled black hair, the princess suddenly found herself thinking of Kashina alone with him, far from home, using her considerable attractions to seduce him just for the pleasure of it, the way a naughty child smashes something rare and precious out of a selfish desire to satisfy a whim. Kashina was capable of it. Anya knew that. And Auntie Lisa had given the ballerina ample reason to hate the Sviridovs by exposing her to shame and ridicule. A woman as proud as Kashina would remember that forever and take suitable revenge when the opportunity presented itself.

Lisa was no longer around to suffer the consequences. She was. All her instincts told the princess to beware of the ballerina even when she appeared at her most charming, for that was when she was especially dangerous. Adam didn't seem able to see it. Perhaps he had a reason.

No, thought Anya. That was unreasonable. Her faith in him was strong; he had never given her cause for doubt. But left alone with a woman like that, a collector of broken hearts, adrift in a war zone, what kind of chance did he have?

And if he ever betrayed her with Kashina, could she ever feel the same way about him? It was a terrible thought, almost as dreadful as the prospect of his death, for if he ever became Kashina's lover, she knew their marriage would be finished, no matter how passionately she loved him. She wasn't made of the same cloth as Gigi Grekov, betrayed time after time by Natalya, who pretended there was nothing wrong. My God! That wasn't a marriage! It was a living death.

As Anya lay in her husband's arms, she thought of those long-ago days in Paris when she had been close to killing herself, shattered by Ivanov's attack and its consequences. It was Adam who had restored her to life and given her a better future than she could ever have hoped for.

On the very day he'd arrived to become her fiancé, he had been delayed by Kashina. How ironic. The ballerina's love affairs then had been amusing, something out of a Parisian comedy, involving characters whose hearts were too tough ever to break. Now it all seemed different. Anya knew *her* heart was fragile. It would take so little to shatter it forever. As she nestled closer and closer to Adam in their silken bed, she only hoped he knew it too.

◆   ◆   ◆

When Princess Anya saw her husband off on another of his visits to the Polish front, she was accompanied by her three beautiful children, Aunt Ksenia, Uncle Andrei and even Tatiana Sergeevna, the clan resplendent in white summer linens, the women carrying fluffy lace parasols against the July heat, Andrei in his straw boater. All were concerned about Prince Sviridov's safety in the crumbling sector he was about to tour.

"Don't take any unnecessary risks," murmured Anya, kissing him as he boarded the train, despite the hundreds of soldiers regarding the family with interest. Their wives and families were far away and just as worried. A few of the younger men patted Byelochka shyly on the head as they passed by, remembering small sons left far behind in Kazan, Smolensk or Tyumen, possibly forever.

Some of them were observing with bitter satisfaction that this war could make even the *boyars* suffer. It was their sole comfort.

26

From the atmosphere in the briefing room, Prince Sviridov realized things were a lot worse than the army would admit. The Germans were breaking through along the Narev River, and Stavka, army headquarters, had decreed a retreat to the Vistula. Poland was being taken from them piece by piece, against a background of immense human suffering.

"All civilian operations will cease immediately in the areas being evacuated. Prince Sviridov, you will destroy any of your stations in the affected areas, in keeping with official policy."

"But what about our supplies? Surely the army can make use of them."

The elderly general glared at Adam. "The army," he said icily, "has enough problems of its own. It doesn't need to be bothered with the debris of civilian establishments. Destroy everything in the path of the enemy."

"General, Russian soldiers are dying in every sector of this war because they lack precisely what I'm offering."

"Prince," replied the general, "the army doesn't have the necessary equipment to transport your supplies. We can barely move our wounded. All we can do now is prevent the Germans from getting their hands on anything useful."

The army was being routed; they no longer controlled the situation in Poland. It controlled them, and it was becoming more dismal by the day. Warsaw was rapidly filling up with civilian refugees fleeing the fighting in the rear areas, with transports of wounded due for shipment out of the war zone and with tons of dismantled machinery slated for destinations in Russia, too precious to be left to fall into the hands of the Germans. The entire city was a turbulent swarm of humanity, hot, frightened and prepared for disaster.

When Adam returned to his hotel suite at the Rossiya, which served as bedroom and operational headquarters for the Amer-Russians in Warsaw, he was startled to find a letter awaiting him, addressed in a very elegant feminine hand.

Opening it quickly, the young man learned that Kashina was in Poland with the grand duke in spite of his previous objections and was visiting the troops—Adam knew she meant officers—on a morale-boosting round of appearances. She was to make a stop at Zegrze, thirty miles from Warsaw on the morrow and would be delighted if Adam Mikhailovich could come out to see her.

My God, thought the prince, that's crazy. The front is about to disintegrate and Constantine Andreevich allows his mistress to go to Zegrze. It was in a dangerous area, quite close to the fighting. No man in his right mind would agree to let a woman go there. But perhaps Constantine knew nothing about the ballerina's decision. She didn't strike Adam as a timid woman; she'd very likely do exactly as she pleased.

No wonder Sandro had loved her so much. She was a lot like his own ladies, beautiful, brave and stubborn. Damned stubborn.

For a minute Adam hesitated. The thought of seeing Kashina was enticing, especially since he had been thinking of visiting Zegrze anyway to check on the condition of the front. He had a warehouse full of supplies to ship back to Russia and wanted to know just how much time he had to get them out of Warsaw before he lost them. Conditions at Zegrze should be a reliable indicator. If a breakthrough was imminent, he'd better get them out as soon as possible.

Lying down on his bed, the prince threw the letter on the night table and stared up at the plaster work of the ceiling, studying the swirl of moldings around the crystal chandelier. Kashina was very foolish to do this. She was used to traveling great distances for her prewar engagements, so perhaps she found nothing unusual about it. Still, the idea of a woman venturing so far into a war zone appalled Adam. The civilian corpses he had seen in the countryside included women as well as men, a sight that never failed to horrify him.

Thinking of that grim vision, Adam Mikhailovich Sviridov was extremely grateful Anya was safe at home in the Sviridov Palace on the French Embankment, surrounded by their three children and a house full of servants. Whatever happened here in Poland would never touch her.

It was the only comforting thought he had at the moment.

The next day, borrowing a car from the agency's motorpool, Adam set off for Zegrze. He was one of the few drivers on the road heading in that direction, though traffic was fairly heavy coming into Warsaw from the outlying regions, with all sorts of peculiar vehicles pressed into service to bring civilians in from areas recently overrun by the Germans. Adam saw everything from two-wheeled donkey carts to shiny French automobiles. It was a pathetic parade streaming into the Polish capital. Families trudged alongside carts piled high with the few belongings they had managed to save from the invaders. Old carthorses staggered in their harnesses as they clomped doggedly along dusty roads, exhausted by the journey and the pace they were forced to keep. One farm family had a cart loaded with a huge pile of potatoes; the grandmother was sitting on top of the heap, looking forlorn and weary, her cotton kerchief wrapped around her head like the kerchiefs of Russian peasant women Adam often saw at Byelaya Beryozka. A bundle of belongings was clutched in her hands.

"Don't go to Zegrze, Monsieur," cried a Russian officer cantering past on a tired-looking black horse that was covered with sweat. "The Germans are close by! I've just come from that area."

"How close are they?" shouted Adam, desperate for information.

"A few kilometers away," replied the officer, repeating a false rumor. And then before the American could question him further, he repeated his warning and rode off in the direction of Warsaw.

Shocked, Adam calculated that army headquarters was either misinformed or lying like hell. Official reports placed the Germans much farther away than that. But the reports had possibly been put out to forestall panic in the city until the very last minute—at which point the chaos would be nightmarish.

Glancing at a bunch of ragged travelers who were staring with great interest at his new automobile, the prince asked in what he hoped was a semblance of Polish, "*Nemtsy à Zegrze?*"

Screwing up his weather-beaten face in an effort to understand what the foreigner was trying to say, a Polish peasant suddenly understood and nodded emphatically. "*Nemtsy,*" he agreed, gesturing in the direction Adam was taking. Germans. He attempted to indicate many Germans.

Hesitating, the well-dressed young man in the motorcar glanced up the road, then back at the Poles. "Thanks for the warning," he said to the puzzled farmer. Then fishing a large can of American cookies out of the back seat, he tossed them to the man, drawing cries of delight from the fellow's family.

He was going to Zegrze, even though it appeared to be a very bad idea that was getting worse by the minute.

When Adam approached the army outpost at Zegrze, he found almost total chaos. A meeting of officers was being held in a wooden peasant hut. The wounded were being evacuated to the nearby railroad station and from there to Warsaw or farther north to Russia. Two horses had managed to break away from their hobbles and were giving several soldiers a hard time as they tried to rope them. The whole place was hot and dusty in the July sun and utterly disorganized. To his surprise, nobody challenged him as he drove into the camp, unauthorized and alone.

Heading for the officers' hut, Prince Adam saw a familiar figure standing outside, smoking a cigarette—Major Volodya Grekov, Countess Natalya's ex-husband, Gigi's brother.

"Adam Mikhailovich! What the hell are you doing here? Are you crazy? The whole area's about to be overrun."

"When did it start to heat up?" asked the American. "I just received a letter from a lady who said she was about to pay you a visit."

Volodya grimaced. He knew Adam had to be referring to Madame Kashina. She had arrived the previous night to visit an old friend of hers—his colonel—and had found herself a lot closer to the enemy than she had ever planned to be. The colonel had insisted upon telegraphing Grand Duke Constantine for the best way to get Kashina back to Warsaw unscathed and hadn't yet received an answer. That meant either trouble with the wires or German sabotage. Now Kashina was demanding to be put on a train with the troops and returned to Warsaw, even in a third-class coach if necessary. But the colonel wouldn't consent to that, not wishing to bring down her protector's wrath on his head. Still, he hadn't been able to come up with a better suggestion.

"Where is she?" asked the prince, rather amused.

"With some of the wounded who are about to be shipped out," replied Volodya.

When Adam located the ballerina, he was surprised to find her in the makeshift field hospital, talking animatedly to the patients and doing her best to calm their fears of the trip to Warsaw through what was rapidly becoming German territory. It was a revelation. As the prince stood in the doorway, watching Zenaida banter in the rough-and-ready slang of Moscow's working class, talking with these men who had surely never had the chance to see her at the Maryinsky or at any European opera house, Adam felt he was seeing her for the first time. Relieved of the necessity to be an inauthentic *grande dame* among the aristocracy, Zenaida was allowing herself the luxury of being what she was before she'd become an idol—a tough girl from Moscow's slums who still retained enough of the vernacular to make her listeners howl with laughter as she described her own experiences in the war zone.

These men didn't know who the hell she was; they just thought she had a lot of nerve and they liked her for it. Enjoying her performance, Adam liked her too, surprising himself. Without her usual jewelry, makeup and couture gowns, with her dark hair in a single plait down her back and her expression relaxed and cheerful, Zenaida looked like a young girl, so different from her usual pose of guarded grandeur. Adam wondered if Sandro had ever got to see this side of her. He rather doubted it.

When the ballerina realized she was being observed, she turned around with a little start, not knowing how long the prince had been watching.

At the appearance of the *barin,* the soldiers stopped talking and regarded him with curiosity.

"I received your letter," said Adam, a little awkwardly as he and Kashina strolled outside. "It was a very bad idea to come here. The Germans are closing in."

"They weren't so close when I decided to make the trip. And now I'm having a difficult time leaving. My friend, Colonel Saltykov, is afraid Constantine Andreevich will have him court-martialed if he doesn't get me back to Warsaw in one piece, but he hasn't yet found a good way of doing so."

"You don't seem too frightened."

The petite dancer looked up at the prince and smiled. "I'm concerned," she said.

When Adam found his way to the colonel's office, he discovered the cause for the uproar. The Germans had cut through the Russian lines unexpectedly and were in the process of being repelled by a Russian force that needed reinforcements fast. Colonel Saltykov had just received orders and was doing all he could to move his men up to the front, transfer the wounded to Warsaw and send Kashina safely back to her grand duke.

When Adam offered to take responsibility for getting Madame Kashina back to the Polish capital, Saltykov sized him up as reliable, gave him a hearty handshake and turned Kashina over to him. They had been lovers a long time ago, and he still worried about her. He would trust this foreigner to take care of her. He would have to.

As Adam and the ballerina were about to get into the agency's motorcar for the ride back to the capital, a messenger came sprinting toward them from the direction of the headquarters hut. The Germans had been spotted on the Warsaw road. It was an unconfirmed but very scary rumor.

"My God," murmured Kashina. Suddenly, she was afraid. She had heard the horror stories about boche brutality and didn't wish to verify them personally.

Adam saw Volodya in the group of officers just preparing to mount up and he ran to catch up with his friend, hoping he might be able to help. The prince had one hope of getting out of there without traveling on the Warsaw road.

Unknown to anyone but a few Russian officers in Poland, Prince Adam had flown on several dangerous noncombat missions, bad eye notwithstanding. If anyone had ever found out about this foolish and decidedly unneutral practice, Adam's head would have been on the line. As it was, everything had gone well thus far. But there was always the possibility of detection if the Germans shot him down. That, he hoped, would never happen. At the very least, it would probably be the end to his diplomatic career. Still, he only felt guilty whenever he thought of how horrified Anya and the family would be if he were to be reported shot down over some Polish cabbage patch when he wasn't even supposed to be flying in the first place.

"Volodya," Adam said now to his friend, "would you do me a favor before you go?"

"Name it."

"Get your friend Captain Danilov on the line and tell him I need one of his airplanes. I have to get back to Warsaw without taking the main road, and his pack of Spads are my best bet."

Unauthorized use of military equipment, thought Major Grekov. A very serious offense. He wondered what Adam Mikhailovich was going to offer Danilov for that.

After a few unsuccessful tries, Volodya managed to get in touch with Danilov, who was in charge of several airplanes at a small airdrome two miles from their camp. "Affirmative," came the reply.

After Adam and Kashina had said their brief farewells to the departing officers, they headed toward the motorcar and set out for the airdrome located at the edge of a small forest of fir trees.

Despite the fierce fighting not too far away, the crews at the airdrome were relaxing, having received no orders to engage the enemy in the skies. No Germans had shown themselves overhead and the Russians weren't about to go looking for them. The squadron was still recovering from their last encounter, trying to repair the planes after a particularly savage dogfight that had taken the lives of two of their best pilots.

Adam knew Danilov slightly, having met him in Warsaw with Volodya. That both men had participated in the St. Petersburg-to-Moscow air race had created a certain camaraderie between them, a fact which the prince was going to rely on right now. And he hoped the captain was a lover of the ballet. As it turned out, Danilov, a small wiry fellow with curly dark hair and blue eyes, was overwhelmed to encounter Prince Adam's precious cargo, and he delighted her when he expressed his admiration for her Esmeralda, which he said he'd seen in St. Petersburg, Paris and Warsaw.

While Kashina was making conversation with Danilov and the men of his squadron, Adam was checking the condition of the planes, which left a lot to be desired. After a year of use, they were ready for the scrap heap. Even the newest was damaged—but it would fly.

While Adam was talking with the mechanics, Madame Kashina was casting suspicious glances at him. He actually expected her to fly in one of these things. Close up, it really didn't look like a good idea.

"There must be another way to get back to Warsaw," said Kashina as the prince cheerfully announced he had found their means of escape.

"Not the main roads. Too risky. And they're no longer sure about the railways either. This is the best way out today."

Kashina stared at the tall prince who looked absolutely serious about this bizarre notion. She did not want to die young. She had a palace on Liteiny Prospect, a dacha near Peterhof, a large bank account and a vault crammed with precious jewels. Plus a career that kept bringing in more of the same.

"Are you quite mad?" she demanded, staring at Adam Mikhailovich. To think she'd planned on seducing this madman to spite the Sviridovs! Let Anya have him. He was dangerous.

Looking down at the dark-haired ballerina, Prince Sviridov was al-most glad to find something that intimidated her. After hearing all the stories from his wife and her aunt, one would think the woman had horns. "I know how to fly these," said Adam. "Believe me, it's the best way to return to Warsaw today. Don't be afraid."

Standing there in the middle of the airdrome, with the pilots looking on and envying Adam Mikhailovich, Kashina felt lost. Trains were her usual method of travel, especially private railway cars. She had covered all of Europe and the Balkans by rail and had even ventured into places like Constantinople to entertain the Russian ambassador, but she had never tried leaving the ground, and she didn't plan to start at this late date. "I'm not getting into that thing," replied Kashina. "There *has* to be an-other way."

Adam looked down at Kashina, glowered a little and, without warn-ing, scooped her up and carried her to the plane. Her bloodcurdling screams had him half-expecting the Russians to come running after him to rescue their favorite ballerina, but to his amusement they didn't. They knew what the roads were like. They considered Adam's plan a lot safer.

"I'm going to tell Constantine Andreevich what you did to me!" screamed Kashina as the prince placed her in the rear seat and buckled her in. One of the pilots tossed him a jacket, which he told her to put on, and someone else offered caps and goggles.

"Fly this to the airdrome outside the city," shouted Danilov. "I'll let them know to expect you."

"Will there be a problem?" Adam shouted back.

"No. Leave that to me."

"Danilov!" screamed Kashina. "This man is crazy. Don't let him do this to me!"

"*Nichevo,*" replied Danilov with a grin, using an all-encompassing phrase which signified that everything was fine. "Trust him. He's good. I wouldn't let him borrow the plane if he weren't!"

These men are all crazy, thought Kashina, crossing herself with a fervor she hadn't displayed in twenty years. Silently invoking the help of the Kazan Madonna, she felt the motor start to roar. She clung to the seat as Adam began to taxi the small airplane down the runway—a grassy field. Three placid sheep were grazing peacefully as the old Spad began to gather speed, its body reverberating with every bump in the terrain. They didn't even raise their heads.

As Adam gave the Russian pilots the thumbs-up sign and began his ascent, Kashina gasped at the sight of the ground getting farther and farther away. The group of pilots on the field became smaller and smaller as the plane rose into the blue sky high above the countryside, a noisy olive bird racing toward the clouds.

My God, thought the ballerina, it looks so strange, like the maps she had seen laid out on Constantine Andreevich's desk. Or a peasant quilt made up of patches of green, yellows and browns. It was fascinating and gorgeous at the same time. And she was looking at it from God knows how many feet above the earth.

"This is extraordinary!" she shouted, more delighted than frightened now. "I love it!"

Adam heard some sort of sound drowned out by the roar of the motor and hoped Madame Kashina wasn't still threatening him. She'd probably raise hell with her grand duke, but at this point he didn't care. He wanted to get back to the city as fast as he could and this was the best way. If he hoped to salvage his supplies, every minute counted.

As the airplane flew peacefully on its way toward the Warsaw airdrome, the prince saw something in the distance that made his heart skip a beat—a Fokker E III.

"Damn," muttered Adam. What were the Germans doing this close to Warsaw? None had ever been reported in this sector. Just his luck they had decided to make the trip now.

Thinking of his ambassador's reaction if he was discovered piloting this plane, he decided he had only one choice—outrun the boche. Gunning the engine for all it was worth, Prince Sviridov silently prayed Danilov's mechanics did good work. He was about to push this plane to its limits.

In the rear, Kashina had become quite relaxed, although she clutched her seat harness each time a gust of strong wind buffetted the plane. It was a little terrifying but undeniably exciting. Men had done a variety of peculiar things to her in her career, but nobody had ever abducted her by airplane. This was a first!

In the clear blue sky, the German had seen the Spad with Russian markings just as Adam had spotted him. To the boche's surprise, the Russian showed no desire for combat and seemed to be doing his best to get out of his range. The German was on a lone reconnaissance mission, spying on Russian troop movements; nobody had challenged him in what ought to have been Russian airspace. It annoyed him. He had one kill to go before he could be officially classified as an ace.

Why not? he thought, smiling a little at the sight of his fleeing enemy. It wouldn't even be too difficult. And putting on a burst of speed, the boche flew after the Russian, determined to become an ace that afternoon.

As the Fokker came closer, Adam knew he would have to fight. There was no escape. He thought of that Berliner who had sent him to the hospital and cursed him for damaging his eye. If ever he needed perfect vision, it was now. He wouldn't even allow himself to think of the woman in the back. If he did, it would make him cautious, and right now, he was going to need every bit of nerve he possessed.

Catching up with the Spad, the German made a swoop that brought him near Adam's side. He fired rapidly, then dove to get his bearings and try again.

"Son of a bitch!" The bullets had pierced Adam's wing in several spots but had done no harm to either occupant of the plane. Now the bastard was going to have another go at them.

Taking the Spad down in a sudden dive, Adam spoiled the other pilot's pass and fired off a burst from the plane's machine gun straight at the boche. To his amazement, the gun worked. It was the first time he had ever used one.

Encountering unexpected resistance, the German tried another approach, this time attempting to fly at the Russian straight on, firing like mad.

As he saw what the German intended, Adam began to climb, gunning the motor for all it was worth. If he could get above this maniac, he could shoot at him from above, a safer position than the one the German intended for him.

In the back seat, Kashina felt numb with terror and almost breathless with excitement. It was insane. She might die in the middle of this blue Polish sky in a ridiculous accident that nobody would ever be able to understand. If she did, it would be the ultimate joke of the war. It would also be lovely revenge on the Sviridovs—dying under suspicious circumstances with Prince Adam. But Kashina preferred to enjoy her revenge!

"Come on, damn it," Adam was muttering to the Spad. "Climb!" As the plane rose to soar above the Fokker, Prince Sviridov started firing, then watched in fascination as the bullets tore holes through the wings and body of the German's plane. To his surprise, both pilot and plane seemed unharmed. Then suddenly Adam saw a plume of black smoke wafting upward from the Fokker. The plane started to lose power and began falling.

"He's hit!" shouted Kashina, her voice drowned out by the noise of the motor. "He's going down!"

As if they were watching the scene in slow motion, Adam and his passenger saw the Fokker slowly lose control, plunge rapidly and finally hit the ground, crashing into several pieces in a Polish meadow and bursting into flames.

"Get out of there!" the prince found himself screaming as he watched helplessly from the air. He had gone through the same thing in a Moscow meadow, and the memory made him go white as he saw no sign of the pilot emerging from the wreck. The bastard had tried to kill them. Why hadn't he just allowed them to continue on their way? The fool. He had probably considered them an easy target.

Watching the black cloud of smoke rising higher over the burning Fokker, Adam saw several small figures rush toward the plane—Polish peasants. If the German wasn't already dead in the wreck, he soon would be, thought the prince. Well, he had chosen his fate himself.

Prince Sviridov was silently grateful another German pilot had once been his teacher, and dipping his right wing in a gesture of farewell, he continued on to the airdrome outside Warsaw without further delay.

Danilov had already sent word ahead to prepare the Warsaw pilots for Adam's arrival. When the Spad landed with bullet holes in its wing, everyone wanted to know all the details. After giving Prince Sviridov a stern reprimand for his foolish disregard for American neutrality, the commanding officer ordered champagne all around and enveloped the prince in a bone-crushing bear hug.

For once in her life, Zenaida Kashina was willing to relinquish center stage to someone else.

As Adam and Kashina were driven back to Warsaw, courtesy of the airdrome's pilots, the prince felt as if he were emerging from a strange, distorted dream. He had nearly been killed that afternoon and he had shot down another pilot. It was the sort of thing that happened every day in this war, but it was the first time it had happened to him and he found it disturbing. He wasn't sentimental. It had been a question of his death or the German's, and luckily his number wasn't yet up.

But he didn't have any business being up there, a citizen of a neutral country in a Russian plane engaged in a dogfight with a German over Poland. If he and not the German had gone down, the State Department would have had a lot of explaining to do to the Wilhelmstrasse. Christ!

What an embarrassment that would have been. Dying with Zenaida Kashina would have been the icing on the cake.

Arriving at Kashina's hotel, Adam intended merely to deposit her
safely inside the lobby and leave, but he was surprised to receive an invitation to join her for dinner.

"I'm not really hungry," he said, glancing around the crowded lobby.

Kashina smiled. "Neither am I. But I'm still shaking from the fright you
gave me this afternoon and the least you can do is keep me company."

The Moscow accent was gone, replaced by Kashina's perfect St. Petersburg drawl. Once again she was the self she had worked so hard to create
over the years. After her experience this afternoon, her quick recovery fascinated the prince.

The ballerina looked up into his eyes with a touch of wickedness as
he faltered, tired and hesitant among the tall white columns and potted
palms of the hotel lobby.

"I'll tell your fortune, prince," smiled Kashina, taking his hand.

"Are you afraid of anything, Zenaida Felixovna?" Adam murmured,
thinking of the dogfight that afternoon, their survival and the absurdity of
it all.

Smiling into his dark eyes, Zenaida gently shook her head. "Not of
men," she said.

"I don't doubt that."

Amused, Zenaida took his hand. "Come," she said. "Let's find out
just how fearless I am."

Fascinated by the delicate creature who had nearly perished with him
that afternoon, the woman who had captivated Sandro Sviridov, numerous
princes and one very susceptible member of the imperial family, Adam forgot
about the driver waiting outside and the crowd of people in the lobby, some
of whom knew him. All there was at that moment was Kashina.

Without a word he followed her up the marble staircase and down
several corridors until they came to the white-and-gilt-paneled door of her
suite. He was moving like a man in a dream. This isn't real, he thought.
No.

As the ballerina paused on the threshold, waiting for her maid to let
them in, she looked up at the prince. "Do you remember that day we
made arrangements for the gala? The day I read your palm?"

"Yes," murmured Adam, seeing nothing but Kashina's gorgeous dark
eyes. Was he insane? he wondered. He no longer knew. Why didn't he
leave?

"I said there would be three loves for you. Would you say I was a
prophet?"

Whether there was a gleam of triumph or simply affection in those beautiful eyes, Adam wasn't quite certain. He was so wild to bury himself in the woman's arms that he murmured something incoherent and remembered very little afterward, except that he and Kashina were both very excited, grateful to be alive and desperate to forget the afternoon and its terror.

But as Prince Sviridov lay nestled in Zenaida's bed, caressing her tenderly after their lovemaking, he knew love had very little to do with his actions. The woman he loved was hundreds of miles away.

And he was a disgrace.

27

Petrograd

The July weather was pleasant and warm in Petrograd's Letny Sad, Peter the Great's Summer Gardens, now a public park for the enjoyment of the citizens. Princess Anya was strolling there with her brother-in-law, accompanied by her small son and his new nurse—not a Russian *nyanya*, but an authentic British nanny with several years' experience in the households of the aristocracy. Princess Anya wanted her children to be able to speak their father's language fluently and was taking steps to ensure it. Although Adam would have preferred to hear his offspring speak to him in his own Boston accent rather than in Nanny's British tones, the difficulty of transatlantic travel these days had made it hard to acquire a Boston girl. So Nanny had been hired to preserve the young Sviridovs' English-speaking heritage, but there were French and Russian girls to tend them and speak to them as well.

Right now, Princess Anya had other things on her mind besides her children's upbringing. Billy had just received an urgent wire from his brother in Warsaw ordering him to send him a train to help in the evacuation of men and supplies from their establishments in Poland. Without delay.

"But why won't the army give him top priority?" demanded Anya, glancing at Byelochka, who was walking ahead of them with Nanny, chattering gaily as he pointed out his favorite spots in the park. He was a beautiful little blond child, as fair as his mother, with just a trace of Adam in his features, although none of their relatives ever noticed it. The baby girls were acknowledged to look like their father though, in spite of their blonde hair and blue eyes.

The American looked worried. It wasn't like him and it bothered the princess. "The army is giving Adam a hard time because he wants to cart off a trainload of our equipment instead of destroying it, as they wish."

"But why would they want to destroy it?" Anya asked, puzzled.

"Because if it's left behind, the Germans will make use of it. And

326

because a certain clique of officers in Warsaw never liked the idea of the Amer-Russian War Relief Agency to begin with. We've run into this attitude many times, more than I'd like to remember. It's all politics. And jealousy."

Anya knew that was true. She had seen trainloads of wounded arrive at Petrograd's Warsaw Station, dirty, still wearing bloodstained uniforms and lying in their own filth. That was how the government was tending its wounded. Men who were lucky enough to be taken to the Amer-Russian facilities near the battlefields came home in much better shape. And it had caused resentment. Gentlemen at parties in Petrograd were beginning to make remarks about "foreigners meddling in Russian affairs," which exasperated Princess Anya. What Adam was doing for the Russian war effort was more than most of her Petrograd friends were doing, and she felt they should be grateful.

"Adam doesn't deserve to be treated like this," said Anya, thoughtfully twirling the lacy white parasol she carried. "We'll just have to make sure he gets his train."

Billy glanced at his lovely sister-in-law. She appeared to be serious.

"Anya," he reminded her, "the people who oppose our organization are the same ones in a position to deny him a train."

"Nonsense. We have very good connections. Without them, you and Adam could never have undertaken your work in the first place."

"True," acknowledged her companion, "but don't forget, the problem is centered in Warsaw. We'll have to find a way to get around it."

The princess paused in her stroll and surveyed the peaceful scene: children playing near a small basin, frolicking gaily in the sunshine, her little boy chasing a butterfly under the watchful eye of his nanny. She could only imagine what her husband faced in Warsaw, far from home and family. Terribly close to the Germans. And Madame Kashina.

"We'll try getting in touch with Grand Duke Constantine. He's inspector-general of the military hospitals. Wouldn't his signature count for something? And the minister of war, Polivanov. He's on good terms with you, isn't he?"

"But they're far from where the trouble is."

"If we could get them to order a train to be placed at Adam's disposal, that would carry a lot of weight."

"It would certainly be difficult for a local commander to dispute a direct order from the minister of war," agreed Billy. "Especially in a time of crisis."

"Then that's what we'll do. I'll try to see the grand duke. You go after Polivanov."

"Constantine Andreevich is at army headquarters right now. He won't return to the capital for several days. Polivanov might see me, though. I'll do my best to get an appointment."

"Good," nodded Princess Anya as she stood watching her son, enjoying the child's carefree happiness, thinking of what his father must be up against in Warsaw. Why did he have to be there? It wasn't right. He should be here with his family, not hundreds of miles away presiding over the destruction of his agency. There were others who could have taken care of that.

Suddenly, glancing down the pathway, the young woman saw a crippled officer coming toward them, walking painfully, supported by a cane and a young woman. His wife? His fiancée? For a minute Anya felt ashamed of herself. There were other women who loved their husbands and they hadn't been spared by this war. What made her think she was special? The sight brought tears to her eyes. The young woman was looking at the man the way she'd looked at Adam after his plane crash, with tender concern—so worried about him, so anxious to help him.

"Billy," said the princess. "Do everything you can to get him that train. Offer bribes if necessary. Big bribes. Just get him out of that place as soon as possible."

All levels of society were feeling the effects of war, from the highest in the land to the lowest. Prince Andrei was informed by his butler that a peasant had arrived from Byelaya Beryozka to request a meeting with His Highness. He was in the kitchen, being fed, as was the custom of the house.

"Who is it?" demanded the prince, surprised and fearing something extraordinary had taken place out there, perhaps a new rebellion. Boris was driving his people to despair with the decisions he and the war mobilization committee were making.

"The man's name is Lev Petrovich, Highness. And he wouldn't tell me anything else."

When the peasant was called into the prince's presence, he removed his cap and kissed Andrei Nicolaievich's hand, overwhelmed by the surroundings. Byelaya Beryozka was impressive, but this Petrograd mansion was as long as a city block and looked like a palace the tsar himself might live in. Wherever the tracker glanced, there were servants in odd uniforms hanging about doing nothing except opening doors—or giving him strange looks. Hadn't they ever been to the country? wondered Lev. Out there, these dressed-up monkeys would be the butt of everyone's jokes.

"Lev Petrovich," said Andrei, looking concerned, "how are things with you? Is there trouble at Byelaya Beryozka?"

"Highness," replied the man, "it's my boy Petya. He joined the army, and the Germans shot him as soon as he got to Poland. He's lying in the hospital there, wounded. Andrei Nicolaievich," he said, tears in his eyes, "we've lost one son. We don't want to lose young Petya as well."

Stunned, the prince stared at the man. Little Petya. Good Lord. He was just a boy. He couldn't be more than sixteen. But as young as he was, he was a tiger. He had tried to fight off Ivanov that day in the forest to protect Anya. They owed him for that.

"Lev, I'll do whatever I can to help get him home. Anna Nicolaievna's husband is in Warsaw right now helping to evacuate the wounded. We'll send him a telegram. Do you have the name of the hospital?"

He had, in a letter sent by Petya and written by one of the nurses in his ward. The Emperor Paul Military Hospital, Alexander Street. The fact that Petya was unable to write it himself worried both men. They knew the boy was literate, a great achievement for a peasant. Andrei had seen to it that the youngster had taken lessons with the local priest. If he were unable to pen a letter himself, it could only mean his wounds were bad.

The peasant's tired eyes welled with tears. "If Petya dies, it will kill his mother," he said. "He's our youngest. They had no business taking him. It wasn't right."

But the recruiting officer wouldn't have cared. With the heavy losses among the troops, he would have been delighted to sign up a healthy youngster like Petya without checking too carefully to see if he was really as old as he claimed. He would have been a prize.

"Lev Petrovich," said the prince, "I'll use every contact I have to bring your son home. You have my word."

The peasant nodded gratefully.

When Anya heard of Lev's visit to the Malyshev Palace and the news he brought, she was horrified. Little Petya wounded in the fighting. It couldn't be. He wasn't old enough. Thinking of that day at Byelaya Beryozka when he had tried to protect her against that madman, she wept. He might die. She had seen the condition of the wounded brought home from the army hospitals. They had to get him out of Warsaw and into a decent clinic here at home. Now there was another reason to get Adam that train.

The minister of war, Polivanov, proved to be no problem. Quite willing to order the dispatch of one of the Amer-Russians' own hospital trains to Poland to recover the wounded, he warned the young American to move quickly. If he hesitated, there wouldn't be any point because the Germans would have overrun the Russian lines and the prince would be trapped. The minister signed the necessary papers, handed them over with a flourish and sent Billy on his way happy, but he had little conviction that Adam Mikhailovich would be able to carry out his plan before the city fell to the boches.

The night before the train was to leave for Warsaw, Princess Anya was up late, composing a letter to be delivered to Ksenia Alexandrovna once Anya had left Petrograd. Uneasy at Adam's continued presence in the Polish capital amid reports of an imminent German breakthrough, the young woman had decided the best way to hurry him home was to go there herself with the train. That would give him all the incentive he needed to get out of there.

It would also be extremely foolish. She knew how dangerous the situation was. If she and Adam weren't able to leave immediately because of a German attack on Warsaw, they would have to endure a bombardment, with the famous German field guns pounding the city to rubble. It wasn't a fate she would have wished on anyone.

"I am going to accompany the train to Warsaw in my capacity as a Red Cross nurse," wrote the princess. She paused. What a lie! She had qualified as a nurse at the beginning of the war, or rather as a sort of assistant to real nurses, like many other Petrograd society ladies, but this was pushing the truth beyond its limits. Ksenia would laugh as she read this, thought Anya in embarrassment. Well, what else was she going to say? Dear Auntie, I'm so worried about Adam being in the same city as Zenaida Kashina that I'm about to risk my neck to rush off and drag him home?

Sighing, Anya glanced at her reflection in the gilt-framed mirror of her dressing table, intricately draped with lovely swaths of pink tulle and, trimmed with silk rosebuds. The crystal prisms of the candelabra tinkled softly on either side of her on the wall, gently stirred by the breeze coming through the open window. She was a jealous woman. It even showed in her face, she thought, looking sternly at her pretty image, a slim blonde girl dressed in a pale-green silk charmeuse negligee with a frill of Belgian lace at the throat and elbows. She was so jealous she was about to risk what no reasonable woman would ever do—venture into a war zone to take back what was hers before it was too late.

My God, thought the princess, Adam will think I've gone mad. Let him. If he wasn't so determined to worry me into an early grave, I wouldn't even have to think about doing this.

At this moment she hated Zenaida Kashina with all the fury she was capable of—not for seducing her husband, because Anya wasn't sure Adam would succumb, but because Kashina presented such a threat that it made her dare such a mad gesture as this. "Damn her!" muttered Anya, using unaccustomed language. "Why does she have such an effect on them?"

Grand-père, a man of refinement and culture, admired for his erudition here and in Europe, had been as weak as water in Kashina's hands. Anya would never forget seeing him waiting for the ballerina at the train station in Paris as if he were a mere nobody, a ridiculous old man consumed with passion for a young tart. It was humiliating.

Could Adam ever behave that badly? she wondered. She hoped not. She would never accept that from him. She was much more beautiful than Zenaida Kashina. She was younger. She was Princess Sviridova. That ought to be enough for any man.

But as Princess Anya studied her face in the mirror, she had a grave suspicion that whatever Kashina could offer was somehow independent of beauty, youth or lineage. And whatever it was, it was probably so unspeakably wicked and immoral that it would continue to drive men wild for years to come.

Modestly pulling up the lace ruffle at the neck of her negligee, Princess Anya thought of Adam stranded in Poland and shuddered. She loved him so much that if she had to make a choice between knowing he was safe and well in the vicinity of Kashina and knowing he was alone and wounded, she wouldn't hesitate to put him in Kashina's company.

But, thought the princess, throwing a golden hairbrush across the room, why didn't he simply come home so she wouldn't have to think of these hideous possibilities? Did he love excitement more than he loved his wife and family? More to the point, could he be seduced by Kashina and forget his responsibilities to them? The idea made her tremble with dread.

You ought to be ashamed of yourself, thought the princess as she stared into her mirror. Adam was an honorable man, not like the men she observed in the salons, war profiteers and vermin who preyed on people's misery, making fortunes in the black market, hoarding scarce materials only to sell them at inflated prices. No. He was a good man, a wonderful husband, a loving father.

But he was human and that made him vulnerable.

Picking up her pen once more, Princess Anya decided to tell Ksenia that she was entrusting her children to her in case of disaster. She was determined to go to Poland to ensure their father's quick return home and nothing could stop her, but if anything prevented her from coming back, she wanted Ksenia to tell Byelochka and his sisters that it wasn't because she didn't love them that she was doing this, but because she loved their father so much more than she could ever express.

"It's all you ever have to say, Auntie," she concluded, adding as a postscript that she wished Ksenia to have the use of her personal jewelry until her daughters were old enough to wear it.

Well, there. It was done. And now all Princess Anya had to do was say goodbye to her children. Early the next morning, while the nurse-maids still slept in their narrow beds near the twins' cribs, Anya slipped into the room and stood for a long time looking down at her two daughters, all blonde curls and pink cheeks, their little hands clutched into tiny fists, sound asleep and snoring like little animals, warm, drowsy and pro-tected in their silky nests.

Gently stroking their fluffy curls, Anya smiled, remembering their Berlin adventure when they were still being referred to as "he." They were good babies. She wanted to see them grow up.

Moving silently to her son's bedroom, Anya made a gesture to quiet Byelochka's nanny, who had been startled out of a sound sleep by the princess's light tread on the parquet floor. Nanny, a gray-haired woman of substantial proportions, wondered what Her Highness was doing here so early in the morning but said nothing, preserving a respectful silence.

Bending over her sleeping son, Princess Anya kissed him softly on the forehead and stood up again, admiring him as he lay curled up in his narrow white bed of Karelian birch. She had given the Sviridovs a prince. If she were to disappear in Poland, at least they had that. She hoped the family would speak well of her to her son when he no longer remembered what she looked like.

No. That was ridiculous. Of course she was coming back. And she was coming back with Adam. And young Petya as well. She had too much to live for to allow any Germans to prevent that.

Glancing around the gaily painted nursery with its gorgeous murals of ancient Russian folk heroes, Princess Anya bent down to kiss her sleep-ing son once more and departed with a cheerful smile for Nanny, who was wondering just what was going on.

Meeting her chauffeur in the courtyard of the Sviridov Palace, Anya got into the automobile and headed for the Warsaw Station, looking back at the large butterscotch-and-white neoclassic building until it was out of sight, still thinking of those small blond children who were going to awaken in a few hours and wonder where Mama had gone. Was she heartless? Could a mother do this to her children and be forgiven? And if she never came back, did she *deserve* to be forgiven?

The young doctor and nurses waiting for Anya at the station were a somber group. They had been talking with a railroad man who had just returned from Warsaw. He was giving the city two weeks before the boches took it. Nobody looked eager to go. The four nurses stared mournfully at the platform; the doctor was trying to make conversation to cheer them up but was failing to improve their mood.

Greeting Princess Anya respectfully, Dr. Malevich introduced his nurses and informed Her Highness that the news from Warsaw was not good. The nurses, three blondes and one redhead, Sonia, Natasha, Maria and Olga, wondered what could possibly inspire this young lady to risk her neck in this way. They were being well paid for this run. So was Malevich. From the look of her, this young aristocrat didn't need anybody's money.

"Anna Nicolaievna's husband is the director of our agency," murmured Dr. Malevich to his nurses.

"Ah," replied Sonia, fixing Anya with an astonished stare. So this was what the wife looked like. Of course she would have been a beauty. And devoted too.

As the long black train rattled and hissed, creaking into view, the nearly deserted platform vibrated a little beneath their feet. Whistles screeched, steam came whooshing out from the great iron wheels and the uniformed railway officials told Malevich to start boarding.

Glancing at the large round clock above the door of the first-class waiting room, Princess Anya noted the time—6:10. It was the first time in her life she had ever been up so early. Odd. The whole scene appeared to Anya as if she were in a dream—the railway men rushing about, the uniformed nurses next to her, the steaming, clanging locomotive itself.

In a matter of seconds, Anya would be climbing aboard the train, bound for Russian Poland, ready for whatever awaited her there. As she glanced around the grimy station, the princess suddenly quickened her pace and hurried aboard the train, eager to get going. Rushing toward the travelers was a familiar figure, shouting at the top of his lungs—Billy.

Horrified to see his sister-in-law in the group of nurses about to leave for Warsaw, Billy was determined to keep her in Petrograd if he had to carry her off the train. Adam would kill him if he allowed her to do this mad thing.

To his distress, the train was already moving, beginning to gather speed. He ran as fast as he could, shouting so hard he was afraid his lungs would give out. Damn! He was too late. She was actually leaving!

Leaning out one of the windows, Princess Anya waved goodbye and tried to look cheerful, but she was unable to say anything to this fellow with the blond hair who looked as if he were about to collapse. What could she possibly tell Adam's brother? What had brought him here? Perhaps he always checked on his trains. Perhaps Nanny had called him. She didn't know.

"Anya!" he shouted, cupping his hands around his mouth as he called

after the departing train, "don't go to Warsaw! Get off at the next stop.
I can meet you there! I'll take you home!"

"Embarrassed to be the object of such a public disturbance, Princess
Anya shook her head stubbornly and waved once more before ducking
inside and disappearing from view.

"My God, she's crazy to do this," he gasped, trying to catch his breath
as he looked down the tracks to the plume of smoke coming from the
locomotive's engine, while one of his railway acquaintances looked on sympathetically. The young American *barin* had lots of ladies. Perhaps one of
them had just jilted him.

"Petrograd has lots of pretty girls," he joked. "There are plenty of
others to make you forget about this one."

Billy had gone white, terrified at the possible consequences of Princess Anya's trip. Nobody was giving Warsaw any chance of holding out
longer than a few weeks. If anything was to happen to her, his brother
would hold him responsible for her safety and would probably kill him.
Adam loved that woman.

And with him, there wouldn't be any chance of appealing to a kind
heart. It was ironic that Adam shared at least one trait with young Tasha.
Cross either one and you'd pay for your mistake forever.

Turning to the railwayman, the American asked brusquely, "Will this
train make any stops before leaving the Petrograd area?"

"None, *barin*. It's an express, specially routed through to Poland."

"Is there any way to flag it down?"

The railwayman had visions of an immense accident ensuing, with
his superiors all holding him personally responsible.

"Out of the question, *barin*. It's gone."

Billy shook his head. He couldn't believe Anya had done this. She
was a married woman with three small children. Her place was home with
them, not racing off to Poland, for heaven's sake.

No man was worth that kind of devotion. He knew damned well *he*
wasn't.

As Princess Anya watched the industrial outskirts of Petrograd start
to blend into long stretches of green fields, she saw groups of peasants
fanning out along country roads, scythes and rakes in hand, ready to begin the day's work. There were more women than men in these parties,
the reflection of the war's toll on Russia's peasants.

As the long black train rumbled on across the fields and meadows, its
shrill whistle drawing delighted cries from the youngsters it passed on its
journey south, Princess Anya thought of Adam's descriptions of the war
going on and wondered how she would react if she found herself a lot
closer to the front than she planned to be. It was a real possibility, and it

made her apprehensive. She had no wish to see any more Germans. Those she had encountered in Berlin were quite enough for her. All she wanted to do was deliver this train to her husband, find Petya and take both of them safely home to Petrograd with her.

Staring out the windows at the green, peaceful Russian countryside, Anya suddenly felt very young and very lonely on board the train with its crew of strangers.

The sooner she arrived in Warsaw and found Adam, the sooner she could return home. She already missed it terribly.

Warsaw

The long columns of terrified civilians streaming out of Warsaw made the trip to the beleaguered city a nightmare. Russian troops, retreating from various sectors of the front were interspersed with lines of refugees, their automobiles, carts and farm animals clogging the gritty roads and raising thick clouds of dust along their path, lingering in the hot July air like a funeral shroud over the fate of Poland. It was a scene of the most pathetic desperation—fear was driving the people forward like the sting of a cossack's whip.

In the distance, heavy German seige guns released a symphony of destruction that could be heard miles away. Women wept, children shrieked, and everyone kept on going despite their terror, for the Russians had told the Poles horrifying stories of boche brutality, and nobody wanted to let his wife or daughter fall prey to the lusty and degenerate Germans. The enemy, it was alleged, made soap from their victims after raping them repeatedly.

Nobody knew how the soap story got started, but it was taken for gospel and repeated so many times along so many fronts that it came to be an article of faith among civilians that the kaiser's men came equipped with giant portable vats. Nuns were said to be prized by the soapmakers, as well as very young girls and babies. Nothing was sacred to these beasts.

In the lead of a convoy of trucks, Prince Sviridov was heading into the city while nearly everyone else was fleeing it. Having purchased the vehicles at an outrageous price from a Warsaw firm, Adam had them loaded with the staff and patients of his recently abandoned field hospitals. He also carried a cache of medical supplies which would have brought a fortune on the black market—which is precisely where it would have ended up if he had been naive enough to allow the army to dispose of the agency's goods. These trips were now almost a daily occurrence, his final effort.

If Billy had done his work at home in Petrograd, Adam would find a means of transport waiting for him in Warsaw. If not, it was going to be *sauve-qui-peut*, with a mad scramble for survival that would make scenes

from the "Inferno" appear tame. Putting his faith in Billy's powers of per-
suasion and his own determination, Adam steeled himself to face whatever awaited him in the city. Meanwhile, the Germans advanced steadily,
creating havoc in their wake.

In Oleg's establishments, the girls were close to hysteria. The lack of customers led to long periods of inactivity, which in turn, led to anguished
discussions of what to do when the first boche soldier appeared on the
doorstep. The general consensus was to run. The girls had heard all the
soap stories. Not being babies, nuns or virgins, they ought to have felt
secure, but they didn't; and they were eager to flee the city at the earliest
opportunity.

One morning, Oleg sauntered downstairs as usual, only to find the
place strangely quiet, with not even the soft tapping of high-heeled slip-
pers on the parquet floors. Wandering through the debris of the night's
revels, Monsieur Mossolov was irritated at the disorder everywhere. Things
were getting too lax, he muttered. It was Wanda's fault and he intended
to let her know about it as soon as possible.

"Where are you, you Polish cow?" he roared, kicking a broken vase
out of his way. "This place is beginning to look like a third-rate flophouse
in the slums. What's the matter with you?"

No answer.

Angrily, Oleg raced back upstairs, pounding on all the doors as he
searched for his partner, shouting for her to come out and face him.

Finally, at the end of the second-floor hallway, the angry Russian
saw the swish of a fluffy white tail as Koshka darted into the last room on
the corridor, taking shelter from his enemy.

"Ah, so there you are," he bawled, planting himself firmly in the
doorway as Wanda and her cat glared at him. The woman was seated at
her dressing table, her nightgown falling off her shoulder, an empty bottle
of Moët lying on the Chinese carpet at her feet. "I have to talk to you,
Wanda, and you'd better listen if you know what's good for you."

"Go to hell," replied Mademoiselle Zumbrowska as casually as if she
were speaking about the weather.

"What?" bellowed Oleg, the veins standing out on his forehead.
"What did you say to me?"

"I said, 'Go to hell,'" repeated Wanda, not at all disturbed by either
his tone or his presence. "Whatever you want to tell me can wait till later, because I have some news for you. We're ruined. The girls ran away
last night. It's all over."

Startled, Oleg couldn't believe his ears. He just stood there staring at

Wanda, his peasant face large and stupid in the doorway. And then he lunged at her, knocking her off her chair and onto the carpet, a pile of blonde hair, flying arms and legs and disheveled silk.

"Damn it! What do you mean the girls ran away? Why didn't you stop them? Why didn't you tell me?"

Towering over the woman, Oleg kicked her furiously before she could protect herself, making her shriek with pain as she staggered to her feet, tripping over her nightgown. Koshka hopped out of her way, spitting at Oleg, his back arched with fear.

"You animal!" screamed Wanda, clutching her side as she took cover behind an armchair, her face distorted with rage and pain. "They ran away because they're all afraid of the Germans. How could I have stopped them?"

"You could have told me. I would have stopped them!"

"Don't be an idiot! They ran off after I was asleep. So what? If we stay here, we're all going to be killed anyway!"

Staring at the bald Russian as he came towards her, glaring at her with that terrifying expression in his light-blue eyes, demented, filled with hate, Wanda was frightened out of her wits. My God, she thought, trembling with fear, he's starting again. He's getting that crazed look on his face. And now she was alone in the house with him, with no one to come to her aid if he attacked.

Advancing on Wanda as she cowered behind the armchair, Oleg picked up her heavy silver hairbrush from the dressing table. He stared at her intently as he approached. He felt as if the pretty room with its mirrored ceiling and white-and-gold-paneled walls, thick pink damask drapes, white lace curtains and oriental carpets were changing before his eyes to a forest clearing where a young blonde girl was standing with a skirt filled with mushrooms.

"Anna Nicolaievna," he muttered.

He was calling her by that woman's name again, thought Wanda, thoroughly frightened. Oleg's expression was so strange, so demented, it made the Polish girl wish she had a weapon handy right now. He hated the woman he called Anna Nicolaievna. And he was acting as if he were out of his head.

"You bitch," muttered the bald, ugly Russian. "Little aristocrat."

Aristocrat, thought Wanda. Hell, she was a lot of things, but nobody had ever thought of calling her *that*. He had to be crazy.

Shaking with fright, the blonde pushed the armchair straight into Oleg's middle as he got within striking distance, the silver hairbrush upraised. As he staggered in pain, she let out a screech and fled the room, little Koshka racing along behind her, his white fur standing on end, his large green eyes wide with fear.

"You think you can abuse me," shouted Oleg, venting his fury on the large mirror above Wanda's dressing table, shattering the glass into splinters as he hurled the silver brush into it. "I'll show you this time! I'll kill you!"

"Oh, God!" wailed the girl, frantic with fear. "He's really lost his mind!"

Frantically stumbling down the stairs, her long nightgown hampering her movement, Wanda ran panting toward the kitchen, desperate to reach the drawer where the cook kept the knives. If the Russian was really as crazy as he seemed, she had to protect herself.

"You can't escape this time!" roared Oleg as he pursued her, smashing vases, mirrors, small china objects as he ran, leaving a trail of destruction behind him, careless of the cost. All he wanted to do was get his hands around Anna Nicolaievna's neck this time. Everything else was unimportant. Now she was finally afraid of him. Good. She ought to be. He was about to kill her at last.

Tearing open the drawers in the kitchen, Wanda searched for the knives in a frenzy as Oleg barged into the room, grinning like a madman.

Just as he was about to seize Wanda by the hair, the woman spun around to confront him, a sharp twelve-inch butcher knife in her hand, pointed straight at his throat.

"I'll use it if you touch me," she gasped, white with fear, her full bosom rising and falling beneath the flimsy silk gown. To her surprise, Oleg backed off a little, raising his hands in a placating gesture that did nothing to deceive the woman. He would kill her in a second if he sensed she was weak enough not to use the knife on him.

"Little aristocrat," he sneered, "do you know how to use that thing? Don't you know you can get hurt with a knife like that? Especially if someone snatches it from you."

"I know how to use it on you," replied Wanda, her eyes on his, not letting him get any closer.

In the crowded kitchen, hot and miserable in the late July heat, perspiration running down their faces as they faced each other across a space of less than four feet, Wanda glared at her partner. He grinned at her like a lunatic, waiting for her to make her move so he could overpower her.

"Try to use that," he taunted her, pretending to grab at it, scaring Wanda so that she jumped backward, nearly colliding with Koshka in her terror.

"Keep away from me. Don't get any closer!" she ordered, almost sobbing with fear. Why wasn't anyone else in the house? How could they do this to her? she thought frantically.

Without another word, the bald Russian took hold of a wooden kitchen chair, sent it crashing into Mademoiselle Zumbrowska and grabbed the knife as it fell to the floor. Wanda cried out in pain and fear as she tried to get to her feet, struggling with the overturned chair.

Lunging at the woman, Oleg slashed wildly as Wanda tried to escape the gleaming blade. She covered her face and ran from him, screaming with fright.

Leaping over the overturned chair, Oleg ran after his prey, managing to block her exit as he flung himself on top of her. He seized Wanda by the arm as they both tumbled to the floor, taking the tablecloth and several dishes with them.

Hissing with fear, Koshka watched the large Russian grasp Wanda by the neck, pinning her to the floor. Oblivious to her thrashing, he raised the knife high overhead, preparing to drive it deep inside her.

Shrieking with terror, the woman clawed at her attacker as he aimed the blow. She threw him off balance just enough for her to dodge the main thrust, taking a slash across her upper arm. Both were covered with a bright red trickle of blood as they fought savagely for the weapon, rolling on the floor, biting, kicking, screaming as they went at it, each desperate to kill the other in a no-holds-barred contest.

Grunting with the force of his effort, Oleg ripped away most of the woman's nightgown as he pulled her across the floor, aimed the knife and caught her right on target this time, slashing her throat from ear to ear, nearly severing the head from the body with the momentum of his thrust.

Still panting heavily from the effort as he knelt over Wanda's body, Oleg began to retch, seeing the whole room through a blurry red mist, disoriented and frightened. For a moment he didn't know where he was. Then he glanced down and saw the mutilated body of his partner, the woman who had come to Warsaw with him and who had helped him make his fortune.

"No!" he howled. Scrambling to his feet, the Russian staggered to the sink, looking backward in horror as he did, unable to believe what he saw. Suddenly it occurred to him that he was the one responsible. He had done this. There was no one else around.

Shuddering with revulsion, Oleg stared at what he had done to Wanda. Unable to think clearly, he vaguely recalled talking with a woman— Anna Nicolaievna—and then going after her. It wasn't Wanda he had wanted to kill. It was that little aristocrat. And now she had made him kill his partner. He wouldn't have killed Wanda. He almost liked her, in a way.

Trembling with fright, the Russian glanced down at his bloodstained hands, at the knife lying on the floor, at Wanda, and he retched again, bending over the sink as he emptied the contents of his stomach, choking and gasping, violently ill.

Koshka, watching the altercation from behind the safety of a chair, peered at the man bent over the sink, padded carefully across the tiles to where Wanda lay, touched the corpse with a tentative white paw and pulled back, twitching in disgust, wading in a puddle of blood.

As Oleg staggered away from the sink, wiping his mouth on his bloodied sleeve, he paused in midstride at the sight of Koshka arching his back at him, hissing furiously, his tiny fangs bared like a wild beast.

He hated that cat. Stunned by the sight of what he had done to Wanda, Oleg was still having a difficult time coming back to reality, but he had absolutely no doubt about the cat. The little furball was real, and so was his hatred for it. "Come here, you," he said quietly, bending over to make a grab for the cat.

Still hissing, the cat backed up on tiny, bloodstained paws, its tracks little red imprints on the floor. As the cat edged away from Oleg, it emitted a low, eerie growl, cringing and hissing as it went, knowing it was being stalked by a larger, crueler beast than itself.

"Come here, damn you," muttered Oleg, following it into the hall, gesturing angrily as he tried to waylay the animal, trailing it into the corridor beyond the kitchen.

Forcing the cat into the far end of the hall, then cornering it with the aid of an overturned chair, Oleg seized the clawing, hissing animal by its fluffy white tail and smashed it viciously against the wall until all that was left of his small, furry enemy was a limp and broken ball of bloodied fluff.

Flinging Koshka's remains aside in disgust, Oleg told himself poor old Wanda wouldn't want to be without his company in whatever place she now inhabited. She had loved the little furry bastard in life; he might as well go with her on her last trip.

In his entire life, Wanda was the only woman Oleg had ever felt superior to, the only one he'd ever really liked. Now, still reeling from the shock of his mad act, Oleg had to dispose of the body and make plans to flee the city before the Russian authorities, or the German invaders, caught up with him.

❧ 28 ❧

I n the headquarters of the Amer-Russian relief agency, Prince Adam Sviridov had already received news of his wife's departure from Petrograd from his worried brother, who begged him to believe that he'd known nothing of her plans and had, in fact, tried desperately to prevent her from traveling. It didn't matter. Adam was furious with both of them—Anya for risking her life and Billy for failing to prevent her from leaving. Any man who could stand by and allow a woman as sheltered and naive as Anya to venture into such danger ought to be horsewhipped. Billy was a fool. Or worse.

Worst of all, the prince had gone to the railway station to meet the train and had been told of a delay up the line due to troop movements. God only knew when Anya would arrive in Warsaw now. Everything was in a fantastic uproar, and Adam was so busy arranging for the evacuation of men and supplies that he wasn't able to wait for his wife's arrival. A Polish employee was left at the station to meet her and escort her without delay to the agency's headquarters.

As the Polish capital prepared to face the coming of the Huns, the hospital train from Petrograd, shunted to a siding in a small town north of Warsaw, was forced to spend three hours awaiting orders to move on, while trainloads of dismantled factory equipment headed toward Russia, taking precedence over everything else that day.

As the princess and her companions waited for permission to go on, sweltering in the hot sun pouring down on the roof above their heads, they witnessed a pitiable procession of refugees trudging north, carrying what little they could, terrified of falling into the hands of the Germans.

When the train finally got going once again, Princess Anya was praying nothing more would delay it. The sooner she was reunited with Adam, the safer she would feel. Along with the worn-out refugees, she was starting to notice an unnerving amount of violence in the area. If she felt it was necessary, she wouldn't hesitate to use the revolver she carried in her purse.

To her distress, when Anya and her group arrived at Warsaw's main station Prince Adam was nowhere in sight. However, the presence of his emissary was reassuring. Dr. Malevich volunteered to stay with the train to keep an eye on things while it was taken to a siding to be rerouted back home in exactly four hours.

"Is that all the time we have?" demanded the princess. "What if we aren't ready by then?"

The dark-haired young Pole looked grim. "We will have to be. It may be the last chance we have to get out of this hellhole. That will make us hurry."

Shocked by his tone, the princess clung to his arm as he escorted her through the crowded station, loaded with Poles trying desperately to bribe anyone in uniform into giving them a clearance to board the trains going north. The military had preference and they seemed to be evacuating everything that wasn't nailed down—with the exception of Polish civilians. They were the lowest priority, and very few Russians were sparing them a second thought.

After a nerve-racking journey across town through streets jammed with military vehicles, farm carts, automobiles and dozens of horses, all of them creating terrific confusion as they jockeyed for position in the narrow and congested streets, Princess Anya and her escort arrived at the hotel where Adam had his headquarters.

Inside was a similar pileup of people all over the lobby, the stairways, the restaurant, huddled by their baggage, all hopeful of finding a way out of Warsaw before it was too late. For most, escape was an illusion. It was Russians first, with hardly anyone else in second place.

As Princess Anya carefully picked her way across the packed lobby, she happened to glance through the glass doors of the hotel's restaurant to the left of the lobby. There, seated at a table close to the door, smiling into the dark eyes of a woman who was stroking the palm of his hand was Prince Adam. Smiling! How could he?

Zenaida Kashina was not only a threat, she was apparently a successful one. The sight infuriated the princess. She turned bright red.

"Madame Kashina was very brave to remain in Warsaw this long," said the Pole, trying his best to calm this excitable Russian princess as he saw her head straight toward the couple. "She's been very supportive of our agency."

"You don't have to tell me. I have eyes in my head."

"*Barinia*," stammered the young man. "I don't think...."

Before he could finish whatever he intended to say, Princess Anya was standing in front of her husband, rigid with anger, glaring at him and totally ignoring the small, dark-haired woman with him.

"Anya! Thank God you've arrived safely. Whatever possessed you to do it?" Adam was shocked to see his wife.

"Concern for my husband," she replied icily.

Madame Kashina looked on in barely disguised amusement. She had just settled her score with the Sviridovs. Now, bored, she could move on to other pursuits.

Staring at his angry wife, who had never in her life looked at him with such cold fury, Adam felt guilty to the bottom of his soul. He had done what she was no doubt accusing him of in her heart. He had been clutching at life, not falling in love. And he would never be able to explain it away. He loved Anya. She was his life. Kashina was an aberration.

"I can see I'm wasting my time in Warsaw," said Anya bitterly. "I should have stayed home."

"Anyushka!"

To Adam's horror, she turned on her heel and stalked out of the room, too angry to continue the conversation and unwilling to cause a scene in front of all these people who seemed to expect something of the sort.

Let them stare, thought the princess as she made her dignified exit.

Before Adam could rise to follow her, Anya was out the door of the hotel and racing for the first cab she saw, desperate to get away.

How could he? she thought, fighting the tears that came to her eyes. She loved Adam more than anyone. He had always been faithful. He had told her she was the only woman he ever wanted. And now he did this!

Well, she thought with fury, he had been born Adam Lowell, and Adam Lowell he was going to be again. Anyushka was glad the Orthodox religion permitted divorce. She'd have divorced him even if she were Catholic.

After ten minutes of unaccustomed jostling on a crowded street around the corner from the hotel, where she was hoping Adam couldn't spot her, the princess finally managed to find the owner of a hackney carriage who agreed to take her to the Emperor Paul Military Hospital, where she knew Petya was supposed to be. If her trip to Poland was a failure from one point of view, at least she could help Petya. If he were still alive.

As the cab carried the princess to her destination, she observed with distaste that the vehicle was dirty, the driver was dirty, and from what she could see of Warsaw, that was dirty too. And hysterical with fear of the Huns.

"There's the hospital, *barinia*," announced the cabbie finally, reining in his horse alongside the curb.

The building he indicated was a weather-beaten wooden structure with a leprous coat of green paint. A giant Red Cross flag underneath a sign that announced its military name and serial number seemed to be its sole adornment.

"Will you wait here for me?" asked Anya. "I'm going to bring someone out of there, and I need a cab to take us back to the station."

"They could make you wait here all day, *barinia*. I'd lose money."

"I'll pay you fifty gold rubles. That should make it worth your while. Just stay here and don't let anyone move you."

"Pay me half now," he said firmly.

"The whole thing when you've brought us to the station."

"*Barinia,* you owe me something for the trip from the station."

"Oh, all right," she muttered, greatly annoyed with the fellow. "Here are twenty gold rubles. You'll get the rest when you've completed your trip."

"Thank you, excellency," replied the cabbie, ceremoniously handing her down from the rickety vehicle. "I'll be waiting here when you come back outside."

Princess Sviridova wasn't so sure, but she tried to be optimistic as she headed toward the hospital's entrance, armed with a sheaf of official papers bearing impressive signatures. The building was a mess. She hoped the inside was more prepossessing than the outside, since the exterior appeared to be in danger of sudden collapse. Once she entered, she saw that the interior was infinitely worse.

"Halt," snapped the sentry on duty near the door, startled by the visitor.

"I am Princess Sviridova," announced the tall lady. "Take me to the director."

That sounded official enough to the youngster on duty, so he led her down the creaking corridors until they arrived at a door bearing a metal plaque marked DIRECTOR: COL. ORLOV.

"He's in there," said the lad.

"Please knock."

"What the hell do you want?" came the reply. "I'm busy here. You know better than to interrupt me at this time."

Blushing with embarrassment in front of this visitor who seemed very grand, the youngster shrugged and tried again, gritting his teeth.

"What's going on?" grumbled Colonel Orlov, quite exasperated by all the racket. Couldn't the louts follow orders? he wondered. Or was it their idea of a joke?

"Soldier," he roared, as he flung open the door, "bother me again and I'll put my foot up your ass."

"Good day, Colonel," said Princess Sviridova looking down onto the officer's bald spot.

Colonel Orlov stood in the doorway, his shirt off, pants half-undone, boots missing. He had been in the midst of his afternoon dalliance with one of the nurses and seemed quite put out.

"Good God," exclaimed Orlov in near shock. "Excuse me."

Slamming the door shut, he dressed at top speed, cursing hysterically as he struggled to pull on his boots while his lady slipped out through a side door expressly created with such an emergency in mind. When he appeared at the office door several minutes later, Colonel Orlov looked the soul of dignity. "Madame," he said, ushering the tall lady into his office, "what can I do for you?"

Princess Sviridova looked about with an air of hauteur that would have done justice to the Empress Alexandra and delicately plucked a silk stocking from the colonel's chair before sitting down, dropping the evidence of the colonel's playtime onto the rug.

Orlov turned a deep shade of crimson, gnawed on his drooping mustache, and mumbled something about shiftless cleaning ladies not doing their job.

"I am Princess Sviridova," announced Anya, ignoring the colonel's discomfort. "I have a letter signed by the minister of war releasing one of your patients, Petya Nikolaiev, to my care. My hospital train is at the station now, preparing to leave Warsaw as soon as I arrive with the boy."

That was stretching the truth a bit, but at this point, Anya didn't care. Polivanov *had* signed the papers ordering the train through. That was enough. It would cover whatever she chose to let it cover.

"My husband is Prince Sviridov," added Anya, trying not to grit her teeth as she got the words out. "I'm sure he and the Amer-Russian agency are familiar to you."

"Yes," nodded Orlov, smiling. "I met him once. But I regret to tell you, Princess, that your trip out here was unnecessary."

For a moment, Anya felt the room start to spin. Petya was dead. She was too late. Faltering, she forced herself to ask the colonel if they had sent the body home yet.

"Oh no, dear lady. Nothing like that. The lad was shipped out two days ago. On a stretcher, but very much alive."

"Oh!" Overwhelmed, Anya buried her face in her hands and tried to control herself. Her whole trip had been useless. She was grateful Petya was alive, overjoyed in fact, but she felt like an idiot. There was no earthly reason for the foolish trip she had taken. Her marriage was over and Petya didn't need her help. What a splendid joke.

"Are you all right?" asked Orlov gently. "It must have been a terrible journey for you. Will you be able to get home safely?"

"Yes. I'm to leave Warsaw this afternoon. And," she sighed, "I have to hurry if I want to be on time."

"Don't delay," advised the colonel, looking serious. "It's too dangerous."

Princess Sviridova left the shabby hospital, silently damning the unpredictability of the Russian Army—and fate.

"To the railway station," Anya ordered her driver. "And hurry."

"What? No extra passenger?" he asked, flicking the whip over his horse's left ear.

"They sent him on two days ago," replied the princess in disgust.

As the cabbie made his way with great difficulty through an even-greater traffic jam than before, Anya noticed that people seemed to be carrying the oddest bits and pieces with them. One woman drove an ox cart loaded with her family's clothing and a magnificent pair of bantam roosters, both of which were screeching noisily above the cries of the people in the street.

"Isn't anyone remaining in Warsaw?" asked Anya.

"Not if they can get out. The Russians are telling them the Germans will murder them if they stay."

"They probably will."

"You Russians lie a lot," smiled the cabbie.

Anya gave him a sharp glance. "So do the Germans," she responded.

When they finally reached the station after an overly long drive, Anya paid the man the gold rubles she owed him and received his blessing in return. The driver was certain the crazy Russian *barinia* would never make it back home alive and he was rather sorry. She was young and pretty, a great loss to some man.

At the railway station, the chaos was even worse than in the streets. With the cries of desperate people mixing with the sounds issuing from the trains, the noise was deafening. Flourishing her travel papers in order to get inside, Princess Sviridova had to push her way through the crowds, a shocking experience for Anya who was used to preferential treatment. Peasants probably behaved like this, thought the princess, struggling to make her way to the departure platform from which the hospital train was to leave for home.

Ksenia Alexandrovna would never believe this. Then again, who would have believed Adam capable of such behavior? This war was giving everyone an excuse to behave like an animal.

As the lovely blonde girl in the white uniform of the Amer-Russian agency rushed past a group of wounded Russian soldiers near the open departure platform, she could have sworn she heard someone call out her name. Impossible, thought Anya, halting for a split second. As she picked up her pace, heading for the train, she heard it once more, desperate, fearful, as if the person was in terror for his life.

This time she stopped and turned around, curious to see who could be calling her. There was no mistake. It was "Anna Nicolaievna" and the voice was disconcertingly familiar.

Spotting his wife on her arrival, Prince Adam had just turned the loading of the train over to Dr. Malevich when he saw her pause, turn to a pathetic-looking group of soldiers and slowly walk toward one of the men, a heavily bandaged fellow lying on a stretcher on the platform.

Princess Anya let out a cry, covered her mouth briefly with her hands and raced to where the soldier was lying, practically flinging herself on the ground next to him. "Petya!"

There, dirty, weak and lying unattended in a pile of straw was Petya Nicolaiev, the boy who was supposed to have been shipped out two days earlier. Anya was so horrified to see him like this, she was speechless, staring at him with tears streaming down her face, clutching his bandaged hand. The boy was crying, so grateful to see someone from home in this frightening hellhole that he forgot all about trying to be brave and sobbed like the terrified sixteen-year-old he was.

"Anna Nicolaievna," he pleaded, "they're going to make us wait until tomorrow before they send us home. We won't last that long. Please make them get us out of here now. Please."

Looking at the group, all as badly wounded as Petya, Anya was filled with disgust at the authorities who would do this to their own men. Adam was right when he said his agency was important. From what she could see of the army's care of its wounded, they needed all the help they could get. She couldn't leave them to their fate. They were going with her. Now.

Turning to a couple of officers who were standing not far from the group of wounded, Princess Anya said crisply, trying to control her voice, "Start loading these men onto that hospital train, the one with the insignia of the Amer-Russian agency. I'm with them. They can leave with us."

"Who the hell are you?" replied the officer closest to Anya, grinding out his cigarette beneath the heel of his polished boot as he approached, eager to get a better look at this arrogant girl who was trying to give him orders. No woman told *him* what to do.

"I'm Princess Sviridova," replied the woman. "Now find someone to help us. Our train is about to leave."

As the men watched, the officer grabbed Anya by the arm and gave her a rough push that nearly sent her crashing into the wall.

"Get the hell out of here," he warned. "And mind your own business. These men move when the army says to move them. They're all going to die before they ever reach Petrograd. Let the ones who can make it go home. All this bunch will do is take up valuable space."

Watching Anya from a distance, almost afraid to approach her after their confrontation in that restaurant, Adam had just about decided to go back to his work, assured now that his wife would return to Petrograd. But when he saw the officer take hold of her, he sprinted toward him in fury, ready to tear him apart. Rushing the man, the prince grabbed his arm and doubled him over with a punch to the stomach that sent him sprawling on the platform, breathless with astonishment.

"Keep your hands off my wife," shouted the prince, looking like a wild man. "And start loading these men onto the train. Now."

"You can go to hell," replied the officer, a heavyset man with a drooping blond mustache and a red face. "You don't give orders to a Russian officer. Foreigner."

And then he lunged at the slim prince, throwing a punch that would have landed Adam on the ground if he hadn't ducked. Adam seized the opportunity to hit the man with a sharp jab to the jaw, momentarily stunning him. Recovering, the fellow landed a good shot at Adam's ribs while a crowd started to gather, calling out advice to one or the other of the combatants.

Using the fracas to best advantage, Anya signaled to Malevich to get the wounded onto the train. While her husband went at the officer with a fury she had never seen before, she pressed the nurses into service to carry Petya's group onto the train. Let them die here? Was he crazy?

"You're going home today," declared Anya to the men as the train began shooting steam out onto the tracks. To tell the truth, they were all in such bad condition from two days of wretched neglect that she knew some of them wouldn't make it. It didn't matter. They were leaving.

"Anna Nicolaievna," whispered Petya, "you're an angel."

Looking down at the boy, she gently stroked his hair. And then she raced back to the station platform to where Adam was still battling the red-faced officer. Gasping for breath, the men were trying to kill each other. And the officer was bigger than Adam. A lot bigger.

"Damned foreigner," panted the Russian, striking out at Adam. He nearly brought Adam to his knees with the force of a fat right fist. As Adam reeled, Princess Anya felt her heart nearly stop. The train was set to go. The whistle was sending shrieks of steam up into the clear blue summer sky. Every man was on board—except her husband, his escape blocked by the officer.

"Adam! We're leaving!"

Wonderful, thought the prince, dodging a powerful punch. If he didn't take care of this character, he might never get out of Warsaw. Out of the corner of his eye he could see the approach of some military police, who could only be arriving to help the officer and probably arrest *him.*

As the train began to move forward, Dr. Malevich shouted to theengineer to halt. Impossible. They had immediate clearance. If they let the opportunity slip by, it might not come again. They were off.

"Princess!" shouted Malevich. "Board the train!"

Looking at the crowd gathered around the two men, Anya saw her husband stagger, exhausted from the fight but still on his feet. The train's whistle screeched a warning. It was now or never.

Desperate at the thought of losing Adam—in spite of her anger, in spite of his bad behavior, in spite of everything—Princess Anya suddenly had an inspiration. Reaching into her handbag, she withdrew the revolver. If she failed to rescue Adam now, he would be left there and probably arrested.

"Stop this right now," shouted Anya, rushing toward the crowd, who scattered at the sight of the weapon. Pausing, the officer stared at her, looking as if he thought she was crazy. So did Adam.

"Get on the train," ordered the princess. "Hurry!"

As Adam gaped at his wife, Anya stamped her foot in fury. "Hurry! Or do you want to stay here forever?"

Summoning up his last bit of strength, Adam dodged the Russian, who was attempting to get in one last punch, and staggered toward his wife, who was shouting at Malevich for help. As Adam leaned on Anya, she practically dragged him toward the already-moving locomotive. It was picking up speed now. If Malevich didn't come to her aid, they would both be left behind.

"Jump up there," ordered Adam. "You can still make it."

"You first," replied the princess, shoving him toward the steps.

Then Dr. Malevich and one of the nurses appeared on the platform of the train and reached down to yank the princess on board. They pulled her up beside them, then quickly released her and reached out to grab Prince Adam's hand. He was running as fast as he could, out of breath, gasping, desperate to make the train. With the red-faced officer and some of the military police chasing after him now, the prince had no alternative but to leave town, and he knew it. But the fight had sapped all his strength and he was staggering.

"*Adam!*" Anya was terrified.

With an enormous effort, Dr. Malevich braced himself against the railing, grasped Adam's hand and lifted him off the ground, hauling him aboard the train. Gasping from the unaccustomed exertion, Malevich sat down hard on the rattling platform as Adam Mikhailovich fell into his wife's arms, clutching her frantically as they both clung to the railing.

"Come inside," said Anya, pulling Adam after her as she made her way into her private compartment, nearly colliding with some of the wounded packing the train.

Still a bit dazed from their race for the train, the Sviridovs were grateful to be out of the madhouse they had just left. But Princess Anya had more on her mind than her relief at escaping from Warsaw. There was the matter of Kashina.

As she glared at her husband, Adam felt his knees go weak. She was still furious.

"Anyushka," he stammered, "forgive me. I love you. In spite of what you seem to think...."

"Oh stop! You were with that woman, Adam. I know it."

To her surprise, he didn't deny it. She almost wished he had. Looking intently at her handsome, dark-haired husband whose lip was split from the fight he'd just waged to protect her, Princess Anya wondered if divorce was such a good idea after all. He had seen her in danger and had come rushing to her defense without even a second's hesitation. That counted for something. And the officer had been a big fellow, built like a prizefighter. Not too many men would have taken him on without a good reason—which Adam certainly had.

As the father of her three children, Adam couldn't be cast aside too lightly. That would create a terrible scandal and reflect badly upon the family. Was she going to let that little dancing tart destroy her family just because Adam Mikhailovich had been weak, foolish and probably desperate with loneliness? Looking grave and very beautiful at the same time, Princess Anya gave her worried husband a thoughtful glance.

"Please forgive me," he repeated. "I promise I'll never give you cause for unhappiness again."

The princess's beautiful blue eyes registered skepticism.

"Anya, do you want me to plead with you?"

To his surprise she merely shook her head. "No. I just want you to promise you'll stay far, far away from Zenaida Kashina as long as you live. *I mean it,*" she added, with icy emphasis.

"I will. You have my word on it."

He looked thoroughly contrite. He could have posed for a portrait of the repentant sinner, thought Anya. And his lip was bleeding.

"Here," she offered, taking out a clean handkerchief. As she watched him dab at the blood, she looked at him from under a fringe of lovely, long dark lashes and smiled.

She loved Adam Mikhailovich, wicked or not, and would never forget seeing him rush to defend her from that dreadful man.

Petrograd

After the Sviridovs returned from Poland, everyone noticed a change in Princess Anya; it was as though she had aged several years in the space of a few days. No longer was she merely the pretty young mother of Byelochka, Sashenka and Tory. She had evolved into a woman who no longer believed in happy endings.

Russia was losing the war. Anya had suspected things were bad from some of Adam's stories, but the nightmare in Warsaw was the brutal confirmation of her worst suspicions. There was no hope now. They were done for.

Come what may, Anya swore her three little ones would never suffer the fate of Poland's children, whose small corpses Anya had seen lining miles of railroad tracks. Even if Russia itself failed to survive the deadly conflict, Byelochka and the girls would never be exposed to such desolation, not as long as their mother had breath in her body. In fact, if any good could be said to have derived from her recent recklessness, it was that faced with a danger to someone she loved, Anya now knew she was capable of courage rather than passivity. Adam knew it too, and he would never forget it.

Prince and Princess Sviridov reached Petrograd a mere six days before Warsaw fell to the Germans, making Anya mistrustful of military predictions forever afterward. But they had managed to rescue a trainload of wounded soldiers as well as a huge cache of supplies from under the nose of the enemy—a tremendous coup.

Billy, taking advantage of the opportunity to promote his agency, had the foreign press corps waiting at the station when the train arrived—and then had to prevent his brother from throttling him for having failed to prevent Anya's departure. It was the forcible intervention of the American ambassador that saved Billy's neck. Instead of appearing in a photo destined for the front page of *The New York Times*, he had to take refuge in the bar at the Hotel Astoria for several hours, hoping Adam would cool off and not come looking for him. It was one of the low points of his diplomatic career.

More adroit than her lover, Tatiana Sergeevna graciously consented to pose for pictures with the wounded, upstaging Princess Anya. To everyone's astonishment, Tasha turned up on page 1 of the leading New York dailies as the brave Russian princess who had risked her life to snatch her wounded countrymen from under the noses of the Germans. She blandly attributed the mix-up to the difficulties of translation.

Moved to tears by his son's arrival home, Lev Petrovich swore hewould repay Princess Anya's extraordinary kindness. Andrei's peasants looked upon the boy's return as a sort of miracle. Prince Malyshev's family took care of their own, they murmured. All the other estate-owners ever did was bleed their peasants. Especially Count Scherbatkin. Anya's exploit entered into the local folklore with a great deal of embellishment in the retelling that made it even more exciting each time it came up.

Despite an occasional bit of good news, life in the wartime Petrograd was deteriorating markedly. Prices were rising faster than salaries and scarce commodities were becoming even scarcer. The atmosphere was chaotic— gloom and utter cynicism one moment, frantic gaiety the next. The night-clubs were prospering and so were the coffin makers. The most unlikely people were quietly talking treason with shadowy figures who crossed the borders from Scandanavia, some very highly placed.

Half of Russia was wishing their tsar would find a way to lead them out of the quagmire he had got them into; the other half was already talk-ing of the day there would no longer be a tsar. The old year gave way to 1916 with renewed hope for the future and numerous prayers for peace— none of which had the slightest effect on the troops who were mauling each other to death along the many fronts of the Great War.

The Polish debacle was such a disaster it cost the jobs of several Rus-sian generals—and led to a growing estrangement between Adam and his brother. No matter what argument Billy used on his brother, the fact re-mained—he had failed to prevent Anya from undertaking a dangerous jour-ney while he had remained safe in Petrograd. There was no way Billy could have known of Anya's plan, but Adam didn't care. He had failed his brother again. In Adam's cold eyes, Billy could see his reflection labeled "coward, wastrel, buffoon," and he was now doing his best to live up to Adam's bad opinion of him, spending all his free time drinking with his cronies or in bed with Tasha. Both were dangerous addictions.

Since Russia's summer campaign of 1915 had been so dismal, it was dropped from all official conversations as if the mere mention of it would summon up further disasters. This being the case, Prince and Princess Svir-idov were greatly surprised to receive a request to present themselves at the Alexander Palace in Tsarskoye Selo in early 1916 to accept the grat-itude of the government for their actions on behalf of the wounded.

Along with a dozen others, the Sviridovs were lined up in one of the white and gilt reception rooms and presented to the tsaritsa, who greeted them stiffly, exchanging formalities in thickly accented Russian, and left them feeling they had somehow annoyed her. On the way home, Anya wondered what the point had been. She felt almost as if she had been reprimanded by Alexandra, who had once been so kind.

Speculating on Rasputin's influence over her, Anya was starting to believe Volodya had been right all along. The entire Rasputin clique, from the tsaritsa right down to the harmless hangers-on like Natalya, were all insane in some mysterious new way that was unlike all other forms of insanity and peculiar to Russia and its women. Volodya had once used those words to Ksenia, and she had smiled in amusement. Now nobody would find the idea amusing; it seemed to be eerily accurate.

Princess Anya nestled against Adam, her beautiful dark sables brushing his face, both of them silently watching the frozen countryside, the icy fields, the small peasant villages and the boarded-up summer dachas of the affluent slide by as they sat in a first-class compartment of the Petrograd train, heading for the capital.

"Anya," said Adam at last as he held her gloved hand, "it's all over for them. Russia's slipping further and further behind. She's lost momentum."

"We're losing the war, you mean."

"Yes. I consider it lost, and believe me, I'm no quitter."

"Do you think we might have a chance of recovering what we've been forced to concede this past year?"

"Not unless a miracle occurs. Do you know Volodya told me 90 percent of the officers from his regiment have already died? That's only one regiment. Multiply it by dozens. This war is bleeding the country to death."

"Then," replied his wife, "we must step up our shipments to Stockholm. Our children's future may depend on it."

Putting his arm around Anya, Adam nodded. "This time," he said, "I'd like you and Ksenia to go through your collections and pick out the best. I have a feeling we'll find the Germans on our doorstep before the end of the year."

Leaning her head on Adam's shoulder, Princess Anya remembered the terrible things she had seen in Poland. The idea of fleeing her homeland was dreadful, almost unthinkable—but in light of the risk to her children if they remained in the midst of a battleground, it seemed the only logical choice. If the choice had to be made. They would always remain Russians; a brief exile wouldn't change that. Besides, every war, no matter how dreadful, had an end.

As the train carried them noisily back toward Petrograd, Anya was already beginning to make her selections.

29

In the capital, Tatiana Sergeevna was having her own thoughts about the future. As she and Billy Whitmore lay entwined in his bed, jostling each other among the lynxes, the young countess suddenly jabbed him with an elbow. Sighing a little, the American pushed his hair out of his eyes and sat up, waiting for her next demand. With Tasha there were always demands.

"What is it, darling?" he asked wearily, leaning on an elbow as the girl pulled the furs up over her bosom and looked serious.

"I want you to do me a favor," she announced. "In Paris."

"What?" he exclaimed. "Are you out of your mind? There's a war on. One can't simply rush off to Paris as if it were the old days."

"You're lying! You always lie! I know a friend of Auntie's who just returned from a diplomatic conference there."

"But, Tasha, that's government business. One can always find special ways for something like that."

"All right," replied the girl, glowering at him. "Find one. I want you to go there for me."

"Impossible. The best I can do is get myself sent to Stockholm."

"Stockhom isn't Paris. I want a gown from the house of Poiret. Just because there's a stupid war on doesn't mean I ought to be deprived of looking beautiful on the night of my presentation. It's important to me."

Ah, so that was it, thought Billy smiling almost in spite of himself. The little thing was looking ahead to her presentation ball. She had probably already calculated the exact amount of time it would take for the couturier and his staff to put together her gown and didn't want to waste a minute. When it came to looking out for herself, Tasha was second to none.

"I want my gown from the house of Poiret," repeated Tasha, beating the bed with her fists.

"How are we to go about getting you this gown? Monsieur Poiret can't measure you, after all."

Pulling the lynxes closer around her in disgust, Tasha gave her lover a look of venomous disdain. "I can send him my measurements and a good dressmaker's dummy. He can work from that. It's been done."

Rolling his eyes toward the ceiling, Billy lay back in the bed and sighed. The sooner Tasha came out in society—or whatever was left of it—the sooner he could begin to court her openly. He was determined to marry her and acquire Seriozha's millions, and if it meant he had to find a way to get her this damned dress, he'd try. "How soon can you get me this dummy?" he asked at last.

"Tomorrow if you wish."

Making a few calculations in his head, the American sat up again and looked at the girl, who was still regarding him as if he were an unreliable servant.

"I know a Swedish lady who might be able to help."

"I don't care who gets me the dress," shrugged Tasha. "But I have to have it in time for my ball in January."

"Fine. You'll have it. That's months from now."

"What I want will take months."

Naturally, thought Billy. He'd never known the girl to ask him for anything simple like other girls. No. Former girlfriends used to be overwhelmed with things like flowers, candy, romantic poems. Tasha lived in a palace decorated with more out-of-season flowers than three florists' shops, nibbled one piece of candy out of a box and flung the rest to the servants and detested all poetry except for some of Pushkin's more comical pieces.

Billy's sole means of appealing to her was through his willingness to indulge her odder whims. Like this one.

"I want to be the most beautiful woman in the ballroom that night," declared Tatiana Sergeevna with determination. "Remember, most of Auntie's friends are homely, but Ksenia and Anya will be there, and of course, they'll be absolutely dazzling, so I'll have lots of competition from them. I don't want anyone to spoil my evening by outshining me."

"You'll be the most beautiful woman there, darling. Never fear."

"Yes," agreed Tasha. "If you get me that gown from Poiret."

"I will," he promised. "Word of honor."

Sneering a little, Tasha retorted, "You haven't got any."

"That," he pointed out, "is a very cruel thing to say to the man who loves you."

Tasha decided to humor him a little longer. He was a bit like a dog; he needed an affectionate pat every once in a while. She thought it was rather amusing. And she despised him for it.

◆ ◆ ◆

One of Petrograd's newest residents, a businessman who had fled Warsaw shortly before the Germans broke through, was beginning to make a name for himself in his adopted city, catering to a wealthy and discriminating clientele weary of wartime deprivations.

In his new establishment on a street off the Fontanka Canal, Monsieur Mossolov, né Ivanov, was doing much better than he had ever hoped. He felt safe from the war and was convinced the authorities would never bother Mossolov. The building itself had a nice facade, all neoclassic cornices and caryatids and a lovely interior using fine *faux-marbre* work. Attractive as that was, there was something even more appealing about the Garden of Eden, as Oleg had named the place. Downstairs it had one of the largest cold-storage rooms in the city.

In a land famous for the bitterness of its winters, most Russian houses had cold-storage rooms, but the sheer size of this one made it truly exceptional. Now Oleg had become a flesh peddler in every sense of the word, with live meat upstairs in the reception room and frozen black-market goods in the cellar. Life was marvelous, not to mention profitable.

Everything would have been splendid if it hadn't been for the frustration he felt each time he thought of his suffering at the hands of the aristocracy, one family in particular. The mere thought of his pursuit by those fiends from the Okhrana, hired by Prince Malyshev to kill him, made him grind his teeth with rage. If it hadn't been for them, he would never have been forced to flee to Poland with that cow Wanda. When Oleg thought of Wanda, he felt somewhat guilty, so he tried not to think of her too often. Her death was all the fault of Anna Nicolaievna, anyway. The little aristocrat had been using poor Wanda's body to haunt him and he had been forced to take action. The thought of it made his skin crawl.

Oh, he loathed them all, but he hated Prince Andrei's family more than any of the others, and when the opportunity presented itself, he would destroy them. Of course, he knew he might have to wait a bit, in order to seize the perfect moment when it came, but he had time. He had been forced to learn patience in his life.

Roman V. Petrov had nearly lost contact with his former operative Pavel Scriabin after he had been called upon to work the bodyguard detail for Rasputin, but he had passed Scriabin along to another colleague, praising him as a reliable informer.

In late 1916, with Russia losing most of her battles, most of her regular army and all of her faith in the government, Pavel reported to his boss that the workers at his place of employment were planning a massive strike and had every intention of spreading as much dissent as possible throughout the heart of Petrograd's industrial center. He was instructed to go back and try to talk them out of it, but in the confrontation that ensued at the factory—a Derzhavin plant—it soon became obvious to Pavel that he must participate or lose his credibility with his comrades.

With grave misgivings, Pavel placed himself at the head of the strikers and led them out—straight into a trap. In the riot that followed, Pavel Scriabin was one of the first to be cut down by the rifles of a waiting band of cossacks.

As Countess Derzhavina explained it at dinner that evening, she and the manager of the plant had set the whole thing in motion with a telephone call to the city commandant. Her only regret was missing the show herself. Andrei Nicolaievich reflected with a wince that in another era she probably would have had a box at the Colisseum. And enjoyed it immensely, too.

Nineteen sixteen was the year people finally gave up hope and began to ask for an end to all the things that were making their lives miserable. They called for an end to the war and usually included demands for the abolition of the autocracy. The war was the cause of most of the misery and was literally bleeding the country to death. In a land of great inequality, only death was democratic.

For Prince Adam, it was a time of extraordinary activity. He was feverishly planning to transfer his family's treasures to Stockholm, while supervising the shrinking network of agency field stations. By the fall of 1916, the red, white and blue insignia of the Amer-Russian War Relief Agency was hanging only over small hospitals in the major cities, far from the front. And each of these establishments was filled to capacity with the wounded, who arrived in a uniformly wretched state.

Despite Princess Anya's insistence that Billy had known nothing of her trip to Warsaw before the moment he discovered her at the station, the brothers continued to treat each other with elaborate coolness, rarely speaking unless it was absolutely necessary. That pained the princess. Her chief joy was her family, and she spent hours with Byelochka and his sisters, but especially with her son, who was now four and old enough to be a small companion to her.

Accompanying Mama on her daily drives down the Nevsky, the little prince chattered gaily about everything that came to mind and loved to watch the patrols of cossacks that seemed to be appearing with greater frequency than ever on the city's busiest boulevard. As Byelochka waved to them and occasionally received a smile in return, Princess Anya wondered if the government was foreseeing trouble. Cossack patrols were the autocracy's traditional response to signs of rebellion in the capital. But so far, there was little to worry about. If anything, the people were too numb with despair to create any disturbances. The young princess marveled at Russian stoicism.

For Anya and Ksenia, the main event of the winter was to be Tasha's presentation to society shortly after the New Year. The ladies were sparing no effort. Although Princess Ksenia had enjoyed mothering Anya and had raised her quite successfully, Tasha's nature was so different from Anyushka's that it drove her beautiful aunt to distraction to deal with her. At times, she could almost understand why Lisa had had so few maternal feelings for this odd little creature whose coldly beautiful blue eyes looked out upon the world with such cynicism. Princess Ksenia couldn't wait to find her a husband—poor fellow.

By winter, Tatiana Sergeevna had succeeded in getting her gown from Poiret and she was ecstatic.

"Oh Billy," she gasped. "It's magnificent. Absolutely perfect. Thank you!"

Tasha flung her arms around Billy's neck and kissed him several times, genuinely delighted with her gown. Early January was to be the date of the great event and it was essential to have the gown ready early in case of any last-minute alterations. Aunt Ksenia would be impressed.

"Now, darling," smiled Billy, "wrap up the package so I can bring it to the house and present it to you in the bosom of your family. They'll all want to see the famous gown that caused so much trouble."

"All right. Let them envy me."

"Tasha?"

"Yes?"

Those beautiful blue eyes looked so innocent, it was difficult to believe this sweet young girl could easily surpass any whore in Petrograd in bedroom abilities. Billy wondered how she could still manage that air of unsullied purity. She would have been a hell of an actress, he thought with a smile.

"When you come out this winter, we can start to see each other openly. Your aunt won't object to that, surely."

"I won't have the time," replied Tasha. "I have to find a husband to get me out of her house. We're going through all the young titles who are still able to walk. With this stupid war, it's going to make things very difficult to find someone in good condition."

"Well, does your husband have to be a young title?" Billy was dashed.

"I'll be a wealthy woman," Tasha reminded him. "I don't want to be bothered with a sponge."

"Tasha," Billy said quietly, "what about marrying a man who loves you? Isn't that important?" As he regarded his young mistress with tenderness, the young man bent over and gently kissed her neck, stroking her lovely cheeks, still glowing from the winter chill outside. "I have a great deal of affection for you," he whispered. "I really do. If I hadn't, I never would have done what I did."

"You did it because I threatened to blackmail you," she was quick to remind him.

Taking her gently in his arms, Billy said softly, "I've always found you irresistible, Tatiana Sergeevna. And if possible, I'd like to marry you after you've had your season."

Countess Derzhavina pulled roughly away from the slim, young man and began packing her presentation gown. Billy lifted an eyebrow, startled by her brusqueness.

"I'm sorry. I didn't realize marriage to me was such a distressing thought," he said.

Tasha steadfastly ignored him. She hadn't even thought about marrying him; the suggestion came as a total surprise. "I don't think so," she replied finally, "I don't think I can marry you."

Billy smiled bitterly, watching her. She wore a lovely red wool suit with black mink trim and neat little fur-lined boots. With Tasha's dainty figure, she looked like one of the dolls one could find on display in the finer toy shops. And like a doll, she had beauty but no heart, no warmth, only the illusion of humanity.

"Things are going to explode if this war continues much longer," warned the young American. "And Mrs. Billy Whitmore would be a lot safer than Countess Derzhavina if all hell breaks loose in Petrograd. You know that as well as I do."

Picking up her large black muff, Tasha looked carefully at her reflection in the mirror. "I know," she nodded. "It's true."

"Well," he said, "will you consider my proposal?"

Turning toward her lover, Countess Derzhavina shrugged. "I don't know," she demurred. "Sometimes you remind me of my father."

"Is that such a bad thing, darling?"

Flinging the muff angrily across the room, Tasha replied, "I hated the little monster with all my heart, Billy! Do you think I'd ever want to marry his replacement?"

And with that, Countess Derzhavina fled the room, leaving her astonished lover staring after her, absolutely dumbfounded. It was the last time he ever asked her anything about the dear departed. He didn't have the nerve.

By December, all Petrograd was ready to explode. The hopelessness of the war combined with the helplessness of the tsarist government made daily life a bad joke. Cossacks patrolled the Nevsky, looking for the first signs of trouble; housewives lined up at dawn in subzero weather for their daily bread—when it was available—and the soldiers of the Petrograd garrison grew more and more cautious about using force against the growing crowds of demonstrators on the city's broad boulevards.

Now composed almost entirely of reluctant draftees from the capital's working-class districts, the soldiers were sympathetic to the complaints of their brothers and sisters and rather hostile to the orders of their officers. They still obeyed, grudgingly, but soon they might not. And their superiors knew it.

"I'm predicting an all-out disaster," Volodya Grekov informed Prince Andrei one day shortly before Christmas. "The trash they have in the army now is so unworthy of the uniform, it makes me sick to see them. They've begun to draft strikers, you know. That's insane. It's totally unrealistic to expect them to fight for the government."

"They're scraping the bottom of the barrel."

"Hah!" snorted Volodya, "worse than that. We've had cases of men surrendering wholesale to the enemy rather than keep fighting. We've had cases of men shooting their officers!"

At that, Andrei looked startled. "I thought those were just rumors."

"I wish they were. I've known two officers who died like that."

Pouring Volodya a shot of vodka from his prewar supply, the prince sat silently staring out of the window. At last he said, "Do you think Nicholas will put us all out of our misery and make a separate peace with Germany? It was a stupid, senseless dream even to think we could wage war like this. Doesn't he realize people are talking about deposing him?"

"God knows what our tsar thinks. I heard a rumor he sent one of his ministers to a secret conference in Sweden to negotiate with the Germans. I have no way of knowing whether or not there's any truth in the story."

Prince Malyshev settled back in his armchair and smiled oddly. "Natalya says her Siberian friend has given the tsar a special icon to carry with him when he confers with his generals. It's supposed to make him invincible."

"Nicholas had better get something to make him bulletproof," replied Volodya. "I've heard all sorts of plots, even among those who wouldn't strike anyone as remotely disloyal."

"A coup d'état?"

"Anything's possible."

Since Volodya's return to Petrograd as a training officer for the newly drafted factory workers, his mood was gloomy regarding the future. From what he could see, the brave, loyal fellows who had gone off to war without a second thought were all dead and had been replaced by a newer kind of animal, a sullen product of the sprawling urban slums. This new recruit was as likely to shoot a Russian officer as he was a German, perhaps even more likely since he hated his officers for putting his life on the line to fight their war.

And lately, poorly produced pamphlets had begun to appear in the mess halls to drive home the point that the people of the so-called proletariat had more in common with each other, no matter the nationality, than they ever had with the officers who commanded them. To Major Volodya Grekov, such Bolshevik propaganda was a disturbing sign of the government's weakening grip on the army and a chilling reminder of the worst excesses of 1905.

Worse than that, in 1905 the army had remained stable and steadfast, loyally backing the government. In these final days of 1916, nobody could count on anything, least of all from the querulous riffraff of the Petrograd garrison, the government's only hope of defense in case of civil unrest.

"Let's drink to a better year ahead in 1917," suggested the prince, refilling Volodya's glass.

Major Grekov smiled as he proceeded to toss down the vodka. "Let's just drink to making it through this year," he said. "We can worry about 1917 if we're lucky enough to reach it."

At that point Prince Andrei decided to ask Adam to use his influence at the embassy to outfit the whole family with American passports—just in case.

30

For Oleg Ivanov, nothing mattered except the nightly turnover in his fashionable establishment on the Fontanka, where his girls heard ad nauseam their officer-clients' fears for the future while they drowned their worries in frantic pursuit of pleasure. Requests for the most bizarre triple or quadruple combinations were becoming the norm as staggering losses at the front cut a man's life expectancy to near-zero in some sectors. Frantic for distraction, the survivors burned themselves out in the whorehouses and theatres of Petrograd while they awaited their own deaths in the vast charnal house the war had become.

Rich beyond his wildest dreams, Oleg found success a mixed blessing. From behind his impressive French antique desk he directed a luxurious *maison de plaisir* that was being mentioned as a worthy rival to the great Parisian houses, but in his heart he knew he was a man living on borrowed time, for if any of his enemies discovered the truth about Monsieur Mossolov, he would die. Or worse than that, he would be sent to prison to languish while some rival took over his business, enjoying all that he had worked so hard to accumulate.

On those days or nights when he felt the urge to spy on his enemies, savoring the pleasure of watching their movements unseen, Oleg would take himself to the French Embankment, never actually strolling in front of the Sviridov Palace, but skirting it, pausing to lean over the Alexander Bridge as if he were watching the ice skaters while he fixed his small, piglike eyes on the huge neoclassic building, searching for any sign of Princess Anya.

Sometimes he would be rewarded with a glimpse of her; more often than not he would return to his bordello unsatisfied, cheated of his odd pleasure. Fearing her, yet somehow fascinated by her, Oleg lived for those moments when he could observe her, all the while trying to ascertain the proper time for another attempt at killing the woman who tormented his dreams. With a demon like Anna Nicolaievna, one had to be very careful.

The sight of the children never failed to rattle him. They resembled their blonde, blue-eyed mother so closely it seemed to Oleg he was seeing her in triplicate. They looked nothing like the tall, dark-haired man who sometimes accompanied Anna Nicolaievna on her drives; they were all tiny replicas of the mother, three little enemies who would hate him just as she did, who would probably try to kill him just as she had. Their presence made him feel threatened, vulnerable. Now there were so many of her, he was clearly outnumbered. He would have to choose his next method of attack with the greatest care.

One gray, windy afternoon in December, Oleg stood watching as the whole family drove out of the courtyard of the great mansion in a fine, shiny black sleigh drawn by a pair of prancing trotters, silver sleigh bells jingling merrily as they made their exit. The children were shouting gaily; Anya waved at a neighbor as the sleigh raced down the embankment heading for the Alexander Bridge.

Turning to stare curiously as they approached the bridge where he was standing, Oleg saw Anya with her arm around her husband, both of them bundled into thick sables, the children sitting next to them. The man was of no concern, thought Ivanov. He was the same one who had fought with him in that French museum, the one Oleg would have finished off if it hadn't been for that demon. He almost pitied him for having to live with her. She must be ten times worse than Wanda had ever been.

Following the sleigh with his squinting eyes as it made the turn and headed down Liteiny Prospect away from him, Oleg felt almost overwhelmed by a frustration that nearly took away his breath. It hit him so hard he had to lean against the railing of the bridge to steady himself as the fierceness of his emotions swept over him, infuriating him, making him feel impotent before fate. He wanted her to feel powerless in his presence as he humiliated her, degraded her, tore her children from her arms and laughed in her face—and killed her.

Then he would be satisfied—only then.

"Damn," muttered Oleg as he strolled toward the tram stop. With the state of things as bad as they were, how long was it going to be before the citizens of Petrograd decided to erect barricades as they had in 1905, battling the police, shutting down all city services and providing the right opportunity for what he intended to do?

With an opponent as evil, cunning and clever as this blonde witch, a man needed all the help he could get. And in his case, nothing less than total anarchy would give him the nerve to act.

But when would it happen? As Oleg climbed aboard a tram loaded with tired, badly nourished housewives, clutching the loaves of bread for which they had stood in line for hours, he wondered when these stolid, docile countrymen of his would say, *Enough.*

◆ ◆ ◆

In the white columned halls of the Duma—parliament—opposition to the monarchy was almost at the same level as it was in the breadlines on the boulevards. While Oleg Ivanov was standing on the Alexander Bridge speculating about his fate, the deputies in the Duma were deciding to force the hand of Gregory Efimovich Rasputin. Almost to a man, they rose to call for his removal from the tsar's court—meaning by now the tsaritsa's. Nicholas was constantly away at army headquarters, having left the reins of government in the hands of his loving wife.

Deputy after deputy approached the speaker's platform, denouncing the hated *starets*, but it was in Vladimir Purishkevich, the tsar's staunchest supporter, that the Duma found its most eloquent voice. The deputy, a man so violently reactionary as to be an extremist even by tsarist standards, was disgusted. Looking around the great hall, Purishkevich affirmed his devotion to his tsar—and his bitter scorn for Nicholas' inner circle. He then commenced a blistering vilification of the tsaritsa's evil clique who had led the monarchs down the path of folly and who had degraded the autocracy with their villainy, lust for power, and treachery to the tsar and Holy Russia. Now, he declared, if the country was to survive, every patriot must tell Nicholas to assert himself and cast out the vermin who had dared to come so close to his throne.

Gregory Efimovich Rasputin was at the head of the list of vermin.

When Purishkevich had finished, the hall was so carried away by its unanimous agreement with him, it was difficult to hear above the roar of the applause. Men were screaming as they called for the death of the *starets*, and some of them wished the same fate for the tsaritsa.

One youthful member of the audience took the message so personally he promptly paid a call on Purishkevich and pledged himself to help carry out the execution. Prince Felix Yusupov, dilettante, playboy, husband of an imperial princess and sometime companion of Rasputin was about to become a murderer out of dedication to the monarchy.

In the Grekov mansion, Count Gigi was becoming murderous too. His warnings to Natalya to give up the *starets* had produced no visible effect over the years; finally, in despair, he had decided to use force.

On a snowy evening toward the end of December, he encountered his wife ready to leave the house alone, a sure sign of a visit to her mentor. "If you see him again, I'll kill you and that bastard brat of yours," he announced quietly. "This time, Natalya, it will be the end."

The countess barely glanced his way. Throwing on her sable coat, she glided out the door and into the waiting automobile, telling her chauffeur to take her to 64 Gorokhovaya Street, the *starets'* address.

Gigi watched the car pull away, then went to the study, poured himself a double whiskey and with slow determination, mounted the stairs, heading for the nursery where his two sons lay sleeping, their nursemaid nearby.

Opening the door, the count walked silently into the room and over to the bed where Nicky lay, clutching the large plush bear Ksenia had given him.

"Bastard," muttered Gigi. But he didn't do anything except stare at the sleeping child.

When Natalya reached the doorway of her mentor's second-floor apartment, she was startled to find him on his way out. The last time they had spoken, Gregory Efimovich had been depressed and worried about the future—especially after hearing reports of Purishkevich's recent speech in the Duma—but tonight he seemed almost a different man. He was plainly in high spirits, seemingly anxious to get rid of her so he could leave for a party.

As Natalya stared at her mentor, she wondered if she had ever really known him. She looked at him carefully as he asked her if she had come to say farewell, all the while decking himself out in a splendid red silk Russian blouse embroidered by another aristocratic admirer.

"It's a strange time to come calling," he said jovially, pleased with his reflection in the mirror. "Much later than usual for you."

Suddenly the countess recalled his opening question. "Why should I be coming to say goodbye? I don't really understand," she said.

"I thought perhaps you were leaving for the Crimea. A lot of people are going there until Petrograd calms down. You were talking about it a few weeks ago."

Natalya shook her head in bewilderment. If she had been leaving the city, she hoped he would have been more upset over her departure. Really, his behavior was quite peculiar. He was not himself this evening.

"Gregory Efimovich," she said, "I have to talk to you."

To her astonishment, he replied with an edge in his voice, as if she were a troublesome child he had to endure. "Not tonight, little dove. I have an important meeting with someone, an unfortunate young man who is a great sinner. He's asked me to help him in his struggles against the Evil One and I couldn't find it in my heart to refuse. After all, who knows more about sin than Gregory Efimovich, eh?" he smiled, giving Natalya a wink. "It will take a great deal of prayer."

But he certainly didn't look like a servant of God about to save souls; he looked more like a man about to set off for a good time with bad company.

"Pray for me, Gregory Efimovich," pleaded Natalya, putting her arms around him. "Please."

"I always do, little Natalya," he replied, kissing her softly on the lips. "Always."

Leaning against him, Natalya whispered, "I love you more than anyone. And I'm so afraid for you right now."

"Why?" he smiled.

"We need you so very much," she hurried on. "Without you there is nothing, no hope, no reason to go on living. We look to you in our time of trial."

Rasputin gently stroked her pretty blonde hair. "No," he murmured, "that's wrong. All men die. So will I, and perhaps sooner than you think."

"No!" protested the countess, violently shaking her head. "That can't be!"

"I will not live to see the new year. I was told this by my holy mother, the Virgin of Kazan. I cannot escape my fate."

She couldn't believe she was hearing her beloved mentor say these words. His apartment looked strange, as if it were part of some hazy dream, ready to vanish forever if she so much as blinked.

"One thing I will promise, Natalya," said Gregory Efimovich as he caressed her beneath her warm furs, "I will not abandon you, even in death. I will never forsake you, little dove, not through all eternity."

"Then take me with you," she whispered fiercely. "I want to go with you."

"You will," he nodded, "but your time has not yet come. You must wait and prepare."

As Natalya left the *starets'* apartment, she turned toward him one more time. Kneeling in the snow on the outside landing, she begged for his blessing, her blonde hair dusted with the sparkling snow as it fell softly to the ground, glittering like a thousand little diamonds in the night.

"Goodbye, little dove," smiled Rasputin, raising his hand in the Christlike pose of so many cherished icons. "God keep you."

As she departed in the falling snow, leaving her tracks across the courtyard, the *starets* returned to his preening in preparation for his rendezvous.

When Natalya returned home, she found Gigi waiting for her.

"You went to him," he said coldly. "In spite of my warnings, you went to that filthy swine and shamed me as you always do."

"I'm going to bed," replied Natalya, scarcely glancing at him. She was too tired to argue. "Goodnight, Gigi."

"No!" Her husband didn't even give her time to take off her coat. In an instant he had her by the arm and was dragging her, protesting furiously, upstairs to where her sons lay sleeping.

Nearly throwing his wife into the boys' nursery, Gigi headed for the bed where Nicky lay.

"What are you going to do?" demanded Natalya, quite frightened.

"I'll show you, you slut!"

To Natalya's horror, he seized Nicky as if he were a rag doll and flung him viciously out of bed and across the room, while little Kolya screamed.

"No!" shrieked the countess as she ran to shelter her injured son. "You must be insane. Don't hurt the child!"

"Hurt him?" laughed Gigi, reaching for a poker from the fireplace. "I intend to kill the little bastard!"

Taking the poker in hand, Count Grekov brandished it menacingly at his wife, who clutched her son, sobbing with terror as she tried to lift the child off the ground and carry him out of harm's way.

Laughing at Natalya's fright, her husband saw he had finally made an impression on her dense little brain. Pity it was so late in the game.

"Don't hurt the child," she wailed, trying to shield Nicky with her body. "Kill me, Gigi, but don't hurt the boy! Please leave him alone. He hasn't harmed you!"

By now half the house was awake and curious to see what was happening in the normally quiet nursery. Daria, the maid, arrived in time to see the master knock his wife to the floor with a single blow and stand menacingly over the frightened child, poker in hand, ready to brain him. Devoted to her small charge and unmindful of the consequences, Daria crept up behind the master and smashed him over the head with a bronze doorstop just as he was about to bring the weapon down on his son's head. Nicky stared in shock, seeing both parents lying in front of him. He began to sob over Natalya, trying to revive her, afraid Papa had really killed her.

Daria lost no time in fleeing the Grekov household with the terrified children. She took shelter at the Malyshev mansion on the Moika, where Princess Ksenia assumed responsibility for the children and Prince Andrei called his doctor to attend the fallen parents.

On his way to meet the doctor at the Grekovs' home, Andrei found himself marveling that Gigi's self-control had lasted so long before snapping. He may have tried to murder the silly girl, but at least he had waited long after most people would have already gotten it over with. For that, he ought to be congratulated, thought the prince with a bitter smile. But Lord! what a disgrace to the family.

Countess Grekova was judged to be suffering from unspecified trauma and sent to a private clinic in the Petrograd suburbs. There she spent a week trying to understand what she could possibly have done to drive Gigi to commit such a mad act. It was the final proof of his innate wickedness, she decided sadly. From now on, they must live apart. It was a decision gladly endorsed by Gigi, who took Kolya, leaving Nicky with Prince and Princess Malyshev, and left town for his estate in central Russia.

Rasputin was less lucky than Natalya that night. Lured to the Yusupov Palace, he was murdered by his aristocratic host with the aid of various nervous friends, dumped into a hole in the ice-covered Neva and discovered there by police divers. Fished out of the river, his corpse looked like an apparition from an icy hell.

After Rasputin's murder, hopes were raised that the monarchs would return to sanity. But the tsar and tsaritsa continued as before, out of touch and determined to persevere in the spirit of the dead *starets*. People lost all optimism and went back to talking about a coup d'état.

31

On the day of the great event, Countess Tatiana Derzhavina decided that Princess Ksenia's maid was hopelessly out of touch with the latest hairstyles and proceeded to wail as if her heart would break, declaring to her aunt that if that woman did her hair, she'd ruin the whole evening for her. Ksenia and the maligned servant exchanged glances and inquired just who would suit Tasha.

"Anyushka's maid," replied the young countess.

"Then who will do Anya's hair?"

Tatiana Sergeevna didn't care.

Tapping her foot on the parquet floor of her bedroom, Princess Ksenia considered the request. She had worked long and hard to ensure the success of her niece's presentation at a time when social events were losing a bit of their luster because of wartime shortages and a growing tendency to save on nonessentials. Even in her circle, people were starting to cut back on electricity. And friendly contacts with butchers and bakers were carefully cultivated.

She did not want several months of meticulous planning to be sabotaged by Tasha's temper tantrums. The girl was so stubborn, she'd sulk all night and ruin her aunt's hopes of getting rid of her. The eligible young men in Petrograd must not see her like this. What she revealed after she had a wedding band on her finger was up to her.

"All right, darling," agreed Ksenia. "I'll call Anyushka and ask if she minds lending you Sonia for the afternoon."

"Good," nodded Tasha. "Daria is much better at doing older people's hair anyway."

Daria, the princess's maid, decided the best course of action was to keep looking relentlessly at the floor. Princess Ksenia was a beautiful and elegant lady. If she were to reach over and slap the little witch, Daria would be quite pleased. "Older people" indeed!

To Daria's surprise, Ksenia chose to ignore the remark and merely went to her boudoir to make the telephone call. She was in no mood to waste energy or emotion in a ridiculous verbal battle with this child. She had better things to do. And plenty of them.

At her bidding, the city's leading florist had transformed the gilded rooms of the vast Malyshev Palace into an enormous garden, with arches of white roses, cascades of other flowers and trails of smilax creating an illusion of springtime in the midst of one of the harshest winters Petrograd had ever known. The florist's assistants were largely female, the young men having long since departed for the front. And the flowers they were so carefully draping all over the foyer and ballroom were from the Sviridov hothouses at Tsarskoye Selo, not the Crimea. But at least they were available, thanks to Princess Anya.

Ksenia Alexandrovna wished she could say the same about the young men she had invited—or had wanted to invite. Three of her friends had lost sons within the past four months, cutting down Tatiana Sergeevna's list of possibilities still further. If this war lasted any longer, there wouldn't be any young men left.

Out on the Nevsky, cossacks, tall, bearded men on stocky horses, armed with steel-tipped lances, patrolled the wide boulevard, determined to keep any rebellious citizens in line. Looking at the cossacks with a mixture of respect and dislike, citizens muttered about the implied threat of violence from the soldiers and hurried on their way, muffled against the biting wind and snow flurries blowing in from the Neva, adding a few more inches of ice and snow to the streets.

Early in the day, Adam had made inquiries about the possibility of trouble in the streets, and while his contacts didn't foresee anything out of the ordinary, he thought it best for Anya to take her gown and jewels to the Malyshev Palace as early as possible and dress there. The children were taken along as a lark, playmates for little Nicky Grekov, who was staying with Ksenia until his mother could pull herself together.

Once Sonia arrived with her mistress, Tasha was quite content to spend the rest of the time that remained before the ball closeted with her maid and Anya's maid, arranging and rearranging her long, shining black tresses, leaving Auntie Ksenia and Anyushka to do whatever they wished to complete the final preparations for her presentation.

Anya, deprived of a similar ball several years before, was almost as excited as a young girl herself. Delighted with the flowers, the feverish anticipation, the heady scent of springtime in the snow, Princess Sviridova wandered through the halls, hand in hand with her twins, breathing in the perfume of flowers, recalling that day in the garden of Grand-père's Paris residence when she had so tremulously asked Adam to be her husband.

Looking back on that day, the young woman found herself nostalgic for those first moments with Adam when she realized just how much he cared for her. She couldn't even imagine how terrible her life would have been if it hadn't been for him. His *yes* had come without a moment's hesitation, and he'd known full well what filth the gossips were spreading about her. Adam Mikhailovich was a treasure.

As Anya stood before a huge gilded mirror in the foyer, Sashenka and Tory clutching her skirts, she smiled, glancing down at her two small daughters. She adored them and their brother who was upstairs with little Nicky playing under Nanny's supervision. Looking at her girls' pretty little faces, she wondered uneasily if she would ever have the pleasure of presenting them to society against the lavish background of the Sviridov Palace, or would she, her daughters, even Russia itself be swallowed up in the cataclysm already forming outside? The thought made her fear the future more than ever. And it made her determined to enjoy what might very well be last great ball any of them was likely to give for quite a while.

While Princess Anya was having her hair done, once Tasha had released Sonia, Prince Adam was making his way to the Malyshev Palace to join his relatives and dress for the great event. St. Petersburg balls always started early and just because the capital had changed its name, society saw no reason to alter its habits. Therefore Adam was leaving the offices of the Amer-Russians in plenty of time.

As he met his driver outside the building, the prince noticed that the man seemed preoccupied. Upon questioning, the fellow said he had seen several detachments of cossacks heading down the Nevsky, looking as if they were headed for a scrap. Did the *barin* think it might be a good idea to avoid that route this afternoon?

Adam hesitated. He certainly had no wish to find himself in the middle of a free-for-all, but Nevsky Prospect offered the shortest route to Ksenia's home on the Moika. If they used the back streets, it would take forever. And he didn't dare to be late for this.

Shaking his head, the tall, dark-haired *barin* seated himself in the sleigh and ordered his driver to use the Nevsky. The city was full of rumors; if there was trouble, they would have seen some evidence of it by now.

"Yes, Highness," nodded the driver, and the sleigh began its trip across town, scattering chips of ice all around.

Heading down Liteiny Prospect to make the turn onto the wide Nevsky, Adam saw the usual sights, lines of housewives outside food stores, schoolchildren heading home from classes in the afternoon dusk, playfully throwing snowballs at each other as they raced for the tram, officers in the shiny black sleighs of general staff headquarters—nothing out of the ordinary.

And then halfway down the Nevsky, Adam and his driver saw where all those cossacks had been heading.

"Should I turn back, *barin?*" shouted the driver to his passenger.

"Keep going. They don't appear to be halting traffic yet. We can get through."

At Kazan Cathedral, all around the statue of General Kutuzov were demonstrators, mostly women, chanting angry slogans against the war, the autocracy, and especially against the lack of bread in Petrograd. At this point the soldiers were merely onlookers, awaiting further orders. But as Adam and his driver both knew, that could change momentarily.

"Khabalov is determined to rid the city of all demonstrators," offered the driver, flicking his whip lightly over his horse's head. "He's got *his* orders too."

General Khabalov, the city commandant, had the unenviable task of trying to keep the lid on trouble in the streets, while the citizens grew more and more restless each day. They were just waiting for the signal to start something. At this point, nobody knew what that "something" was, but the tension was almost palpable, keeping the military in a perpetual state of nerves. Right now, each street-corner agitator was being looked upon as a grave threat who ought to be supressed to preserve the stability of the government. If several citizens congregated in one spot, it was regarded as imminent revolution.

As Adam's driver raced his sleigh past the soldiers in front of the cathedral, the prince turned around to see what was happening. Just as the sleigh was safely past the danger spot, Adam could hear the sound of a shout from the officer in charge, ordering the people to disperse.

"Faster," ordered the prince, looking back at the scene. The demonstrators were standing their ground, he could see, while innocent pedestrians were fleeing to the other side of the street, to huddle in curious clusters on the corner where the Singer sewing machine building, marked by the distinctive globe atop the roof, was located. "The cossacks are getting ready to rush the crowd!"

He had scarcely uttered the words when the officer at the head of the detachment raised his sword and shouted to his men, leading them against the demonstrators at a gallop. Some of the citizens were sent sprawling on the icy ground beneath the hooves of the horses. The prince, who was seeing a cossack charge for the first time, was shocked.

Lashing out at the largely female group with steel-tipped whips, the soldiers dispersed the main body without too much difficulty and then went in furious pursuit of anyone they saw running for safety, knocking girls to the ground with a playful savagery that turned Adam's stomach. If the government was so afraid of its angry, hungry women that they had to resort to force to silence them, it was in even worse shape than he thought it was. It was losing confidence in its own power to deal with problems in a normal fashion.

At moments like these, he felt his foreignness more than ever.

"It's the way things are, *barin,*" said the driver, seeing the expression on his passenger's face.

Maybe, thought Adam, but it was a hell of a way to deal with people whose main complaint was lack of bread. And it was giving them a lot more to protest.

When Prince Adam reached the Malyshev Palace on the Moika Canal, Anya was almost finished dressing in the room she had used as a young girl, the one where she and her husband had spent their first night together. Seeing her here brought him back more than five years, to a far happier time. It was almost hard to believe they were still in the same city.

"You look beautiful," he said, admiring her elegant figure in a new evening gown, pale-pink silk charmeuse edged with swansdown and embroidered all over with tiny seed pearls. "I'm afraid you may outshine our little debutante."

"Oh, no," laughed the princess. "I know better than that. This is Tasha's night. You ought to see her. She's positively radiant."

But he noticed that Anya liked his compliment.

When Adam had bathed and changed into evening clothes, the Sviridovs went into the dressing room that was serving that night as a bedroom for the children and tucked them in. Byelochka was dazzled with Mama's profusion of jewels, the most jewelry she had worn in months, since so much of it was already reposing in a bank vault in Stockholm. This display of rubies and diamonds was to follow the rest within the week.

When Anya and her husband joined her aunt and uncle in their sitting room on the second floor, they found Tatiana Sergeevna with them, wearing what must have been every diamond her late mama had owned, sparkling like an electric light from the collection of brilliants around her neck, on her arms, at her ears and scattered through her hair.

"Tasha," said Adam gallantly, "you are magnificent."

Princess Ksenia smiled diplomatically. She was afraid he was about to tell her niece she looked like one of the blazing chandeliers in the ballroom. Diamonds were all right, but young girls didn't usually wear the entire contents of their jewelry boxes. That practice was best left to courtesans. However, Ksenia no longer cared to offer unsolicited advice to this creature. If she wished to glitter, let her. It was her night. And the gown was truly elegant; nobody could fault her taste there.

As Adam looked at the ladies, he was struck by the strong family resemblance. All were beauties, all were elegant, all shared the same in-definable air that marked them as Sviridovs. Anya and Ksenia had the height as well, one of the outstanding marks of the line. Tasha didn't. She was smaller, more like the Derzhavins in that respect. But when one looked at her face, she was a Sviridov through and through, the finely chiseled features and extraordinary eyes so much like Ksenia's and Anya's.

Almost seventeen, Tasha was surely going to develop into one of the great social successes of the season. Prince Andrei, exchanging glances with his wife, read her mind and was worried about that very thing. Tatiana Sergeevna was destined to become a great source of anxiety until the day she was safely and extravagantly married. And the sooner the better.

Before the family went downstairs to begin receiving their guests, there were two small details to attend to—the presentation of the Malyshevs' and Sviridovs' gifts to the young debutante and the group photograph Ksenia had arranged with one of Petrograd's leading photographers.

To commemorate Tasha's coming out, Ksenia and Andrei had pur-chased a fine bracelet of large pearls set off by an emerald clasp from Bolin, the court jeweler. Anya and Adam had commissioned a beautiful pair of pearl and diamond earrings from the same source. For once, Tatiana Ser-geevna appeared to be truly touched. She opened the little velvet boxes with great care, gasped in genuine surprise and looked quickly up at her relatives, who were watching to see if the presents met with her approval.

"Oh thank you," whispered Tasha, hugging Anya and Ksenia. "They're so beautiful."

The ladies were astonished to see tears in her eyes. And when she hugged them, it was with real warmth. It was the first time they had seen her let down her guard.

"Please put it on," asked the countess, holding out her hand to Ksenia.

Delighted, the princess fastened the pearl bracelet around Tasha's wrist and removed one of Lisa's; she stood back to admire the effect. "Very el-egant, darling," she smiled.

Not to hurt Anyushka's feelings, Tatiana Sergeevna was gracious enough to take off her diamond earrings and replace them with the new ones, two rather large baroque pearls capped with a cluster of brilliants.

Looking magnificent—Tasha in sparkling white georgette loaded with seed pearls, Anya in palest pink and Ksenia in deep emerald-green with a parure of emeralds and diamonds—the ladies had their pictures taken to-gether, separately and with the gentlemen.

That formality dispensed with, off they went to the ball, leaving in their wake an admiring gaggle of ladies' maids and footmen in the gilded corridor.

♦ ♦ ♦

In a season marked by a great lack of notable parties, Countess Derzhavina's presentation ball was the grandest of the winter. While snow fell softly outside the glittering windows of the Malyshev Palace, guests arrived in elegant sleighs, wrapped in sable, fox, mink and chinchilla, the ladies escorted by gentlemen in the gold-braided full-dress uniforms of the Guards' regiments or in the civilian equivalent—white tie and tails.

As fascinated passersby stood gaping in the snow, hoping for a glimpse of this countess or that princess, they could see a little of the activity inside the mansion through the brilliantly illuminated tall windows that offered them a peek at the guests dancing beneath huge, glittering crystal chandeliers. Ladies in Paris gowns from prewar days and decked with a fabulous variety of jewels looked like elaborately made-up dolls waltzing with gentlemen who appeared equally exotic. To the citizens gazing in with a kind of rapture at the spectacle before their eyes, it looked like something out of never-never land.

To those familiar with prewar balls, it was an unexpected stroke of luck to discover this one. They knew from past experience that the great houses frequently gave away leftover food to the poor, and they were hoping the custom would continue with this one. Many of those watching on the street had had little to eat. Scraps from Princess Malysheva's golden plates would represent an unimaginable feast, to be taken home and consumed with pleasure.

Under the blazing crystal chandeliers in the ballroom, Countess Derzhavina had arrived in an icy sparkle of diamonds, made a spectacular curtsey to her Auntie, Grand Duchess Maria Pavlovna, Grand Duchess Xenia, Anyushka and the rest of the elite before opening the ball on the arm of Prince Andrei, who was representing the late Count Derzhavin.

"She's absolutely ethereal," gushed one lady to Princess Ksenia, fluttering an ostrich fan. "Beautiful child."

Smiling graciously, the princess acknowledged the compliment and suggested that the lady's son might be interested in getting to know her. She was Derzhavin's sole heir.

"Ah," murmured the dowager, looking even more carefully at the little angel. "I see."

Dancing with all the uncles and family friends for the sake of politeness, Countess Derzhavina almost forgot about one gentleman in particular who was genuinely eager to hold her in his arms. Much to his chagrin, he had had to work hard just to get his name on her dance card.

As Tatiana looked up into Billy Whitmore's blue eyes, she gave him

the kind of smile that always made him want to take her directly to the
lynxes, which was a very naughty thought at the moment.

"You're beautiful, Tasha," he murmured, enjoying the sight of her in
the gown. It really was a masterpiece.

As Prince Adam watched his brother sweep Countess Derzhavina into
a tango, his mouth tightened almost imperceptibly. Anya saw it and had
to hide a smile. Her husband was acting like a dinosaur—or a disapprov-
ing parent.

"One would think Billy was an old roué the way you act," she murmured. "If you're really concerned about Tasha's virtue, I'd suggest you
keep an eye on that fellow over there in the hussar uniform. They say he's
caused several highly placed papas to keep their daughters under lock and
key."

The prince smiled. "I think Tasha could give Houdini a run for the
money if anyone tried that with her. She'd break out in record time."

"Yes, she probably would," giggled Anya, watching her little cousin
glide elegantly through the tango, one of the latest crazes. She and Tasha
had spent hours practicing together in Grand-père's now empty Gallery of
the Ottocento, especially while Adam was away. Now the young countess
was giving a remarkable demonstration, drawing raised eyebrows as she
and her partner executed more and more daring turns. As Anya looked
on, she suddenly realized that Billy and Tasha were too perfect together.
This was not the sort of dance one could do well with a strange partner.
They had spent a lot of time on this. But where? And how?

Catching Ksenia's eye across the ballroom, Princess Anya wondered if
her aunt was thinking the same thing. If what she suspected had the least bit
of truth to it, Billy was indeed as wicked as his brother said he was. Blushing
slightly as she watched Tatiana Sergeevna and her partner, Princess Anya
hoped that nobody else in the ballroom was of the same opinion.

When the company went in to supper at midnight, they found elegant tables set up in the gallery, laden with all the delicacies Ksenia's cook
had worked so hard to prepare—after spending a fortune in bribes to ensure the arrival of all ingredients. Service plates of gold gave way to fine
porcelain, heavily encrusted with more gold, flanked by goblets and champagne flutes of St. Louis crystal, all set out on table linens that came from
the finest French establishments. Silver bowls held charming arrangements
of spring flowers, perfuming the air with their dewy fragrance.

After dining splendidly, the guests went back to the ballroom, where
footmen were waiting to hand out little nosegays of baby's breath, daisies
and roses to the ladies, who accepted them with delight. It was a charming touch in the midst of a Petrograd winter.

As the ball finally drew to an end at five in the morning, after an evening of unsurpassed splendor, Countess Tatiana was still too excited to go to bed, so she kept her aunt and cousin up for hours afterward, reliving the whole thing until all three ladies simply collapsed together. Adam and Andrei had retired to their rooms at five-thirty, too tired to listen to another word.

As Princess Ksenia glanced outside into the late-morning gloom before going to bed, she gave thanks that no riots had prevented her guests from coming and noticed uneasily that there seemed to be Cossacks riding in a single file below her windows, an unusual occurrence.

If soldiers were patrolling this area, it couldn't mean anything good.

But at that moment, her highness was so exhausted that all she wanted to do was sleep. If the revolution itself had begun on her doorstep, she wouldn't have heard it.

In the weeks that followed Tatiana Sergeevna's presentation, there were quite a few alarms, if nothing concrete, as the demonstrators on the Nevsky became bolder and less willing to obey the soldiers and mounted police who were supposed to maintain order. The bridges of the Neva were now being carefully guarded, with an eye to preventing large groups of factory workers on the Vyborg side from crossing over. It was an atmosphere in which one man's bad temper would be enough to start a riot, with fearsome consequences.

Major Volodya Grekov, now on garrison duty in Petrograd, was extremely pessimistic on his visits to the Malyshev Palace between patrols. A reliable shipment of frontline troops was the government's best hope right now, he maintained. In a confrontation with the citizens, he fully expected his own men to shoot him in a rather flamboyant mutiny.

General Khabalov, the city's nervous commandant, had no grand design for dealing with the situation. He was losing ground each day and knew it, forced to rely on troops who were themselves workers drafted with great unwillingness into the army. In any large-scale uprising, they couldn't be counted upon to uphold law and order if they found themselves facing their own friends and relatives across the barricades. And trained officers were a breed that was almost extinct by now, having been killed off at a terrifying rate since the outbreak of hostilities. Major Volodya Grekov was a very rare bird indeed, a survivor of East Prussia in 1914 and Poland in 1915. Andrei was calling him indestructible, but Volodya wasn't so sure. There was always tomorrow and another fight; his luck couldn't hold out forever.

The one thing that gave Molyshev, Grekov and their friends cause for optimism was the news that Nicholas II was due to visit the Duma on the following day and address a special session, giving rise to rumors about reversing certain imperial policies. If the tsar could rid himself of the remnants of the Rasputin clique who were still surrounding the tsaritsa—and influencing the throne despite the death of the *starets*—perhaps progress could be made. It was everyone's wish.

But in light of all the past mistakes and wrongheaded blunders made by his government, it seemed a lot to expect.

In Princess Ksenia's bedroom, her maid Daria announced a telephone call for Her Highness from Countess Grekova at Tsarskoye Selo. The countess had gone there to resume her duties at court after her release from the clinic, and little Nicky was with her, a very unwise move, according to Ksenia. But Natalya was devoted to Alexandra and wouldn't abandon her post.

In bed with a dreadful head cold, Princess Ksenia flung off the heavy pink silk comforter and headed for her boudoir to take the call on the telephone next to her dressing table.

As she sank down in the satin-padded chair, Ksenia sighed, thinking of little Nicky with his ridiculous mother. If she had been able, she would have kept the child with her instead of returning him to that foolish girl. Natalya wasn't fit to raise sheep, let alone Nicky. But she *was* his mother, and Andrei said she had the law on her side. Stupid law.

Now Ksenia was startled to hear the countess say there was trouble at Tsarskoye. Her heart nearly skipping a beat, the princess asked if it was a coup.

"Oh no," replied Natalya. "A measles epidemic."

Princess Malysheva made a face in disgust. Another false alarm.

"Her Majesty advised me to send my son back to Petrograd before he catches them. All her girls have them, and it's very difficult for her right now since she's all alone. I have to help her nurse the invalids."

Even in her fevered state, Ksenia knew there was something wrong with that statement.

"What do you mean?" she demanded. "Nicholas is at Tsarskoye. I wouldn't consider that being alone."

The countess was impatient. "Not since last night," she replied. "That was when he left for Stavka. She really is all alone."

"What?" exclaimed Ksenia. "He wasn't due to return to army headquarters! He's expected at the Duma tomorrow to address a special session. Has he lost his mind?"

The whole town was anticipating his address to the Duma, desperate for some sign of renewed vigor on the part of a monarch who appeared to be lost and floundering, unable to choose a proper course for the nation. This was madness!

As if to confirm that opinion, Countess Grekova said that their majesties had had a conference with the minister of the interior, Protopopov, a Rasputin appointee who "communicated" with the late *starets* by means of seances; Protopopov had advised an immediate return to Stavka.

"It's done," said Natalya, rather petulantly. "Now can I expect to see you today? I'll send someone to meet the 10:15 train at the Tsarskoye Selo station. You can bring Nicky back with you."

Dazed from the fever as well as from the shocking news that had just been relayed so casually, Ksenia shook her head as she told Natalya it was impossible for her to venture out of doors at the moment. Still, she hated the thought of leaving Nicky with his mother under the circumstances. Ksenia didn't trust her to take care of herself, let alone a young child. Desperate for a solution, Ksenia thought quickly and suggested that Tasha could make the trip and return with the boy.

"Wonderful," agreed the countess. "Goodbye, darling. Thank you."

Glancing at the small Fabergé clock on her dressing table, Ksenia gasped. If Tasha was going to Tsarskoye, she had better be on the train in forty-five minutes.

"Daria!" cried the princess. "Find Countess Derzhavina at once. It's important!"

A search of the house failed to locate the young lady; in despair, Ksenia called Anya, explained the situation and asked her to go get Nicky. So far, there was no trouble in the streets; if they waited another day, the situation in town might make it impossible to leave and return easily.

Ascertaining that Nicky didn't actually have the measles—a threat to her own three youngsters with medical supplies running low in Petrograd in the midst of an epidemic—Princess Anya agreed to go to Tsarskoye and get the child. She shared her aunt's low opinion of Natalya's fitness to care for him and knew he would be better off in Petrograd with Ksenia Alexandrovna.

"All right, Auntie," she replied. "I'll leave for the station at once. See you this afternoon." It might entail some risk, but having survived the Polish debacle, Anya was unafraid.

With that, Princess Sviridova glanced out the window to check on the strikers on the Vyborg side of the Neva, saw nothing more unusual than the ordinary crowds of protesting workers, flung on a sable coat and called downstairs to the servants' pantry to prepare an automobile for her. She was going to the Nicholas Station.

Making their way through streets filled with soldiers on patrol, crowds of workers carrying banners, and rather nervous-looking mounted police,

Anya and her chauffeur had a few bad moments on Liteiny Prospect when snowballs were flung at their motorcar. And there was a chorus of angry shouts from a cluster of female strikers who called the princess a "rich pig" as her automobile was forced to wait in traffic while an army convoy passed. But apart from such incidents, the trip to the station was fairly calm.

Arriving just in time to dash inside and pay for a ticket two minutes before the train departed, Anya felt peculiar at traveling by herself under the present conditions. But she hadn't wished to burden herself with Sonia for a companion. Sonia had been frightened by the angry workers who had recently attacked her outside the Sviridov Palace as a "food hoarder," a designation that was a total lie; they had pelted the maid with chunks of ice, terrorizing her beyond belief. Now she was afraid to leave the house, a great problem for Anya.

Listening to the conversations of her fellow passengers on the way to Tsarskoye, the young princess heard the same theme repeated over and over. The cause of all the trouble lately was the lack of fuel. If the fuel could only get through, the bakers could bake. If the bakers could bake, the people wouldn't be out in the streets demanding all sorts of nonsense from the government.

"But it's all quite hopeless," sighed someone in back of the princess. "Nothing is being done to solve the problem."

"Or any other problem," replied a deep voice. "It's all a dreadful muddle."

"It's incompetence at every level."

Princess Anya shivered in her sables and silently agreed.

Arriving at the Tsarskoye Selo station, the princess looked around for a familiar face, saw none, and was wondering what had happened when she was approached by one of the countess's servants, who quickly led her to a waiting motorcar. After a short drive, she found herself in the vicinity of the Imperial Park, not too far from a small stone chapel.

"But I don't understand," said Anya as her companion stopped the automobile. "This isn't the area where Countess Grekova lives."

He smiled sadly. "Highness," he replied, "Natalya Alexeevna spends all her time here now. It's become her obsession."

Following the servant across a well-worn path of hard snow, Princess Anya found herself at last on the doorstep of the chapel. As the footman opened the thick wooden door to let her in, she was overwhelmed by a sense of unease; she felt as if she ought to turn around and leave at once.

"Natalya?"

Her eyes unaccustomed to the darkness, Anya stood in the small, icy chapel, aware of Natalya's presence, but unable to see her. At the sound of light footsteps running toward her, the princess turned around quickly, nearly colliding with little Nicky.

"Auntie!" he cried, burying his face in her thick fur coat. "You came!"

"It's Auntie Anya, darling," she said tenderly, caressing him as he clung to her. "Auntie Ksenia doesn't feel well."

"I want to see her. Will you take me to her?"

"Of course, Nicky. That's why I'm here."

"Good," he replied. "Mama doesn't want me anymore."

"Natalya?"

"Ssh! He doesn't want to be disturbed. He's angry." It was Natalya's voice.

"Who, darling?" asked Anya as she held Nicky's hand. There wasn't anyone else in the tiny chapel.

"Gregory Efimovich," replied the countess. "This is his tomb, and you're an unbeliever. He wants you to leave immediately."

Repulsed, Princess Anya approached the spot where Natalya knelt, a little bundle of fur on the cold stone floor, her forehead almost touching the ground as she groveled beneath a flickering row of candles, facing a photograph of her dead mentor. The countess glanced up.

As Anya looked into her friend's face, eerily white in the light of the candles, she shuddered. It was difficult to believe this ravaged-looking woman had been considered the loveliest bride of her year.

The large brown eyes that used to be so expressive were ringed with dark circles; all human warmth was gone. The fine complexion that had once invited envy had long since turned chalky. Deep lines creased her forehead and traced a pattern of misery from nose to mouth, a testimony to her grief at Rasputin's loss.

"My God," breathed Princess Anya, "you're ill. Come home with me, Natalya. You musn't stay here or you'll surely kill yourself."

"Nonsense. This is where I belong," replied the countess, looking away again. "I must stay here to be ready when Gregory Efimovich calls me. He promised to send for me on the night he was taken from us. I know he won't disappoint me."

"Natalya!"

"Take my son," replied the countess. "Ksenia will be good to him. Gigi ran off with little Kolya but that's just as well. I haven't the time to devote to my boys any longer. I have more important things to do."

"You must come back to Petrograd with me, Natalya. Adam knows a doctor who can help you. We'll care for you until you feel better."

"I don't need a doctor. I don't need anyone but him," responded Countess Grekova, pointing downward.

"He's dead, Natalya. He can't do anything more for you."

Holding Nicky close, Anya watched in surprise as Natalya finally rose and came toward her. Embracing the girl, Natalya Alexeevna kissed her formally on both cheeks, kissed her son farewell and silently returned to her prayers, having taken care of her last important business on earth.

Wordlessly staring at the countess, Anya knew there was nothing short of sheer brute force that could pry her loose from this insane cult to a dead monster. She wished Adam were with her; together they might have been able to do something.

"I'll take Nicky to Ksenia," Anya promised, pausing before she opened the door. "He'll be all right."

The only answer she received was a slight nod of the head as Natalya bent closer to the floor in an intensely private prayer, a pathetic figure completely out of touch with reality.

"*Do svidanya, Matushka,*" said the little boy, running back to embrace her for the last time.

At that moment, Anya hoped desperately that Natalya would get to her feet, seize Nicky and come with them.

"*Do svidanya,*" murmured the countess, releasing the child. "Go with Auntie."

As Princess Anya stood watching Natalya in that chilly house of death and madness, she shuddered violently at the pitiful human wreck before her, wasting all her love on a dead charlatan. Even in death, the *starets* refused to relinquish his amazing power over the susceptible.

"I'm ready, Auntie," announced Nicky, pulling on Anya's sables.

Ignored by Natalya, Princess Sviridova and the child opened the heavy oak door and crossed over into bright sunlight, the snow glistening like billions of diamonds in the sun.

"Goodbye, Natalya," said Anya as she left. But she never received so much as a wave of the hand in return.

On the way back to Petrograd, the princess wondered if their majesties were in the same sort of mental state as Countess Grekova. If they were, there was no hope for Russia. As she and Nicky sat quietly in their compartment, Anya was struck by the timeless quality of life at Tsarskoye. Nothing seemed to have changed since her last visit to the Alexander Palace, many months ago. Looking at this lovely and peaceful haven only fifteen miles from the rebelliousness of Petrograd, it was difficult to believe the tsar's capital was on the verge of open revolt.

Nothing like that ever happened at Tsarskoye Selo. It wasn't permitted. All that was permitted was a measured and mannered way of life, based on protocol that allowed not the slightest threat of reality to intrude on its delightful existence.

Do they understand what is going on in the country? wondered Anya, her chin on her hand as she gazed out the window at the snow-covered countryside speeding by. Do they care?

While the young woman was brooding over the fate of Russia, little Nicky was making himself a nest in her thick fur coat. Suddenly Anya felt a soft thud accompanied by a sort of peaceful grunt at her side. Staring down at the seat next to her, Anya saw Nicky, snoring like a little animal, comfortable and content in her sables.

"Poor child," she sighed, caressing him as he slept, "what's going to become of you?"

Then, with an uneasy heart, the princess began to wonder the same thing about her own little ones. Just how long did they have left in this country which had suddenly become so fiercely antagonistic to them and all their kind?

32

The next day, Princess Anya was awakened by a kind of distant roar, as if the ocean had suddenly moved to her doorstep. Startled, she leaped out of bed and called for Adam. Then, quickly remembering that he had left for Stavka with Billy, she opened the draperies to get a clear view of the Vyborg district across the frozen Neva. What she saw made her blanch.

Thousands of workers were milling around the streets on the opposite shore and great swarms of shouting, angry men were crossing the ice, despite the best efforts of the police to hold them back.

"What's the matter today, Sonia?" Anya asked as the girl entered bearing her breakfast.

"Nobody seems to know, Highness. A few of the servants are going across the bridge to have a better look and talk to the people."

Dressing as fast as she could, Anya telephoned Princess Ksenia to ask her if she had heard any new rumors. According to Ksenia's best sources, there had been more bread riots, and a neighbor, recently returned from his estate in Moscow province, reported a general stalling of railroad traffic all along the main line last night. Everything was in a thoroughly miserable condition, including Princess Ksenia who was still suffering from fever. There was no food in Petrograd—no fuel, no bread and no great respect for the law, either. People were becoming savages.

Ksenia advised her niece to stay inside and keep the doors bolted. Volodya Grekov had called earlier to inquire about Natalya and little Nicky, hoping they were no longer at Tsarskoye. The latest rumor in the barracks district was of a planned rebel attack on the palace. He was relieved to learn that the boy had been taken to Petrograd, although Natalya's stubborn determination to remain with Alexandra disturbed him greatly. The tsaritsa was the target of so much hatred, he feared for her life in any encounter with disaffected troops.

Leaving Anya with that gloomy thought, Princess Ksenia told her she was going to try calling several friends who might be able to give her more information on the situation on the streets. She'd call back later with more details.

Deciding to prepare for the worst, Anya headed for the nursery and a conference with Nanny. If any of the mob across the Neva took it into their heads to storm the Sviridov Palace, she had to work out an escape route for her little ones. With Adam far away at Stavka, responding to an imperial summons, Princess Sviridova had taken control of the household's defense.

In Okhrana headquarters across town, the police were among the most nervous citizens in town. For months, the loyal agents of the Okhrana had been filing reports warning of widespread rebelliousness and hostility on the part of the tsar's subjects. Now, with the capital just this side of armed insurrection, many of the police were wondering how to survive the coming street battles. Many were putting their faith in strategically located machine-gun nests. Others had less bellicose intentions in mind, with no plans for sacrificing themselves on the altar of tsarist incompetence.

In a well-hidden niche on the second floor of police headquarters, Roman Vasilievich Petrov sat talking with an old friend of his from years before. The man had been assigned to the Warsaw office for a decade and was back in the motherland out of circumstances beyond his control—the German invasion in 1915. After a stint in the Kiev branch, he was once again in Petrograd and was shocked by the collapse of morale at home.

Sipping tea from a chipped and stained glass, Petrov's friend, Anton Nicolaievich Kuzmin, stated gloomily that it all reminded him of Warsaw just before the debacle—heads of departments running amok like wild men, screaming at subordinates, blaming all their mistakes on others. Oh, it was so familiar. He had got out by the skin of his teeth, after delaying his departure because of a girl.

"A girl?" inquired Roman Vasilievich. "She must have been something to have kept you there while the Germans were about to march in."

Smiling in pleasant recollection, Kuzmin replied she was. Her name was Wanda Zumbrowska, she was a madam in one of the city's fanciest bordellos, and he adored her, even if she had the bizarre habit of sleeping with her damned white angora cat beside her.

He sighed over his fond memories of Wanda, but his face clouded as he revealed that she had vanished from sight shortly before the Germans took the city—despite his promise of safe transportation to Russia. The pass he had wrangled for Wanda he'd left with her partner in case she returned. As far as Kuzmin knew, pretty Wanda had simply vanished from the face of the earth, a great loss to mankind.

Petrov, always the policeman, suggested foul play, which Kuzmin denied. Sheer panic, more likely. The partner had reported her disappearance, along with that of her beloved cat, on the night the girls had all fled the establishment. Nobody'd seen any of them afterward.

Except for the partner, a Monsieur Timofey Mossolov. He had turned up in Petrograd, had opened a new place called the Garden of Eden. But he had no news about poor Wanda, lamented Kuzmin. A great tragedy.

Smiling sympathetically, Petrov suddenly glanced at his friend in surprise. The partner was here?

Kuzmin nodded. In fact, Monsieur Mossolov had invited him to his new place—a very high class house off the Fontanka Canal. For old times' sake, he said.

Would Petrov like to pay it a visit with him?

Roman Vasilievich shrugged. All his life he had been in contact with lowlife trash like Mossolov; he'd kept men like Rasputin under surveillance while they amused themselves at establishments like the Garden of Eden—or less elaborate houses. And he had rarely crossed the threshold.

Now with the city about to disintegrate into chaos, Roman Vasilievich decided to permit himself an unusual debauchery. Sins of the flesh were not his weakness. They came in a very distant second to what one might call sins of acquisition—Petrov would undertake almost any loathsome task if it put money into his retirement fund. But at this particular moment, with all hell about to break loose in Petrograd, the inspector had no reason not to indulge himself.

And he had always wished to experience the comforts a place like the Garden of Eden could offer, if only for an hour.

Shrugging, he accepted Kuzmin's offer. Why not? It might be their last chance for a good time before they all vanished like his friend's Polish lady.

"Roman Vasilievich, do you mean to tell me you don't intend to fight to the last for tsar and country?" smiled Kuzmin.

"I intend to fight as long as we can count on winning," replied Petrov frankly. "And then when the tide begins to turn, I plan on making my exit with my hide intact."

Raising his glass to his companion, Roman Vasilievich suggested he do the same.

En route home from Stavka, Prince Adam Sviridov was thoroughly exhausted and acutely depressed by what had transpired there.

Summoned to the presence of the tsar, he and Billy had been praised in Nicholas's perfect English for the good work of the Amer-Russian War Relief Agency, honored at a luncheon by General Brusilov, thanked, congratulated, toasted in endless rounds of vodka—and then informed the agency would cease to function on Russian territory. From now on, the government was assuming control of all such work, the better to coordinate the war effort.

Stunned by the completely unexpected decree, Prince Adam Sviridov had come close to undiplomatic fury. It was ludicrous, he'd protested. His organization had done more than any other civilian agency to help the war wounded. And it had done a hell of a lot more than the Russian Army ever did to help its men. Or was that the reason it was being disbanded? he demanded, recalling the hostility of the officers' clique at the time of the Polish fiasco.

Trying to restrain his angry brother, Billy had advised caution. The agency had been a tremendous benefit to his career, and he was desperate to salvage anything that could be retained. The hell with the humanitarian aspects. It had been a wonderful way to gather intelligence!

"We think Russians can do a better job," growled a colonel whose chest was heavy with campaign ribbons from Tannenberg to Galicia.

"That's utter rubbish and you know it," snapped the prince, treading on dangerous ground. "Our agency has a record second to none."

Billy had to intervene a few moments later when the tone escalated and both men appeared ready to come to blows.

"You damned foreigners are like vultures," shouted the colonel. "You're all the same—Germans, Americans, French! I hate you all!"

Several of the colonel's friends managed to pull him away from the American before he could damage Amer-Russian friendship further. But in their hearts, they felt the same.

On the way back to Petrograd, Adam and his brother were silent, staring out the train windows at the darkened landscape. They were accustomed to mutual silence, and there was nothing unusual about it. But tonight Adam felt compelled to speak.

Quietly, he said, "They're ready to crack. That colonel is only one of hundreds feeling the strain. The country's seen too much blood spilled to be able to bear it any longer. And they want to blame it all on something they can understand. They want their sacrifices to have counted."

He shook his head sadly. It was all lost. Worse than that, the whole mad adventure had wrecked the country, putting its economy, its government, its citizens under such tremendous pressure that a volcanic eruption was due—the only relief in sight.

"Billy," said the prince, startling him with the brusqueness of his tone, "I'm finally going to call in a few debts. I want your help."

"Of course. Anything I can do." He really didn't like the tone. It meant trouble.

"Well, that's good to hear, because I want a lot."

Now Billy was thoroughly nervous, glancing at Adam, who sounded like a man with a long list of grievances. What the hell was he about to ask?

"We both know Russia's headed for disaster. Perhaps even civil war."

"Yes."

"Well, I intend to protect my family from the worst of it."

"Naturally."

"And you're going to help me. In fact, you and I are about to export the largest shipment of our glorious careers—several million in gold bars."

"Christ! That's impossible. You must be mad, Adam. We could be shot for something like that!"

"You have to get caught to get shot, and we won't because you're going to arrange embassy cover for our little operation. Use anyone who can help. But don't breathe a word of what's going on. It's too sensitive."

"Sensitive! Hell, the word is illegal! Illegal in huge capital letters! No. It's too risky."

Grabbing his brother by the coat collar, Prince Sviridov nearly pulled him out of his seat.

"Listen to me, you little bastard," he hissed, "it was too risky when my wife showed up in Warsaw and you stayed home and went whoring after a fifteen-year-old countess. But now you're either going to develop some nerve or the ambassador's going to have Princess Malysheva in his office, demanding your head for seducing her niece. And Anya would be right behind her. They'll ruin you."

Billy was so astonished, his heart began to race. How could Adam have known? Tasha wouldn't have told. Or would she? The damned girl was so peculiar, he wouldn't put anything past her. "I don't know what you're talking about," he stammered.

"I'm talking about all those times you and Countess Derzhavina were alone together at the apartment on the Millyonaya, that's what."

Adam had spied on him! The hypocrite! The idea wounded him deeply. His own brother had become just like one of those snoops from the secret police who kept track of comings and goings at the embassy. He was now more Russian than the Russians.

After a lengthy and embarrassed silence, Billy said, "I didn't seduce her. It was more like mutual satisfaction. Besides, I plan to ask Countess Derzhavina to marry me."

"You bastard," replied the prince. Like Anya, he had had his suspicions ever since the night of the ball, but the accusation had been only a shot in the dark. Until his brother admitted his guilt, Adam couldn't have proved a thing. "You're despicable," he muttered, disgusted with Billy.

"Don't tell anyone about this. It would be a disaster for me."

"I'll give you a good way to avoid trouble," retorted Adam. "But as for marrying Countess Derzhavina, I wouldn't put my hopes on it. Her aunt has someone else in mind."

"Who?" he demanded in genuine shock.

"A textile millionaire from Moscow whose mother is an old friend of the family."

"She never told me!"

"She never considered you a serious prospect," Adam answered, somewhat cruelly. And if you ever caused her any trouble, she'd be merciless."

Looking his brother in the eye, Billy knew he was not going to win. It galled him to think he had underestimated Adam all these years. The man was not only unforgiving, he was sly as well. "I'll try my best to do what you want," declared Billy, bitter at the prospect of disgrace because of a fickle woman. He had worn himself out trying to please that girl! And this is the thanks he got.

"I know you'll do your best," replied Adam. "You don't have any alternative."

When Adam returned to the great mansion on the French Embankment, he had to pound on the door for a good ten minutes before anyone came to let him in. People at the Nicholas Station had spoken of workers on strike by the hundreds, demonstrating all over town, scaring the police and rioting outside bakeries on Kamennoostrov Boulevard and Bolshoi Prospect. It was dangerous in the city, they said, more riots were expected at any moment. Obviously the servants had heard the stories too.

When he reached his apartment on the second floor, Adam found Anya seated on the floor in front of the fireplace, reading to Byelochka while his sisters lay curled at her side, snoring peacefully on the oriental carpet.

"What a pretty sight, darling," smiled Adam as he stood watching them. "It was well worth the trip home."

"Adam!" Springing to her feet, Anya raced across the room, threw herself into her husband's arms and kissed him wildly, murmuring her joy as they hugged each other in the glow of the firelight, with Byelochka pulling at his father's coat, begging him to tell him what happened when he and Uncle Billy met Tsar Nicholas at Stavka.

"I'm so happy to be able to hold you again," whispered Anya as she clung to him. "I was dreadfully frightened for you when I heard the news about the trains."

"Oh, that wasn't too bad, darling. The really bad news came at Stavka. I'll tell you about it when we're alone."

After regaling Byelochka with tales of Stavka, showing him a beautifully framed presentation photo of His Majesty, and promising to let him keep it, Adam carried the child off to the nursery while Nanny and a maid followed with Sashenka and Tory, both sound asleep in their arms.

When the prince rejoined his wife, who was drawing him a warm bath in their onyx-and-silver tub amid the art-nouveau decor of her marble bathroom, he eased himself into the water, sighed and announced the end of the Amer-Russians.

"What?"

"It's all over, darling. The Russian government is taking full responsibility for all such work, the better to coordinate it. We've been phased out."

"That's insane. You worked like a slave for them. Our soldiers know what they owe you. The government is disintegrating!"

Adam gently kissed Anya's hand. "Are you afraid?" he asked.

Nodding seriously, she admitted she was. With three small children to protect, the prospect of an angry mob on the doorstep was chilling. If those demonstrators had already reached the stage where they no longer cared to listen to the police, then the Sviridov Palace could expect very little protection from the forces of law and order.

Recalling the peasant uprisings in Moscow province when she was a girl, Princess Anya knew just how savage the people's hatred could be. Byelaya Beryozka had been lucky. Other estates hadn't.

And the atmosphere in Petrograd now was horribly similar to that of 1905.

Later that night as they lay in bed, nestled in each other's arms, safe and warm, sheltered from the riots, the war, the quickening revolution taking shape on Nevsky Prospect, on Bolshoi Prospect, in the factories of Vyborg and in the barracks of the Petrograd garrison, Prince and Princess Sviridov forgot this bleak reality as they made love, shutting out everything but each other. For a brief moment in time, nothing else existed. Reality was worthless in comparison.

Later, when they were lying sleepily among the disheveled silk covers, caressing each other in the aftermath of their lovemaking, Adam announced quietly that he was about to take out one of the largest shipments of valuables he'd ever attempted.

"What?" murmured Anya. "Most of my jewels are already in Stockholm."

"Not jewelry, darling—gold. A freight car full of it."

Startled, Anya sat up and stared at her husband in the light of the fireplace, fearful for his sanity.

"That's too dangerous, Adam. Jewels are one thing. Exporting gold in the middle of a war on such a grand scale would look bad."

He looked up at her and clasped both hands behind his head. "I don't have any other choice if I want to safeguard your future and our children's. When the rebels start the revolt here in Petrograd, the banks will be the first institutions they'll attack. I'll be damned if I'll let them get their hands on what belongs to your family."

Leaning on an elbow, Anya gazed at her husband and sighed. "What will become of us, Adam? Where will this terrible war take us?"

"I don't know, darling," he replied, "but wherever it is, I want you and the children with me."

They both knew the exodus had already begun, with many illustrious names heading the list of those who found the capital too dangerous now. Country estates in central Russia or the spas of the Caucasus were favorite destinations. The farther from Petrograd, the better. Some members of the imperial family had headed east before the choice was taken away from them.

Thinking of possible destinations, Princess Anya wished they could go back in time to before the war. That would have been her choice. Unfortunately, it was utterly impossible. Pulling the covers around her, she sighed. Finally she said, "I'd like to go to Switzerland. Byelochka was born there. And it's the most peaceful place in the world. Could we go there, do you think?"

Adam hadn't thought about Switzerland; his plans were running more in favor of Sweden—at least for the time being. He wondered. "I'll look into it," he promised. "In the meantime, I must make this trip before we run out of time. When I return, I want you and the children ready to leave at a moment's notice. Tell nobody about our plans. And don't do anything to attract attention to yourself."

"What about Ksenia and Andrei?" she asked. "I'd want to tell them."

"Of course, we'll tell them. I'll speak to Andrei myself and advise him to come with us."

Later that night Princess Anya's sleep was disturbed by a succession of nightmares filled with hordes of workers streaming across the ice-bound Neva, hurling themselves against the walls of the Sviridov Palace, screaming for the blood of her children. As they poured into the white and gilt foyer, overpowering the servants and flinging family treasures out the broken windows, the scene changed to a forest, abruptly as such dreams do, and Anya found herself near a group of birches, searching for mushrooms, careless of the man racing toward her, pursuing her, desperate to reach her. When the sound of heavy boots crashing through the underbrush finally intruded on her thoughts, the princess saw herself reach into her basket, take out a knife and stand facing the peasant coming toward her, ready to protect the children behind her, determined to defend what was hers. As the man lunged for her, Anya woke up with a start, shaking with fear, her eyes wide and frightened, reaching for Adam in the dark.

Dear God, she prayed, trembling at the memories she thought she had overcome, why must that day come back to haunt me now, when things are bad enough?

In his office in the Garden of Eden, Monsieur Mossolov was having a bad night. With the general uneasiness in the city, some of his best clients were staying at home nights, although he still drew the army officers who preferred his brand of hospitality to the depressing atmosphere of their quarters, where their peers were earnestly discussing what to do when the Bolsheviks finally won over the troops. Things had reached the point where most of them were fully expecting the worse; the only question that remained was when.

Shimmering in the light of Oleg's expensive Venetian chandeliers, the girls in their satin gowns had the same sort of glimmer one could find on putrifying meat—rotten and shining at the same time. Ascending and descending the long, curving staircase on the arm of one client or another, all of them were interchangeable to Oleg, all of them expendable.

As the evening's activities reached a peak at around one o'clock, Monsieur Mossolov heard the bell ring and saw the maid hasten to admit two more gentlemen, rather shabby types in comparison with the other clients, but unmistakably worthy of special consideration. Everything about them shouted "policeman."

Watching surreptitiously from behind a cluster of girls and clients, Oleg saw his old acquaintance from Warsaw, Kuzmin, smile cheerfully as he gazed in the direction of the reception room, where a gypsy violinist was serenading a pretty blonde in honor of her birthday. Champagne corks were gaily popping as couples eyed each other, paired off and disappeared up the stairs, heading for brief, commercial passion.

Standing next to Kuzmin, Roman Vasilievich shifted uneasily from side to side, taking in the scene. So this was what a high-class bordello looked like inside, he thought. Very nice decor. Odd to walk into a house as fancy as this and pick out a girl as if she were a loaf of bread. Somehow it seemed revolting in a refined way. Looking at these women, he felt like an alien. He couldn't imagine his wife, Vera, doing anything like this. And although he had agreed to accompany Kuzmin, he knew this was not his kind of entertainment.

"Good evening, gentlemen," smiled the maid, steering them toward the girls. "Which one of our ladies is waiting for you?"

"This is rather a spur-of-the-moment visit, actually," confessed Kuzmin.

"Ah." Afraid the visit might be more official than amorous, the girl, Marta, went to speak with Monsieur Mossolov. He would know how to handle this.

Seeing Marta walking toward him, Oleg slipped out the door to his left and headed for his office, not wishing to give himself away. By opening the door to his office, he had a good view into the gilt-framed mirror that was strategically placed to allow him to see into the outer room, the better to keep an eye on things without intruding too obviously.

As he stood there, questioning Marta about the purpose of Kuzmin's visit, he kept staring at the other man, a short, nondescript type with the round, owlish face and gleaming round spectacles. Damn it, that face was familiar. But why? It really wasn't the sort of face that would stick in anyone's mind.

As Marta spoke to her employer, she was suddenly startled to see Monsieur Mossolov's mouth drop open. The bespectacled fellow had turned around, allowing them an unimpeded look at his plain, round face, the spectacles glittering brightly as he surveyed the scene.

"Christ!" whispered Oleg in shock. "It can't be."

There in the middle of his blue and gilt reception room, basking in the lights of his huge imported chandelier, was Roman Vasilievich Petrov, his unsuccessful executioner. In his whorehouse! Worse than that—in his whorehouse, looking for a free night of pleasure. Damn him to hell!

Looking sharply at the girl, who was now staring at him, Oleg pulled himself together sufficiently to tell her to send Kuzmin up to the blue room with the new Finnish blonde. "Plenty of champagne and caviar," he ordered. "Keep him happy and out of our way."

"And the other one?" she asked. "Where shall I send him?"

Straight to hell, thought Oleg, although he didn't say it. Instead he replied, "Have Olga take him to the room with the four-poster. And tell her to use the special equipment—whether or not he wants it."

Glancing nervously at her boss, Marta nodded and departed, a good little soldier.

His heart pounding with violent emotion, Oleg could scarcely believe his luck. Fate had handed Petrov over to him like a sheep for slaughter. There was only one drawback. He was not alone.

Pacing his office behind the closed door, allowing Roman Vasilievich time to get himself settled upstairs, Oleg tried to plot his moves. Killing two agents of the Okhrana might be foolhardy. On the other hand, if he were to kill only Petrov, the other one would certainly want to know what had become of his companion. He couldn't allow that.

"So it's both," he muttered to himself. "All right. I'll have to do it that way. There's no getting around it."

Thirty-five minutes into his session, Roman Vasilievich was lying in Olga's arms, his face buried between her large breasts, making the ecstatic sounds of an infant with his favorite plaything. As a concession to romance, Petrov's spectacles were sitting on a bedside table where they couldn't get in the way of passion. Without them, Olga and the extravagantly overdecorated room were a voluptuous sort of blur.

"Ah, Romanchik," murmured the girl as Petrov's hands roved merrily over her silken skin, "would you like to have a surprise?"

"Only if it's a delightful one." he replied, kissing her all over. "Will it be nice?"

"Oh yes," she laughed. "You'll enjoy it."

With that, Olga raised herself on an elbow and leaned over him to press a malachite button on the wall behind the English four-poster, a pretty lavish affair hung with blue silk swags.

"Am I dreaming?" demanded the inspector, "or is the bed moving?"

"You'll see," smiled Olga, proud of her toy.

To Petrov's astonishment, the floor seemed to rise as he and the girl descended slowly to a lower level, a soft whir in the background attesting to the presence of a hidden hydraulic lift, rather like an elaborate dumb-waiter.

"Close your eyes," ordered the girl, quickly binding them with a black opaque silk scarf.

"Is this part of the surprise?" he smiled gamely, wondering what else she had in mind.

Suddenly Petrov started, unnerved by the sudden contact of cold steel around both his wrists. Unseen hands grabbed him roughly and pinned both arms together behind his back, then seized his legs and tied them at the ankles. Despite his frantic struggles and sharp cries of protest, his hands and ankles were joined together in an expertly knotted bind, bending him backward in a vicious curve.

"Olga! Stop this. It's not amusing. It's painful!"

Putting his finger to his lips in a gesture for silence, Monsieur Mossolov motioned to the girl to leave. He was going to return her client to the room, and he was taking over.

Smiling at their strange joke, Olga left without a sound, leaving her gentleman trussed up like a roasting bird. Silently, Oleg took her place on the bed, pressing the mechanism for its return to the upstairs room, enjoying his old enemy's blind panic; Petrov was as helpless now in his hands as he had once been in Petrov's hands.

When he killed this one, Oleg thought, it would be a fine warning to all the rest. Even if Wanda and Katia were still in league with Anna Nicolaievna and the Okhrana, this corpse would demonstrate his contempt for all of them—living or dead. Let them all see how he could strike back!

When the bed reached its destination, the motor suddenly shut off, making an abrupt choking sound. Now thoroughly apprehensive, Roman Vasilievich was still thrashing wildly in his bonds without being able to budge an inch and silently cursing Kuzmin and his idea of a good time.

"Olga," he said, trying to sound patient, "be a good girl and let me loose. Let's do something else."

"If you like," said a strangely familiar voice, a deep, raspy masculine one. "I'm tired of the game myself."

Freezing at the sound, Petrov felt the bottom drop out of his stomach. No! His mind must be playing tricks on him. It wasn't possible, he thought in confusion. It couldn't be possible. He knew that voice!

When Oleg ripped the black bandage from his eyes, Petrov knew he was dead. His vision blurry from the band pressing against his eyes, he slowly began to make out the heavyset, bald figure before him, grinning at him as he approached with a length of silk cord, a smiling executioner.

"Ivanov! Christ, I can't believe it!" he squeaked, wriggling like a fish out of water as he rocked back and forth on the bed, still helpless in his bonds.

"Oh, it's true enough, Petrov," smiled his host, snaring his neck in a loop of cord, twisting it viciously as Roman Vasilievich gagged, rocking back and forth in a frenzy as he tried to escape the inevitable.

Twisting with all his might, Oleg knelt on top of the trussed inspector, pressing him into the covers as he choked the life out of him, making his eyes bulge and his tongue hang out in a grotesque image of terror, choking him again and again to make certain he'd achieved the desired end. Petrov's own sloppiness five years earlier had been a lesson to him. He wasn't about to make the same mistake now.

Panting from the hysteria of his labors, Oleg finally let his victim fall limply to the floor, the life drained from him, a threat no longer.

"You bastard," grunted the peasant as he surveyed the lifeless form of Inspector Roman Vasilievich Petrov. "You tried to murder me as if I were a mad dog, you turned me over to those Scriabin morons, you let them cut off my finger...."

Oleg's anger mounted steadily as he kept remembering the horrors Petrov and the others had inflicted on him that terrible night. They were worse than wild beasts. They had done it for the money Prince Malyshev had offered them, all at the urging of that devil woman, Anna Nicolaievna.

"You thought you were so clever. I only wish you could get a look at yourself right now," sneered Oleg, giving Petrov's limp body a swift kick. "Little bastard!"

Loading Petrov back onto the bed, Oleg pressed the button and descended once again to the lower level, where he covered the corpse with a blanket and locked it in the room until early in the morning, when the girls had retired for the night. Then, dragging the body from there to a dumbwaiter in a nearby room, Oleg took it to the cold-storage chamber in the cellar, unlocking the heavy wooden door with his key, the only one in existence.

As he opened the door to his collection of frozen meat, Oleg was seized by a playfulness. Stringing Petrov up by his bound wrists and attaching them to a steel meathook on the wall, he reflected that his old enemy was now the most unprepossessing piece of beef in the house. It was a private joke that kept him chuckling for hours. Now all he had to do was find a suitable dumping place for the inspector's corpse; until then, this could serve as a temporary morgue, hidden from all prying eyes and accessible to him alone.

Kuzmin, having been drugged earlier in the evening, was in pitiful shape when Oleg loaded him into a sleigh and sped off into the night with him, well after the staff had gone to sleep.

Driving to the slum neighborhood of Narva, Oleg found a cul-de-sac near a factory, carefully slit his passenger's throat and hauled him down the nearby riverbank to a hole in the ice large enough for his purposes.

Shoving Kuzmin beneath the icy Neva, with no witness except a prowling cat, Oleg wished him a good journey, swiftly clambered back up the bank and drove furiously home, well pleased with the night's work.

This had been so simple it gave him a new idea, or rather new thoughts about an idea that had never really left his mind. If killing Petrov was so easy, perhaps his luck had changed. He was rational now. He knew what he was doing. With Wanda's death had come a period of tranquility that had reassured him of his sanity.

The tide had finally turned in his favor. And he wasn't about to pass up the opportunity it offered.

❦ 33 ❦

Finland Station was crawling with soldiers bound for one distant front or another when Adam and his brother arrived, wearing heavy dark overcoats and Russian fur hats. They were dressed for a rough trip, allegedly a mission of mercy, repatriating the remains of British advisers killed in the service of the tsar.

"Wiped out in the fighting in the Baltic provinces?" the stationmaster had asked when Adam called to inform him he needed two of his agency's cars attached to the express bound for Finland.

"No. It was an epidemic of typhus that carried them off. Pity."

Upon hearing that, the stationmaster had gulped, looked agitated and promised to ship those coffins out as quickly as possible, advising his people to act with all due caution toward the perilous cargo.

"Do you think they'll suspect?" whispered Billy as he and Adam strolled under the station's floodlights while they supervised the loading. "These boxes are damned heavy."

"Not to worry, Billy. This looks perfectly legitimate. King George himself couldn't receive a better send-off."

This was one of Billy's finest hours. The entire spectacle had been concocted with the aid of an embassy colleague who loved a good joke. The fact that he owed Billy Whitmore a large amount of poker money also entered into it. The bagpipes were pure inspiration.

As astonished Russians watched the little show, the directors of the Amer-Russian agency stood at respectful attention for the loading of the "British dead" aboard the train, while Johnny MacNamara from Boston, who had learned how to play the bagpipes from his father and uncles, puffed manfully away in full regalia, creating an ungodly racket in the Petrograd night air. The onlookers were speechless.

"Just don't let anyone drop those coffins," prayed Billy as he and Adam watched the loading. Inside each sturdy oak casket were bars of gold bearing the Sviridov family crest, secretly removed from the vaults of the Bank of Azov and the Don. Only the highest official of the bank knew of the transaction, and he wasn't about to reveal his part in it.

"Our man in Stockholm will oversee transport to the Warburg Bank once we arrive at the station," murmured Billy, shivering in the biting wind. "The only problem is getting it there intact."

"We've moved valuables before."

"Yes, but never such a heavy shipment at one time. We could be undone if one of these boxes breaks open in transit. They're going to be loaded and unloaded several times before they reach their destination."

The trip across Karelia to Finland and then by sledge to the Swedish frontier wasn't the most comfortable journey one could choose, but it was the only route available at the moment, and the only way to export Adam's gold. Wartime limitations on travel made trips abroad extremely difficult, but the prince knew the route by heart after many such jaunts.

"Damn, it's cold!" lamented Billy as the last coffin was hauled aboard and the mournful squeal of the bagpipes had faded to a dull whine. "It makes me feel as though spring will never come."

"Cheer up, Billy. Spring is on its way and so are we. Let's get going!"

And smartly saluting the detachment of Russian railway officials, Billy and Prince Sviridov thanked the exhausted railway workers who had overseen the loading of the "heroic British dead," clapped each other on the back and sprang on board the steaming train.

"Tell your mistress I'll be home as soon as possible," Adam shouted to the valet who had accompanied him to the station. "I'll be back before she even has a chance to miss me!"

"Yes, Highness."

"And make certain you guard the entrances carefully. The city's becoming a jungle."

"Yes, Highness," he nodded. "Godspeed."

Then the train began to shudder and rattle, shooting out great bursts of steam as it slowly headed down the tracks, bound for Finland.

The following day, the weather was cold but clear and Petrograd's citizens were out in force on the streets, despite repeated warnings from the city commandant not to congregate. Nobody paid attention to General Khabalov these days, and the Nevsky was flooded with strollers and demonstrators, including a large group of people listening to a speech in front of Kazan Cathedral, a traditional gathering place for antiwar protests.

As a fiery Bolshevik street orator urged the crowd to rise up and put an end to the tsar's war, a unit of the Pavlovsky Regiment appeared, confronted the people and ordered them to disperse. When no one moved, the officer in charge, a nervous little man, barked the order to fire. Within minutes, the scene was a horrible confusion of rearing horses, bloodstained snow and shrieking, hysterical citizens, some of them badly wounded and attempting to flee for their lives.

"Murderers!" screamed a woman, hurling a chunk of ice at the troops.

She slipped on the bloodied snow and was trampled beneath the hooves of the rearing horses as the soldiers struggled to maintain discipline amid the chaos they had just created. Some of the troops looked as shaken as the demonstrators, and some could be seen to ignore further orders to fire as their officers shouted at them above the noise of the crowd.

While people were still fleeing the scene, a second detachment of the Pavlovsky appeared, broke ranks and overwhelmed their comrades, furiously protesting the shooting of civilians. In minutes, the newly radicalized troops had shot the nervous officer who had ordered them to fire on the people and were attacking a patrol of mounted police, sent in to help suppress the demonstrators. The mutiny had begun.

That afternoon when Prince Andrei heard the news at his club, he thought uneasily of Volodya's gloomy assessment of the garrison troops. His predictions were eerily accurate.

From now on, anything was possible.

That night in the great barracks district, fiery young agitators from factories of the Vyborg and Narva regions infiltrated the mess halls and called for their comrades in uniform to follow the example of the Pavlovsky, rid themselves of their officers and join the workers in forming soviets as the revolutionaries of 1905 had done.

"Comrades!" they shouted to the young draftees, "seize the power! You have weapons. Kill your officers if if they dare to oppose you; put an end to this senseless war. You don't have to obey any longer. Seize the power from them and have them follow *your* orders! Russia's fate depends on you!"

That was impressive enough, but the men were still not won over. Those rebels among the Pavlovsky were now in prison awaiting execution on charges of treason. Mutiny, as they well knew, was still a capital offense, and nobody wanted to die for a cause that seemed so uncertain—yet. But they were listening.

At nine-thirty the next day, Princess Ksenia was awakened by the sound of running feet outside the Malyshev Palace. Startled, she got up and was peering through the draperies when Prince Andrei entered to announce bad news.

"Darling," he said, "don't go outside today. Volodya just telephoned to inform me the army's turned to mass mutiny. The city's filled with all sorts of rebel troops spoiling for a fight with any remaining loyalists."

Shocked, she parted the silk draperies to see a crowd of soldiers racing along the Moika, right below her windows.

"Good Lord. It looks as though the worst has finally come to pass."

When Nicky Grekov appeared in Auntie's room to say good morning, he told her he had seen lots of men running across the bridge down the street and they were all carrying rifles. It was exciting, he said.

"This is the revolution," declared the prince, quite disgusted. "Volodya told me the Volinsky Regiment mutinied at dawn this morning, and shot their colonel. They're roaming the city now, looking for trouble."

Shaken by the news, Ksenia hugged little Nicky as he climbed into bed with her. She rang for the maid to bring breakfast and glanced nervously at her husband, who was at the window watching a group of rifle-toting soldiers with red armbands racing across the bridge a bit farther down the street.

"It's going to be total insanity in the streets today, milochka. I'm going to have the servants barricade the doors. I'd also advise you to stay away from the ground-floor windows. There's no telling what might set these people off."

"Yes," replied the princess, suddenly thinking of friends and family at various locations across town. My God! What would become of Volodya Grekov in this uprising? He was scarcely the sort to lie low and allow a band of mutineers to dictate to him. And Anya? Good Lord! Adam had just left on another of his trips west. What a disastrous time to leave a young girl and three babies on their own. And Tasha....

"Where's my niece?" asked Ksenia. "I hope she hasn't decided to go outside to view the excitement."

"No, darling. She has more sense than that. The last time I saw her was fifteen minutes ago, sitting with a couple of the maids in your music room, piecing together the largest red flag I've ever seen. She informed me she intends to raise it over the house in case of imminent attack."

"Andrei! Would you permit that?"

The prince chuckled. "Darling," he smiled, "if the situation gets much worse, I may help her hoist the damned thing."

Leaving Ksenia to get dressed, Prince Malyshev made a telephone call to the Sviridov Palace, informing the butler of events in his part of town and ordering him to take appropriate precautions to safeguard Princess Anya and her children. If things looked risky there, Andrei offered to escort her to the Malyshev Palace, but only as a last resort. His home was a lot closer to the center of the rebellion than Anya's was, and barring anything extraordinary, she and her little ones would be safer where they were.

Receiving a promise of cooperation from the butler, Andrei descended to the ground floor to supervise the erection of his defenses.

Around ten-thirty, Princess Anya, her children and their Nanny were gathered in the winter garden, having cocoa and biscuits, when Matvei the butler entered, quite out of breath, requesting the princess's company in the hall. He had something urgent to communicate.

"What's happened?" Anya demanded nervously. "Is it Adam Mikhailovich?"

"No, Highness. Please come and look. It's dreadful."

Following him on the run, Anya entered Sandro's denuded Gallery of the Ottocento and looked out onto the wild scene in the snowy streets. Hundreds of soldiers were pouring across the nearby Alexander Bridge, shouting wildly and waving rifles as the troops on the other side faced them with drawn weapons, holding their ground. Then as the rebels reached the Vyborg side, the Moscow Regiment suddenly caved in, threw down their rifles and noisily embraced their brothers, one more group won over to the cause.

In the wake of the surrender, several bodies—all officers—went sailing over the railing of the bridge and landed on the frozen Neva.

Horrified by what they had just seen, Princess Anya and her butler stared first at the bloodied corpses and then at each other, silent and shaken. The revolution had come to Petrograd.

This is what we've been dreading, thought the young princess as she looked across the frozen river to the mass anarchy on the far shore. The people have had their fill of war, shortages and incompetence, and now they're going to have their revenge. My God, how they must hate us.

The bitter, angry faces of the women who had recently thrown snowballs at her automobile came to mind. They hated her for being able to afford something they could not. *Rich pig.*

And now the city was about to be overwhelmed by these angry, hungry people who had suffered so much for so long. With a shudder, Princess Anya wondered how long it would take them before they attacked the Sviridov Palace. She wished Adam were home, standing beside her right now. Despite the presence of the servants, Anya felt horribly alone in the face of riot and revolution. She found herself recalling that dream of the other night; at this moment it wasn't so farfetched.

"Will that be all, Highness?" asked Matvei, intruding on her thoughts. "I'd like to check the entrances."

"Yes. Thank you."

As the old man departed for the ground floor, Anya glanced once more at the dreadful sight on the ice. Several dead officers were lying like so much debris as an excited crowd of soldiers and workers raced across the frozen river, as wild and unrestrained as the waters of a burst dam. This was anarchy. Now they've lost the army, the princess thought as she gazed out onto the scene. It was their only hope. And ours.

And she returned to the winter garden to tell Nanny the bad news, wishing she and her children were with Adam, wherever he was, far from Petrograd and revolution.

Major Volodya Grekov was one of the few loyalists to rally to the city commandant's call for officers to lead troops against the spreading rebellion. Disgusted by the murderous behavior of the Petrograd trash, as he called the rebels, Volodya set out with a couple of other bitter-enders to tame the trash and show them how a real Russian officer behaved in a crisis. Proceeding on horseback into a zone completely controlled by the mob, Volodya and his colleagues found themselves shouted down, disregarded and finally overwhelmed by sheer numbers.

"Join us, brothers!" cried the rioters, surging around them, swamping officers and horses alike.

"Go back to your homes, back to your barracks!" shouted Volodya as he drew his sword, the family heirloom Gigi had brought him before he left for the front in 1914. Its blade gleamed brightly in the winter sun as he waved it high above his head, trying his best to charge them.

"Go to hell!" replied the mob.

And down went Major Grekov, rudely yanked out of his saddle by a dozen strong arms and thrown neatly over his horse's head as the crowd stomped by, without so much as a further glance in his direction.

Dazed, bruised and lying in the gutter, Volodya merely stared at his attackers in amazement. By the time he could get himself off the ground and back on his feet, the rioters had veered off down another street, leaving him nearly alone, except for the presence of another officer lying about ten feet from where he now stood.

As he called to his fallen comrade-in-arms, he realized with a shock of horror that the fellow was dead, stabbed in the heart and left in the gutter as a souvenir of the encounter.

"Christ!"

Bereft of his sword, his horse, even his fellow officers, Count Grekov limped painfully onto the sidewalk and headed in the direction of his mother's house on Sergeivskaya Street, the nearest possible shelter.

◆　　◆　　◆

At Okhrana headquarters, nobody ever had a chance to miss Petrov and Kuzmin after their night on the town. They were too busy trying to defend themselves from the wrath of the populace.

By noontime, the rebels had attacked Petrograd's prisons—freeing a quantity of Bolsheviks languishing there—had set the law courts on fire and were preparing to put the torch to the stronghold of the detested secret police. Amid scenes of hysteria in the corridors, Okhrana officers were frantically burning files, breaking out stores of weapons and, in some cases, quietly changing into civilian clothes for a quick escape.

By the afternoon, Okhrana headquarters had fallen to the rebels and was roaring like a bonfire under the cold winter sky, only one of many of the hated symbols of tsarist rule to be put to the torch.

In the streets of Nicholas's capital, it was open warfare on those who had served him well.

Not far from the great barracks district sat the Tauride Palace, the home of the Imperial Duma—at the moment the one place in town where both rebels and monarchists were heading, some to justify their revolt, others to take refuge. As mutineers poured in at the head of their regiments, looking for someone to take charge of the revolution they had just started, detested tsarist ministers buttonholed deputies, begging for protection.

For some reason everybody had faith in the Duma, and that was good. It gave people some sort of badly needed stability in the midst of so much disorder. Not to be outdone by the parliamentarians, the Bolsheviks arrived in droves—some of them just liberated from prison by the riots— and demanded equal space, setting up a countergovernment in one of the unused wings of the building and biding their time.

In the city's great mansions, the revolution had created a growing climate of fear and panic. Arrests of prominent officials had sent their friends and relatives scurrying out of Petrograd as fast as possible.

One of the most sensational arrests following the revolution in Petrograd was that of the ballerina Zenaida Kashina, detained as she was about to board a train going east. She was taken to a different destination, the grim Petropavlosk Fortress, where she was questioned at great length by several stern-looking gentlemen about the source of her finances. And about the prewar rumors of involvement with "agents of foreign governments."

To Kashina's fury, Grand Duke Constantine Andreevich had already fled the city, leaving her to face her inquisitors alone, after having promised to take her with him. It was rumored that in retaliation the vindictive woman was providing the government with enough information about her lover's shady dealings with German agents on the eve of the war to justify his arrest as a traitor—if they could catch up with him.

Facing the panel of deputies from the Duma who were charged with investigating her case, Kashina treated them with the contempt she had formerly harbored for princes. If there was anything she detested more than princes, it was a bourgeois, and these were bourgeois to a man.

Reviling the leader of the pack, Alexander Kerensky, as a man living on illusion if he thought he was going to be able to control the revolution, Kashina informed him the people were out for blood and wouldn't rest until they had murdered them all.

Kerensky demanded to know just what category Kashina would claim to be in, a woman notorious for her many—he stressed "many"—aristocratic liaisons.

Without blinking for an instant, Zenaida Kashina replied that she was merely an exploited working girl, trying to pursue her art as best she could in a corrupt and graceless world.

"Well, that's the limit," exclaimed the deputy. "Madame Kashina, you are the most brazen woman it's ever been my misfortune to meet!"

Pompous little twit, thought Kashina, eyeing Kerensky with disdain. At least her princes had style. It was the first time in her recollection that a man had failed to appreciate the quality that had endeared her to so many others. Glancing around the room, Zenaida Felixovna knew that whatever they did to her, she would survive. She had a feeling they wouldn't. It was the only thing that comforted her as they sentenced her to an unspecified amount of time in prison, pending further investigation of her alleged traitorous activities. And Constantine's.

Nicholas II, surprised at Stavka by the *fait accompli* in his capital, was forced to abdicate, thereby ending 300 years of Romanov rule in Russia. Graciously granted permission to return to Tsarskoye Selo and his family, the former tsar headed home to await the pleasure of the new provisional government.

When the ex-tsar arrived at the Alexander Palace in Tsarskoye Selo most of the court had vanished, choosing not to share their sovereign's arrest. Only a few loyalists remained, including Countess Natalya Grekova, who couldn't bear to be separated from her adored *starets*, interred in the Imperial Park.

The night Nicholas arrived home, Natalya took it into her dazed little head to pay the *starets* a visit to inform him of the newest developments and to ask for his intervention with the Bolsheviks. Stumbling out an unguarded side door, clad in a magnificent sable and her sapphires,

Natalya scampered along the dark paths leading to the chapel, avoiding the newly posted sentries, staggering a little in the heavy snow, her coat catching on the branches of bare birches and thick pines.

Finally arriving at the small stone chapel, Natalya was outraged to find it locked. How could it be locked? She needed him. He had always promised to help her. Pounding frantically on the oaken door, shrieking for Gregory Efimovich, her hands bleeding from the force of her efforts, half-freezing from the cold, Natalya spun around in fright when she found herself caught in the glare of headlights. She faced a noisy mob of soldiers driving straight for the chapel, a band of Reds from Petrograd who were out to have a little fun with the dear departed.

"Out of the way!" yelled someone. "Out of the way. We're going in!"

Impatiently, one of the soldiers leaped from the open truck and dragged the woman clear of the door as his comrades gleefully smashed it in.

"*No!*" wailed Natalya, restrained by two men from flinging herself across the open door to protect Gregory Efimovich from these monsters. As she watched in horror, three or four of the khaki-clad soldiers forced their way into the crypt where Rasputin lay buried, smashed it open and after a moment's hesitation, due mainly to the unprepossessing state of the corpse, lifted the mortal remains of Gregory Efimovich out with the aid of large wooden icons and carried him outside in a triumphal procession liberally fueled with alcohol.

"*No!*" sobbed the countess, observing this desecration in terrified disbelief. "You can't do this to a servant of God!"

Nobody listened.

Hastily throwing pieces of broken branches together to start a fire and lacing it with gasoline from jerry cans they had brought with them, the men howled with delight as the *starets*' pallbearers lugged him into position, then tossed the decomposing mess onto the fire, amid a shrill chorus of obscenities.

Dropping to her knees in the snow, her eyes wide with horror, Natalya stared as the remains of her beloved mentor landed with a thud and a great scattering of sparks. The flames rose high into the night air, casting a hellish red glare over the soldiers, the surrounding fir trees and the curious peasants who had crept into the woods to see what was happening.

Shouting with delight as each splash of gasoline sent the flames shooting higher into the sky, the men sent the dead *starets* to hell with their best wishes, as they staggered drunkenly around the funeral pyre, while a skinny private solemnly mimicked a benediction.

As the countess knelt in the sooty snow, sobbing in despair, she looked into the depths of the blaze and said quietly, "Yes, Gregory Efimovich. You know I still believe in you."

"I'm going to keep my promise, little Natalya, the one I made on the night I was taken," said the voice from the flames, speaking in the rough accents of his native Siberia. "You will be united with me for all eternity, my dove. Nothing will ever separate us again. Nothing. Are you ready?"

It was all Natalya heard, drowning out the shrieks and the roars of laughter all around her. She no longer saw the soldiers in their army great-coats or heard their obscenities as they raced drunkenly round Rasputin's pyre. Everything else had ceased to exist for her. All she saw was the *starets*, warm and welcoming, reaching out to take her hand and lead her to a better world.

"*Barinia,* don't!" A soldier spotted the woman running toward the bonfire. All of them heard her screams as she flung herself on it, becoming engulfed in a sea of fire with Rasputin, the orange and scarlet flames rising higher and higher in the midnight blackness.

Some of the younger men put their hands over their ears to block out her cries of anguish; others poured more gasoline onto the bonfire. And then, as the screams became unbearable, one bearded fellow took out his service revolver and, aiming carefully, sent the poor lunatic hurtling toward eternity, out of her misery at last.

When the ashes of the bonfire were discovered the next day, Natalya was burned beyond recognition, but Volodya, who had expressed concern about her welfare in a visit to the new commander of the palace guard, was able to identify the body through pieces of jewelry, including her sapphires, her wedding present from his brother.

"I'm so sorry," babbled the officer in embarrassment. "There will be a full investigation, I assure you."

Volodya looked at him patiently and then abruptly turned his back, departing through the office door and out of the gate forever, waved on by the sentries who were now in charge of access to the former tsar's residence.

It doesn't matter, he thought. None of it matters any longer. She's where she wants to be and nobody could have prevented it. It was what she was headed for since the first time she ever laid eyes on the bastard. And there on the train platform at Tsarskoye Selo, Volodya Grekov broke down and wept.

Fellow passengers eyed the tall sandy-haired man who sobbed and assumed that he had just lost someone in the war. In a way, he had.

❧ 34 ❧

On the day of the great army mutiny, Monsieur Mossolov né Ivanov, seeing the soldiers running amok, had barricaded his front door against intruders and sternly warned his girls about giving anything away gratis.

"This is a high-class house," he declared. "Our clients get the best, and they pay for it. No free samples."

His staff, a collection of native Russians with a sprinkling of foreigners, nodded solemnly and swore they'd uphold the house's reputation.

Then Oleg retreated to his office to try to think of a good way to dispose of the corpse in his cold-storage room. With the general level of disorder in the city, there had to be a reasonable way of getting rid of Petrov, especially since the Bolsheviks had declared open season on the Okhrana, but somehow it just wouldn't look right to be caught tossing him out the front door, revolution or no revolution. It would lead to too many awkward questions, and Oleg wasn't the sort of businessman who could afford to let any red-hot revolutionary peer into his basement. Murdering a member of the detested Okhrana might be viewed as a public service, but hoarding black-market meat was a failing those starving bastards would never forgive. That would send him straight to the gallows.

Oleg decided to let Petrov linger a while longer among the sides of beef. When the city calmed down, he could deal with him. Until then, he would throw on a little more ice and do as little as possible to attract the attention of the Reds.

With the whole town caught up in a violent revolutionary fervor, things were becoming quite tense at the Garden of Eden. The girls had had a run-in with one of their more respectable neighbors, and out of spite, the woman had informed a group of roving Red Guards that Oleg's ladies wanted to make a donation to the troops.

Horrified when a dozen dirty soldiers showed up to accept the offer,

Oleg had kicked them all out and made it quite clear what the house policy was on *that*.

"Couldn't we drop our prices along with our drawers?" asked a practical French girl. "Half a crust is better than no crust at all."

"Absolutely not," snapped Monsieur Mossolov, eyeing his staff in dismay. Inactivity was making them willing to compromise their integrity and allow riffraff to soil his silken sheets and oriental carpets. If he had wanted a low-class clientele, he would have set up shop in the Haymarket, not off the Fontanka. Christ!

"Nobody's been here in two days," stated one of the girls. "They're all afraid."

"Or under arrest," said another one.

"Well, it doesn't matter. Once you let in common soldiers, it's all downhill, and I've worked too hard to allow that to happen. This is a *maison de luxe*, not a meat market."

At that, the girls giggled, amused by Monsieur Mossolov's little joke. If this place wasn't a meat market, what did he think it was?

Offended by their mirth, Oleg retired to his office to take solace in a bottle of prewar vodka.

That night, while the girls stood around the reception room, chatting and exchanging stale gossip with each other, someone actually rang the doorbell.

Monsieur Mossolov brightened, surveyed his staff and dispatched the maid to admit the guest. As the girl opened the door to see who was there, she found herself facing a crowd of sturdy soldiers, all ready for a good time.

"Monsieur Mossolov!" she screeched, roughly shoved aside by the incoming tide of khaki. "Help!"

Dazzled by the blue and gold splendor of Oleg's reception room, the soldiers gawked at the elegant furniture, the large crystal chandelier, the oil paintings, the girls. And then they started to take off their coats.

"Out!" shouted Oleg, stopping them cold. "No soldiers here!"

"Oh?" inquired the leader of the pack. "Is this how you citizens treat your liberators?"

"This is a high-class house. We only accept clients who can pay."

Grinning, the sergeant unbuttoned his ragged greatcoat, signaling for his men to follow suit. Dirty and bedraggled, they brought with them a stench that was impressive even by army standards.

"We heard you wanted to donate your services to the revolution," he leered at the girls. "Well, here's your chance."

The staff, accustomed to a more refined clientele, took one sniff and ran for the exits. Unfortunately for them, the soldiers were thoroughly determined to enjoy what they considered the spoils of war, and blocked their escape.

"Stop!" shrieked a blonde as she was thrown down on the carpet. "My comrades and I are calling a strike!"

"Is that so?" inquired her admirer, unbuttoning his fly. "Good luck to you."

And that bit of labor unrest promptly came to an end.

Oleg was in near-shock as he saw the khaki-clad horde take over his establishment, smashing his Lalique vases, dirtying his oriental carpets, breaking his antique furniture, shooting his gilded mirrors, raping his whores. It was a heartbreaking sight, the destruction of his business, the ruin of his investment, the crumbling of his niche in the world of commerce. God! How he hated this stupid revolution.

Working their way through the building, the soldiers went from girl to girl, floor to floor, looking for new opportunities for destruction. Unable to endure the appalling vistas of devastation and the bloodcurdling screams of the whores, Oleg ran to his office to take refuge with a bottle of vodka. The demolition of his house was one thing, but if those animals ever got downstairs, he was a dead man.

"Damn!" he shouted at nobody in particular as he sent the bottle flying against the wall in a fit of rage. The liquor splattered over the room, his two oil paintings and himself—a shower of broken glass and 80-proof vodka. "Why does it always happen to me?" he screamed, pounding on his desk in fury, cutting his hands on the bits of glass and not caring.

Pausing to listen to the sounds issuing from the outer rooms, Oleg cursed, slightly out of breath from his exertions, and despaired.

"Damn!" he repeated, sinking down into a chair, smashing a small Fabergé clock in his frustration.

They'll kill me if they find that meat, he thought frantically, trying to estimate his chances of concealing it. No. It was well hidden.

He had been a fool to antagonize those damned soldiers; he knew that now. If he hadn't been so particular, he could have appeased them and sent them on their way happy. No, he had to think of his investment, like some fat bourgeois! Him, a member of the bourgeoisie! What a joke! Oleg the revolutionary ruined by Reds running amok in his whorehouse.

"God damn them to hell!" he roared, throwing another *objet d'art* against the wall. "All of them—Katia, Wanda, Anna Nicolaievna. All damned cows! It's all their fault!" he raved. "Worse than the soldiers!"

From his reception room, Oleg heard the sound of shattering glass as somebody's pistol shot out half the lights in his imported Venetian chandelier. Shrieks of glee echoed through the rooms as the savages began smashing the mirrors, the small inlaid tables and the tiny, precious objects lying on them.

From the carved staircase, the soldiers were flinging furniture from the upstairs hall—tables and chairs that had cost a fortune at Meltzer's, where Petrograd's rich merchants bought the magnificent reproductions that aped the antiques in the city's palaces. Now thousands of rubles' worth of kindling lay at the foot of the stairs, trodden underfoot by rampaging proletarians.

Just as Oleg was reaching for a pistol from his desk drawer, unsure of anything but his need to protect himself, his door buckled, rammed by two corporals and a heavy cabinet from the reception room.

"Christ!" he bellowed, quickly grabbing the weapon, ready to use it.

"One, two, three—go!" roared the intruders, throwing their backs into the work.

One more try and the door came crashing in, swiftly followed by the soldiers. As they stepped over the smashed door, they approached their host, grinning like children at the mess they had created.

"Well, brother," chuckled one as he wrestled the weapon away from Oleg, "that thing's no good against all of us. Now tell us. Where's the liquor?"

Pulling out a long bowie knife, the corporal grabbed Oleg around the neck and giggled wildly as he held him. Oleg struggled like a roped calf.

"I'm all out of liquor," he gasped, straining against the man's arm. "Damn it, I don't have anything left."

"We know that's a lie, brother. Think again. Or you lose your ear."

Sweating now, Oleg swallowed as the knife pressed close enough to his throat to make him blanch. The blade was sharp as a razor and twice as deadly.

"Downstairs," gulped Monsieur Mossolov, closing his eyes as he felt the sharp steel against his vulnerable throat. "I have crates of it downstairs."

"Ah, good," smiled the corporal, glancing at his comrade. "Very hospitable of you."

"It's all yours."

"Did you doubt that?" asked his friend, flashing a smile remarkable for its gaps.

"Take it all," said Oleg, still in the corporal's grip. "You deserve it."

Releasing Oleg, the soldiers didn't even glance backward as they headed for the cellar, intent on liberating his vodka.

In a complete panic, Oleg knew he had to flee. Rushing to his office safe, he hastily twirled the combination, cursing in hysteria as he had to dial twice before he got it to open, then began stuffing wads of rubles into his pockets, dropping some of them on the floor in his panic, not caring at this point, frantic to get out.

When he heard a loud scream from the cellar, he knew the time had come for his exit. "Damn!" he fumed. Even in death, Petrov might yet get him killed.

Racing out of his office, clutching an overcoat and whatever he had managed to take from the safe, Oleg sprinted out the door, through the wreckage of his reception room and into the night before anyone knew enough to stop him. They were all too busy rushing to the cellar to gawk at the ghoulish display their comrades had discovered.

"Shit! Oh shit!"

Clustered around the door of the cold-storage vault, peering inside with a blend of fascination and horror, the soldiers shuddered as they beheld the grisly exhibit. There beside several sides of beef hung a naked human corpse, strung up by its wrists, its eyes wide with terror.

"Mother of God!" shouted the corporal in utter horror. "Do you suppose all these are people?"

His comrades turned to him in astonishment then turned back to take a second look at the meat dangling from meathooks in the vault. Christ! There could be anyone's mother or father up there. The men were speechless with shock. They had heard stories of cannibalism in remote peasant villages, but none had ever seen it firsthand.

"Cannibal!" screamed the corporal who had battered open the door, drunk and excitable. "He's a cannibal!"

"Get him! Don't let him escape!"

In a panic, the soldiers fled the fiend's storage vault as if from a pestilence. By the time they reached the ground floor of the bordello, everybody in the place was crying "cannibal" and shouting for Oleg's blood.

"Don't let him go. He's a killer. There's a man's body downstairs along with a whole collection of human parts!" they bawled drunkenly. "Kill him!"

Marta the maid, shocked at what the soldiers were saying about her employer, picked herself up from the floor and staggered downstairs, curious to see for herself. What she saw convinced her she had been working for a madman.

"Mother of God!" exclaimed the girl, recognizing Petrov as one of their last gentlemen callers. "So it's true! Monsieur Mossolov was butchering them!"

And then just before she collapsed in a faint on the cellar floor, Marta wondered briefly about the origin of her dinner the night before.

◆ ◆ ◆

Prince Sviridov and his brother had encountered a little bit of trouble on the return leg of their journey when the Russian railway workers shut down the main lines for forty-eight hours. Now they were on their way home from Stockholm after a delay in Karelia and frantic about the fate of their women. Stories coming down the line made it sound as if aristocratic Petrograd were being butchered in the streets.

Adam had nightmares about his family's fate, made worse by Billy's nervous references to the September massacre of another revolution.

Billy, despite his recent animosity, was genuinely worried about Countess Derzhavina and brooded incessantly about his lady of the lynxes.

In Petrograd, Princess Sviridova was worried about Adam's unaccustomed delay and imagined the worst. Nanny was a great help with the children, telling them the huge demonstrations were actually parades and spending hours with them at the windows of Sandro's vacant Gallery of the Ottocento, pointing out the tsar's different regiments as they crossed the Alexander Bridge nearby, on their way to pledge allegiance to the new provisional government.

Across town, on the Moika Canal, Tasha was bored and restless. Aunt Ksenia refused to allow her to venture outside the gates of the Malyshev Palace while bands of armed and dangerous Red Guards roamed the streets. And she was complaining so bitterly about the lack of freedom that when little Nicky asked if they could build an old-fashioned ice mountain in the gardens, Ksenia readily agreed. It was harmless and wholesome and it would shut Tasha up and occupy her and Nicky while the princess kept in touch with her friends by telephone—although in the spirit of rebellion, the women at the telephone exchange were no longer putting through calls to certain numbers.

The whole situation exasperated Ksenia and kept her awake nights wondering how the world had changed so disastrously and worrying about the growing tendency of the provisional government to placate the Reds. Three government ministers she knew had been sent to the Petropavtosk Fortress—like Kashina—and Princess Ksenia was grateful Andrei had never gone into government service.

She feared the day when the new government would start a raft of idiotic agrarian reforms, turning her husband's vast estates over to the peasants. The Reds were screaming about all land going to the people and in its weak-willed and frightened way, the new government of bureaucrats and lawyers might very well give in to their demands. The idea sickened Princess Ksenia and made her wish she had been born in another century, in a Russia whose tsar had known how to rule.

One morning, behind Ksenia's back, Tatiana Sergeevna rang up Anya to ask if she could bring little Nicky to visit Byelochka and the twins. Things were very much calmer, she declared, not a Red Guard in sight.

Princess Anya hesitated. "Darling," she said, "you know I'd love to see you and Nicky, but I don't think it's very wise to go out yet."

Tasha made a grimace of annoyance. If she had to stay cooped up in the Malyshev Palace, she'd lose her mind. And at this point she really didn't give a damn if she met up with an entire regiment of wild and reckless Red Guards. At least they wouldn't be boring.

"Oh, Anyushka," she lied, "it's perfectly all right. The Reds have stopped parading and city traffic is almost back to normal. There aren't any problems today."

On the other end of the line, Princess Anya hesitated. From her vantage point overlooking the Vyborg area, she couldn't see any trouble either, but it still didn't seem like a good idea to leave the house if one didn't have to.

"If it's all right with Aunt Ksenia, then it's all right with me. Ask her and call me back."

Replacing the telephone on its cradle, Tasha rolled her eyes. Anya really had such a trusting nature. Tasha certainly was *not* about to ask Ksenia; she wasn't simpleminded.

Going to fetch Nicky, Tasha ordered him to get his hat, coat, gloves and boots without letting the maids see him, and announced they were off to visit his friends.

"Is my new mama coming?"

The girl looked at him in amusement. Nicky had started calling Ksenia his "new mama" ever since they told him the old one had gone to heaven.

"No," replied Tasha. "And we can't let her see us leave, either, or she might not let us go. You *do* want to see Byelochka again, don't you?"

The blond child with the peculiarly light-blue eyes nodded solemnly and set off to collect his things. In his dark-blue sailor suit, he looked just like any other upper-class child in town, but those eyes were a fascinating reminder of the gossip surrounding his origin. It would be comical, thought Tasha, if Auntie Ksenia were mothering Rasputin's son.

As she and the child were ready to leave the house, Tasha telephoned Anya and said she had Auntie's approval. They were on their way.

♦ ♦ ♦

In a seedy hotel in the notorious Haymarket district, Monsieur Mossolov né Ivanov sat staring at the peeling plaster on the walls and cursing. He was a ruined man. All he had left were the clothes on his back and whatever he had managed to stuff into his pockets when he was forced to flee his house, now a sacked and pillaged shell, utterly destroyed by fire and plunder. And he had heard of the charges of cannibalism. Somehow that rattled him.

"They called me a cannibal," he muttered to his image in the cracked mirror. Me! Christ, what a joke. And all because of Petrov!

He couldn't escape them, could he? Petrov had managed to track him down—God knows how—right to his new establishment, still a good little lackey of the regime, a servant of the corrupt aristocracy, a man who lived on the blood of the people. Even on the very eve of revolution, he was still the loyal bloodsucker he had always been. But he had been outwitted once and for all. That gave Oleg some satisfaction, but only briefly; there were still others with whom he had a score to settle, and the general atmosphere of chaos and uncertainty was now his best ally.

He had been preparing for this, waiting for the exact moment to strike. Now the soldiers had forced his hand. It was time to clear out, leave this mad town, put this life behind him. He was no pimp. That had come about because of Wanda. Wanda had entered his life because of Katia and Kiev. And Katia had ensnared him following that fiasco with Anna Nicolaievna. He sometimes saw them together, talking about him, mocking him.

Now Anna Nicolaievna was the only one who was still alive. But not for long.

Wanda's murder had freed Oleg from his illusions that the princess was haunting him through the Polish girl, although he occasionally felt Wanda's presence near him, speaking through him at times. That worried him. But it didn't frighten him the way Anna Nicolaievna had frightened him when she used to take possession of Wanda, turning her into a pseudo-aristocrat and using her to make his life miserable.

No. He could deal with Wanda. She was nothing.

And now Anna Nicolaievna would be helpless and terrified while he extracted his revenge, repaying her for all those years of misery.

While Tasha and Nicky were sneaking downstairs to tell the prince's old coachman to prepare a sleigh, Prince Andrei was leaving for the Nicholas Station to take the train to Byelaya Beryozka. Roving bands of deserting soldiers were ravaging the countryside, and Andrei wanted to organize his men under Lev Petrovich to meet the threat.

"I don't know why you have to go," Ksenia told her husband as he put on his overcoat and fur hat. "It's dangerous."

"That's precisely why I have to go. I can't ask people to risk their lives on my behalf if I'm not prepared to join them. And," he added, "I'll be damned if I'll ever allow some band of thugs to steal even one square foot of my land."

"It's not worth dying for."

"I don't plan to die yet," replied the prince, kissing his lovely wife.

"The cemeteries are filled with people who've said just that."

Andrei Nicolaievich embraced her, holding her very close as she caressed him, gently stroking the soft gray tufts at his temples, evidence of the war's effect. He smiled at his wife's touch, and was grateful he didn't have more gray hairs. He kissed her gently. "I'll send you a telegram from Byelaya Beryozka when I arrive to let you know how things are."

"Don't stay too long," whispered Ksenia, burying her face in his chest. "I'll miss you."

"Don't worry, darling. Nothing exciting ever happens in that backwater. My peasants are too lazy to rebel."

That was a lie and they both knew it. As Princess Ksenia watched her husband leave, she felt overwhelmed by fear. The city was bad enough, but the countryside was beginning to blaze with old, half-forgotten feuds and vendettas that had their origin in quarrels so remote the causes were buried in speculation. But people remembered whom they hated. Ksenia Alexandrovna prayed that Andrei had more friends than enemies at Byelaya Beryozka.

When Tasha's sleigh reached the Sviridov Palace, she and little Nicky were waved through the inner courtyard and admitted by old Matvei, the butler, who was waiting at a little-used side entrance.

Byelochka and the twins were delighted to see company once again, and in honor of the occasion, Nanny arranged a children's party in the nursery while Princess Anya and her cousin had a light luncheon in the Gallery of the Ottocento, the room with the most exciting view in the house.

Tasha, Anya noticed, was wearing only a pair of gold earrings and a bracelet, a far cry from her former splendor. Her dark-blue suit was an older one and quite subdued. Things were so bad that even this glittering butterfly had adopted protective camouflage.

"The situation is impossible, Anyushka," declared the countess as she spooned rich sour cream over her blini and sprinkled it with the last few grains of the Sviridovs' supply of caviar, offered in honor of the visit. "That fool Kerensky who's taken charge of the provisional government has to exert his authority over the Reds or they'll eat him alive. If he had any brains, he'd round up the leaders, cart them off to the Petropavlosk Fortress and stand them up against the wall. If he doesn't, they'll do it to him one day."

"For a young lady, you have very bloodthirsty ideas."

Tasha gave her beautiful cousin a disgusted pout. "It's them or us. Their Russia or ours. There won't be any middle ground now."

Princess Anya's attention was suddenly drawn to a group of men on the embankment directly across from her home. The sight of men gathering in a crowd always made her apprehensive, even more so than did the sight of demonstrators. They at least kept moving.

"Anything wrong?"

"No, I suppose not. I do wish Adam were here, though. I don't like being alone now."

"Where is he?" asked Tasha, curious. She'd thought he *was* here.

Anya smiled. "In Sweden. He and his brother had to go to Stockholm in connection with their organization. It's been disbanded and there are loose ends to tie up."

Yes, thought Tasha. That was one way of putting it. Billy had already shipped out a lot of loose ends for her. Judging by the bare walls of the Sviridov Palace, Adam was doing the same for Anya. Looking around the beautiful gallery with its exquisite boiseries, painted ceiling, magnificently draped windows and totally denuded walls, Tasha thought it seemed a perfect symbol of present-day Petrograd—a gilded shell overlooking a scene of through disintegration.

"I hate real life," announced the countess as she smiled into Anya's light-blue eyes. "What we used to have before the revolution was so much nicer."

Princess Sviridova laughed at that. "You're right," she agreed. "It was a grand party while it lasted."

And unfortunately, it didn't show any sign of starting up again any time soon, reflected the princess.

Outside, across the street from the mansion, a small cluster of soldiers had gathered around a heavyset man in a thick wool coat. Some of them were sympathetic. He seemed to be one of them, as down and out as the rest of them, speaking in the rough accents of Moscow province, not in the refined drawl of the St. Petersburg gentry.

"Brothers," he inquired, "what has this revolution brought us? Food? Warm houses? Pretty women?"

His audience managed thin smiles. As far as they could see, all it had given them was a new set of rulers who were as obstinate about continuing the hated war as the Romanovs had been.

"The great revolution hasn't brought us a damned thing," replied one of the soldiers, a young fellow with wavy dark hair peeking out from under his cap. "It's cheated us."

"Exactly," nodded Oleg. "It's become just another way for the politicians to keep us under their thumbs. What it ought to mean is a reward for men like us."

The soldiers' interest was aroused. "What kind of reward?" asked one.

"Anything you feel like taking. It ought to be ours for the asking."

"Right," agreed the men. "But when you start taking things, people begin to threaten you with the police, just like the old days."

Oleg chuckled. "You can have anything you want if you act quickly enough. I'll prove it." Yes, he thought. These fools would help him.

"How?"

"Just follow me." There, it was easily said. They took the bait.

The men glanced around at each other and at their new acquaintance and gazed in the direction he was indicating, the huge yellow-and-white palace across the street. If he thought he could break into that place, he was crazy. But if his plan succeeded, they would be just as crazy not to go with him, for it was as gorgeous as anything the tsar himself might possess. And it must contain acres of rooms to plunder.

"I'm with you," announced the dark-haired boy, setting off in step with the stranger.

After a few seconds, the others, too fell in line.

Inside the Sviridov Palace, Anya and Tasha had rejoined the children, who were all begging to play a game of hide-and-seek with Mama and Auntie. At first Tasha demurred, but in the end she relented and let Byelochka drag her off downstairs while Nicky, Sashenka and Tory were restrained by Anya in order to give the quarry a good head start.

As soon as Tasha and the child reached the ground-floor salons, they heard a loud noise like something crashing. Thinking it was ice falling from one of the cornices outside, they ignored it. Then all at once there were screams from the footmen on duty in the foyer and the angry sound of men's voices shouting abuse at the servants.

"My God!" shrieked Tasha. "It's the mob! Run!"

The girl took the youngster by the hand and raced for the long, curved white marble staircase, desperate to warn the others. At that point, the soldiers and their leader burst through the barricades of furniture thrown up by the staff and crossed into the main hall, racing after the young girl and boy.

Terrified of being molested or murdered by these animals, Countess Derzhavina pulled Byelochka after her as if he were a rag doll, scampering along with him in tow, frantic to escape the intruders. They had almost reached the second-floor landing when one of their pursuers tackled the girl, sending her and the child tumbling to the ground, frightened and quite out of breath.

"No!" shrieked Tasha as she felt someone grab her from behind. "Don't touch me or my child. I'm a poor widow."

Gasping for breath, she scrambled to her feet to confront nearly half a dozen peasant soldiers in long, dirty army greatcoats and fur hats. To Tasha, they appeared thoroughly degenerate and utterly filthy; they were probably lice-ridden too. She was terrified, convinced she was about to be raped by the whole pack.

Tasha used Byelochka like a human shield as she faced down the invaders, a small and dainty figure in the midst of so many large ones. The men looked embarrassed as she stared at them, clinging to the little boy.

"We're not going to harm you, *barinia*," mumbled one of the soldiers. "We just wanted a look round. It's a nice house," he added, rather sheepishly.

And evidently they were trying to make themselves at home, by the look of them. Protruding from coat pockets were an interesting variety of knickknacks and small objects, looted from the foyer and several first-floor rooms.

Tasha thought fast and decided to brazen her way out. What were they, after all, but a bunch of peasants? She wasn't about to be ordered about by peasants. And these were already hesitating, probably afraid she'd call the police and report them for housebreaking.

Drawing herself up to her full height, Countess Derzhavina said briskly, "Out of this house, all of you. Leave me and my little boy alone. What sort of men are you to molest innocent mothers and children? You ought to be ashamed of yourselves."

Feeling foolish and vulnerable to punishment for their lark, the men were about to turn around and leave with their souvenirs when the heavyset man who had led them into the place elbowed his way to the head of the pack and said angrily to Tasha, "Who the hell are you? Where is Anna Nicolaievna?"

Astonished that this scum knew Anya, Tasha was frightened all over again. Perhaps Adam was about to be arrested with all his family, she thought suddenly. Everybody was being arrested these days.

"I don't know anyone by that name," lied the countess, digging her nails into Byelochka's arm. He took the hint and kept quiet, wincing as she nearly drew blood.

Surprised that their new comrade actually knew someone who lived in this place, the soldiers halted and watched the interaction between him and the small, dark-haired girl with the blond child. Whoever she was, this Anna Nicolaievna must be very grand. This mansion was the most fabulous place the men had ever seen, nothing but white-and-gold-paneled walls, oriental carpets, loads of statues—some small enough to carry away. It was like heaven. And this fellow with the rough face and missing finger knew one of the family.

"You must be insane," replied Tasha. "There isn't anyone called Anna Nicolaievna in this house. Try farther on down the street."

She was lying and she and Oleg both knew it. Frightened by the strange, demented gleam in his eye, Tasha looked toward the soldiers, hoping for help.

"This man is crazy," she declared, trying hard to look confident. "We're a law-abiding family and we've lost people in the war just as you probably have. I don't know this man and I don't know anyone named Anna Nicolaievna. Now will you please leave and take him with you? You're frightening the child."

Abashed by the reasonableness of the young lady's tone and the over-whelming beauty of the surroundings, the soldiers felt out of place and increasingly ill at ease under the curious gaze of the boy, who stared at them as if they were something let loose from the zoo.

"Let's go," muttered one of the men, eyeing the servants watching from the foot of the staircase. Penalties for hooliganism were severe—if the civil authorities could catch the culprits. These men did not want to chance being caught.

"Let's go, brother," repeated the soldier, taking hold of Oleg by the arm and starting to propel him toward the door. "Leave this girl in peace."

Protesting violently, Oleg tried to pull away from his new friends, who seized him roughly and began dragging him away. They almost had him half-way out the door when another blond child scampered down the stairs; he came to an abrupt and startled halt on the landing when he saw the visitors.

"Auntie!" cried Nicky, "it's the revolution!"

When Princess Anya reached the landing a moment later, the crowd turned to gawk at her as she grabbed Nicky and stood facing them in dead silence, too shocked to speak. And then she ran to grab Byelochka.

With a cry of triumph, Oleg pulled away from the soldiers and raced up the stairs, recognizing Anna Nicolaievna, Prince Malyshev's niece, the cause of all his troubles. Coming face to face with the woman who had terrorized him, who had shot at him, and who had caused him to kill Wanda, Oleg was almost intimidated. She was beautiful. Up close, clutching the two children, she didn't seem to be as wicked as he remembered her. But his mind had a way of playing tricks on him. He knew that. It frightened him. It made him think he was crazy. For a minute, he saw Wanda and Katia standing by her.

As Oleg reached for the children, Anya screamed in horror, recognizing the intruder now for who he was. Tasha looked on in astonishment as Princess Anya struck the man across the face as hard as she could, knocking him off balance. Before he could recover from the blow, Anya was hitting him again, wild with fury, beating him like a madwoman, outraged that her home had been violated, no longer in control of herself.

When Oleg staggered again, losing his balance on the stairs, the princess snatched her frightened son and ran up the stairs with the child, heading for the second floor. She had a revolver there, hidden in the drawer of her dressing table. Her only thought was to get it and shoot him. Out of breath, hysterical, wild to kill him, Anya forgot everything else in the world except her son and this madman who had to be killed before he harmed her child.

Where was Adam when she needed him? thought Anya clutching Byelochka. Well, she would do what had to be done. By herself. There was no one else.

As the princess ran up the stairs, Ivanov ran after her, shouting with fury. At the first sign of trouble, the soldiers had taken their loot and fled, leaving Tasha and the useless servants to watch the drama on the staircase. Little Nicky was holding onto the countess's hand and sobbing, terrified for his Auntie and Byelochka.

"Help her!" shouted Tasha at the servants. To her fury, nobody moved, too afraid of the lunatic to approach him.

"I'll call the police," offered one fellow.

"Idiots!" shrieked the girl, shaking herself loose from Nicky. "Go after him!"

When they still hesitated, Tasha screamed at them and raced up the stairs after her cousin, unwilling to see her harmed by this madman. She was in such a rage, she seized the first object that came to hand on the landing, a large malachite and ormolu vase, and hurled it straight at the man's head, striking him in the back, making him scream in pain.

Princess Anya and Byelochka had made it halfway down the hall, heading for Anya's bedroom, when Ivanov had caught up with them. Then, as Tasha struck him with the vase, Anya pulled free. But before she could break completely away, he recovered and seized her arm, pulling her back.

"Let her go, damn it!" screamed Tasha, looking around wildly for something else to use on the man, while Anya fought like a wild woman, using her nails on him, punching, screaming, beside herself with rage.

Byelochka stood several feet from his mother, frightened for her, terrified the crazy man would kill them both.

"Tasha!" panted the princess as she and Ivanov struggled, "get the gun. It's in the dressing-table drawer! Hurry!"

Practically knocking the child over, Tasha ran to the bedroom and headed for her cousin's dressing table; screams from the corridor made her desperate to find the weapon and use it. Pulling out several drawers from underneath the dressing table's frothy skirt, Tasha dumped them on the floor. Where was the revolver? "Damn, damn, damn!" wailed the girl, searching frantically through the pile of odds and ends on the carpet as the screams outside got worse. He'll kill her, she thought. Then he'll kill the child. Then he'll kill me.

Like hell he will!

In the corridor, Ivanov had grabbed Anya by the throat and was holding her against the wall, grinning like a lunatic, enjoying the spectacle of this woman helpless at last, totally at his mercy.

She was out of breath, glassy-eyed from the fight, still trying to hit him, feebly now, too worn out from their struggle to do him any harm. He felt superior, almost for the first time in his life; she could no longer dominate his mind, force him to think of her, take over the souls of those around him.

She was just a woman. But she had children. They were hers and therefore dangerous to him. To save himself, to preserve his last remnants of sanity, he had to kill them all. If not, he would never feel free of her. She would haunt his sleep for years to come, mocking him, tormenting him, laughing at him. This would put an end to that.

As the princess tried for the last time to throw him off, Oleg began to squeeze her white throat, grunting with the force of his anger, choking the life out of her, grim and desperate to kill.

Byelochka cried out and ran at the man, beating him with little fists, distracting him long enough to make him take his hands away from Anya's throat. As he released her, she slumped to the floor at his feet, a threat no longer.

The child let out a piercing shriek and threw himself over his mother, terrified that the man had killed her. And then, as Tasha burst out of the bedroom, Ivanov grabbed the little boy and raced with him down the stairs.

Holding the revolver, horrified at the sight of her cousin and the spectacle of the lunatic running off with Byelochka, Tasha rushed to the railing of the staircase; she would shoot him before he could abduct the boy.

As Ivanov paused to pick up little Nicky, Tatiana Sergeevna aimed her weapon and fired a shot, chipping away at the marble beneath his feet. Releasing Nicky, Ivanov let out a cry of shock and started for the door with Byelochka slung over his shoulder, screaming with fear. A feeble effort by two footmen failed to halt his progress as the intruder thrust them aside and escaped to the street, heading in the direction of the Alexander Bridge and the tram that was just about to make the crossing. Before anyone could run after him, the man had boarded the tram and disappeared from sight, still carrying the little prince.

Terrified by everything that had happened, Nicky scampered up the stairs to where Tasha was now trying to revive her cousin, the child sobbing as the girl knelt on the floor, patting Anya's face, trying to bring her to her senses, hysterical with fear that she was too late already.

When Anya opened her eyes, she looked up into Tasha's face and grabbed her arm. "Where's my son?" she demanded. "Where's Ivanov?"

"Gone," replied the girl, her face nearly as white as Anya's. "Both of them."

"He's taken my son?" gasped the princess. "And no one stopped him?"

This was the revolution, she thought bitterly. For years her family had supported dozens of servants, taken care of their children's education, fed them. And this was their thanks. They had stood by and watched a lunatic steal her child.

Somehow it didn't surprise her to learn that Tasha had done her best to shoot Ivanov. For some reason, it seemed quite in keeping with her character. But her effort had failed.

Weak from the attack, Anya waved away a footman's help and got to her feet unaided, angry and in pain. If the man had tried to help her before, she might still be holding Byelochka in her arms, not trying to think of where that madman had taken him.

"Get out of here," she hissed at him. "And take the others with you. Don't ever show your face in this house again! Cowards!"

Staggering from the attack, Anya leaned on her cousin as she made her way down the staircase, demanding to know which direction the man had taken.

"Highness," said one of her footmen, "it's too late. He jumped on board a tram and vanished. You'll never find him."

"And why didn't you stop him? How could you have just stood there watching?"

"We tried to stop him."

"Then you should have tried harder. A lot harder!"

Flinging on a fur coat, Anya headed out the door, not really knowing where she was going. All she knew was the danger Byelochka faced alone with Ivanov. The man was insane. She could tell it by his eyes. He hated her and he had tried to kill her. Now he would try to kill her son.

"Anyushka!" shouted Tasha. "Where are you going?"

"After him."

"But you don't know where he's gone!"

Still shaken by her fight with Ivanov, Anya was no longer thinking clearly. She didn't care about logic, she didn't care about her pain. All she cared about was her son.

He was in danger. She was going to find him.

And she was going to kill Oleg Ivanov when she did.

35

After several hours of wandering the rough streets of Vyborg with Tasha in a dazed and futile effort to find the madman who had taken Byelochka, Anya returned to the Sviridov Palace to find Princess Ksenia in one of the ground-floor salons with Nanny, Nicky and the twins, all of them fearful of another attack and grieving over Byelochka's abduction and his mother's and cousin's disappearance. Ksenia was convinced her niece had lost her mind if she had actually gone off to try to track her son's kidnapper.

With the women and children were two representatives of the Red Guards. Charged with maintaining order in the neighborhood of the French Embankment, they had been alerted by the servants at the height of Ivanov's attack. They were standing now beside Princess Ksenia, listening to her descriptions of Anya, Tasha and Byelochka, writing it all down in little notebooks, all the while stealing glances around the beautiful white-and-gold-paneled salon.

When Princess Anya and Tasha entered, Ksenia rushed to her nieces and embraced them, horrified at the bruises on Anya's face. The children started to cry, glad to see Mama and Tasha and quite upset to see Mama looking so dreadful. The Reds looked silently at the young princess and at each other. This must be the one whose son was taken.

"Anyushka," said Ksenia, indicating the two men in worn greatcoats and fur hats, "these gentlemen belong to the local Red Guards unit. They're charged with protecting this neighborhood. Now that you've returned, you can tell them what happened."

From Ksenia's tone of voice, Anya and Tasha could sense something not quite right. The meaning became quite clear the moment the first Red began to speak. For some reason, he seemed to take the entire episode as a personal affront—a complaint that his unit was not providing adequate protection to the residents. Serious rivalries between units had made people very touchy lately. The last thing he wanted to hear about was a complaint about housebreaking and abduction. It wouldn't do him any good; it would, in fact, cause him serious embarrassment.

"There were soldiers with that man," said Anya. "And they helped him break into my home. He tore my son from my arms and carried him off God only knows where. Is this how your revolution protects the innocent?"

The elder of the two Reds looked around the sumptuous room and coldly eyed the young woman who was castigating the revolution and regarding him with barely disguised anger and contempt.

"Citizen Sviridova," he replied evenly, "I can appreciate your anger over the abduction of your child, but I would suggest you watch your tongue when you speak of the revolution. If it weren't for people like you and your family, there wouldn't have been a need for revolution in the first place."

"If it weren't for people like me and my family, Russia would still be a country of ignorant peasants, rooted in the dark ages," she flung back. "My family represents the best in our culture. What can you say about the animal who stole my child?"

"Anya, *assez*," murmured Princess Ksenia, gently taking her niece's arm. "*Ne sois pas bête. Ce monsieur commence à se fâcher.*"

The representative of the people didn't understand what Princess Malysheva was saying, but he could catch her meaning. She was more reasonable than the young girl, he thought. Good.

"We will try our best to find your son, citizen," he said, somewhat placated. "But it's going to be difficult. The city is filled with troublemakers. There are more pressing problems confronting us."

"Not for me."

The man smiled coldly. "Citizen," he said, "when I was a child, I saw three of my brothers die from hunger. We were poor. It was our fate. This might be your child's fate."

Shocked by the brutality of that suggestion, Anya flushed bright red, glared at the man and realized just how much Byelochka's survival depended on her and her alone.

Later, after the representatives of the new order had left, Anya, Ksenia and Tasha had a conference in the small green and gold salon on the second floor. Princess Sviridova was so furious she had no time to be fearful any longer. She had fought Oleg Ivanov and had spent three hours walking the streets of Red Vyborg and survived. She would survive anything and everything else she had to do to get Byelochka back. She swore it. The thought of Ivanov with her child drove out every other emotion except cold, fierce rage.

"I'm going to Byelaya Beryozka," announced Anya. "Ksenia, I want you to take my daughters, Nicky and Tasha, to Stockholm. This city is too dangerous for children now. You heard that animal. His kind would exterminate us all, babies first."

Princess Ksenia was startled. "Anya," she protested, "I don't think you're in any condition to track someone like that. He's a madman. He'll kill you."

"He's already tried three times and failed. But he will surely kill Byelochka if someone doesn't stop him. Do you think I'll stand by and let him succeed?"

"But what makes you think he'll head for Byelaya Beryozka? He hasn't been there in years."

Tasha agreed with Anya, claiming Petrograd would be too hot for Ivanov right now. He'd want to put as much space as possible between himself and those Red Guards. They might not wish to acknowledge his crime in their district, but they'd probably put him up against the wall just for spoiling their reputation if they ever caught him. And for someone like Ivanov, looking for shelter in the midst of such turmoil, why not return to where his family lived? They might be the only ones he could count on for help.

"She's right," said Anya. "It would be the ideal shelter for a man on the run. And he'd never expect to see any of us in the middle of Moscow province. Things are too unstable there at the moment."

Yes, thought Princess Ksenia. That's what I told Andrei.

"Anyushka," she said gently, it sounds quite reasonable, but remember, Ivanov is a madman. His destination may be the Crimea for all we know. Or even the very place in town where he lives. We just can't be certain."

"Ksenia," cried Anya, "I have to find my son! Let me believe there's *some* logic I can rely on to help me! My God, for all we know, he's already murdered Byelochka and left him in some filthy alley like a dead dog! Don't you think I've already thought of that?".

Princess Malysheva put her arms around her niece and held her close for a minute, thinking of that dreadful day six years earlier. Things had gone full circle and had come back to Oleg Ivanov and Anya.

"Anyushka," declared Ksenia, "I think you're right to want to send the children to Sweden. Tasha and Nanny can go with them. Petrograd is far too dangerous for youngsters at the moment."

"What?" exclaimed the countess, whirling around. "How shall we get there?"

"By Adam's regular route," replied Princess Sviridova. "The train to Finland, sleds through the Finnish forests and across the frontier at Haparanda. It's not comfortable, but it's our one way out of Russia right now. Are you game?"

Under the curious gaze of both princesses, who were still astonished and touched by Tasha's rush to Anya's defense in the fight, the countess shrugged, glanced at her cousin's bruises and said, "Why not?"

Petrograd was lost. The animals had taken over and Tatiana Sergeevna had no desire to live among them any longer.

"Good girl," smiled Ksenia, knowing how her niece's mind worked. "By the time we see you again, you may have become a Swedish baroness."

Yes, thought Tasha, thinking of tall blond gentlemen. That was a very definite possibility. She liked blond men.

"Ksenia," said Anya, "I don't want to put you in any danger. Please go to Stockholm with the children. Adam will help me when he returns."

"Darling, we can't afford to wait that long. If we hope to rescue Byelochka, we'll have to start moving this afternoon. Besides, I'm not about to run off and leave Andrei by himself at Byelaya Beryozka. Tasha and Nanny will have to look after the children."

The thought of entrusting her babies to Tatiana Sergeevna was a daunting idea. However, since Nanny would be with them, that meant they would be in safe and loving hands. They would simply have to stay at a hotel in Stockholm until their parents could rejoin them. It would be safer than allowing them to remain even one day longer in revolutionary Petrograd.

"I've always wanted to see Stockholm," declared Tasha. "This could be quite a lark."

"Start packing," ordered Anya, about to deliver the news to Nanny. "I want you and the children out of Petrograd by this afternoon. The sooner you leave, the sooner you'll arrive in Sweden. Besides, you may be able to intercept Adam and tell him what's happened."

With that, Princess Sviridova headed for the nursery to announce her astonishing decision.

Nobody paid much attention to the heavyset, bearded man as he sat with a blond child in the second-class coach of the Moscow train. The little boy was wearing a shabby overcoat and knitted cap, but the fine leather boots he wore seemed odd in comparison with the rest of his outfit. The bruises on his face added their own jarring note.

The little one had just been given a hell of a beating, and now he was sobbing softly, making the sounds of a weak kitten. No one felt free to say anything since his large companion didn't look as if he cared about anyone's opinion. And these days, people were very touchy. One didn't start up with fierce-looking strangers if one had any sense at all.

Surrounded by peasants and soldiers, raucous, grubby figures, some carrying bundles, some bearing small wooden cages filled with live fowl, Byelochka stared in bewilderment. He didn't understand how he had come to be sitting here beside this bad man who sounded like Uncle Andrei's peasants. He knew the man had broken into his home and knew he had fought with Mama. He knew that the man had carried him screaming out into the street and onto that tram. But Byelochka didn't really comprehend any of it. All he knew right now was fear and pain—fear of this bad man who had taken him to a dark and dirty place with strange, loud, bad-smelling people all around and pain from the beating he'd received when he had asked to be taken home.

"I'm going to do better than that, you brat," the man had said to him, hitting him angrily across the face. "I'm going to take you back to the place where it all began—all my troubles are because of your family. And you're going to help me put an end to them."

Frightened, the little boy had begged to go back to his mama. He wasn't able to understand what this man said. His rough peasant speech grated on Byelochka's ears, accustomed as he was to his family's polished tones. And what the man said made no sense.

But it all terrified him, especially when the wild ravings were accompanied by slaps, aimed straight at Byelochka's face. What was worse, the man seemed to enjoy hitting him, making him cry, calling him names he'd never heard in his life. The things he said about Mama were even worse. When Byelochka heard him call his mama bad names, he stubbornly put his hands over his ears and refused to listen, and it had made the man even angrier.

Now he and the strange bad man with the missing finger and no hair were on board a horrible train, heading toward Byelaya Beryozka, Uncle Andrei's estate. That was the one thing that offered a tiny spark of hope to Byelochka. He knew Uncle Andrei would take him away from this man when they got there and punish him for the wicked things he had done to Mama. To Byelochka it seemed strange his captor didn't understand what would happen to him once he found Uncle Andrei, but the child wasn't about to tell him. He wanted it to be a nasty surprise. At the thought that his uncle might not be there, the little boy started to cry. He had to be there. If he wasn't, who would rescue him?

And how would he ever get back to Mama? He loved her more than anyone, even more than Papa or Auntie Ksenia or the twins. She was the one who took him for drives while Nanny stayed with the babies, ice-skated with him on the pond in the gardens, read to him at night before he went to bed, let him fasten her pretty sparkling jewelry around her neck and wrists when she was going out. If he never found her again, who would do those things for her? And he knew she would miss him, even with the twins. He was the one she loved best, her favorite, her little squirrel.

He couldn't imagine life without her. Or comprehend why this ugly man hated her so. All he knew was that if Uncle Andrei didn't take him away from the bad man, the man would kill him. He had said he would and the child didn't doubt it for a minute. In the meantime, the little prince put his hand to his bruised cheek and hoped his companion wouldn't hit him again.

It was snowing lightly when the Sviridovs' private railway carriage was rolled out onto the tracks at Finland Station and linked up with the regular train. Imperial grand dukes were having a hard time with the railroad these days, but Adam still enjoyed good relations with the workers because of his war work, and his wife and children could depend on their goodwill—at least for the time being. Anya decided to make the most of it. Her babies deserved to travel in comfort while they still could.

As Countess Derzhavina, Nanny, Nicky and the two-year old twins boarded the train, Anya had to fight back tears. She and Ksenia were a lot less certain about sending them off now that the time had actually come for their departure. And the children sensed their fear, clinging to Mama and Auntie as the train began to rattle, ready to move out.

"Nanny, you have enough money with you to provide food and shelter for you and the children for at least six months," said Anya, having sewn several thousand British pounds-sterling into her corset three hours earlier. "Put it in a bank once you get to Stockholm and withdraw what you need on a weekly basis. Book yourselves into a suite at the Hotel Angleterre and wait for us to join you. Stay there as long as it takes."

"Yes, madam," replied the British nanny, amazed at Princess Sviridova's mathematics. She had given her enough for over a year, living in grand style. Nanny hoped the separation wasn't going to last *that* long.

"I'll keep careful accounts, madam," she replied. "And I'll see to it that the little ones eat well and get their exercise."

"And keep an eye on the young lady," added Ksenia. "She's not as grown-up as she thinks she is."

"Auntie!" laughed Tasha. "I don't need a keeper."

Nanny could see there were going to be stormy times ahead with that one.

"Nicky," said Ksenia to the little boy, enveloping him in the scent of her perfume and the warmth of her fur coat, "I love you very much and I'm going to come get you. After all this is over, you, Uncle Andrei and

I will be together again, although I don't know where. That's a promise," she said, kissing him gently as tears fell on the soft, golden fur. "You be a good boy for Nanny and wait for me, will you?"

Nicholas Georgievich buried his face in his new mama's sables and put his arms around her, smelling the scent of roses coming from her soft white skin. It was his favorite scent in the whole world. When he looked into Ksenia's eyes, he was remarkably calm, his own light-blue eyes solemn and quite serious. "Don't cry, Matushka," he said, patting her cheek the way she'd often done with him. "I'm not afraid."

"Good boy," laughed Princess Malysheva, hugging him once again.

Anya kissed her daughters, caressing them tenderly, hoping she'd see them again and not terribly certain she would. Those pretty little faces looked at her so trustingly she could hardly bear the thought of their crossing the frontier without her, two small blonde creatures alone in a fierce world that had grown so hostile so quickly.

"I love you, darlings," murmured Anya, hugging them. "I love you very much. Never forget that, no matter what happens."

As the whistle blew to signal departure, Countess Derzhavina suddenly threw herself into Auntie's arms, although Ksenia couldn't quite tell whether it was from emotion or from the abrupt movement of the train.

"Goodbye, Auntie," whispered Tasha, kissing her quickly on both cheeks. "And thank you for everything you did for me. Or tried to do," she smiled, rather sheepishly. "You and Anyushka are the only people who have ever really been good to me. And I don't even know why."

Ksenia embraced the girl as the train began to move. For some reason she was even more concerned for her niece than she was for the youngsters. This girl was so vulnerable, so close to the edge that the princess dreaded sending her off. But she had no choice.

"Goodbye, Tasha," she whispered, kissing her once more. "We'll come back for you too."

And then Ksenia and Anya had to rush to descend the stairs before it was too late to leave.

"Goodbye, darlings!" called Anya, waving at them as they began their trip to Finland and the frontier. "Be good for Nanny!"

In response, three small blond heads appeared at the window, waving wildly, calling their goodbyes, bewildered about leaving Mama behind. Behind them stood Tasha and Nanny, their hands raised in farewell, hovering over the children.

When the train had finally cleared the station, out of sight and heading west, Anya took her aunt's arm and set off for the Nicholas Station across town.

Byelaya Beryozka

"It's very bad, Highness," reported Lev Petrovich, Andrei's best tracker. "The soldiers raided several estates and killed a few of the landlords. They tortured some of them first and made them suffer a long time, the bastards, before putting them out of their misery. They're scum."

"Then we'd better make sure they don't pay us any surprise visits. I want men posted round the clock on sentry duty. Fire a warning shot at the first sign of trouble."

"Right, Highness," nodded the weather-beaten peasant, looking much older than his years as he cradled his Winchester rifle. "My boy Petya is out there right now, scouting for any sign of them."

"He's a good son, Lev. And a fine tracker."

"He had a good teacher," grinned the peasant.

Since being invalided home, the boy had helped his father and older brothers, trying to keep up his studies with the help of the local priest. With the outbreak of trouble in the capital, Andrei's plans to send him to school in Petrograd had to be put off until things were calmer. Meanwhile, there was plenty for Petya to do at home, especially since the old man was relying on him more and more. Even Praskovaya Feodorovna deferred to his judgment on occasion, a rare compliment. Or a sure sign she was aging.

Andrei smiled and clapped the grizzled peasant on the back before heading into the study to take inventory of his weapons and ammunition. If it came to a pinch, he'd have to arm those who had no rifles. He only hoped he had enough. Reports from the neighboring estates were appalling. A battle for Byelaya Beryozka was a certainty.

Two days before, a band of army deserters had descended on a manor house not far from Andrei's and murdered the owner, his wife and children after having tortured them for hours. The unspeakable savagery, especially the butchering of two innocent children, had struck fear into everyone in the area. Andrei Nicolaievich was not about to fall prey to the same group—at least not if he could help it. If he found himself under attack, he was planning on taking as many of them with him as possible.

As the prince took stock of his weapons, he wondered if his neighbor, Count Scherbatkin, was doing the same. Boris had long been hated for his work on the war mobilization committee and had recently been threatened. Lots of peasant boys Boris had sent off to war had never returned, while his healthy son-in-law had never been called up. People knew that and resented it, some of them bitterly.

"Highness, would you like tea?"

Andrei turned around to see Praskovaya Feodorovna, his housekeeper, standing in the doorway bearing a shiny copper samovar on a tray. She looked worried.

"Yes, thank you," he smiled. "Nice of you to think of it."

"It's too dangerous for you to be here, Andrei Nicolaievich," she declared sadly. "You know you shouldn't have come."

Praskovaya looked so old all of a sudden, thought the prince. The war had been hard on everyone.

He shook his head. "No. With those animals loose in the area, I think it would have been foolish to stay away. My people have to be protected."

"Some of the peasants are ready to join the soldiers," replied the woman as she seated herself beside the prince. "People are angry at everyone and especially at the landlords. What happened at that house west of here will happen again. They say the sight was so terrible that grown men wept to see the bodies."

"Yes, I heard," murmured Andrei, staring into the fire in the hearth before him.

"Don't let it happen to you, Andrei Nicolaievich," said the woman. "I would be so sorry to see you end up like that."

"Don't worry, Prashkosha. I don't intend to," he said warmly.

"Yes, and I'll bet that was just what the other fellow said too."

Yes, thought the prince. It probably was.

When Oleg arrived at the Byelaya Beryozka station, he would have passed unnoticed except for the little boy. He was too obviously a little *barin*, even with the shabby coat. He just didn't belong to the bulky peasant, and to prove it, he cried out to everyone in sight that he wanted to go back home to his mama, Princess Sviridova.

Slapping the boy viciously across the face to shut him up, Oleg hauled him off before anyone could question him, but not before a few loafers began to speculate about the truth of his claims. There was a Princess Sviridova who often visited the area and she *did* have a son, although it seemed peculiar that he'd be in such rough company. Who could tell?

Later, the carter who transported Oleg and the boy out to the Ivanov place remarked to friends that the man had been so angry with the child for making a spectacle of himself that he had hit him several times on the way out. He was a strange one, thought the carter. Those eyes of his were enough to send chills down a man's spine.

Farther west, Nanny, Tasha and the children had reached the end of the line in Finland at a small village called Tornio and were beginning to bargain with colorfully dressed Lapp drivers to take them through the forests in their sturdy reindeer sleds. In the middle of nowhere, Tornio looked like the end of the world to the ladies, especially to Tasha, who swore she would never again complain about backward Russian stations after seeing this place.

At their first sight of reindeer, the children began to clap with delight; the creatures came prancing up to the station, tiny bells jingling and oddly garbed Lapp drivers shouting to them in a language nobody could understand.

"Heathenish, isn't it?" giggled Tasha as the men helped Nanny and the fur-coated, laughing twins into one sleigh, while Tasha and Nicky were bundled into the following one. Nanny didn't reply; she merely smiled at the outlandish foreigners and held the children very close.

Sashenka and Tory were utterly fascinated by the reindeer and called back to Tasha and Nicky that it would be nice to have them in Petrograd. Nicky replied *no.* Reindeer didn't like cities.

The Lapp driver grinned at the little boy, winked wickedly at the pretty young lady and chirruped to his animals as they sped through the snowy forests.

When Tasha's party reached the Swedish-Finnish border at Haparanda, Nanny appointed herself leader of the pack. That was fine with Countess Derzhavina. The tall British nanny had a genuine British passport and the manner of a sergeant major. Let her take care of the border guards.

"*Anglaise?*" inquired the fur-hatted inspector as the party approached his desk in a tumbledown shack, Russia's border outpost.

"*Oui,*" replied Nanny, an imposing figure in a fur coat and hat, looking twice as large as she usually did, owing to the bulky fur.

The man eyed the women carefully and Nanny responded in kind. She normally had all the hauteur of a duchess, so it was easy to fix him with a cool stare, indicating she was a straightforward person with absolutely nothing to hide. Tasha silently said her prayers as the two of them locked eyes over the desk.

The guard glanced sharply at the group of children. "*Famille?*"

"*Ma fille,*" replied Nanny, indicating Tasha, "*et ses enfants.*"

Nodding at the fertile lady, the man put out his hand for their passports. His eyes showed a sleepy sort of surprise when he saw the diplomatic stamps—one of Billy's last gifts to Tasha.

"*Votre mari?*" he asked. "*Où?*"

"*A l'ambassade américaine à Petrograd,*" replied Tatiana Sergeevna.

"Ah."

The guard glanced at his second in command, exchanged shrugs and politely handed back the ladies' passports. "*Au revoir, mes dames. Bon voyage.*"

As the fur-coated group filed out of the customs station, silent and weary, Nanny realized they had been lucky. The next fellow in line, a Russian, had his bags dumped all over the floor and was being closely and aggressively questioned by the same officers who had been civil to them.

When they had crossed over to Sweden and were able to board a train for the long ride to Stockholm, everyone curled up in the comfortable seats of their first-class compartment and promptly fell asleep, Nicky with his arm around Tasha and the twins nestling close to Nanny, their sole link with normal life in the midst of so much agitation.

To everyone's distress, when they finally reached Stockholm and the Hotel Angleterre, they learned they had missed Prince Sviridov by mere hours. He was already on his way back to Petrograd with Billy.

"Damn," muttered Tasha, thinking it would have been fun to let Billy take her to dine at one of the city's elegant restaurants, making up for the recent deprivations in Russia's revolutionary capital. "I might have known he'd disappoint me."

Nanny settled the children into a pretty suite of rooms, assured them Mama and Papa would soon be joining them and prayed she wasn't lying to the poor things. What they had left behind in Petrograd was a nightmare, and Prince and Princess Sviridov were still in it.

With a shudder, the Englishwoman thought of her small charges alone in the world with Countess Derzhavina as their only living relative. She hoped fate wouldn't be that cruel to them.

God knows they didn't deserve *that*.

When Oleg arrived at his father's house, he and the child were hastily dropped off at the entrance gate by the carter, who told them about the recent troubles, leaving them to walk the few hundred feet of freezing, rutted courtyard to the door.

Once Oleg arrived at the long wooden porch, he knocked loudly, then waited, looking uneasy. There was no discernible sign of life in the place.

To Byelochka, it was frightening, a dark and forbidding place with creaking stairs and loose planks of wood in the porch, probably as bad inside as that place in Petrograd the man had taken him before they went to the train station. Looking up at the ugly man with the scruffy beard and the missing finger, the little prince shivered, as much from fright as from cold.

After a few minutes of steady pounding on the door, it opened a crack, and someone peered out from behind the barrel of a gun. He looked as if he meant to use it on them.

It was Ivanov senior.

"Father!"

"Oh Christ!" exclaimed the old man. "Look at this."

He glared at his son in astonishment, his face registering as much disgust as anything else. This was the last person he expected to find on his doorstep, and he didn't want to be bothered with him.

"I thought you were dead," he said at last, disappointed.

"Well, damn it, you look as if you're sorry I'm not."

The little boy stared at the ugly old man and wondered if he was going to let them in. He hoped not.

"Can I come in?" asked Oleg. "Or do you mean to keep us out here in the cold?"

"Do whatever you want. Who's the boy?"

Pulling the child after him, Oleg entered a house that had plainly seen better days. Peeling paint was scattered like dandruff over the carpets. Dirty plates decorated tables in the front parlor. Nowhere was there evidence of Maria Andreevna's loving care, and that puzzled Oleg.

"Where's Mama?" he demanded suddenly.

"Dead four years, God rest her soul. She hoped you would come back and see her before she died, but you disappointed her there, too. I don't know what brought you out here now," added the old man with contempt. "There's trouble, you know."

"What kind of trouble?"

"Murder. Robbery. Arson. Take your pick. They burned a manor house west of here and killed all the people in it. My men and I are waiting for them to come here."

"Christ!"

As Oleg looked around the room, he saw six sturdy men, peasants like himself, all armed with guns and ready to use them at a moment's notice—his father's few loyal workers, two of them overseers. Ties to old man Ivanov made them marked men. They had no choice but to stand together now.

This all looks bad, thought Oleg. It was just like Petrograd; there was no escape. Finally he said, "I have nowhere else to go. I'm destitute."

You fool. It doesn't surprise me. I always told your poor mother you'd end up badly. You know, you're still wanted for trying to murder that girl. They'll be after you in a flash if they know you're back."

"Well," laughed his son, "at least I'm lucky there. There's no more law in this country. Now it's every man for himself."

Ivanov senior grimaced. Then he glanced down at Byelochka and looked wary. "Who's the boy?" he repeated, peering closely at him, fingering the fine material of the sailor suit under the child's overcoat.

The boy looked up at the mean-looking old man and backed away, repelled by the strong odors of home-brewed spirits, cheap tobacco and cabbage soup emanating from Ivanov senior. The smell made his stomach turn.

Oleg hesitated, staring down at the child who looked so much like Anna Nicolaievna. Suddenly a thought came to mind. This child was his. The boy was the embodiment of all the evil that had pursued him since that encounter in the forest with his mother. He was Oleg's own creation. And if he could take him back to the spot where all his problems had started, back to the clearing where he had first tried and failed to kill that blonde witch, he could put an end to all his bad luck, to his misery.

Yes. That was the answer. He would sacrifice him on the very spot where it had all begun. The little prince's death would free him from the evil Anna Nicolaievna had cursed him with. It would break the vicious cycle.

Looking the old man in the eye, Oleg replied, "He's my son."

"God in heaven!" exclaimed Ivanov senior. "That's just what I need. Another mouth to feed!"

"Yes. And we're both staying here until I feel like leaving, so get used to the idea, old man." As he said the words, he believed them.

The boy seated himself on the creaking sofa while the fat man argued with the old man, both of them equally frightening to him. This house was freezing, he noticed, and ugly too. Nobody he knew lived in a place like this.

Worst of all, Uncle Andrei wouldn't know where he was, hidden here with these people. And he had to find him, otherwise he would never see Mama again. The idea frightened him more than ever. The child shivered uncontrollably. To underscore his dissatisfaction with the place, Byelochka, accustomed to the oriental carpets, crystal chandeliers, Chinese vases, oil paintings and gilded furniture of the Sviridov Palace, began to howl with grief, wailing so loudly that he began to annoy old Ivanov, who slapped him hard.

"What's the matter with him?" he demanded.

"I want my mama!" replied Byelochka, pounding on the sofa so hard he raised a cloud of dust that made him cough. "I want to go home!"

"Christ!" snorted the old man, "I might have known your son would turn out like this."

"He's never been away from home before, I guess."

"You guess?" laughed the old man. "It sounds as though you don't know his mother too well."

"I knew her well enough to father him," replied Oleg, angrily. "What difference does it make to you? You were never what I'd call a good father yourself. Christ, how I used to hate you!"

"And now you've come back to sponge off me, haven't you? That's the only thing you ever did well, you fool. I'm ashamed you're my own flesh and blood."

"Bastard!" cried Oleg as he lunged at him, knocking him backward onto the floor.

The old man didn't stay down for long. Like a cat, he was on his feet, ready to take Oleg apart despite their difference in age. Years in the fields had toughened him to a point where he was twice as likely to win the scrap as the fat, lazy oaf he had fathered.

To even the match, Oleg grabbed a club from the hands of a servant and struck his father full in the face, sending him to the floor, stunned.

Breathing heavily, the son looked around the room, waiting for one of the men to come to their boss's defense. Nobody did. Family fights were off-limits to outsiders. Taking advantage of the opportunity, Oleg was about to beat in the old man's brains when a shot spoiled his concentration.

"Shit!" said one of the onlookers. "More trouble. It's been like this almost every night."

"What's going on around here?" demanded Oleg, forgetting the old man momentarily.

"The peasants are trying to burn us out. They've been here every night and they have army deserters with them now. It's bad," said one of the men, the one who seemed to take charge now.

"Boy, lie down on the floor under the sofa. Don't raise your head. Oleg, do you still know how to use a rifle?"

"Yes. Give it here."

Old Ivanov was barely conscious but nobody appeared to care. He was almost universally detested, so no one gave much thought to his welfare in the midst of all the commotion.

Oleg received his instructions from his father's foreman and took up a position at a dark parlor window, waiting for a chance to shoot.

A shot turned a windowpane into splinters of glass. Oleg flinched as the shreds covered him.

"What about the Malyshev estate? Is it bad there, too?" Oleg asked the foreman.

"No. That's the quietest place in the district. So far."

An indistinct yell from a faceless raider was accompanied by a chorus of catcalls from the yard.

"Ivanov, are you there?"

"You'll sleep in hell tonight, landlord!" The tone was mocking.

"All land to the people!"

"That one's from our village," noted the foreman. "Listen to his voice."

"Hell, you'll find the same slogan all over Petrograd and not a peasant in sight."

The yelling began all over again.

"We'll cut your throat, landlord!"

"Get your coffin ready, Ivanov!"

"Prepare to go to hell, old man!"

Suddenly a fiery object crashed through the windows, igniting the threadbare curtains, then spreading the flames to the worn sofa and finally to the floor.

"Get the boy out!" screamed Oleg.

But Byelochka didn't wait to be helped. He rolled out from under the sofa and ran into the next room to take shelter behind an armchair. In the decrepit parlor, the men were fighting the fire and trying to repel the attackers at the same time, while in the center of all this chaos old Ivanov lay rigid and helpless.

"Cover the back of the house!" shouted the foreman. "They're going to try to break in through there!"

Byelochka saw a husky man in a sheepskin coat grab a rifle and race down the darkened hall, followed by a second man. The child became frightened by the noise and attempted to escape by running upstairs. From the railing, he could look down into the foyer and see men firing rifles, screaming wildly and beating the flames, all at the same time. It was a terrifying spectacle.

Meanwhile, outside the house, a new group had joined the battle; these were not ragtag peasants with old hunting rifles but soldiers, veterans of the front, with two machine guns mounted on flatbed trucks, purchased in the United States by the tsarist army.

"Ivanov, you have one final chance," shouted a deep bass voice. "Come out now or we'll kill you!"

"Go to hell," replied the foreman, picking off one of the peasants.

"Open fire!"

The crackle of machine-gun fire ripped through the night air like fire through gauze. Screams from inside the house let the gunners know they had scored well.

"Christ! What have they got out there?"

Oleg ran to the place where his father lay and shook him to see if he were still alive. Not a sign. He had been shot through the head in the commotion.

His heart beating wildly, Oleg looked around the semidarkness of the parlor and tried to control his emotions. He was terrified. What did they want? What could he give them that would buy them off and send them on their way? Why, it was obvious. The landlord.

As Oleg reached this conclusion, someone from the outside bellowed, "Give up or die. We'll kill you if you don't surrender now."

Nobody answered. The men were too intent on reloading their rifles. Byelochka lay on his stomach, his breathing coming in sharp, panicky spurts, his heart racing as if it were about to burst with the effort. Too bewildered to understand it all, the child wailed for his mama and beat his fists on the floor, sobbing in terror.

After a brief pause, Oleg and his companions heard a voice with a Moscow accent give the command, "Commence firing!"

Down they went, hugging the charred floor while bullets tore chunks from the walls and sent glass splintering over their heads. Upstairs, Byelochka watched this scene of destruction from behind the railing and started to crawl farther back into the hall, flat on his stomach like the men downstairs and sobbing as he went. Stray bullets were kicking up dust not three feet from where he lay.

"Cease fire."

The only sound in the parlor was the heavy breathing of the trapped men as they waited for the next move by the soldiers. By this time, there were only a few of them left; the rest were dead.

"Surrender and you can walk away!" roared the fellow with the Moscow accent. "All we want is old man Ivanov."

"So, what are you waiting for?" demanded Oleg. "Throw out his body."

The foreman shook his head, still flat on his belly amid the debris of the devastated parlor. "They're liars. They'll kill us all. These are the deserters who murdered those people a few days ago."

"We're not landlords," replied Oleg, "and they want the landlord. So let's make them happy and hand him over. You know he's dead anyway."

The survivors looked at each other.

"Throw him out," repeated Oleg, edging toward the corpse. "Come on!"

"Wait," warned the foreman. "We'd better let them know what we're about to do. Otherwise they'll shoot for sure if they see the door open."

"Right," muttered Oleg, crawling toward the shattered window.

He raised himself up slightly and peered outside. There in the courtyard was a ragtag mob of peasants and soldiers standing beside two trucks, that carried mounted machine guns. Shouting to get their attention, he called out, "Don't shoot! We're going to turn over the landlord!"

A ragged chorus of cheers greeted that announcement.

"Hurry," Oleg grunted as he took hold of his father's feet. "You grab him by the shoulders. You," he said, indicating another peasant, "open the door so we can toss him out. Quickly. And then slam it shut as fast as you can."

With the foreman's help, Oleg dragged his dead parent out into the foyer, waited for his assistant to open the front door and then heaved the body out, sending it clear over the wooden railing of the porch for good measure.

In the harsh glare of the trucks' headlights, old Ivanov was a pitiable object, his gray hair and beard caked with blood, his shirt ripped by bullet holes. No one in the courtyard was in a mood to feel pity. A loud cheer greeted landlord Ivanov as he landed with a thud in the half-frozen slush.

"Bunch of pigs. Listen to them. And not even half are from these parts," muttered the foreman, trying hard to put out the flames.

In the courtyard, the soldiers and peasants were just beginning the evening's entertainment. Quickly they stripped the corpse, expressed their displeasure at not finding any valuables on it and began to hack it to pieces with their knives.

Blood spurted over the dirty snow as the gang went to work with a viciousness that bordered on the insane, tearing apart the old man as if they were a wolf pack dispatching a deer in the forest.

When they had finished, they propped the headless, eviscerated corpse against a tree and shouted for the landlord's men to come out and take a look.

"Like hell."

"We'll kill you inside the house if you don't come out and play!"

"Try!" came the reply.

Oleg felt his stomach flutter with fear. They weren't going to be satisfied with their prize. They were out to kill them all. As he looked at the man nearest him, covered with blood and grime, he felt terror take hold of him, turning his knees to cotton. He couldn't escape them.

Anna Nicolaievna was behind this, he thought wildly. That child upstairs had called up these savages to torment him. The sooner he could kill that boy of hers, the better off he'd be.

But he had to kill him properly, he told himself. It had to be at the exact spot where his troubles had started. Otherwise his torment would never end. It would continue forever, haunting him until he drew his last breath.

As the voice with the Moscow accent gave the order to fire, the machine guns ripped chunks from the facade, tearing holes in the men at the windows.

"Damn it," cursed Oleg, flattening himself on the floor. "They're maniacs!"

Racing up the stairs during a lull in the firing, he grabbed Byelochka and ran with him to the cellar, where he burst open a locked door and pulled the child in after him, putting an end to his terrified screams with a succession of blows. Upstairs the noise was deafening, like a symphony from hell, and it was obvious the landlord's men were getting the worst of it.

Staring at Ivanov and trembling with fear at the hideous sounds coming from overhead, Byelochka frantically obeyed when his captor ordered him to help him tear some shelves away from the cellar wall. Not knowing exactly why they were doing this, the child sensed it might be a way to flee the house without being seen by those madmen outside. Upstairs the last man left alive was howling like a wild animal in the deadly rain of gunfire. The little boy clawed at the shelving, sobbing and panting as he heard the gunfire finally drown out the man's last cries, the final human sound in the pandemonium.

Working feverishly alongside the child, Oleg searched for the entrance to the tunnel his father had constructed following the troubles of 1905. After four or five unnerving minutes, Oleg managed to uncover what he had been looking for and joyfully tore open the door, a low thing half-hidden by twelve years of accumulated dust, cobwebs and grime.

Taking a lantern from the hook on the wall, Oleg lit it, took hold of the boy and shoved him into the entrance. Something with large yellow eyes peered back at him, sending Byelochka screaming back into the cellar. He didn't get very far.

"Shut up and get moving! You've seen rats before."

"No, I haven't!"

"Well, you'll see them now," Oleg grunted, pulling the door shut after them, forcing the child to move ahead of him into the entrance once more.

After a frightening journey through a long, damp, dark tunnel, musty with stale air and littered with the occasional skeleton of a dead rodent, they came to a trapdoor and opened it to find themselves staring into the cold night sky. They were deep in the woods behind the house, far enough away from the fighting to enable them to make good their escape.

Hoisting the boy onto his shoulders, Oleg climbed out of the tunnel by means of a ladder and ascended into the snow-covered forest. He had outwitted those maniacs, but for how long?

As he lurched through the woods, dragging the child after him, Oleg felt ghostly hands clutching at his throat, tearing at his coat; he heard a woman's shrill voice calling after him, taunting him. As he kept on running, stumbling in his fright in the moonlit forest, he had only one thought—to find the right place for the deed and kill this child, the witch's baby.

If he didn't, he was lost forever.

The soldiers had finished shooting now and were mutilating the bodies of the landlord's men as a warning to others in the area. The whole gruesome collection of corpses was to be displayed in a neat row on the long wooden front porch, with old Ivanov's headless corpse at a short distance from the rest, leaning against a tree.

As a final touch, Ivanov's head was impaled on the hitching post in front of the steps. His heart was pinned to the door with a knife. By noon the next day, there wasn't a landlord within a twenty-mile radius who hadn't heard the story of the savage slaughter. By dinnertime, the peasants were already making bets on who the next victims would be.

36

When Adam returned to Petrograd, he was outraged to hear of the abduction of his son. And he was fearful for his wife and children. The girls' trip would be rough, but Anya's and Ksenia's might be fatal. Moscow province was starting to flame up again as it had in 1905, and this time there was no authority capable of containing the growing disorders.

Adam wasted no time in setting out for Byelaya Beryozka. If things were as unstable as people said, they would need him. At least they would be together at the end. It wasn't a comforting thought, but it was the only hopeful one at the moment.

When Anya and Ksenia arrived at the Malyshevs' country home, they created a sensation, shocking Praskovaya Feodorovna who thought they were out of their minds to have chanced the journey.

After embracing both ladies, the housekeeper called in the direction of Prince Andrei's study, her voice nearly cracking with emotion, "Highness, look who's come to join us!"

Prince Andrei was not pleased. Shock and astonishment were the emotions he felt at seeing his beautiful wife and niece standing before him, having risked God knows what to make the trip.

"My God! I thought you had more sense than this," he exclaimed. "The whole countryside is going wild. The attacks have already begun."

Ksenia and her niece kissed Prince Andrei and headed directly for the fireplace as the housekeeper went to fetch tea. They were tired from their journey and didn't feel like being lectured, having had to endure all sorts of revolutionary drivel on the train out of Petrograd.

Both ladies were still recovering from that experience. Forced to take the train like the rest of the world—no private railway carriage on this trip—Anya and Ksenia had found themselves sharing a first-class compartment with several rowdy soldiers on their way home to *izbas* in the hinterlands after declaring themselves through with "Kerensky's damned war."

Saying nothing, the ladies had pulled their brightly colored print shawls over their heads and turned away. That had been a mistake. It seemed to incite the men to expound their philosophy of life, which amounted to going home, drinking lots of strong spirits and chasing all the girls available.

But that could have been borne in stoic resignation if it hadn't been for their desire for company. When one of the men reached out to put his arm around Princess Anya, Ksenia had firmly pushed it away, drawing roars of laughter from the men who took her for the young girl's mother and proceeded to joke with her over the availability of her pretty daughter.

Since that was the natural response they would have got from anyone's mother, the soldiers hadn't held it against the feisty mama with the lovely green eyes and, in fact, had directed a lot of their conversation to her. A little rattled to be addressed on such familiar terms by drunken peasants, Princess Ksenia had wedged herself between her niece and the soldiers and prevented them from doing anything more than looking.

It wasn't an experience she would want to go through twice, even if the Reds were merely drunken, overly friendly boys who were out for a good time. She considered herself and Anya fortunate to have escaped anything more serious and didn't want to press her luck.

"Andrei," she said abruptly, "we came here because Oleg Ivanov broke into Anya's home and took Byelochka. We think he might have come here to seek refuge at his father's house. We want you to round up a search party and go out there. It's our only hope."

Stunned, the prince could only stare at his wife and her niece. It was his fault, he thought bitterly, all his fault. There was truly a punishment for one's sins, thought the prince. It was as inescapable and inexorable as the tides. But why did his punishment have to involve Byelochka, the little jewel of their family? It was almost more than he could bear now to hear Ksenia describe the abduction and to hear how Anya had tried to fight Ivanov off.

"Anya, *milochka*," he said, "things are very bad here right now. It's unbelievable."

"What, Uncle?"

Taking her hand, Andrei made her sit down. "Anyushka," he said, "last night a band of renegade soldiers attacked the Ivanov estate. They killed the old man and every other soul they found with him."

"No!" screamed Anya, rising from her seat. "It's not possible!"

"*Milochka*," said Andrei, holding her to try to calm her, "all the corpses were adults as far as we know. Nobody said a word about finding a child there."

Princess Sviridova stared at her uncle, wild-eyed, not knowing what to think, still fearful for her son. She was almost ready to accept the idea that she had been wrong about Ivanov's flight when young Petya, practically a grown-up now, entered the room, excused himself in embarrassment for bursting in on them and blurted out, "Highness, Dimya the carter just told me a man and young boy were dropped off at the Ivanov place just before the soldiers attacked. He said the child looked like a boy from a good family, and the man could have been Oleg Ivanov!"

Turning to stare at Petya, who was out of breath from excitement, Princess Anya demanded, almost shaking with emotion, "What description did the carter give of the man and the boy?"

"A fat, bald, bearded man wearing a gray coat and a blond boy with long curls in a shabby coat and very fine boots. No more than five years old."

"Petya, that has to be Ivanov," breathed Princess Anya. "He abducted my son in Petrograd and I know he's come here with him."

Shocked by the princess's statement, the young fellow glanced at Prince Andrei, waiting for orders, his blond hair falling in his eyes.

Springing out of his chair, Andrei said, "I'm rounding up the men and going out there to take a look. Petya, get me about half a dozen men with rifles. I'm going to the Ivanov estate to take a look around. You come too."

"Saddle up a horse for me," ordered Anya. "I'm going with you."

"No, *barinia*," pleaded the boy. "It's too ugly for you to see these things."

"So was Warsaw," replied Anya with a grim smile. "But if I hadn't gone there, you wouldn't be standing here today."

She was right. There was no answer to that argument.

"Anya," said her uncle, "if your son was there, you wouldn't want to find him."

Princess Ksenia watched her niece. She had a strong stomach, but she found herself shuddering violently at what those corpses must look like. Remembering the bodies in the aftermath of 1905, the princess couldn't bear the thought of finding Anya's son murdered by those renegades.

To Ksenia's surprise, Anya was adamant. The girl walked straight to Andrei's gun cabinet, unlocked it and selected a Purdey rifle. When the men were ready, so was she.

"Lev," shouted the prince to his head tracker, "you stay here and look after my wife and the other women. If the soldiers arrive, do what you have to do. We'll be back as soon as possible."

"Yes, Highness," he replied, and watched Petya and Princess Anya riding off next to Prince Andrei, the men following at a canter as they headed down the drive. "Good luck," he called after them.

But he didn't like the idea of the young *barinia* going out there to the Ivanov place. Lev was quite sure her son wasn't there, since nobody had said anything about finding a child's body with the rest. Still, he didn't blame her for wishing to make certain.

It was just that it would be easier to protect her if she were back at the manor house with the rest. A pretty girl like that was practically a magnet for the kinds of men who had come calling on old Ivanov. Why go looking for trouble by making her presence known?

Standing behind Lev Petrovich as the party rode away, Princess Ksenia was already planning Byelaya Beryozka's defenses in the face of an invasion. "Lev," she said casually, "do we still have that anchor and chain from Prince Andrei's sloop?"

"I think so, Highness," he replied, puzzled.

"Let's find it. I'll show you what I have in mind."

"Yes, Highness."

Knowing Ksenia Alexandrovna as he did, Lev was intrigued. Even if she was a St. Petersburg lady, she was clever enough to come up with something ingenious in a crisis, and right now he needed all the help he could get. From what he heard about the massacre at the Ivanov estate, if they didn't outwit those renegades, they wouldn't live long enough to worry about their mistakes.

An hour later, when Andrei, Princess Anya and six of their men reached the Ivanov place, they beheld a scene straight out of hell. Nobody had moved the bodies, and they were still laid out like the carcasses of slaughtered animals taken in a hunt. Nauseated by the sight of the mutilated corpses on the porch, the prince and princess averted their eyes as they walked past them through the shattered front door.

To Andrei, who had been inside Ivanov's house the night Anya was attacked, nothing was as he remembered it. A plaster coating over everything made it look ghostly. Walls were pockmarked with bullet holes, furniture was shredded, lamps smashed. And over all the rest was the blood—splattered on the walls, floors, furniture, a gruesome reminder of the massacre.

Her heart beating quickly as she poked among the wreckage of Ivanov's home, Anya tried hard not to think about what had happened to these people. All she wanted was some sign of Byelochka—alive. If she received a sign he was alive, in the area, capable of being rescued, she would never again ask God for another favor. Just let his mother find him!

"Anya," called Prince Andrei from another part of the house, "let's try the cellar."

When the prince and his niece descended to the lower level, they saw nothing that would encourage them. Although the soldiers appeared to have spared it, there was no sign of a child's presence.

Then suddenly Prince Andrei bent down to examine something that caught his eye.

"Anya! Could this belong to your son?"

Staring at the red silk scarf he held, Princess Sviridova tore it from his hands, screaming in her excitement. "Yes!" she exclaimed. "Yes! It's the scarf from his sailor suit. Here are his initials!"

Throwing her arms around her uncle, Anya began to sob, relieved that she finally had some trace of her son, still fearful for his safety.

The prince held her close, trying to comfort her. Then he pulled back, distracted by something against the wall.

"What is it?" Anya asked.

"I don't know yet. Let me take a look."

Curious to explore what appeared to be a small door, half-hidden by a shelf, Andrei pushed aside the debris in his way, opened the door and found himself inside a narrow tunnel.

"Anya, come here. What do you make of this?"

Entering the passageway, the young woman looked around cautiously, glancing at Andrei, who was staring into the darkness, trying to figure how far it went.

"Get me the lantern, will you, *milochka?* I'm going to do some exploring."

"I'll come too," replied the princess, right beside him.

Oleg staggered through the forest, dragging the frightened boy after him, searching for the spot where the five birch trees spread out into a circle. Disoriented by the snow, the patches of pale moonlight, the fear of the soldiers, he had walked in the wrong direction. Now he and the child were lost, and he was furious, beating the helpless boy. It was his fault, a trick of Anna Nicolaievna's. She had done this to him. Confused him. Cheated him of his victory over her.

"It doesn't matter," he muttered, throwing the child down on the snow-covered ground. "I'll kill you right here. It's all the same. And when you die, you'll free me from that witch's power over me."

Terrified, the little boy looked up to see Ivanov take a large butcher knife from under his coat and raise it high over his head. Before the knife could strike him, Byelochka rolled over and out of the way, screaming as loud as he could, his piercing shrieks echoing among the ice-draped fir trees of the forest, reverberating like the terrified cries of a bird through the moonlit woods.

"Help!" screamed the boy, scrambling to his feet. "Help!"

Dodging Ivanov, Byelochka scampered into the woods, taking shelter behind a large cluster of snowy pines while his pursuer lurched after him, shouting and cursing.

While Byelochka clung to the trunk of a tree, hidden from view by the deep shadows and low-hanging branches, Oleg wandered through the woods, his knife poised to strike, talking to himself as he staggered in the snow, his feet catching in the dead vines of the underbrush.

Not far from where Oleg was searching for Byelochka, Count Scherbatkin's men, prowling the forest, looking for any sign of the rebels, heard the screams and were off and running, heading in their direction. As they approached, Oleg grew frightened and flattened himself on the ground, deep in the shadows, just a few feet from where the boy was hiding. Byelochka's breathing was shallow and irregular. Afraid of Ivanov and afraid of the strangers, the boy was nearly paralyzed with fear, not knowing if these men would rescue him from his captor or become new captors.

And then Byelochka saw the shifting moonlight fall on the blade of Oleg's knife. As the peasants in rough sheepskin coats and fur hats turned away, on the verge of heading off in another direction, he took a deep breath and shouted, "Help!" startling them so much, they nearly collided with each other in the semidarkness.

"Help!" screamed the boy, doubling over with the force of his effort. "He's going to kill me!"

As a man reached out to grab the screaming child, Oleg scrambled to his feet and tried to run but succeeded only in heading straight into the waiting arms of two other men. They sent him sprawling to the ground and kicked him several times to keep him there.

"Who are you, boy?" asked the leader of the group. "What are you doing out here at this time of night? And who is he?"

Sobbing with a mixture of fright and relief, the child told them he had been taken from his home in Petrograd by this bad man who had then taken him to a place where all the people were shooting at each other. He was tired and he wanted his mama.

"Christ!" exclaimed the peasant as he glanced at the fellow on the ground, not quite knowing what to make of this information.

"Let's take them back to Count Scherbatkin," suggested one of his men. "He'll know what we ought to do with them."

"Right," nodded the first man. The whole story was peculiar, it seemed to him, and Count Scherbatkin would want to take a look at the pair in any case.

Forcing Oleg to his feet, the men marched him off between them, with another peasant bringing up the rear, his gun pointed straight at the stranger's back. One false step and Oleg was finished.

Byelochka clung to his rescuer and thought of his mama, so far away. How was she ever going to find him if strangers kept carrying him off?

"It's all right, youngster," smiled the fellow who was carrying him. "We'll get you back to your family."

"I'm his father," said Ivanov.

But nobody believed that story.

When Andrei's party returned to Byelaya Beryozka, they found Adam waiting for them, anxious to see Anya and to hear of Oleg's attack firsthand.

"Adam!" cried his wife, rushing to embrace him, "thank God you've come home! Do you know what happened? Oh Adam, I was so worried about you," she murmured, burying her face in his chest. "I was afraid something had happened to you too."

"Don't worry about me," he replied, wrapping his arms around Anya. "Just tell me what happened to you? My God, you're bruised."

Going into the house, the prince and princess gathered in Andrei's study with Andrei and Ksenia to hear his news and hers. Adam was horrified to hear the details and astonished to learn that Tatiana Sergeevna had come to her cousin's defense.

Ksenia smiled weakly. "When we were saying goodbye," she sighed, "Tasha told me Anyushka and I were the only two people who had ever been kind to her. I think she was paying off a debt."

"She fired a shot at him as he was running down the stairs," added Princess Anya. "She nearly got him too. The twins are in Stockholm with Nanny by now," said the young princess. "I gave her enough money to tide them over until we can join them."

Ksenia hastened to call Praskovaya to bring them some tea. Anya was cold and weary, grateful to be reunited with her husband but bitterly disappointed not to have found her son. She looked exhausted in the flickering light of the fireplace.

"Did you have any luck at the Ivanov place?" asked Princess Malysheva, looking at her husband. "Any trace of Oleg or our nephew?"

"Tell them," Anya murmured wearily.

The prince looked at Adam and then at his wife. "We found Byelochka's scarf. That means he and Ivanov were there. But then they must have vanished before the soldiers came; otherwise they would have been among the dead."

"Ivanov brought Byelochka back here?" exclaimed Adam. "*Here?*"

"To his father's home. Where else would he have found a safe spot? It was logical."

Anya took her husband's hand and pressed it against her cold cheek, enjoying his warmth. "There was a slaughter at the old man's house, but I know Ivanov escaped with our son. And that means Byelochka is alive."

Everyone in the room fervently wished Princess Anya was correct in her supposition. They couldn't bear to think of the only other possibility: that having escaped the massacre at the house, Ivanov had taken the boy away to kill him somewhere else. That thought went unexpressed.

As Adam, Andrei and Ksenia silently looked on, Princess Anya gently caressed her son's silk scarf and prayed he was safe.

"Lev Petrovich and Petya have been told to take a group of our men back out to continue the search," Prince Andrei informed Adam. "They have orders to bring Byelochka straight to us as soon as they find him." That was hopeful, thought Adam. He only hoped the optimism was justified.

"And as soon as they deliver Ivanov to us," said Princess Anya, "I'm going to shoot him. It's my right, and I'm going to do it myself and at close range."

That shocked Adam and her uncle but they said nothing. There was plenty of time to take over when they were holding Oleg at gunpoint behind some building, out of sight of the women.

Knowing how their minds worked, Princess Anya knew she'd have to move quickly once he was in their hands or Adam and Andrei would prevent her from taking the vengeance she had been denied for six years.

Let them try, the princess thought. She had been Oleg Ivanov's helpless victim and she had been forced to suffer again when he abducted her son. Now, if there was justice under heaven, she would be his executioner.

In the woods near Byelaya Beryozka, Lev and his party scouted for Ivanov and the boy and for any sign of the soldiers, while Andrei and Adam began supervising the erection of a line of defense stretching from the entrance gate to the front door of the manor house.

Since there was nothing sophisticated about the *modus operandi* of the marauders, there was no reason to believe they wouldn't use the same tactics at Byelaya Beryozka as they had at the Ivanov house: simply drive up to the main entrance and start blazing away.

Adam and Andrei decided to let them enter unmolested while their own armed men crouched behind the piles of snow flanking the drive, waiting for them to head into an ambush. Then when the soldiers were halfway up to the house, they would be forced to halt by the thick iron chain Princess Ksenia had ordered strung across the *allée,* stalling them at a safe distance from the door, confused and momentarily helpless. At this point the signal would be given to open fire, and—God willing— they would be quickly and neatly dispatched before they even knew what hit them.

To even the score further, sharpshooters on the roof of the manor house would start pouring down a murderous stream of gunfire the second the trucks hit the chain, pinning them to the spot and making it almost impossible for the soldiers to use their dreaded machine guns on the defenders.

It sounded good, admitted Ksenia, but she was going to reserve her judgment until after Byelaya Beryozka had weathered the storm. "If your strategy is successful, I'll congratulate you," she smiled. "And if it isn't, I don't imagine we'll live to complain about it."

From now on, the ladies informed the men, they intended to wear riding breeches, boots and revolvers. This was war.

"Good Lord," murmured Adam, "you'll start looking like those Red harpies in Petrograd!"

"Nobody bothers those harpies," replied Anya, and off she went with Ksenia to ransack her old wardrobe, hunting for her tweedier outfits.

After the women left, the men glanced at each other and reached for a bottle of prewar vodka.

"What do you think our chances are?" asked Adam. "Truthfully."

"I think if we can ambush them in the drive, we'll carry the day. If we don't stop them in their tracks then and there, we're lost. Remember, these are soldiers with combat experience and machine guns, so we're going to be outgunned in any kind of regular battle. But with a surprise attack we can shift the balance of power. Really, it's our only hope."

Prince Sviridov nodded. "We better make damned sure we win," he said.

"Yes," agreed Andrei. "I wish the women weren't here. Win or lose, the fight's going to be a bloody one."

"I only want one thing before I die—if I have to die soon," said Andrei. "That's to kill Oleg Ivanov."

Silently Adam raised his glass to Andrei's and tossed the vodka down.

Then both men sent their glasses crashing against the wall of the fire-place, sealing the toast.

In the woods several miles away, a military conference was taking place in a deserted peasant's hut, not too far from Boris Scherbatkin's estate. The soldiers and their local allies were holding a strategy session, discussing plans for the evening's foray.

"Scherbatkin's his name," said one fellow whose only brother had been sent off to war by Boris. "He killed my young brother. Now I want to kill him."

"Any women there?" asked the leader of the soldiers, a sergeant with a strong Moscow accent.

"A wife and daughter. But," he added, "the Scherbatkin ladies have been sent by the count to the Crimea."

"Damn," remarked the sergeant. "And I was hoping to get my hands on a countess tonight."

The men laughed in appreciation of their leader's humor and wondered what delights lay in store for them at the Scherbatkin estate. An aristocrat always had plenty of things to steal, heaps of things. It was something to look forward to.

These men were deserters like so many others fanning out across Russia in the wake of the revolution. A combination of skill and luck had saved them from being killed in the war, and the revolution had provided them with the opportunity to seize the trucks and machine guns from a depot outside Moscow. Now they were out to wage a war of extermination against landlords wherever they could find them. It was Boris's turn tonight. The luck of the draw.

When Boris's men brought Oleg and the child into the manor house for the master to take a look at them, Oleg prayed that his host had a poor memory; he had often got into trouble with him when he was young, and his back still bore the scars of Boris's lash—punishment for poaching on his property. This was the worst possible place to end up and he knew it.

Escorted into the front salon where Count Scherbatkin sat with one of his servants, cleaning rifles, Oleg felt his throat go dry.

"What's this?" demanded the count, looking hard at the shabby man with the rough beard and the pretty blond child with long curls.

"Trespassers, *barin*. We found them in the woods. The boy claims this character snatched him from his home in Petrograd."

Startled, the count motioned to the little boy to come toward him so he could take a good look at his face. There was something vaguely familiar about him. Odd.

"He's my son, *barin*," Oleg lied, trying to keep his face down and look humble. "We were traveling across the fields when a band of soldiers attacked us."

"That's not true, uncle," declared Byelochka, using the polite term children used with adults. "This man came to our house in Petrograd and hurt my mother and took me with him. I want to go home and he won't let me."

Nervously, Ivanov shook his head at the child's accusations and tried to look as meek as possible. Inwardly he was terrified. These aristocrats would kill him without blinking if they ever realized who he was.

"Is this true what the child says?" demanded Boris, looking sternly at the ruffian in front of him.

"Of course not. The brat's lying."

"I'm not lying. My name is Prince Mikhail Adamovich Sviridov, and I live in Petrograd with my mama and papa. I don't know this man."

"Jesus!" exclaimed the count, staring at the child. It couldn't be. Gently taking the little boy's face in his hands, he turned his head to get a better look at him in the light of the gas lamp. "Little one," he said, "what is your mama's name?"

"Princess Sviridova," replied Byelochka.

"No. I mean her Christian name and patronymic."

"Anna Nicolaievna," replied the child, "but Papa calls her Anya or sometimes *dushka.*"

Boris smiled. "Well, Prince Sviridov, I don't know how you came to be in such bad company, but I do know your mama and I'm going to see to it that that she gets you back."

Oleg protested violently. "The brat's a liar! He doesn't know any princesses. He's mine."

"No, uncle," replied Byelochka. "This is a bad man. He hurt my mama at our house and then he brought me out here to a bad place where people were shooting each other last night."

At the mention of people shooting each other, Count Scherbatkin and his men exchanged looks.

"The Ivanov estate?" murmured one of the men.

Rising, Boris stepped forward to examine the ruffian more closely. "Who are you?" he demanded, taking a rifle from one of the men and pointing it at Oleg.

"Just a poor man who was attacked by the soldiers, *barin*, that's all," he mumbled, staring into the barrel of the rifle.

Nose to nose with Oleg, Count Scherbatkin felt as if he knew him.

"Dimitri," he said to one of his men, "go get some hot water, soap and a razor. We're going to take a look at our friend without his beard."

"No!" protested Oleg. "You can't do that!"

But they did. And as soon as the last clump of hair was gone from Oleg's face, Boris ordered his servants to tie the visitor's hands securely behind his back, tie his ankles together and link the hands and ankles so the prisoner couldn't move.

As he heard Count Scherbatkin give the order, Oleg attempted to bolt from the room, but he was stopped at the door by a blow from a rifle butt that sent him sprawling on the floor, unconscious.

"Don't you recognize him, men?" asked Boris as the peasants began to truss him up. "This is old Ivanov's son, *Oleg,* the one who tried to murder Princess Anya six years ago, the same one who used to stalk deer on my land when he was a boy."

"Well, *barin,*" smiled Dimitri, "I know one of your neighbors who will be glad to hear about this. Prince Malyshev's come to stay at Byelaya Beryozka. We'll have to let him know at once."

"Andrei Nicolaievich is back? Are you certain?"

"His housekeeper told my wife yesterday. She was surprised to see him, with all the trouble now."

"Marvelous," declared Boris. "We'll make our neighbor a happy man on two accounts then," he smiled, patting Byelochka on the head, "although for the life of me, I can't imagine how that fellow ever got close enough to this child to abduct him. He's had a price on his head for six years."

"It's that mess in Petersburg," said Dimitri. "It's making all the scum very brave now. It's bringing them out of the sewers."

Boris supposed so. At any rate, this particular bit of scum was not going to bother anyone any longer, not after Andrei Nicolaievich got done with him.

"Keep him under guard and tied up," ordered Boris. "I'm going to put a telephone call through to Prince Malyshev and tell him the good news."

"Why don't we just kill him now, *barin,* and save the prince the effort?"

"Because," replied Boris, as he took Byelochka with him to telephone his uncle, "he'd be heartbroken to miss doing the honors himself. He's been waiting a long time for this moment."

When Praskovaya Feodorovna answered the telephone, she was almost beside herself with joy. Out of breath with emotion, she ran into Andrei's study and announced Boris's call telling Princess Anya her son was safe.

"Where?" cried Anya, rushing to take the call. "Who found him?"

With her husband and relatives close behind her, Anya spoke to Byelochka on the other end of the line. When he heard his mother's voice, the boy sighed with relief and asked her plaintively to come take him home. He missed her.

"Oh, darling," laughed his mother, nearly in tears. "Of course I'll come. Nothing could keep me away from you. Are you all right?"

"Yes, Mama. But the crazy man took me to a terrible place where people were shooting each other. I was afraid."

"You don't have to be afraid any more, darling. You and I will be together in an hour. Papa is here and so are Uncle Andrei and Aunt Ksenia. We'll all be together."

"Let me speak to Boris," whispered Andrei.

Relinquishing the telephone, Anya embraced her husband and her aunt while Andrei tried to get some information from his neighbor.

Yes, Boris had Oleg Ivanov tied up and ready for delivery. No, the child was unharmed. And yes, they could hold the execution when Andrei and his party arrived.

"Good," replied the prince. "We'll be on our way."

As he replaced the receiver, Count Scherbatkin patted the little boy on the head and led him off to the kitchen where the cook promptly got out some ham from the larder and offered the child the first meal he'd had in two days.

After half an hour had gone by, Boris heard the sound of automobiles and looked out the window, puzzled to be greeting Andrei and Princess Anya so soon. What he beheld nearly made his heart stop.

"The deserters!" shouted Count Scherbatkin. "Everybody to his battle stations! Girl, take the child to the cellar and stay with him. Hurry!"

Shots rang out from down the drive as one of the count's men exchanged fire with the intruders, then more shots were heard as windows began to shatter, sprinkling everyone with bits of glass and wood.

Furniture was slammed up against windows and doors. Lights were extinguished as master and servants rushed to their prearranged positions in preparation for a last stand.

"You in the house," shouted someone from the courtyard, a stranger, "open up. Give up your money and we'll let you live. Put up a fight and you die!"

Not a sound came from the darkened house. A few of the soldiers exchanged glances. They knew that nobody ever rushed to open the door for them until they had first been softened up by a pounding of gunfire. It was a mere formality.

"Don't leave me helpless," pleaded Oleg, just beginning to regain consciousness. "I can't move bound like this."

One of the men gave way to a misguided notion of kindness and pushed Oleg, tied hand and foot, into one of the small rooms off the salon, out of harm's way for the moment.

"If we come in shooting, you'll die," shouted the sergeant.

Boris and his seven men replied to that with a volley of rifle fire from the windows of the facade. In a second, the marauders were running for cover, firing back as best they could from behind any available shelter.

This one wasn't going to be easy.

Inside the house, Count Boris and his men were aiming with care, trying to catch the glint of light on metal buttons or on rifle barrels to use as targets in the semidarkness. With the trucks' headlights turned off, only the light of the moon illuminated the courtyard, and it wasn't enough for the deadly accuracy needed right now. Tonight, every bullet counted.

After the first couple of rounds, one or two or Scherbatkin's men had suffered wounds, not from bullets but from splintering glass. The soldiers had lost two men to Boris's fine Remington rifle. Downstairs, the maid trembled with fear as she held the little boy in her arms. She had no illusions about her fate if the soldiers took the house.

A little farther down the road, a party of nearly a dozen horsemen was making its way toward the beseiged manor house, still unaware of the fighting. It was Lev Petrovich who first heard the sounds of gunfire and reined in his mount, making the others do the same.

"Highness, listen. Someone's shooting."

"Where?" demanded Andrei, reaching for his rifle.

"At the Scherbatkin estate or pretty close to it."

"Byelochka!" cried Anya. "My God!"

The horsemen all stood still to listen. It was unmistakably gunfire. The peasants all knew the sound.

"It must be Boris's house. What shall we do?"

"You do nothing, Highness," replied Lev. "I'll go have a look. Then we can make plans. And Highness, if I were you, I'd send Princess Anya back to Byelaya Beryozka to rejoin her aunt. This is no place for a woman."

"No," said Anya. "My son is in danger if the soldiers are there. I won't leave until I can leave with him."

"Go back home," Adam ordered. "Lev is right."

"I don't care what you say. I'm staying."

"This is no time to be mulish," snapped Adam, taking the reins of her horse. "Get out of here."

"No, Adam! I will not!"

Andrei's men watched Lev ride off toward the Scherbatkin estate to scout the area; to their annoyance, Princess Anya insisted upon remaining with them in spite of all good sense. Even her husband couldn't dissuade her, a terrible thing in their eyes. A woman was made to take orders, not give them.

When Lev returned, a solitary figure in the moonlight, his breath puffs of steam in the cold night air, he reined in his horse beside the prince's mount. "It's them, Highness. They're attacking the house."

"And Boris's men?"

"Returning fire for all they're worth. It's a fierce fight."

Glancing angrily at his wife, Adam said once more, "Will you go home and wait there?"

"Not as long as my son is in that house. You know that."

"Anya," said her uncle, "go back to Byelaya Beryozka and stay with Ksenia. The people there have to be warned about the soldiers. Believe me, you'd be doing them a service."

"You'll have to send someone else, Uncle. I won't leave until I know what's become of Byelochka."

"God Almighty!"

"I will not turn tail and run. Not while my child is in danger. How could I?"

Lev Petrovich looked at Prince Andrei. "Shall we join the fight? Scherbatkin's men are going to need all the help they can get."

The prince glanced at his niece, worried for her safety.

"Yes," he replied. "We can't leave those people at the mercy of the savages. Come on."

At the Scherbatkin estate, the count and his men seemed at first to have the upper hand, firing from first- and second-floor windows at their attackers and inflicting real damage. Then suddenly the soldiers brought their machine guns into play, cutting the facade of the house into chips of flying plaster and spraying the windows with deadly slugs of lead.

Splinters of glass flew through the rooms like snow in a blizzard. Unable to return fire under this murderous barrage, Boris's men had to fling themselves on the floor to avoid being cut to pieces. With the defenders pinned down, a group of the renegades forced their way in through the front door, surprising and capturing the entire contingent.

Upstairs Scherbatkin's men had already ceased firing, having been wiped out by the first lethal blast of machine-gun fire from the soldiers. Their corpses lay sprawled across the floor, bloodied and battered.

Not far from the scene of the fighting, Andrei's party was approaching the manor house, cautiously reconnoitering before joining the fray. Tethering their horses, they proceeded on foot, able to make out the figures of several soldiers and peasants near the entrance, caught in the glare of the headlights of the two trucks.

"This is peculiar, Highness," muttered Lev. "The firing's stopped."

"Hold your fire," Andrei warned his men softly. "We'll see what's going on."

Keeping Anya firmly in his grasp, Adam followed Prince Andrei and Lev as both men headed in the direction of the house, taking cover behind a long row of hedges as they tried to see what was taking place inside.

The once-elegant facade was pockmarked with bullet holes, mute testimony to the fury of the battle. It was horrifying to picture what had happened to the defenders.

"Quiet," cautioned Lev, "and keep your weapons ready."

Several hundred yards down the road, Andrei's peasants waited with the horses, standing guard and wishing they had more men with them. If His Highness did anything foolish, he would have to be rescued, along with the *barinia*. It was a bad business, they grumbled. These *boyars* were too easy with their women; they let them defy them at will.

As Andrei and his party crept closer to the house, they could see still more battle scars. In the harsh light of the trucks' headlights lay several corpses, all in khaki uniforms. Boris's house was a near-ruin.

Inside, all hell had broken loose—shouts of soldiers running through the rooms, shooting at survivors, mingled with cries from the dying. The deserters were ready to enjoy the spoils of battle and were prepared to loot anything still in one piece. Boris, identified as the landlord by one of the peasants, was about to face a tribunal of revolutionary justice.

Downstairs in the cellar, the terrified maid screamed as two burly ruffians burst in through the locked door and scrambled down rickety wooden stairs. In their lust to rape the girl, they completely ignored the child, allowing him to flee upstairs while they pursued her around the cellar.

Disoriented by the noise, the acrid smell of gunpowder and the wild men rampaging through the house, Byelochka managed to find himself an exit and scrambled out a window, nearly cutting himself on the jagged bits of glass all around. Heart pounding, he began to race across the courtyard, desperate to escape, not knowing where he was running.

Both the soldiers and Anya spotted him at the same time. Prince Sviridov had to clamp his hand over Anya's mouth and physically restrain her as she saw the precious figure of her son sprinting toward her; he was terror-stricken and still unaware of her presence in the nearby shadows.

Suddenly, just as the child seemed on the point of escaping, a single rifle shot tore through the cold night air, leaving a hideous echo in the darkness.

"*Byelochka!*" Anya screamed, clawing her way free of Adam and racing toward the child, desperate to rescue him. As she attempted to pick him up and carry him to safety, a burst of machine-gun fire blazed across her path, rooting her to the ground.

Adam was about to spring out of the bushes after his wife when Lev Petrovich whacked him in the ribs with the butt of his rifle, sending him sprawling, winded, on the ground. As the prince fell, Andrei saw another soldier leap onto the truck and aim a second burst of gunfire straight at them, pinning them to the ground.

Anya saw it too, threw her son to the ground and fired at the soldiers with her revolver, distracting them enough for their fire to go wild above the heads of her companions. But just barely.

Taking the opportunity, Lev aimed his rifle and managed to score a direct hit. The gunner fell backward, lost his balance and toppled over the side of the flatbed, fatally wounded.

"Run, Anya!" shouted Adam, writhing in pain, struggling to rise.

But Anya didn't seem to hear. She had fallen to the ground, covering Byelochka with her body, and now appeared unable to move. As Adam was on the point of rushing out and pulling her to safety, a barrage of gunfire from the soldiers forced him to rejoin Andrei and Lev among the bushes.

By the time the men were ready to try again, Anya and her son were gone, as if they had never been there at all, taken prisoner by the rebels.

Inside the manor house, the sergeant with the Moscow accent was delighted to greet the two new captives. He casually shoved Princess Sviridova into an armchair while he continued his interrogation of Oleg and Boris, two suspected enemies of the people.

Taking her son on her lap, Anya held the child close and felt desolate. Her captors looked every inch the degenerates they were supposed to be, and they were in fact discussing various ways to torture the prisoners, no holds barred.

"I'm frightened, Mama," whispered Byelochka as the man with the Moscow accent pulled Boris to his feet and kicked him viciously in the groin.

Gently caressing Byelochka, Anya hoped Adam and Andrei wouldn't disappoint her. She expected nothing less than rescue and prayed it wouldn't come too late. It had become horribly obvious to her that the soldiers were going to kill Boris right before her eyes. They had him spread-eagled on the floor now, held down by sturdy arms, though he fought like a calf bound for the slaughter.

"Stop it!" shouted Anya as the sergeant was about to slice off two of Scherbatkin's fingers.

"Why? We asked him for his money before and he refused to tell us where he keeps it. So we'll have to keep asking until he decides to come clean."

"Boris has no money. He's bankrupt."

"Liar," replied the sergeant. "This is a fancy house. It reeks of money."

"He lost most of his fortune in the war. The rest he threw away on women and horses. If you notice, there's no Countess Scherbatkina. She left him when he went bankrupt. Anyone can tell you he's one of the biggest gamblers in Moscow province, and the most unsuccessful one, too."

Anya was lying. She looked the sergeant directly in the eye and re-stated her story, depicting Boris as a wastrel, a womanizer and a man who couldn't keep two rubles in his pocket without wanting to bet on something. Then suddenly, without warning, Anya spun around and pointed straight at Oleg.

"Look," she said, "this is your rich landlord. He's also a well-known hoarder. Ask anyone who lives around here."

"No!" screamed Oleg. "She's a damned liar. I don't come from these parts."

"Listen to him," Anya said scornfully. "He's one of the wealthiest men for miles around, and now he's trying to hide it."

"She's lying. I swear on my mother's grave she's lying. She's Princess Sviridova and she has more money than God. Start peeling off a couple layers of skin and you'll find out how much gold you can get from her."

"Princess Sviridova?" laughed Anya. "What a good joke! She died of influenza two weeks ago in Petrograd. Ask Count Scherbatkin."

"Yes," agreed Boris, still pinned to the floor. "It's true."

"She's a lying bitch! She's Princess Sviridova and her relatives own an estate near here. Go there and you'll find plenty of money."

The sergeant didn't know whom to believe. The woman could very well be a princess. She had a lot of style, even in her outlandish riding breeches, while the man was plainly trash, even though he might be rich.

Suddenly one of the soldiers who was staring hard at Oleg let out a cackle and spun him around, shoving him toward the sergeant.

"I'll bet this one's a food hoarder. Look at the gut on him! If we started to go through his house, I'll bet we'd find plenty of good food there."

Food hoarders were scum. The soldiers all turned to give the suspect a hard, appraising stare. He was certainly fat enough. Any decent person was nothing but skin and bones these days.

The sergeant seemed perplexed by it all. He took out his sharp knife and held it close to Anya's throat as he asked, "What's your name, *barinia*? No lies. And don't try to be clever."

Anya looked him in the eye. "Maria Petrovna Narishkina. This is my son."

The blade pressed uncomfortably close to her throat, and Anya was afraid to breathe, convinced she was about to be killed.

"Don't hurt Mama," ordered Byelochka. "She hasn't done anything. Hurt this bad man."

Looking the sergeant calmly in the eye, Anya suggested he use his knife on more profitable endeavors—like prying the rich landlord away from his money.

"Don't listen to her. She hates me. She'll tell you anything."

Pausing, the sergeant put his knife away and pushed Anya back into the armchair, turning his attention on Oleg.

"I won't deny hating him," declared Anya, speaking to the soldiers in a conversational tone. "He stole money from me and made me lose everything I had in this world. If you want him dead, I'll kill him for you and spit on his corpse. Just give me the knife."

Startled by the venom in the woman's tone, the soldiers appeared to believe her. After all, they could tell the man was a lowlife. Who would believe such a person?

"Don't torture Count Scherbatkin," said Anya. "It's pointless. That's the one with the money, and he lives only a few dozen *versts* from here, down the road at Byelaya Beryozka. If you go there, you'll be wealthy."

"That's where her family lives," roared Oleg. "Don't listen to her."

Anya looked straight at the sergeant and said confidentially, "He has a strongbox so heavy, they say it takes four men to lift it."

"You lying bitch!" screamed Oleg, raging in his bonds. "I should have killed you the first time! You've brought me bad luck ever since that day six years ago."

Anya sprang from her seat and slapped him furiously across the face, momentarily silencing him.

"You animal! You tried to murder me, you tried to murder Adam and you dared to take my child! I swear to you, Ivanov, I'll see you dead for what you've done to me and my family! And if these men don't do the job, I'll find a way to kill you with my own hands!"

"I hate your kind," replied Oleg, his face reddening from the slap. Looking fiercely at Byelochka, he said angrily, "I wish I had been able to kill this little bastard too. Even your son is a typical little *boyar*. I hate your whole damned lousy race!"

Taking the bewildered child in her arms, Anya laughed in Oleg Ivanov's face. Byelochka clung to his mother, frightened by this crazy man who wanted to kill them all. The soldiers watched curiously, wondering whether the *barinia* was about to slap the angry lowlife once more.

"Give me a revolver," demanded Anya, turning to the sergeant. "I want to shoot him." Putting her son down, she extended her hand.

Smiling benevolently, the sergeant patted the excitable lady on the shoulder and murmured, "Later. First we're going to pay a visit to this strongbox of his. Then we'll see what we're going to do about you."

As he stood before her, the sergeant smiled, his small eyes gleaming with lust as he put his arms around her, sliding his dirty paws into the front of her blouse, roughly caressing her breasts, humiliating Anya in front of her young son.

"Don't touch me," she said coldly, pushing him away. "I'm not your woman."

Amused, the sergeant ripped open the blouse, grabbing at Anya's full bosom under its white satin corset. "You wear too damned many clothes," he grinned, giving her a playful slap on the backside. "But after we get done with the fat trash here, *barinia,* they'll come off and you'll find out what loving's like with a real man."

"I already know what it's like with a real man," the *barinia* replied coolly. "All I see here are animals."

Slapping her face in anger, the sergeant threw Princess Sviridova back into the armchair and began to bark orders at his men to get ready to move. They were on their way to Byelaya Beryozka.

From outside the house, hidden by a growth of bushes, Petya had been observing what was taking place inside. He had seen the confrontation between Princess Anya and Oleg, and he had seen the sergeant put his hands all over the princess. Now at the mention of attacking Byelaya Beryozka, he was on his way back to warn his father and Prince Andrei.

"*Barin,*" he gasped, "the young princess has told them Ivanov lives at Byelaya Beryozka and has money there. She's trying to send them into an ambush. We have to help her, otherwise she's dead, and the little boy too."

"Is she hurt?" demanded Adam. "Have they harmed her?"

"No, *barin.* She tried to kill Ivanov but they wouldn't let her. They want this money she's telling them about."

"Jesus," murmured Andrei, amazed at Anya's nerve, realizing her intentions but heartsick that it was necessary to leave her with these monsters one second longer. "Let's get started. We'll take the route across the fields. I've already sent two of our men to warn the people of an attack. The soldiers will have to stick to the roads because of their trucks. We'll get there first and be waiting for them. When they reach the drive, we'll attack with everything we can hurl at them."

Quickly rejoining the others, Adam, Andrei, Lev and young Petya announced their plan, ordered the men to mount up and raced with them across the slushy fields to Byelaya Beryozka, ready to give battle.

At home, Ksenia had already received the news of the attack on Boris's estate and was arming every man who declared himself willing to fight. She and Praskovaya Feodorovna were determined not to disappoint Prince Andrei. Byelaya Beryozka would not fall before an onslaught of savages, no matter what; they had too much to lose.

"Highness," said one of the peasants, "we have our men in place along the drive and on the roof. The chain ought to stop their trucks before they realize what's happened. Even if they manage to break through after a few minutes, we'll have them where we want them just long enough to do what we have to do."

Nodding her approval, Princess Ksenia solemnly shook hands with the bearded old man in the worn sheepskin coat. "Thank you," she said. "If this works out, I want each of those renegades killed. If it doesn't, I don't want to be taken alive by those beasts. Promise me you'll shoot me before I ever fall into their hands."

Remembering the accounts of the slaughter at other places in the district, the peasant looked Ksenia Alexandrovna in the eye and silently nodded.

"Thank you," she said quietly. Turning to her housekeeper, the princess enbraced her wordlessly, then handed her a rifle.

"We survived 1905, Highness. We'll survive this."

"We must," replied the princess. "We have no alternative."

At the Scherbatkin house, the soldiers and their peasant allies were preparing to leave, taking the *barinia,* the child and the fat, cursing Ivanov with them.

"What are we going to do with the landlord?" asked the corporal, indicating Boris, who lay on the floor with both hands tied.

"Shoot him," replied the sergeant, on his way out the door, dragging Anya and her son with him.

"No!" cried the princess, struggling with her captor. "Don't!"

Byelochka cried out in fright as the gunshot rang out, sending most of Count Scherbatkin's head over the walls. Frantically, his mother held him against her so he couldn't turn around and see.

"If you give me a hard time," smiled the sergeant, "that's what will happen to your son."

Wisely, Anya said nothing this time, praying Andrei and his men had their ambush well prepared at Byelaya Beryozka, not knowing where they were now, but certain they were out there, just waiting for the right moment to attack.

Surrounded by soldiers and peasants, who were joking about what they intended to do when they got their hands on all that money, Princess Anya thought grimly that they'd be in the farthest corner of hell long before they ever saw so much as a kopek from Byelaya Beryozka.

Of course, she thought with trepidation, clutching her young son, once the ambush was underway, there was a very real danger she and the child might be shot along with the invaders, simply because her men wouldn't realize she was in the thick of it.

"Well," Anya murmured to herself as she and Byelochka were ordered into the small cab of one of the trucks, "let's hope we live to see the morning."

Right now, she was no longer certain.

Holding Byelochka on her lap, Anya found herself seated beside the corporal who had accused Oleg of being a hoarder.

In the back, clinging to to the removable side panels of the flatbed was a group of about six or seven soldiers with one of the machine guns that had been mounted on the truck. Oleg was ordered into the other vehicle, now freed of all bonds except for his hands.

"I tell you, you're making a bad mistake," he shouted, receiving a blow from a rifle butt to shut him up. "The woman is a liar."

"Get in," ordered the soldier behind him, striking him once more. "And shut your mouth. You have nothing to say to us."

Thrust into the cab of the truck, Ivanov nearly despaired. If the soldiers didn't kill him, Princess Sviridova certainly would, right in the courtyard of her uncle's home, surrounded by her loving family.

One way or another, he had to get out of there before either group had a chance to use him for target practice. He began to work at loosening his bonds, urged on by blind panic.

As the small convoy began rolling toward Byelaya Beryozka over the half-frozen, slushy country roads, Anya wondered where Andrei and his men were. She was counting on them.

"Mon petit," murmured the princess, using French, a language her son knew and the guard did not, "we're going to see a lot of shooting when we get home. Slide down on the floor and stay there. Whatever happens, don't raise your head. Understand?"

"Oui, Maman," he replied. "What will you do?"

"Don't worry," she smiled, trying not to alarm him too much. "I'll be all right."

"Speak Russian," ordered the corporal. "You sound like a damned German."

"Sorry."

In the other truck, Oleg was desperately trying to loosen the rope that was tying his wrists together. The soldiers had done such a good job it was almost impossible to work free. Then suddenly, just as he was about to despair, he felt a slight bit of give.

Ah, he thought, his hope renewed. Now all he had to do was work fast enough to get the hell out of there and kill the guard in time. Christ!

By now Andrei and his party had returned to Byelaya Beryozka and warned their people of imminent attack. Everyone was in position, rifles ready for the first sign of the renegades.

The only thing that troubled the defenders was the fact that the young princess and her son were going to be right in the middle of the battle, helpless and unprotected as her uncle's men fired everything they had at her captors. In a fight like that, nobody could guarantee their safety.

"It was Anya who gave them the idea," said Adam. "She knew the risk she was taking. We can't fail her now."

Figuring that the *barinia* and the child would most likely be inside the cab of one of the trucks, Andrei's men agreed to hold off firing directly at that part of either vehicle. Everything else was fair game.

From the darkened upstairs windows, Princess Ksenia and her housekeeper also waited with rifles, keeping watch for any sign of lights approaching from the distance.

Suddenly, Ksenia let out a cry, shouting down to her husband from the open window. "Andrei! Get ready! I see something that could be them!"

Two seconds later, the men on the rooftop confirmed the *barinia*'s report.

"This is it," murmured Adam, his heart beginning to pound. Within half an hour he would be holding his wife and son in his arms or they would all be dead together.

"Good luck," said the prince to his men. "You know what you have to do."

As soon as the first truck began its approach to the driveway, the men hidden behind trees and bushes aimed their weapons, waiting for the prearranged signal—the moment of collision with the heavy iron chain stretched tightly across the path.

Rolling up the driveway with all the arrogance two mounted machine guns bestowed upon them, the soldiers saw no sign of life at Byelaya Beryozka. It was as if the inhabitants had fled in terror before them.

Anya wasn't fooled; she knew her people were out there.

"Byelochka," she said in French, "Remember what I said. Keep down."

At that moment, their truck encountered some heavy obstacle, forcing it to a halt despite all the efforts of the driver to move ahead. His wheels spun uselessly on the pebbled *allée*. Failing to stop in time, the second vehicle, carrying Oleg and the sergeant, plowed into the lead truck. The ambush was on.

"Fire!" shouted Andrei, picking off the first casualty.

Screaming in fury, the sergeant was about to scramble out of his truck when Oleg overpowered him, grabbed him from behind with the rope he had been bound with and garroted him, flinging the body out the door before anyone could notice what had happened. With all the commotion, nobody even glanced his way.

Panicking at finding themselves in the middle of a trap, fired upon from several directions at once, the soldiers and peasants tried to return fire, but found themselves hopelessly outgunned. No one could get close enough to the machine guns to use them, pinned down as they were under a murderous barrage of bullets. Within minutes, most of the men were already dead or wounded, picked off by Andrei's sharpshooters, who fired from the rooftop from both sides of the drive and from the upper stories of the house.

Anya, crouching down nearly on top of her son, flinched as the driver of the truck suddenly slumped forward, taking a direct hit in the head. At least that was one who wouldn't be giving them any more trouble.

"Mama!"

"Don't worry. I'm all right. Papa will save us."

Seizing the shotgun the soldier had brought with him, Anya pushed his corpse out the door, shouting for Adam and Andrei. Upstairs Ksenia saw the body roll out the door and screamed for her husband to help Anya and her son.

Andrei heard his wife, sighted Anya in the truck and alerted his men.

While the defenders were busy pursuing the last of the soldiers, hunting them down as they tried to escape across the broad lawn, slippery with slush and half-frozen mud, Oleg Ivanov saw his last chance to avenge himself. In the semi-darkness of the courtyard, illuminated only by the glare of the trucks' headlights and the glow of a full moon, Oleg saw Princess Sviridova and her son step out of the vehicle in front of him, perfect targets.

But he wasn't the only one to see them. Adam spotted his wife and child and called for them to get back inside the truck until the fighting was over.

"It's too late for you, *barinia!* Too late for the boy, too!"

Freezing at the sound of that hated voice, raspy with rage and venom, Anya pushed her son behind her and ordered him not to move.

Sixty yards down the drive, Adam saw Ivanov, heard him menace his wife, and raced toward them.

"It's going to be a pleasure to kill you," grinned Ivanov, pointing a stolen shotgun at the woman and child. He was freeing himself from her forever.

Suddenly, the peasant faltered. Pointed straight at his middle was another shotgun, this one in Anya's hands. As shots rang out in the distance, Oleg and the woman began circling each other like animals before a fight, heedless of the danger.

"Run, Byelochka," Anya ordered, releasing the safety catch of her weapon.

Adam and Andrei had halted where they were, raising their rifles to get a good shot at Oleg. As the American was about to pull the trigger, Prince Malyshev jostled him roughly aside. "This is my duty," he said, speaking in a strange, choked voice. "I failed Anya once before. I ought to be his executioner!"

Adam could only stare as the prince aimed carefully and pulled the trigger, his face taut with unspeakable emotion.

He was too late.

Covering her son's escape, Anya had raised her shotgun, aimed and fired instinctively. As Andrei's bullet struck Oleg he was already dead from the shotgun blast fired by Anya from a distance of less than ten feet. Coldly composed, Anya had just extracted her revenge.

As Oleg went flying backward from the force of the bullets, the young princess threw down her weapon and rushed toward her husband and son. Ivanov was a threat no longer.

In the strange, swirling maze of light from the trucks' headlights and the lanterns carried by men rushing to round up the intruders, Anya stared at the hideous sight of Oleg Ivanov stretched out before her. She alone had accomplished what neither her uncle nor her husband had been able to do, just as she had once sworn she would. As she stood there in the courtyard, holding Adam and Byelochka close to her, she knew justice had finally been served. She had no regrets.

As the Sviridovs embraced, Prince Andrei walked a little unsteadily toward the corpse of the madman who had tried to attack him through his young niece. Oleg was finally dead. But it was Anya who had killed him.

As the prince stepped over Oleg's lifeless body, he called to Lev and Petya to round up the last of the renegades still alive. They executed the men with their own machine guns, dumping both the corpses and the dismantled weapons into the swiftly flowing currents of the River Moskva.

Andrei himself threw in Oleg's body, the last to go, after checking thoroughly for any sign of life. This time he was taking no chances on anyone else's bad judgment.

Later, as he embraced Anya, holding her silently in his arms, Andrei was grateful it was all over and even more grateful they had survived. His young niece had been the joy of his life and Ksenia's, and he looked forward to seeing her children grow up.

❧ EPILOGUE ❧

Despite their success at repelling the marauders, Anya and her family knew the old Russia was dead and that the new one had marked them for extinction. They were now being referred to as the ex-prince or ex-princess, just as Nicholas II had become their ex-tsar. It was oddly comical and strangely sad, as if a mere shift of vocabulary could erase centuries of history.

Sadder yet was the quickening disintegration of life at Byelaya Beryozka. Proud of his men who had stood by him to fight off the renegades, Prince Andrei was unprepared for what was to follow—Lev Petrovich's murder at the hands of a jealous peasant who resented his long friendship with the *boyars* and the alleged privileges he had accumulated over the years.

It happened two days after the attack and nobody came forward to identify the murderer. Petya and his one surviving brother wept bitterly as they stood with the Malyshevs and Sviridovs at Lev's grave. And then they went looking for the killer. When they found him, they buried him so deep in the woods that nobody ever found the body. But the break-down of old habits and old ways had already started and everybody realized it.

Anya decided not to waste another day delaying her trip to Stockholm to rejoin her two daughters. Along with Adam, Byelochka, Andrei and Ksenia, the young princess made her way back to Petrograd—the fastest way out of Russia—only to find a Bolshevik commissar waiting for her and her husband, intent upon nationalizing the Sviridov Palace. Orders from the new government.

That same night, after a conference with Andrei and Ksenia, the Sviridovs and Malyshevs threw some clothing together and headed for the American Embassy on Morkhovaya Street where Billy had been alerted to launch Operation Repatriation. To his credit, he hadn't hesitated.

Moving too quickly for any member of the new government to put out an order to detain them, the party assembled in Billy's office, where he handed out the diplomatic passports Adam had stored there for just such an eventuality, along with clothing bearing labels of New York and Boston stores for these "American diplomats" to wear on their journey to Finland that night.

Counting on the generally poor communications between various government factions and the pervasive spirit of disunification, Adam decided to risk a bold move. Calling up the stationmaster at Finland Station, an old ally from the days of the Amer-Russian War Relief Agency, he asked him to roll out a private car for the American ambassador and attach it to the 11:45 train going west. Urgent business required him and his party to get to Helsingfors by daybreak.

Hesitating a little, the man finally said, "Be there at 11:45 on the dot and you'll have it."

"Is he reliable?" asked Anya as her husband announced the plan.

"I hope so."

Since Adam was too well known to pass himself off as the American ambassador, it fell to Prince Andrei to play the part. He did so with great dignity, a tall, imposing figure in an astrakhan coat and fur hat, both bearing labels attesting to their manufacture in New York. Ksenia, wearing a blonde wig, was his distinguished spouse, bundled up in a fox-trimmed wool coat with silver fox hat and muff.

Following these two were the ambassador's secretary, Mr. Adam Lowell, and his secretary Anya, who brought up the rear with the ambassador's "grandson."

Escorted to the station by Billy and an honor guard of Marines, who were wondering what sort of joke Billy Whitmore was playing now, the party passed rapidly and silently through the station, filled even at this hour with soldiers and peasants, some of whom had been waiting at the depot for hours or even days.

Greeted warmly by the stationmaster, the "Americans" were quickly rushed on board the private car, with the Marines standing at attention as they pulled out, looking resolutely official. No one got near them.

As the train picked up speed, Anya was overcome with tears. She waved at Billy until she could barely make out his figure among all the others. If this was her last view of Petrograd, it would have to remain with her for as long as she lived.

As she held Byelochka close to her, watching the station fade from sight, Anya was grateful she had managed to save her son from the animals who were taking over the once-imperial city, even while she was filled with bitterness at the thought of being forced to abandon what remained of St. Petersburg.

Having let it be known their destination was Helsingfors, Adam and his party deliberately avoided it, instead choosing the forest route to Stockholm. They were aided on their trip west by some of the same Lapp drivers who had once helped him export the treasures of the Sviridov Palace.

Deciding not to chance rejection at the border by suspicious Reds, the Sviridovs and Malyshevs let the Lapps lead them across the still-frozen river to Swedish territory. They arrived at Haparanda, easily passing the scrutiny of Swedish border patrols, who weren't turning away anyone who showed diplomatic passports and claimed to be fleeing Bolshevism.

About the same time Anya was helping her son onto the train to Stockholm, her old butler in Petrograd was explaining to a very angry commissar that Her Highness, the ex-princess, seemed to be sleeping late and absolutely refused to be disturbed.

Furious, the man shouted he'd arrest her if she didn't come down to speak to him. After waiting five minutes, he raced up the long white marble staircase under Matvei's horrified gaze to personally awaken her.

All he found was an empty room in a palace that had been stripped of every precious object. The best he could nationalize for the revolution was a small group of paintings by several minor artists.

There was, however, one magnificent formal portrait left behind, a breathtaking likeness of Princess Anya placed at the top of the stairs, looking as if she were preparing to greet her guests at one of her splendid balls. Leaving it behind was Anya's way of maintaining a link with all the members of the family who had lived in this great house.

"Are you going to take the painting?" Matvei asked as he saw the Bolshevik study it with interest. He hated the thought of Her Highness's beautiful portrait leaving its proper place. Especially with this type.

"No," replied the commissar after a few seconds. "It has no value whatsoever for us. The revolution has no need of princesses." And then he departed to swear out a warrant for the arrest of Princess Sviridova.

Hundreds of miles to the west, on board a first-class coach of the Swedish railway, Anya was holding Byelochka in her arms and drowsily staring out the window. One part of her life was over today. To her surprise, she was quite calm. There was always the chance of returning to Russia once the turmoil was over. Revolutions generally brought forth counterrevolutions, didn't they? She could always hope for that.

And if the unspeakable happened and there was no counterrevolution, at least she had taken the road to exile in the company of those she loved best. As long as the family remained together, they would survive.

As she sat gently stroking Byelochka's curls, Anya thought that no matter where they were, they would flourish.

That was a pledge for the future. And a promise to keep.